THE SMUGGLER KING;

OR,

THE FOUNDLING OF THE WRECK.

A NAUTICO DOMESTIC ROMANCE.

BY THE AUTHOR OF

"GALLANT TOM;" "ELA, THE OUTCAST;" "ANGELINA;" "EMILY FITZORMOND;" "MANIAC
FATHER;" "MARTHA WILLIS;" "MARY CLIFFORD;" ETC., ETC. ETC.

"There's a brave little barque stealing out in the dark
From her nest in the bustling bay;
The fast mist meets on her dingy sheets,
And swiftly she darts away.
She never must run in the eyes of the sun,
But along with the owl take wing;
She must keep her flight for the moonlight night,
For she carries the SMUGGLER KING!"   SONG.

LONDON:
E. LLOYD, 12, SALISBURY SQUARE, FLEET STREET.

1844.

THE SMUGGLER KING;

OR,

THE FOUNDLING OF THE WRECK.

A NAUTICAL DOMESTIC ROMANCE.

BY THE POPULAR AUTHOR OF "GALLANT TOM," ETC.

EPOCH I.—CHAPTER I.

THE TEMPEST.—THE SHIPWRECK. — THE RESCUE FROM DEATH. — THE
CONFLAGRATION.—THE YOUNG MURDERER. — THE ABRUPT DISAP-
PEARANCE.

THE "Spirit of the Storm" held predominant sway both by sea and
land on the night of the 24th of August, in the year 1774, and for the time
it lasted seldom were more disasters heard of, especially at sea. In all
parts were to be heard the cries of lamentation from the widow and the
fatherless, and the numerous shipwrecks that had occurred in that fearful
tempest had caused incalculable distress among the poorer classes, and
created an universal panic among the shipowners and underwriters, whose
losses were immense.

That benevolence which characterizes the British public was never
exerted with greater energy than on the occasion to which we have alluded,
in order to relieve the wants of those whom the perils of the deep had con-

signed to sudden misery and despair. Public subscriptions were opened in every quarter, and many hundreds of humble hearts were lightened of half their cares by the munificent aid afforded by the hand of philanthropy.

It was at this calamitous period that the " Terrible " British frigate was on her homeward-bound passage; but she had not been many hours from Gibraltar ere the weather, which had before been promising, became violent and tempestuous; fogs and storms rapidly succeeded each other, and driving her from her course in the fury of a storm of hail and snow, while the wind blew a perfect hurricane, the frigate struck upon a rock and divided her keel.

The utmost alarm was now excited in the minds of the passengers on board, but the officers maintained their usual coolness and intrepidity, and endeavoured to calm the minds of those on board, in which they partially succeeded.

It was not without the greatest difficulty that the vessel was got off; but when she again floated, the water poured in through her yawning timbers, and all possibility of saving her from her perilous and dreadful situation seemed to be at an end.

Awful was now the despair and consternation that prevailed. Nothing was to be observed around but horror and confusion, and it was several minutes ere even the officers themselves, who hitherto had displayed such presence of mind, could so far govern their feelings as to act with prudence and promptitude.

At length reason asserted her sway, and, in the wild uproar of oaths and prayers, self-preservation prompted the getting out the boats; and the captain helped several of the principal passengers into them, among whom were several females and children.

Quickly the wind and the waves hurried them from the sinking vessel, and the unhappy companions of their voyage. In the hurry and confusion to preserve their lives, no one had thought of a compass, and they drove before the wind the whole of the night, which was not cheered by the twinkling of one of Heaven's silvery orbs, and during the whole time, the rain continued to descend in a perfect deluge, drenching their shivering limbs, and freezing their very life's blood, making the horrors of their situation still more terrible.

Thus awfully situated, they continued, while the wind swelled the surrounding billows into mountains, till the morning dawned, and then was presented to their despairing eyes a wide expanse of agitated and foaming sea.

Among them a very small portion of biscuit had been shared and three of the few inmates of the boat were found to have expired through the effects of terror and the fatigue they had undergone. Their bodies were immediately consigned to the deep.

And now the dread of famine was adding fresh horror to the minds of the survivors, when one of the sailors, who had sought safety in the boat, overcome with sleep, from having applied too frequently to a rum keg, fell on the knees of one of the females, and, in the effort to raise him up, owing to their crowding too much on one side, the boat was in an instant capsized.

All sunk to a watery grave but two; they heard the last despairing and agonizing shrieks of their companions, although one of them, a child, a fair boy, was too young to understand the meaning of them;—the dreadful plunge of the wretched beings to eternity hissed in the ears of that one;—he felt the foaming waters close over him, and that was the last he heard or felt.

The storm had now abated, and the golden beams of the sun illumined that ocean in which so many human beings had recently been summoned to their last awful account. The billows had sunk into a comparative calm, and no one to look upon that beauteous expanse could have imagined that so recently had been enacted a calamity of such fearful and destructive consequences.

Under a beetling rock during the night a poor fisherman and his son, a fine, hardy, promising, and intelligent lad, had been constrained to shelter their little vessel, and when the wind had subsided, were preparing in the morning to put to sea with their freight.

While they were thus occupied, they observed drifting towards them a strange object. They instantly backed their sail, and waited till they could plainly see it was a boat, which dragged after it the body of a child, whose clothes were tightly held between the timbers of the boat, which the violence of the storm had driven over each other. Stretched insensible, and apparently dead, at the top of the boat, was the form of a handsome-looking youth about seventeen, attired as a midshipman, and who had lashed himself to the shattered boat as well as he was able, and which had been the means of keeping him afloat.

Humanity impelled the fisherman to take up the bodies, in the hope that life was not quite extinct; and with the greatest difficulty and danger himself and his son secured the boat, and got the still senseless beings on board their own little vessel, where, fancying they felt a faint pulsation about the heart of the child, which was a boy, and the lad evincing evident signs of life, they exerted themselves to restore animation, in which, after the lapse of some time they succeeded; but the child, when it opened its eyes, and beheld its preservers, and the difference of the scene to that from which he had been preserved, became again insensible through confusion and terror.

At that moment a low feeble groan intimated that the young midshipman still lived, but when the fisherman turned towards him, and compassionately inquired after his health, he stared at him so wildly, and uttered such strange incoherences, that, though they understood from his ravings that a ship had been wrecked, and that his father and all his friends had perished, he could not bring his mind to believe otherwise than that the melancholy accident had turned his brain, and that he knew not what he uttered.

Twilight had only just set in the following evening, when the fisherman and his son moored their little vessel in safety. They had reached their home, and they bore the beauteous child and the young midshipman to the comfortable cottage where they dwelt.

No sooner had they arrived there than the females were ready to bestow upon them their tender care (the wife and mother of the fisherman), and their curiosity was not a little excited to know where the fisherman and his son had found them.

The child appeared not to be more than four years of age; its countenance was extremely beautiful and intelligent, and its beautiful flaxen hair fell over a neck and shoulders fair as alabaster, and of a symmetry sufficiently delicate to have belonged to one of the other sex.

Its eyes were of a Heaven-like blue; and even now sparkled with a brilliancy which could not fail immediately to win upon the admiration of the beholder.

The young midshipman was a very handsome lad, yet there was something in the expression of the general contour of his features peculiarly striking, and calculated to leave anything but a favourable impression upon the mind of the beholder.

"What a sweet pretty child," said the wife of the fisherman; "I never saw a lovelier one in all the course of my life. Where did you pick it up, Ben?"

"Why," replied the fisherman, "we picked them both up at sea, floating after a boat, which belonged, I suppose, to a ship that went to the bottom. May the Almighty extend His mercy to the poor souls that went down in her. And now since you know all that I've got to tell you, go and put the poor creatures to bed, and make them both something comfortable to take, and to-morrow morning I will send Harry to the chateau of Monsieur Aumaile, and make him acquainted with the circumstance, and I warrant he will take them both under his protection for the present, and endeavour to find out who they belong to; but of this I feel certain, that they are neither of them the children of humble parents."

"Poor things," said Marie, the fisherman's wife, "perhaps lost all the friends and relatives dear to them, and in that case, how terrible will be their situation."

"Ay, poor dears!" ejaculated her mother; "but come, let us convey them to a chamber, and see what can be done towards their restoration."

With the assistance of Harry, the fisherman's son, the insensible unfortunates who had been so miraculously preserved from the wreck, were borne to a comfortable apartment, and being undressed by the old woman and her daughter, they were both put into an homely but clean bed, where they, appearing to sink into sleep, Marie and her mother retired.

Ben Backstay, the fisherman, as his name will explain, was a native of England. He was a man now in the prime of life, and with a heart overteeming with every honest and generous feeling. He was an honour to the station he moved in, and would have reflected no discredit on one much loftier. But Ben was as contented and happy as the days were long. He coveted no more than the common enjoyments and necessaries of life, and peace and content; and with those it had pleased Providence to bless him. His acquaintances were but few, but those he had were honest, and esteemed him as a sincere friend, and were always proud of his society, when a relaxation from their laborious avocations would permit them to meet together.

Early in life Ben Backstay had been left an orphan, without a relation or friend in the world. He was forced to go to the parish poor-house, from whence he was apprenticed to the sea, and served in the battles of his king and country for many years, always gaining the utmost respect and approbation from his commanders, and the esteem of his messmates. At length, after being severely wounded, he was taken prisoner by the French, and remained in confinement for three years. On an exchange of prisoners, Ben was transmitted once more to his native land, where, having passed before the Board of Admiralty, and being considered past service, he was discharged; but, as many a brave fellow had been served before him, he was juggled out of that pension he had so bravely earned.

During the time that Ben had been in France, he had formed an acquaintance with Marie, his present wife, and their attachment soon became of the most mutual and ardent character.

Marie was a pretty, innocent, intelligent, and kind-hearted girl, and honest Ben felt confident that he could never select another with whom he should better like to plough the ocean of life. She was the daughter, and the only child of a poor, but industrious fisherman, who was already as much attached to Ben as if he had been his own son.

Ben having taken a few hundred pounds, prize money, that were due to him, and for a time feeling a sort of disgust at his own country after he had been so scurvily treated, and anxious once more to behold the object of his affections, returned to France, where, finding that Marie's sentiments were unchanged, but that, on the contrary, time and absence had rather strengthened her love, he proposed for her hand—was accepted, both by her and her parents, and in a short time afterwards they were united by the rites of the Protestant church.

Happy was the marriage of this humble but honest couple, far greater than that which is often the result of marriages of rank and station. The loves of Ben and Marie were pure, sincere, and devoted, and years of felicity seemed to be promised to the weather-beaten and neglected seaman, for the many vicissitudes he had undergone. He joined his father-in-law, and became a partner with him as a fisherman. Fortune favoured their exertions, and they managed to gain a comfortable and respectable livelihood.

Thus passed away several years, and Marie bore her husband two children, the boy Henry, before mentioned, and a little girl, now about five years old, and shortly after whose birth the father of Marie breathed his last, thus leaving the whole of his business and the support of his aged widow to the exertions of Ben.

Fortune still continued to favour the honest exertions of Ben, and there was not a comfort which the humble ambition of himself and his dear relations coveted that was not gratified.

After Marie and her mother had seen the two shipwrecked boys safe in bed, they quitted the chamber, and having felt an inclination to examine the drenched clothes of the child, they were convinced on the investigation that he must be the child of some great personage, because his linen was so very fine, and his clothes altogether of the richest description. Besides, if any further proof were wanting, he had a gold chain round his neck, from which was suspended a very handsome locket, and Marie was convinced that no common person wore such fine clothes and such rich jewels.

"What a beauteous child it is!" exclaimed Marie to her husband; "I declare, as it lies sleeping, it looks for all the world like a little angel. Oh! Ben, we will never part from this little innocent; I am sure I could love it as fondly as if it were my own offspring."

"And so could I, lass," replied Ben, "but it is our duty to endeavour to find out who the child belongs to, for doubtless it has friends who will be rejoiced to discover that it has been preserved from the dreadful fate that threatened it. In this I have no doubt that Monsieur Aumaile will most readily assist us, and when the young midshipman recovers his senses, he may be able to give us some information about him."

"I wonder if they are related," said old Clotilde; "there certainly is a great likeness between them."

"There is," coincided Ben; "but yet a vast difference in the general appearance of the figure-head of the two. Heaven pardon me, if I judge wrongfully, but there is something about the jib of the young reefer, which, although he is only a boy, is far from pleasing."

"He is very handsome," observed Marie.

"He is," answered Ben, "but handsome is that handsome does—and—but, it is not fair for us to pass an opinion at present. I am only happy to think that I was enabled to snatch him from Davy Jones's locker."

"Oh!" exclaimed Marie, "how very happy am I too; thank Heaven that they were not drowned."

"Yes, wife," returned Ben, "it was Heaven's will to save them: but it is sad to think how many poor souls have been lost; and if ever they recover their senses, it will be a sorrow to weep for their friends that are gone!"

"Heaven forbid that they should not recover their senses," said old Clotilde; "for time would wear away grief, and they might yet live to enjoy every earthly happiness and fortune."

"To-morrow morning," said Harry Backstay, who was an intelligent lad, "I will depart to the chateau, and tell Monsieur Aumaile about this calamity, and I am certain that he will soon learn who they really are, and exert himself for their benefit."

"Aye, Heaven bless him," ejaculated Ben. "Monsieur Aumaile is a Christian if ever there was one cruized the ocean of life. His sails are ever spread for the port of humanity, and he never weighs anchor from doing a good action. Never shall I forget how kind he was to me, when I fell down before the door and broke my leg ; and how he watched and tended you and Marie when you had the ague."

"There is not Monsieur Aumaile's equal in the whole world for kindness and humanity," observed Marie, who heartily joined her husband in his praises of Monsieur Aumaile.

" Yes," said old Clotilde, " it's all true, for he gave us this snug pretty cottage after the death of my poor husband, and bought Ben the fishing smack."

" Yes," said little Fouchette, who was present when this conversation took place ; " and the good gentleman has always been so kind to me, and bought me so many pretty things ; and his pretty daughter Mademoiselle Ninette is always kissing and caressing me whenever she sees me, and has promised when I get bigger that I shall go and live at the chateau. Oh ! how I do long for that time to come."

"What, to leave your parents and your brother Fouchette?" said her mother.

"Oh ! no," said the sweet child, " that certainly would grieve me very much ; but you know that Monsieur Aumaile and Mademoiselle Ninette would always be most happy to see you whenever you thought proper to come."

Marie and her husband kissed the little prattler affectionately, and then Ben, turning to his wife and mother said :—

" You look carefully after your patients, and see that they want for nothing ; Harry will depart as soon as possible to the chateau of Monsieur Aumaile, and acquaint him with all the particulars. I must now away to dispose of my fish."

Honest Ben Backstay then departed for Dieppe, revolving in his mind as he proceeded the extraordinary events of the last few hours.

It was yet early in the morning and there were but few persons stirring in the villages which Ben had to pass through. He had not, however, proceeded any considerable distance, when he was startled from a deep lethargy into which he had fallen, by hearing loud cries of alarm and distress, and looking up, he perceived a lurid reflection in the heavens, which momentarily spread into a large expanse of ensanguine reflection, while dense volumes of smoke ascended from a short distance to the clouds, and informed him that there was a terrific conflagration close at hand. The next moment a crowd of persons from the adjacent village rushed past him, shouting " Fire ! fire ! it is the chateau of the good Monsieur Aumaile." Ben Backstay now, for the first time, perceived that it did indeed come from that direction, and immediately entering the first cottage he arrived at, he left his fish in the care of an acquaintance, and followed, with all the speed he could, the crowd in the direction of the flames.

Too soon it was evident that the suspicions at first entertained were correct ; it was indeed the chateau of the benevolent Monsieur Aumaile that was burning, and before any assistance could reach it, the flames had reached such a fearful ascendancy, that all hopes of saving the building were at an end.

The anxiety and attention of every one was now devoted to saving Monsieur Aumaile, his daughter, and the rest of the inmates from the flames, for it was yet so early in the morning that it was not probable the family had arisen, and they might have fallen victims to the fury of the devouring element before they had an opportunity of effecting their escape.

We need not attempt to describe the agitation of honest Ben Backstay, as he contemplated the scene of devastation, and thought of what might probably be the fate of those who had been the benefactors of the poor and needy of the whole neighbourhood, and of whose assistance and counsel he, at the present time, stood so much in need. He rushed towards the burning chateau with the speed of lightning, and no sooner had he reached it, than the most frantic screams of terror met his ears, and, raising his eyes, he beheld at the casement of one of the rooms situated at the very top of the building, Monsieur Aumaile, standing in an attitude of frenzy and despair, with the form of his insensible daughter supported in his arms.

The destructive element was crackling and hissing close around them, and its fury was spreading rapidly towards the spot on which they stood, but yet was there no prospect of assistance to rescue them from their perilous situation.

"Oh! help! help!" cried Ben Backstay, "or our good benefactor and his daughter will perish!"

"Help!" said several of the persons assembled, in a breath, "alas! there is none. The flames have gained too powerful an ascendancy, and to attempt to reach the unfortunate gentleman and his daughter could only be attended with inevitable destruction."

The voice of Monsieur Aumaile was now heard in piteous accents, exclaiming,—

"God of Heaven!—oh! save my child, my Ninette. For myself I care not. But, oh! save my only one from so terrible a death."

"Clear decks, and prepare for action," shouted Ben Backstay, "at the hazard of my own life, I will make the attempt to rescue them whose lives are of so much more value than my own."

Before any one could attempt to prevent him, Ben rushed towards the entrance of the chateau, but terrific volumes of flames met him and drove him back, and he then perceived that to attempt to enter the burning pile would be madness, as it was all one entire mass of flame.

The next moment he was startled by a loud cry from the assembled multitude; and, raising his eyes once more towards the casement, he beheld, to his horror, that the flames had reached the spot where the unfortunate Monsieur Aumaile and his daughter were standing.

The glare of the conflagration fell awfully upon the features of Monsieur Aumaile, which were ghastly pale, and marked by the most livid and terrible despair. He still clasped the form of his daughter firmly in his arms; death seemed already to have put a period to her sufferings. Then he made one motion towards the casement, as if he would leap from it. The flames met him, and a frightful and appalling shriek followed, which was responded to by the persons assembled below. The flames had caught the light dress of the ill-fated Ninette, and the destructive element quickly enveloped the forms of her and her father.

It was an awful sight; but it was only for a moment; a loud, yet death-like crash was heard, immediately afterwards the rafters gave way, and Monsieur Aumaile and his daughter sunk into the midst of the burning pile, and were seen no more.

For a few minutes every person was paralyzed to the spot with horror, but at length, completely heart-sick with the dreadful sight he had so unexpectedly witnessed, poor Ben Backstay turned away from the place, and with a more melancholy heart than he had for many a day before experienced, he slowly retraced his footsteps towards his humble dwelling to apprize his family of the dreadful event that had taken place, and which had so suddenly deprived them and many others of such kind benefactors.

It would be impossible to describe as it deserves the grief and consternation of Marie and her mother, when they were made acquainted with the destruction of the chateau, and the appalling fate of Monsieur Aumaile and his daughter. It was a long time before it in any way abated, or Ben could find fortitude to converse with them on any other subject; but at length when he had become a little more composed, he inquired eagerly after the boy he had saved from the wreck.

"We have visited their chamber several times since you left the cottage," said Marie, "and they still appear to be wrapped in a refreshing sleep."

"Would that they would awake so that I might question the eldest of the two," said Ben, "who no doubt can afford me all the information I require, and which may afford me the opportunity of restoring them to their friends and relations, if they have any surviving. This calamity has deprived me of the aid and counsel I thought of obtaining; but I have no doubt that they are highly connected; and ——"

"Should you restore them to their relations," hastily added old Clotilde, "who knows but if they are wealthy people, it will make your fortune. I dare say they would very handsomely reward you."

"Reward!" cried Ben, "shame on you, mother, to think I seek any reward for the service I have done! No, shiver me; I should be unworthy the name that always attaches to the British sailor, if I was not always ready to perform my duty as a man ought to do it, from motives of Christianity, and not for gain. But this frightful adventure this morning has quite unmanned me; my nerves are all unhinged. Give me a glass of brandy, Marie. Poor Monsieur Aumaile and his unfortunate daughter! I shall never get them out of my eyes again, the longest day I live, and the terrific shriek they uttered when the burning rafters sunk beneath their feet ——"

"Oh! horrible! horrible!" groaned Marie, shuddering and covering her face with her hands, "I cannot bear it."

"Hark!"

"What has alarmed you now?" demanded his wife.

"It was like the piteous cry of some one in agony."

"No; no; it was only your imagination," said Marie.

"I tell you, woman," returned Ben, hastily, "it was no imagination. It seemed to proceed from the chamber up stairs. I heard it plainly."

"Ah! perhaps they have awakened and need our aid."

"There again!" said Ben, listening, "do you not hear it now?"

Marie and her mother answered in the affirmative, and, indeed, the sound was now plainly discernible. It was like the low moaning, the half stifled groans of some person in great pain, and seemed to proceed from the room up stairs in which the two shipwrecked boys had been placed; but it lasted only for an instant, and then all was as still as death.

Ben and the others looked at each other for a few seconds in astonishment.

"Something up stairs is wrong," said the former, "let us hasten and see what it is."

He immediately rushed out of the room as he spoke, and the others followed him. They opened the door quickly and entered the chamber, and what was their astonishment to behold the child rolling about the bed apparently convulsed and in great agony, while the elder one had dressed himself and quitted the place.

The window was standing wide open, with a portion of the bed-clothes attached to it, and which plainly showed that he had made his escape that way, but whatever could have been his motive for so doing they were at a loss to imagine.

They all hastily advanced to the bed, and there beheld the poor little fellow writhing in great pain, and apparently gasping for breath.

"The child is dying," exclaimed Ben; "there must have been something wrong here. Ah! see the black marks on his throat! Murder has been attempted."

"Murder! oh, by whom?" gasped Marie and her mother in a breath.

"Whom should we suspect but he who has fled?"

"One so young and attempt a crime so monstrous—impossible."

"Here are plainly the marks of fingers in the child's throat," said Ben; "the young villain has attempted to strangle him. Do all you can to save him, and I will hasten in pursuit of the young assassin, and to alarm the adjacent village. Should he escape justice will be defeated of her rights, and the secret of the poor little fellow's birth for ever remain in obscurity. I have already mentally vowed to be a protector to 'the foundling of the wreck,' and I will not be worse than my word."

Thus saying, Ben Backstay quitted the cottage in a great hurry, while Marie and her mother flew to look towards the recovery of the suffering child, completely paralyzed and horror-struck at the extraordinary and almost incredible character of the event.

CHAPTER II.—EPOCH II.

CHANGE OF SCENE AND CIRCUMSTANCES.—THE MARINER AND HIS FAMILY.—
THE PROTEGE.—THE SMUGGLER KING.—THE ALARM.

TWENTY years had elapsed since the events recorded in the previous chapter had taken place, and great was the change that had come over the different characters that have already been introduced to the reader O

Clotilde had been dead many years, and a distant relation of Mrs. Backstay's having died, bequeathed her a handsome annuity, and Ben having a wish to return to his native country after an absence of so many years, purchased a small farm in one of the pleasantest parts of Hampshire, where he determined to settle for the remainder of his days. Henry was married to a neighbouring farmer's daughter, and was very well to do in the world, and Fouchette had grown a very fine and lovely girl, with a countenance bewitching as her heart was virtuous. Great pains had been taken with the education of Fouchette, and possessing natural qualities of her own, she had profited well by the care that had been bestowed upon her. She was beloved by her parents and her brother, and admired by every person who saw or knew her.

But was the poor foundling, the child that Ben and his son had so miraculously preserved from the wreck still living? He was, and from that time had been brought up by his kind protector, and looked upon him as a father.

A few days after the abrupt departure of the lad, who had been saved with him, and who had made an attempt upon his life, the child was perfectly restored to health, but he was too young for them to be able to elicit anything satisfactory from him. All that they were enabled to gather from him was, that, "he had lost poor papa in the great house upon the water, and that he wore pretty clothes, with gold and silver all over them." But when they questioned him about the young midshipman who had been saved with him, he seemed at a loss to answer them, and appeared very much alarmed, saying, "he had pinched him," which left no doubt upon their minds that he had made an attempt to murder the child. But what motives could induce a lad of such tender years to try to commit a crime of such atrocity, they racked their brains in vain to endeavour to imagine.

Weeks, months, passed away, and notwithstanding all the inquiries made by Backstay and others, they did not succeed in ascertaining the least clue to guide them to the friends and relations of the foundling, nor was there anything found about him that might lead to the discovery of to whom he belonged, although there could not be the least doubt but that he was the child of wealthy, if not noble parents, who had in all probability perished in the ill-fated vessel, which had gone to pieces entirely, and not the smallest particle was seen of her afterwards, and thus everything seemed likely to be for ever involved in mystery.

The fisherman and his wife did not repine at this extra burthen upon their limited means, but on the contrary, the engaging manners of the little foundling quickly endeared him to them as much as if he had been one of their own children, and Harry and Fouchette were taught to call him their little ocean brother.

From the child they learned that his Christian name was William, and after the lapse of a year or two, he was recognised by every one as William Backstay, or by others he was called, "The Child of the Wreck!"

William grew apace in beauty, and early evinced the noble virtues that predominated in his mind. He was generous, spirited, and with a cheerfulness of disposition that never suffered anything to interrupt it. He was the delight of Ben and his wife, and the never-tiring companion of Henry, and the playmate of Fouchette, who was dull and unhappy when her little "foundling brother" was out of her sight.

Old Clotilde had sunk peacefully into the grave about two years, when a brother of hers, who had for many years been estranged from her, and had amassed a considerable fortune, also expired and left to Mrs. Backstay a very liberal annuity for life, which was afterwards to descend to her children. It was then that her husband proposed retiring to England, being anxious to pass the remainder of his days in his native land, and moreover, he could not divest his mind of an impression that had long taken possession of it, that he should there at some future period be fortunate enough to trace the origin of his adopted child, and probably be able to restore him to his friends and that rank in society which he felt confident he was born to fill.

Mrs. Backstay, who had now no tie, no kindred to find in her native land, willingly assented to this arrangement, and in a few weeks having arranged all their affairs, they departed for England, where they arrived safe, and shortly afterwards Ben Backstay purchased the farm in which we have now seen him comfortably situated. He had chosen a spot where he was well known, and he soon had many of his old acquaintances around him, among whom were several of his old shipmates, and after the labours of the day were over, the honest farmer's greatest delight was to smoke his pipe in his pretty and well arranged garden, in company with these old sons of the ocean, exchanging yarn for yarn ; recounting the adventures they had shared together, and detailing the particulars of those great naval victories that had stamped the fame and glory of Old England, and achieved for her a superiority over all other nations of the globe.

During these times, it was young William's greatest delight to be present that he might listen to the many spirit-stirring narratives his adopted parent and the veterans his companions would recount. They fired his young and ardent spirit, and filled him with a burning desire to mingle in similar scenes to those which he heard them describe, and to brave the perils of that boundless deep, with which he had in childhood become associated.

In this manner many years had rolled away, and many material changes had taken place in the family of Ben Backstay, as we have before stated.

It was a beautiful afternoon, in 1797, a few weeks after the victory obtained by Lord Duncan at Camperdown, when Ben having mustered together a few of his chosen friends, among whom was his old particular, who was known by the cognomen of " Commodore Jack," was seated as usual in the garden attached to his farm, and enjoying the luxury of a pipe and a pitcher of excellent ale. On his right hand was seated his comely-looking dame, busily occupied in knitting, but at the same time paying every attention to the conversation that was going forward. On a garden-seat, round which twined the honeysuckle, were seated Henry Backstay and his handsome young wife, in company with Fouchette, while, leaning gracefully over the elbow of the seat was a female form of such grace and loveliness, that the eyes must swim in rapture and admiration that gazed upon her.

This was Flora Clarendon, the younger sister of Henry's wife, and the admired and beloved of the neighbourhood in which she resided.

All the charms and graces that nature could bestow upon one human being, were combined in the mind, the form, and features of Flora Clarendon. Her countenance was the very perfection of beauty, and at the age of eighteen bloomed forth in all the rich luxuriance of lovely womanhood. Her clear blue eyes brilliantly sparkled with every kindly and virtuous feeling, and the long silken lashes that shaded them, and the beautifully arched brows that surmounted them, would have defied the pencil of the most skilful artist to have done justice to. But who shall describe the beauty of those auburn tresses, that without the aid of art, flowed in such graceful and luxuriant ringlets over one of the whitest and most sweetly moulded necks that human eyes ever feasted on ? And then the delicate blossom of her cheeks ; the rosy richness of her lips, round which a myriad of little loves and fascinations ever played ; the transparent whiteness of her teeth ! But language, however eloquent, must fail to pourtray as they merit, or give even a faint idea of the transcendant beauties of the simple, the noble-minded, and generous Flora Clarendon.

Such was the fair maiden that formed one of the party on this occasion, and who shed a lustre upon all around her. But her countenance was now sad, and tears might be observed occasionally (as painful thoughts arose) trembling in her eyes ; while the agitated heaving of her bosom, showed that some heavy sorrow lay deep at her heart.

Her sister and Fouchette watched her looks with the deepest solicitude and affection, and every now and then ventured to whisper words of love and consolation to her ear.   Her intelligent eyes beamed the expression of her gratitude, but it was evident that her sorrow was too poignant to admit of that comfort which they so affectionately sought to impart.

Old Ben Backstay had been reading the account of the Battle of Camperdown, to which his messmates, as he still called the old tars that were gathered round him, listened with the most profound attention and lively interest, and the other persons present with the deepest emotion, particularly Flora, whose tears as the former proceeded with his account, in spite of all her efforts to restrain them, burst forth, and she sunk into the seat by the side of Fouchette, and hid her beauteous face in her bosom.

"Poor girl ! poor girl !" said Ben Backstay (as he still liked to called) in a voice of the deepest sympathy ; " she has lost the rudder and compass of hope and consolation, and is tossed about on the rough sea of doubt and apprehension.   But cheer up, Flora, my lass ; he will return—he will return, never fear.   The Almighty Commander who rules everything, will not suffer the happiness of one so young, so pretty, and so innocent, to be wrecked entirely on the shoals of adversity !"

Poor Flora sobbed bitterly, but could not speak ; her heart was too full,— and her emotions were far beyond the power of consolation.

"Heaven send it !" said Mrs. Backstay, in reply to her husband's observations, and looking up from her knitting as she spoke, " poor noble-minded lad ; I dare say he has fought hard in the battle, and won golden opinions from his officers."

"Ay, ay, dame," said Commodore Jack, " I'll warrant he has made some of the enemy skip abit ; for he was a neat trim-built lad ; jist sich another as myself, when I first went aboard the " Thunderer," 'under'd and twenty. I know'd no danger, feared no trouble then ; I was all red hot as a cannonball for mischief among the enemies of Old England, and, as my captain used to say, 'Jack,' says he, 'Jack' ——"

"There, there, Jack," interrupted another of the old seamen who were present, " belay your palaver for th' present about that, don't yer see th' young lady get's paler at every word yer say? Ah ! poor thing, I do not wonder at her being sorrowful, for a sweetheart's a sweetheart arter all, and when we come to think of the perils of the battle, how many a brave fellow's head's laid low, how many a lad unprepared is called to his last reckoning aloft, in this here engagement, we ——"

"Avast! avast! Harry Spritsail !" interrupted the farmer, "don't you see how you are torturing the poor thing? Come, Flora, lass ; look up, that's a dear, and smile again like the bright golden sun upon the ocean after a storm. When I was at sea, they always used to reckon me as good as a prophet ; I was always as merry as a grig, and when I saw any of my messmates downhearted, which was not often the case, for sailors are not the chaps to despair at trifles, I used to cheer them up by predicting good fortune, and somehow or the other it always used to turn out pretty correct.   Now on this point I will assume my old character, and prophecy that poor William will not only return safe with the fleet that is expected in a few days, but crowned with honourable promotion, and what a happiness that will be I know to my pretty Flora, to what it would have been for a lad of her lover's mettle to have remained idling at home, while the fair forms and sparkling eyes of his countrywomen were pleading to him to lend his aid in resisting foreign invasion."

The words of the farmer animated the noble mind of Flora ; her bosom swelled at the mention of her lover's name, and the idea of the promotion and honour he had no doubt won, if he lived to survive the battle in which he had been engaged, and smiling through her tears, she warmly returned the pressure of Ben Backstay's hand, and, although she was unable to give expression to her feelings, her brightened countenance spoke more eloquently than language could have done.

"Your protege has now been some time at sea, Ben," observed one of the sailors.

"A matter of thirteen years."

"And during that time you have never been able to discover who his parents were, or with whom he was connected?"

"No," answered Ben, "and I suppose I never shall; and to tell the truth, only that it might be the means of bettering the lad's fortune, I have no wish, for, I need not say that I, and all of us love him, as if he were our own, and it would break all our hearts if we were to be deprived of him."

"Ay, ay, I have no doubt of it," observed Commodore Jack; "but you have made him acquainted with all the particulars of the manner in which you found him?"

"Everything," answered Ben, "and I verily believe that if he was to discover himself to be the son of a lord or a duke, such is his attachment to us, that he would willingly resign wealth and rank rather than part from us, if he could not share his good fortune with us."

"He is a brave lad, an excellent lad," said another of the tars, "and worthy of being a commander instead of a common blue jacket."

"From a child," resumed Ben, "he conceived the most enthusiastic notions of a seaman's life; he had heard us talk of the perils of the deep; the moving scenes of the ocean's storm, and the battle's fury, and his natural brave young heart glowed. Nothing would do but he must go to sea, and mingle in all those scenes he had heard described. I could not check his laudable desires, and to tell the truth, neither had I the desire; and I am certain that should we ever discover his real friends and connections, let them be ever so situated in the world, they will have no cause to regret that he has learnt in the vicissitudes of life, and in the struggles for his country's rights and liberty, to estimate more powerfully the blessings which it may please Providence in future to bestow upon him."

"Well said Ben, my hearty," observed Commodore Jack, "a man-o'-war's th' best in th' world to teach a young man morals, and d—me, talk about boarding-schools, where's there a better boarding-school than a line-o'-battle-ship in a hot engagement. Hurrah! for Admiral Duncan."

"And hurrah for Sir John Jervis, whose glorious victory off Cape St. Vincent, has added another gem to the brilliancy of British valour," exclaimed a grey-headed veteran, of benevolent and healthy aspect, who, engaged in the luxuries of his pipe, had hitherto contented himself by listening to the conversation that was going forward, without making any remark of his own.

"Ay, he is a brave fellow, and made the Spaniards cry peccavi, as well as Duncan did these fat hided rascals, the Dutch, at Camperdown," said Commodore Jack.

"So Basilwood Hall is at last sold and occupied," said Henry Backstay, who saw that the present conversation was too painful for his sister-in-law, and was anxious to change the topic.

"So I hear," replied his father, "and the present possessor is ——"

"One Sir Julian Mordlington, a man of great wealth."

"And his character?"

"From all that I have heard, he bears no good reputation," answered Henry. "He is what is called a man-of fashion, a *roue*, generally the nicknames of arrant scoundrels, who make use of the fortune Providence has lavished upon them, to tyrannise over the more humble but honest of their fellow creatures, and consider their property a *carte blanche* for all kinds of villany, dissipation, and profligacy."

"A very pretty character to enter upon a man's log-book," remarked Commodore Jack, "but I have no doubt a very true one, for I have in the course of my cruise through life experienced some'at of these here gew-gaw, gingerbread land-lubbers."

"From his name he is an Englishman," said Ben.

"He is," answered his son. "He has for some time been sojourning among the giddy scenes of London, and the frivolities of Paris ; but I have heard that he has been many years at sea, and there is that in the appearance of his sunburnt countenance which carries out the report."

"You have seen him then ?"

"Several times since he has been at the hall."

"And what description of man is he ?" inquired Ben.

"Tall, about thirty years of age, and rather handsome," answered Henry ; "but still there is something about his eyes, the curl of his lip, and the general expression of his countenance, which is extremely disagreeable. He has the appearance of a naval officer."

Flora uttered a cry of emotion which attracted the attention and excited the curiosity of all present. They beheld her pale and trembling, and clinging to Fouchette for support.

"Why, child, child," said Mrs. Backstay, "what is the matter with you, my love ? What is it that thus agitates you ? Bless me, how very pale you look."

"That man—that man !" gasped forth Flora, "the very mention of his name——"

"What man do you allude to, my lass ?" inquired old Ben Backstay, kindly.

"This—this Sir Julian, the new lord of the manor, that Mr. Henry, your son, has been mentioning," replied Flora.

"You know him then ?"

"No, no ; but——"

"But what, my poor girl ?" said Ben, hastily ; come, come, do not be afraid to speak, for Ben Backstay is not yet too old to see you righted, if occasion should require. What is it that causes your emotion at the mention of this Sir Julian Thingembob's name ?"

"This morning I met him as I was crossing the lawn near the hall, and —"

"And what ?" demanded old Ben, his feelings, from suspicion, beginning to be aroused, and the colour mounting still more powerfully to his usually rubicund visage."

"He—he insulted me !" said the maiden, in a timid voice, and she drooped her head.

"Insulted you !" shouted Ben and his son in a breath, and starting to their feet, while indignation inflamed their countenances.

"D—n me !" continued the former, after a pause, "he shall pay dearly for this, though he be Sir Julian Mordlington, Baronet, or if he were even fifty Sir Julians. Insult the daughter of my dearest friend, the—the—d—n him for a scoundrel and a villain !"

"Nay, my dear sir," said Flora, "perhaps I have been too hasty—have judged too hastily ; Sir Julian might have meant no harm. He merely stopped me, and passed some fulsome compliments upon me, which he, mixing as he has done in the world of fashion, might have thought ——"

"Confound what he thought," said the honest farmer, passionately ; "he knew that such empty compliments as those he might use to the senseless victims of adulation, the votaries of fashion and vanity, would be insults to rustic simplicity and virtuous innocence, and his real character may be discovered in a moment. He is evidently an unprincipled villain; but he may find himself deceived if he thinks to carry on his base practices here, and—but you are agitated, my poor girl, and we will e'en drop the subject for the present. You are safe under the protection of your parents and your friends, and should the new lord of the manor repeat his insults, he may find that even his rank and wealth may not be sufficient to protect him from the just vengeance of honest poverty and virtue."

The good old man pressed tenderly the delicate hand of the fair maiden as he spoke, who, with tear-bedimmed eyes, beamed upon him her most heartfelt gratitude and love.

Flora evidently regretted that she had spoken what she had done, for although her strict sense of virtue rendered her tenacious of the slightest insult, her generous nature led her to put at all times the most favourable construction upon the intentions and actions of her fellow-creatures.

"You say," observed Joe Helm, after a pause of a few moments had ensued, addressing himself to Henry Backstay, "that this Sir Julian What-do-you-call-him, has the appearance of a seafaring man?"

"Yes," replied Henry, "and I have also heard that he has been many years at sea."

"And his age?"

"He appears to be about thirty, or he may be more."

"Handsome?"

"Yes."

"Tall?"

"And commanding in appearance."

"Noticed you a scar on his left cheek?" demanded Joe Helm.

"I did," answered Henry, "and from the hasty glimpse I had of it, it appeared to be a sabre wound."

"Ah! the very same; I'd lay my life on it."

"The same," said Ben Backstay, "who—who—what mean you by the questions you have put to my son, Joe?"

"Have you never heard of the Smuggler King?" inquired Joe.

"Ay, ay," answered Ben and the other old seaman.

"He who for the last ten years has been the sovereign of all the smugglers and pirates that infest the bosom of the deep blue waters?" added Joe Helm; "their regular elected monarch, whose word has guided all their actions, and whose very name has struck terror to the mind of the mariner, and afforded subject for all the gossips and wonder-mongers in the universe?"

"We have! we have!"

"He is supposed to be a person of noble birth and fortune," continued Joe, "whom a love of the adventurous, and a natural propensity for scenes of plunder and bloodshed, have plunged into his present course of life."

"Well, Joe," inquired Ben Backstay, "and what has that to do with the subject we have been talking upon?"

"The description your son has given of this Sir Julian exactly corresponds with that of the Smuggler King," answered Joe.

The persons present all started, and looked at Joe in amazement.

"What," said Ben Backstay, "a baronet, a man of wealth and rank, a fashionable lounger among the follies of London and Paris, to be mistaken for the sovereign of smugglers and pirates?"

"Ay, Ben," returned Joe Helm, "such is the character of the Smuggler King. He mingles in the fashionable world, without any one being aware of who he is. He is the accomplished villain, the gentlemanly cutthroat, the adept in every species of refined villany!"

"You have seen him then?"

"Once only, to my cost, when every soul on board but myself and a black cook were sacrificed, and we only escaped by a perfect miracle, after leaping overboard."

"Why, what a monster he must be."

"The blackest scoundrel that ever escaped a gibbet."

"And yet so young!"

"True."

"But you say he is not always on the ocean?" said Commodore Jack.

"No," answered Joe, "his movements are so secret and so well contrived, that it is impossible to form an idea where you may expect to find him."

"But should you know him again if you were to see him?" asked Ben.

"I think I should."

"My eyes, Joe," said Commodore Jack, "if this lubber, this land-shark, this Sir Julian, or whatever you may call him, should turn out to be the —"

At that moment the observations of Commodore Jack were interrupted by a loud scream of terror from Flora Clarendon, who had walked to the gate of the garden, and had been for a few moments leaning listlessly over it. They all flew towards her in a moment, and she sunk pale, trembling, and violently agitated in the arms of the trembling Mrs. Backstay.

"For Heaven's sake, my dear child," said the old woman, "what has thus alarmed you?"

Flora endeavoured to speak, but could not; she pointed towards the lawn, beyond the garden wall, and they all looked eagerly in that direction, but could not observe the least thing to account for her excessive terror.

"Tell me, lass," said old Ben, "what is it that has frightened you so much?"

"A form—a frightful form," replied Flora, with difficulty, "appeared before me, and scowling upon me, retired with the speed of a phantom, uttering a malicious laugh."

"Imagination, child," observed Marie.

"Or, mayhap," remarked her husband, "it was Crazy Marian, the poor witless woman, who for the last four years has infested this neighbourhood, subsisting on the benevolence of the inhabitants of the village, and singing those wild ditties that have never failed to excite the deepest sympathy. Poor creature, she must have suffered greatly to have reduced her to her wretched state."

"Oh, no," returned Flora, "it was not her, or I should not have been alarmed; for, poor unfortunate, she would not harm anybody. It was a man!"

"A man?"

"Yes, of the most ferocious aspect, and habited as a smuggler."

"Oh!" observed Ben, with a half smile, "the story that Joe Helm has been telling of the Smuggler King has preyed upon your imagination."

"No, no, my dear sir," answered Flora, "I am positive I was not deceived. I saw the man as plainly as I now behold every person present."

"Indeed," ejaculated Commodore Jack, "then come, my lads, let us weigh anchor, and spread all our canvass in pursuit. We are not yet so old but that we can prove that we are still a match for any piratical rascals we may come athwart of. Good evening, Ben, good evening, dame—good evening all!"

Ben Backstay heartily responded to the good evening of Commodore Jack, and the latter and his companions immediately took their departure. The farmer and his family, with Flora, who had become more composed, then retired into the house.

CHAPTER III.

AN UNEXPECTED GUEST.—A MANLY HEART.

AFTER some conversation, and when the feelings of Flora Clarendon had become pretty tranquillized, she took her departure from home, accompanied by Henry Backstay and her sister. They had not been gone more than a quarter of an hour, when the bell that communicated with the farm was pulled violently, and in a few minutes the servant entered the parlour in which Ben and his family were seated, and informed his master that a singular-looking gentleman requested to see him.

"Did he not leave his name?" inquired the farmer.

"No, sir," replied the servant, "he said he was an entire stranger to you."

"An entire stranger," returned Ben Backstay; "then what the devil can he have to say to me? What sort of a man is he, Jemmy?"

"A very funny-looking man," replied Jemmy, "and with such a curious way of talking—oh, I never!"

"Well, hoist all sail, and convey him hither, Jemmy," commanded Ben Backstay, "and let us see what sort of a looking craft he is, and hear what it is he wants."

Jemmy departed in obedience to these instructions, and in a few moments returned, escorting in a middle-aged man of very respectable exterior, but certainly altogether, as Jemmy had described, of rather singular appearance.

He was attired in a travelling coat, not made very fashionable; he carried a small portmanteau under his arm, a broad-brimmed straw hat surmounted his head, which was further secured to the same by a number of handkerchiefs that were tied under his jaws. His countenance was redolent of health, good humour, and an honest and kindly heart and although

No. 3

Ben Backstay was certainly surprised at his visit, he was far from being un-prepossessed in his favour.

"Your pardon, ladies—your pardon, sir," said the stranger, speaking with a rich Irish brogue, and bowing very politely; "your pardon for thus intruding upon you. I am Patrick Fitzpatrick, Esq., solicitor, of London. I have been absent on business for some time, faith, and have come here upon mighty big business. The inn being entirely full, and being anxious to put up somewhere for the night, I was recommended to apply to you, sir, who I was assured would be happy to afford me every accommodation in your power."

"To such accommodation as I can offer you, sir," replied Ben Backstay, "you are most cordially welcome. Pray be seated, sir. Jemmy, take charge of the gentleman's portmanteau. Fouchette, prepare the supper."

"Och! and by my sowl, then, I am in England again," ejaculated Mr. Fitzpatrick, seizing Ben's hand with a fervent grasp. "Och! and many thanks to you, my dear sir; you are the pleasantest fellow I have met with since I left this country. Och! botheration! and may it never fall to the lot of my own dear self to travel from this beautiful land again, unless it be to my own dear native isle."

The gentleman whom we have thus introduced to our readers, as Mr. Patrick Fitzpatrick, was a man of unimpeached character, who had grown rich, not by the chicanery of the law, but by its honest, honourable exercise. He was a bachelor, something past the middle age, and had many peculiarities in his disposition, among which was the pride of being a branch of a very ancient Milesian family. He had been absent from London for several years, on matters of importance, and in the prosecution of that business he had lately visited France, of which, its manners, and inhabitants, he entertained the most profound disgust and contempt. During his absence he had left the management of his business and his affairs to his confidential and faithful clerk, Flym, and he expected and hoped in a short time to be able to rejoin him.

Having disencumbered himself of his hat, and the superfluity of hand-kerchiefs, Mr. Fitzpatrick, taking a seat in the chimney corner opposite Ben Backstay, seemed to feel himself as much at home as if he had been acquainted with the farmer for years, and had been on the most intimate and visiting terms; and Ben, for his part, was as much prepossessed in favour of the solicitor as it was possible he could be with him.

"Have you travelled far, sir?" inquired Ben.

"Faith, no," answered the solicitor. "The farthest place I have been to is France; and bad luck to me if ever I was in such a scurvy country before, wid their *parley woos* and *Jenny Squaws*. Och! botheration! and didn't I wish myself in old England again, and with my confidential clerk, Flym, who is stuck up in my office, I dare say fretting himself as thin as the skin of parchment he is engrossing, with impatience at my long stay and thinking when I get back to find me metamorphosed from a plain, blunt Irishman, into a French jackanapes, all fluster and frothy palaver, bowing and scraping, and nodding their heads like so many Chinese images on a mantel-piece."

"Then you do not like the mounseers, sir?" said Ben Backstay, laughing, while his wife certainly evinced no very good humour at the description which Mr. Fitzpatrick gave of her country and countrymen.

"Och! botheration! the devil burn the whole kit of them," returned the solicitor. "I never was among such a set of nondescripts before in the whole course of my life. Tunder and turf! and yet it is from these fantastic skipping monkeys, that Englishmen go to learn elegance and politeness. But by my sowl, it is only a mutual exchange of compliments, that's all; for many a time have our brave lads of the land and the ocean taught them to dance to another tune. But bad luck to the fashion, for it is a monstrous one, which induces our countrymen to be pouring over to France and other parts of the continent in shoals to waste and lavish the money upon foreign fripperies that would be of so much service if properly circulated to the starving population at home."

"You are right, sir," said Ben, "and I commend your honest feeling. But have you long returned to England?"

"I only arrived yesterday," answered Mr. Fitzpatrick; "and by my sowl, glad enough I was when I once more set my foot on these precious shores. Bad luck to me, what a voyage I had, to be sure. Och! botheration! I never was among such a set of spalpeens in my life. There was one lady entreating that the captain would keep the vessel from rolling, and another insisting on being set on shore; one calling for a pail, another for a glass of cogniac; some eating, some smoking, some snoring; there was groaning in one corner, and praying in another; children squalling, sailors swearing; poultry cackling, and pigs grunting. Och! botheration! the confusion of Babel, sure, was nothing to be compared with it."

"Ha! ha! ha!" laughed Ben; "a very pretty description you give of it, sir. But here is Fouchette with the supper. Now, sir, pray take your seat at the table, and make yourself at home, for you are heartily welcome."

"By the powers!" returned the solicitor, "I see I am; and as I am as hungry as a hunter, there is no doubt but that I shall do full justice to your excellent fare."

Mr. Fitzpatrick kept his word, and having made a hearty meal, he once more took his seat in the chimney-corner.

"Is Basilwood Hall far from here?" inquired the solicitor.

"It is little more than a mile," replied the farmer.

"Indeed, so near?" said Mr. Fitzpatrick; "if I had known that I might have proceeded on my journey; but as I am here, by my sowl, I will intrude upon your hospitality for to-night."

"To which you are quite welcome, sir," said Ben. "Basilwood Hall is then the place of your destination?"

"It is," answered the solicitor, "and if I am informed rightly, it has lately been purchased, and is now occupied by one Sir Julian Mordlington?"

"True," said Ben.

"And know you what sort of a man he is?"

"I have never seen him," replied the farmer; "but I have been informed that he is about thirty years of age, tall, and handsome; but with a countenance upon the whole not very prepossessing. He has the appearance of a man who has passed some years at sea."

"Och! sure! and it must be himself, the description answers in every particular," observed Mr. Fitzpatrick.

"You know the baronet then, sir?" said Ben.

"To be sure I do," returned the solicitor, "and, by the powers, he is likely to know a little more of me than he will fancy before I have done with him."

"If report speaks truly, he bears no very good character!"

"Och! then that is him, his own dear self, to a dead certainty. Report in that same thing has been no liar, or I am much deceived. Och! and won't he be flabbergasted when he sees me! Och, splithereens and tenpennies! Basilwood Hall shall be honoured by my own darling self tomorrow morning, if I live as long. But I am tired, and will feel obliged to you if you will show me to my chamber. Good night, ladies, and sweet repose to you. Mr. Backstay, if you please, och, you and I must become better acquainted."

"I shall be most happy, sir," replied Ben; "you will find me an honest man, although only an humble one."

"Och! botheration to the humbleness, man!" exclaimed the warm-hearted Irishman, "isn't an honest man the noblest work of God? I attend you, Mr. Backstay. Once more, good night, ladies, and pleasant dreams and many of them to you!"

Bowing politely to Fouchette and her mother, Mr. Fitzpatrick followed Ben to the clean and comfortable chamber that had been quickly prepared for his reception; and again shaking him cordially by the hand, and reiterating his thanks for his hospitality, he bade him good night, and Ben left him.

The farmer returned to the parlour, and after having some conversation with his wife and daughter upon the eccentricities of their unexpected guest, and as to what could be his business at the hall, they also retired to rest.

CHAPTER IV.

SIR JULIAN MORDLINGTON.—FAMILY SECRETS.—THE SEA-DEVIL.—CON-SCIENCE.—THE SMUGGLERS.—THE MEETING.

In an elegant apartment in Basilwood Hall, on the morning after the events just related had taken place, lounging upon a sofa, in fashionable dishabille, was Sir Julian Mordlington, apparently wrapped in deep meditation. His brows were contracted, and there was an expression about the curl of his lip, which plainly indicated that his mind was occupied by some important and painful thoughts. Suddenly he arose, and placing one hand in his breast, he paced the apartment in a state of great mental agitation.

"I cannot get it from my thoughts ever since I have heard the name mentioned," he at length muttered to himself;—"Ben Backstay! yes, I am certain it was so they called him; and should it be he—but, pshaw!—Why do I torture myself?—Should this farmer really prove to be the same man, what have I to fear from him?—Have I not power, wealth, everything to protect me from any danger that might threaten me? Besides, it is not likely that, after the lapse of so many years he would recollect me now, especially as I was but a boy when—but I dare not think of that crime! After all the atrocities I have since committed that one rises paramount in my conscience, and freezes my blood! I began my career of bloodshed by times! Oh, it was a hellish deed! and in the midst of all the scenes of revelry I have flown to, to banish thought, the writhing agonies of that little innocent, as I pressed my fingers upon his throat, have been ever present to my eyes, as if the deed had only that moment been perpetrated!—But it was a bold deed!—a daring deed, and procured me wealth in abundance! He must have died,—he must have died, for I could swear that I saw him heave his last gasp before I made my escape. But let me not think of it! Where can that fellow, Sam Raker, be?—I expected to see him last night, and he is usually so punctual. Ha, ha, ha! little do those who court my society, who lavish upon me their flattery, and exhaust all their powers of adulation, suspect my real character. I have played my cards with admirable skill, and have now more power than ever to become a very devil. But I must use caution, and for awhile the boundless ocean must not be graced by my sovereign presence. This goodly hall will suit my purpose well; suspicion dare not light upon me, and here my victims may move among the very splendour of which they have been plundered! ha, ha, ha! I like the life of the debauchee on land, and the sovereign on the deep. Fools bow to me on shore, while those who plow the ocean tremble at my name. I am powerful, terrible everywhere; and yet, am I happy? Yes, yes, I will be so. It is the coward only that suffers himself to be subdued by the bugaboo, and it is the province of a man of my desperate character to laugh such fools to derision, not to yield to the same weakness myself. That girl—that fair, that beauteous girl, whom I yesterday saw, has haunted my imagination ever since. Never did I, among all the beauties with whom it has been my good fortune to be favourably received, ever behold one to approach her in loveliness and fascination. She realises all that I have heard of those ideal creatures of immortality. Such grace, such simplicity, such angelic sweetness of countenance. By Heaven! she has set my very blood on fire! she haunted the visions of my slumber last night, and will continue to occupy my thoughts until I gain possession of her, which I am determined to do, even though it cost me my life in the effort. Once on board one of my bonny craft, she is mine—mine beyond the power of redemption. Fit maiden is she to become the Queen of the Ocean, and once possessed of her, who will then be so proud, so triumphant as the Smuggler King?"

The baronet traversed the apartment for a few minutes in silence, and wrapt in deep thought, the principal portion of which was devoted to Flora Clarendon, and the means to be adopted to get that lovely damsel in his power, and force her to yield to his vicious propensities.

Sir Julian Mordlington had mingled with the gayest of the gay, and received the favours of the most beauteous of the sex, and had seldom came off without a triumph in his amours; but although such conquests had flattered his vices, and given him a most unmitigated and unlimited opinion of his own powers of fascination, he felt a certain sensation of awe in approaching Flora Clarendon, which was strangely at variance with his real character. He believed her to be humble, and might have flattered himself with an easy conquest, but still there is something about genuine virtue that possesses the power of daunting the most daring spirits of villany. He felt his own weakness before the strength of that fair maiden's invulnerable shield of purity, and doubted, while at the same time he made sure of his triumph. Possessed of natural good sense and acquirements, which, if devoted to a proper use, would have calculated him to shine in an elevated position in society, Sir Julian could not but warmly admire the brightest perfections of human nature, but at the same time his principles would not allow him to do justice to them in his own conduct. By accident he had early been left to the guidance, the unrestricted control of his own passions, which being naturally base, and thus divested of the only means of arresting them, deprived of every means of guiding and advising him, he had become as it were, naturalized with every bad feeling, and given unlimited indulgence to his wicked propensities. Not contented with all the advantages that fortune could bestow, he had sought a still wider range for the indulgence of his vices, in which he had succeeded to an extraordinary degree, as will be shewn in the course of this narrative. He had basked in the smiles of the courtezan until he was completely satiated, and now he looked to the destruction of female innocence as his greatest triumphs. Splendid offers of matrimony had been made to him, but he rejected them with contempt, and that in spite of the mystery, the unfathomable mystery that was attached to his character, and which often formed the topic of conversation in the different fashionable circles in which he was wont to mingle, and where he used to predominate as a perfect star.

In London and in Paris, Sir Julian was the courted, the admired of the fashionable circles, and wherever he went, a brilliant train of the *elite* of the aristocratic world was sure to follow. Sometimes he would disappear for months, and no one could tell what had become of him. His establishment would be broken up, and the greatest mystery prevailed as to where he was gone, or whether it was likely that he would again appear amongst that society of which he had formed the ornamental, and the chief magnet of attraction. Suddenly, however, Sir Julian would drop among these brilliant coteries again, like a star from the heavens, shining forth in greater splendour than ever, and always living in a style of princely magnificence. No one ventured to make an inquiry as to where he had absented himself, for they knew that they could never obtain any satisfactory answer; and while he gave splendid banquets, feasted the great, pandered to the taste of the gay and the dissipated, catered for the tastes of the giddy votaries of fashion, and flattered the fair sex, they cared very little what he did while he was away from them, and had he even been a second Jack Sheppard, Paul Clifford, or Claude Du Val, it would, no doubt, have been treated as a matter of equal indifference by them.

Sir Julian, as has been seen, was a handsome man, possessed of innumerable accomplishments, and everything to advance his views in the world, and well did he avail himself of them. Of his early history only this was generally known :—He was the son of General Harlington, by his first wife, who claimed no affinity with rank or title. She was the youngest daughter of a wealthy merchant, who falling in love with the handsome Colonel Harlington at a fashionable ball, yielded to his proposals, and bestowed her fair hand and thirty thousand pounds upon him.

It was on the colonel's side, a match of prudence; he was the younger son of a family of rank, and had at that time, of worldly possessions, little more than his pay. But though he was not passionately attached to the lady who bore his name, he made an exemplary husband, paying her every attention during a long illness, of which she died, just as Julian, their only child, had attained his sixth year.

Colonel Harlington paid every respect to the memory of his wife, yet he was not inconsolable for her loss, which was rendered still lighter by his becoming heir at this time, to his maternal uncle, who left him two estates in the north of England, and this accession to fortune was soon followed by a baronetcy, and his promotion to the rank of general.

Hitherto Sir Clarence Mordlington (as he was now by title and name) had escaped the all powerful influences of the little blind deity, but that delectable hour, which sooner or later is sure to arrive, was swiftly approaching.

At the Court of St. James's, when he went to be presented on his promotion, he encountered the beauteous and accomplished Lady Emmeline Montobello, at that time in her eighteenth year. In her he beheld the modest grace of unconscious loveliness, the blushing timidity of innocence; and these charms made an instant impression upon his heart, and convinced him, that, of all her sex, Lady Emmeline could alone make him happy.

It was not long ere an introduction was brought about, and mutual affection united the tie, that connected this amiable but unfortunate pair.

But a few months after Lady Mordlington had given birth to a son, their happiness was overturned by a circumstance which will be explained in the course of this narrative. Whether the unfortunate lady was guilty of the errors laid to her charge was at that time a matter of speculation, but a separation was the consequence, and General Mordlington being appointed Governor in India, departed from England with both his children, and left his beauteous wife to misery and despair.

In a short time afterwards Lady Mordlington disappeared, and notwith-standing the anxious and indefatigable inquiries of her friends, nothing whatever could be heard of her, and it was generally supposed that she had either died of a broken heart in some place of obscurity, or that she had laid violent hands on herself.

General Sir Clarence Mordlington had only remained little more than three years in his appointment, when he was recalled to England by govern-ment, in consequence of a change in the administration. The vessel was wrecked on its voyage home, and of all that were supposed to survive that calamity was Julian Harlington, now Sir Julian Mordlington, the son of the general by his first marriage.

He was then not more than fourteen years of age, and related a wonderful story of the manner in which he had been preserved from the wreck, which was generally believed. He placed himself under the care of a lawyer, Mr. Patrick Fitzpatrick, who had had the management of his father's affairs, supplying him with all proper necessaries for his rank and station.

The young baronet, destitute of those natural feelings that belong to our common humanity, rather exulted than bemoaned the loss of his affec-tionate father, believing himself the sole possessor of his immense wealth, as he knew not that his father had left a will, and if he even had, he ima-gined that he had rid himself of the only obstacle to the full enjoyment of all his wealth, and he looked forward to the future with the most sanguine hopes and proudest ambition.

Mr. Fitzpatrick he had seen but two or three times, the business of that gentleman calling him to London, and in fact, he dreaded his society, for there was something in the manners of the honest Irishman, which led him to look upon him with suspicion, and at times the uncertainty of the death of his brother, and the existence of a will, although he had never ventured to question the lawyer upon the subject, and the latter had never thrown out the least hint upon the matter, caused him much anxiety and uneasiness of mind.

At length, much to his relief, the solicitor left England, and his means being unlimited, he resolved to give no more indulgence to painful thoughts. At an early age he mingled in every possible scene of extravagance, folly, and dissipation, until his fortune became considerably impaired, at the same time he received an intimation that no farther assistance could be rendered him until the return of Mr. Fitzpatrick to England, when he would have arrived at an age that it would be prudent a proper adjustment of his affairs should take place.

This was terrible news for Sir Julian, and he cursed and swore for several days, almost without intermission; but at length finding that any satisfactory arrangement was at that time impossible, and that his affairs were in a most desperate state, he flew to other resources, the nature of which will be explained at a future period. He was absent from England for several years, but where he had been to no one could imagine. He was strangely altered in his personal appearance; the slight figure of youth had ripened into the muscular grace of manhood; and his countenance seemed burned by the sun of a tropical climate. From his observations he had been engaged during the principal portion of his absence, at sea, but in what capacity, no one had any opportunity of ascertaining, and whenever any hint was given upon the subject, he most sedulously avoided it, and only returned such answers as served to involve the inquirers in still greater doubt and perplexity.

He brought with him several companions of no very interesting appearance, and took up his residence at a suburban village, in a handsome cottage villa, within a few miles of London. He seemed to be possessed of immense wealth, for his expenditure was conducted on the most extravagant scale; he entered into every scene of festivity and aristocratic magnificence; entertained sumptuous parties, and for some months was the lion of the day.

Then he again as suddenly disappeared as he had done before, and so also his companions; his establishment was disposed of through the means of an agent, who knew not, or pretended not to know anything of the character of his employer. He was now lost sight of for a period of three years, and his name was almost forgotten among the circle where he had been the rage, the all presiding planet; when suddenly he burst forth again as a luminary in the giddy city of Paris. Here for months he was the courted, the admired of all, when he again as abruptly disappeared as he had done in England.

Prior to this period, a perfect panic was created in the maritime world by the daring deeds of an individual who was recognized by the title of the Smuggler King, and who was supposed to hold every smuggling craft and piratical vessel that ploughed the ocean, to the injury of the honest mariner, under his dominion. His desperate actions, his unconquerable courage, the mystery of his proceedings, and the manner by which he effected his object, and set at nought the powers sent against him, had commonly gained for him the appellation of the sea-devil; and, certainly, if he was deserving of one quarter of the acts of atrocity that were attributed to him, he well merited the unenviable title.

No one, unless it was any of his own crew, was supposed to have seen his features, for in all the engagements that had taken place with him, they were invariably concealed by a frightful black mask, and he wore a dress of a corresponding colour, covered with skulls and cross-bones, and other unearthly devices. His head was surmounted with a coronet formed out of choice and rare shells, and, altogether, his person was tall, athletic, and commanding. He never spared an enemy; a lingering death of torture, and then the ocean deep for his grave, was sure to be the portion.

He was supposed to have vessels in every part of the globe, and so well were they manned, and so desperate were the characters of the wretches under his command, that they had but to hoist the black flag, with the terrific name of the Smuggler King inscribed upon it, in whitened human bones, to excite the utmost terror in the minds of even the stoutest hearts, and those who had encountered all sorts of perils and dangers, in fighting the battles of their country.

No one had had an opportunity of forming even the slightest conjecture of the actual character of the Smuggler King, and there were many who were even weak enough to suppose him to be a supernatural being, some the Flying Dutchman, and others the very devil himself.

That he was very rich there could not be the least doubt, for his successes were almost certain, and had been for several years, and many were the rich prizes of merchandize and specie that had fallen into his hands. Where his haunts were, after quitting the deep, it had been impossible to discover, though thousands of pounds would have been gladly given to purchase the information.

Such was the romantic and daring character of this nautical marauder, that he was the theme of conversation on every lip, and among all ranks and classes of society. Children shuddered when they heard his name

mentioned, and even the hardy-hearted mariner feared not half so much the battling of the waves, or an engagement with the enemies of his country, as encountering the Smuggler King, and his desperate, blood-thirsty crew.

Various were the stories that were circulated concerning his daring deeds, and the muse of the poet had been taxed to record his actions, as the following song will testify :—

There's a brave little bark, stealing out in the dark,
　From her nest in the bustling bay,
The fresh mist meets on her dingy sheets,
　And swiftly she darts away.
She never must run in the eyes of the sun,
　But along with the owl take wing;
She must keep her flight for the moonlight night,
　For she carries the Smuggler King!

A monarch is he, as bold as can be,
　Of a strong and daring band ;
The bullet and blast may go whistling past,
　But he quails neither heart nor hand.
He lives and he dies with his tearful prize,
　Like a hunted wolf he'll spring
With trigger and dirk, to the deadliest work,
　And fight like a Smuggler King !

Back from the wave, to his home in the cave,
　In the sheen of the torches glare
He reigns the lord of a freebooter's board,
　And never was costlier fare.
Right firm and true are the hearts of his crew,
　There's a faith in the shouts that ring,
As they stave the cask, and drain the flask,
　And drink to the Smuggler King !

No. 4

But to return to the young Sir Julian Mordlington. After another absence of about two years, he once more alighted upon fashionable society in London. Much was the wonder excited at his long absence, and unexpected appearance, but no one took the liberty of questioning him whither he had been, or the motives for his singular conduct, especially as he was, if possible, more gay and liberal than ever.

Wherever he went he was followed by a numerous train of admirers, especially the fair sex, with whom his gallant conduct, flattering address, and handsome gentlemanly exterior, had made him an universal favourite.

He kept up a most extravagant establishment for a single gentleman, having a full retinue of servants, and giving the most gorgeous and expensive *fêtes.* In fact, he appeared by some means or another to have gained possession of Pandora's box, so great seemed to be his wealth.

At length Basilwood Hall being for sale, and he having got tired of town, became the purchaser; and thus we bring him down to that period of our history from which we have so long digressed.

Another quarter of an hour the baronet paced his apartment with disordered steps, and at length his impatience increased beyond endurance.

"Where can the fellow be?" he said; "what can detain him? He surely cannot be sporting with my feelings. No—no—he knows his master too well to venture that. I have many questions to ask him, and—but hark! some one comes."

At that moment there was a knock at the room-door, and on being commanded to do so, a servant entered.

"How, now!" hastily demanded Sir Julian; "what do you want, fellow?"

"Strange man waiting below, Sir Julian," returned the servant, "who wishes to see you."

"Show him up stairs immediately," said the baronet.

"What, here, Sir Julian; here, in this very apartment, and —"

"Begone! and do as I order you;" said Sir Julian, and when the servant had vanished, he added, "'tis Sam Raker, I have no doubt; better late than never."

He had scarcely thus spoken when the individual he mentioned unceremoniously entered the room.

He was a tall uncouth-looking man, with huge black whiskers, and forbidding looking aspect. He had on a broad brimmed leather hat, and was otherwise attired in a shabby seaman's suit.

"Oh! you have come at last," said the baronet.

"Yes, cap— "

"Silence," interrupted Sir Julian, sternly, "we are not on the blue waters now, that title must not here be mentioned. Why did you not come before?"

"Because accident prevented me," answered Sam Raker; without any further ceremony seating himself in an arm chair.

"Accident! what do you mean?"

"Why, I accidentally got a glass too much grog aboard last night cap—I mean Sir Julian."

"Ah! your old tricks," said the baronet; "but you might have avoided it when you knew you had other and such important business to attend to."

"Business is business, and drinking is drinking, Sir Julian," replied Sam Raker, "but the whole of it is I attended to both."

"And what have you learnt?"

"Much more than I think you will like to hear."

"What mean you?"

"You shall know all in good time."

"Be brief."

"I will."

"Shut that door."

"Ay, ay, cap—, Sir Julian I mean," said Sam, going towards the door.

"There is no one outside?"

"No."

"No listeners?"

"No."

"Then proceed. Have you seen the girl?"

"Yes, and a lovely craft she is; just such a one as I —"

"Psha! this is no time for idle trifling," said Sir Julian, impatiently; "have you ascertained who she is?"

"I have."

"And her name?"

"Is Flora Clarendon; she is the daughter of a farmer in this neighbourhood."

"And on my estate?"

"I presume so."

"'Tis well; where did you behold her?"

"In the garden of the farm belonging to one they call Ben Backstay."

"Ben Backstay!" exclaimed the baronet, turning pale, "that name—you—you must be mistaken."

"No—no, I am not though; and, moreover, I am certain he is the very man you have cause to dread."

"Impossible! you must be mistaken, Sam."

"Oh, no, I am not though," answered Raker, "I listened to all the conversation, and am satisfied of the fact."

"Well, well," observed Sir Julian, after a pause, "and should it indeed prove to be so, what have I to fear? Twenty years have now elapsed, he saw not much of me, and it is not likely that he would now recognize me."

"He might not;—but that boy!"

"What boy?"

"The boy you thought you had —"

"Silence! what of him?"

"He lives!"

"Lives!"

"Aye!"

"Liar!"

"And no thanks for your politeness, cap—, Sir Julian, I mean."

"Don't tire my patience," said the agitated baronet; "how heard you this?"

"From the lips of Ben Backstay himself."

"Perdition!"

"Ay, it is rather awkward."

"Lives—where?"

"He is daily expected home from sea. He has been fighting the battles of his country."

"Ah! then he may have fallen among the slain."

"He may."

"But even should he not," continued Sir Julian, "I have still nothing to fear. He cannot have the means of proving his origin."

"But he may have the means of proving you —"

"What?"

"A villain!"

"Ah! so bold."

"Nay, I meant no offence."

"Should he even be able to prove who he is," observed Sir Julian; "Mr. Fitzpatrick is out of the way; I do not believe that there is any will in existence, and therefore I can still claim the whole of my father's fortune."

"I wish you may get it. But I am thinking that it is likely you will have more trouble than you at present calculate upon."

"Should he return we must find some way of disposing of him. It might be done."

"Oh, yes, I dare say it might."

"As he is a seaman, he might be found of some service on board one of our craft."

"He might," returned Sam Raker; "but the thing is to catch him."

"That must be contrived. But this girl—the lovely Flora Clarendon."

"Her and William Backstay, as he is called, are lovers," answered Sam Raker.

"Lovers ?"

"Aye."

"D—— n !"

"Ah, it is no use to swear about the matter; such I have heard is the fact."

"I detest him more than ever for that."

"And so I think you have very good reason, cap ——, Sir Julian, I mean," said Sam.

"She must be mine."

"How ?"

"You say she is the daughter of one Farmer Clarendon ?"

"Yes."

"And that he resides in the vicinity of this mansion ?"

"Very true."

"She is in the constant habit of visiting the farm of Ben Backstay ?"

"I dare say she is," replied Sam Raker.

"And might easily be waylaid ?"

"Ah, that might be done."

"It must."

"How is it to be accomplished ?"

"You must watch her father's farm, having some of our comrades close at hand to assist you, and when you see her reach a fitting spot, pounce upon her, and stifling her cries, bear her to this hall, whence at midnight she can be conveyed on board the craft which we have at present lying close to this spot in a place of security."

"It shall be done, if possible," said Sam Raker; "but when shall we attempt to put it into execution ?"

"The sooner the better," answered Sir Julian, "if it were even this very night. I am all impatience until I get possession of the beauteous damsel."

"Well—well, cap ——, Sir Julian, I mean, I will lose no time in ——"

"Who's there ?" hastily demanded Sir Julian, as a knock at the room-door alarmed and startled them both.

"It is only I, Sir Julian," replied Simon, the servant, as he popped his head in at the door.

"And what do you want now, booby ?" demanded his master, wrathfully.

"Strange gentleman waiting below, Sir Julian."

"Another strange gentleman ! Who is he, and what does he want ?"

"He desired me to deliver this card to you, Sir Julian," answered Simon.

The baronet hastily snatched the card from his hand, and as his eye fell upon it, his eyes became distended, and his countenance changed.

"Mr. Fitzpatrick!" he exclaimed.

"Another of your friends," said Sam Raker.

"Confusion! is it possible that he still lives, and has found me out? Never did I expect to behold him again. D——n!"

"Shall I tell the strange gentleman to walk up stairs, Sir Julian?" inquired Simon.

"No—yes, idiot. I suppose I must see him. Would that some friendly hand had taken the old lawyer's life. But I must be calm, and meet him with the air of an hypocrite."

"Which you know so well how to assume, cap ——, Sir Julian, I mean," added Sam Raker.

"Bah!" ejaculated Sir Julian; "you are too bold, Sam. Retire into the next room; I may need your aid."

"Aye—aye, cap ——, Sir Julian, I mean," returned Sam Raker, as he opened the door to which the baronet had pointed, and hastily made his exit.

"This unexpected visit from the man whose power and interference I may have too much reason to fear," said Sir Julian, "quite unnerves me; but ——"

"And it's up stairs he is, you say?" now remarked Mr. Patrick Fitzpatrick, as he made his way up to the room, following the servant.

"It is his hated voice," muttered the baronet to himself; "but I must compose my feelings, and meet him in a manner that may further my views, and conceal from him my real character; it is not possible that he can have learnt it. He is here."

At that moment the solicitor was ushered into the room, and Sir Julian advanced towards him with apparent cordiality, and grasped his hand.

CHAPTER V.

THE INFAMOUS PROPOSAL. — THE WILL. — AN HONEST LAWYER. — THE INTERRUPTION.—BAD COUNSEL ACCEPTED.—THE TWO VILLAINS.

"Is it possible, my dear Mr. Fitzpatrick," said the baronet, "that I have the pleasure of again seeing you after the lapse of so many years?"

"Arrah, now!" answered the solicitor, "and much pleasure may the meeting afford you, Sir Ju-Julian, that is your title, I believe. Faith! and it is my own darling self that you see, returned to England once more to adjust affairs and other important business, and glad enough I am of it."

"Most happy I am to see you, Mr. Fitzpatrick," said Sir Julian, with well-affected friendship and pleasure; "pray be seated. You were the friend of my lamented father, and ——"

"Ah! poor General Harlington," interrupted the solicitor; "faith, and he was a gentleman and a good man, and I hope his son may prove as good a man as his father."

Sir Julian frowned, bit his lips, and could scarcely suppress a word of indignation.

"Och!" continued Mr. Fitzpatrick, taking no notice of the baronet's displeasure, "sure, and the general was a brave man, and I should have been far better reconciled to his death, had he lost his life fighting nobly for his country, sure, than being swallowed up by the waves. Then the poor child that his heart doated on, your brother, to be cut off at so early an age, both food for fishes. Och! and the melancholy event was enough to have he breaking of your heart, Sir Julian"

Although Mr. Fitzpatrick made use of these observations, he felt convinced that the heart of the baronet was not made of such tender materials. His father's estates were safe on terra firma, and that consideration had at the time more than consoled him for his loss. He scarcely knew what answer to make the solicitor, whom his keen and penetrating eye could discover was looking upon him with suspicion, and who he felt convinced, liked him not in his heart.

"Yes, it was an unfortunate circumstance, Mr. Fitzpatrick," he at length said, "and you, I believe, lost something considerable by my father's death?"

"Och! indeed, and it's myself that did do that same thing, Sir Julian," returned the lawyer; "let me see, as near as I can guess, it was six hundred a year or thereabouts. By my conscience now, and that was no trifle to be taken out of a man's pocket all at once, as clean as a tenpenny. But, och! botheration and buttermilk, what the divil's the use of fretting about it at all, at all? All men are liable to losses, and I have managed to make myself contented with the little I have scraped together, which, to be sure, will be sufficient for the support of my old age, and having been got honestly will be enjoyed without any upbraidings of conscience, which is more than many in the world can say; what is your opinion, Sir Julian?"

The baronet felt confused, and knew not what answer to make. He took two or three strides across the room, and then returned and resumed his seat.

"This is a very illigant Hall that you have purchased, Sir Julian," remarked the solicitor.

"Yes, it is a pleasant place," replied the baronet; "but my dear Mr. Fitzpatrick, to what may I attribute the honour of your visit?"

"To what? arrah! now! and is it all surprising that, after so many years absence a gentleman should feel anxious to see the son of his old friend?"

"No, certainly not, Mr. Fitzpatrick," returned Sir Julian, "and I'm sure I feel honoured ——"

"Och! tunder and turf! hold your blarney about being honoured, and all such nonsense; it reminds me too much of them scarecrows the French, bad luck to them! and it is yourself Sir Julian, that ought to feel mighty glad to see me, too, for your affairs cannot be exactly in order without me, and——"

"Ah!" interrupted the baronet, hastily, "that is a point upon which I would immediately speak to you."

"All in good time, Sir Julian, all in good time," said the solicitor; "I have scarcely got my breath yet, and by my sowl, a glass of wine would not be at all disagreeable at the present moment."

"My dear sir," exclaimed the baronet, with the greatest assumption of politeness, "I'm sure I apologize a thousand times for not thinking of that before, but ——"

"Och! botheration and buttermilk," interrupted Mr. Fitzpatrick, "botheration and buttermilk to apologies where a gentleman has committed no offence at all, at all."

Sir Julian having rang the bell, the servant appeared, and the wine being ordered was immediately brought; Mr. Fitzpatrick partook of a glass, smacked his lips in token of his approval of it, and then observed;—

"Faith, Sir Julian, although it was a very melancholy sad piece of business, it was a fortunate job for you that your brother also perished."

"But what if he lives?"

"Lives! lives! arrah, be aisy now, or you will drive me mad with joy at the bare supposition of such a thing."

"I have lately heard that my brother survived the wreck, and that he is still in existence," said the baronet, fixing a keen glance upon the lawyer.

Mr. Fitzpatrick bounded from his chair, with a sort of view halloo.

"Lives! lives! och! och!" he cried, "how—where?"

"I know not," answered Sir Julian, "and after all it may be but an idle report."

He walked away from the solicitor for a few moments, and muttered to himself ;—

"Cursed fool that I was to mention anything about it."

"Hurrah ! hurrah ! och ! by the holy St. Patrick," cried the solicitor, "this is the happie intelligence, sure, than I ever expected to hear. The darling, sedate little honey ; the powers be praised for his preservation ; hurrah ! hurrah !"

The baronet coloured, frowned, and bit his lips, and mentally cursed himself again for an egregious fool to mention anything at all about the matter. He could have expressed his indignation to Mr. Fitzpatrick for the ecstasy he evinced, but was too cautious to give way to passion at a time when he wanted the lawyer's connivance in a scheme which suddenly darted across his brain.

"You will recollect, Mr. Fitzpatrick," he observed, "that what I have stated is only a report, a mere idle rumour, and doubtless, if there is any one in the world that has the effrontery to call himself my brother, he is only an impostor."

"Botheration to that word impostor," returned the solicitor, impatiently, "the world is full of wickedness sure, but if William Harlington has escaped drowning, he must now be about twenty-four years of age. I shall make it my business to try and find out this individual, faith, and he must be clever if he deceives me."

"And may I ask, Mr. Fitzpatrick," said the baronet, unable to conceal his anger, "may I ask, sir, what purpose your seeing this person may answer? William Harlington was not many months old when the general left England, and it would, therefore, be impossible for you now to recognize him."

"Och, botheration, man, and isn't it myself now, that have as clear a recollection of the darling's features as if I had only looked at them this morning? He had three pretty moles on his neck, and was marked with a strawberry on his wrist."

The baronet muttered to himself a curse against the lawyer's tenacious memory.

"Yes, that he had, by the powers," continued Mr. Fitzpatrick; "three brown moles, about the size of small peas, and sure, now I come to remember, his mother, Lady Emmeline——"

"Mention not the name of that degraded woman to me, sir," interrupted Sir Julian, passionately; "her, whose shameful conduct but too well justifies the belief, that the child General Harlington was so fond of, might have claimed another father."

The anger of Mr. Fitzpatrick was evidently rising, for his face coloured, but acting with prudence, and wishing to elicit all he could, he restrained the expression of it.

"Arrah, now !" he said, after a pause, " sure, and it's very true, that a child must be mighty wise that knows his own father ; but, Sir Julian, be after letting me take the liberty of informing you that I never heard of any suspicion attaching to the character of Lady Emmeline; no, not so much as a whisper against her, till the very year in which she was divorced from her husband."

"Well, well," replied the baronet, becoming more cool, " but after all, Mr. Fitzpatrick, you must allow that it is far from impossible that Lady Emmeline might have been guilty, long before her misconduct was discovered."

"To be sure, and that is true enough," said the lawyer.

"And, if such was the case," continued Sir Julian, "and this child should really be living, would it not be monstrous that a spurious child should inherit any part of the fortune of a deceived and dishonoured husband ?"

" Whist ! whist a bit, honey,l" cried Mr. Fitzpatrick, " your father, General Harlington, never entertained any doubts of his wife's fidelity, till the unfortunate circumstance that occasioned their divorce. Your father, sir, had no doubts, he was convinced that William Harlington was his child, dearly and tenderly beloved as yourself; which will be proved by the will he signed, and left in my keeping, previous to his going abroad." .

The baronet started, and fixed upon the lawyer a withering look, as he shouted,

" A will ! a will ! Did then my father leave a will ? or ——"

" He left a will, sir, which is in my possession ; and a fortunate thing it was, that the general was so thoughtful, being so young a man when he left his native country."

" Would that the will was at the bottom of the sea with my father," muttered Sir Julian to himself, as he hastily traversed the room, unable to conceal his agitation ; " but it may be destroyed—yes, it must be destroyed, and a new one made entirely in my favour. I must calm my passion, and make the proposal."

" He then walked again to Mr. Fitzpatrick, and said, .

" You say, sir, that my father's will is in your care ?"

" Faith, and that's thrue, now," answered the lawyer, " all properly sealed, signed, and attested."

" And the witnesses, are they forthcoming ?"

" Arrah ! and that is a puzzler."

" The witnesses are not to be found ?"

" Whist ! whist, man. I did not say that," returned Mr. Fitzpatrick, " but the will has been made four-and-twenty years, and in that time death and other circumstances may have wrought many other changes. But no dispute about the validity of the will can possibly arise, and now I recollect, that you having already received fifty thousand pounds, should your brother be really living, you have nothing at all to do with the residue of your father's property, the whole remainder being bequeathed to William Harlington."

" D—n !" cried Sir Julian, unable any longer to control his rage. .

" Nay, nay, arrah now, man," said Mr. Fitzpatrick, coolly ; " do not be after flying into a mighty big passion. I dare say you would be too happy to find your own darling of a brother living, to begrudge him his father's fortune."

" But he lives not. It is only some base imposter ! I myself saw him sink in the deep and fathomless ocean."

" Faith ! and that I shall make it my especial business to ascertain."

" Officious fool !" Sir Julian was about to utter, but he repressed the words, and added,

" And why, sir, have you kept this will so long a secret ?"

" Faith ! and I had my motives for so doing," replied the lawyer, " which I do not now at all regret, since it is not unlikely but it may lead to the most fortunate results."

Again Sir Julian paced the room with disordered steps ; he could have pressed his fingers in the lawyer's throat, and have murdered him on the spot, but he knew the deed would only involve him in ruin, and suppressing his rage, he determined to try what artifice and persuasion would effect for him.

" Mr. Fitzpatrick," said he, " should my brother be really living, he has probably been brought up in the most humble, vulgar, and illiterate manner ; he would never be received and countenanced by the higher orders

of society; therefore, to invest a complete clown with so much wealth, would be only setting him up as a mark for the unprincipled and designing."

"Och! botheration!" replied the lawyer, "justice is justice, all the world over, and law is law; and if William Harlington is still alive, and does not know great A from a pig-sty, I see no way of preventing him from inheriting his father's property."

"But I do," hastily returned Sir Julian, and catching hold of the lawyer's arm; "it is in your power, Mr. Fitzpatrick, and if you will only consent to promote my interest, twelve thousand pounds shall be immediately paid into your hands."

"Twelve thousand pounds," repeated the lawyer; "faith now and that's a very handsome sum, and of what nature are the services you require for that illegant gratuity, I suppose I must not call it a bribe?"

"A trifle, my dear sir," replied Sir Julian, eagerly, and his eyes at the same time gleaming upon the countenance of the lawyer as if he would penetrate to his very soul; "you can effect it without the least difficulty; all that I ask of you is that you immediately destroy —"

"What?"

"That accursed will!"

"Tunder and turf!" shouted Mr. Fitzpatrick, starting to his feet and his honest face turning as red as fire with indignation. But before he could give utterance to another word, there was a knock at the room door, and Simon announced " Sir Gregory Ballandale."

"Perdition seize this interruption!" cried Sir Julian; " hasten, tell him I am not within, I —"

"Arrah! be aisy now, honey!" interrupted the warm-hearted Irishman, who the moment before was half inclined to crack every bone in Sir Julian's body, for the villanous proposal he had dared to make to him; " I would

No. 5

not interrupt your business with Sir Gregory Ballandale, for the world! I shall return to honest Farmer Backstay's, and —"

" Backstay !" cried Sir Julian, unable to conceal the agitation under which he was now suffering, " Backstay !"

" Aye, Backstay, jewel," returned Fitzpatrick ; " but arrah, man, how strange you look ; it is a plebeian name certainly, but one, I dare say, that the owner is not ashamed of."

" Do you know him ?"

" I never had the pleasure of seeing him before last night, but I hope that will not be the last of our acquaintance."

" Of course, Mr. Fitzpatrick, you will say nothing to him of what has transpired between us at this interview ?"

" Botheration, man," said the honest lawyer, " and do you suppose that he would feel any interest in it? I wish you good morning, Sir Julian, and I hope when next we meet, I may have heard something of your brother, which will probably save you the twelve thousand pounds that you was so liberal to offer as a bribe for —"

" Shall I see you again, Mr. Fitzpatrick ?" hastily interrupted Sir Julian, unable to conceal his confusion, agitation, and vexation.

" Och! yes," replied the lawyer, " and I wish you joy, darling, of the meeting when it takes place." And thus saying, the solicitor, whose fingers were itching to give the baronet a sound drubbing, bowed himself out of the room, and quitted the hall.

" What an infernal scoundrel," soliloquized Mr. Fitzpatrick, as he left the threshold of the hall ; " what a blackguard, to wish to rob his poor brother of his rights. Och! botheration! would that I could discover whether the darling still lives, which I am induced to believe is certain from the manners and the observations of this spalpeen ; but if he is, leave Patrick Fitzpatrick, Esq., alone to find him out. Och! that great big blackguard, Sir Julian, has given me the gout in my stomach! The villain! the rascal! the thief, to presume to offer Patrick Fitzpatrick a bribe to destroy his father's will, and cheat his poor brother, if he be still alive, his fatherless and motherless brother out of his just right! Who ever heard before of such an insult being offered to a gentleman that has pure Milesian blood running in a red stream through all his veins ? Och! by the powers! if it had not been for the interruption caused by the arrival of this Sir Gregory, old as I am, I would have thrashed him soundly for daring to believe me as big a scoundrel as himself. He ought to be committed to prison, and punished like other robbers, for the design is as bad as the act ; already, in his mind, he has defrauded and plundered his own brother. But I will learn where the wronged, deserted orphan is to be found. His brave, generous father was a friend to me, when I had a plentiful lack of everything but misfortune, great honour to his memory! He was a true gentleman, and had a heart as warm, and as tender, and as liberal, as if he had been born an Irishman ; and now, when is darling son his likely to be living, and stands in need of a protector, blood and tunder! shall I sneak like a spalpeen from the charge ? Och! by the powers! but my blood rises and boils at the thought. But I will soon let Sir Julian see that the orphan son of General Harlington has a protector, when I find him, who will establish his rights to the very letter of his father's will, sure! and it will not be long before I teach him what it is to offer a dirty bribe to a Milesian ! I will let him know, that though in the law, as well as in every other profession, men of base and dishonourable principles have established themselves, yet it boasts hearts that would rather never so much as lay by the value of a tenpenny, and prefer to live all their days upon butter-milk and potatoes, rather than accept a bribe to defraud an orphan, and grow rich by means that ought to purchase them a halter. Och! botheration, sure, and I never thought that I had rogue written in my countenance before!—but never mind, what Sir Julian Mordlington fancied he saw written on my forehead—my heart denies, and my conduct shall give it the lie; and when I have finished my course in this life, my friends, as they read the inscription on my tomb, shall have it in their power to add, ‘ Patrick Fitzpatrick was an honest lawyer.’ ”

Thus soliloquising, and in a state of great mental excitement, the worthy lawyer bent his way to the farm of Ben Backstay.

In the meantime, Sir Julian, after Mr. Fitzpatrick’s departure, was in a state of mind of which the reader may easily form a conception. He reproached himself for being an arrant idiot in having divulged what he had heard respecting the existence of his brother; but in a moment afterwards he consoled himself with the idea, that, notwithstanding the at present apparent repugnance of the solicitor to take the bribe he had offered him, he would at last accede to his proposals, and if he did not, some other and more desperate means must be adopted to carry his nefarious designs into execution.

He was in no state of mind to meet Sir Gregory Ballandale, who was an easy, wealthy young spendthrift, of whom he had made a considerable dupe at the gaming table, and after some trivial conversation, he pleaded a prior engagement, and contrived to get rid of him.

He then released Sam Raker from the room in which he had been concealed during his interview with Mr. Fitzpatrick.

“ You overheard all that passed,” said Sir Julian.

“ I did,” answered Sam ; “ I did, cap— Sir Julian, I mean ; and allow me to make so bold as to tell you that you acted the part of a complete fool.”

“ Ha !” ejaculated Sir Julian, frowning.

“ Nay, it is the truth,” returned Sam, “however unpleasant it may be, and I think you know it. Why should you have intimated anything to the lawyer about the supposed existence of your brother ?”

“ That was wrong, very wrong, I admit,” said the baronet.

“ The old lubber, it is a chance, would never have heard anything about the matter, and the whole of the property would have been yours without any further trouble.”

“ But the will !”

“ Psha ! The boy was supposed to be no more. The opinion of every one of any influence was that he had perished with your father. The claims of your brother, brought up in obscurity as he doubtless has been, could have been easily overruled by the means of gold and your power, and you would have gained possession of your father’s property without any further trouble. Do you mean still to offer the lawyer the bribe ?”

“ What other alternative have I ?”

“ I will tell you,” answered Sam. “ The lawyer might be waylaid, taken on board one of our craft, from thence tossed overboard as food for sharks, and there would be an end to the business.”

“ But the will would still be in existence.”

“ True ; but that is no reason that your brother should long remain so ; and then what becomes of the danger you apprehend ?”

“ Ah, Sam !” exclaimed Sir Julian, hastily ; “ you are a capital fellow ; my best adviser.”

“ You flatter me, cap—Sir Julian, I mean.”

“ That is an excellent thought,” continued the baronet ; “ it must be acted upon. Should this William Backstay return from sea, we must contrive some means to get him in our power, and then he is safe.”

“ Yes, and the whole of your father’s property also.”

"Exactly so. But the girl—this Flora Clarendon."

"What of her?"

"She must be mine."

"She shall, if possible."

"You remember my instructions?"

"I do."

"Let them be executed with all expedition," said Sir Julian, "this very night."

"I will be on the look out, and will soon give you intimation if I am successful."

"To-morrow night I will be on board with you."

"Aye, cap—Sir Julian, I mean, we need your presence; it is some time since you ——"

"Enough," interrupted Sir Julian; "get you gone, and obey with promptitude my orders."

"And let me advise you also, Sir Julian," observed Sam Raker, "to mind how you act with the crafty lawyer. Pay him the twelve thousand pounds bribe, if he will accept of it,—get the will; we will soon have old Latitat in our power, make him refund the cash, give him the salt sea for a cooling-bath, and all will then be safe."

"Your advice is excellent," said Sir Julian; "it has made me more easy than I have been for some time past. You shall be handsomely rewarded for this, Sam."

"Oh, I have no doubt of that, cap—Sir Julian, I mean," returned Sam Raker; "but there is one thing, I always take good care to look after myself."

"What paper is that you hold in your hand?" demanded Sir Julian.

"Oh, I had almost forgot; look at it, I dare say it will prove rather interesting to you."

Sir Julian took the paper from the hands of Sam Raker, and unfolding it, read:—

"'Five thousand pounds reward for the apprehension of the notorious pirate and smuggler, commonly known by the title of the Smuggler King!'"

"Ha! ha! ha!" laughed Sir Julian, scornfully. "They must catch him,—they must catch him!"

"A goodly sum, that, for a single life," said Sam Raker; "a very decent sum, that, to make a fellow comfortable for the rest of his days."

"But who would venture to attempt to earn it?"

"Not one of the daring crew of the Smuggler King, for ten times the amount, would attempt to betray their sovereign," answered Sam Raker.

Sir Julian took the hand of the ruffian and shook it vehemently.

"Read the description of his person."

Sir Julian once more glanced at the paper, and read:—

"'A man of tall and athletic mien; his features concealed by a black mask; his head surmounted with a coronet of shells; his dress black, and covered with numerous unearthly devices!'"

"Ha! ha! ha!" again laughed Sir Julian, "so they may find the Smuggler King on the deep blue waters, but let them know him on land, where alone they may dare to meet him. Ha! ha! ha! This for their reward!" and he immediately thrust the placard in the fire.

"This, night, then, cap—Sir Julian, I mean," observed Sam Raker, advancing towards the door.

"You will be upon the look out for the damsel," returned the baronet; "and if possible, seize her, and bear her on board The Devil Skipper; but use no more violence than is necessary."

"Your orders shall be obeyed."

"You will give me immediate intelligence as t show you have succeeded?"

"I will."

"Then, farewell," said Sir Julian; "begin, and lose no time in arranging the business entrusted to you."

"I will attend," answered Sam Raker, and the two worthies separated.

CHAPTER VI.

THE WOOD.—THE SAILOR'S RETURN.—THE MINIATURE.—THE COMBAT.—CRAZY MARIAN.—THE RECOGNITION.

IT was a beautiful evening; such an evening as lifts the soul to Heaven, and will lead the most insensible to adore the wondrous works of Omnipotence. The moon rode in brilliancy, unobscured by a single cloud, splendid was the sky and calm the sea; just like the human mind as it is stamped by nature; so lovely, so tranquil is the bosom of youth, before the passions, bursting from the control of reason, destroy its peace.

The scene was a romantic wood on the borders of the ocean, and at that peaceful hour, when all around was so lovely and so bright, the beams of the clear-faced empress of the night converting every leaf that fluttered on the branches of the trees into silver, the stillness that reigned around was suddenly interrupted by the cheerful tones of one apparently in the most exuberant mirth.

It was the voice of a man, and although it was unadorned by any of the superfluous embellishments of art, it possessed that melody and soul heartiness that must have rendered it pleasing even to the most fastidious ear. The individual who could give utterance to such tones must have known little of care, and the conscience must be as clear as the face of the bright moon that shone so chastely above him. The words the traveller was chaunting with so much gusto were those of the immortal Dibdin, and ran thus :—

"Here I am poor Jack,
    Just come home from sea,
With shiners in my sack,
    What d'ye think of me ?"

But quickly the singer changed it to the following, seeming to have forgotten the words of the song he had first commenced :—

"When scarce a handspike high,
    Death with old dad made free;
So, what d'ye see, does I,
    But packs it off to sea !
Says I to sweetheart Poll,
    If ever I comes back,
We'll laugh and sing tol-de-rol,
    If not—remember Jack.

'I'd fortin smooth and rough,
    The wind would chop and veer;
Till hard knocks I'd nabb'd enough,
    On board of a privateer.
Propp'd with a wooden peg,
    Poll I thought would bid me pack;
So, was forced d'ye see to beg,
    And it was—pray remember Jack!

"I axed as folks hove by,
    And showed my wooden pin;
Young girls would sometimes sigh,
    And gaping lubbers grin.

> In vain I'd often bawl,
>   My hopes were ta'en aback;
> My share of coppers small,
>   So pray remember Jack!
>
> " One day, my lockers bare,
>   And togs all tattered grown,
> I twigged a pinnace fair,
>   Well rigged, a bearing down.
> 'Twas Poll, she look'd so spruce,
>   ' What thus,' says she, ' come back?'
> My tongue forgot its use,
>   And, pray remember Jack.
>
> " What matters much to prate,
>   She'd shiners saved a few;
> Soon I became her mate,—
>   Warn't Poll a sweetheart true?
> Then a friend I'd serv'd before,
>   From a long voyage trips back,
> Shar'd his gold with me galore,
>   For he well remembered Jack!
>
> " So though I lost my leg,
>   It seem'd to fortune mend,
> And when forced, d'ye see to beg,
>   I gained a wife and friend.
> Here's the King, Old England, Poll,
>   My shipmate just come back;
> Then laugh and sing tol-de-rol,
>   And pray remember Jack!"

Heartily was this characteristic ballad sung, but the individual who the next moment made his appearance, corresponded not in the least with the character represented in the song. He was a tall handsome young mariner, apparently about two-and-twenty, or he might have been a year or two older. His countenance beamed with intelligence, good humour, hope, buoyant hope, and every generous feeling; and yet there was a general expression about his features that seemed to say that he was born to fill a far higher station in society than that of a humble blue-jacket. He was graceful in form, and attired with that degree of neatness, which the sons of the ocean would have agreed became a taut and trim-built seaman.

He carried in his hand a stout cudgel, which served him for amusement, as well as a protective in case of the attack of any " nasty customers."

" Hilloa! hilloa!" shouted the tar, " what latitude am I steering in now? I am all aback, as if I had been cast on an unknown island; but avast! avast! No grumbling, Will, your heart bears a rudder and a compass that is sure to guide you to the girl you love, and the dear friends you left behind you. How my heart throbs; it is going at the rate of twenty knots an hour since I have set my foot once more on the shores of Old England! Dear friends!— darling Flora! Are you all well, and baffled and weathered the gales of life since your poor Will has been ploughing the ocean deep, and contending with the enemies of his country? Oh! yes, ' there's a sweet little cherub that sits up aloft,' that assures me you are all floating as gaily as a seventy-four. Friends! Flora!—bless, bless your hearts! Father, mother, Fouchette, Harry, all, all! Oh! how full my heart is with joy! How glad you will be to see me again! My eyes! what a merry meeting there will be! Won't their scuppers run over?—I—I d—e! I am as soft as a child—I could cry —I could laugh!—I could sing! Ha!—there is the bell of the old village church! Eight o'clock! Oh, well do I remember the tones of that old church bell: many a time have they met my ears as I and Flora rambled to— yes, 'tis the very spot!—I recollect it well now; and every breeze that wafts seems to bring with it the odour of her sweet breath! Dear, dear Flora, how rejoiced you will be to see your William once more safely moored in his old quarters. I would not let my dear friends or Flora know of my safe arrival, because I thought I would give them a joyful surprise! What a lovely night, just like the one on which Flora and I parted! Dear, dear Flora! I could almost imagine I saw your eyes beaming love and welcome to me from two of those bright stars, only your's can even surpass them in brilliancy. Chaste moon, the weather-beaten mariner greets thy welcome to his native shores. Here beneath thy radiant light, let me once more gaze upon the likeness of her whose image is treasured in my heart's deepest recesses!"

The young sailor as he thus spoke, took from his bosom, where it had been treasured since his absence from home, a miniature likeness inclosed in a locket. It was that of Flora Clarendon, and skilfully had the artist performed his task. With transport William contemplated it beneath the bright beams of the moon, and pressed it again and again with rapture to his lips.

"How like her," he said; "I could imagine she was standing before me! What a happy fellow I ought to be to be sure, to possess the love of such an angel as this. Bless you, Flora—bless you! bless you. Your William hopes soon to enfold you in his arms, and once more breathe his vows of love in your ear. You are well, I am sure; hope tells me that you are."

He was suddenly started by a loud, wailing, and piercing cry, which made the wood re-echo again.

"Hilloa!" exclaimed William; "what was that? A signal of distress? Where did it come from? I see no one, or I would slip my cable, and steer off to their assistance. What a queer sound! What could be the cause of it? All is still now, and —— but hark! Some one is singing."

It was the voice of a female, but so impressively plaintive and melancholy, that it almost melted the heart of the young sailor to tears as he listened to it. His whole soul was absorbed in the profoundest attention, and at length he elicited the following words :—

> "Gone, gone, beneath the billow,
>   Where I ne'er shall see them more;
> No cypress green, no drooping willow,
>   Canopy their tomb on shore!
>   Gone! gone!
>
> "Husband!—hush the word—deserter,
>   Yet unto my heart how dear;
> Child! the name my heartstrings sever,
>   All—all is gone! while I am here!
>   Gone! gone!
>
> "Dead! dead! each one I loved so,
>   Left, left, to weep alone.
> Death! oh! why not now relieve me,
>   Hope—comfort! gone, all gone.
>   Gone! gone!"

The voice ceased, but such was the impression that its musical tones had made upon the young mariner, that they seemed still to be ringing in his ears, and his soul was melted almost to tears.

He looked around him, but as far as the bright moonbeams would allow him to observe, he could not distinguish any object from whom the melancholy notes could have proceeded.

"Unhappy, melancholy wanderer," he exclaimed, "where are you? Whoever you are, too surely has your mind been split upon the rock of adversity. Would that I could see you; there is something in your voice that almost sets my pumps agoing. What can be the meaning of this feeling? Hilly yeo! hilly yeo!—unhappy woman, if you want assistance, here is a ready hand and a willing heart to tender you that aid!"

William shouted at the top of his voice, but no answer was returned to him,; and all remained as silent as the grave. He advanced farther into that part of the wood, from whence the sounds appeared to have issued; but, although the brightness of the moon rendered it as light as at noonday, he could not distinguish the least object to excite any particular attention.

While he thus stood wrapt in amazement and confusion, he was startled by a loud and piercing scream that proceeded from another direction of the wood.

The sailor turned hastily round, and grasping the cudgel more tightly than before, he endeavoured to penetrate into the deepest recesses of the wood.

"Ah!" he cried, "another signal of distress! Clear decks, and prepare all hands for action! D——e, where are they? 'Twas a woman's voice, and that appeal nerves my heart with the strength of a lion. Who dare insult a female while Will Backstay is at hand? Where are ye, ye lubbers, why do you not show yourselves and let me pour a broadside upon you? D——e! no skulking! All fair and above board, that's the way a British seaman likes to meet his enemies. There, ag•in!"

A second and a third shriek followed, and then a piteous cry of—

"Help! help! for Heaven's sake, help!"

"Help!" ejaculated William; "and in the supplicating voice of a woman! Hold on! d——e! You have a friend at hand, who will stick to you while he has a timber to float with."

Quickly William Backstay bounded towards the spot from whence he could now plainly distinguish the cries to issue, and forcing his way through the deep cluster of trees to his right, a broad and open space was before him, and in a moment he beheld the form of a female struggling in the grasp of a tall and powerful-looking ruffian, and calling loudly for assistance.

It was only the work of an instant for William to rush to the spot, and immediately snatching the female from the villain's grasp, she fainted on his shoulder, while at the same instant he felled the ruffian to the earth by a heavy blow from his cudgel.

The fellow soon recovered himself, and attacked the sailor fiercely with his sword, but William repelled all his attacks with the greatest courage and the most cool intrepidity, and finding that he was likely to be defeated, he was about to place a whistle to his lips, which William perceiving, he immediately knocked it from his hand and trampled it under his foot.

The combat was now renewed with redoubled fury on both sides; the ruffian, worked up to a pitch of the most ungovernable fury, and dealing the most terrific blows with his sword, the cudgel of William was at length hewn to pieces in warding them off, and he was left entirely at the mercy of his antagonist.

The ruffian had torn the insensible form of the female from his grasp, and William's foot having slipped, he sunk on one knee, and the ruffian had raised his deadly weapon in the air, with the intention of cleaving the sailor to the earth, when in an instant a loud female voice was heard to cry "Hold!" and directly afterwards the tall and majestic form of a woman, with wild and dishevelled hair, and in apparel of the meanest description, rushed precipitately in between them, and presented a pistol at the villain's head.

Confused, surprised, and alarmed, the fellow immediately resigned his hold of the fair form he had snatched from William, who sprung upon his feet in an instant, and once more took her under his protection.

The ruffian made an attempt to spring upon the woman, and to wrest the deadly weapon from her grasp; but she sprung back a few paces, levelled it at his head, and laughed aloud in the most scornful derision.

"Ha! ha! ha!" she laughed. "Come on—serpent—reptile—you do but rush on certain death! Ha! ha! ha! see how bravely poor Crazy

Marian can yet defend her own sex. Off—off—villain—monster! I have been betrayed, deceived, wronged, deserted! They are all gone—gone—but I have yet strength and courage left to defend the innocent. Away—or I will stretch thee a ghastly corpse at my feet!"

The ruffian growled forth a bitter curse, and, fixing a look of deadly revenge upon William, he plunged hastily into the thickest of the wood and was immediately lost to sight.

For a few moments William Backstay was so confused and astonished at the event which had within the last few minutes taken place, that he was unable to move or speak, but continued to support the inanimate form of the damsel, to whose protection he had so fortunately flown.

Crazy Marian also seemed transfixed to the spot, and gazed upon William and the maiden who hung over his shoulder alternately. Her eye was wild, yet brilliant, and there was an expression in its very wildness which was sufficient to create the deepest interest in all who beheld it.

"A sailor, and so young too," she at length uttered, in melancholy accents; "of noble mien and generous aspect—such—such would he have been had he been living—such—such was his father—but they are gone—gone—both gone! Go, seek for them at the bottom of the deep—go, watch for them in the bright blue Heavens! You will meet with them there—yes, there—and 'tis there poor Crazy Marian will again see them! They cannot divide us there—they cannot tear the infant from the mother's throbbing breast! The poisonous breath of calumny enters not there—no—no, they are gone—gone! But there we shall meet again!"

"Poor creature!" said William, "her reason is a wreck."

"A wreck—yes!" exclaimed Marian, and her countenance underwent the most powerful emotion; "it was a wreck; and, oh! a dreadful one, that deprived a mother of her husband and her only child! Husband!—no—no—

No. 6

they tore him from me—they forced him to abandon me! They reviled me—they calumniated my name; but they could not change his heart. No, no; I know he loved me—and yet was it not cruel to force my infant from my breast, and consign him to the merciless deep? Gone—gone—gone—and poor Marian left alone to weep and wail. Weep!—no; I'll laugh. Ha! ha! ha! Oh, it is a good thing to be merry in despair. Ha! ha! ha!"

And before William had time to utter a single word, the poor witless one rushed away from the spot, and was soon hid from observation by the deep clustering trees.

For a short time the sailor was completely inactive through the astonishment which this adventure, and the abrupt departure of Crazy Marian had occasioned. But at length he turned his gaze upon the insensible burthen in his arms.

"Poor girl—poor girl!" he said; "the ruffianly treatment of that d—d piratical swab has quite overcome her. What a beauteous form, and now, by the bright beams of the moon, let me gaze upon the features of her who is so unexpectedly thrown upon my protection. I wonder who she is—here's tresses, like flakes of gold. Ah! what do my eyes behold? Can there be two angels alike? I—I—avast—avast! I shall choke myself with joy. How my heart throbs—would that I could look into her eyes! But those features, those lips, that look of innocence, all—all tell me that my heart's pulsations have not mistaken the recognition. It is—it is, kind Heavens, I thank thee! Flora—my own dear darling Flora! Look up—speak to me! It is thy William, thine own William, that enfolds thee to his bosom!"

At the sound of her lover's voice, the senses of Flora returned and she opened her beauteous and sparkling eyes, and turned them upon him.

"William!" she screamed in a tone of franctic joy. "William—safe?"

"Flora, my own fond Flora! it is your faithful Will who now clasps you in his arms, and presses kisses of the warmest love upon your rosy lips! My love, my sweetest!"

"Oh, this joy is too great," sighed forth the maiden; and, overcome by the power of her emotions, she once more fainted in his arms.

Again and again did the young mariner kiss the beauteous cheeks of her from whom he had been so long separated, and whom he had met so opportunely; then raising her in his arms, he fled with all the speed he was able in the direction which he knew led to the village.

CHAPTER VII.

THE JOYS OF THE SAILOR'S RETURN.—MORE VILLANY OF SIR JULIAN MORDLINGTON.—CRAZY MARIAN.—THE WILL.—THE REJECTION.—THE QUARREL.—THE PLOT.—THE SEIZURE.

LIGHT appeared to be the lovely burthen which William Backstay bore in his arms. His heart was filled with the most unbounded delight, and he flew along with the speed of an arrow, until at length the tall spire of the village church met his gaze, and shortly afterwards the neat and well-known farm of his foster parents met his view.

It would be impossible to describe the extatic sensation that now filled the breast of the young seaman; it was like the bright vision of past days rushing upon his recollection as a flood of gold, bringing with it rare instances and associations as clear and as brilliant as the most lucid beams of the moon. And then the form he held in his arms, the form of her whom he loved even beyond those who had been to him as parents, added to the extasy of his feelings. He could have danced and sang with rapture, and yet there were certain sensations that restrained the expression of those feelings. But to know that he held to his heart his Flora—his own Flora, his treasured one;—the beauteous innocent that had, during the time he was encountering all the perils of the vasty deep, that he had by Providence been permitted to arrive at the very moment when her peace, her happiness, her very life, perhaps, was placed in the most imminent danger, increased his joy, and rendered even the charms of home as perfectly insignificant when compared with them.

He paused, and resting the inanimate form of the lovely individual he supported, on the blighted trunk of a tree near the spot, he first gazed with admiration on her countenance, illumed as it was by the chaste beams of Diana, and then again and again pressed his lips on her pure but lovely cheeks.

"My Flora, my own Flora," he soliloquized, "how it joys my heart to be able thus again to press thy little sylph-like form once more to it. Poor girl, poor girl! and to preserve thee from the ruffianly grasp of the villain who might have borne thee from me. Bless thee, bless thee, Flora! But who could the miscreant have been that committed the outrage upon thee? He must have been employed by some other individual. He could not of himself have had the presumption to aspire to one so fair, so lovely, so innocent. Poor girl! still insensible. Cannot the kisses of your William recall you to life? And yet his heart, faithful as it has been to you, throbbing as it does now with the warmest sensations against your own, ought to impart once more vitality to it. My eyes! what a happy fellow I am to possess the love of such an angel as this! Bless thee! bless thee, Flora, again, and again. The seaman returns to his native land, and finds every happiness in store for him. Happiness! what greater happiness can there be, than to find the girl of his heart, the beacon of his peace, with a heart and affection bounding towards him, like a bubbling sea, only twice as lovely and healthful. Would to Heaven that she would again open those eyes of light, that they might beam upon me their lustre, and receive the recognition of my own. There's my home! home! how delightful the sound, when we know that we have anxious hearts and friendly hands to greet us. Home! 'tis the haven of peace and love to the weather-beaten mariner. I gaze upon you, home of my more than parents; dancing merrily in the bright beams of the empress of the night. You are happy, living, joyous, all; father, mother, Fouchette, Harry. My hopes convince me that you are. The aspect of the spot of my childhood tells me that ye are. Dear, dear, friends. There, there's the ivy-mantled old church; there stands the pretty farm, the happy abode of honest industry and integrity. Oh, how delighted they will all be to see me once more. But my poor Flora, she still remains insensible. The joy of our unexpected meeting, together with the alarm which that d—d swab has caused her, have quite overpowered her. Let me bear her into the house, and they will soon recover her."

Once more the young sailor kissed the rich ripe lips of his lover, while the most extatic bliss ran through the current of his veins, and pervaded all his senses. He raised her gently in his arms again and then moved on towards the farm. Most eagerly did he fix his eyes upon every well known spot, and, as he gazed upon the farm, he could almost imagine he saw the eyes of his dearest friends fixed upon him, and that he could already hear their merry and cordial tones of welcome and of joy. What changes might not have come over them all, during his absence? Upon this subject, however, he could not venture to dwell, although hope, sanguine hope, still flattered him that he should find them all well.

At the gate that opened upon the little well-laid out garden of the farm, he once more paused, and his heart throbbed violently against his side, with the strength of his emotions. He opened the gate, and entered the garden, and, as he approached the house, loud sounds of merriment greeted his ears, and the hearty laugh of the farmer was plainly distinguishable from the rest.

"Thanks to Providence!" observed the young mariner, "they are well, or they would never be so cheerful. Little do they imagine the cargo of joy that is about to be unshipped for their benefit."

Mr. Fitzpatrick had returned to the farm, after the visit he had made to the young baronet, his honest heart swelling with indignation at the infamous proposal that had been made to him, but determined by every means in his power, and at all hazards, to thwart the diabolical plans of the villain.

"The spalpeen—th—th—the dirty young blackguard!" soliloquised the lawyer, as he proceeded on his way, "to presume to offer Patrick Fitzpatrick, esquire, a bribe. Tunder and turf, and it's me ownsilf that, old as I am, would no more mind knocking him into smithereens than I would about tossing off a noggin of whiskey. Twelve thousand pounds! a very dacent sum that; but it is not twelve times twelve thousand pounds that would induce Patrick Fitzpatrick to have any hand in any such dirty job, and by which the darling son of my old patron, if still living, would be plundered of his just and lawful rights. Oh! bad luck to that thief of the world. He's a bad one, I can tell by the look of his eyes, in a pig's whisper. But he will only have one more to conquer if he triumphs over me. The will is now safe in my possession, and there it shall remain, until I am convinced that the poor boy is really no more. Och! and isn't it a strict search I'll be making after the darlint? There sha'n't be a nook or a corner but what I will examine, and bad luck to that Sir Julian if I should happen to come across him. What a simpleton the young baronet must have been to mention anything about the supposed existence of his brother, and then I might not have heard of it, and he would have had no occasion to betray his villany at all, at all, by wishing me to destroy the will. But he shall find that the old lawyer will prove one too many for him, or my name is not Mr. Patrick Fitzpatrick."

Thus cogitating and ruminating within himself, the lawyer proceeded on his way, fully resolved to use every means in his power to ascertain whether the report was true, namely, that the foundling of the wreck was still in existence, and to reinstate him, if he was, in those rights of which he had been for so many years, and under such unfortuitous circumstances, been deprived of. To his own breast, however, he at present resolved to keep all that he had heard and the interview he had had with Sir Julian, confined, lest it might mar the progress of his designs, and retard the accomplishment of his wishes.

The return of Mr. Fitzpatrick to the farm was greeted with pleasure, for there was that simplicity and soul-heartiness in that gentleman's behaviour, that he seldom failed to make an impression of the most favourable description upon those with whom he came in contact; and his peculiarities and eccentricities, added to his never failing good humour, rendered his society particularly amusing and agreeable.

He found the farmer, his wife, daughter, son, and two or three veteran mariners, as usual, seated by the fireside, and in the cheerful conversation which ensued, and the strange yarns that were spun for their special amusement, his mind soon became abstracted from the disagreeable scene he had so recently witnessed at the hall.

The most excellent humour predominated, and it was hard to distinguish which among the company was the merriest. There was but one circumstance that tended to dampen the mirth of the evening, and that was the absence of Flora Clarendon. It was seldom that she missed paying her customary visit to her friends at the farm, and they could not conjecture the reason. She was well enough when Henry and his wife quitted home, but still she might since have been seized with indisposition; and anxious to set their doubts at rest Henry was about to leave the farm and return home for that purpose, when they were all startled by a loud knocking at the door.

"Ah!" ejaculated old Ben, "there she is at last! Better late than never. Open the door, Henry."

The knocking was repeated, and it was then succeeded by the voice of a man, who shouted aloud:—

"Ship a hoy!—Who's on board there?"

"It is a man," observed the farmer, "and from the nature of the observations he made use of, I should say he is a seaman. He must have a hearty welcome. Perhaps he brings us news of our poor Will."

Henry flew to open the door, but no sooner had he done so than there was a simultaneous exclamation of astonishment and delight, on beholding William, supporting Flora in his arms, standing in the threshold. Hastily William placed the lovely girl in a chair, and in a moment every one flew to greet and welcome him. It was such a scene as may be imagined, but which cannot be done justice to in description. The young seaman's heart was too full,— his joy was too unbounded to allow him to speak; but he alternately pressed old Marie, Fouchette, and the wife of Henry to his bosom, and pressed the hands of the males again and again.

"Oh! William," exclaimed Marie, "the joy of this meeting is too great."

"Great, mother!" repeated William; "it is indeed; I could dance, sing, laugh, fight, do anything, my heart is so full with pleasure. Father! Fouchette! Marie! all—all here! The same old faces! The same happy looks, the—I—I—I can scarce believe that I have even quitted this happy dwelling for an instant, only for the ten-fold joy I now feel on my return. Amid the battle's fury,—the dangers of the deep;—the thoughts of home, friends, and my dear Flora, have ever sustained me, and made me smile at danger, and now —"

"But Flora," interrupted the farmer; "what is the matter with her?"

"Bless her pretty face," answered William, "she has only fainted, overcome I suppose by the power of her feelings after meeting with the lad of her heart, safe and sound once again. Look to the poor girl, mother, Fouchette; she will soon recover again."

The females flew to the aid of the still insensible Flora, but all their efforts were, for a time, completely ineffectual.

"Surely something must have occurred to alarm her," said Marie.

"Alarm her," repeated William; "why, yes, to be sure, there was something took place which was enough to frighten her."

"Ah!"

"Yes; I had almost forgotten that," continued William; "had it not been the will of Providence to guide my footsteps to the very place where my presence was so much needed, and at a very critical moment too, I don't know what might have happened to the poor girl. I found her struggling in the arms of a black-looking piratical rascal, and screaming aloud for help. Little did she expect that her William was so close at hand to fly to her rescue."

"Who dare insult Flora Clarendon?" said honest old Ben, with indignation and resentment glowing on his countenance; "ah! it must have been that villain, the baronet."

"Baronet!" reiterated William; "well, if it was, he was the strangest looking baronet I ever beheld. Black as a tar-bucket, and ten times more frightful than the figure-head of the Gorgon."

"One of the creatures of Sir Julian, I have no doubt," observed the farmer.

"Sir Ju—Julian!" demanded William, "who the devil is he? Insult my Flora!—my—my—d—e! let him be either a baronet, a duke, lord, marquis, or an archbishop, if he dare to attempt anything to her injury, or offers to molest her in any way, I will blow him to the very devil. But see, she opens her eyes! she recovers! Flora, dear Flora, look up, it is your own William that is near you."

"William, William," repeated the damsel, her senses for a moment wandering, and her brilliant eyes fixed on vacancy; "yes,—yes; hasten to his succour, or he will perish. He is struggling with the ruffian, and in another moment ——"

"Flora, my own one," interrupted her lover, "do you not know me? Look up; I am safe, quite safe."

Flora looked at the young mariner for a second or two, in the most earnest manner, then uttering a frantic cry of joy, she exclaimed,—

"William, dear William, safe! oh! God! I thank thee!" and she immediately sunk overcome by her emotions, sobbing on his bosom; while he pressed her with the most unbounded fervour to that heart over which she exercised the most unlimited sway.

During the whole of this time, Mr. Fitzpatrick had been a deeply interested spectator of this joyous scene, but he observed William with feelings such as he had not experienced for many years before. His fine, muscular, and manly figure was nobility itself, and there was something in his handsome countenance which appealed immediately to the worthy lawyer's heart. In a moment he felt for William the same ardent friendship as if they had been intimate for years; a friendship which he was convinced, neither time nor circumstance could alter.

We will pass hastily over the scene which now ensued to greet William's return. It was soon known all over the village, and many were the old friends that came to grasp the hand of an old companion, and to bid him once more welcome to his native shores. The former requested that he would give them an account of the meeting between him and Flora, and the particulars of the outrage, to which she was so near falling a victim. William immediately complied with this request, and then related the narrow escape he had had of his life, and the manner in which he had been saved by the sudden appearance of the wandering woman.

"Ah!" remarked Ben; "from the description you give of her, it must have been mad Marian."

"Ay, too surely her reason was a wreck;" observed William. "Poor creature, it was quite piteous to hear her talk; and then she looked so wild, and sang such a melancholy song, that it was enough to wring the stoutest heart to hear her. Has she been long in this neighbourhood?"

"Ever since you left England," answered the farmer.

"Poor thing," said William, "and where lives she?"

"A wretched hovel in the wood forms her only shelter," returned Ben; "but she is frequently absent from it, and wandering about the country for days together."

"And how does she subsist?"

"Upon the charity of strangers. No one will refuse poor Crazy Marian a portion of their humble fare."

"I wonder what bitter misfortunes could have driven her from society," said William; "and caused such a tempest in a mind that probably once was cheerful and happy?"

"I know not," replied Ben Backstay; "but I have heard it repeated that she was formerly crossed in love; others seem to think that she has been married and suffered some terrible injustice from her husband. It must have been indeed no ordinary circumstance that could cause such ruin and desolation in her bosom. And then the song she is generally heard singing, is— Hark! that is her voice—do you not hear it?"

They listened attentively, and the sweet, yet melancholy tone of the still mellifluous voice of Crazy Marian, might be heard floating on the stilly night air. Every person present listened to it with the deepest attention and interest, and at length as the poor maniac seemed to approach nearer, they could plainly distinguish the following words, that were sung to the same tune as William had overheard her give utterance to in the wood, previous to her hastening to his rescue and that of Flora?—

"Mourn, mourn for those departed,
Weep scalding tears for those no more;
Mourn for the poor broken hearted,
Left her sorrows to deplore!
                    Mourn! mourn!

"But 'twas to lose them harder,
Harder far fell scandal's tongue;
To lose them all—a husband, father,
And still does life my woe prolong!
                    Mourn! mourn!

"Gone! gone! beneath the billow,
Where I ne'er shall see them more!
No cypress green, no drooping willow,
Canopy their tomb on shore!
                    Gone! gone!'

"Can anything be more plaintively beautiful?" said Flora; "unhappy wanderer! could we induce her to enter the farm, so that we might seek to impart consolation to her deeply lacerated mind."

"The appearance of so many persons," remarked the farmer, "I am doubtful would alarm her."

"Poor darlint!" said the compassionate lawyer, who had been for a short time immersed in deep rumination, although it was quite evident that he was paying every attention to each syllable that Crazy Marian was giving utterance to; "poor darlint! Och, and it's her own self that has surely suffered something very dreadful. There is an expression in the tones of her voice, too, that also makes my heart thump against my ribs like a paviour's rammer when I come to dwell upon them. I should like to see her and ascertain whether I have before beheld her. Does she ever venture into the immediate precincts of your residence, Mr. Backstay?"

"She has frequently done so," answered the farmer, "and I have afforded her relief; but, after uttering some wild and incoherent speech, she has abruptly made her departure. Careworn as her countenance is, and haggard as is her form, she yet retains all the traces of having been formerly handsome, and to have moved in some superior station of society. Hark! I hear her frantic laugh outside; I will endeavour to prevail upon her to enter."

The farmer went to the door, and, opening it, the poor witless wanderer was fully revealed to every person in the room, as she stood in the broad beams of the moonlight that fell full upon her countenance and person, her large and brilliant eyes glaring vacantly upon the objects before her.

"Ah! that countenance, those features," exclaimed the lawyer, suddenly springing from his seat, and advancing towards the door; "can two human beings so much resemble each other? Unhappy woman, tell me your name and ——"

The maniac waved her hand in a commanding manner, and arrested the further progress of Mr. Fitzpatrick, then, uttering a strange and almost supernatural laugh, she ejaculated—

"Back! back! back! Approach not Crazy Marian—she knows ye not. Back—back, I say, for mankind has now nothing to do with the be-

48 THE SMUGGLER KING.

reaved—the deserted one. Gone — gone! all gone! Dead! dead! dead! The angry billows did it all. They left me nothing to treasure on earth. It was very cruel!—very hard to leave poor Marian alone in the world! Why have I been suffered to live, the wretched wreck of what was once fair and happy? What has Crazy Marian to do with the world now? Gone—gone! all gone!"

"Poor unfortunate!" said Backstay, in a voice of the greatest commiseration; "come in and comfort yourself. Here will you find hearts that can and will sympathise with your sorrows."

"I never beheld so great a likeness," continued the lawyer, still gazing intently on the features of the maniac; "her words, too, and yet it is impossible!"

The other persons in the room gazed at Mr. Fitzpatrick, and listened to his words with astonishment, but no one offered to interrupt him, and the lawyer, apparently awed and bewildered by the manner of the maniac, did not attempt to advance nearer towards her, although his curiosity was wrought up to the highest and almost insupportable pitch.

Poor Marian stood for a minute or two, and gazed with wondering wildness upon the lawyer and the other persons present, and then giving utterance to another loud and unearthly laugh, she turned suddenly round, and darted from the spot with the speed of lightning, and was in a moment lost entirely to observation.

"Poor creature," remarked Marie; "is it not terrible to see human nature visited with such a fearful calamity?"

"Alas! it is," said Flora, whose tenderest sympathies had been excited by the words and behaviour of the wandering woman; "who and what can she be?"

"The features of poor Marian, and the words she spoke, appeared to strike you most forcibly, sir," remarked the farmer; "think you, you know her?"

"Whist! whist! farmer," replied Mr. Fitzpatrick, "by my sowl I scarcely know what to think about the matter, at all, at all. Her countenance very much resembles one that I knew in former days, but yet I cannot for the life of me, make up my mind to believe that this is her. I must endeavour to see her again."

"I am afraid, sir," returned Backstay, "that although you may find it a very easy matter to behold her again, you will find it much more difficult to obtain an interview with, or to elicit from her strange wanderings, anything that may gratify the curiosity you feel to ascertain whether or not she is really the individual you may take her to be."

"Faith," answered Mr. Fitzpatrick, "and I am very much afraid of that same myself; but I am determined to do my best towards elucidating the mystery, and should she really prove to be the unfortunate I have imagined, och! and it's not a little bit of a hubbub that there will be among some parties before long."

After some further conversation upon this subject, it was changed, and the rest of the evening was passed in the most cheerful manner, William giving a vivid description of the engagements he had been in, and Flora listening to him with feelings of the utmost pride and admiration, at the same time that she mentally returned thanks to the Almighty, who had mercifully guarded her faithful lover from the dangers by which he had been surrounded, and restored him to her in safety and health.

It was the happiest evening that had been spent at the farm for many months, and when they at length separated, it was not till after they had made arrangements for celebrating the safe return of the Foundling of the Wreck to his native land, on the following morning.

Leaving the party at the farm for a short time, we will return to Sir Julian, who, after the departure of Sam Raker, traversed the apartment he was in for a short time, with folded arms, and immersed in deep thought.

"This crafty lawyer," he at length soliloquised, "cannot be disposed of in a readier manner than Sam Raker has suggested, and for which I have every means. The will then becomes mine, and I am safe. Ha! ha! ha! little do the fools imagine that in the person of Sir Julian, the aristocratic man of wealth, the courted of society, the fashionable *roue*, they behold the much-dreaded and terrible Smuggler King, for whose apprehension rewards are offered in vain, and ingenuity and vigilance set at defiance. Oh! it is good to be a man of notoriety, and yet remain unknown. Even now my bonny bark, the Devil Skipper, rides at anchor in the port, known only as an honest trader, and suspicion of her real character never so much as enters the mind of any person. Five thousand pounds for the Smuggler King! Ha! ha! ha! —fools. The sovereign of the deep bids you all defiance; laughs you to utter contempt. Catch him—catch him if you can!"

He paused, and once more paced the room with hasty strides, but yet with inward feelings of exultation and determination.

"Can it be true," he at length continued, "that this William Backstay, as he is called, is that hated brother whom I had hoped that I had, when he was a child, murdered? If so, he must be disposed of, should he return from sea, although I know not that I have much to fear from him, unless that officious old fool, Fitzpatrick, should discover him, before I can complete my designs against him. But that must be accomplished: idiot that I was to mention anything of the matter to him; then he might ever have remained in ignorance. But, pshaw! why should I torment and alarm myself thus?

Sam Racket has suggested, they can both of them, without much difficulty, be waylaid and conveyed on board the Devil Skipper; once there, there is

No. 7

an end to the business, and who will dare dispute the integrity or power of Sir Julian Mordlington? That girl, too, Flora Clarendon, she must she—shall be mine, a fit partner for the Smuggler King. Sam Raker will not fail to put the commands I have given him into execution the very first opportunity, and I have every confidence in the villain's determination and ability. He is one of the most invaluable of my crew. Thus, then, every prospect of success in my designs smiles upon me, and why should I trouble myself with groundless fears? I must, however, act with caution; I must give no cause for suspicion to light upon my real character, or it might cost me more trouble than I am disposed to encounter. The abduction of the girl, and my future departure to join the prize obtained, must be conducted with the greatest care and secrecy. They will not dare to accuse me of being in any way connected with the deed, and I must still appear to be the same charitable and amiable Sir Julian I have hitherto assumed to be. Oh! I will seem a very paragon of virtue, integrity, and philanthropy, while in secret I will hesitate at nothing to gratify my utmost wishes. I will feast my tenants, relieve their wants, redress their wrongs, lower their rents, and appear to do everything that a man and a Christian ought to do, to cajole them into a good opinion of me. Ha! ha! ha! how famously I have laid my plans. How the fools will admire me, laud me to the skies, and lavish upon me every species of adulation. There will be none more admired or praised than Sir Julian Mordlington."

He was interrupted by a low and scornful laugh; and, turning round, he perceived that the room door had been cautiously opened, and standing before it was a figure whose eyes were fixed stedfastly upon him, and whose general appearance filled him with a mingled feeling of astonishment and awe. He started back several paces, and stood gazing at it with amazement for several minutes; while the woman, for such it was, looked at him with a determined expression of hatred and contempt.

It was Crazy Marian; but how she had gained admittance into the hall, or what purpose had brought her there, was beyond the power of conjecture.

Sir Julian would have spoken, but he was so much taken by surprise, that his tongue refused its office, neither could he move a step from the spot on which he was standing.

Marian continued to gaze at him in silence for some time longer, and then she laughed aloud in bitter contempt. Sir Julian was completely confounded: he knew not whether to believe her human or not, and yet his rage at the boldness of the intrusion exceeded all bounds.

"Ha! ha! ha!" laughed Marian at length; "Sir Julian Mordlington talks boldly—bravely; oh! yes; his hopes of triumphing in his villany are most sanguine; but shall they be realized? Oh, yes, for a time they may, but Crazy Marian prognosticates that the time will come when it shall be for the innocent, the oppressed, to triumph only."

"Woman! who are you?—and for what fell purpose have you dared thus to obtrude yourself on my privacy?" demanded the baronet, in a hoarse voice.

"Ha! ha! ha!" repeated Marian, and her fine commanding figure appeared to dilate itself, and her eyes shone with greater brilliancy than ever. "The guilty must fall, they must perish, and innocence at last assert its proper place. I have been wronged, deeply wronged—they have made a wreck of poor Marian's mind; but the darkness will vanish, the clouds will disperse, and all will once more be sunshine. Sunshine—oh! what a summer's day I once experienced!—how fair my prospects, how I loved, how I worshipped; but they calumniated my name, they traduced my fair name, and they told me he believed it; but I cannot think so, after all his vows of love, after all the love I lavished upon him. And yet would you think it? Oh, yes, for who shall deny that men are cruel deceivers—all? But his own wife, to desert her—tear the innocent babe from her breast, and then to suffer it to be consigned to the pitiless deep. But he perished also, he could not perpetrate so cruel a deed! I will not encourage the base scandal, although poor wandering Marian met with such justice and mercy. But they are gone now, all gone—gone!—and Marian is left behind to weep and pray for death. All gone—all gone! Oh! my poor heart—heart, I have none, or it must have broken ere now. All gone—all gone!"

There was something in the words, the voice, the manner, and the features of the wandering Marian that filled the bosom of Sir Julian with the most powerful emotion, and yet he was unable to account for it. Nor could he move or offer to eject her, for there was that about her which awed him in her presence, and made him hesitate to approach her. He had some recollection of having before seen her, but when or where he could form no idea.

"Wretched maniac, for such you are," he at last said, "of what business are your sorrows or wrongs to me? Why came you hither, and who gave you admittance to the hall?"

"Maniac! ha! ha! ha!" returned Marian, "yes, yes, yes; true—true—very true. I am poor Marian, the witless one. My brain is wrecked, as have been all those that I so fondly loved. All gone—all gone—all gone!"

"Leave the house. I like not your presence; but would not use harsh measures. Begone!"

"Ha! ha! ha!" laughed Marian. "How merciful is *the Smuggler King!*"

Had a thunderbolt at that moment have fallen upon the head of Sir Julian, he could not have started more than he did at those words. His countenance changed—his lips quivered; he fixed his eyes upon Marian as if he would penetrate into the innermost recesses of her very soul, and then he felt in his bosom for a knife, as a dreadful thought rushed upon his brain. All these emotions the maniac observed with the utmost composure, and without altering her position the least in the world, at the same time maintaining the greatest coolness and intrepidity.

"The Smuggler King!" he repeated; "who is it that dares thus to—but, idiot that I am to notice the wild ravings of a wandering maniac. Begone! wretched being, I again command you, or, by hell, even you shall not escape the fury of my rage and revenge."

"The Smuggler King delights in the shedding of human blood," replied the unfortunate woman; "who should marvel were he to add the murder of poor Crazy Marian to the list of his other bold deeds?"

"To be taunted thus, and in my own house," shouted the enraged Sir Julian, unable any longer to control his ungovernable frenzy. "Hag! maniac! devil! whatever you are, away, or I will press my fingers in your throat, and stop your babbling for ever."

"Ha! ha! ha!" scornfully laughed the maniac, as Sir Julian rushed towards her, and the next instant she darted from the place, and closed the door after her with a loud bang.

The baronet first re-opened the door of the apartment, and then looked out, but he could not see anything of her. He returned to the apartment and rang the bell violently for the servant. He made his appearance.

"Saw you anything of a strange, wild-looking woman?" he demanded.

"She just this minute passed me in the hall, Sir Julian," answered the man.

"Ah! why then did you not secure her?"

"Secure her, Sir Julian?" repeated the servant; "what necessity could there be for that? It was only poor Crazy Marian, who would do no harm to any one, I'm sure. She used frequently to come to the Hall, I have heard, when ——"

"Idiot! knave!" passionately interrupted the baronet; "am I to have my privacy broken in upon by every wandering wretch?"

"I ask your pardon, Sir Julian, but ——"

"How gained she admittance?"

"I know not, Sir Julian."

"If she again makes her appearance near the Hall, I command you to see that she is immediately taken into custody, or beware of my anger."

"Oh, Sir Julian, surely you cannot mean what you say?" returned the servant, with a look of amazement; "take poor Crazy Marian into custody? For what—and —"

"It is my pleasure, and I will be obeyed," sternly interrupted his master; "get you gone, and mind what I have said to you."

The servant could not help shrugging his shoulders, and muttering something to himself; but as the baronet had turned his back towards him, he did not observe him, and the servant vanished, secretly determined not to attend to one tittle of the mandates that his master had given to him.

Sir Julian paced the room with uneven steps for a few minutes after the servant had disappeared, and his feelings were worked up to a pitch of the greatest agitation by the event which had taken place, and the words that Crazy Marian had given utterance to.

"Am I awake?" he ejaculated, when his surprise and confusion had somewhat abated; "known—taunted—mocked—threatened, at the very moment when I fancied myself in the greatest security. It seems scarcely possible, and yet there was no madness in the accusation she made use of. Who can she be? Her features are familiar to me, and struck me with a feeling almost amounting to horror, and yet I have no recollection of where I have before seen her, or how she should have arrived at the knowledge she possesses of me. Had I not been worse than idiot, I should never have permitted her to leave this place alive. But there are more times than one to secure her. Should she in the meanwhile betray me! But no, she —a wandering maniac, would not be believed. She would only be laughed at—I am safe enough, if the secret rests only with her."

He felt somewhat more composed, after having come to this conclusion, but still the strong impression that the features of Marian had made upon his mind, he could not so easily banish, and he was fully determined to leave no means untried to endeavour to discover who she really was, and to ascertain whether there was any actual danger to be apprehended from her.

He now threw himself on a chair, and for an interval gave way to rumination. He was impatient until he should see Sam Raker again, and learn from him the result of his attempt to secure the person of the beauteous Flora Clarendon, and whether or not he had learnt any more particulars of William Backstay. He was also most anxious to make him acquainted with what had taken place, and the words of Crazy Marian, which had left so powerful an impression upon his recollection.

Hour after hour passed away, however, and Sam came not, which greatly increased the impatience of the baronet, who began to be afraid that something had happened to him, although he knew him to be generally so cautious and designing, that he seldom failed in his object, and always contrived to keep out of the way of danger.

Evening now set in—it was the evening on which William arrived at home, and Sir Julian was beginning to despair of seeing Sam Raker that night, when the before-mentioned Simon, the servant, made his appearance in the room, with his usual announcement,—

"Strange man below, Sir Julian, wants to see you."

"Who do you mean?" demanded his master; "have you seen him before?"

"Yes, Sir Julian," answered Simon; "but it is not the strange little Irish gentleman, who called before, but the strange man with the ugly whiskers and the gruff voice."

The baronet frowned, and then muttered to himself,

"It is Raker;" adding aloud, "conduct him up stairs."

It was easy to perceive by the countenance of Sam Raker when he entered the room that he had no very satisfactory news to impart; he made a slight, sullen inclination of his head to Sir Julian, took off his hat, wiped his forehead as if he had been walking fast, and then threw himself carelessly into a chair.

"You seem out of temper, Sam?" said Sir Julian.

"I am," was the brief reply.

"What has disturbed you?"

"Perhaps you have more right to feel disturbed than I have."

"Ah! what has happened?"

"Why, that I have failed," answered Sam Raker.

"Ah! in what do you mean?" demanded the baronet.

"The girl."

"Have you then made the attempt?"

"I have, not more than an hour since," replied the smuggler, "and I almost got a leaden pill for my pains."

"D——n!"

"Hear me out."

"Be as quick as you can, then," returned Sir Julian; "for I am all impatience to hear these particulars."

"In the first place," observed Raker, "I watched the girl according to your instructions, saw her leave her home, and dogged her cautiously to the wood."

"Well."

"There I seized her. But she screamed and struggled violently."

"What could that avail against your strength?" inquired Sir Julian.

"It brought to her assistance a young sailor."

"A sailor!" repeated the baronet, changing colour.

"A sailor! and he proved to be ——"

"Who?"

"The girl's sweetheart."

"The miscalled William Backstay?"

"The same!"

"Confusion; but are you certain it was really he?"

"I am positive."

"Curses light upon him. But did you suffer him to defeat you?"

"He fought with the fury of a young Nick," answered Sam Raker, "but still I had felled him to the earth, and the next moment I should have had his life, but misfortune in the shape of a woman or the devil started forth to frustrate my purpose."

"A woman?"

"A wandering maniac; Crazy Marian, I have heard they call her."

"Crazy Marian!" repeated the baronet, biting his lips; "the same that, but this afternoon forced her way into my presence, and taunted, upbraided, and accused me of being the Smuggler King."

"Can you speak the truth?"

"I do. But proceed."

"Just as I was in the act of completing my purpose," continued Sam

Raker," the maniac rushed forward, and presenting a brace of pistols at my head, threatened me with instant death if I did not retire."

" And you obeyed?"

" What could I do ; I was disarmed."

" And where were your comrades?"

" They had somehow or other mistaken the instructions I had given them, and had secreted themselves in the wrong place. And even had they been there, I should have been deprived of their aid, as the whistle with which I intended to have given the signal was knocked out of my hand by my antagonist, and having no means of defence, I had no other alternative than to take to immediate flight, or to lose my life."

" Curses light upon this disappointment!" exclaimed Sir Julian, passionately ; " there will now perhaps be such a strict watch placed over the girl, that she will elude all the schemes we may invent to get her in our power."

" But she shall be your's," answered Sam Raker, resolutely, " or my name is not what it is. But we had better let the business rest for a few days."

" Every moment of delay is insupportable," said Sir Julian, " and had you acted with more prudence, the girl might even now have been on board our craft."

" It was no fault of mine," returned Raker, " and therefore it is of no use to upbraid me."

" Well, and how do you suggest that we should now proceed?" inquired the baronet.

" I have told you. We had better wait patiently for a few days, until the present excitement has in some degree abated, and the friends of the girl may become confident that we have abandoned our designs."

" Well ; I suppose it must be so," said Sir Julian, in dissatisfied tones.

" I see no other course to be adopted."

" But this young sailor, my ——I can't say the word."

" We must keep a sharp look out for him," answered Raker.

" I shall not rest until we get him in our clutches."

" Which he will doubtless soon be," said Sam.

" You say he is a resolute young fellow?"

" He is."

" When we once get him on board, we will see whether we can turn him to any account ; if not, the sooner we get rid of him the better."

" Ay, ay," coincided Sam Raker. " But I cannot help thinking of poor Crazy Marian."

" She has never been out of my thoughts since the unexpected interview I had with her this afternoon," observed Sir Julian. " Think you she is really mad ?"

" I have my doubts, but time will show ; at any rate, I owe her a grudge, and shall not forget to pay her off at the earliest opportunity."

" That will be matter for after consideration," said the baronet.

" It will," was the answer of Raker ; " however, I never forget those who offend me."

" I know it."

" We have plenty of business on our hands, cap—Sir Julian, I mean."

" We have ; but I have no doubt but that we shall be able to accomplish it."

" It shall be no fault of mine if we do not," remarked the smuggler. " But about the lawyer ?"

" Fitzpatrick ?"

" The same. He is staying at Ben Backstay's."

" That is very awkward," returned Sir Julian ; " for, should the old the secret will be divulged in a minute, and all my plans thwarted."

"Not so; we must devise some plan to prevent that, should such an accident as you apprehend occur."

"The likeness which William I dare say bears to my father, and the marks which the confounded memory of the old lawyer brings to his mind that he bears upon his person, may betray him."

"Psha! you always anticipate difficulties where there is no occasion."

"It is always better to be on your guard than to make yourself too confident."

"True; and so we can. Had you never mentioned the circumstance of your brother's supposed existence, old Latitat's suspicions would not have been excited."

"No," replied the baronet, "there I admit I acted with thoughtlessness and imprudence."

"To-morrow you expect to see him again?"

"If he has not altered his mind. How would you propose that we then should act?"

"I will tell you," replied Sam Raker; "first be sure that he has the will in his possession, then let him be secured and placed in confinement until midnight, when he can with secresy and safety be conveyed on board our craft, where no one will think of looking for him. Once there, of course you understand how to dispose of him."

"I do," said Sir Julian, with a fiendish smile. "He shall not live long to tell tales."

"It will be your own fault and bad policy if he does," said Raker.

"You and two or three more of our fellows had better come here secretly, and conceal yourselves in the hall in case your aid should be required."

"Exactly—those orders shall be obeyed."

"How are our daring crew?" inquired the baronet.

"All in excellent spirits," answered Sam Raker, "but impatient for business."

"They shall soon be gratified. The Smuggler King will have plenty of work for them by and bye. But you have not heard anything to cause you to believe that any suspicion is entertained of the real character of our vessel?"

"None; or, of course, as we are always on the look out, we should soon have timely notice of them."

"Ha! ha! ha! who plays so deep a game as the Smuggler King, and his bold and intrepid crew?"

"None," returned Sam Raker, "and that under the very noses of the land-sharks. But have you any more commands for me, cap—Sir Julian, I mean?"

"Only to be punctual to-morrow."

"I will not fail."

"And to keep a sharp eye on Flora Clarendon, and my—her lover."

"Ay, ay, you may rest assured of that."

"I do not doubt you."

"I think I may take the credit to myself to say that you have never had any occasion," said Raker.

"You may. But, good night. Leave the hall by the back way, so that you may not attract observation."

"You shall be obeyed; for I know very well that I certainly am not one of the best looking fellows in the world, and do not carry any of my amiable qualities in my countenance. Good night, Sir Julian."

The baronet waved his hand to the smuggler, but returned him no answer, and Raker quitted the room and the hall, making his exit, as he had been ordered, by the back way.

The failure of the evening caused considerable vexation and disappointment to Sir Julian, but he entertained hopes that their future attempts would be attended with greater success, and had every confidence in the craft and determination of the villain Sam Raker, who he was certain would not stick at anything, in order that he might gain the accomplishment of his nefarious designs. Sam was a miscreant of the most diabolical sort. He was never so happy as when he was engaged in some deep-laid scheme of villany, and he exulted and gloried in the miseries of his fellow creatures. He had been engaged in some of the most desperate and daring schemes both on sea and land, for many years, and never had Sir Julian found a more ready or invaluable creature in his hands. Together they had ploughed the ocean deep, and had fought side by side in the determined and bloody affrays in which it was frequently their lot to mingle, and the baronet had ever found him a faithful and ready accessory. He had made him his confidant above all others of his crew, and Sam seemed not a little proud of the distinction, for Sir Julian in every sense of the word, was looked upon as a sovereign by the pirates and smugglers he commanded.

It was therefore owing to this, and notwithstanding the disappointment we have before mentioned, that Sir Julian reconciled himself by the opinion that Sam Raker would be more successful on his next attempt, and that Flora Clarendon would as surely be placed in his power, as if he at that moment held her within his grasp.

The return of his brother, whom he had hoped would have perished at sea, certainly troubled him somewhat more, especially as Mr. Fitzpatrick was staying at old Backstay's; but yet he trusted that he should also be able to get him into his power, and then all his apprehensions on that score would be at an end. The most ungovernable hatred did he feel towards that injured relative, whom he thought he had long since silenced for ever; yet was he most anxious to see him, in order that he might convince himself; for, in spite of the number of years that had elapsed since he had made the attempt to assassinate him, and William was then but a mere infant, he felt certain that there must be something in his features that would assure him of his identity. He would have ventured near the farm in the hope of seeing him; but he was fearful of doing so, lest he should excite suspicion, and especially while the lawyer was staying there, who he knew it was impossible could entertain any very great opinion of his character, particularly after the interview that had taken place between them.

If possible, he detested William more than ever since he had heard that he was betrothed to Flora Clarendon;—but at the same time, from that very circumstance he was half-inclined to think that old Ben Backstay had not made him acquainted with his history and the probability of his origin.

He longed impatiently for the arrival of the following day, when he trusted that Mr. Fitzpatrick and the will would fall into his hand, and that Sam Raker would also bring him some intelligence respecting Flora and her lover.

"Yes," he muttered to himself, as a feeling of certain triumph took possession of his mind; "they must, they shall be mine; the Smuggler King never fixes his thoughts and wishes upon anything but they are sure to be gratified. His power is almost unlimited; it hesitates at nothing to accomplish his designs; he spares neither sex nor age; all—all must succumb to the power of the Smuggler King. Ha! ha! ha! it is a bold life, a merry life. How I long to be once more on board the *Devil Skipper*, where the beauteous Flora

Clarendon shall reign supreme mistress! But I must not yet venture from the hall, only to pay the lads a visit. It would baffle all my views, and moreover, might expose me to danger. That woman, that Crazy Marian, as they call her; her I like not; there is something about her features which strikes almost a deadly horror to my heart, and makes me inwardly shudder. And then her threats! She evidently knows me, and I cannot help believing that she is not the maniac she pretends to be. Where can I have before seen her? In vain do I rack my brain to endeavour to recollect; it is to no purpose! Then again her strange appearance to Sam Raker; her defence of the lovers, and the manner in which she threatened him, all convince me that she is my most bitter enemy. She must be looked to, or she may cause some trouble, and work me evil. Let me but get the other business settled, and Crazy Marian shall not live long to alarm me!"

The villain's countenance had a most savage and unnatural appearance as he gave utterance to these words, and he walked from the room.

The following morning was ushered in by the inmates of the farm, with every demonstration of rustic joy to welcome the return of the young mariner to his native home. A number of the former companions of William, with their sweethearts, had been invited, and flocked at an early hour to the place of merry-making. All was happiness and innocent mirth, and none partook more of the pleasures of the day than the family of old Ben Backstay, who loved William as well as if he had really been connected with them by the ties of consanguinity.

Flora never could have appeared more lovely than she did on that occasion, and in the rapture of the moment, she forgot the alarming adventure of the previous night; and banished from her bosom all idea of how quickly, in all probability, her lover would again be torn from her presence to plough the deep

No. 8

blue ocean, and to encounter once more all those perils from which he had so recently escaped.

Mr. Fitzpatrick would fain have remained at the farm and have joined in the festivities of the occasion, to which he was most warmly invited by them all, but he had made up his mind to go to the hall, burning as he was at the conduct of Sir Julian, and to convince him that the honesty of Mr. Patrick Fitzpatrick was not to be purchased by a bribe, even though it were so goodly a sum as twelve thousand pounds.

He, therefore, although he was convinced of the villany of Sir Julian, did not apprehend any immediate danger, especially as he knew not the manner in which he was connected with the smugglers, and felt no hesitation in seeking his presence, and moreover, in taking the will with him. He apologized to Backstay and his family, from whom he had experienced so much kindness and hospitality during the short time he had been staying at the farm, and then immediately took his departure for the Hall.

We have before mentioned how forcibly struck Mr. Fitzpatrick was with the appearance of William, and, in fact, he had not been able to get him out of his thoughts during the whole of the night. His noble bearing and fine handsome countenance; his fine and intellectual forehead, and intelligent eyes, all reminded him of one whom he never expected to meet with again, and seemed to place him far beyond that station of society in which he at present moved. Notwithstanding that Ben Backstay, as has been before shown, was a very sensible man, and endowed with natural talents superior to those that generally belong to persons of his humble origin, William was so unlike any of the rest of the family that he could scarcely believe him to be the farmer's son; and although it was out of no curiosity, but for other reasons that will be hereafter explained, the worthy lawyer had resolved before he quitted that neighbourhood to question Backstay more particularly on the subject, stating his reasons for so doing. Had not circumstances occurred to prevent it, this would have at once been the means of revealing that which he was so anxious to know; have satisfied him of the identity of William, reinstated him in his rights and frustrated the diabolical designs of the villain Sir Julian. But such a happy consummation of affairs was destined not to be brought about at present. The guilty for awhile were allowed to triumph, and misfortunes crowding quick upon each other, were in store for the innocent and the oppressed.

The honest lawyer proceeded leisurely on his way, ruminating upon the disappointment which Sir Julian would experience, when he became acquainted with his determination, and the reproaches it was his intention to heap upon his head.

He had reached the centre of the wood immersed in these thoughts, and taking no notice of anything around him, when he was suddenly startled by hearing a deep and apparently heart-drawn sigh, proceeding from some person near him, and naturally surprised, he hastily looked up, and his astonishment was in some degree abated, when he beheld standing near him, the form of poor Crazy Marian, who was contemplating him with a vacant yet melancholy look, and listlessly playing with some wild flowers which she had gathered in the course of her solitary wanderings.

Mr. Fitzpatrick gazed at the poor witless one, with feelings of the deepest interest and sympathy, and the more he looked at her the greater did he feel his curiosity of the previous evening increased. There was that in her features, careworn as they were, which made him more anxious than ever to become acquainted with her history, and to ascertain who she really was, and he advanced a few paces, but as he did so the maniac retreated in apparent alarm, and waived her hand for him to keep back.

" Poor darlint creature," said the worthy Irish gentleman, in tones of compassion, " you need not fly me, for it's myself that would not harm a hair of your head."

At the tones of his voice, a change came over the countenance of Marian, and a sunny ray of pleasure for a moment irradiated it. But quickly it passed away, and re-assuming all her usual melancholy and wildness of demeanour, she exclaimed,—

"Back! back! approach me not. Mankind are all the enemies of wandering Marian, but she is their friend. They admired me once, they flattered, they deceived, and abandoned me to misery. Was it not cruel? they heaped scandal upon my name; was it not base and ungrateful in those whom I had never injured? I had those that loved me,—whom I loved—oh! how I loved them! but they are all gone! gone! gone!"

"Who are gone, poor thing?" inquired Mr. Fitzpatrick.

"Gone!" repeated the maniac; "they are all gone; yes, all;—all, and left poor Marian in the wide world alone."

"Those tones!" ejaculated the lawyer; " tunder and turf, but I am certain I have heard them often before. Unfortunate woman, tell me, I beseech you, who are you?"

"Who am I? have I not told you? I am poor wandering Marian, the deserted. Deserted by all; yes, they are gone! gone! all gone!"

"Poor thing," repeated Mr. Fitzpatrick; " if you have been deserted by those who pretended to be your friends, think not so harshly of the world as to suppose that there are not others in it who can pity you, and ——"

"Pity!" interrupted the maniac, " name not the word, it is many years since I before heard it, and then it was used by the lips of hypocrites; by those who had blasted my peace of mind, and loaded me with shame and opprobrium. Pity! ha! ha! ha! it is mockery all. I seek not pity now, but hatred; the word is more congenial to my ears."

"Unfortunate woman," said the lawyer, " there are yet hearts that can feel for the distresses of their fellow creatures, and I ——"

"Back! back!" ejaculated Marian, as Mr. Fitzpatrick again made a motion to advance towards her; " back! back! I say! poor Marian will not trust you. She trusted one, and he deceived her; oh, how cruelly he deceived her; but back, back, I say, Marian will not be deceived again."

She retreated backwards as she spoke, and the lawyer, fearful that she would leave him altogether, and yet seeing no prospect of his being able to gratify his curiosity, once more stopped and gazed at her with looks of the utmost commiseration.

"Mysterious woman," he at length ejaculated, " would that I could learn thy dismal history, that I might convince you how ready I would be to render you all the assistance in my power."

"Assistance!" repeated Marian, with another wild laugh; " yes, yes,—the poor wanderer is now obliged to seek assistance and charity from strangers; but she once had it in her power to afford assistance to the needy herself; and did she ever refuse it? no, no; they well knew this heart, and yet they traduced me,—wronged me,—scouted me. But 'tis all over now; they can scorn me, persecute me if they like, for all I loved are gone! gone! all gone!"

Marian passed her delicate hands across her pale brow, sighed heavily, and then made a motion as if she would depart.

"Stay! stay! poor unfortunate!" cried Mr. Fitzpatrick, " do not leave me thus; I would pity and serve you, if possible."

"Come not near me," said Marian, still retreating from him; " approach me not, I will not trust you. And yet," she continued, after a pause, " you seem kind, and it is many years since I have before experienced kindness; I would serve you."

" Serve me ?"

" Yes ; scorn not my offer."

" What would you ?"

" Whither are you going ?"

" To the Hall."

" Ah! the haunt of villany ;—shun it, shun it, shun it."

" And why should I fear to visit it ?"

" Because danger lurks beneath its roof," answered Marian.

" How know you that ?"

" Ha! ha! ha! poor wandering Marian knows more than they think.   She will shew them that she does."

" Your mind still wanders."

" My mind! I have no mind now; it is gone, gone entirely."

" Of whom would you warn me ?" asked Mr. Fitzpatrick.

" Of he who lurks in darkness to perpetrate deeds that cannot meet the light of day," replied Marian.

" Whom do you mean ?"

" Sir Julian Mordlington! oh, it is a noble name, to perform deeds of villany under.   Ha! ha! ha! beware of Sir Julian."

" Why should I fear him ?"

" Because he may seek your life."

The lawyer started, and looked earnestly at Marian, and then murmured to himself,

" Poor wretched creature ! but she knows not what she says."

" Will you not take my warning ?" demanded the maniac.

" I thank you for it."

" Thank me ! No, no, no, you should not do that ; there is One above who speaks through me, and whom you should thank."

" That One will protect me from danger," said the lawyer vehemently.

" If you are innocent He will ; poor, wandering, witless Marian tells you so. But I must away, I seek those wilds consonent with my mind."

" Leave me not yet."

" Seek not to detain me, or you may make a friend your foe."

" By all the friendship you have asserted for me, explain more fully what you mean."

" I have stated to you enough," returned Crazy Marian ; " shun the Hall, beware of Sir Julian Mordlington, beware of *The Smuggler King !*"

" The Smuggler King !" repeated Mr. Fitzpatrick, with a look of the utmost astonishment.

" Beware of the Smuggler King !" once more exclaimed Marian ; " beware of Sir Julian Mordlington,—beware of *The Devil Skipper !*"

And as she uttered these words, waving her hand, and uttering another loud laugh, Marian the Maniac fled from the spot, and was out of sight in an instant, leaving the lawyer in a state of the utmost bewilderment and astonishment.

" Fait !" he ejaculated to himself after the pause of a few moments, " and this is an adventure, any how !   Beware of Sir Julian Mordlington !   Beware of the Smuggler King !   Beware of the Devil Skipper !   Tunder and turf! What's it all mean ?   But what have I, Mr. Patrick Fitzpatrick, to fear while I have an honest heart throbbing in my bosom ?   Besides, she is only a poor wandering, witless creature, and divil a word does she know of what she's uttering at all, at all ; so, how silly I am to take any notice of her.   Sir Julian Mordlington, I have very good reason to have no great opinion of, but deuce a bit do I fear him, if he tries any of his scurvy ticks wid me, the spalpeen ! As for the Smuggler King, I have heard of him before, but I never remember to have seen the gentleman, and it is not likely that he will have any business wid me! Then as to that Devil's Skipper, jump me to Beelzebub, if I ever so much as heard the name mentioned before in all my born days, and I don't care if I never hear it again! Poor creature! how strangely she talks, and yet sometimes there is a good deal of reason in her madness, and there is that in her manners, conversation, and features that has made an impression on me, I shall not easily forget. I must see her again after I have settled this business with Sir Julian, and then it shall not be my fault if we are not better acquainted. I am all impatience to know who she is, and to see whether I can do anything to serve her, and to restore her from her present wretched condition to her senses and happiness."

Having thus spoken the truly excellent man, nothing daunted by the warning he had received, hurried on his way, and soon afterwards came within sight of the Hall.

Sir Julian Mordlington had arisen at an early hour that morning, for his mind had been too much occupied with perplexing thoughts to allow him to sleep much on the preceding night, and he also expected that Sam Raker and his companions would arrive soon; also he was uncertain at what time the lawyer might take it in his head to visit the Hall, if he really should make up his mind to come there at all.

He had not been arisen many minutes when he heard a low tap at the room door, and it being the signal they had agreed upon the day before, also having provided him with the key of the back entrance, he concluded at once that it was Sam Raker and the other smugglers.

He went to the door and opening it, Sam Raker entered alone.

"You are punctual," observed Sir Julian.

"When did you know me otherwise?" demanded Raker.

"True! but where are the others?"

"In the adjoining room," answered Sam, "where they will be ready to peep out in an instant. I thought you might not wish them to overhear all that we had to say."

"That was right," observed Sir Julian. "Did any one observe you enter the Hall?"

"No."

"That is better still," said the baronet; "so far you have managed this affair very well."

"I am glad I have pleased you, cap—Sir Julian I mean," returned the smuggler.

"Heard you anything more about the girl, Flora Clarendon?"

"No, I have had no opportunity."

"Nor her lover, the hated William?"

"No more than that they are all making jolly this morning at the farm, to celebrate his return from sea."

"If fortune does not frown upon us," said Sir Julian, "we shall shortly spoil their mirth."

"I trust we shall. But think you old Latitat will come?"

"I scarcely know. But it will be very awkward if he does not."

"It will at any rate, spoil our scheme for the present."

"And before we may have another opportunity of putting it into execution, Fitzpatrick may have quitted the neighbourhood."

"That we must endeavour to prevent."

"I know you will do so, if possible, Sam," said Sir Julian, "but for my own part I do not see how it is to be done."

"Oh, leave me alone; I am more than a match for a lawyer at any time."

"Ha! ha! ha! you are an indefatigable fellow, and, I trust, you may not fail on this very particular occasion."

"But should he come?"

"Offer not to make your appearance until I give the signal by stamping with my foot."

"Very good," said Sam Raker.

"Then you and your fellows rush forward and seize the old dotard."

"That shall be done in a business-like manner."

"Gag him, to prevent his cries reaching the ears of any of the servants," remarked Sir Julian. "He can be safely confined in the room where your companions now are, till midnight, when he must be conveyed with all expedition on board the Devil Skipper."

"He shall."

"Is all prepared on board?"

"Oh, yes, everything for the lawyer's warm reception," answered Raker.

"Ha! ha! ha!" laughed Sir Julian, triumphantly; "how surprised he will be to find himself amongst such unexpected company."

"He will," returned Raker, "and it won't afford him any considerable gratification."

"No, it will not, and I dare say he would then be very happy to give up the will without the twelve thousand pounds, and be suffered to depart."

"No doubt of it; but we know better than to do that."

"Certainly; the Smuggler King is not the man to part so easily with his enemies."

"He has proved so at any rate," replied Sam. "But should he come without the will?"

"Why, that would be rather unpleasant," said Sir Julian; "but still we must not suffer him to slip through our fingers."

"To be sure not. He is the principal witness, and, once removed, the validity of the will might be easily disputed."

"And with your power—capt—Sir Julian, I mean, as easily maintained."

"It might," coincided Sir Julian; "I do not think that there are many that would have the boldness to support it."

"If they had, your wealth and influence would easily crush them, if all other means should fail."

"True; I do not think there is much to be apprehended. But, hark, some one is ascending the stairs. Retire; you must not be seen."

Sam Raker nodded assent, and immediately entered the room in which he had secreted his villanous companions.

He had no sooner vanished than Simon entered the apartment, bowing very low to his master, as was his usual custom.

"How now?" demanded Sir Julian, hastily. "What want you?"

"Strange gentleman with the Irish brogue below, sir," answered Simon.

The baronet could scarcely repress a smile of gratification.

"Show the gentleman up-stairs directly, Simon," he said.

Simon departed instantly, in obedience to this command.

"Is it old Latitat?" observed Sam Raker, popping his head out at the door when the servant had gone.

"Yes," replied Sir Julian, in an under tone, "it is all right."

"It soon will be, if you play your cards well," added the smuggler.

"Leave me alone for that."

"Don't forget the will."

"No, no."

"Nor the signal?"

"Yes, yes; but retire again—he comes."

This little colloquy was scarcely ended when Mr. Fitzpatrick was ushered into the room. He had contrived to re-assume his usual air of composure, and Sir Julian received him with a bland smile as he extended his hand towards him, which the lawyer (although it went much against his feelings) accepted, and bowed politely to the baronet in return for the greeting he had given him.

"Pray take a seat, Mr. Fitzpatrick," said Sir Julian ; "I am very glad you have come."

"Thank you for the welcome," returned the lawyer, drily.

"You are looking extremely well, Mr. Fitzpatrick," said the baronet.

"Fait ! and you do me great honour by the compliment," answered the lawyer.

"Is it too early for you to take wine, sir ?"

"Fait ! no ; it is never too early for me to take a glass or so of good burgundy or champagne, Sir Julian."

The baronet again smiled blandly, for it was just the condescension on the part of Mr. Fitzpatrick that he wished for. He therefore immediately rang the bell and ordered wine, which was quickly brought into the apartment by Simon. Sir Julian filled their glasses, and pledging Mr. Fitzpatrick, they both quaffed off the contents.

"Excellent wine that, Mr. Fitzpatrick ?"

"Och ! capital,—capital," agreed the lawyer, squinting into the glass he held in his hand with one of his little bright and intelligent eyes, and at the same time smacking his lips in admiration of the beverage he had just done justice to.

"You will take another glass, Mr. Fitzpatrick? It won't hurt you."

"Fait ! and I don't think it will," returned the lawyer. So the glasses were replenished, and the contents swallowed with the same apparent relish as before.

"And now, Mr. Fitzpatrick," said Sir Julian, having taken a seat by his side, "if you please, we will proceed at once to business."

"To business ?"

"Yes ; the business upon which we have met," said the baronet, looking narrowly into the countenance of the lawyer, who still maintained the utmost coolness and unconcern.

"Och ! humph ! Fait ! and I have got such a bad memory at times, that I quite forgot that I had called upon you for any business at all, at all, unless it was to bid you good-bye before I quitted this neighbourhood, and to inquire whether you had any commands."

"Leave this neighbourhood ?"

"Yes, fait !" answered the lawyer.

"So soon ?"

"My presence, I dare say, is wanted in London," answered the lawyer.

"But I must certainly request that you will stay a few days longer, and honour me with your company."

"Much obliged to you, Sir Julian, much obliged to you for the invitation, but I really must decline."

"I am sorry for that ; but you surely do not forget what we were talking about when we last met ?"

"Och ! I come at you now, Sir Julian ; you mane about the probable existence of your brother ?"

The baronet frowned.

"I must request, Mr. Fitzpatrick," he said, "that you will not call the impostor who may seek to pass himself off as such by such a name."

"Impostor ! Sir Julian," replied the lawyer ; "arrah ! now, be after holding your whisht until you see the young man."

"That must never be. But enough of this. Again I ask you, Mr. Fitzpatrick, whether you have maturely considered the proposal I made to you?"

"About what ?"

"The will."

"Och! och! I smell what you would be after now; I have."

"And have come to the determination to ——"

"To do what?"

"To take the twelve thousand pounds, and ——"

"And what will I do for arning that very handsome sum?"

"You a lawyer and ask such a question?" said the baronet, impatiently.

"Tunder and turf, man! how the divil should I, although a lawyer, know your wishes before you express them?"

"The will must be mine."

"When I have ascertained that your brother is no more."

Sir Julian muttered a curse between his lips, and traversed the room for a few moments before he could again speak, the lawyer in the meantime whistling a tune to himself, with the greatest psssible coolness, and thinking of a volley to salute the villain with at the fitting opportunity.

"The will must be destroyed," at length said Sir Julian.

The lawyer indulged in a very long whistle, and could scarcely resist the temptation of giving vent to his indignation in an oath.

"Twelve thousand pounds will amply repay you for such a trifling deed, Mr. Fitzpatrick," added the baronet.

"And is it a trifle you call it, Sir Julian?" demanded the lawyer.

"A mere trifle; who can reproach you with it afterwards?"

"My own conscience."

"Conscience!"

"Yes."

"Psha! Mr. Fitzpatrick, I am surprised to hear you talk so."

"Indeed! Lawyers sometimes have consciences as well as other people."

"This is nonsense. We must understand each other better."

"I do perfectly understand *you* now, Sir Julian."

"What mean you?"

"That I know you."

"For what?"

"A most consummate scoundrel!" replied the honest lawyer, rising from his chair with an air of dignity, and his countenance flushed with resentment.

"How," passionately demanded Sir Julian, "dare you ——"

"I dare do anything but become dishonest," retorted the lawyer.

"This in my own house? But no matter, I will not be offended. You were my father's friend."

"I was your father's friend, and he was mine. Think you, then, that I would insult his memory by being guilty of an act that only a villain could suggest and a monster perpetrate. Blood and tunder! all the blood of a true Milesian rises in my veins to fever heat to think that I should live all those years and then be taken for a scoundrel. Our interview is at an end, Sir Julian, and thank your lucky stars, fait! that you are the son of my friend, or this might chance to be exposed to the world. Destroy the last will and testament of my friend, my benefactor, and disinherit that unfortunate child whom I now firmly believe to be in existence, and whom I am determined to find out, if I search the most remote corner of the globe? Tunder and turf, I ——"

"Mr. Fitzpatrick," said Sir Julian, conquering his passion, and acting with more coolness until he had ascertained that which he wanted to know —"Mr. Fitzpatrick, we must not part thus. I admire the strict integrity of character you have evinced, and ——"

"Bad manners to your compliments," interrupted the plain-speaking lawyer, "I want none of them."

"Well—well," replied Sir Julian, biting his lips, "I will not, then, in-

sult you by what might appear fulsome flattery. Your pecuniary loss by the death of my father was very great, and perhaps the small remuneration I offered you was not adequate to ——"

"Were it even twenty times twelve millions that you were to offer to Mr. Patrick Fitzpatrick for the perpetration of such an infernal deed, it would not purchase his consent. Keep your lucre; I have sufficient to keep me comfortable for the rest of my days, and I feel that I possess that which is far beyond all earthly treasures—an honest and upright heart."

Sir Julian was quite confounded at the boldness and determination of the lawyer, and paced the room backwards and forwards for a short time, not knowing what to say. As for Mr. Fitzpatrick, he was so enraged that he scarcely could resist the temptation he felt to inflict summary punishment on the baronet, for the insult he had so audaciously offered him.

Sir Julian at last having in some measure regained his equanimity, and being still in ignorance as to whether or not the lawyer had the will with him, turned to him and said,—

"It is a great pity, Mr. Fitzpatrick, that we cannot agree upon this important point; but still there is no necessity for its making us any the worse friends. At the same time you will, perhaps, allow me to have my opinion?"

"And what is that?"

"Why, that you would not have been so over scrupulous, had there been really any will in existence."

"But there is a will in existence!" indignantly returned the lawyer.

"Where?"

"Here!" answer Mr. Fitzpatrick, taking it from his pocket, and unfolding it before the eager eyes of the baronet; "here is the will, properly signed and attested in a manner so that it is beyond the possibility of a chance for any person in their senses to dispute it!"

" That will must be mine!"

" Never!"

" What would you do with it?"

" Keep it until I find your brother, if living;" answered the lawyer, as he folded up the will and replaced it in his pocket; " good morning, Sir Julian Mordlington, perhaps at some future period we shall meet again, when we may enter into a further explanation on this subject."

" You go not hence!" exclaimed the baronet, advancing hastily to the door, locking it, and putting the key in his pocket.

" How?" cried the astonished lawyer, " you will not dare forcibly to detain me? Beware of what you do, Sir Julian."

" You know me not yet, but will perhaps, by and bye."

" Villain!"

" Ha! ha! ha!"

" I will alarm the inmates of the Hall."

" I have the means of soon silencing you. Will you not now give me the will?"

" Never!"

" Then I must e'en have you, will and all, I suppose," said Sir Julian, as he stamped his foot, and Sam Raker and two or three other armed ruffians made their appearance and advanced towards him.

" Villains!" cried the lawyer; " you cannot surely mean murder? Oh! help! help!"

" Gag him! stifle his cries!" commanded Sir Julian; and the villains immediately surrounded the unfortunate Mr. Fitzpatrick, and after doing as they were bid, dragged him into the room and bolted and locked the door.

" 'Twas well done!" observed Sam Raker, " we have got old Latitat secure now, at any rate."

" We have," answered the baronet; " but somebody comes—quick! retire by the same way you entered the hall, and be careful that no person observes ye. At midnight return hither, when you know what you have to perform."

The smugglers instantly departed by the back way, and the next moment Simon, and one or two others of the male domestics rushed into the apartment in a state of great trepidation.

" What do you want now, sirrah?" demanded Sir Julian of Simon.

" Somebody called for help, Sir Julian."

" 'Twas I! The Irishman you opened the door to this morning, attempted to rob me. He fled from yonder window, when I called. Pursue him!"

Away scampered Simon and the others, as fast as their legs could carry them, by an opposite door; and left Sir Julian laughing and exulting in the apartment.

~~~~~~~~~~~~~~~~

CHAPTER VIII.

THE SMUGGLERS.—THE CAROUSAL.—THE DISCLOSURE.—THE DEATH-DOOMED.

It would be impossible to describe the rage, and not to say alarm of Mr. Fitzpatrick when he found himself thus made so unexpectedly a prisoner, and at the mercy of Sir Julian Mordlington, whom he now believed to be a villain of the blackest dye. His hands had been bound together, therefore he had no means of releasing his mouth from the gag, and he had the utmost difficulty in breathing, much more to call out for help, which, in fact, he considered would be useless, as he had very little doubt but that all who inhabited the Hall were merely the creatures of the baronet, and ready to do his bidding, let it be a crime even of the greatest atrocity. He tried the only window there was in the apartment, but it was fastened, and then the rage of the honest Irish gentleman found in some degree vent by his kicking at the room-door, and stamping on the floor, making all the noise he could in that manner, but no person came to his assistance, and the prospect before him became exceedingly gloomy. After the disposition which Sir Julian had evinced, and his determination to get the will, he could expect no mercy from him, but in what manner he intended to dispose of him he could not form any conjecture, unless he meant to murder him, and yet he could not imagine that he could become so atrocious as that. Had he known the baronet's real character, he would have entertained a very different opinion of him, but as it was, his reflections were not of the most pleasant description, although amidst all his anxiety, he felt the satisfaction of a clear conscience in having rejected the bribe offered by the villain in whose power he now found himself.

The warning of Crazy Marian now rushed upon his memory, and he regretted that he had not taken it, and abandoned all idea of coming near the Hall, and seeking another interview with Sir Julian. Her allusion to the Smuggler King, however, he could not yet understand.

Having paced the room in which was confined, for some minutes, in a state of the utmost disorder, he listened at the door. The laughter of the baronet on the departure of the servants, met his ear, and then all subsided into silence, and he imagined he had quitted the room.

We will leave the prisoner for a short time, and return to Sir Julian Mordlington, who, after having quitted the apartment in which his interview with the unfortunate but honest lawyer had taken place, retired to his study, where he could alone give free indulgence to his feelings of exultation at the success of his infamous stratagem, and augur the same for the future schemes he had in contemplation.

Closing the door, he threw himself upon a sofa, and leaning his head on his hand, he gave way for a while to the pleasurable thoughts that crowded upon his imagination.

"So," he at length ruminated, "the cunning lawyer is at last entrapped, and with him the will, from which and him alone I had cause to apprehend any particular danger. Ha, ha, ha! this plot, at any rate, has been well contrived and executed, and with the aid of my invaluable creature, Sam Raker, my other stratagems will, I dare say, be crowned with equal success. Flora and her lover shall be in my power,—and then will my triumph be complete; and I may, as I have hitherto done, bid defiance to discovery. The old lawyer will this night be on board the Devil Skipper, where he will quickly become acquainted with whom I am, and afterwards to prevent any chance of his ever betraying me, he shall be tossed overboard. There will an end to Mr. Patrick Fitzpatrick and his honest heart. Fool! had he at first yielded to my proposal, he might have saved his life, and pocketed the bribe into bargain. But Raker prevented me from so far committing myself, and persuaded me to adopt the safest and the cheapest course. Oh, that Raker is a capital villain! an excellent scoundrel! I do not know what I should do without him. But the will, now that I have the means, let me secure it without any further delay, in case of accidents. I will go and visit my prisoner."

He rose from the sofa as he spoke, and taking the keys of the room in which Mr. Fitzpatrick was confined with him, quitted the apartment and bent his steps thither.

He listened at the door, and could hear the prisoner pacing the room heavily, and evidently in great agitation. This afforded the villain the most infinite satisfaction, and he smiled again in the exultation of his feelings. He withdrew the bolts and unlocked the door, and then all once more became silent.

On his entrance, Mr. Fitzpatrick started back a few paces, and exhibited otherwise some emotion, but it was quickly succeeded by an air of becoming dignity, resolution, contempt, and hatred. Sir Julian smiled triumphantly upon him.

"Well," he said, "my very honest lawyer, I suppose by this time you begin to perceive that you are an arrant fool, and that Sir Julian Mordlington is not the man to be trifled with, or to have his schemes frustrated. You are now securely in my power, from which nothing can release you."

Mr. Fitzpatrick raised his eyes piously and significantly towards Heaven, and then once more looked upon Sir Julian with utter contempt and defiance.

"Ha, ha, ha!" laughed the miscreant; "I understand you; but you may appeal in vain. Have I not the means to stretch you this moment dead at my feet? Oh, how much better would twelve thousand pounds and liberty have been than thus to be placed in jeopardy. You honest lawyers certainly make most consummate asses of yourselves, to suffer we humble traffickers in crime to out-wit you."

Mr. Fitzpatrick averted his head; his feelings of indignation and disgust were worked up to the highest pitch, but he determined not to let his persecutor perceive that he was otherwise agitated or daunted.

"But you do not know me yet, *honest* lawyer Fitzpatrick," continued Sir Julian; "but this night may make you and I rather better acquainted than we have hitherto been, and I trust the introduction will afford you much pleasure. In the meantime, I will release your mind from the natural anxiety it must feel in having the safe custody of such a precious, such an invaluable document as my late father's will."

The lawyer looked at the taunting villain with the greatest abhorrence, and frowned fearfully upon him.

"Nay," resumed Sir Julian, "you may frown; it is all useless here, and in my presence. The will is now mine, and without paying twelve thousand pounds for it. Ha! ha! ha! Come, if you please, I will just take the liberty of putting my hand into your pocket. It is the very acme of the art of thieving, to be able to pick a lawyer's pocket."

Mr. Fitzpatrick bit his lips, and in spite of all his efforts, could not conceal his ungovernable resentment, as Sir Julian approached him, and deliberately placing his hand in the pocket where he knew he had placed the will, took it forth.

He unfolded it, and for a short time read it in silence, then burst forth into a derisive and triumphant laugh.

"So," he said, "how generous! my father was really too liberal, and no doubt has met his reward in Heaven, for thus so kindly providing for his bastard, and almost forgetting that he had an elder and lawfully begotten son. Most generous, truly, and it is a pity that his designs could not be carried into effect. However, I will see whether I can't make as good use of his estates and his superfluous cash, as this worthy brother would have done. The will is now mine, and for the present I leave you to ponder o'er the gratification it must undoubtedly afford you. We shall see each other again to-night, but under very different circumstances to what we have hitherto met."

With these words, Sir Julian secured the will in his own pocket, and with the same sardonic and disagreeable grin as that he had assumed when he entered, he retired from the room, bolting and locking the door after him, and leaving Mr. Fitzpatrick to his own cogitations.

We need not attempt to describe minutely what these ruminations were, but it will probably be sufficient to observe that they were of the most painful and tormenting description, and that it required all the reason he possessed, to enable him to support them with any degree of patience. The heartless revilings of Sir Julian, had wounded his pride more than all, and to know that he was completely, as he was now situated, powerless, augmented in no small degree the indignation he felt. But the loss of the will tortured him more than all, and even the uncertainty of his own fate, which from the base character of Sir Julian, he had every reason to imagine would be the worst that could be conceived, all faded before the pangs this one circumstance excited in the worthy man's breast. He longed, yet dreaded the approach of night, to know what would be the result of his next interview with the tyrant, in whose power he entirely was, and whether it was his intention to remove him to another place, or to suffer him to remain where he was; but after a little deliberation, he had no doubt but that it would be the former, as Sir Julian had informed him, that when they met again it would be under very different circumstances.

Tired at length with thought, he threw himself on a couch in the room, and endeavoured to banish painful reflection from his mind, but that was a task he found it was impossible for him to accomplish. The weight of care, anxiety, and suspense, that pressed upon his heart, was almost more than he could bear, and entirely precluded the possibility of that.

*　　*　　*　　*　　*　　*

The moon had arisen in majestic splendour, and her beams were reflected with the most infinite grandeur on the surface of the ocean, while thousands of stars lent their lustre in spangling the broad expanse of the heavenly firmament. Numerous vessels were riding at anchor, their pennons streaming in the wind, that blew a gentle and refreshing breeze.

Somewhat apart from the rest was another ship, a handsome taut-built craft, which was supposed to be a fair trader, and known as The Mermaid. Little, however, was it imagined what the real character of that vessel was. Little was it supposed that this was no other than the much talked of and much dreaded Devil Skipper, one of the favourite vessels of that desperate and blood-thirsty man, called The Smuggler King, for whose apprehension a reward of five thousand pounds was at that time offered, and who had hitherto set the law at defiance, and triumphantly thwarted every scheme to detect him.

Some of the crew were certainly not the most interesting or prepossessing looking individuals, but they were seldom seen on shore, and then they never attracted any particular attention, being always attired as other seamen, and seeming to be attending only to the ordinary duties. There certainly must have been most culpable neglect on the part of some or other of the authorities, or the real character of the ship would undoubtedly have been discovered, and it must have been, situated as it was, captured, and most likely its daring captain apprehended; but whether any of the said authorities were aware of the fact, and winked at the circumstance, of course from not disinterested motives, is another question, which we have no means of answering here.

It was now about the hour of eleven, and a portion of the smugglers were assembled together in one of the cabins, and, having got the grog aboard, had become pretty moderately jolly. All at once, at the suggestion of a black-whiskered gentleman, whose countenance very much belied him if he had not the heart to perpetrate any crime, however atrocious, they started forth into the following characteristic chorus :

"Hurrah for the Smuggler King!
  Hurrah for his daring crew!
Before them fear takes wing;
  No power can them subdue.
In their gallant bark they sweep,
  'Neath midnight's sable wing,
O'er the wide and boundless deep,
  And a booty rich they bring
            Then hurrah for the Smuggler King!
              Hurrah for his daring crew!
            Before them fear takes wing;
              No power can them subdue.

"Supreme is his power on sea,
  And mighty his power on land;
He prowleth in secresy,
  With his staunch and daring band.
No dungeon can him appal,
  No force that his foes can bring;
Neither fire, nor sword, nor ball,
  Can daunt the Smuggler King!
            Then hurrah for the Smuggler King!
              Hurrah for his daring crew!
            Before them fear takes wing,
              No power can them subdue."

" Well sung!" shouted the black-whiskered individual before alluded to, when this chorus was finished; " our bold captain, the Smuggler King, will be on board with us to-night."

" But not to stop with us, Will Hemlock?" said another of the smugglers, who was seated by his side.

" No," returned Hemlock; " he cannot yet arrange matters on shore to join us at present, Harry. I wish he could."

" Ay," observed the other smuggler, " so do I, for I am tired of leading this lazy life."

" Ay, we are quite dull without our monarch," said Hemlock; " besides, there may be danger if we remain here much longer. Already I begin to think that some of the swabs look at us with suspicion."

" Yes, I have noticed them," observed a third ruffian; " and I think our captain is to blame, daring as he is, and invincible as he has ever hitherto proved himself to be, to run so much risk."

" As to that," remarked Will Hemlock, " we had better not be questioning our captain's conduct. I dare say he knows well what he is about, and keeps a sharp look out for any danger that may threaten."

" Ay, ay, leave him alone for that," remarked another of the crew; " they must be deep, indeed, who can detect the Smuggler King."

" Yes, notwithstanding the reward of five thousand pounds that is offered for his apprehension," added Will Hemlock.

" Ha! ha! ha!" laughed Harry; " these land-lubbers must be fools, indeed, if they imagine that ten times the amount of five thousand pounds would tempt any of his faithful subjects to betray the Smuggler King."

" Death would be the certain portion of him who should attempt it," remarked Hemlock. " But knew you where Sam Raker and the rest of our companions have gone at this late hour, Harry? Is it to escort hither our captain?"

" No," answered Harry; " he will come alone: but I believe that Sam has another and important job to perform. You know he never makes us acquainted with his secrets. But let us upon deck, and see whether any of them are approaching."

"Ay, ay," cried two or three of the smugglers, and they immediately hurried upon deck. They had not been long there when they heard the paddling of oars, and, casting their eyes in the direction from whence the sounds proceeded, they beheld, by the bright moonbeams, a boat approaching the ship, but containing only two individuals, one of whom alone was rowing.

"It is not Sam," remarked Hemlock; "I could tell his figure-head a mile off."

"Ah, now I see," said Harry, straining his eyes eagerly after the approaching boat, "it is our captain. Prepare all hands to give him a hearty welcome."

"Hurrah!" shouted the delighted crew of the Devil Skipper; "all hands and tongues for action!"

In a few moments the boat was alongside, and Sir Julian and one of the smugglers immediately mounted the deck. No sooner did the former make his appearance, than the crew were going to give a simultaneous shout of welcome; but he motioned them to silence, and, shaking them all cordially by the hand, he passed directly to his own cabin, beckoning some of the crew to follow him.

"Our captain is very silent to-night," said Hemlock.

"He always is," answered Harry, "when he has got any important business on his mind. Something more than we know of is about to happen, depend upon it."

"I shouldn't wonder," coincided Will; "well, all I hope is, that we shall have some business to perform, for, being so long out of practice, I am afraid I shall quite get my hand out."

"Oh, never fear, Will," retorted Harry; "you will not forget your old tricks, I dare say. Like myself, I believe you take it quite natural."

"Ha! ha! ha! that's very true. But see, there is another boat approaching; and I can see plain enough that this contains Sam Raker, two of his companions, and something which appears to be concealed beneath a large black mantle."

"This no doubt is the particular business we anticipated," observed Harry; "and now they approach nearer, I can perceive that the object beneath the mantle is some human being."

"Some person whom our captain had cause to suspect meant him wrong, I dare say," said Hemlock, "and whom he has, in consequence, caused to be trepanned."

"That is just the very conclusion I came to," coincided the other smuggler. "But here they come; we must prepare to help them on board."

The other boat, containing Sam Raker, two of the smugglers, and the unfortunate Mr. Fitzpatrick, now pulled up by the side of the vessel, and, as Sir Julian and his companion had done before, they were quickly assisted on board.

The curiosity of the smugglers was excited to know who the individual concealed beneath the black mantle was, and immediately flocked about Sam Raker and the others, in the hopes of catching a glimpse of the stranger's person. But at present they were not doomed to be gratified, for Raker and one of his companions, taking each an arm of the lawyer, were leading him away, when Sam turned to Hemlock, and inquired whether the captain had come on board yet.

Will Hemlock replied in the affirmative.

"'Tis well," returned Raker. "Follow me, Hemlock and Harry Grampus, below—our captain may need the presence of ye all."

At the mention of these words, and when the certainty of the wretches into whose power he was thrown, flashed upon his brain, the unfortunate Mr. Fitzpatrick for the first time felt really alarmed; but being gagged, he had not the power of uttering any complaint, and even if he had, he knew it would be perfectly useless. He was therefore hurried below, by the ruffians who held him, not certain whether they were not leading him to certain death. Again the warning of Crazy Marian rushed upon his memory, to beware of the Smuggler King; but although he regretted that he had not attended more seriously to the caution, he could not reconcile it to his own reason that the smuggler, daring even as he was, would venture into a port like that, and to remain there even in the very midst of his enemies. And who was the Smuggler King, as he was called; and what could he have to do with him? These were questions that he rapidly asked himself. However, he was not long kept in suspense. Suddenly the men who were leading him stopped, and the mantle being removed from his head and body, the lawyer started back with astonishment and alarm, when he beheld himself in a large cabin, and surrounded by a number of the most ferocious looking fellows it had ever been his lot to gaze upon, and whose dresses, and the manner in which they were all armed, left him no room to doubt their real characters, and the nature of the vessel he was brought on board of.

The smugglers on beholding the grotesque figure of Mr. Fitzpatrick, and the consternation he so plainly exhibited, set up a simultaneous coarse laugh, and seemed to enjoy his dilemma amazingly; while the poor lawyer, although he was nearly bursting with indignation, repressed it as well as he could, and returned their laughter and derision with a true Milesian frown of sovereign contempt.

Sam Raker now removed the gag from Mr. Fitzpatrick's mouth, and allowed him once more the liberty of speech, the first use he made of which was to demand where he was.

"In the Devil's Skipper," answered Sam Raker.

"Th—the—the what?" stammered out the lawyer.

"The Devil's Skipper," replied Will Hemlock; "one of the finest free-traders that ever scudded the face of the ocean."

"Blood and tunder!" exclaimed the Irishman; "here's a lucky divil I am now. Smugglers?"

"Yes," answered Raker, "smugglers, and pirates if you like, old Lati-tat. We are not ashamed of our title."

"Och hone! och hone!" ejaculated the lawyer, "and is it myself that was ever born to live to get among such a set of spalpeens as this. Och, then, bad manners to ye all. Mr. Patrick Fitzpatrick don't care for you; he has done his duty, and can confidently put his trust in Providence, who will help him out of this trouble."

The only reply which the ruffians made to this speech was another rude laugh; and the lawyer clenched his fists, and stamped about the cabin in a state of the most furious and ungovernable rage, apparently very much to the amusement of the smugglers.

"Bad luck to ye all, you infernal rascals!" he cried; "and is it bravery you call this to be all upon one man. For what purpose am I brought hither?"

"That will our captain answer you," said Sam Raker.

"Your captain, you dirty fag-end of a villanous bog-trotter!" exclaimed Mr. Fitzpatrick, "and who the divil is your captain, now?"

A shrill whistle was now heard to proceed from an inner cabin, and Raker observed,

"'Tis our captain's signal; he comes, and you will very soon have an

opportunity of scraping an intimate acquaintance with him, old six-and-eightpence."

The door of the inner cabin at that moment opened, and a tall and commanding figure, habited entirely in black, with numerous frightful devices thereon, wearing a black mask, and his head surmounted with a coronet of shells, stalked into the centre of the cabin, and extending his hand to the astonished lawyer, he exclaimed :—

"Welcome, Mr. Patrick Fitzpatrick, to *The Devil Skipper !*"

"Ah !" exclaimed the lawyer ; "blood and turf! that voice ! Where have I before heard it ? Say who are you ?"

"*The Smuggler King !*" shouted a dozen voices in reply, and the announcement was received with loud cheers from all the smugglers, which their daring captain, however, speedily checked by a motion of his hand.

"The Smuggler King !" repeated the lawyer; "bad luck to you, and what the divil have you to do with me ?"

"That you shall quickly know, *honest* Mr. Patrick Fitzpatrick," answered the smuggler chief.

"As soon as you like," observed Mr. Fitzpatrick, regaining all his usual courage and self possession ; "1 am never afraid to become acquainted with my enemies, if you are not ashamed to show your features."

"Behold then," exclaimed the captain of the smugglers, tearing away the black mask that concealed his countenance, and Mr. Fitzpatrick started back with an expression of the most unbounded amazement when he recognized Sir Julian Mordlington.

"Sir—Sir Julian Mor——" he faltered out.

"No—no—on land Sir Julian Mordlington," interrupted the baronet, with a smile of triumph ; "but here the Smuggler King ! Ha ! ha ! ha ! You seem surprised, Mr. Patrick Fitzpatrick."

No. 10

"Tunder and turf," cried the lawyer, scarcely able to credit the evidence of his senses, "Och? musha! musha! And do I see with my own eyes?"

"Indeed you do, *honest* Mr. Fitzpatrick," sneered the Smuggler King, "and hear with your own own ears, too!"

"Och, bad luck to it; and it's a dead man you are, to a certainty, Patrick Fitzpatrick!"

"You seem to possess the gift of prophecy, my worthy lawyer. I told you that you and I should soon be better acquainted."

"The divil's skewer to the acquaintance," said the lawyer, "Och, hone! och hone! and can it be that I behold the flesh and blood of my late venerated friend in this divil's darling?"

In an instant the smugglers surrounded him, with savage looks, and twenty swords were immediately pointed at his breast.

"Hold! stand back!" commanded Sir Julian, waving his hand authoritatively; "the first who dares to act without his sovereign's orders shall be stretched dead at my feet! The poor idiot is in our power, and I give free license to his tongue!"

The smugglers drew back immediately in obedience to the dreaded will of their captain, and watched the proceedings with sullen looks of submission.

"Yes, Mr. Fitzpatrick," resumed the captain, "in me you behold the son of your *late venerated friend*—Sir Julian Mordlington, and the dreaded of the ocean—*The Smuggler King*. Now, what think you of my power? Will you accept the twelve thousand pounds, now, good honest Mr. Lawyer, for the will? Ha! ha! ha!"

"Villain!" exclaimed Mr. Fitzpatrick.

"Proceed with you invective," said Sir Julian, scornfully; "it is all the power you have now to do, and I grant you for awhile that privilege. Idiot! had you at first accepted of my proposal you would have been at liberty and out of danger."

"Sooner would I have a clear conscience than the liberty of which you remind me."

"We shall shortly put that to the test."

"You will not detain me?"

"Fool! think you the Smuggler King parts so easily with his enemies? You have heard little of his character if you imagine so. Has not his name struck terror all over Europe? Do not the mariners fear him as a supernatural being, females shrink aghast at the mention of his name, mothers use it to frighten their fractious children into obedience? Has he not set at defiance all human laws? Have not thousands been offered for his detection in vain? Is not the sacrifice of human life his sport? Is he not in every part of the globe unknown, and courted, and admired? Think you then that you who have seen his features, who know him, who possess a certain power over him, will be suffered again at large?"

"Sir Julian Mordlington," said Mr. Fitzpatrick, "in the name of your late lamented father, what would you do with me?"

"What mercy do you expect from me?" demanded the Smuggler Captain.

"You would not take my life?"

"My own would be in jeopardy while you lived," returned the villain.

"I am an old man, Sir Julian."

"You are an old idiot, and the world would not suffer much by your loss."

"You surely would not murder me in cold blood?"

"I would swim in blood to gain my ends."

"Oh, monster! monster!"

"I do not object to the title."

"Have you not one spark of pity in your nature?" said the despairing lawyer.

" Can you expect to find it in a monster ?"

" To what fate do you doom me ?"

" My bold crew shall answer the question," replied Sir Julian ; then turning to Sam Raker and the rest of the smugglers, he demanded,—

" What would be the fate of the enemy of the Smuggler King ?"

" Death !" replied the smugglers in a breath, and they looked more ferociously than ever upon Mr. Fitzpatrick.

" What should be the fate of him who despises your sovereign's power ?"

" Death !"

" What should be the fate of he who mocks and reviles your captain ?"

" Death !"

" What doom would you inflict upon that man who would rob your monarch of his rights ?"

" Death !"

" What should be the fate of a myrmidon of the law ?"

" Death !"

" What is the inevitable fate of that being who has seen the Smuggler King's features ?"

" Death !"

" You hear," added Sir Julian, with a malicious grin, and addressing himself to Mr. Fitzpatrick ; " you hear, your doom has been pronounced by the terrible crew of the Devil Skipper, six-fold. What think you now of your situation, my *honest* lawyer ?"

" But you will not kill me ?"

" You have heard your doom."

" My age will surely plead for me ?"

" Nothing can revoke the sentence. You die !"

" Beware ! beware !" said the lawyer, " my fate will be inquired into, and a terrible punishment descend upon you."

" Ha ! ha ! ha !"

" My blood will recoil on your own head."

" Be it so."

" Think not for ever to triumph in your monstrous crimes ; vengeance most dreadful will overtake you when you least expect it."

" That vengeance the Smuggler King has long braved, and will do so still."

" Repent ! repent !"

" Repent ! ha ! ha ! ha ! the Smuggler King will continue the same that he has always been to the last moment of his existence," said the heartless miscreant.

" Oh ! spare me ! spare me !"

" You appeal in vain ; the waters of the deep shall silence your tongue for ever."

However well a person is prepared for the change, death is awful when it approaches, and the heart quails at the certain prospect of it, but to die a death of violence brings with it additional terrors, and the stoutest fortitude must sicken at the bare thought.

There were few individuals who had led a life of greater rectitude than Mr. Fitzpatrick. His whole career had been eminently distinguished for probity, virtue, benevolence, and Christian charity ; his conscience acquitted him of having ever wilfully or indirectly offered the slightest injury to his fellow creatures ; in fact, he was in every sense of the word, a good man. But now, when the certainty of death, and that an awful one, appeared before his eyes, even he shrunk appalled, and he mentally prayed to Heaven to frustrate the plans of his diabolical and implacable enemy, and to avert the fate with which he was threatened.

"Sir Julian Mordlington," he solemnly observed, "much as you may at present scoff at and revile the truth, believe me there is an all just God above, who watches all our actions, and much as we may appear to triumph in our iniquities for a time, will not fail to punish us according to our deserts. Again I earnestly exhort, I supplicate to you to repent, and not to add to your manifold crimes, by the cold blooded and deliberate murder of one who never injured you."

"Fool!" exclaimed Sir Julian, "think you I will trust one who has it so much in his power to injure me? Again I tell you your doom is sealed, and that the deep bosom of the ocean shall be your grave, before many hours shall have passed over your hoary head. The Smuggler King is not the man to be moved by threats, by canting religion, or by supplication. *He* never breaks his word."

"Once more, Sir Julian ——"

"Bear him hence, and see that he is properly secured."

"Man of the iron heart, the spirit of your father will look down and curse you for this cruel deed."

"Away with the old dotard!"

The smugglers seized him.

"Then my blood be upon your head; my dying curse pursue you to perdition, and ——"

"Bear him hence, I say again," shouted the inflexible miscreant, stamping furiously; "am I or not to be obeyed?"

The unfortunate Mr. Fitzpatrick fixed upon his deadly foe a look, which made even his stout heart tremble, and he was then forced by the smugglers from the cabin.

"All but Sam Raker leave me," commanded Sir Julian, when the lawyer was gone.

The smugglers immediately obeyed, and then the captain, turning to Raker, said,

"Thus far my plans have succeeded."

"You have acted with prudence and determination," answered Sam; "the old lawyer does not seem to relish his fate."

"No, his *honesty* will soon be cooled," observed Sir Julian, with a malicious smile; "thus perish all the enemies of the Smuggler King!"

"Ay, ay, captain, and thus they shall perish. But when shall his business be settled?"

"To-morrow night."

"So soon?"

"Ay, why not?"

"Had we not better delay the execution of the deed until we sail from this port?" inquired Raker.

"No; I cannot rest while he lives," returned Sir Julian.

"It might not be safe to perpetrate it here," suggested Sam.

"It would not be safe to let him live while we remain here. Inquiries might be made after him, which would lead to unpleasant discoveries; besides, we have other business to perform and he might form some obstruction."

"When shall the deed be performed?" asked Raker.

"At midnight, when no one will be upon the look-out."

"In what manner shall it be done?"

"Secure old Latitat in a sack," answered the wretch, "then you and another at midnight can convey him in a boat to some distance from home, and toss him into the sea."

"Well contrived, captain," said Sam, "it shall be duly executed. Will you be present?"

"No ; my absence from the hall might excite some suspicion, answered Sir Julian, " I intend giving a fete on the occasion, the better to add to my security."

"Also a good idea, captain ;" said Sam Raker, "the old lawyer once disposed of ——"

" We must devote our thoughts to the securing of William and the girl, Flora Clarendon."

"Sure ; and fear not but that they will soon also be in your power."

" They must ; they shall."

" And when they are secured ?"

" Then let the Devil Skipper, in the darkness of night set sail."

" And will you not join us ?"

" Not at present. It would be imprudent to do so."

" Well, so it might. But whither shall we convey them ?"

" To one of our nearest haunts," replied Sir Julian, "and there in the course of a few days I will join you."

" To the Death Rock ?"

" Ay !—they cannot from thence escape."

" It would be impossible."

" Then that business is arranged ?"

" It is," answered Sam Raker.

" You say that the parents of Flora Clarendon rent a farm on my estate ?" said Sir Julian Mordlington.

" They do."

" That is well ; then I can easily make an excuse to pay them a visit, when I shall at least have the satisfaction of seeing the girl who has made so powerful an impression upon me."

" You may ; observed Sam Raker, " but I would advise you, captain, to act with caution, or you may thwart all our plans."

"Oh ! leave me alone for that," observed the baronet, " who so well knows how to act the hypocrite as the Smuggler King ?"

" True, captain ; I did not question your abilities in that way."

" After you have consigned the old lawyer to the deep, hasten to the hall to inform me of all the particulars."

" But should your guests be present ?"

" They will be gone before then," returned Sir Julian ; " I will be waiting for you at the hour of two, in the room where we have before had our meetings, and you having the keys can let yourself in unobserved, by the back way."

" I will attend to your orders, captain," said Raker.

" Enough then," observed Sir Julian ; " look well to your prisoner ; I will remove my disguise, and then you can row me to the shore."

The baronet threw by the strange dress by which he always disguised himself as the Smuggler King, and having ascertained that all was safe, himself and Sam Raker jumped into a boat, and quickly gained the opposite shore, where Sir Julian once more cautioned his ready creature to act strictly in accordance with the orders he had given him, and then hastily retraced his steps to the hall, ruminating with savage satisfaction on the adventures of the night, and the successful result of them.

In the meantime, the unfortunate Mr. Fitzpatrick having been consigned to a place of security in the terrible Devil Skipper, and the smugglers left him, gave way to that intensity of anguish which the horrors of his situation naturally gave rise to. That Sir Julian would put his dreadful threats into execution, he could not but feel certain, and at the thoughts of meeting with death in such a shape ; murdered by heartless wretches, without a friend nigh to receive his last sigh, his dying request, or to soothe the passage to the grave, his heart recoiled with horror. Mr. Fitzpatrick was a man of the greatest fortitude, and he had the hope of a happy future to reward his well spent life, to console him ; but it would have required more than superhuman strength to calmly contemplate a fate so unnatural, so unforeseen, and so premature ; to meet that fate too, at the hands of the son of his dearest friend, and at a time when the injured and innocent probably stood so much in need of his services to restore them to their rights.

He paced the miserable cabin in which he was confined, with disordered steps and in the most feverish state of excitement, and the low melancholy sound of the waves as they dashed against the sides of the vessel, added to the dismal state of the thoughts that crowded upon his brain. But a few hours then, and he would be no more ! But a few hours, and his lifeless body would be reposing beneath the billows that now washed the sides of his prison! The vital spark of life would be extinguished, and he should be in the presence of his Almighty Judge ! It seemed scarcely possible, and yet all at present assured him that it would be realised. And was this to be the fate of one who had passed so many years without a blemish on his character? Whose whole study had been the welfare of his fellow-creatures, even to the pecuniary injury of himself? Surely that all-merciful God in whom he put his trust, would avert so fearful a destiny.

Independent of these agonizing thoughts, strange ideas crowded upon his brain. The features of the young seaman, that had made so singular and powerful an impression on his mind, and he now regretted that he had not made some inquiries respecting him before he visited the hall. Then he thought of his meeting with Crazy Marian, and the words that she had uttered, also the great interest her countenance had at that time excited in his breast, and a crowd of conflicting conjectures rushed upon him, and added to the anxiety of mind he was already enduring. Had he attended to the poor maniac's warning, he reflected, he should not have been placed in his present situation, but might have been spared to bring about the consummation of great events. He could not but reproach himself severely for his thoughtlessness and neglect ; but it was now too late, and he had nothing else to do than to prepare himself for the apparently inevitable fate that in so short a time awaited him.

What would his faithful clerk, who had been with him from childhood, think of his protracted absence ?—and there was no one to inform him of his untimely end. How would the poor fellow dispose of his affairs, and he knew not of a relation that he had in the world ? This thought very much disturbed him, not so much in a pecuniary point of view as regarded himself, but his death would place many worthy families in a state of the greatest difficulty, perhaps involve them in utter ruin. It was in vain for some time that he endeavoured to compose his feelings, so that he could bring his mind to a proper condition, placed as he was, in so awful a situation.

He was compelled to pace the cabin, for there was no place for him to seat himself, or to seek rest, if even that blessing had been awarded to him. The hours passed heavily and drearily away, and the only sounds that met his ears was the moaning of the wind, the dashing of the waves, or the occasional rude laugh or heavy tread of the smugglers. He had no means of judging of the time, but he imagined it must be near daylight, and he had no doubt but that the villain Sir Julian had departed.

The boldness of the smugglers in venturing and remaining so near the other vessels in the port, was to him a matter of astonishment. He was surrounded on every side by those who could and would rescue him, did they but know his perilous situation, and yet he had no means of making them acquainted with it, and all chance of escape was entirely hopeless. Despair enclosed him on every side, and he had nothing left but to endeavour to resign himself to his fate. But to meet that fate unmerited, and from the hands of a villain, was a thought almost insupportable, and Fitzpatrick gave vent to his feelings in the most vehement and distracted language.

"God of Heaven!" he exclaimed, "is it possible 'that any being whom you have created after your own image, can be such a monster as to glory in the miseries of his fellow-creatures, and exult in the shedding of human blood? It seems impossible, and yet such a monster is Sir Julian Mordlington, the son of that revered friend who was the very soul of honour, humanity, and virtue. Vile disgrace to that honoured name, never while I live will I again associate it with you. The spirit of his father would declaim against it!—he is a miscreant of the blackest dye, and unworthy of the name of man. But a few hours, but a few short hours, and this form, now abounding with health and almost youthful vigour, will be cold and inanimate. But a few hours, and this heart, which has ever throbbed with feelings of humanity to all mankind, will be still; every pulsation of life will be stopped in the ice-bound fetters of death! Death! how awful is that word to me, and what must it be to those whose days have been passed in crime? Wretched Sir Julian, what will not be the horrors of death to thee? Even now I shudder for you!"

He paused in the horror of this reflection, and with folded arms, more hurriedly traversed the narrow limits of the miserable cabin in which he was confined.

Some time elapsed in this manner, but at length the unfortunate gentleman became somewhat more composed and resigned, and falling on his knees, he prayed to Heaven for pardon for any sins he might in the course of his life have committed, and implored its aid to give him strength to meet the doom with which he was threatened as became a man and a Christian.

He arose from his knees more calm and confident than he had before been, and the terrors of death had lost nearly all their power upon his mind; while a latent hope shed its influence over him, that something would yet occur to rescue him from so untimely an end, and preserve him to bring about those events in which he felt so deep an interest.

CHAPTER IX.

CLARENDON'S FARM.—THE DREAM.—THE LOVERS.—THE SUMMER'S TALE.— THE MANIAC.— THE UNEXPECTED INTERRUPTION.— THE BROTHERS.—THE HYPOCRITE.—THE MURDER.

CLARENDON farm, the happy home of Flora, was a neat-built and well-arranged house, situated but a short distance from the hall. The parents of Mr. Clarendon had held it before him; in it he was born, and every part of it was as dear to him almost as one of his own children.

Mr. Clarendon was a sensible, amiable, and industrious man, about fifty years of age, with one of those countenances that immediately enlist the friendship and esteem of all who behold them, characteristic as they are of health and good humour. Mr. Clarendon had met with many vicissitudes in life, or he might have been rich, but still he was what is commonly called "well to do in the world," was enabled to provide comfortably for his family, and to give his only two daughters a very fair education; and, possessing a contented mind, there were very few happier men in the world than the worthy farmer.

Mrs. Clarendon was just such a wife as such a man deserved; mild, affable, indulgent even to a fault, and possessed, in fact, of all the virtues that Heaven can bestow upon womankind, and which alone is the true essence of all that is lovely in the sex.

She had received a very liberal education, her parents having been persons of some property; but, when she gave her hand to Mr. Clarendon, they discarded her, and at their death did not bequeath her a single farthing.

Mrs. Clarendon had taken the greatest pains with her two daughters, and to her they were indebted for many of those accomplishments and mental endowments they possessed. Never had children a more affectionate mother, and never did children feel greater love and veneration for a parent than that which Flora and her sister evinced towards their parent.

An early friendship had sprung up between the families of Clarendon and Backstay, which nothing could change, they were so strongly associated by manners and virtues; that friendship was, of course, more powerfully cemented than ever by the union of Henry to Clarendon's eldest daughter, and they were never happy but when they were exchanging mutual friendly visits.

Henry and his wife resided at the farm, the former being of the greatest assistance to his father-in-law, and, as we have before said, there was perhaps not a happier family in the whole county than that at Clarendon farm.

Mr. Clarendon and his wife had been quickly made acquainted with the passion which William and Flora had imbibed for each other, and there was but one circumstance that caused them to raise the slightest objection to it. William was everything they could wish for in a husband for their child. He was young, handsome, virtuous, generous, and intelligent; they believed that his love for Flora was sincere, and that her heart was wholly his; but there was one thing that raised an obstacle to their granting at first their consent to their paying their addresses to one another, and that was the mystery of William's birth, and the uncertainty whether his friends and relations were still living, and at some future period might not claim him. Notwithstanding the lapse of time since he was first found by old Ben Backstay, the numerous inquiries he had made without success, and consequently the improbability that he had any relations living, until that fact was ascertained, they could not consider him master of his own actions, or that he had any right to dispose of himself. He might be of noble origin, and would his parents, if they were living, ever consent to his becoming the husband of a humble farmer's daughter? Nay, even William himself, when he made that discovery, might alter his mind, and thus would bring upon poor Flora the most miserable consequences that might embitter all her future days, and probably bring her to an untimely grave. They therefore argued the point seriously and earnestly with the lovers, and would fain have persuaded them to abandon all idea of ever being united; but to think of such a thing was madness to both William and Flora; their's was no evanescent passion, that could be subdued by circumstances, it was one that was deeply engrafted in the heart, the very soul; it was the main spring of all their wishes, their happiness, and they could sooner die than cease to love. What was life, in fact, to them without each other? A dreary waste, a desert not worth living in. What cared they for the pride of birth? What value rested they upon wealth, while they possessed the wealth of each other's affections? Nothing. Nature seemed to have created them for each other—who then should say that they should not submit to Nature's behests? Did not Flora possess all the virtues that Heaven could bestow upon womankind?—and were they not far beyond all the treasures of the earth? Who could object, however lofty might be their rank and station, however great their wealth, who could object to such a daughter? Besides, what fortune, or circumstances, could ever make any change in William's love? Nothing. No; sooner would he even incur the wrath of parents, friends, all, than he could ever, or would ever think of abandoning her upon whom his very soul was fixed. It was an insult to his

nature to suppose such a thing for a moment. He must be a villain, a worse than ten-fold hypocrite could he thus to deceive and betray so much real purity and innocence.

All these points were urged most strenuously and eloquently by William, and Mr. Clarendon was at length forced to admit the strength of them, and, unwilling to oppose the affection of a daughter whom he so much loved, he at length gave his consent to their paying their addresses to each other, on the condition that they would not think of marriage for a period of five years. Notwithstanding the length of the period, the lovers were forced to yield, and the consent of old Ben Backstay having been before obtained, he possessing none of those scruples that had caused Mr. Clarendon to hesitate, the lovers were fairly considered as betrothed to one another, and many were the happy hours they passed together. The only thing that occurred to interrupt their joy was the departure of William to sea, for, in spite of his affection he entertained for Flora, he could not abandon his inclination for a nautical life, and he longed to mingle in the battles of his country, for such he considered England to be.

Their parting was one of the most affecting that could be imagined, for poor Flora dreaded and anticipated the worst, and never expected to behold him again, going as he was to mix in scenes of bloodshed, independent of the dangers of the deep to which he would be constantly exposed. Providence, however, as has been seen, watched over the young mariner, and brought him safe once more to his lover's arms.

The morning after the merry-making at the farm of old Backstay, in honour of William's return, Flora was seated at the honeysuckled casement of the parlour, her head leaning on her hand, while she gazed vacantly at all around her. Her thoughts were evidently otherwise employed; her

No. 11

eye was melancholy; her countenance pale, and occasionally a faint sigh would escape her breast.

Mr. Clarendon and his wife were seated in the room with her. They had for some time watched her conduct but did not attempt to interrupt her, concluding that it was only some trifling circumstance of no moment that had vexed and harassed her, and that mature reflection would quickly banish it from her mind, and reinstate her in her accustomed spirits.

At length, however, seeing that she did not offer to alter her position, her father arose, and gently approaching her he said,—

"Why, Flora, child, you are sad; your eye is dull and heavy, your thoughts are abstracted, and frequent sighs escape your bosom; tell me what is the meaning of this? What has occurred to agitate you?"

Flora, aroused by her father's words, looked up confused, and endeavoured to smile, but it was very evident that the effort was a failure.

"Sad—sad—dear parents," she faultered, "no—no, I was only thinking that —"

She paused, apparently not knowing how to finish the sentence.

"Nay, my love," observed her mother, "it is useless your attempting to conceal it. Those sparkling eyes are never dimmed by tears without a cause. Something has happened to disturb you; and yet, since the return of your lover from sea, one would think you would be one of the happiest of the happy."

"Happy, beloved mother," replied Flora, "oh, yes! I am happy, very, very happy, but —"

"But what, my dear child?"

"I—I—I know you will laugh at me."

"Laugh at you, Flora?"

"I—I am very silly."

"Come, come, my love, tell us all about it," said Mr. Clarendon.

"I wish you would excuse me, my dear parents," said Flora, endeavouring to look more composed; "for indeed it is not worthy of a second thought, and I should not thus have given way to such weakness."

"It may be a weakness, Flora," replied Mr. Clarendon, "but still you should have no secrets from your parents, especially those in which your happiness may be involved."

"I know it, my dear father," said Flora, "and well you know that there has never been a thought of your Flora's that has been withheld from you."

"True, my dear child," observed her father, kissing her affectionately, "and no occasion have you had to do so, for not a thought has ever entered my Flora's mind that was not purity itself."

Flora looked up brightly and fondly in her father's face, and throwing her fair arms around his neck, returned his kiss with one of the utmost affection and gratitude.

"And now, my love," said her mother, also saluting her lovely daughter with every demonstration of maternal affection, "since we thus so well understand each other, and appreciate our mutual feelings, disclose to us what it is that has disturbed your mind this morning."

Flora sighed.

"Weakness, weakness all," she again observed; "melancholy forebodings have come across my mind, and —"

"Forebodings, Flora?"

"Yes, dear father. A presentiment has taken possession of my imagination which I cannot banish, that some fearful calamity is in store for us."

"Calamity, child," said Mr. Clarendon, "this is indeed a weakness."

"I admit it," answered Flora; " but still I cannot conquer it."

" What calamity should you apprehend, Flora?" asked her mother; "has not Providence hitherto provided us with every blessing and comfort? Are we not all in the enjoyment of health and plenty?—Have we not friends to whom we are dear?—Have you not one who loves you with ardour and sincerity?—Are not our prospects all bright and sunny?—Have we an enemy that we know of in the world? What cause then have you thus to encourage these melancholy doubts and presentiments?"

"True, mother, all at present is smiling and promising; but the brightest prospects are often obscured by the clouds of adversity, and who knows but such may be our fates?"

" Flora, child," remonstrated her father, " it is wrong, very wrong, thus to anticipate evil. Were we always to do so, what wretched beings we should make ourselves, and ill deserve the blessings that Providence has so bounteously bestowed upon us."

" The reproof I feel is just, my father," returned Flora; " but again I say I feel it impossible, at present, to conquer this weakness. Last night I had a fearful dream, which has made an impression upon my mind that I fear I shall not be able easily to eradicate."

" A dream, Flora?"

" Yes, dear father," replied the damsel, " a dream, and one of terror,—one that chills my blood when I think of it."

" Compose yourself, my child," said Mr. Clarendon, " and relate it to us."

Flora paused and hesitated, then making a powerful effort, she at length succeeded in partially conquering her emotions, and thus observed:—

" I will relate my dream to you, my parents, and then I can have the benefit of your consolation and advice:—Last night, on retiring to rest, it was some time ere sleep descended upon my eyelids; but I lay tossing to and fro in a state of mental agitation, for which I could not account. At length sleep gradually stole upon my senses, when the following fearful vision presented itself to my imagination:—Methought that the happy day of my union with William had arrived, and all was gaiety and expectation. Fouchette and another beauteous girl were in attendance as bridesmaids, and I, all bounding with delight, was arrayed in my bridal dress. You were all present in this little parlour, and nothing could equal the joy that marked each countenance. Presently my William arrived, looking more handsome and happy than I had ever before seen him. And now the village bells rang forth their merriest peal, and we departed to the church. Oh, how brilliantly shone the sun, shedding around refulgent floods of heavenly gold. How cheerfully carolled the birds on every spray as we proceeded along. To my imagination the path we trod was redolent of roses and other sweet flowers, and the very air sent forth the most odoriferous perfumes. It was, indeed, a morning of joy, of loveliness, and fair promise, such an one as breathes of Heaven and all that is sweet and charming. At length we reached the village church, and entering, approached the altar where the holy minister was already waiting to perform the sacred rites. We knelt before the altar, the ceremony had commenced, but not far had it proceeded, when a loud crashing sound was heard, and a tall figure in black, whose dress was covered with human bones, and who wore a sable mask, rushed suddenly up to us; the minister vanished, and the strange and awful looking being seized me with one hand, while with the other he firmly grasped the throat of William; the earth appeared to sink under us, and the next moment we found ourselves on the deck of a vessel, surrounded by frightful looking men, and battling with the billows that were running mountains high. The awful object who seized us in the church, held me firmly in his arms ; and William, writhing in agony, was held firmly in the grasp of two of the other men : he called piteously upon my name, and implored them to have mercy on me and to spare me ; but rude and scornful laughter was the only answer he received to his supplications, while the monster who held me again and again contaminated me with his odious kisses.   Oh, God ! what a moment of terror was that to me, it is stamped upon my mind with all the power of reality."

"Compose yourself, my dear Flora," said her father, "and proceed."

Flora, after a pause, during which she was endeavouring to tranquillize her feelings, complied, and continued in the following words :

"Suddenly the form of the ruffian who held me appeared to change,—the mask fell from his face,—his dress faded away, and he stood confessed as Sir Julian Mordlington !"

"Sir Julian Mordlington !" reiterated Mr. and Mrs. Clarendon in a breath.

"Yes, it was him;—I saw him as plainly as if it had been reality;—his countenance was expressive of every evil and diabolical passion, and methought I screamed aloud with terror ; but in vain did I struggle to extricate myself from his hold.   'Thou art mine !' I heard him shout ; ' mine, mine ! the bride of *The Smuggler King !'* "

"Wonderful !" exclaimed both Mr. Clarendon and his wife, whose deepest interest and astonishment were now excited by the extraordinary dream.

"Methought," resumed Flora, "that William once more made a desperate attempt to release himself from the ruffians who held him, and to fly to my rescue ; but he struggled in vain, and, at a signal given by Sir Julian Mordlington, he was suddenly raised up in their arms, and, notwithstanding my frantic cries, was thrown over the side of the vessel into the raging deep. I saw his last look of agonizing despair—I heard the awful plash of his body as it was precipitated into the waters — I heard the fiendish laugh of exultation that arose from Sir Julian Mordlington and the other ruffians, and then I thought I became insensible."

"And is that the whole of your remarkable dream ?" inquired her father.

"No," replied Flora.   "When I recovered my senses how changed was the scene !   I was supported in the arms of William, and we were upon a raft, tossed every now and then almost to the clouds by the stormy billows. Awfully the thunder rolled and the lightning flashed, and nothing but death surrounded us on every side.   As far as the eye could stretch nothing save one vast expanse of ocean met the gaze.   But oh ! amidst all those accumulated horrors, I felt a degree of happiness which I am at a loss to describe, for my lover was saved from the jaws of death—he held me to his heart once more, and, if it was our fate to meet with death at that time, we should at least have the consolation of dying together.   For a long while we continued in this awful situation, and without the least prospect of land, or the approach of any vessel that might rescue us.   Still more furiously pealed the thunder, and fiercer still the lightning blazed, while the wind increased in proportion.   At length a dreadful crash was heard, the timbers that formed our raft divided, and I beheld William sinking.   I clung to him—the raft separated from us—we sunk, sunk gradually, until I felt the waters close over my head, and, in the horror of that moment I awoke. These, my dear parents, are the particulars of my awful dream, and I think you must admit that what I have told you was sufficient to make a powerful impression upon my mind, and to fill it with those melancholy forebodings of approaching calamity which I have expressed to you."

Flora ceased, and her father and mother remained silent for awhile, and seemed to reflect seriously upon what she had been relating to them.

"It was a most fearful and extraordinary dream," at length observed Mrs. Clarendon.

"It was, indeed," coincided her husband; "and, after hearing it, I do not wonder at the melancholy of Flora this morning, and the dismal presentiments she has suffered to take possession of her imagination. That Sir Julian Mordlington should form a principal character in it, and the circumstance of his announcing himself the Smuggler King, surprises me more than all, and greatly perplexes me to interpret it. We must be aware of the baronet, for much I am inclined to think that he is a bad man."

"So report speaks of his character, notwithstanding his assumption of virtue and benevolence since he has become lord of this manor," observed Flora. "I never behold him but he excites in my bosom a feeling approaching to horror."

"But he is our landlord," said Mrs. Clarendon, "and we must be cautious and circumspect in our conduct towards him."

"We will pay him all the respect and deference that his station commands," said Mr. Clarendon, "but he holds no power over us; and, by Heavens! if he oversteps the bounds of prudence towards us, he shall find that, humble as Farmer Clarendon is, he has the moral courage to resent an unprovoked insult, even were it offered by the king himself. He has already dared to address himself with unbecoming freedom to Flora, and if it is repeated I will demand and insist upon that satisfaction which an insulted parent, however lowly his rank in society, has a right to insist upon having."

"But I trust he will not repeat it, father," said the damsel; "and I have now William to protect me."

"True, Flora," said her father; "and it will be well for Sir Julian if he does not repeat his offence, for, depend upon it, all his empty power would not screen him from William's vengeance."

"Heaven grant that our worst fears may prove groundless," observed Mrs. Clarendon. "But Flora's dream has made as powerful an impression upon my mind as it can have done upon Flora's."

"And do you not think, dear mother," asked her daughter, "that it prognosticates future trouble to us?"

"Alas! I scarcely know what to think," replied Mrs. Clarendon.

"It is impossible for us to unravel it," remarked Mr. Clarendon. "All that we can do is to act with caution, and we may then be able to thwart the plans of our enemies, if we really have any. In the meantime, my love, endeavour to banish this strange and awful dream from your memory, and to reassume your accustomed spirits."

"I will endeavour to do so, my dear father," replied the damsel, "although I am afraid for a time that I shall have some difficulty in accomplishing the task. Have you ever heard of the Smuggler King?"

"I have," answered Mr. Clarendon, "indeed there are few persons but what have, and who do not shudder when they hear his name mentioned. He is a desperate smuggler and pirate, and appears to hold a complete ascendancy over all other vessels of that character on the ocean, by which he has obtained the title he now bears. The cruelties that have from time to time been inflicted by him, would make the blood freeze with horror to hear them recounted."

"And have they never been able to apprehend him?"

"They have not. Strong forces have been despatched in pursuit of him, but they have always failed in their object; and those who have engaged with him, have invariably been defeated, and the survivors of the crew put to death in the most barbarous manner. He is always dressed in the manner you have described him in your dream, and his features, concealed by a sable mask, have never been seen except by his crew. Immense rewards have been offered for his detection and apprehension, but without effect. Even now five thousand pounds are advertised for that purpose."

"Most extraordinary," observed Mrs. Clarendon.

"It is," said Flora; "and any one would have thought that the offer of so large a sum of money would have tempted one of his own crew to have betrayed him."

"No, they are all faithful to him, and would lay down their lives in his defence," said Mr. Clarendon.

At that moment there was a knock at the door.

"It is William, I dare say," ejaculated Flora, springing joyfully from her seat and going to the door which she opened, and William entered and enfolded her in his arms.

"My own sweet Flora," said the young mariner, "I have sailed along at a rare rate to have the pleasure of once more seeing you, and kissing your pretty lips. God bless you, my lass! I love you better and better every time I see you. Father, mother, for such I shall now call you, I greet you both. But—but, holloa, splice my timbers! there's something wrong here. Why, Flora, my darling Flora, you look as sad as if you were going to a funeral; you have been weeping too; what's the matter?"

"Nothing, William, nothing," replied Flora, endeavouring to smile; "I—I—but my father will tell you all."

"I—I—but my father will tell you all," repeated William; "why, shiver me if I can understand this at all."

"Do not be alarmed, William," said Mr. Clarendon, "nothing serious has taken place, only Flora has been a little frightened."

"Frightened! my Flora frightened! How, by whom? Show me the swab, and —"

"No one has insulted her," interrupted Mr. Clarendon.

"Insulted her," repeated William, "I should like to come athwart the hawse of any lubber in Christendom that would only dare attempt to do such a thing. But just have the kindness to get your jawing tackle on board and tell me all about it?"

"I will," replied Mr. Clarendon, "but you must promise me that you will listen with patience."

"Ay, ay, so weigh anchor directly," said the young seaman.

Mr. Clarendon then, as briefly as possible related the dream which had so much alarmed Flora, to which William listened with the deepest attention, and when he had concluded, said,

"Well, this is certainly a very strange dream, and was enough to alarm the poor lass; but cheer up, Flora, neither Smuggler Kings, nor Sir Julian Bodlingtons or Mordlington, whichever you call him, shall dare attempt to harm you while your William is at hand to protect you. By-the-bye, I have heard no very good account of that Sir Julian, and it strikes me that he knew something about that outrage from which I saved you in the wood."

"Ah!" exclaimed Mr. Clarendon, "that thought never occurred to me."

"If I thought he was connected with the black-looking swab," added William, his cheeks glowing with indignation, "I would pay him a visit and pour such a broadside in upon him as he would not forget in a hurry."

"We are not certain that he is guilty," said Flora, "and you know not, dear William, the danger —"

"Danger," interrupted her lover, "who talks about danger to a British seaman? 'tis a word he does not understand; but there is one thing he understands perfectly well, and that is how to punish, as he deserves, the cowardly lubber that would dare insult a female, especially the girl of his heart. But I will tell you an excellent plan that will get rid of all this bother."

"What mean you, William?" demanded Mr. Clarendon.

"What mean I? do you not read an answer in the pretty eyes of my Flora, and in the expression of my own countenance? What mean I? why, let Flora and I be spliced directly, and then she will be safely moored in the arms of one who will protect her with the last drop of his blood."

Flora blushed deeply, and hid her face in her mother's bosom.

"What say you, father?" demanded William, eagerly. "I know my friends will consent immediately; and what's the use of delaying, if two lovers are to be made happy, which I am certain both I and Flora shall be—why the sooner it is done the better."

"You know our agreement, William," said Mr. Clarendon, seriously.

"Oh, a fig for agreements, unless they are marriage agreements," replied William. "Five years! only consider what a time that is for a man to look forward to, before he can expect to cast anchor in the ocean of matrimony; and there are only three years of the time expired yet."

"William," returned Mr. Clarendon, "I have given you my word that you shall become the husband of my Flora at the expiration of five years, if nothing particular occurs to prevent it, and that promise I will not break. I have every confidence in your sincerity, and the affection you bear my child. I know that you both love each other, and I believe you will be happy together; but I cannot alter my first decision."

"And why not, sir?" asked William.

"That question I should have thought was unnecessary to a man of his word," replied Mr. Clarendon; "but I will give you my reasons for deciding on a delay of that time."

"And what are they?"

"Great changes may take place in the course of that period."

"You are right there, father, at any rate," observed William, with a smile; "for instance, we may all of us be shipped off to Davy Jones's locker in that time, and then, you know, Flora and I should not want to get married."

"Hear me seriously, William, I beg," said Mr. Clarendon. "As I before said, in the course of five years great changes may take place. You may discover your real parents, and ——"

"And think you," interrupted the impatient young mariner—"think you that any discovery I might make of that kind would alter my sentiments as regards my dear Flora?"

"They might be wealthy."

"All the better, then they would be able to supply me with the means of making my Flora more comfortable," returned William.

"They might object to your union," added Mr. Clarendon.

"And so they might," answered William; "but they could not put another heart in my breast, and till they could do that, all their objections would be useless. Let them keep their gold, and their rank and dignity, but they never should rob me of my Flora."

The damsel looked up from her mother's bosom, with a sweet smile, and her eyes sparkled with the most unbounded affection and gratitude upon her lover.

"It would be your duty to obey the will of your parents," observed Mr. Clarendon.

"In all other respects I would," replied William; "but I would not allow them to exercise a tyrannical authority over my heart, especially when the future happiness of my Flora is involved. Besides, that my parents are living I do not entertain the most remote idea. They were, doubtless, in the vessel that was wrecked, and you have heard my foster father say that I and another boy, supposed to have been my brother, were all that were saved."

"That brother may be living."

"If he is, he is a wretch whom I would loathe as a monster," returned William.

"Why?"

"Did he not, even young as he was, attempt to murder me?" said William in reply, "and afterwards disappeared, and was never heard of more."

Mr. Clarendon was about to make a reply, when they were all startled by a piercing scream, and looking towards the place whence it proceeded, they were astonished to perceive the door partially open, and standing on the threshold, apparently in the act of listening to their conversation, they beheld the figure of the mysterious wandering woman, Crazy Marian.

They all started from their seats, and made a spring towards the door; but the maniac no sooner beheld their intention than she rushed precipitately from the spot, and when they reached the door, she was out of sight.

They returned into the room, and, for a few minutes, were so much amazed at what had taken place, that they could not speak a word.

"Well, that is certainly a strange looking craft," at last said William; "and what could she want here?"

"I am at a loss to conjecture," replied Mr. Clarendon. "She had evidently been listening to our discourse."

"She had," returned William; "but if she is a maniac, she could not understand much about it."

"I know not that," remarked Mr. Clarendon; "the shriek she uttered just at the time when you came to the description of the attempt at murder made by your supposed brother, would almost tempt one to believe that her reason has not entirely left her, and that she was shocked by the villany of the deed."

"Well, I should certainly like to know who she really is," said William; "for I cannot help feeling a strange interest and curiosity in her fate. Maniac or not, I owe her a debt of gratitude for saving my life, and probably that of Flora. But to return to the subject upon which we were conversing. You will not consent, then, that I should marry Flora until the expiration of the five years?"

"I have told you so, William," replied Mr. Clarendon, "why then urge the question farther?"

"Well, I suppose I must submit," said the young seaman, "but I must say that it is very hard. Besides, would it not, as I before said, be the surest way of securing my dear Flora from insult from all such lubbers as this Sir Julian Mordlington?"

"It might," answered Mr. Clarendon, "but you must recollect that Sir Julian has power."

"And what care I for his power?" demanded William; "do I not possess courage and honour on my side, and that will always stand against powerful villany; for that this Sir Julian is a villain, I have not the least doubt."

"Of that opinion I am likewise," said Mr. Clarendon, "but time will probably reveal his real character, and in the meanwhile we must be on our guard against him."

"I should like to see this gentleman, as he is called," observed William, "for after what I have heard of him, he has excited in me some curiosity. There is one circumstance, by-the-bye, speaking of this Sir Julian Mordlington, which I forgot to mention."

" What is that, pray ?"

" You noticed the Irish gentleman, Flora," said her lover, " that has been staying for a day or two with my foster father?"

Flora replied in the affirmative.

" Yesterday morning," continued William, " he left the farm at an early hour, to go to the hall, where, it appears, he had some particular business to transact with the baronet ; and although all his luggage is left behind, he has never since returned."

" Indeed !" said Flora, " that is most remarkable. What can have become of him ?"

" That we cannot surmise," answered her lover.

" But have you made any inquiries after him ?"

" We have inquired everywhere in the neighbourhood, but without success."

" At the hall ?"

" Yes, Mr. Backstay went there this morning," replied William, " before I left the farm."

" And what was the result ?" inquired Flora.

" The answer he received was, that Sir Julian was not up, and consequently could not be seen, but that he knew nothing of the individual inquired after, and that he had never been at the hall."

" That surely must be a falsehood, or else the baronet has made a mistake," observed Flora, " for I was present when the gentleman was mentioning that he had been to the hall, and had had an interview with Sir Julian, and that it was his intention to go there again as yesterday."

" There is something very mysterious about the affair altogether," remarked William, " and it must be sifted to the bottom."

No. 12

"Good God!" exclaimed Flora, "I hope that no harm has befallen the poor gentleman."

"I hope not," returned William, "for there was something in his manners that deeply interested me."

"Do you know his name?" asked Mr. Clarendon.

"We never heard him mention it," replied William, "but the name on one of his boxes is Fitzpatrick."

"Fitzpatrick!" repeated Mr. Clarendon, endeavouring to recollect; "I have heard that name before."

William was going to make some reply, but was interrupted by a loud knock at the door, and Mr Clarendon on opening it, was struck with astonishment on beholding Sir Julian Mordlington

The baronet entered without ceremony, but no sooner did his eyes encounter William, than he started back as if he had been stung by some venomous reptile; his countenance changed, his lips quivered, and as he gazed earnestly at the young mariner, his very frame might be observed to tremble with the most violent emotion.

"The very image!" he muttered to himself; "it must be he—curses on him!"

William met Sir Julian's gaze with a steady eye and an air of dignity, but at the same time a tremour passed through his frame, for which he was at a loss to account. Flora shuddered instinctively in the presence of the baronet, and kept closer to her mother.

Sir Julian having recovered himself, once more advanced into the room, and bowed politely to all present, which they returned with all becoming respect, although they were at a loss to imagine what purpose it was that had brought him thither.

Mr. Clarendon was the first that recovered himself sufficiently to speak, and addressing the baronet, he said,—

"To what, Sir Julian Mordlington, may I attribute the honour of this visit?"

"I came here, Mr. Clarendon," replied Sir Julian, in a bland voice, "to offer an apology to you, and the young lady, your daughter."

"Apology!" repeated William, his face colouring, and feeling his indignation rise.

Mr. Clarendon motioned him to be calm, and William obeyed, although it was quite evident that the baronet quailed beneath his penetrating glance, and wished that he had postponed his visit till a future time, when William might not have been present.

"You came here, you say, to apologise, Sir Julian Mordlington," said Mr. Clarendon; "may I presume to ask for what?"

The baronet looked at William, and hesitated. He would fain have excused himself from answering the question, but he could not, and he regretted that he had broached the subject at all. He could perceive the looks of mistrust, if not hatred, that William fixed upon him, and knowing how richly he merited his abhorrence, he shrunk beneath his glances.

"It is a mere trifle that I have to apologise for, Mr. Clarendon," he said at last, in reply to the question the farmer had put to him; "but I fear that it is probable I might have been misunderstood, and that when I took the liberty of addressing your daughter the other morning, she might misconstrue it into a wish to insult."

"Insult! insult offered to Flora Clarendon!" ejaculated William passionately, and advancing nearer to Sir Julian, while his fine eyes sparkled and flashed with indignation. "Dare you in my presence acknowledge that you insulted her?"

The innate pride of the baronet, in spite of the emotion which the presence of his brother excited in his bosom, returned in all its full force, and fixing upon the youthful mariner a look of contempt, he demanded,—

"And who are you, pray, that Sir Julian Mordlington should not dare to speak in your presence ?"

"Well, if you wish to overhaul my log-book," coolly replied William, "you will find it there inserted William Backstay, an honest seaman, poor, but independent; ready in a moment to resent an insult, and fierce as a lion at any time, to stand in the defence of injured innocence. You will also find it there written, that William Backstay is betrothed to one Flora Clarendon, as pretty a little craft as ever floated on the ocean of life, and that the man who dares to say a word in her presence, or offer the least insult that might call a blush upon her cheeks, be he lord or duke, prince, peer, pauper, or baronet, must answer dearly for it to the man who is now addressing you. How do you like that bit of palaver, Sir Julian Mordlington ?"

"The detested viper !" thought the baronet; " curses on my hands that failed in their deadly purpose, when he was an infant. But I must conquer my rage, and play the hypocrite."

"Humph !" he uttered aloud, and forcing a smile, " you are warm, my young sailor, on the subject; but I commend your spirit, and wish you and the fair damsel you have chosen to be your future partner, happy. I shall feel a pleasure in rendering you any assistance in my power."

"Assistance !" repeated William indignantly; " look in my face, Sir Julian Mordlington, and see whether you fancy I very much resemble a beggar ? a British seaman asks not for charity; he can always satisfy his wants in drubbing his enemies, and taking his prize money."

Sir Julian frowned, looked confused, and then turning to Mr. Clarendon, he said,—

"I came here, sir, as I informed you, to see you ; I have told you the business I came upon; do you accept of my apology ?"

"I do, this time, Sir Julian Mordlington," said the farmer boldly, " but I would have you to understand that, although our stations in society are widely different, should such conduct ever be repeated, you may find there are those who have the moral courage to resent it."

"Yes, Sir Julian Mordlington," observed William, " at any rate you will find one that may prove rather more than a match for you, and whose motto is, when he has to encounter a d—d shark, fair play above board, and no quarter. Put that in your pipe and smoke it, Sir Julian Mordlington."

The baronet bit his lips, and could only with difficulty repress his rage. To be thus taunted by the very man he had so much reason to detest, was more than he had prepared himself to encounter; but he consoled himself immediately with the reflection, that he would shortly have both him and Flora in his power, and then he could take ample revenge for all. The looks, the very tones of William's voice, and his whole demeanour so forcibly reminded him of his father, that it filled him with sentiments of dread, and the most powerful emotion, and he felt that he should never be happy while he continued to exist.

During the time that Sir Julian was present, Flora endured the greatest agony of mind ; she recollected her dream, and the prominent part which the baronet enacted in it, and every time she gazed upon his features, her heart sunk, and the blood chilled within her veins.

Sir Julian but once or twice ventured to look towards her, for the presence of William abashed him; but when he did so, it increased the guilty passions that had taken possession of his breast, for the charms of Flora appeared to have increased tenfold, since he had last beheld her.   He was, however, anxious, as the young mariner was present, to make the interview as brief as possible, and therefore once more turning to Mr. Clarendon, he said,—

"Sir, you will find me attentive to your wishes; at the same time if I can serve you in any way, you may command me."

"I never ask favours, Sir Julian," said Mr. Clarendon in reply, proudly.

"Humph!" muttered the baronet to himself, somewhat disconcerted; he then added aloud,—

"It is my wish, Mr. Clarendon, since I have become lord of this manor, to make all my tenants as comfortable as possible."

"I am very glad to hear it, Sir Julian," was the farmer's laconic reply.

"I believe some of them to be too highly rented.   I intend to reduce the rents so as to meet the incomes of the different tenants."

"A very benevolent design, sir," returned Mr. Clarendon, "and one that is very much needed.   There are many of them, God knows, that are but ill able to pay what they are doing at present; but for my own part, I am perfectly contented.   My father before me was enabled to pay it, and realise sufficient to make his old age comfortable, and I trust, with the blessing of Providence, to be able to do the same."

"What a stubborn old idiot," thought the baronet.

"I admire your honest independence, Mr. Clarendon," he said, "and I trust we shall soon be better acquainted."

"Oh, yes," observed William, with a significant smile, "I dare say we shall all be better acquainted by and by."

"We shall," muttered Sir Julian to himself; and he fixed a look upon William, which the latter returned with one of the most supreme contempt.

"At any time," he remarked to the farmer, "I shall be happy to see you or any of your family at the hall."

"No doubt of it," said William, with a sneer.

"I thank you, Sir Julian," replied Mr. Clarendon—"I thank you for the invitation.   Your steward will always see me punctually on the rent-day.   I seldom pay any other visits, unless it is to my old friend, Mr. Backstay."

"Well—well," observed the baronet, confused, "in that, of course, you can use your own discretion.   I have given you the invitation."

"For which I thank you, Sir Julian," replied the farmer.

"Thank you for nothing," added William, with a laugh.

"You are disposed to be jocular, young man," said the baronet, scowling.

"Oh, yes, I am sometimes taken that way," returned William, "especially when I find a fair subject to joke upon."

Sir Julian bit his lips, but he stifled the expression of his anger.

"I wish you all good morning," said he, moving towards the door.

"Good morning, Sir Julian," returned Mr. Clarendon.

"Avast, Sir Julian, a moment, if you please," said William, suddenly advancing towards the baronet.

Sir Julian turned hastily round, and looked with surprise and confusion at the young mariner as he demanded,—

"What would you?"

"I would merely ask you a question, Sir Julian, if I am permitted to do so," returned William.

"What question would you put to me?" inquired the baronet.

"You know a Mr. Fitzpatrick, I believe?"

"What of him?" demanded Sir Julian, with increased confusion.

"Oh, you do know him, then?"

"Yes—no—I never heard of the gentleman."

"Oh, indeed! Well, we shall see."

"I know nothing of him," returned the baronet, sternly. "What of him?"

"He has been missing since yesterday morning," replied William, fixing a penetrating look upon the baronet.

"What is that to me?" demanded Sir Julian, with a look of disdain.

"If all be true that I have heard," returned William, "it has a great deal to do with you, Sir Julian."

"And what have you heard?" inquired the baronet, evincing some uneasiness.

"I will tell you. Mr. Fitzpatrick once called upon you at the hall, upon business, and he left my father's yesterday morning to repeat the visit, since which he has never returned. Of course it is very singular, and as he is a friend or acquaintance of yours ——"

"I tell you, sir," interrupted Sir Julian, "that I am not acquainted with the person you have mentioned, neither have I seen anything of him. Good morning."

Thus saying, Sir Julian abruptly quitted the farm, not very well pleased with the result of his visit.

"It is he," he soliloquised, as he proceeded on his way to the hall—"I am certain it is my brother. So great is his likeness to my late father, that I could almost imagine his spirit stood before me. Oh, how I loathe, yet dread him! And then the bold and taunting language he used towards me. Would that we had been alone, he should not have lived to repeat his words. It is evident that he views me with suspicion, hatred, and contempt. He must be removed. Then his remarks about Fitzpatrick. It was no use my denying that I knew anything of him; it is clear that he suspects me. But he cannot have any idea that I have acted unfairly by the old lawyer, unless—but away with these surmises. I am torturing my mind to no purpose. Had Fitzpatrick mentioned anything of his business with me, this young sailor, I am certain, would have told me of it. But he shall speedily be removed; Flora shall be in my power before many days have elapsed, and then all will be safe."

He moved quickly on towards the hall as he thus spoke, which he arrived at without meeting with any individual that knew him.

After he had quitted the farm, William observed,—

"Well, if ever a man had villain stamped upon his countenance, it is this same Sir Julian Mordlington."

"I believe him to be a bad man," said Mr. Clarendon, "and we must be guarded against him, or he may work us harm."

"Oh, how I shuddered in his presence," said Flora.

"Fear him not, my lass," said her lover, "he will find William Backstay more than a match for him, with all his craft and power. There is something in his countenance which has made an impression upon my mind of a most singular character, and it seems to me as if we had met before."

"That, I think is very unlikely," said Mr. Clarendon, "for he has not been many weeks in this neighbourhood, and you have been at sea, and had no opportunity of beholding him."

"Very true," returned William, "but still his form and features are strangely familiar to me. Did you not notice the emotion he betrayed on entering the farm and beholding me?"

"I remarked it," replied Mr. Clarendon, "but he was doubtless confused at seeing you, knowing you to be the lover of Flora."

"He came here with no good purpose," observed William.

"Of that opinion we must all be," said the farmer, "but I do not think he will repeat his visit in a hurry, after the reception he met with."

"That he knows something about the extraordinary disappearance of Mr. Fitzpatrick, I am certain."

"I think so too," replied Mr. Clarendon, "and his confusion when you mentioned that gentleman's name, and his so stcutly denying any knowledge of him, confirms me more than all in that belief. If he does not return, it will be the duty of Mr. Backstay to make the authorities acquainted with the circumstance, who will not fail to investigate the matter to the bottom."

"That shall be done, depend upon it," said William, "and if Sir Julian has acted anything wrong towards Mr. Fitzpatrick, woe betide him, for his wealth and power will not protect him from punishment."

"Mr. Backstay is approaching the house," said Flora, who had been looking from the window.

"Now then we shall hear what has been the result of his inquiries," said William, as he hastened to the door and gave admittance to his foster-father.

To the questions that were speedily put to him, Mr. Backstay replied that the lawyer had not returned, and that all the inquiries he had made after him had not been attended with the least success. He added, that he should only wait over that day, and then, if Mr. Fitzpatrick did not make his appearance, he should inform the proper authorities of the circumstance, and they, no doubt would institute a most rigid investigation.

"They will," he observed, "I dare say, order his boxes to be opened, in order that it may be ascertained whether they contain any papers that may lead to a discovery of his friends and relations."

"No doubt of it," coincided Mr. Clarendon, "but I hope he will return."

"I hope so too," said Mr. Backstay, "but I cannot help thinking that something has happened to the unfortunate gentleman."

"What can have happened to him?" said Mr. Clarendon; "know you whether he had any considerable sum of money about him?"

"I am not aware that he had."

"Oh," said the gentle Flora, with a shudder. "should he have been way-laid and murdered."

"There is nothing improbable in that," observed Mr. Backstay, "for there are many desperate characters in this neighbourhood, who would not hesitate to do such a deed."

"For instance, that black-looking lubber whom I encountered in the wood, attempting to bear Flora away," said William.

"Ay," returned old Backstay, "and I cannot help still suspecting Sir Julian Mordlington of something wrong, for the very reason that he persists in not knowing Mr. Fitzpatrick, when we are well convinced that it was to see him the gentleman came to this neighbourhood, and that he had one interview with him."

"True," remarked William, "and your suspicions will be strengthened when you hear what we have to tell you."

Mr. Clarendon then related the particulars of the visit of Sir Julian to the farm, and the conversation that had taken place on that occasion, also the manner in which the baronet there denied all knowledge of Mr. Fitzpatrick. Mr. Backstay listened to the account with much attention, and when Mr. Clarendon had concluded, he said,

"This confirms the opinion I have always formed of this Sir Julian Mordlington, ever since he has been in the neighbourhood, namely, that amiable and benevolent as he may appear in his manners, he is at heart a villain, and so, depend upon it, time will prove him to be. I am now more anxious than ever to ascertain what has become of Mr. Fitzpatrick, for if there was any enmity between them, he could not have fallen into worse hands than those of the baronet. But I will not let the matter rest. I consider it my bounden duty, as the missing gentleman was staying at my house, and I was in some manner responsible for his security, to exert myself to the very utmost to discover what has become of him."

"You say right," observed Mr. Clarendon, " and I trust that your efforts will ultimately be crowned with success."

After some further conversation upon the subject, Mr. Backstay quitted the farm, fully determined to lose no time in making all the inquiries he could.

In the meantime, Sir Julian Mordlington, having reached the hall, retired to his study in order that he might endeavour to smooth his ruffled temper, ruffled by the events of the morning, to meet his invited guests.

"That daring youth," he ruminated, " he has all the dignity of bearing and of speech, as if he was acquainted with his origin, and yet that is impossible. I hate him worse the more I think of him, and shall not rest until I have him in my power. It was a fortunate job that I secured the lawyer, or the discovery I dreaded would most assuredly have been made, and ere many days, William would have been in a fair way to have gained possession of the property my foolish father bequeathed him, and I should have been held up to the world as a villain of the blackest dye. It is all mine now, and there is no will, no person to dispute my claim. The stir they are making about the disappearance of Fitzpatrick is rather awkward, but no matter, I am safe enough. There is no one to prove that I know him, or that he has ever been to the hall, and no doubt the excitement will pass over in a few days. At any rate, no clue to his fate, if Sam Raker punctually attends to the instructions I have given him, can possibly be discovered. In a few hours more there will be an end to the *honest* lawyer; ha! ha! ha! I have made quick work with him, thanks to the advice of Raker, and such will always be the fate of the enemies of the Smuggler King."

He paused awhile and paced the room with feelings of exultation, as he reflected on the success that had hitherto attended his schemes.

"Flora Clarendon," he at length resumed, " there is something in the very name of that beauteous damsel that charms my senses. How lovely she looked this morning; and yet her looks and manners convince me that she views me with horror and abhorrence. Strange that people should take such prejudices, and yet I know not of anything particularly repulsive in my person; nay, have I not been courted and admired by some of the loveliest and the wealthiest maidens in Europe? And now to be scorned by a mere rustic girl. But no matter, let me but once obtain possession of her, and I will soon find out the way to cure her of her pride and disdain. Sir Julian Mordlington, the Smuggler King, never suffers his hopes and designs to be disappointed and thwarted. Oh! what a noble bride will she make; my floating palace will receive additional power and attraction by her presence. I grow impatient for the time to come."

Sanguine in his hopes of gaining possession of Flora Clarendon, the villain continued to traverse the room, immersed in similar reflections to those we have mentioned, until the arrival of the guests he had invited, and whom he received with as much ease and courtesy, as if his mind was entirely unoccupied by any other thoughts than those of pleasure.

It was a merry day at the hall, and the festivities were kept up with much gaiety until a late hour. All the principal fashionables of the neighbourhood were present, and did full justice to the hospitality of Sir Julian. There was open house too, to all the tenantry of the baronet that chose to come, and ample fare was provided for their consumption. It was an excellent scheme of Sir Julian's, and it succeeded admirably; every one went away praising the liberality of the new lord of the manor, and full of ad-miration at the urbanity of manner he had displayed on the occasion.

But although Sir Julian had appeared to mingle freely in the festivities of the day, and laughed and joked abundantly, his thoughts were far other-wise directed. He longed for the approach of night, and the arrival of the time when he had appointed Sam Raker to meet him, so that he might learn the particulars of what had taken place on board the Devil's Skipper, and be assured that Mr. Fitzpatrick was no more. Since he had seen William he could not rest until he had got rid of the unfortunate lawyer, so that there might not be the shadow of a chance of his discovering who the young mariner was, and working him any harm, although he well knew that now he was once in his power, there was no cause whatever to ap-prehend the slightest danger from him. But there was another circumstance that rendered him anxious to make away with Mr. Fitzpatrick as speedily as possible, and that was the search that was being made after him; the manner in which old Backstay was busying himself in the affair, and the probability there also was of their suspicions being ultimately directed to his vessel, where, if a search was made, not only would the lawyer be dis-covered, but the nature of the ship become known.

He was extremely glad when the company separated, which did not take place till some time after midnight, and then he entered the room in which he had appointed to meet the smuggler, and impatiently awaited his arrival. The hour of two arrived, but not so the smuggler,—and when another half hour had passed away in like manner, Sir Julian began to apprehend that something had happened.

It was not until nearly three o'clock that the baronet heard a footstep cautiously ascending the stairs, and the next moment he heard a knock at the room-door.

" Who's there ?" demanded Sir Julian, in a low voice.

" Why, who should it be," answered the voice of Sam Raker, " but me."

The door was opened directly, and the smuggler entered. His brow was scowling.

" You seem out of temper, Sam," said the baronet.

" Well," abruptly answered Sam, " if I am, it is not at all surprising, for I have had a hard night's work of it."

" You are late."

" I could not get the business settled and reach here before," answered Sam Raker, very unceremoniously taking a seat.

" Ah! then is it settled ?" demanded Sir Julian, eagerly.

" Yes, old Latitat has made his last voyage," replied the miscreant.

" He is no more ?"

" Have I not told you so ?"

" Then I am safe! I am secure!" exclaimed Sir Julian with a look of the most fiendish exultation.

" And so you were before," observed Raker, sullenly.

" Well, well," returned the baronet, " so I might have been ; I will not dispute that point with you; at any rate, it is better that the old lawyer is put out of the way."

" So I think."

" I owe you many thanks, Sam, for this."

" Why, yes," said the smuggler, with a sarcastic grin, " if you have the ample share of the honour, I think I have my full share of the work, captain."

" You shall not go unrewarded."

" Oh, I dare say not."

"And how did you perform the deed?" inquired Sir Julian.

"In the manner you instructed me," answered Sam Raker.

"And how did he die?"

"Oh, he did not seem to fancy it at all. He struggled most desperately when we went to fasten him in the sack, and I never heard any one beg so hard for mercy in my life before. I was almost inclined to pity him myself, and you know I am not one of the most tender hearted. But I have some recollection of a grey-headed old father myself, and ——"

"Ha, ha, ha!" laughed Sir Julian; "well, this the most amusing thing I ever heard; Sam Raker turned moralizer."

"To be sure, I must acknowledge that I am somewhat out of my element in that line. But the old chap died very hard."

"Ha, ha, ha! old parchment did not like to resign his briefs just yet."

"No; he wanted to live a little longer," replied Sam.

"It is the way with us all, however much we may boast of our honesty and integrity," observed Sir Julian. "But did you take him far from the vessel before you consigned him to deep?"

"I did."

"And you saw him sink ——"

"To rise no more?" added the murderer.

"How could he be off it, when he was sewed in the sack."

"'Tis well, 'tis well," said Sir Julian, in tones of satisfaction.

"As we tossed him over the side of the boat he uttered such a cry that I shall never forget; it still seems to ring in my ears."

"Psha!"

"Well, captain, you may treat it with contempt because you was not there to hear it; but ——"

No. 13

"Nonsense, Sam," interrupted the baronet, impatiently, "you are quite childish this time. One would think it was the first crime of the sort that you had perpetrated."

"It is the hardest job I have ever had," returned Sam.

"Well, well, it is done now, and there is an end to the matter," said Sir Julian.

"I hope there is."

"Hope! what is there to fear?"

"Nothing that I am aware of. But I say, captain, have you anything good in the bottle? for I am greatly in need of something, I assure you."

"Here is wine," answered Sir Julian, "so you can enjoy yourself. I cannot help thanking you for the business-like manner in which you have executed this job."

"Why, I believe I am rather clever at those sort of jobs," returned the ruffian, filling the glass from the decanter, and raising it to his lips. "Your health, captain."

"Two things more accomplished," said Sir Julian, "and then my mind will be at rest, and the Smuggler King will soon join his bold crew again on the deep blue waters."

"And what are those two deeds that you want accomplished, captain?" asked Raker.

"The seizure of the young sailor and Flora Clarendon."

"That shall be done, if you will leave all to my prudence," said the smuggler. "But did you pay the visit you talked of to the farm this morning?"

"I did."

"And saw you the girl?"

"Yes; in the presence of her parents and William."

"Ah! you have seen him, then?"

"Yes."

"And what think you of him?"

"That there cannot be any doubt of his being my brother," answered Sir Julian; "the likeness he bears to my late father is most striking, and his language and bearing correspond with the nobility of his origin. He is a bold and daring fellow, and must be got rid of as soon as possible, and before he has an opportunity of giving us some trouble."

"It is almost a pity to sacrifice so bold a youth."

"Why, Sam," observed the baronet, "you are quite chicken-hearted this morning. Would it not be madness to run the risk of sparing him?"

"Why," replied the smuggler, "I don't know but it would be bad policy, so I suppose the deed must be done. Then, at any rate, you may reckon yourself quite secure, and, with the girl Flora for your companion, the Smuggler King ought to consider himself one of the happiest men in the world."

"And so he will be," returned Sir Julian. "Farewell to this neighbourhood, then, for awhile, until I can return with safety, and without suspicion."

"Suspicion! oh, there is no danger of that, if you only play your cards well. Besides, do you not possess abundance of wealth, and what power has the voice of suspicion against that?"

"True. But how would you advise that we should act, in order to accomplish our designs?"

"That is a question that cannot easily be answered in a moment," returned the smuggler; "it requires consideration, for we must not do things in a hurry, or we cannot expect to meet with any success. One thing, however, I would suggest, and that is, that one or two of our men, disguised as peasants, should be constantly on the look-out, and watching the actions o Flora and her lover, so that they may give us timely notice if any opportunity of action presents itself."

" That shall be done. I will leave everything to you."

" Well, then," observed Sam Raker, " I will lose no time in maturing my plans, and will shortly consult with you again."

" Let there be no more time lost about the business than is possible," said Sir Julian, " for I am, you know, all impatience until all our plans are completed."

" You ought to know me too well, captain, to consider these observations necessary," said Sam Raker. " You are aware that if I am slow I am sure, and that when I fix my mind upon anything it is very seldom that I fail to accomplish it."

" Well, well, that is true," returned Sir Julian. " Take another glass of wine."

Sam Raker needed no second invitation, but quaffed off the contents of a second and third glass very expeditiously, and apparently with much relish, and he then arose from his chair.

" I suppose, as it is now almost four o'clock," said he, " you do not care how soon I depart, captain, for I dare say you require some rest after the festivities of the day ?"

" Let me see you again to-morrow."

" I will."

" There is one thing more I should have mentioned to you. There is a strict search being made after Fitzpatrick ; I have denied that I know him, and therefore you must be cautious."

" I will."

" There is still another being," said Sir Julian, after a pause, " that I would have removed."

" And who is that ?" interrogated Sam Raker.

" That wandering maniac."

" Crazy Marian ?"

" Ay."

" What of her, captain ?" asked Raker.

" She is dangerous."

" Psha ! what is to be feared from her ?"

" I informed you of her strange appearance to me ?"

" You did."

" And that she called me by the title of the Smuggler King."

" Yes ; how could she have known you ?"

" I cannot even conjecture," said Sir Julian ; " but should she divulge it to any other person ?"

" And who would believe the assertions of a wandering mad woman ?"

" I do not believe that she is so mad as she pretends to be," said the baronet.

" That," returned Raker, " we may at some future time have an opportunity of ascertaining. But we must not be too precipitate in these proceedings ; should so many persons at once be missing from the neighbourhood, we know not what suspicions it might excite, or the danger in which it might also involve us."

" True," answered Sir Julian ; " but we will talk of this another time. You will be punctual in meeting me again ?"

" At what time ?"

" Twelve o'clock."

" I will not fail."

" In the meantime, select some of the crew to act as spies."

" That shall be done without delay, captain," said Sam Raker.

" Will Hemlock and Harry Grampus, I think, will understand the business."

" They are the two I thought of choosing."

" Let one of them lurk in the immediate neighbourhood of Clarendon Farm, and the other that of old Backstay."

" It shall be done."

" Then good morning."

" Good morning, captain," said Sam Raker, approaching the table. " I will, with your permission, just take another glass at parting, to cheer me on my way."

Having helped himself unceremoniously to another glass of wine, Sam Raker bowed to Sir Julian and quitted the place.

" So," reflected the baronet, when he had gone, " that job is done in a business-like manner, and the old lawyer is silenced for ever. His fate can never be discovered, for his carcass will lie safe enough at the bottom of the sea. Fool that he was to venture into the jaws of the lion ; but he little expected the man he had to contend with, or in spite of his *honesty,* I think he would have preferred accepting of the twelve thousand pounds to a watery grave. Ha! ha! ha! how well do all the schemes of the Smuggler King succeed. How secretly and securely he conducts all his designs. But his triumph is yet to be completed ; William has yet to become better acquainted with the man he has dared to taunt, and Flora Clarendon must be made to yield to my wishes, and to learn the power of the man whose passions her charms have inflamed. I like the counsel of Sam Raker ; acted upon, it must be crowned with success, and then shall I have all that my most ambitious wishes can require. Wealth, power, sovereignty, and beauty. But it is nearly daylight, I must endeavour to snatch a few hours' repose, to fit me for the business of the day."

Sir Julian took up the lamp as he spoke, and slowly retired to his chamber, where he threw himself upon his couch, and endeavoured to sleep. But for some time he courted it in vain. In spite of his hardened nature, he could not become entirely insensible to the stings of a guilty blood-stained conscience, and thoughts of the most harassing nature would, in spite of himself, crowd upon his brain. The description which the villain Sam Raker had given of the death of the unfortunate Mr. Fitzpatrick, notwithstanding he had pretended to treat it with indifference, and his usual heartless levity, had made a powerful impression upon him, and he tossed to and fro in the most restless manner. The awful cry of the murdered man, as Sam Raker had described it, appeared to ring in his ears, and his ghastly countenance as when he appealed in vain to the blood-thirsty wretches for mercy, arose vividly and startlingly on his imagination. He trembled, and two or three times he arose from the bed, as he fancied he heard low and dismal moaning sounds, as if proceeding from some poor dying wretch in his last agonies, and he looked fearfully around the room, as though he dreaded at every turn to meet the ghastly form of his murdered victim. But all was still ; it was only the excitement of his fevered imagination ; the torturing creations of his heavy laden conscience.

" Fool!" he ejaculated, " to give way to this weakness. I have never before done so, and why should I now ? The account of Sam Raker has quite unmanned me. Away with this nonsense ! It ill becomes the character of the desperate and daring Sir Julian Mordlington. Ah! what noise was that! Surely I heard a groan ? Psha ! what a very child have I suffered myself to become. He is safe enough and will trouble me no more. I will to bed again, and endeavour to sleep off this strange excitement."

Once more Sir Julian threw himself upon the bed, but in spite of all his efforts he could not shake off the thoughts that would rush upon and distract his brain. Awful mutterings seemed to sound in his ears, and ghastly faces to grin and frown upon him. He closed his eyes; but still they were present to his imagination. He placed his fingers in his ears, but he could not shut out the sounds that his fevered conscience had created to torture him. Sir Julian Mordlington the bold, the insensible, at that moment felt all the horrors and apprehensions of coward-guilt. He feared to be alone; and regretted that he had suffered Sam Raker to depart from the hall. All the past crimes, the numerous deeds of blood that he had perpetrated and caused to be committed, rushed upon his recollection, and filled him with the most insupportable horror.

For the first time in his life did Sir Julian Mordlington feel the real terrors of conscience, and as he lay tossing about on the bed, cold drops of perspiration stood upon his temples, and every limb trembled in the most violent manner. He would have arisen and walked from the hall, but fear bound him to the place, and he was afraid to traverse the different apartments at that hour, and with his mind in such a dreadful state of perturbation.

At length nature was exhausted, and the wretched and guilty baronet gradually sunk off to sleep. But that brought with it even accumulated horrors. Dreams of the most terrific description flitted before his imagination, and he awoke at length in a greater state of agitation than ever.

It was now broad daylight, and the sun was shining brightly in at the window of his chamber. He, therefore, immediately arose, and finding that none of his domestics had arisen, he quitted the room, and left the hall by the back and private way. He walked leisurely on towards the wood, wrapped in gloomy meditation on the occurrences of the night, and the tortures he had for several hours endured.

" What means this weakness?" he reflected; " I never experienced it before when I have had far greater cause to feel it than on this occasion. Am I becoming a coward to tremble at my own shadow? Psha!—Sir Julian Mordlington allow himself to become the slave of conscience! By all the infernal host it shall not be. I will conquer it, I will shake it off, and become once more myself. At the present time I need all my presence of mind and determination, to enable me to accomplish the several designs I have in view; and any indulgence in these idle fears may at once thwart all that I have determined on. Why should I fear; have I not removed one of my principal enemies, who had it in his power to ruin me, and are not William and Flora all but within my grasp? They are. Be bold then, Sir Julian, be bold and confident; conscience must have no influence over your mind. You must once more become a man, aye, and a happy one, too."

He was startled by a rude laugh of derision, and looking up, his eyes fell upon the figure of poor Crazy Marian, who was standing at some short distance from him, and gazing at him with her usual wild expression of countenance, but the most deadly hatred was also mingled with it.

Notwithstanding his vaunted courage, Sir Julian Mordlington was then in no state of mind to meet unmoved the mysterious wandering maniac. A strange tremor thrilled throughout his veins, his eyes became distended, and, starting back several paces, he stood transfixed to the spot, and trembled with the most violent emotion.

Marian seemed to notice the agitation he betrayed, and a singular smile of satisfaction passed over her pallid features. She advanced nearer towards him, and then her almost supernaturally brilliant eyes became fixed upon him, as though they would penetrate into his very soul.

" Maniac!—hag!" at length the baronet found strength and courage to articulate, " again do you appear before me? What want you now?"

" The Smuggler King, the desperate, the blood thirsty, trembles," replied

Marian; "ha! ha! ha! Conscience is an excellent thing to make the stoutest heart tremble; but thou wilt have cause to tremble more anon, when the long-lost one shall be placed in a position to claim his rights, and seek redress for his wrongs. They are not all gone: I thought they were—they told me so; but they lied, as they have often before done, to torture the mind of poor Marian. There is still one left—one that is precious and noble, brave and virtuous. He lives—lives! Ha! ha! ha!—yes, he lives, to thy confusion, Sir Julian Mordlington, and ere long will hurl thee from thy seat of usurped power!"

"Cursed fiend in female form!" hoarsely shouted Sir Julian, while his eyes were perfectly bloodshot with rage; "thou art no maniac, though thou pretendest so to be; who and what art thou, that thou darest thus talk to Sir Julian Mordlington?"

"I am Crazy Marian," said the maniac, in her usual wild and wandering manner; "dost thou not know me? Thou wilt do so soon, and so shall the world become better acquainted with Sir Julian Mordlington. But he ——"

"Babbling wretch!" interrupted the infuriated baronet, snatching a pistol from his bosom; "thus do I prevent thee from putting thy threats into execution. Die!"

He discharged the contents of the pistol at Marian as he thus gave utterance to the rage which convulsed his whole frame; but the state of excitement he was in would not suffer him to take a sure and steady aim—the maniac escaped unhurt, and, laughing scornfully, immediately plunged into the thickest part of the wood, and instantly vanished from the baronet's sight.

In a moment he recovered himself, and hastily he pursued the way she had taken; but it was all to no purpose—she was gone, and he could not discover any traces of her. He paused to reflect upon the circumstance, and the more he did so the greater his agitation and confusion increased, and the certainty of his own danger, while Marian existed, became more apparent to him. Whoever she was, it was evident that she knew him, and was aware of the existence of his brother; and he had no doubt, from what she had said, that she was determined to do all that she could to reinstate William in his rights, and bring himself to ruin and disgrace. That she was no maniac he was certain, and, therefore, while she lived, he had everything to apprehend, and must immediately depart from the hall, or else by some means get Marian in his power. Had he not been so unsteady in his aim, his fears would have been ended, and Marian been no more. A thousand times he cursed his precipitation, and then again he regretted that he had not immediately sought some means of securing her after their first meeting, and when her words had fully convinced him that she was well acquainted with his real character.

"Fool!" he exclaimed, "to be so sanguine in my hopes. I thought, now that the lawyer is removed, I was perfectly safe, but I had forgot that I had even a more dreaded enemy in existence. I am now, even now, surrounded with danger while she lives. But who can she be? How can she have come to the knowledge of my real character, how have made herself acquainted with my family history and the origin of my brother? All this must be elicited. She must, she shall be in my power before many hours have passed away. She may easily be seized upon, as her haunts are well known. I must arrange this business with Sam Raker when I see him to-day. Strange feeling that comes over me, I tremble when I think of her. It seems as if she was more closely connected with me than I can at present imagine, and I long, yet dread for the mystery to be unravelled. This cursed event will quite disarrange my plans, and probably I may have to quit this neighbourhood before I have an opportunity of putting them into execution. But no, that must not, shall not be; I will act with promptitude, prudence and determination, and all may yet be well. This Crazy Marian, as she is called, must be secured without any further delay. Had I not acted worse than an idiot, she could not have escaped me when first she came to me in the hall. But then she was seen to enter, and had she been missed, suspicion might have fallen upon me. I am tortured with conflicting thoughts and fears. Fear!—Yes, 'tis useless to deny it, Sir Julian Mordlington, the Smuggler King, is afraid. Let me return to the hall, for I have not patience to walk here longer."

He turned his steps towards the hall, and returned thither in a state of greater agitation than when he had left it. The more he ruminated upon the words of Marian, the more did he become involved in mystery, and tortured his brain to no purpose to endeavour to form a probable conjecture as to who she really was. There was something in the caste of her features that was extremely familiar to him, and he was certain that he had seen her in former days, and under peculiar and very different circumstances, but he taxed his memory in vain to try to recollect where he had seen her, or in what manner he could be in any way identified with her history. In this state of mind he continued for some time, and he most impatiently awaited the hour at which he had ordered Sam Raker to attend him.

The adventure with the maniac had partly driven the other thoughts from his mind, but still the ghastly form of the murdered lawyer would occasionally flit before his imagination, and fill his soul with the utmost terror.

"Some powerful change is certainly about to come over me," he said, "or why these unusual apprehensions? I never shrank and trembled at the thought of crime before, when it has even been perpetrated by myself, and I have been an eye witness to the atrocities of my crew; why then should I now fear? Fear! is it fear? Yes, by what other name can I call it? Shame on you, Sir Julian; shake off this childish weakness, and be once more the reckless villain that thou hast hitherto been. If I thus indulge in these sad and cowardly thoughts, I shall unfit myself for that which it is so necessary I should perform, and promptly. I wish Sam Raker would come. He is the man upon whom I can alone depend, when I cannot trust even to myself. He will quickly advise me how to act under this emergency, and will, no doubt, not only advise, but speedily put his plans into execution. He will find some means of getting Marian into our power, or else of despatching her at once, although I would much rather that it should be the former, as I should then have the means of ascertaining who she really is, and of satisfying the doubts that have at present arisen in my mind. Yes, I must not entirely despair, but, on the contrary, I will endeavour to compose myself."

Somewhat recruited in spirits, he walked into the library, and selecting a book, after having partaken of his morning's repast, he endeavoured to abstract his thoughts from the subjects that had hitherto engrossed them, and to wear away the time until the hour when he expected to see Sam Raker.

In this he succeeded better than he had anticipated, and at length twelve o'clock arrived, and, punctual to the very moment, Sam Raker made his appearance.

"I am glad you have come," said the baronet, when he entered; "I have been most anxiously awaiting you; I have much to say to you."

"Indeed!" said Sam, looking keenly at him; "I am a rare man of business, captain; what would you do without me, eh?"

"I really can't say;" answered Sir Julian, "but you know I fully appreciate your value."

"You look pale."

"I have slept little."

"You seem agitated."

"I have been harassed with painful thoughts."

"Thoughts! captain! ha! ha! ha! can this be you? And only this morning you were upbraiding me for ——"

"Do not mention that circumstance," quickly interrupted Sir Julian; "it is that which has racked my brain more than any deed that I have perpetrated for years."

"Indeed?"

"Yes; yes;—I don't know what has come to me; I feel as weak as an infant, and cannot shake off the feeling for the life of me."

"Come, come, captain," said Raker, "you must not give way to this, or what will become of our plans?"

"True; but I shall soon be better."

"I have placed Will Hemlock and Harry Grampus upon their duty," said the smuggler.

"That is all right."

"But what agitates you?"

"I have met with another adventure this morning to disturb me."

"Another?"

"Yes. Listen."

Sir Julian then recounted to him the particulars of his meeting with Crazy Marian, her singular behaviour and the words to which she gave utterance, and when he had concluded, Raker paused for a short time and reflected.

"This is strange!" he said, "who can the woman be?"

"I have been in vain endeavouring to conjecture," said Sir Julian, "but her features are familiar to me."

"Hump!"

"It is evident she is an object of danger;" added the baronet.

"She is."

"Her words convince me of her knowledge of my real character, and likewise of the existence of my hated brother."

"She must be removed."

"She must, and with as little delay as possible."

"Yes; or else she might tell some unpleasant truths, and render it necessary for us to weigh anchor from here much sooner than we intend, according to our present arrangements."

"True," said Sir Julian, "and I feel certain that she is not really a maniac, and therefore is she the more dangerous, for credit will be attached to her statements."

"I will lose no time in preventing that accident, by stopping the tongue of Crazy Marian for ever."

"If she could be secured without hurting her, I should prefer it," observed Sir Julian.

"That must all depend upon circumstances," returned the smuggler; "and in such emergencies, you know, it will not do to stand upon niceties."

"Exactly so;" remarked the baronet, "but I am anxious that her life should be spared until some future opportunity, so that I may be enabled to elicit from her who she really is, and by what means she acquired the knowledge she evidently possesses."

"That shall be done, if there is a chance without running any risk of danger," observed Raker.

"When will you set about your task?"

"This very day."

"'Tis well."

"Know you any of her haunts?"

"She sometimes inhabits a wretched hovel in the wood," answered Sir Julian, "but she is frequently away from there for several days together, I am informed, and wandering over different parts of the country."

"If she is to be found I will discover her," said Raker, "and I warrant, captain, that when I once lay my grappling-irons upon her, I will not let her slip her cable as you did this morning."

"Had I not been confused and excited," said the baronet, "the contents of my pistol would have reached her heart."

"Confused! excited!" repeated Sam Raker, "psha! captain, I am surprised at you; why do you not take it as I always do, take things cool and comfortably. This Crazy Marian will not prove so troublesome a customer as you seem to imagine, I think. She will be easily secured."

"I hope she may."

"Well, captain, we have plenty of business on our hands at present."

"We have, but I hope we shall be able to accomplish it all."

"Oh, never fear; we have always been successful hitherto, and fortune will not forsake the captain and crew of the Devil's Skipper yet."

"I wish all our business was over, and we were once more on the deep blue waters," said Sir Julian.

"Ay, ay, captain," returned Sam Raker, "and so do I; for I begin not to like the looks of some of the land sharks; and it would not be very pleasant to have them upon us while we are in this port."

"True," said Sir Julian, "but think you they begin to suspect the character of our vessel?"

"I can't say what they suspect, but as I said before, I do not admire the manner in which some of the fellows eye us when we leave the ship."

Sir Julian walked backwards and forwards across the room for a few moments, and was evidently in no very pleasant state of mind.

"D——n!" he at length ejaculated; "it seems as if everything should occur to torment and perplex me."

"Do not put yourself out of the way, captain," said Raker, "all will yet

No. 14

be well, I dare say, and your wishes gratified to their fullest extent. But have you anything more to communicate to me?"

" I have not," answered the baronet. " I have told you all the particulars."

"Then I think the sooner I leave you the better," said the smuggler; "there must not be any time lost over this part of the business, and if we are as lucky as we have been with the old lawyer, we shall very soon have our fears set at rest, and Crazy Marian will be at rest also."

"I trust she will," remarked Sir Julian Mordlington. " Whither do you intend to go in search of her?"

" In the place where you say she sometimes shelters herself, of course," answered Raker.

" You will not go alone?"

" No, no ; I shall be attended with two or three of the lads, so that we may secure her, if possible ; for from what I could see when I encountered her in the wood, and she rescued your brother and Flora from my power, I should say that she is nothing better than a regular she-devil."

" But she is but woman, after all," said Sir Julian, " and it would be strange indeed if you could not easily take her."

" Oh, I do not fear anything about that," returned Sam Raker ; "but woman or not, it is always as well to be on your guard, as there is no knowing what friends she might have at hand to fly to her aid."

" Right," coincided the baronet ; " but I will no longer detain you ; make your way with all expedition to the ship, and taking with you two or three of the crew, depart on your search directly."

" That order shall be punctually obeyed, captain."

" You will give me timely notice should anything favourable occur," said Sir Julian.

Sam Raker replied in the affirmative, and then took his leave, and left Sir Julian to compose his feeling, which the smuggler had never seen so ruffled before during the whole time that he had known him. The baronet shortly afterwards departed into his study, where he resumed the book he had before been perusing.

CHAPTER X.

THE FRUITLESS SEARCH.—THE MANIAC AND WILLIAM BACKSTAY.—THE APPOINTMENT. — THE SECRET.—THE DISCOVERY. — THE SURPRISE.—THE CAPTURE.—THE FATAL SHOT.

IN vain were all the inquiries that Mr. Backstay, assisted by William, made after the unfortunate Mr. Fitzpatrick ; they could not discover the least clue to him, and the apprehensions of every person were naturally increased, and it was feared that something of a serious nature had really happened to him.

Mr. Backstay now considered it necessary that he should make the magistrates acquainted with the circumstance, and he therefore repaired to the house of the principal one for that purpose.

The magistrate heard the account which the worthy old farmer gave with the deepest interest, and immediately gave instructions to the constables of the place to institute the most rigorous inquiry into the mysterious affair. He also ordered bills to be printed, stating his name, and describing his person, offering a reward to any individual who could give any information respecting him.

At the suggestion of Mr. Backstay, a constable was despatched home with him, in order that Mr. Fitzpatrick's trunk should be forced open, to see whether it contained any papers that might lead to the discovery of his friends or relations. This being done, the profession of Mr. Fitzpatrick was discovered, also his address in London, and the constable and Mr. Backstay having returned to the magistrate with this information, he immediately addressed a letter to his confidential clerk, informing him of what had taken place, and requesting his attendance as quickly as possible.

Mr. Backstay now informed the magistrate what the lawyer had said about his interview with Sir Julian Mordlington, and that on the day he disappeared he had distinctly told him that he was going on business of importance to the Hall. He also told him of the positive manner in which the baronet had denied all knowledge of the missing gentleman, and the confusion he had evinced when William put the question to him at Clarendon Farm.

"It is very strange," remarked the magistrate; "there certainly must be some misunderstanding in this; I must see Sir Julian and question him upon the subject."

He then instructed one of the officers to repair immediately to the Hall, with his compliments, and to request the attendance of the baronet at his house at his earliest convenience.

Mr. Backstay and William were desired to wait till Sir Julian's arrival, which they were anxious to do, to hear the answers the baronet would return to the interrogatories of the magistrate, and likewise to see how he would behave when confronted with them.

In a short time the officer returned from the Hall, with a message from Sir Julian, stating that he regretted, as he was very much engaged, he could not comply with the magistrate's request that day.

"This certainly looks like an evasion," observed the latter gentleman; "however, this investigation will not admit of any delay, consequently I will myself repair to the Hall and seek an interview with Sir Julian."

Mr. Backstay and William thanked the magistrate for his polite attention, and promising to attend at his house on the following day, they returned home. The magistrate then mounted his horse, and instantly rode off to the Hall.

Sir Julian was in the study when the officer came to the Hall with the message from the magistrate, and when Simon informed him, he started in the greatest confusion, and muttered a curse between his teeth.

"An officer from the magistrate," he ejaculated, "and want to see me?"

"Yes, Sir Julian," replied Simon, "strange looking officer, with a carbuncle nose, and a cast in one of his eyes, he ——"

"What can he want with me?" said the baronet; "ah! Fitzpatrick! hark ye, Simon, you saw that gentleman who—who called upon me the day before yesterday?"

"Strange little gentleman, with the Irish brogue, Sir Julian? he who attempted to rob you and then bolted?"

"Yes—yes."

"They haven't taken him, have they, Sir Julian," asked Simon, "and want you to appear agin him?"

"Yes—no—I don't know," stammered the baronet; "but you haven't mentioned that circumstance to any one, have you?"

"Oh, dear no, Sir Julian, not a syllabub," replied the man.

"You are sure you have not?"

"Oh, quite sure, Sir Julian."

"Hark ye, sirrah," said his master; "if you mention a word to any one that that individual has ever been to the Hall, I'll wring your neck."

Poor Simon started back at this awful threat, and trembled very much.

"Do you hear what I say, knave?" demanded Sir Julian, sternly.

"Oh!—ye—yes, Sir Julian," faltered out Simon.

"Not a word, mind you."

"Not a syllabub, Sir Julian."

"You never heard his name?"

"Never in my life."

"You understand me?"

"Oh, dear yes, Sir Julian," answered Simon.

The baronet then despatched him with the message to the officer, which that functionary afterwards delivered to the magistrate.

The request of the magistrate caused Sir Julian much uneasiness, and he scarcely knew how to act. But after mature consideration, he thought it would be better for him to see that gentleman without delay, as his conduct might otherwise cause some suspicion, and he had just put on his hat, and was about to leave the Hall for that purpose, when Mr. Ingleford, the magistrate, himself was announced.

Sir Julian had by that time regained his self-possession, and was resolved to brave out the inquiries of the magistrate, with all that tact and effrontery which he so abundantly possessed. He received him with a very courteous smile, and then requested to know the business upon which the magistrate wished to see him.

Mr. Ingleford informed him, and the baronet listened to him with the most perfect composure, and when he had concluded, Sir Julian observed,—

"I am most happy to see you, Mr. Ingleford, and it was my intention to have called upon you immediately, although I sent the message I did by the officer, as I was not aware at the time that I should be so shortly disengaged. May I beg leave to inquire what is the nature of the business that you requested an interview with me upon?"

"I would merely ask you, Sir Julian," replied the worthy magistrate, "whether you were acquainted with one Mr. Fitzpatrick, a solicitor?"

The baronet repeated the name two or three times, as though he was endeavouring to recollect, and then replied in the negative.

"That is singular," remarked Mr. Ingleford, "for I have from very credible witnesses, that he had an interview with you the day before yesterday, and that he left the place at which he was staying yesterday morning for the purpose of having a second meeting, by appointment, with you."

"Oh, that is impossible, my dear sir," returned Sir Julian, with perfect ease and coolness; "but who pray, are your informants?"

"Mr. Backstay and his son, Sir Julian," answered the magistrate.

"The individual who holds a farm on my estate, I believe?"

"The same."

"I hope, Mr. Ingleford," said the baronet, in a tone of offended dignity, "that you do not suppose that I can be on such terms of intimacy with a person of Mr. Backstay's description, that he should be acquainted with my business?"

"Certainly not, Sir Julian," replied the magistrate, "but this Mr. Fitzpatrick was staying with him, and he told him that he had seen you, and that he had come to this neighbourhood for the very purpose of transacting important business with you."

"That is very extraordinary," said the baronet, with affected surprise, "but there must certainly be some mistake in this. What is your motive for inquiring of me after this Mr.—Mr. Fitzpatrick, I think you call him?"

"He has disappeared in a very mysterious manner," answered the magistrate.

"Indeed?"

"Yes, and as it has been asserted that he was a friend of your's, Sir Julian, and that the Hall was the last place he was known to be going to, I thought you might be able to give me some information respecting him."

"Astonishing that such rumours, entirely without foundation, can have got into circulation," said Sir Julian.

"Of course, sir, you could have no reason for denying the fact, if you were acquainted with the missing gentleman, and he had visited you at the times mentioned?" said the magistrate.

"Certainly not, my dear sir," replied Sir Julian, "what motives could I have? Has it been ascertained whether the gentleman had in his possession any money at the time you say he left Farmer Backstay's?"

"It has not."

"There are many bad characters in this neighbourhood, Mr. Ingleford," continued the baronet.

"True."

"And the gentleman might have been knocked down and robbed, probably murdered."

"But he left the farm at broad daylight, and such an attempt would not then be made, I should imagine," observed the magistrate.

"Have you strictly examined Mr. Backstay and his son?"

"I have, and their answers were perfectly satisfactory."

"The gentleman was staying at the farm, you say; they might have known that he had property about him, and—and—the temptation—the temptation, you know, Mr. Ingleford, to persons in humble circumstances, is very great."

"Sir Julian Mordlington," said the magistrate, with indignation, "I have known Mr. Backstay for years, as a worthy, industrious, upright man; his character is beyond reproach."

"Well," observed the baronet, "that may be; but—but as you have remarked, the disappearance of the gentleman is very extraordinary and mysterious; it requires the most searching investigation, and as my name has been made use of in a most unwarrantable manner, I have an undoubted right, in vindication of myself, to make the inquiries I have done."

"Certainly, Sir Julian," coincided Mr. Ingleford; "and I trust that you will, for the sake of humanity, persist in those inquiries."

"Of that you may rest assured, sir," returned the baronet, with a complacent smile; "I shall make it my business to institute every inquiry after the fate of this Mr. Fitzpatrick, in which I now, naturally, feel a very deep interest."

"I am obliged to you, sir," said the magistrate, "then you still deny knowing the unfortunate gentleman?"

"On my word and honour as a gentleman," returned the baronet, placing his hand upon his heart, "I never heard the gentleman's name mentioned before."

"That is enough, Sir Julian," said the magistrate; "of course, after such a protestation, I cannot doubt your word."

"I should think not, Mr. Ingleford."

"However," continued the magistrate, "I have no doubt that we shall shortly gain more information on the subject, for we have found from the contents of one of his boxes, the connections of Mr. Fitzpatrick; I have written to his confidential clerk, in London, making him acquainted with what has happened, and I dare say I shall speedily receive some communication from him."

Sir Julian could not help looking confused at this intelligence, and he muttered a curse to himself.

"I trust that your endeavours may be crowned with success, sir," he at last observed, "and that something will quickly transpire to clear up this extraordinary mystery. For my own part, I am determined that I will do all that lays in my power to elucidate it."

"I am much obliged to you, Sir Julian," said the magistrate, who was satisfied by the candour and apparent sincerity of the villain's manners; "I am much obliged to you for your politeness and attention, and hope you will excuse the liberty I have taken in calling upon you?"

"Oh, do not mention it, my dear sir," returned the baronet; "in the cause of humanity, in such a case as this, where life may have been sacrificed, and justice calls aloud for the punishment of the guilty, it behoves us all you know to exert ourselves to the very utmost."

"Very true, Sir Julian," coincided Mr. Ingleford; "I admire and commend your principles very much."

"You pay me a very high compliment, sir," said the hypocrite, "I trust during the time that I reside in the neighbourhood, that we shall become better acquainted."

"I shall be most proud," replied the magistrate, who was completely deceived by the plausibility and urbanity of Sir Julian's manners.

"The honour will be conferred on me," said the baronet.

Mr. Ingleford bowed most politely, and again apologizing for intruding upon Sir Julian, he wished him good morning, and was about to retire, when there was a knock at the room-door, and before the baronet could inquire who was there, it was thrown open, and Sam Raker partly entered the apartment, but beholding the magistrate, and the confusion of Sir Julian, he hastily retreated, not, however, before Mr. Ingleford had observed him, and evinced no little surprise at the coarse and unprepossessing appearance of the visitor. He turned a penetrating look upon the baronet, and then again politely bowing, he left the room, and retired from the Hall.

"Curses light on this unexpected appearance," said Sir Julian, when the magistrate was gone, "I noticed the looks of surprise and suspicion of this meddling magistrate. Sam Raker."

"I am here," replied that individual, stepping into the room; "I am sorry I interrupted you, captain, Sir Julian I mean."

"It was a confounded misfortune," said the baronet.

"It was no fault of mine," replied Sam, "as I came in the back way I had no opportunity of knowing you were engaged."

"Engaged, yes," returned Sir Julian, "and with no very pleasant customer."

"May I take the liberty of inquiring who the gentleman is, that you were talking to?"

"A magistrate."

"A magistrate?"

"Yes."

"The name always makes me feel a strange sensation about the neck. What could he want with you?"

"That babbling fellow Backstay has been busying himself about the lawyer, and informed Mr. Ingleford all about his having been to the Hall."

"And what came he here for?" asked Sam Raker.

"To inquire whether I know anything of him."

"Which you, of course ——"

"Stoutly denied," rejoined the baronet; "moreover, I pretended to take great interest in the affair, and promised to use my exertions in endeavouring to unravel the mystery."

"Very prudent behaviour," said Sam Raker, "and how did the old beak seem to take it?"

"Oh, as well as could be wished," answered Sir Julian, "I flattered his vanity with compliments, and ——"

"There is an end to the business, I suppose; you are now safe."

"I am afraid not."

"Why so?"

"I am doubtful that we shall have to decamp from here more suddenly than we anticipated, and before we have any chance of accomplishing our designs."

"What for ?" demanded Sam Raker.

" The magistrate," replied Sir Julian, " has written to the confidential clerk of old Fitzpatrick, and no doubt he will furnish him with the particulars of the connection between his master and me."

" That is very awkward," observed Sam.

" It is," returned the baronet, " and I know not how to act ; can you advise me ?"

" Not at present."

" There is one thing certain."

" What is that ?"

" That it will not be safe for me to remain here after the magistrate has received a communication from the clerk of Fitzpatrick," answered the baronet.

" And leaving here," said Raker, " would be nothing less than a confirmation of your guilt. You must remain and brave it out."

" How ?"

" Adhere to the statement that you have already made," observed Sam Raker, " swear that you neither know the clerk nor his late master, and your word, as a baronet, will weigh down a million from such as those who are arrayed against you."

" I like your counsel, Sam," said Sir Julian, " and will act upon it, although I wish it could be avoided."

" You have nothing to fear, captain," said Raker, " if you only observe your usual precaution."

" But Crazy Marian ?"

" I have been upon the watch for her."

" And have not discovered her ?"

" No ; but the lads are on the look out near the hovel, and should she return, she will be secured immediately."

" But should she in the meantime have any communication with the magistrate," said Sir Julian.

" And what then ?"

" She would disclose my real character, undoubtedly," answered the baronet.

" And what if she should ?" said Sam Raker ; " think you the magistrate would pay any serious attention to the statements of a maniac ?"

" She might convince him that she was not really one," suggested Sir Julian, " and I have too much reason to believe that she really is not."

" I cannot for the life of me, captain," said Sam Raker, " conceive what has come to you lately ; for you indulge in nothing but idle surmises and apprehensions."

" And not without cause, Sam," returned the baronet, " this visit of the magistrate has ruffled my temper."

" Why should it do so," demanded Raker, " when according to your own account, you have evaded all his questions in a business-like manner, and it is not likely that he will trouble you again."

" I wish he had not seen you."

" Why, that certainly was unfortunate. But he had scarcely a glimpse of my person."

" He saw quite enough of you to ——"

" To what ?"

" To convince himself, if he was any judge of countenances, that you are an arrant scoundrel," replied the baronet.

" Upon my word, you get very complimentary, captain," said the ruffian, with a smile ; " but, certainly, I believe that my countenance is not decidedly handsome."

" Should Marian, after hearing of the disappearance of Fitzpatrick, repair to the magistrate, which she will probably do," observed the baronet, " not-withstanding the character she is supposed to be, he may be inclined to listen to her story, and unpleasant suspicions may be excited against me."

" That must be prevented, and speedily," said Sam Raker.

" How ?"

" Why, Crazy Marian must be secured, this very night, if possible."

" If that could be done, my mind would be somewhat set at rest."

" At rest altogether, captain, I should think."

" Not so."

" Why ?" demanded Raker.

" The communication of Fitzpatrick's clerk may unfold some unpleasant truths," answered Sir Julian.

" I have before told you, captain," said Sam Raker, " that your own in-genuity may easily and satisfactorily dispose of them. The protestations of Sir Julian Mordlington will certainly be taken before the bare assertions of a lawyer's clerk."

" They may be, but I like not to run the risk," said the baronet.

" But you must," returned Raker ; " we cannot accomplish all our designs in a few hours ; besides, if you should leave the Hall under such circumstances, and in so abrupt a manner, you could not return again at any future period, for it would be a tacit acknowledgment of guilt, and look at the sacrifice you would thus have to make."

" True, true," returned Sir Julian, after a moment's reflection, " I must brave it out, and leave it to chance."

" And your own prudence, captain," added Sam Raker.

" Decidedly so. But we waste time. Have you anything more to suggest or communicate, Sam ?"

" I have not."

" Then the sooner you depart the better," observed the baronet. " Exert yourself to the utmost to discover Marian."

" That you may be certain I will, captain," replied Raker.

" And if you cannot capture her without, be sure that you silence her for ever," said Sir Julian.

" My pistol will not fail to do its office, captain," returned the smuggler. " I will see you again to-night."

" 'Tis well ; at what hour ?"

" That it is impossible for me to say. But should success crown my de-signs, I will give you immediate notice of it. Adieu, captain."

" Farewell ; be vigilant, for you see the necessity of prompt action," said the baronet.

" I do," answered the smuggler, moving towards the door, " and you will find that Sam Raker will not only talk, but act. Something tells me that Crazy Marian will be in our power before many hours have elapsed."

" I shall be a happy man if your predictions are verified, Sam," replied the baronet.

" It shall be no fault of mine if they are not, captain. Farewell."

" Farewell."

And the two worthies separated, Sam Raker retiring by the same way that he had entered.

Sir Julian Mordlington was more at ease after his interview with Sam Raker, but he was still apprehensive that Marian, before they could have an opportunity of seizing upon her, would be induced to see Mr. Ingleford, the magistrate, and communicate what she evidently knew of him. That she

was well acquainted with his whole history he was thoroughly convinced, though by what means she had acquired her knowledge, he was at a loss to conjecture, or in what manner they had before met previous to her coming to the Hall. The collected manner in which he had met the magistrate, he was convinced had at present satisfied that gentleman, but he was vexed that Sam Raker had made his appearance so inopportunely in the room before his departure, as he had noticed the looks of astonishment and suspicion which Mr. Ingleford had cast upon the smuggler, and he might be induced to entertain no very high opinion of him (Sir Julian) in having such visitors. This circumstance, however, he did not suffer to trouble his mind long, and in order to rally his spirits and collect his thoughts, he walked from the Hall, and bent his footsteps towards the wood.

In the meantime, Mr. Backstay and William, after leaving the house of the magistrate, separated, and the day being fine, the latter felt inclined for a ramble. Buried in profound and interesting meditation on the prospect of his future happiness when Flora should have become his wife, he wandered on, almost unconscious whither, until, suddenly looking up, he found himself in a dell in the midst of the wood which has been so often mentioned in the course of this narrative. He now regretted that he had not walked to Clarendon Farm, and was turning into a beaten track that led from the dell for that purpose, when he was surprised to hear some one call him by his name, and turning towards the spot whence the sound preceeded, he beheld Marian standing close by him, and gazing at him with looks of affection and the deepest interest.

"Shiver my timbers," said the young mariner, "here is this poor stranded vessel again. How pitiful she looks, and—and—what a strange feeling I have at my heart. What can she want with me?"

No. 15

"Yes, yes," observed Marian, approaching him nearer; "how like, how very like;—I could imagine that he stood before me. Oh! how like!—It is —it must be he."

"Who, my good woman?" demanded William; "of whom is it you speak? Whom do I resemble?"

"One," answered Marian, in a voice of the deepest melancholy, "one, who to this wretched heart was dear,—oh, how dear! But he is gone, now;— gone, gone—they tore him from me; they made him desert me, hate me!— Hate me! Oh, no, no, no,—they could not make him do that! they could not make him do that."

"Poor creature," said William, in accents of pity, "what would you with me?"

"I will tell you," answered Marian; "they say I am mad; I was so once, but am not now. A sudden light has burst upon my reason, and dispersed the dark clouds that before obscured it. Yes, yes; they shall soon know that poor Marian is not mad. They shall know it all; they have reason to fear and dread her."

"Of whom do you speak?" asked William.

"Of those who too long have triumphed in their iniquity," replied Marian. "But the day of my triumph is approaching—the day of reckoning is at hand. Oh; it will be a terrible reckoning to them. Ha! ha! ha! Won't they tremble at poor Crazy Marian, then? Follow me, William Backstay, as you are called."

"Whither?"

"To my wretched hovel."

"What would you with me?"

"You do not fear me?"

"Fear you! oh, no."

"I would render you a service."

"What mean you?" inquired William, with astonishment; "cannot you reveal your business here?"

"No," answered Marian; "but will you comply with my request?"

"I scarcely know how to act," answered William, astonished at the altered manners of Marian, and at the request she made. At the same time an indefinable feeling predominated in his mind; he gazed at Marian with a sentiment approaching to love and veneration, and an instinctive power seemed to urge him to comply with what she desired; still he hesitated, and was undecided how to act.

"You cannot surely doubt me?" at last appealed Marian.

"Why should I?" asked William, "and yet your request is a strange one."

"You will not repent granting it," observed Marian; "will you attend me?"

"I know not how it is," returned William, "but some inscrutable power seems to urge me to comply."

"It is the voice of nature appealing to your own heart," said Marian; "do not disregard its impulse. Come, come."

"Lead on, mysterious woman," said William. "I am ready to obey your wishes."

Marian smiled sweetly and gratefully upon him, and beckoning him to follow, she led the way from the dell into the thickest part of the wood, and proceeded with such rapidity that William was obliged to walk quick to keep up with her.

As they went on, William became more and more wrapt in amazement to conjecture what it was that Marian wanted with him, and what she had to reveal. That her senses were restored, the rational manner in which she talked quite convinced him, and his curiosity was excited to the highest degree.

Every now and then she looked back to see if he was following her, and every time she did so she smiled more sweetly and encouragingly upon him.

The feelings which at that time predominated in William's breast were such as he never recollected to have felt before, and for which he was at a loss to account. There was something in the looks and the character of poor wandering Marian, that appealed immediately to his heart, and a presentiment crossed his mind that something was about to happen to him upon which his future happiness and prospects in life in a great measure depended.

Marian led the way through the gloomiest and most thickly interwoven part of the wood, and they proceeded so quickly that they had soon left the dell far behind them. At length forcing her way between a thick cluster of wide-spreading trees, they came in sight of the miserable hovel in which poor Marian sought a temporary shelter.

"This way," said Marian, "you will soon be in the *palace* of poor wandering Marian."

William made no reply, but he looked with a feeling of the utmost compassion upon that female who had so deeply and so singularly excited his sympathies, and then followed her into the wretched abode, if such it could be called, which formed the mausoleum of all her cares and secret broodings.

He started back aghast when he viewed it—it certainly was a miserable receptacle. The timbers of the place were shattered in every direction, through which the rude blast might penetrate : over what had been a mantel-piece were sketches of portraits, worked with great skill and delicacy, and upon which the eyes of the young mariner immediately became fixed. One in particular attracted his attention. It was that of a general officer in the army, of benevolent aspect, and which at once appealed to the young man's heart. He felt a sensation pass through his veins, for which he could not account, and which filled him with mingled sentiments of pleasure, admiration, and surprise. The features appeared to him familiar, and yet he could not conceive where he had before seen them.

Marian watched his emotions with evident interest, although she did not attempt to interrupt them. Her mind was apparently made up for some great object, and she allowed the young sailor to give free indulgence to the thoughts that crowded upon his brain. He looked around the place, and its wretched aspect the more and more filled him with pity and disgust. An old stool, and a straw mattrass, formed the only articles of furniture in the hovel, while in all other facts it seemed scarcely possible to afford even temporary shelter to a human being.

"And has this, then, been the shelter of ——"

"The wandering maniac," rejoined Marian, with a laugh of wildness. "Yes ; here she has brooded over her sorrows, and learned to hate mankind. Do you not think it a sightly dwelling ?"

"What could have driven you to such a wretched retreat ?"

"You shall know," said Marian ; "be seated, for I have much to say to you, and many questions to put, which I expect you will answer me, for your future happiness and prosperity depend upon it."

"What questions can you have to put to me ?" inquired William.

"Do you not feel any sensation at your heart ?" demanded Marian, at the same time fixing her full and penetrating eye upon his countenance.

"I do," answered William ; "a feeling has came over me, for which I cannot account. I feel that I could worship, love, venerate you, as if you were my parent."

"Parent !" repeated Marian. "Ha ! ha ! ha ! Parent !—oh, that is a word that is long since a stranger to me. The impulses of all-glorious, all-wonderful nature work well. I was mad once, but I am not now ; no, no, I am not now, and so shall the guilty find, to their cost. My manners may appear strange, but heed me not. Oh! boy, did you but know the tumult of feelings, the ungovernable sea of affection that at present rushes tenderly through this bosom, you would pardon me for any discrepancies that may appear in my conduct. I look upon you as a being of another world, for you are the image of one who is now a saint in Heaven. Bless you! bless you! dear resemblance of one so loved, of one so cruelly torn from me."

And thus saying, Marian threw her arms around William's neck, and kissed him again and again.

Surprised, confused, astonished, William knew not what to say, or how to act. His heart responded to the caresses of the maniac, as he had been hitherto led to believe her, but it was with a feeling he had never before experienced. He loved to adoration Flora, but at that time he felt that he could have worshipped Marian. And then the expression that beamed in her eyes; it was one of such maternal fondness, that it sunk into his very soul.

"Mysterious woman!" he exclaimed, "I know not how it is that you have gained such a powerful ascendancy over me, but for what purpose have you brought me hither?"

"To reveal to you the truth, and defeat the designs of villany," answered Marian.

"You are not what you seem to be?"

"I am not."

"You have moved in other scenes—in a far different station of society?"

"I have mingled with the noblest of the noble, the gayest of the gay," replied Marian. "I have been surrounded by all the splendour of rank—have been the object of admiration, and fulsome adulation; but it was all hollow; I found it out, and have suffered. Those that pretended to be my friends turned round upon me, and proved to be my greatest enemies. They scandalized me, traduced my fame, banished me from my husband, the husband of my heart; they tore from me my child. Oh, God! let me not think, or my senses will again leave me."

"Compose yourself, I beseech you," said William, who was deeply interested by the observations of Marian, and wondered what could be the reason of her seeking an interview with him.

"Yes—yes," replied Marian; "I must, I will be composed; for I have much to explain, and justice demands the immediate restoration of the innocent to their rights, and the punishment of the guilty."

"What have you to reveal to me?" asked William; "and why have you brought me hither?"

"You saw me this morning?"

"I did."

"You noticed my agitation?"

"Yes—yes."

"Oh, could you but have entered into my feeling at that moment, how would you have pitied me!" said Marian.

"What mean you?" inquired the astonished William.

"You are not the actual son of Backstay the farmer?"

"Why do you ask the question?"

"Be explicit; your own happiness and that of more than one depends upon your answer," said Marian, eagerly, at the same time fixing upon William a look that penetrated to his very soul. "Your real name?"

"I know not."

"You are no relation to Backstay?" hastily demanded Marian, and her bosom heaved with the most intense emotion.

"I am not," answered William.

"How then came you under his protection?" inquired Marian.

"The story has been told to me," replied the young mariner; "but what matters it now, I would willingly forget it all, and believe myself the son of him who has ever acted towards me with even more than the affection of a parent."

" But it must not be so," observed Marian ; "justice demands a full explanation, and you know not how much the happiness of others beside yourself may be involved in the disclosure. You say that Mr. Backstay has revealed to you the manner in which you came under his protection ?"

" He has."

" Name it."

" He rescued me from a wreck when I was little more than an infant," answered William, " and a lad at the same time, who appeared, from the resemblance he bore to me, my brother."

" Ah !" ejaculated Marian, her eyes sparkling with uncommon interest, and her bosom throbbing with the deepest agitation ;—" and what became of that lad ?"

" He fled after having attempted to take away my life, as is imagined ; for I was found writhing as if in the last convulsive agonies of death, and with the impression of fingers upon my throat."

" Monster !" ejaculated Marian, with a shudder of horror, " and you have never heard of that lad since ?"

" I have not."

" And his appearance ?"

" Was that of a young midshipman," answered William.

" Ah ! everything serves to convince me," said Marian.

" Why do you ask these questions ?" demanded William, his feelings becoming more excited as he noticed the evident emotion which Marian was evidently undergoing.

" Proceed, proceed," she said ; " what was the person whom you call your father at this time ?"

" A fisherman."

" And how was you dressed ?"

" In clothes that proved that I must have belonged to some person of distinction," replied the young seaman.

" Oh, my poor heart !" exclaimed Marian, as she approached William nearer ; " it will burst its humble tenement."

" What mean you ? what excites you thus ?" said William, and his own agitation increased.

" Does not your own heart respond to my feelings ?" demanded Marian, with a look of the most intense feeling.

" It does, it does !" replied William ; " what can this mean ?"

" The name of the vessel that was wrecked ?" asked Marian. " Quick, quick !"

" I know not."

" And how many years is it since this took place ?" inquired Marian.

" About twenty."

" The very time. Every circumstance corresponds," observed Marian ; " approach me nearer, young man."

William, filled with astonishment, and his heart palpitating heavily with suspense and anxiety, obeyed, and Marian looked more narrowly into his countenance.

" Oh God !" she cried, " those features ;—I—I cannot be mistaken ; it is—it must be he. Let me examine your neck."

" There are three marks upon it," said William.

" Moles ?" almost screamed Marian.

" They are," was the reply ; and in an instant Marian, with an hysterical laugh, enfolded the young seaman in her arms.

" Again let me look into those eyes," said Crazy Marian ; " they remind me so much of days gone past, when all was happiness and peace ; come hither, young man, be not afraid of me ; they have called me mad, so I have been ; but Marian, poor Marian, is restored to her senses, and will yet bring retribution upon her oppressors."

As Marian uttered these words she placed her yet fair and delicate arms around William's neck, and looked at him with an intensity of feeling that no language can describe. The young mariner, at the same time, felt a sensation of an unaccountable nature creeping through his veins, and he looked at the hitherto supposed maniac with sentiments that he had never before experienced.

" Mysterious woman," he said, " why do you thus embrace me ?—What is it you would say to me ?—Why have you called me hither ?   I—I feel as if I could worship you ; and—and yet, shiver my timbers, I am making a complete lubber of myself !"

" You are realising Nature's works and Nature's God," solemnly returned Marian ; " you *should* love me."

" I do, I do," replied William, completely bewildered, his interest more and more increasing ; " and yet, why these peculiar sensations ?"

" I have heard you say that you were a foundling ?" said Marian.

" I was," answered William ; " as I before stated to you, the kind man who has acted more than as a father towards me, took me and another, a lad, from the portion of a wreck."

" True, true, and the name of that vessel ?" demanded the supposed maniac.

" I have before told you that I know it not," said William.

" The boy preserved with you, of what age did he appear to be ?"

" About thirteen."

" And habited as a young midshipman ?"

" Yes."

" Oh, God !"

" Why this agitation ?"

" You feel the same ?"

" I do, and yet I know not wherefore," answered the young seaman.

The eyes of Marian became even more brilliant than they had been before, and the agitation of William increased as she pressed closer to him, and looked into his eyes with such an expression that seemed as if she would dive into his very soul, and hug him to her heart with all the strength of maternal affection.

" Why, oh, why have you called me to this interview ?" at length said William ; " and why these questions ?"

" They originate from no idle curiosity, young man," said Marian in reply. " Oh, did you but know the feelings which at present rend this heart—did you but know the claim which I am convinced you have upon its warmest pulsation, you would not marvel at the emotions I evince."

" You torture me with suspense," returned William ; " my own heart beats at the rate of thirty knots an hour."

" Oh, it joys me to hear it," said Marian, and her looks became even more intensely affectionate than before.

" Mysterious woman, explain yourself, I entreat. Why this strange, this unaccountable feeling that pervades me, and leads me to reverence—almost worship you ?"

" Oh, this is bliss to the poor, seared heart of Marian," ejaculated the wanderer ; " she has still one left to love—one who can love her. She is not the lone one she supposed herself to be. Boy, thine heart but responds to the feelings of nature. It bounds at its powerful throbs."

"Is it nature that prompts the feelings I now experience?" asked William, as he gazed with increased interest at Marian, and sensations of a description that language cannot pourtray predominated in his bosom.

"It is," replied Marian. "Oh! how like he who had my soul's whole devotion. Such was he when first my heart owned his influence—such that noble contour of countenance. Oh, my heart! this meeting will be too much for me."

"Again I implore you to inform me why you have sought it," said the youthful sailor. "Know you anything of me?"

"Know you!" repeated Marian, with singular emphasis. "Knows the mother her own offspring? Cherishes the parent its own blood? Oh, God! oh, God!"

"Parent!" exclaimed William. "What mean you? I never knew a parent but he who saved my life."

"And he was a fisherman?"

"He was."

"The same kind and benevolent man whom you call father?"

"The same."

"Blessings, Heaven's choicest blessings, be showered upon his head!"

"They are—they will be."

"And at that time he lived near Dieppe?"

"He did."

"And the lad preserved with you?"

"Made an attempt on my life."

"The base, the heartless wretch! How like the character he has since maintained," said Marian.

"You know him, then?" said William, with a look of astonishment.

"I cannot be mistaken in him."

"Lives he yet?"

"He does."

"Ah! then to whom, if you thus know so much of my history, do I belong?"

"You shall know. But my heart is full. I fear that I have imposed upon myself a task that I shall not at present be able to accomplish. Leave me alone but for a few moments."

"This suspense is torturing, and I cannot understand you," said William.

"Again let me look at your neck," said Marian, eagerly, as she approached the astonished young seaman, and placed her yet fair and delicate hands upon his shoulders.

William once more loosened the collar of his shirt, and exhibited the three moles upon his neck. Marian fixed one intense look upon them, and then, with a frantic shriek, she pressed William convulsively to her bosom.

"The same—the same!" she cried. "These proofs convince me that my heart was not wrong. Oh! gracious Heaven! thou art still kind. Thou art too good to the so long persecuted and deserted one. Boy—boy, she who now clasps thee to her bosom—she whose scalding tears fall upon thy cheek—the despised, the deserted, the lonely one, gave thee birth!"

"Mother!" shouted the young mariner, with an intensity of feeling that no language can describe, and he hugged the poor wanderer to his heart, as if she had been a thing of Heaven.

"Mother!" repeated Marian. "Oh, blessed sound! Never did poor Marian expect to hear it from the lips of her own offspring. Son—son! dear relic of a beloved, but ill-fated husband! 'Tis indeed a mother's heart that beats responsive to thine own—a mother's arms that enfold thee. Oh, God! when can my gratitude to thee cease for allowing me to live to see this day ?   Years of suffering, of bitter and heart-rending anguish are more than repaid by this circumstance.   Thou art my son—my own one—my only one.   Does not thine own heart tell thee that I speak but the truth ?"

Strange and tumultuous feelings rushed through the young seaman's veins, and he looked into the animated countenance of Marian with all the strength of affection and amazement.   It was like a vision to him ; he could not believe it scarcely to be reality, and yet an inward, an instinctive power convinced him that Marian spoke the truth.   Mother ! the name brought with it a flood of ecstacy that was hitherto unknown to him.   Mother ! there is a magic in the name which touches the tenderest chord of our feelings, and supersedes the tenderest of all other sentiments.   Mother ! oh, the Heaven conveyed in that title, especially to one who has been for so many years led to imagine that he has no one in the world on whom he could probably bestow it.   William again and again strained Marian to his heart, but his feelings were too powerful to allow him for some time to speak, and those of the hitherto wandering maniac were of a corresponding character.   The force of nature had its full sway ; it burst its channels ; tears of joy, of wonder, of ecstacy streamed from the eyes of William, he pressed his lips to the pallid cheek of Marian, and sobbed aloud ; manhood gave way to the more potent feelings of the child.

If we are permitted a foretaste of Heaven, William and Marian experienced it at that moment.   They both gave free vent to their emotions, for they felt that they emanated from a genuine source ; and they mingled their tears and their sobs together.

At length William recovered partially from his emotion, and, gently releasing himself from the embraces of Marian, he once more repeated the name of " mother."

" Mother !" cried Marian ; " yes, yes, that is the name ; that is the title thou owest me, although Providence until this time has not permitted our fond endearments.   I am thy mother, boy, thy poor, deeply injured, calumniated mother !   She who bore thee in her womb, and had thee snatched from her by her cruel foes.   Merciful God ! thou knowest that I speak the truth !"

" My mother !" exclaimed the astonished young man, " and in this wretched state ?"

" Yes ; yes !"

" I can scarce believe the evidence of my senses," said William ; " but are you convinced that you speak the truth ?"

" Oh, yes," answered Marian ; " the marks upon your throat ; the likeness you bear to your father, and the circumstances of the manner in which you were found, independent of the inward feeling that I now experience, all serve to confirm the blissful fact.   Thou art indeed my son, the son of the unfortunate, wandering Marian."

" Mysterious Providence ! can it be ?" ejaculated William.   " Oh, who then art thou really, and who is my father ?"

" That is a secret which I cannot, at present, entrust myself with the disclosing," answered Marian ; " another time, and all shall be revealed."

" And why not now ?" asked William, urgently.

" No, no ; not now, not now ; my heart would burst in the effort," replied Marian.

" But how is it that I see you thus ?"

" Cruelty and scandal have brought me to it."

" Am I the child of shame ?"

" The child of shame !" reiterated Marian, and her countenance glowed ; " the child of shame ! oh, boy, boy, how could such an idea enter your

mind? No; thou art the child of virtue, although they endeavoured and succeeded in calumniating me."

" Who ?"

" My bitterest enemies," answered Marian ; " but I forgive them, although they deprived me of my husband and my only born."

" And why have you so long kept this a secret locked within your own breast ?"

" Because I viewed all mankind as my enemies, and was fearful of confiding it to any one," replied Marian.

" And what led you to imagine that I was your son ?" inquired William.

" Your likeness to your father, and what I heard you conversing about at Clarendon Farm."

" But after all, you may be mistaken," observed William, although his heart at the same time told him to the contrary, and every feeling prompted him to hope that his doubts might not be realized.

" Was there anything upon your person when the fisherman found you, that you have since preserved ?" eagerly inquired Marian.

" There was."

" What was it ?"

" A small silver locket."

" Ah !"

" Inclosing a lock of hair."

" Oh, my poor heart ! The confirmation becomes still stronger," said Marian ; and her heart heaved and throbbed as if it would burst its tenement. " Have you that locket by you ?"

" 'Tis here." said William, as he took the locket from his bosom, and placed it in the hand of Marian.

No. 16

No sooner did she behold it than she uttered another cry of frantic joy, and once more pressed the youthful seaman convulsively to her heart.

"The same! the same!" she sobbed, hysterically. "This—this is proof beyond disputation. My son! my son! my long lost, only one!"

Overcome by his emotions, yet lost and bewildered in the excitement of the unexpected occurrence, William returned the embrace of Marian with all the warmth with which she pressed him to her bosom, but utterance for a time was denied him. He felt he was certain that he was in the arms of her who had given him being; but yet the discovery was so joyful, so unexpected, that he could scarcely dare trust himself with a conviction of its certainty.

"That locket," said Marian, after a pause, during which her emotion had somewhat subsided, "that locket was mine, and when you were born I placed it around your neck, little thinking at the time how soon you were to be torn from me."

"Strange mystery!" exclaimed William; "why, oh, why should you hesitate to unravel it?"

"Not now; I dare not—I cannot," returned Marian, with a deep sigh.

"And who was my father?"

"He was noble by birth, by station, and intrinsic worth."

"His name?"

"That, on another occasion, you shall know."

"And he loved you?"

"Oh! none could love more fondly—ardently."

"And what, then, could cause your separation?"

"The deep, insidious plotting of a set of fiends in human shape. But Heaven knows my innocence, and in that conviction, amid all her many misfortunes, poor Marian has been happy!"

"But surely the cause must have been powerful," said William, "that could have induced a husband of the affection you have described yours to possess to abandon you, and to tear your infant from your breast."

"Oh, the wretches worked their infernal plans well," answered Marian; "they triumphed for awhile; but it will yet be Marian's turn—the time will come and that shortly, when her innocence will be proved, and justice be done to her wrongs and those of her child."

"And can I indeed be that child of whom you speak?" said William, "or is your brain still wandering?"

"No, no—not now, not now," returned Marian; "I was mad once, but reason has again asserted her sway, and I speak the truth. Oh, my son, these feelings could not predominate in my breast, unless Nature told me that you were indeed my son. Oh, how my heart throbs towards you, and your eyes convince me that your sentiments are the same. There is no mistaking the feeling; it is one that will assert its sway beyond all other."

"Mother, dear mother, if such you really are," said William, "we will never again part."

"Yes, yes; we must this day," said Marian; "but to-morrow we will meet again, when all shall be satisfactorily explained."

"And why not this day?"

"It cannot be; I must collect my thoughts, and prepare my mind to disclose the melancholy incidents of my life."

"But to leave you in this wretched hovel," said William.

"Yes, wretched indeed it is," replied Marian; "but it possesses no horrors to me—I am used to it, and its gloom and misery best associates with my mind. The stranger who was staying at the farm of Mr. Backstay?"

" He is missing in a most mysterious manner," answered William ; " and we cannot conceive what has become of him."

" Sir Julian Mordlington can best answer that question," observed Marian.

" But he denies all knowledge of him."

" He is a liar."

" Knew you this stranger?" inquired William, eagerly.

" His features were perfectly familiar to me," replied Marian, " and it was on beholding him, that reason first again dawned upon my mind, and the memory of the past rushed back with greater tumult to my brain. But I know not his name."

" It is Fitzpatrick."

" Fitzpatrick!" repeated Marian, and her countenance exhibited greater emotion than it had done for the last few moments before; " Fitzpatrick! that name. Then the mystery is all explained. Good, kind-hearted man ! oh, what feelings do the mention of thy name create in my bosom. Alas! what has been thy fate?"

" Then you did know him?" eagerly demanded William.

" Know him ! oh, yes. He was my best, my dearest friend; the friend of your father. Oh! could he but have known me, how happy he would have been ; he would have been the principal instrument in gaining me and you restitution of our rights, and in redressing the wrongs of the innocent. But, alas ! I fear he has fallen beneath the hands of villany, and here I swear, that even at the hazard of my own life, I will ascertain his fate. Would to Heaven that he had taken my advice, and not have gone to the villain Sir Julian Mordlington."

" But are you convinced that he went thither?"

" I am positive, my son," said Marian; " I watched him enter the Hall."

" Then Sir Julian Mordlington must know what has become of him, or what motive could he have in so firmly denying all knowledge of him ? He must answer for this."

" He shall," returned Marian ; " but, alas ! I fear it is too late to save Mr. Fitzpatrick."

" Think you, then, he has had violent hands laid on him by the baronet?"

" I do."

" What motives could the baronet have for doing so?" inquired William.

" The miscreant had reason to hate and fear him," answered Marian ; " but he shall find that there is yet another whom he has more cause to fear, and who will ultimately bring him to that punishment which his crimes deserve."

" What mean you ?"

" The time is not yet come for explanation," replied Marian.

" Oh, what necessity can there be for keeping me thus in suspense?" asked William.

" It might thwart my plans to disclose more at present," answered Marian, " but to-morrow you shall know all. We must now part. One more embrace, my son; bless you, bless you, and in your prayers, do not forget your poor mother."

Once more did Marian throw her arms around the neck of William, and kissed him fervently. The most powerful feelings of love and veneration filled his bosom, and he returned the caresses of her he now firmly believed to be his mother, with equal ardour. It was a sentiment that was entirely new to him, but so powerful that it by far exceeded all that he had before experienced.

After a few moments spent in this manner, Marian gently withdrew herself from the young man's embraces, and fixing upon him a look of the most indescribable tenderness, and repeating her blessing, she was about to leave the hovel, when William gently detained her.

"Mother, dear mother," he exclaimed, "but just to know each other, and to part thus, it must not be."

"To-morrow, at the same hour and in the same place, my son, we will meet again," said Marian; "let he who hath fostered you with fatherly love accompany you, and from my lips hear a confirmation of that which I have asserted, and listen to my melancholy history of wrongs."

"Oh, why delay?" eagerly demanded William, "my foster-father will most gladly receive you, and I cannot, dare not think of leaving you in this melancholy wretched place. I pray you attend me to the farm."

"No, no," answered Marian, "I have important business that must be performed; besides, my heart is too full to-day to suffer me to collect my thoughts. Begone, my son, and to-morrow do not fail to meet me again at the time I have appointed."

"I must obey you, dear, dear mother," said William, reluctantly, "but ere I go, there is another question I would put to you."

"Name it."

"You questioned me about the boy that was preserved with me from the wreck?" said William.

"I did."

"You asked me his age, and his description?"

"True."

"And evinced extreme emotion when I answered you."

"And, oh! good reason had I so to do," answered Marian.

"Think you that you knew the lad?"

"I do."

"Who was he?" eagerly inquired William.

"Your brother!" answered Marian.

"My brother!" repeated William, with a look of the most unbounded astonishment. "How can you reconcile these discrepancies? I thought you told me that I was your only born?"

"He was the son of the same father by a former marriage," answered Marian, with a deep sigh; "oh! bitter remembrance!"

"Does he still live?" asked William.

"He does," replied Marian, "and is a villain of the blackest dye."

"His name?"

"Hark ye, my son," returned Marian, "that brother, should he know you, would seek your life, and never rest until he had obtained his infernal object; he possesses power, greater power than many can imagine, but yet his very life is in my hands. Even at this time he resides not far from the very spot on which we at present stand, but his home is on the bright blue waters."

"And his name?"

"His name is —— "

Before Marian could finish the sentence, the report of a pistol was heard, and in an instant she fell staggering on the floor.

"Ah!" she groaned, "we are betrayed; the assassins are at their work. I am shot. Oh! my son, my poor boy, how will you escape?"

"Mother, dear mother," cried the distracted William, as he rushed towards the wounded Marian, and raised her in his arms; "oh, who has done this hellish deed?"

But Marian had become insensible and heard not what he said, and William had only just time to look around him, when the place was filled with armed ruffians with Sam Raker at their head.

"Villains!" exclaimed William, supporting the form of Marian in one arm, and looking round for some means of defending himself. " What would you here ?"

" By Lucifer!" said Sam Raker, " my mark this time has proved sure, at any rate, and the babbling of that old hag is silenced just, fortunately, in the nick of time."

" Murderers, stand back!" shouted William, as he wielded a large cudgel which he found in the room ; " stand back, I say, or I will pour a broadside into some of you. You have a furious lion to deal with."

" Ha! ha! ha!" laughed Sam Raker, scornfully, " the furious lion may roar, but we will soon find a way to tame him. Seize him, my lads."

" The first that approaches me is a dead man!" returned William, courageously.

" Fool!" answered Sam Raker, " of what use is it your offering resistance to us. Do you not see our numbers?"

" I would resist twice the number of such infernal swabs!" said the young man; " you have already committed murder, what more would you now ?"

" You must go with us," answered Sam Raker.

" Go with you, where ?"

" That you will shortly find out. So you had better go quietly."

" If I do I'm d——d !" determinedly uttered William. " At any rate you shall have a tussle to secure me."

" Seize him, my lads," commanded Sam Raker; " why do you stand listening to his empty prate ? Are you to be bullied and frightened by one man ?"

" Come on, you lubbers!" cried William, as two or three of the smugglers rushed upon him, and flourishing his cudgel above his head, two of them were felled to the ground in an instant. Furious with rage at the young seaman's obstinate resistance, Sam Raker and the others now rushed simultaneously upon him, and not until he had dealt them all some pretty severe blows, did they succeed in disarming him, and securing him, bound his arms with a rope, and prepared to drag him from the hovel.

" Villains! murderers! release me!" he cried.

" Away with him !" commanded Sam Raker.

" What shall we do with the woman ?" asked one of the ruffians.

" Oh," returned Sam Raker, kicking the body of Marian with his foot, " she is dead enough, and so it is no use being bothered with her carcase. Let us leave her here for her friends to dispose of her, if she has any."

" Oh! wretches! miscreants!" cried William, as he gazed with the most intense agony on the apparently lifeless body of her he had so lately discovered to be his mother; " for this monstrous crime surely the vengeance of Heaven will overtake you!"

" Ha! ha! ha!" laughed Sam, " we have done our business to perfection this time. Away with the young spitfire; we shall soon find a way to cool his courage, depend upon it."

William cast one more look of bitter anguish on the insensible form of the unfortunate Marian, and was then forcibly dragged by the smugglers from the hovel.

In addition to William's surprise and doubt as to what the ruffians by whom he was seized intended to do with him, he experienced all the intense agony of horror and grief at the dreadful fate of her who had claimed him for a son, and at the very moment when she was about to disclose that on which so much of his future happiness in all probability depended. Then did he also feel most keenly for the sufferings that Flora and his friends would undergo at his disappearance, and the uncertainty as to what had become of him. Still he was determined to make another effort to

escape from the hold of those who detained him, although that was perfectly useless, as his single arm, could he have released himself, would have
effected little against numbers.   He was held more securely than ever, and
in order to silence his cries, which might give the alarm to some travellers
or other, they gagged him, and then with tauntings and other vexatious proceedings, they continued to drag him by the least frequented way towards
an old building in the midst of the forest, which had been untenanted for
several years, and which Sam Raker and his companions had speedily become acquainted with, where in case of danger of his being seen, the
smugglers had determined, on the suggestion of Raker, that they would
keep him until night should have set in, when they might with greater
safety convey him on board the Devil Skipper.

It was a gloomy pile of building, although it had formerly, no doubt,
been a place of some consequence; but notwithstanding it had been for so
many years deserted, there were several of the rooms that were in a perfect
state, and into one of these they conveyed the young mariner.   Having
secured the door, they removed the gag from William's mouth, and he was
again allowed the liberty of speech, the first use of which he made was to
turn round and reproach in the bitterest terms those whom he supposed to
be the murderers of his mother, and whom he now began to think had
brought him to the place where he was at present confined, for the same
purpose.   But yet what motive could they have to induce them to such a
deed, unless it was robbery, and then surely if that had been their design
they had had the opportunity of doing so in the wood without taking the
trouble to bring him thither.   Another thing, he could not be mistaken as
to the real characters of the ruffians after the words they had made use of.
That they were smugglers or pirates he was convinced, and, therefore, he
had every reason to believe that they intended him some wrong of the most
desperate nature.

Sam Raker having called one of the men aside, whispered something to
him, and then turning to William, he said,—

" You will remain here, my young shark, until night, when you will be
safely stowed away on board our craft, and then a long adieu to England."

" Shiver my timbers!" cried William, " it is then, as I suspected.   You
are pirates, smugglers ——"

" Ay, ay," interrupted Sam Raker, " both if you please; we are not
ashamed of our titles."

" Why, you blood-thirsty set of murderers ! ——"

" Hold !" shouted Sam, " you must use better words than that, or you
may chance to have to pay dearly for it.   Besides it is no use your getting
out of temper now you are in our power ; you cannot help yourself, and
you will act wise if you keep a civil tongue in your head."

" Villains !" resolutely returned the young seaman ; and his fine handsome countenance glowed with indignation, while an icy death-like chill
ran through all his veins when he thought upon the untimely fate of
Marian, the voice of Nature, which could not be mistaken, strongly pleading
within him.   " Villains ! heartless wretches !   What harm could that
poor creature have done you that you must seek her life ?"

" That is our business," returned Sam, with a look of exultation ; " but
at any rate so far, we have triumphed, and silenced her for ever."

" But the atrocious crime must and will be avenged," said William ;
" the great Commander above will not suffer it to go unpunished, and that
in the most terrible manner."

" Ha, ha, ha!" laughed Sam, " I dare say not; but we must take the
chance of that ; we are not the sort of fellows to tremble at trifles."

" You must be a cowardly, blood-thirsty set of scoundrels," boldly remarked the young seaman, and his features fully evinced the anguish of mind he was enduring, not so much on his own account as for his sympathy in the untimely end of Marian, and the distraction of mind under which poor Flora would suffer, and the rest of those so dear to him.

" Beware, young spitfire," said Raker, frowning and pointing significantly to his pistol ; " I have before cautioned you that that sort of language will do you no good, and that it may be visited in a manner that will not be very palatable to you."

" Unpinion my arms," demanded William, " give me something to defend myself with, and you shall soon find to your cost, many of you as there are, the true blood of the British man-o'-war's-man that flows within these veins."

" Ha! ha! ha!" once more laughed Sam Raker; " that's a very likely thing. But trust me, my young swab, we shall find out a way to cool your courage by and bye, or I am much mistaken."

" Never!" resolutely answered the youthful mariner; " in the cause of innocence and justice, William Backstay will never flinch even to the shedding of the last drop of his heart's blood."

" The boast of all headstrong fools like yourself," retorted the smuggler.

" The time may come when you will find to your cost that it is no empty boasting on my part," said William.

" It may," observed Sam; " but it may also happen that you may be shipped off to Davy Jones's locker before you have the opportunity you speak of."

" For what purpose do you seize upon me ?"

" That you will not long remain in ignorance of."

" I have never injured you."

" Perhaps not," replied Sam Raker, " although I have not forgotten the encounter we had together a day or two ago, when, what between you and that cursed Crazy Marian, you managed to frustrate my designs just as they were upon the point of being accomplished."

" And think you that I would be lubber enough to stand by and see one of the fair craft borne down by such an infernal black-looking, piratical rascal as you ?" said William, and his manly bosom swelled at the thought, " that damsel my own Flora too ; my—my—oh, damme! I shall choke with rage."

" It will be something very strange to me if ever the girl becomes yours."

" Liar !"

" She is destined for another," said Raker, with a look of the utmost derision and triumph at the agony which William was evidently undergoing.

" 'Tis false !"

" Thou wilt find it is not so, or Sam Raker never was more deceived in his life."

" My—my Flora the bride of another !" repeated William, his emotion increasing every moment ; " but what a lubber I am making of myself to pay any attention to what such a black-hearted swab as you say. It is only done to mock me."

" Perhaps the truth of my words will be proved rather sooner than you anticipate, my bold young mariner," returned Sam Raker ; " in the course of a few hours the girl may be in the power of he whom I say again is destined to become her future companion."

" Companion !" repeated William, while at the moment he felt all the rage of the aroused lion at the dark insinuations of the smuggler ; " oh ! beware! beware! villain as you are, do not attempt to say or do anything that may injure that innocent girl, or surely the vengeance of Heaven will immediately descend upon your head, and all those miscreants with whom you are connected."

"Heaven !" mocked Raker, "what have we to do with that ? But I waste time, I must leave you for awhile in the care of three or four of these gentlemen ; no doubt you will find them very agreeable companions. Look well to your prisoner, Will Hemlock, and if he lets his tongue run too fast, you must resort once more to the gag. Do you hear me ?"

"Ay, ay," answered Hemlock, "leave him alone to me, and I will manage him, I warrant."

"As soon as it is dark, I shall return hither," added Raker ; "myself and the others now go upon other business."

With these words, Sam Raker, once more fixing a look of scorn and ex-ultation upon William, and then attended by the remainder of the smugglers, quitted the place.

Finding it would be quite useless to expostulate with or upbraid the villains in whose power he was, William, after traversing the room for some time with the most disordered footsteps, threw himself at length upon part of a broken bench which was in the room, and gave way to the deepest melancholy of reflection.

It is a task we would fain not undertake to attempt to describe the state of mind the young seaman now endured, and indeed his situation was one of the most painful, and at the same time fearful character. He was in the power of villains who were blood-thirsty enough to perpetrate any crime, no matter however monstrous, as the supposed murder of Crazy Marian fully testified ; but it was not, as we have before said, so much on his own account as those of Flora and his friends, who must be undergoing even now the most dreadful agony of mind on account of the mystery of his disappearance, and he was certain that if he should not be restored to them it would prove a blow to the fair damsel who owned his purest and most ardent affections, from which she would never be able to recover.

Then the observations of Sam Raker respecting her, convinced him that she was threatened with some danger, and he not to be at hand to protect her was more terrible than all. But surely, villains as they were, they could not offer violence or insult to one of so much innocence and beauty as Flora Clarendon ? And yet had he not had a convincing proof that they would not hesitate to do so. The idea was torturing in the extreme. What astonished him more than all was, that, smugglers and pirates as they admitted themselves to be, they should have been able to have eluded the vigilance of the preventive service, or should have ventured boldly into the very midst of their enemies.

There certainly appeared to him to be some very extraordinary mystery in the affair, and he thought the pirate captain, whoever he might be, was a person of considerable power, and that he was in all probability connected with some of the authorities, or otherwise he could not have ventured so daringly into the very jaws of those he should have most cause to dread.

The unaccountable disappearance of Mr. Fitzpatrick next occupied Wil-liam's thoughts, and he could not help imagining that the honest-hearted lawyer had met with some violent end ; and when he recollected all that Marian had mentioned about him, and the words Sam Raker had given utterance to, when he discharged the contents of the pistol at her, he firmly believed that the present wretches had done the deed, but at whose bidding he had no means of deciding, although his strongest suspicions rested upon Sir Julian Mordlington, and the remarks of Marian showed plainly that she suspected the same.

But, if possible, more intense than anything else were the dreadful

thoughts that crossed and distressed the mind of William, when he dwelt upon the untimely end of Marian, and just at the critical moment when the whole secret of his birth seemed upon the point of being unravelled. That she was now perfectly rational he had every reason most firmly to believe, and that she had spoken the truth, as regarded their consanguinity, he had likewise no reason to doubt. There was an instinctive voice within him, a feeling at the heart, which convinced him of that fact; besides, what motive could she have in telling a falsehood upon the subject? But, to be restored to the arms of a parent only a few minutes before he was destined to lose her for ever, and that in a manner which made the very heart's blood run cold at the thought, was too dreadful for even the most insensible to endure; and the manly heart of the youthful mariner was so overpowered that he could have wept.

There were moments, however, when he could scarcely believe that Marian was no more, that the wound she had received could have proved mortal, and then a hope would dart across his brain that she would be discovered by some person and assistance rendered her in time to save her life, and that Providence might afterwards restore them to each other, and all terminate happier than there was at present any prospect of. This hope was, however, but transient, and the mind of William, although he possessed an ample share of fortitude and patience, gave way to the influence of misery and despair.

The smugglers enjoyed themselves in their own way, with singing and ribald jests, and as William made use of no observation they did not offer to interrupt him in his meditations, although from the observations which frequently escaped them, he was not long in ascertaining that they belonged to a most desperate and determined gang of smugglers and pirates that the ocean could be infested with, and would not hesitate at the perpetration of the most atrocious deed; therefore, once on board their vessel, he had little to hope from them, unless he would join them; which he could never consent to do. The name of the ship, however, he could not learn, neither that of the pirate captain; but he could gather from the different hints that fell from the smugglers, his power was very great, and he was considered to hold almost unlimited sway over the ocean, and to set at complete defiance all attempts to take him, and to laugh and mock at the government. He was lost in bewilderment upon this subject, and knew not what to think; but one thing was certain, namely, that he had little, or in fact nothing, to hope from the mercy of wretches so inured to crime.

In this state of suspense and misery the hours passed tediously away, until at length the shadows of evening fell upon the earth, and William awaited the arrival of Sam Raker and the other smugglers to convey him to the place of his destination, in a state of mind we have attempted to describe, but which may be more readily imagined by the reader.

And now would the alarm of Flora and the others, he felt certain, have attained the utmost pitch, and he pictured to himself the mental agony of them all, especially Flora, whose delicate nature was so ill calculated to support so severe a trial.

"Poor, dear girl," he reflected, "little did you this morning expect so severe a misfortune to befal us all. Alas! I fear that should Providence ordain that the designs of the wretches, in whose power I now am, should not be frustrated, this will prove your death blow. Never could you survive the loss of one who is so dear to you. But surely Heaven will not permit so great a misfortune to take place."

He was interrupted in these reflections by Will Hemlock observing,

"Sam tarries; it is now past the hour at which we expected him, and yet there are no signs of his appearance. I hope no accident hath befallen him."

"Oh, no," answered another of the smugglers, "Sam is right enough, depend upon it; leave him alone for keeping out of danger. The business he has gone upon has most likely detained him longer than he expected it would have done; but there is little fear but that he will be with us soon."

"I do not care how soon then," remarked Will Hemlock, "for I don't much fancy this place, and never feel happy but when I am on shipboard. I hope it will not be long before we quit this part altogether, for should we be discovered, we should have hot work of it."

"Ay, ay," said the other villain, "but we have hitherto escaped detection, and I do not think there is much fear of it now."

"There may not be," said Hemlock, "but it is not because we have been lucky all along, that we should continue to remain so. These preventive men have keen eyes, and the excitement which the disappearance of ——"

"Hush! be on your guard," interrupted a third smuggler, "you remember the necessity of using precaution, and the warning our captain gave us?"

"True," replied Hemlock, "but I am afraid that so many adventures one upon the other, may place us in rather an awkward predicament."

"Oh! I do not see anything to apprehend, and it will not be many days before we slip our cable, and then hurrah once more for the bright blue waters."

"Ay, that's what I long for," said Will Hemlock, "but know you, Harry, the nature of the business Sam Raker has gone upon?"

"I do."

"What is it?"

"Can't you guess?"

" Oh ! the ——"

" Enough ; do not mention any more. I see you understand me. But think you he will succeed ?"

" It is very seldom Sam fails."

" Should he indeed meet with success, we shall have made a pretty good day's work of it."

" And are sure of our captain's gratitude."

" Yes, and something else into the bargain, of a more substantial description."

" I understand you. The captain of our gallant barque never fails to reward us handsomely when we deserve it."

" Miscreants !" thought William, " if you had indeed the reward you merit, it would be the gibbet-post."

He did not, however, offer to make any observation, for he knew that it could do him no good, but perhaps, on the contrary, bring down upon him the vengeance of the smugglers, and tempt them to commit some violent outrage upon him. The darkness increased, and as the smugglers had no means of obtaining a light, the place was particularly dismal, and well calculated to excite the most gloomy and painful thoughts, even if William had been placed in far different circumstances than those he was. But still Sam Raker did not make his appearance, and William began to think that something had indeed happened to him, or that the business he had gone upon had failed. He strongly suspected from the hints that had partially escaped the smugglers, that that business had probably some connection with Flora, and that Sam Raker and the other, had been employed to seize her, which they had now a better opportunity of doing, as they had him in their power. This idea filled his mind with the most insupportable anguish and suspense, and again he walked the room with hasty and disordered footsteps, mentally offering a prayer to Heaven at the same time, to avert the danger he apprehended. The smugglers evidently observed his emotion, and they exchanged glances with each other, that shewed they exulted in it.

" It is no use waiting here any longer, I think," said Will Hemlock, " for I do not think that Sam Raker will come here to-night, and time wanes apace, and as the coast is likely to be clear the way we are going, I think the sooner we depart with our prisoner to the ship the better."

" Yes," observed one of the smugglers, " that is my opinion, Will Hemlock, and should Sam come here after our departure, he will make sure that all is right, and where we have gone."

To this proposition the smugglers all agreed, and they prepared once more to place the gag in William's mouth. He resisted this indignantly.

" Wretches !" he said ; " why do you want to add to my misery ? Have you not got me securely in your power ?"

" We don't know that, my young spark," answered Will Hemlock. " Were you to raise any outcry on the road we might be interrupted, and perhaps that would not prove altogether agreeable or convenient."

" Come—come," observed another of the smugglers, " it is no use to be obstinate, or to offer any resistance. You must submit, and so you may as well do so at first as at last."

" Oh, villains !—cowardly villains !" ejaculated William. " For this, depend upon it some day or other you will be severely punished."

A rude laugh was the only reply the smugglers made to this, and the gag being placed in the mouth of William, he was led from the building, guarded on each side by two of the wretches, and the next minute was in the wood, and being led on at a rapid rate towards the place where the Devil's Skipper was riding at anchor. How anxiously did William look around him as far as the almost impenetrable darkness would permit, in the hope of seeing some persons who might be induced to attempt to rescue him; but not an individual could he see, and all was as still as the grave. The smugglers had taken good care to select a way that was very little frequented, and they had every opportunity, as it at present appeared, of reaching the vessel in safety, and without encountering any person from whom they could have cause to apprehend any danger.

They proceeded on for some distance in the same manner, when the heart of William throbbed violently, and the smugglers looked around them in astonishment, when their ears were assailed by the piercing shrieks of a female, which seemed to proceed from the same direction as that in which they were going.

With the utmost anxiety William listened to these sounds that were repeated, and he could almost have sworn that in them he recognised the tones of Flora. What would he not have given could he have released himself from the cords that bound him, and flown towards the spot to the relief of the distressed damsel.

"What sounds are those?" said Will Hemlock.

"They are plainly those of some female in distress," said one of his companions. "But that is no business of our's. What have we to do with distressed damsels?"

"True," returned Hemlock; "but the sounds came from the same spot as that in which we are going, and we might run ourselves suddenly into danger when we least expected it."

"Let us wait here awhile, Will, and then the danger may be over, if there really is any at all."

"What if it should turn out to be Sam Raker," said Hemlock, "and that this should prove to be the female he ——"

"Ah! the thought never occurred to me before," said another of the smugglers. "It is not at all unlikely; but still I should have thought that Sam would have contrived better than not to have stopped her cries."

The agitation of William increased, and he could with difficulty contain himself, more especially when he heard the sounds repeated, until they gradually died away in the distance and were heard no more.

Stronger than ever was the impression upon William's mind that the voice was that of Flora, and his heart sunk with despair, at the same time that he was in a state of the greatest suspense to have his doubts satisfied one way or the other.

"All is silent now again," said Will Hemlock; "they have managed to quiet the squaller, at any rate, at last."

"Yes," said one of his companions; "and I think we may now proceed with safety. There does not appear to be any one near at hand."

"At any rate," observed Grampus, "it is useless our tarrying here, when we may lose the chance of securing the prisoner we have already."

"Who is to rob us of him?" demanded Hemlock.

"The preventive service may be on the alert," rejoined Grampus, "and come down upon us in numbers that we cannot cope with. Come on, and if it is really Sam Raker and his companions who have seized upon the girl, we may rest assured that she is safe, for he never easily resigns his prey."

"Villains!" reflected William, "would that those you dread would now encounter you, not only for my sake, but for her ——"

He was interrupted in these meditations by a repetition of the shriek, which died away in an indistinct murmur upon the air. The smugglers looked at each other significantly, and then once more seizing William by the arms, he was hurried along at a more rapid rate than before, and at length the wide expanse of the ocean burst upon his vision.

The smugglers took him round to an obscure part of the coast, where they found one of their own boats fortunately awaiting, in which William was placed, and the villains seating themselves by his side, they rowed off rapidly towards the vessel which rode at anchor a short distance off.

We need not attempt to describe William's feelings as they proceeded, carefully avoiding the other vessels, and at every stroke of the oars, despair sinking deeper into his heart. To be in the power of such wretches was as bad as certain death, and what mercy could he expect from them? Then the awful events of the night; his interview with Marian; the extraordinary assertions she had made use of, and her dreadful fate, all crowded in rapid succession upon his brain, and increased the agony and suspense he was enduring. The motives of the smugglers were very evident to him, but his fears for the safety of Flora, and the anguish which she and her friends would be sure to endure at his mysterious disappearance, tortured him even more than all. That Sam Raker had gone with the design of seizing Flora he could have no doubt, from the conversation of the ruffians, and should he succeed in meeting her, she would be lost. Then the screams he had heard in the wood recurred to his memory, and increased his apprehensions that Flora had really fallen into the villain's power.

Never had William felt such deep, almost insupportable anguish before, and all hope of rescue was completely banished from his mind when the boat came alongside of the Devil Skipper, and he was handed on board, where he was quickly surrounded by a number of the crew, whose looks, as they were rudely fixed upon him, convinced him that they were men who were capable of the most atrocious deeds. They gazed at him with expressions of curiosity which they were going to give utterance to, when Will Hemlock motioned them to silence, and then, turning to two of the smugglers, he commanded them to return to the boat, and hasten to that part of the shore they had just left, so that they might be ready to receive Sam Raker and the others when they arrived. The fellows obeyed, and then William was conveyed below, to a small and wretched cabin, where his limbs were unbound, and the gag removed from his mouth.

"Wretches! villains!" he exclaimed, when he found his tongue once more at liberty, "for what purpose am I brought hither! Depend upon it, my disappearance will be inquired strictly into, and you will all of you have to pay dearly for this outrage upon a British seaman."

"You threaten here in vain, my young sea-shark," returned Hemlock, "and as for the land swabs, they will have a job to find you, and might, if they did, find rather a warm reception from the saucy Devil Skipper."

"The Devil Skipper!" repeated William.

"Ay," answered Will Hemlock, "the terror of the ocean. It is rather a striking name—do you not think it is?"

"Murderers!"

"Come—come, better lingo, my young fellow," said Grampus; "we are not used to accept such compliments."

"For what purpose have you made me your prisoner?" again demanded William.

"Oh, that is a question which our captain will, doubtless, answer when you see him," returned Hemlock; "we have no authority for so doing. But we have no time to waste here palavering with you. On deck, lads."

William turned away in disgust, finding that it was utterly useless to put any further questions to the ruffians, who immediately quitted the cabin, securing the door after them, and leaving him to himself.

When they were gone the young seaman gave free indulgence to the torturing thoughts that harassed his mind, and was almost beyond endurance. He was then on board that terrible vessel belonging to the Smuggler King, and which had for so many years been the dread of the honest trader, and had set every law at defiance. From such wretches he knew it would be vain to expect the least shadow of mercy, and the fate which consequently attended him, appeared to be almost inevitable. To meet with death fighting the battles of his country would have been that of glory, but to perish by the hands of lawless ruffians, whose deeds had entitled them to the name of demons, was revolting to think on, and made the heart sick as the reflection flashed across the brain. Then what had been the fate of her he so fondly loved? It was more than probable that she had also fallen into the hands of the smugglers, and if, indeed, she had done so, that would be to him the most dreadful and the severest blow of all. But what could be their object in seizing her? He was unable, at present, in the bewildered state of his mind, to form any conjecture upon the subject; but should she be taken, he was fully convinced that even her innocence and beauty would not protect her from a fate which was too dreadful to contemplate.

Even should she escape them, her sufferings would scarcely be less at his disappearance, and the uncertainty of what had become of him. How fearful also, would be the anguish of his more than parents, and all his friends, at the event? From these reflections his thoughts turned to his interview with and the fate of poor Crazy Marian, and this was indeed a subject on which he dwelt with the most poignant anguish. Could what she had stated have been correct? It seemed so remarkable and improbable, that he could scarcely credit it; and was half inclined to believe that it was but the wild wandering of Marian's brain; and yet at the time she revealed it to him, she seemed perfectly rational, with the exception of the emotion, which it was natural that the character of the recital should excite. His brain was completely bewildered, and he traversed the narrow limits of the cabin in which he was confined, with uneven and disordered steps.

At length he was aroused from these ruminations by hearing the dashing of oars in the water. A boat was evidently approaching the vessel, and again his curiosity and suspense were excited. Then he thought it was probably Sam Raker and his companions, who had returned to the ship, and the young seaman's heart palpitated with apprehension, lest the villain should have succeeded in his designs, and Flora should also be his prisoner. What would he have given could he but have ascertained that fact? The cabin window was placed so high that he could not get to look out of it, and there was nothing upon which he could stand in order that he might achieve that object.

He listened with breathless attention, and presently afterwards he heard the voice of Sam Raker, speaking to the crew, as he ascended on board, and this was followed by a strange confusion on deck, and then he heard several voices in conversation, followed by indistinct murmurings, as if proceeding from some person in distress. The agitation of William increased, and his fears suggested the worst. Should it really be poor Flora whom the villains had secured and brought on board, his misery would be complete. He beat his breast in the agony of his thoughts, and then he once more listened, but all had become still, and no sounds reached his ears, save the dashing of the waves against the sides of the vessel. Shortly afterwards he heard the boat again lowered, and some persons getting into it, they rowed off.

Poignant reflection and apprehension almost overpowered him, and folding his arms across his breast, he paced backwards and forwards in a state of the most pitiable despair.

CHAPTER XI.

THE MEETING OF THE VILLAINS. — EXULTATION. — FURTHER PLOTS. — THE FRUITLESS SEARCH. — DESPAIR OF FLORA'S PARENTS.

SIR JULIAN awaited the arrival of Sam Raker, in the apartment where they always held their meetings, with the utmost impatience, and as hour after hour passed away without his making his appearance, he began to fear that something had happened to him, and that some danger threatened them.

Unable any longer to endure this state of suspense, he had just made up his mind to go forth from the house to ascertain whether he could see anything of him, when he was gratified by hearing the usual signal at the door, and opening it, Sam Raker entered the room, and without saying a word, he threw himself in a chair, and began wiping the perspiration from his temples. Sir Julian could perceive in a moment, by his looks, that something particular had happened, and he was impatient to be made acquainted with it.

" You have tarried, Sam," he observed.

" Ay," answered the ruffian, " but better late than never ; " I have had a rare night's work of it."

" Your looks bespeak good news."

" I dare say they do, and they do not belie the facts."

" Ah ! what is it ?" demanded Sir Julian, eagerly.

" Nay," answered the other, " you must not be in such a hurry ; I am confoundedly tired, and very thirsty, and cannot tell you anything until I have refreshed myself with a glass of wine, and the sooner you let me have it the better."

The baronet frowned, and was burning with impatience ; but Sam Raker treated it with the utmost indifference, and Sir Julian knowing well his character, was certain it would be useless to urge him, until he had complied with his wishes ; he, therefore, brought forth the wine, and placing it before him, Sam helped himself to two glasses, and then turning to Sir Julian, said,—

" Now that is over, to business."

" Ah ! have you succeeded ?"

" I have, beyond your most sanguine expectations, or my own."

The eyes of Sir Julian flashed with pleasure, as he grasped the hand of Raker, and said,—

" The girl, Flora Clarendon ? What of her ?"

" She is secured."

" Ah ! joyful news. I triumph ! Sam, for this I owe you my eternal gratitude."

" No doubt," said the smuggler ; " but you do not know half what you are indebted to me yet."

" What mean you ?"

" Why, simply this," returned Sam, " that both the girl and her lover are secured, and are now safe on board the Devil Skipper."

" Impossible. This intelligence is too good," said Sir Julian.

" It is not only possible, but true."

" Ah ! then by hell my triumph is indeed complete. You are not deceiving me, Sam ?"

" Psha !" replied the smuggler, " what would be the use of my attempting to do that ? But I have not told you all yet."

" What more successes ?"

" Yes, the woman you dreaded, Crazy Marian, is no more."

" Dead ?"

" Yes, she fell by my hand this night," answered Sam.

"Wonder upon wonder!" ejaculated Sir Julian; "then my fears are at rest."

"They ought to be."

"But could you not get her in your power without taking her life?—I was anxious to ascertain who she really was."

"That you may perhaps imagine from the circumstances. It could not be avoided."

"Tell me all about it, Sam, and be quick, for I am all impatience till I am made acquainted with it."

"I must first have another glass of wine."

Raker unceremoniously filled himself a glass, the contents of which he drank, and then related, in as few words as possible, the murder of Marian, and the seizure of William. Sir Julian listened to him with feelings of astonishment and exultation, and when he had concluded, he once more grasped the villain by the hand, and lavished upon him the most unbounded thanks, at the same time expressing his entire approbation of the manner in which he had acted.

"But the girl, Flora Clarendon, the future bride of the Smuggler King?"

"Shortly after leaving the hovel," replied Sam, "we were fortunate enough to encounter her as she was returning home, and we seized her. She offered a vain resistance, but we stopped her cries, and bore her on board the craft."

"But you did not use her with violence?"

"No more than was necessary."

"Sam Raker," said Sir Julian, "what you have been relating to me is so joyful and extraordinary that I can scarcely believe it. Now, indeed, who shall compete with the Smuggler King! You have, indeed, had a night's work of it, a glorious night's work."

"Ay," returned the ruffian, "Sam Raker is the chap to accomplish his object, in a business-like manner, when he has set his mind upon anything particular."

"But you are certain they are secure?"

"Have I not said so?"

"These events will cause the greatest excitement in the neighbourhood," said the baronet.

"That they are sure to do."

"The voice of suspicion will be excited."

"Probably it may."

"And yet from the station I hold in society, and my real character not being known, I do not see how suspicion can dare attach itself to me."

"One would think not," returned Sam.

Sir Julian traversed the room in thought for a moment or two, and then added,—

"But after all, as a strict search will be made, our vessel might not escape, and therefore, to prevent the danger in time, I think the sooner the Devil Skipper weighs anchor from this port the better."

"I think it would be advisable, captain," coincided Sam Raker; "but you will not embark with us?"

"No, I must remain here for awhile," said Sir Julian, "or my departure in so abrupt a manner might excite suspicion, and perhaps make them acquainted with my real character."

"True," observed Sam Raker; "and that would prevent your revisiting this part."

"Which would be very awkward," said Sir Julian. "No, no, bear Flora to the Death Rock, where in the course of a week or so I will hasten."

"That shall be attended to, captain," answered Sam; "but the young sailor; what shall be done with him?"

"Let him be taken to the same place of security, but mind and keep them apart."

"And will you not see them ere the vessel sails?"

"See them?" repeated the baronet. "Oh, yes, I will immediately accompany you to the ship, and there enjoy my triumph. Oh, Sam, you have made me one of the happiest fellows in the world."

"I told you I should succeed," returned Sam.

"You did," answered Sir Julian, "but I did not expect that your success would be so sudden and complete."

"Oh, Sam Raker does not take long to accomplish anything upon which he has fixed his mind."

"But how seems the damsel?"

"Oh, sorrowful enough, you may be sure, captain," replied the smuggler; "but no doubt she will soon recover from that when you visit her, or you will be to blame for your want of skill."

"She cannot, she dare not resist my importunities," said the baronet. "But how seems William?"

"I left him raving like an infuriated maniac," answered the smuggler.

"And he made a determined resistance?"

"He did, and had he been better armed he might have made his escape."

"Could he be persuaded, he would make a bold acquisition to our crew," said Sir Julian.

"We are already sufficiently powerful," said Sam Raker; "we could never trust him; besides, do you not think it would be better to dispose of him at once, and that would entirely prevent him from being any further trouble to you?"

"On that I will hereafter decide," said Sir Julian; "but that I have him in my power, fully satisfies me; what has the Smuggler King to fear from him?"

No. 18

"Nothing!"

"I am sorry that you could not take Crazy Marian without adopting the course you did."

"I thought it was better to silence her as she was about to reveal your name."

"To my brother?"

"Yes."

"And of what consequence would that have been, since you were sure to have him in your power immediately afterwards?" demanded the baronet.

"I know not that it would have mattered much," answered Sam Raker; "but I acted on the impulse of the moment, and I am certain you have no cause to regret the finish of one who evidently well knew you."

"I do not regret it," said Sir Julian, "no more than that I had hoped to have had an opportunity to discover who she was."

"She seemed not to be the maniac she has ever been supposed to be," returned Sam Raker. "Cannot you call to mind where you have known her before you saw her in this neighbourhood?"

"I cannot—I have racked my brain in vain to recollect; but the more I do so the more do I become bewildered. Overheard you much what she said?"

"I did not," replied Sam Raker; "but what I did, convinced me that she was not what she appeared to be."

"Think you she had filled a different station in society?" interrogated Sir Julian.

"I do. But what surprised me more than all were the affectionate words she addressed to William, and the tenderness of her manners towards him."

"That was most extraordinary," said the baronet; "and for what purpose could she have sought an interview with my brother?"

"That I cannot imagine."

"And what did you with her body?" asked Sir Julian.

"Left it in the hovel where she met her fate," answered Sam Raker. "The dead cannot reveal any secrets, you know, captain; and, therefore, it will never be known how she came by her death, or who was her murderer."

"True; but are you certain that she was no more?"

"Oh, yes," answered Sam; "she died almost immediately."

"She might only have become insensible," remarked Sir Julian; "and should she afterwards revive, and be able to reveal ——"

"Psha, captain," interrupted the smuggler, "you are absolutely becoming as timid as a lubber. This looks not much like the daring and reckless character you have hitherto maintained."

"I am not fearful, Sam," returned Sir Julian; "but it is necessary that the utmost caution should be used, or I might have the landsharks down upon me before I could have an opportunity of leaving this neighbourhood."

"Why, that certainly would not be altogether pleasant," observed Sam Raker; "but I do not think you have any cause to apprehend. What course do you mean to adopt while you remain here regarding the excitement caused by the disappearance of the old lawyer?"

"I have already told you I must brave it out," answered the baronet; "I have already managed the business famously with the old magistrate."

"But the death of Crazy Marian and the disappearance of William and Flora Clarendon occurring so soon after, will add to the excitement and make e inquiry doubly vigorous."

"And what of that? what shadow of a cause have they to fix the least suspicion on me?" demanded Sir Julian.

"None, that I am aware of, captain," answered Sam Raker; "but I would advise you to leave this place for awhile, as soon as possible."

"Ay, that I intend to do, Sam," replied Sir Julian; "for I long to meet my chosen bride, and to be again upon my native element; the bright blue waters of the ocean."

" Yes, captain," returned Sam Raker, " I also wish the same ; for, to tell the truth, I am tired of being a gentleman.   There is plenty of work for us on the deep, and the Smuggler King must not suffer any booty to escape his coffers. How surprised the lubbers will be when they find that the Devil Skipper, the saucy Devil Skipper, has slipped her cable and steered off."

" Yes ; they will begin to suspect her real character," observed Sir Julian ; "and discover that they have been the most arrant fools, and suffered that booty to escape, for which stratagem after stratagem has been devised, and rewards offered in vain."

" Ha ! ha ! ha !" laughed Sam Raker ; " they are indeed fools, or they would have had suspicions before now. But come, when shall we go to the vessel ?"

" This instant," answered the baronet ; " I am ready to accompany you."

" But it is even now so late that I am fearful you will not be able to see Flora," said Sam ; " she will have retired to rest."

" Of that I must take the chance," answered Sir Julian ; " but you will mind and keep her secure if I should not see her."

" Oh ! you well know, captain," returned Raker, " that he cannot find any possible opportunity to escape ; and when we gain the Death Rock, we may safely bid defiance to any one to attempt to discover her."

" Ay, it is a famous retreat," said Sir Julian, " and looked upon with such terror that it as much avoided as if it was a lion's lair."

" And the lion's lair it is when you are in it, captain," observed Sam Raker.

" Ay, the Smuggler King is as much to be dreaded as the most ferocious of the forest inhabitants," said the baronet.

" But come, we still delay," said Sam Raker. " Let us begone, if you are determined that we shall weigh anchor in the morning."

" It would not be safe to remain here any longer," answered Sir Julian.

" Well, it might not, but if you would make up your mind to delay our departure till the day after to-morrow, it would give you an opportunity of the interview you want with the girl."

" No ; I will not run the risk," said Sir Julian ; " besides it will not be many days before I will hasten to the Death Rock, and then all my wishes will be gratified, and nothing can prevent the accomplishment of my design."

They now quitted the hall, and hastened towards the place of their destination.

In the meantime Mr. Backstay felt rather alarmed and surprised on arriving at Clarendon Farm, to find that William had not been there ; but that amazement and apprehension was greatly increased when night arrived and neither the young sailor nor Flora Clarendon returned. Darkness had now completely veiled the earth, and the fears of the Clarendons may be very easily conjectured.   Flora would never have prolonged her walk till such an hour if even she had met with her lover, they were certain, and something must have happened to detain her they were fearful.   This fear was greatly increased when they recollected the outrage she had so lately met with, and from the conduct of Sir Julian Mordlington, whom they were positive was a villain, and that he still harboured some evil designs against Flora, and would, if he possibly could, get her into his power. His visit to the farm, and the offers he had there made, the more convinced them that his desires were just the same, and they at the same time could not help thinking that the ruffian who had formerly seized upon the damsel was employed by the baronet. These thoughts crowding upon their minds, rendered their apprehensions and suspense almost insupportable, and after the lapse of another hour, still seeing nothing of either her or William, they could not await any longer, but Mr. Clarendon, Henry, and Mr. Backstay determined to go in search of them, leaving the females at home in a state of alarm which we need not attempt to describe.

Mr. Clarendon and the others proceeded with heavy hearts, and repaired to all those places to which they knew the lovers were accustomed to resort, but without success ; as the reader may expect, they could discover no traces of those they were so anxious to find. In this manner they wandered about for more than two hours, and now the deepest despair and the utmost alarm predominated in their bosoms, and they concluded that something of a serious nature had happened to both of them, but of what nature they could not form any idea.

"What is to be done?" said Mr. Clarendon ; "our search appears to be entirely hopeless."

"It does indeed," observed Mr. Backstay. "Alas! I fear that some harm has befallen to William, or he never would have absented himself all this time, when he might be certain how uneasy and anxious it would make us."

"Flora, my child," said Mr. Clarendon, in accents of the most bitter anguish, "where, O where art thou. All merciful Heaven, avert the evil I apprehend! but surely she must have fallen into the hands of some villain, or she would have returned home before now. I shall go mad, and dread to return to the farm without her, for the agony it will cause my wife and daughter will be more than they can support. Flora, my darling Flora, what can have become of you?"

"Pray endeavour to calm yourself," said Henry, "for to give way to this despair will not, cannot effect any good. I do not see how we can prosecute our search any further, and, since we left the farm, Flora may have returned."

"Heaven send that she may," said Mr. Clarendon; "but alas! I have little hopes of that. Something tells me that she will not return again, and that some villain holds her in his power, and will heap upon her head the greatest misery and oppression."

"Nay," observed Mr. Backstay; "this is a weakness. Have I not equal cause for apprehension?"

"True," answered Mr. Clarendon ; "it is most mysterious and unaccountable that both William and my poor girl should be missing at the same time."

"It is," coincided Mr. Backstay, "and especially as they did not go out together."

"But they may afterwards have met," said Henry.

"Oh, no; if they had they would have been sure to have hastened home before such a late hour," returned Mr. Clarendon. "Oh! what can be done? What course can we take with the hope of finding some clue to them?"

"I am perfectly at a loss," replied Mr. Backstay, whose countenance fully showed that he was enduring the greatest anxiety and agony of mind.

"There is some nefarious miscreant at the bottom of all this, depend upon it," said Mr. Clarendon. "Oh, God! should my poor child have fallen into the power of some heartless libertine, it will be a death-blow to myself and her mother. That villain, Sir Julian Mordlington, would not hesitate to use any means to accomplish his base designs."

"That he is a bad man, I am quite certain," said Mr. Backstay; "but I do not think he would attempt an outrage of that sort so near his own estates."

"He would think that his rank and power might shield him from justice," added Mr. Clarendon, "and therefore that he could commit such an act with impunity."

"But he might be certain that it would be discovered," remarked Mr. Backstay.

"Oh! no doubt he would adopt some steps to prevent that," replied Mr. Clarendon; "he could remove her to a distant part of the country where we might in vain endeavour to find her. I liked not his visiting the farm, and his fawning hypocrisy. But, by Heaven, should he have worked me harm by insulting my child, I will not rest, in spite of his power, until I have obtained retribution."

"Pray, my dear sir," expostulated Henry, "be more calm, and do not give way to despair before you are certain that there is ample cause for it."

"And have not I already ample cause for it?" demanded Mr. Clarendon.

"The absence of Flora and William is certainly very alarming," replied Henry; "but after all they may have met each other and returned to my father's farm, instead of Clarendon."

"Ah!" observed Mr. Backstay, "that is an idea that did not occur to me. Let us hasten thither, and put our doubts and surmises at rest."

"We will do so," observed Mr. Clarendon, "but I fear it will be to little purpose. Oh! my poor, beloved Flora, should you, indeed, be lost to me, madness will most assuredly seize upon my brain."

"Hope for the best, hope for the best," said Mr. Backstay; "notwithstanding the anguish and anxiety I must necessarily feel, something seems to tell me that they will be both safely restored to us. Let us no longer tarry here, wasting the time in useless presentiments and speculations, but hasten to my residence, where in all probability we shall find them, or otherwise hear of them."

"Would to God that I could entertain the same opinion, and that it might be realized," said Mr. Clarendon, "but, alas! I fear there is but little prospect of it."

They now moved on in the direction of the farm of Mr. Backstay, in the hope of finding that William and Flora had met each other, and were there, or else had returned to Clarendon Farm. The moon shone brightly in the Heavens, and everything around was illumined almost as brightly as if it had been broad daylight. In a short time they arrived near the hovel in which the unfortunate Marian had occasionally sought a shelter, and here, the moon shining brilliantly upon the earth, they perceived that the grass was much trampled and disturbed, as if a violent struggle had taken place.

"There has something happened here," observed Mr. Clarendon, his eyes resting upon it in a moment; "the grass would not have been thus disturbed had there not been a struggle, and that of the most fearful description."

"And see here are plainly the mark of footsteps," said Henry.

"Gracious Heaven!" ejaculated Mr. Clarendon; "and here is blood."

"Blood?" repeated Henry and his father, in a breath.

"Yes, yes—look!" said Mr. Clarendon, pointing aghast at the traces of blood which were plainly distinguishable upon the grass.

"Good God!" cried Mr. Backstay, "what dreadful crime has been perpetrated here? Murder has been committed."

"My heart misgives me!" exclaimed Mr. Clarendon. "Oh, my Flora! my poor child!"

"And William!—where—where is he?" said Mr. Backstay. "Probably he has lost his life in endeavouring to defend poor Flora."

"The marks of blood," observed Henry, "seem to proceed in a direct line to the hovel."

"It is the hovel of Crazy Marian," observed Mr. Backstay, his spirits somewhat reviving ; "perhaps it may be her who has lost her life, if, which Heaven forbid, life be taken."

"Let us immediately examine the place, and very likely we may ascertain the truth.   Oh, how my heart trembles !"

They moved on in the direction of the blood-marks, and at length came to the miserable place in which the unfortunate and ill-fated Marian had at times formed her retreat, heedless of "the pitiless pelting of the storm," to which its dilapidated state so much exposed it.   The door was standing open, and they all three immediately entered, but started back aghast at the sight which immediately presented itself to their eyes.

The moon streamed a full flood of light in at the broken casement of the wretched hovel, and everything was thus fully exposed.   They cast their eyes upon the floor, and there beheld a large pool of blood, and the imprint of a human form, which seemed as if it had been dragged or had crawled from the cottage.

"Oh, dreadful !" exclaimed Mr. Clarendon, clasping his hands most vehemently together ; "our worst fears are then realized.   Murder has been committed !   My child—my child !   Surely Almighty God would not, in his infinite mercy, suffer innocence like thine to fall a sacrifice to some fiend in human shape."

"Pray calm your deeply-agitated feelings," expostulated his son-in-law ; "it may not be as you apprehend.   This is the hovel of Crazy Marian, and it may be her who has been so unfortunate as to meet with so horrible and untimely a fate."

"Oh, horrible !" groaned Mr. Backstay, still gazing upon the blood with looks of the most unqualified horror.   "What monsters must they be who could commit so dreadful a crime as this ?   But, have I not equal cause to fear with you, Mr. Clarendon ?   May not William be the victim, and ——"

"But what should bring William or Flora hither ?" interrupted Henry.

"I am unable to form even a conjecture," answered Mr. Backstay ; "but it might be curiosity."

"Here is something that perhaps may lead to the unravelling of the truth," said Henry, as his eyes rested on a small glittering trinket on the floor.   He stooped and picked it up, and handing it to Mr. Backstay, the latter no sooner beheld it than he uttered a cry of astonishment and horror, and Mr. Clarendon looked eagerly and anxiously for an explanation.

"For Heaven's sake, what is it that thus so powerfully agitates you ?" he inquired.

"It is the locket which William always had suspended from his neck," said Henry, "and which was found on him when my father and myself rescued him from the wreck.   Horror ! horror ! he has been murdered !"

Mr. Backstay could not speak ; he was transfixed to the spot, and gazed upon the locket with an expression of countenance which showed the great anguish he was mentally undergoing.   As for Mr. Clarendon, he was in scarcely any better condition.

"Good God !" he exclaimed, at last, "can this possibly be ?   Who can have done so cruel, so sanguinary a deed ?   And yet it appears but too probable.   But what is the fate of my child ?   Still are we involved in the same dreadful mystery as we were at first."

"How shall I be able to support this terrible blow ?" said Mr. Backstay ; "how impart the intelligence to my wife and Fauchette, who loved the poor lad as dearly as if he had been our own flesh and blood ?"

"But still you are not yet certain that William has met with the fearful fate you anticipate," said Henry.

"Is not this a confirmation of it ?" demanded his father, in a deeply agitated voice, and pointing to the locket which he held in his hand.

" It is not, in my opinion," replied Henry.

" How came it here then?" asked Mr. Backstay.

" That certainly is most extraordinary and mysterious," returned his son.

" Mysterious!" repeated Mr. Backstay; " oh, Heaven! it is all but proof positive. William has fallen a victim to the bloodthirsty designs of some monster in human shape."

" What motive could any one have for such a deed?" said Henry.

" He may have been discovered by some of his relations, who may have been his enemies, and who might have considered it not safe to permit him to live."

" Or," remarked Mr. Clarendon, with a look of horror, " he may have been protecting my girl from outrage, and thus lost his life, and after all not have been able to preserve her."

" You say that Sir Julian Mordlington evinced the utmost confusion and hatred when he beheld William at your house?" said Mr. Backstay, eagerly, and addressing himself to Mr. Clarendon.

" He did," answered the latter, " and I could perceive his countenance changed colour, and his whole frame trembled, as if he had been struck by noticing him to bear a likeness to some person."

" Ah!" cried Mr. Backstay, " all this serves to excite my worst suspicions. Unfortunate young man, I am afraid that I shall never behold you again."

" Nay, my father, do not yet give way entirely to despair," said Henry.

" Alas! have I not ample cause? I have often thought of that Sir Julian Mordlington, and the extraordinary likeness he bears to the lad we rescued from the wreck, and who, there can be but very little doubt, afterwards attempted to murder William. Have you not noticed it, Henry?"

" Now you remind me," said the latter, after a pause, " I do remember that the baronet's features struck me when I first saw them as being familiar to me, but I was unable to form an idea as to where I had before seen them."

" Do you not think that there is a remarkable resemblance to the lad I have mentioned?" demanded Mr. Backstay.

" As well as I can call to mind the features of that lad, after the lapse of so many years, I do," answered Henry.

" If living, the young midshipman would also be about the same age as Sir Julian appears to be," added Mr. Backstay.

" I should imagine he would," coincided his son.

" Should they prove to be one and the same individual," said the farmer, " the fate of poor William may be easily accounted for."

" You know not that William is not yet in safety," observed Henry.

" True," answered his father; " but my heart entirely misgives me when I think of the occurrences of the night, and gaze upon these marks of blood, and this well known locket. He would never have parted with it but by force."

" But may he not have dropped it here by accident?" asked Henry.

" And what business had he in the hovel at all?" asked Mr. Clarendon, who had been for a short time standing in a state of anguish of mind and terrible thought of the most painful description.

" Curiosity might have prompted him to visit the hovel, in the hope of being able to have an interview with Marian, and to ascertain who she was," replied Mr. Backstay.

" The more we endeavour to form a conjecture, the more shall we become involved in perplexity," said Henry. " But let us quit this wretched place, and hasten to the farm to see whether William or Flora have returned."

Mr. Backstay shook his head hopelessly, and then without saying a word, he followed his son and Mr. Clarendon out of the hovel. They were all of them too deeply immersed in thought to permit them to enter into conversation, but their feelings were harrowed up to the greatest pitch of excitement and suspense, and with heavy and despairing hearts they made their way towards the farm of Mr. Backstay. In a short time they arrived there, but they were still doomed to be disappointed, nothing had been seen of either William or Flora Clarendon, and Mrs. Backstay and her daughter had entertained a similar hope to that which had brought them thither; namely, that the young mariner had met with Flora, and had accompanied her home to Clarendon Farm.

On hearing the particulars of their researches, and the disappointments they had met with, Mrs. Backstay and Fauchette were in a state of the utmost alarm. William they were as much attached to as if he had been really connected with them by the closest ties of consanguinity, and Flora was as much beloved by Marie as if she had been her own daughter, and Fauchette looked upon her with all the fervent regard of a sister. They were so closely assimilated by natural good qualities of heart, that no wonder such a mutual regard should spring up between them. What was now to be done? The hour was getting very late, and it was getting quite evident that something particular must have occurred, as they neither of them would have remained absent, knowing the anguish it would cause those who were so dear to them. All parties were in a state bordering on distraction, and the mystery of them both being missing, and yet not having been known to have been in company with each other, increased the perplexity, and added to their worst fears of what might have befallen them. What was now to be done? This was a question which no one was prepared to answer, and the horrors of that moment can be much better imagined than it is possible for the pen to do justice to it, in endeavouring to pourtray it. It seemed very evident to them all that something very particular had taken place; and when they remembered the marks of blood they had seen in the old hovel, and the discovery of William's locket, the most dreadful apprehensions were naturally entertained.

"Oh, my poor boy!" ejaculated Mrs. Backstay, wringing her hands, "you are certainly murdered. My God! the thought will drive me mad."

"And my child—my innocent Flora," exclaimed Mr. Clarendon, his blood running cold at the idea, and every nerve excited to the most insupportable pitch, "is there not every reason to fear that she has met with the same fate?"

"And yet," said Henry, "what monsters could have perpetrated so horrible a deed?—and what could have been their motives?"

"Alas!" returned Mr. Clarendon, "to what purport is it talking of motiv under such circumstances? Are there not plenty of villains who would not hesitate for a moment in committing such crimes from mere thirst of blood, much less the prospect of gain?"

"And what could they hope to gain from William and his lover?" demanded Henry, who, although his apprehensions fully coincided with those of the others, was willing to do all in his power to allay their fears, certain that it was only by maintaining their fortitude and self-possession they could hope to elicit anything like the facts.

"Has not my poor child before been subjected to an outrage, from which it is evident that some miscreant, whose passions have been excited by her charms, wishes to get her in his power?" said Mr. Clarendon; "a second attempt may have been made, and proved more successful."

"And," observed Mr. Backstay, in a state of the greatest mental agony, "should William have met her, it is but too probable, after what we have seen, that he has lost his life in her defence."

"Oh, God!" ejaculated the deeply-agitated Marie and her daughter, in a breath.

"Nay," interposed Henry, "it can answer no purpose to be thus premature in our alarm."

"But the marks of blood in the hovel," observed Mr. Clarendon.

"And the discovery of poor William's locket?" added Mrs. Backstay.

"Oh! are they not enough to create our worst, our most horrible surmises?" demanded Fauchette.

"But it was the hovel in which Crazy Marian seeks a shelter," said Henry.

"What of that?" demanded Mr. Clarendon.

"Supposing the lovers had met," continued Henry, "what could take them there?"

"They might have been forced there by the ruffians who attacked them," returned Mr. Clarendon, "as being a more convenient place to commit their hellish purposes without the fear of discovery. Or William and my poor Flora might have sought shelter there from the storm, which for a short time raged."

"How useless is it to harass our mind by all these dreadful suppositions," retorted Henry; "they can but unfit us for more active measures. Is it not just as likely that the unfortunate Marian may have been the victim whose blood we saw upon the floor of the wretched hovel?"

"But the locket of William," gasped Mrs. Backstay, "how came that there?"

Henry could return no answer to that question, and a pause of several moments ensued, during which the mental agony of all present was equal.

"Even Crazy Marian, as she is called," at length remarked Mrs. Backstay, "may be a guilty party in the plot, a creature belonging to some powerful villain, who only pretends to insanity for the purpose of better furthering her designs, or, rather, the designs of her employers."

No. 19

"Oh, no," returned Mr. Backstay; "I cannot believe that; I will not imagine that any person could so well act the hypocrite; especially a female."

"Alas!" observed Mr. Clarendon, "guilt too frequently obtains an ascendancy in the female as well as the male breast. The thought of Mrs. Backstay never occurred to me; but it is too important to be treated lightly. Should not William or my daughter return, we must endeavour to discover Marian, and try to elicit the truth."

"And what strengthens that suspicion," remarked Fauchette, "is the manner in which Crazy Marian has lately so often appeared before us, and in a manner that seemed as if she was watching our actions. Oh! this torture of suspense and uncertainty is dreadful."

"Have we not reason for the worst fears," said Mrs. Backstay, "after the mysterious disappearance of Mr. Fitzpatrick?"

"It is evident that there are some atrocious villains in the neighbourhood," observed her husband, "and that they will not shrink from the most daring outrages."

"And likewise," added Mr. Clarendon, "that they have some powerful miscreant at their head."

"Sir Julian Mordlington," remarked Mr. Backstay.

"Ah!" exclaimed Mr. Clarendon, "it was he who first insulted my poor child."

"And," added Mr. Backstay, "no doubt it was he who employed the ruffian who afterwards endeavoured to seize her, and from whom William rescued her."

"With the aid of Crazy Marian," remarked Henry, "which, at any rate shews that she was the friend of both, and not the enemy you appear to have taken her to be."

No one present could return any answer to this; the circumstance had for awhile escaped their memory, but the fact was so glaring, that they could not but afterwards admit that they had done poor Marian an injustice. They were completely lost in a dilemma as to the manner in which they should now proceed, but at length they determined to despatch a messenger to Clarendon Farm to ascertain whether anything had been there heard of the lovers. They awaited his return in the utmost state of suspense, and as the lateness of the hour seemed now to preclude all hope, the emotions of all the anxious waiters became most intolerable.

At length, after the lapse of half an hour, the messenger returned with the information that neither of the lovers had been to the farm, and that Mrs. Clarendon and her daughter were in a state of the greatest mental excitement and apprehension, and begged that Mr. Clarendon and Henry would return as soon as possible.

"They are lost! they are lost!" exclaimed Mr. Clarendon, "alas! our worst prognostications are all but verified."

"Compose yourself, I beseech you," said Henry; "if your wife or Helen see you in this state of agitation, it may be productive of the most serious consequences."

"What had best be done?" asked Mr. Backstay.

"Oh! God!" interrupted Mrs. Backstay, as her son was about to speak, "that this calamity should occur. Poor William and Flora are murdered. I shall go mad!"

"Murdered!" repeated her husband, although his fears were as strong as her own. "Nay, nay, it may not be so. We must not put the worst construction on the circumstances, or it will disable us from using that discretion that we should towards the unravelment of the mystery."

"What then had best be done?" asked Mrs. Backstay, in a state of the utmost anguish.

THE SMUGGLER KING.

"Nothing more can be done to-night," observed Henry; "we have searched every place that is likely they might have wandered to, and we must leave it to Providence, whether they return or not, praying that it may not turn out so bad as we anticipate, and endeavouring to acquire sufficient fortitude and self-possession to prosecute our inquiries with success to-morrow, which must be commenced at the earliest hour in the morning. In the meantime, we have heard from the messenger that has been despatched to the farm, that Mrs. Clarendon and my wife are in a state of the greatest alarm, and it is necessary that Mr. Clarendon and myself immediately return thither, in order to quiet them in the best way we can, or we know not what may be the consequences. Should any intelligence reach us, we will give you immediate notice."

"Poor Mrs. Clarendon and her daughter," said Fauchette, "what must be their sufferings?"

"Great as they undoubtedly are," observed Mr. Backstay, who was endeavouring, as much as he could to appease the apprehensions of his wife and daughter, although he laboured under as severe himself, "we must endeavour all we can to be equally composed and collected, to enable us, as Henry says, to meet the morrow with sufficient energy and self-possession. They cannot be greater than our own feelings on this occasion; but let us pray that all may turn out better than we at present anticipate. Return home, Mr. Clarendon and Henry, and as soon as it is daylight, we will meet again."

"Where?" demanded the deeply agitated Mr. Clarendon.

"Here," answered Mr. Backstay; "but there is one thing I would advise."

"What is that?" asked the former.

"That you do not make your wife or daughter acquainted with the discovery we made, respecting the signs of murder in the hovel, or the locket of poor William being found there," said Mr. Backstay.

"A wise suggestion," remarked Henry; "it would answer no other purpose at present than unnecessarily to increase their alarm and agitation, which already is no doubt very great."

"But they must ultimately be made acquainted with it," said Mr. Clarendon.

"I do not see the necessity of it," said Mr. Backstay, "but at any rate, I think it would be good policy at present to act in accordance with my advice."

"I will," replied Mr. Clarendon, "but I fear that I shall never be able to support the dreadful state of suspense into which this unexpected event has thrown me. My poor girl, my artless, innocent Flora."

"Courage, courage," said Mr. Backstay, "and hopeless as everything at present appears, let us trust in the mercy of Providence, who will ever protect the good and innocent from the snares and evil machinations of the guilty, although, for a time, they may seem to triumph."

"True," coincided Henry, "but let us depart, or Mrs. Clarendon and my wife will be alarmed at our protracted absence."

Mr. Clarendon, with a heavy heart, obeyed the advice of his son-in-law, and bidding the other persons a disconsolate good night, they departed to Clarendon Farm.

We will now return to the pirate vessel. It was night, and the moon was sailing through a bright ocean of fleecy clouds, and casting her beams in majestic splendour across the deep, revealing every object as distinctly as at noon-day.

Several of the pirates were assembled in the forecastle, while others were on the look out, expecting the arrival of their captain and Sam Raker.

"So, we sail to-morrow morning, Harry Hemlock," said one of the crew.

"Ay, and glad enough I am of it," answered Harry.

"Where do we sail to?" asked the first speaker.

" To the Death Rock," answered Hemlock.

" Where, I suppose it is the intention of our captain to deposit his fair prize."

" Yes."

" But the young seaman, what is it intended to do with him ?" asked Joe Scupper, as the fellow who had first spoken was called.

" Oh," answered Hemlock : " I don't know ; Sam Raker is our captain's confidant, not I ; but I dare say he will be made food for fishes, like the old lawyer."

" I hope not."

" Why ?"

" Because I believe that no luck will attend us, if we wantonly take the life of that young fellow. He is a brave, honest ——"

" Honest !" interrupted Harry Hemlock, with a look of scorn, " why, you have copied a lesson from the old lawyer."

" It would have been much better for me," said the other pirate, as he felt some qualms of conscience, " it would have been better for me, had I never learnt otherwise than to be an honest man."

" Ha ! ha ! ha !" laughed Hemlock ; " what, were you ever an honest man, Joe ?"

" I was an honest seaman," answered Scupper.

" Indeed,—and in what service were you ?"

" Some years on board a king's ship, and afterwards in the merchant service. I remember the last voyage I served, on board the Nancy Dawson, we met with an adventure with pirates."

" Pirates," repeated two or three of the crew, gathering round Scupper, with curiosity.

" Aye," answered the latter ; " and if you have no objection, my lads, just to while away a few minutes, I will relate it to you."

" Aye, aye," cried several of the crew ; " give it to us, Joe."

" Well, then," commenced Scupper, " you must know that the Nancy Dawson was as fine a craft, for a merchantman, as ever plunged the deep. The last voyage I performed in her, she was bound to India, with a valuable cargo of goods and a considerable quantity of specie. Nothing particular occurred to us, till just before doubling the Cape, when a suspicious looking craft was discovered, dead to windward, under a press of canvas, bearing down upon us. Our captain had a keen eye, and his experience soon enabled him to tell that she was a small light schooner, an acquaintance with which would not be altogether pleasant. We had few arms, and although our crew was true as steel, for a well armed pirate they were no match."

" I should think not," observed Hemlock, " but proceed, Joe."

" Feeling assured of this," continued Joe, " the ship was put away before the wind, and every rag of canvas packed upon her that she could bear. For a time the eye of our captain rested on his bending masts, covered with canvas to the very trucks ; it was then turned upon the gallant crew, who collected, having entire confidence in his skill and courage, and at last settled long and steadfastly on the chase.

" ' See,' he at length exclaimed, ' she gains—she gains upon us, and it will yet be many hours before it is dark.'

" You all know that a ship has the advantage of a small craft with a floating sheet, but yet the pirate gained upon us. The danger was pressing, was most imminent ; and at that moment a new and terrible enemy appeared. Far to leeward a black cloud rose slowly from the horizon, and gave but too surely an intimation of what might be expected shortly. Our ship could not shorten sail, for the chase would be upon her, and the captain's plan was instantly laid. Every man was ordered to his post. The heavens became more threatening every moment, but the pirate did not start a tack or sheet, as our captain hoped he would have done, and thus have allowed him to gain a little before the hurricane came on.

"And now the wind freshened—the masts yielded to the tremendous pressure which they had to sustain—the teeth of the stoutest seamen were set firm, in the apprehension that we should go by the board, while on the gathering tornado the keen eye of our captain was steadily fixed.

"In a short time it came—the ocean in the distance was white with foam, and he who was now before so quiet and unmoved, was now animated to tremendous exertion.

"'Let go all fore and aft,' he sung out in a clear and loud voice.

"In a moment he was obeyed.

"'Clew up and clew down,' he shouted.

"It was done.

"'Lay aloft.'

"This order was obeyed as promptly as the others had been. The flapping sails were quickly secured; the wind lulled, and the tornado was upon us, taking us aback. The ship fell off, she bent to the gale, until her yard-arms were in the waves. She began to move through the water, with a constantly quickened motion. The pirate, who was a clever fellow, and of quick penetration, in a moment saw the advantage he had. He was near two miles dead to leeward of us, and our vessel made greater headway under her poles than he did.

"It was evident that the hurricane could not last long, and when it passed over he would be close on board of us, and we must then have fallen an easy prey to him. Our gallant captain saw it all. There was but one fearful way to escape,—he had a gallant and staunch ship under him; she had not yet sprung a spar nor split a sail; he had an extremely valuable cargo, and his men, he could not see them strung up to the yard-arm on the principle that 'dead men tell no tales.' He therefore set his fore topsail, and close reefed main-top-sail, which urged the ship through the waters with greater speed.

"The little black pirate saw the plan, and attempted to make sail: but all would not do, and he saw that his only chance of safety was, if possible, to elude the shock at the very moment of the concussion which was expected. Our ship came down upon him with terrible precision.

"'Hard to port,' shouted the pirate to the helmsman.

"'Hard to port,' echoed our captain to his. It was a fearful moment; there was but one tremendous, one wild frantic shriek, and the pirates were all hushed in death."

"Poor fellows," ejaculated Hemlock; "they deserved a better fate. And is that the whole of your story?"

"It is," answered Scupper. "Is it not time that our captain and Sam Raker were on board?"

"It is," returned Hemlock, "but the moon shines almost too brightly for them, and they might be observed by some of the seamen on board the other vessels."

"Very true," said Scupper, "and perhaps in a short time the moon may go down again. Ah! by Neptune, no sooner have I spoken than it is done."

The empress of the night, which had before been shining so brilliantly, was indeed at that moment obscured by dense black clouds, and the night became as dark as pitch, and which did not seem likely again for awhile to disperse.

Presently afterwards the dashing of oars in the water was heard, and the dark shadow of a boat was just discernible on the surface of the water, approaching the vessel.

"They are coming," said Hemlock.

"I wish our captain was going to remain with us," said Scupper.

At that moment the boat, containing Sir Julian Mordlington and Sam Raker, came alongside (the former's person entirely concealed in a large cloak), and they quickly stepped on board. The smugglers greeted their captain in silence.

"Send for old Maud," he commanded.

"Ay, ay, captain," answered one of the men, and left the forecastle, almost immediately returning with the woman who had been deputed to attend upon the unfortunate Flora.

"Where is the girl?" he hastily demanded.

"Retired to rest," answered Maud.

"That is unfortunate," said he, "for I cannot see her, and it will be some days before I shall have an opportunity of doing so. But you are certain she is quite safe?"

"She is."

"And how does she bear with her captivity?" interrogated Sir Julian.

"Better than might have been expected, captain," answered old Maud.

"'Tis well," observed Sir Julian; "no doubt I shall soon win her to my will. See that she has every attention paid her, Maud."

"You may depend upon me, captain," answered Maud.

"And now, Hemlock," said Sir Julian, "how is the young mariner?"

"Safe in the cabin where he is confined," replied Hemlock.

"First then, to assume my disguise," said Sir Julian, "and then I must see him. Attend me, Sam."

Having thus spoken, the baronet and Sam Raker hastened to the cabin of the former, which was fitted up with much grandeur; and, having put on the dress which had so long concealed his person when engaged in his lawless traffic, they repaired to the cabin in which William was a prisoner.

William had in vain endeavoured to conquer his emotions at the situation in which he found himself. About his own fate he cared not, only on account of Flora and his friends, who, he was certain, would be in a state of distraction at his disappearance, and that dear girl, who loved him so fondly, would break her heart. Little did he imagine that she was at that time so near him, or his anguish would have been, if possible, even more severe. As it was, the agony of his mind was most intense.

"Poor Flora," he soliloquised, "what are now your sufferings? What the dreadful thoughts and apprehensions that beset thee at the disappearance of him you do so fondly love? Poor girl, poor girl, you will surely break your heart. Father, mother, Fauchette, too; what will be the dreadful agony that you will also undergo? I shudder when I think of it, and with difficulty can find patience to support this torturing captivity."

He paced the cabin with disordered steps, and beat his breast in despair. Then the melancholy fate of Marian, who had proclaimed herself to be his mother, crowded upon his recollection, and the sensations it created in his mind were of the most powerful and conflicting nature. Could she have spoken the truth? What interest could she have in telling a falsehood? Besides, an instinctive feeling told him that they were connected by the strong ties of nature, of consanguinity. But, after being so long deprived of a parent's fostering care; so long separated from her, to meet with but to behold her die an untimely death, and that too at the very moment when she was about to disclose the so long hidden secret of his birth, was more torturing than all. The manly-hearted young seaman was deeply affected by all these torturing circumstances, that he could almost have shed tears; but the agony of his bosom found no relief that way.

Thus for hours did William sit in gloomy meditation, or traverse the cell with hasty and disordered footsteps, while no one came near to interrupt him. He had been informed that he was in the power of smugglers and pirates ; that he was on board the much-dreaded Devil Skipper ; and from wretches like them, from miscreants who exulted in acts of barbarity, he could expect no mercy. He feared not death ; he had often faced it in many a fierce encounter ; but to meet with such a death as that he now contemplated, was more than he could view with any degree of patience. To die in the service of his king and country, he would not shrink from ; but to perish by the hands of murderers, was so revolting to every feeling, that when he reflected upon it, he could not help shuddering with the greatest horror.

At length, placing a firm reliance on the mercy of the Almighty, he became more calm, and awaited the issue of the event with patience and resignation. Hour after hour elapsed, and still no one came near him ; but he could hear from their boisterous laughter occasionally, that most of the smugglers were on board.

It was now night, and the hour was getting late, yet William felt not the least inclined for rest ; but, wrapt in meditation, he continued to pace the little confined cabin with disordered steps. It was most remarkable, he reflected, that the real character of the smuggler's craft had never been suspected, and, as she had hitherto escaped, it was not likely that she would now be detected while she remained in the harbour, and in consequence he had no hope of being released in that way.

The hour of midnight had now arrived, and William suddenly heard a great confusion on deck. It lasted for a few minutes only, and then all was again silent. Presently afterwards, however, he heard footsteps approaching the cabin, and the next instant it was opened, and Sam Raker entered, leading the tall figure of a man enveloped in a cloak. William started on first beholding them, but in a moment he resumed his composure, and, folding his arms, he stood firm and erect, and confronted his enemies with a bold look of contempt and defiance.

"So, my bold young mariner, my haughty brow-beater of those placed by rank above thee, thou art entrapped, caged at last," said Sir Julian Mordlington, for the person in the mantle, as the reader no doubt has guessed, was the baronet. "Thou art now in the fangs of the lion, and will find it no easy matter to escape from them. I come to bid thee welcome to the Devil Skipper."

"That voice !" exclaimed William, with a look of surprise, " I—I have surely heard it before. Tell me, who art thou ?"

"Thy bitter foe," answered Sir Julian, disguising his voice as much as possible.

"You have convinced me of that," said William, " or I should not now be placed under hatches in this infernal hell-craft !"

"You have rightly named it ; ha! ha! ha!" laughed the villain.

"Yes," observed Sam Raker, " and he will find the crew of the hell-craft as desperate a set of devils as Lucifer himself could wish for."

"Ha! ha! ha!" laughed Sir Julian, " well said, Sam Raker. But you have asked me who I am ;—behold !"

Sir Julian threw aside the mantle, which he had covered over him, and the Smuggler King stood before the astonished young mariner, attired in the manner we have before described, and his features concealed by the black mask.

"Need you now to be told who I am ?" demanded he. "Do you not tremble in the presence of the Smuggler King ?"

"I tremble in the presence of no man," returned William, with a look of the most ineffable scorn, " much less a miscreant like you are, whose deeds of bloodshed and the disguise you assume, prove you to be a coward as well as a villain."

"Bold words—bold words, these," said the smuggler, "but they have no effect on me ; you will shortly have reason to tremble before the power of him whose name is terrible to his enemies."

"Why have you brought me hither ?" demanded William.

"Because I hate you, and would sacrifice you to my hatred," replied Sir Julian.

"Villain !"

"True, that is one of my honorary titles," returned the smuggler, "and I glory in it."

"Why should you hate me ?—Why seek my life ?" asked William.

"I will tell you—I will relate to you a few facts," answered Sir Julian, "and then you may judge. A person of noble birth marries a lady of wealth and beauty. One son is the fruit of this marriage, and soon afterwards the lady dies. But a short time afterwards, but a few days after the remains of his wife have been consigned to the tomb, the gentleman becomes acquainted with another female, and a criminal intercourse follows. A second son is the consequence, upon whom the father lavishes the most unbounded fondness, while he scarcely deigns to notice his lawfully begotten offspring. Something occurs which causes a separation between the gentleman and his mistress ; the gentleman goes abroad, taking both the children with him. After remaining some two or three years abroad, he has occasion to return to England ;—the vessel is wrecked, and all perish except the two boys, and they ——"

"Ah !" interrupted William, who had been listening to the words of the smuggler with the most breathless attention ; "can it be possible?—And yet —"

"The story seems to interest you," observed Sir Julian ; "but hear me out. The boys were rescued by a fisherman."

"Gracious Heaven !" again said William, "it must be."

"The interest of my narrative increases," resumed Sir Julian ; "years fly away, and the lawful son naturally expects to come into possession of the whole of his father's wealth, and just at the very moment when fortune appears to be smiling propitiously upon him, he learns that his brother still lives, although he knows not his real name or origin. He also discovers that his father had made a will, in which he bequeathed an equal share of his immense fortune to the bastard."

"Ah !" ejaculated William, "and that boy ——"

"You are that boy, that detested boy," answered Sir Julian.

"And his brother ?"

"Stands before you."

"You—you !" exclaimed William, staring with astonishment and incredulity ; "can it be possible ? But our name ?"

"That will I not reveal," said Sir Julian ; "now see you not why I should have reason to hate you ?"

"But unacquainted with my real name, how could I injure you ?" asked William.

"The Smuggler King always makes his safety doubly secure, by removing those whom accident might place in a position to injure him," said Sir Julian.

"But, as you have admitted that the same blood flows within our veins, although my heart revolts from the association, surely you would not dye your hands in your brother's blood ?"

"I would have done so years ago, but was foiled in my purpose," replied Julian.

"Oh ! villain ! unnatural villain," exclaimed the young mariner, as he thought of Flora, and the dreadful state of anguish she would be in, did she but know the untimely fate with which he was threatened.

"Aye, you can call me a villain or any other name you please ; but, brother, I will never acknowledge a bastard !"

Indignation sparkled in the fine eyes of William at these words, and he clenched his fist, as he said,—

"Dare to utter that again, and even though my death follow the next moment, I will bury my fingers in your throat, and never release my hold until I have had your life. It is true that my birth is enveloped in mystery, but there is a certain feeling within me, that tells me I am no base-born mind; and although I am your prisoner, while my hands are still at liberty, that vile aspersion would give me double strength, and ——"

"Ha! ha! ha!" laughed Sir Julian, scornfully, "hear the idiot talk;— could I not in a moment stretch you dead at my feet? Are you not entirely in my power, and of what avail would all your puny efforts be? But I have something more to say to you. You love Flora Clarendon?"

"Love her," repeated William, and his fine manly countenance glowed with the powerful excitement of his feelings,—and when he thought upon the suffering she must already endure, and that which she was yet doomed to undergo, he exclaimed; "oh! Heaven!"

"There, we have nothing to do with Heaven here," said Sir Julian; "it is for that passion I hate you more than all."

"Why should you do so?" asked William.

"Because the girl has excited passions in my breast, which ——"

"In your breast!" interrupted the young mariner, with the utmost indignation.

"Yes," returned the smuggler-chief, "and those passions will be gratified too."

"Liar!"

"Ha! ha! ha! Fool! What if the girl should be even now within my power?"

"In your power!—No—no, the Almighty would never permit such a calamity."

No. 20

"What if I tell you that Flora Clarendon is already in my power?"

"I will not believe you."

"That she is on board this very vessel?"

"It cannot be."

"But she is. And of that you will shortly have a convincing proof," said the villain, with an expression of the utmost exultation.

William clasped his hands together with the greatest agitation, and then turning towards the smuggler, in a voice which plainly showed the deep mental agony he was suffering, he exclaimed,—

"You cannot speak the truth;—you—you say this only to torture me! But if you have one spark of humanity left within your breast, oh! convince me that Flora, my poor, innocent Flora, is no more, rather than that she is in your power."

"Ha! ha! ha!" laughed Sir Julian; "I thought I should find the way to break your stubborn spirit and to make you quail and tremble at the power of the Smuggler King. This is rare gratification to my soul! Once more I tell you that Flora Clarendon is in my power; that she is on board this vessel, and that in a short time she will become the bride of the Smuggler King. I will e'en permit you to live until after our nuptials, so that you may be present at them."

"Oh! God!" groaned the young mariner, while a feeling of the most horrible description pervaded his whole frame; "surely this cannot be true. Pirate," he continued, "my own life I value not; torture me as you please, fully satiate your vengeance on me; but if that poor girl is indeed in your power, do not, oh, do not harm her."

"Oh! no," returned Sir Julian, "the Smuggler King will not harm his bride."

"Have mercy on her, or rest assured, however much you may at present seem to triumph, the most terrible retribution will at some future period overtake you."

Sir Julian laughed scornfully, and then said,—

"I have now given you all the intelligence which I thought would be of interest to you, and will therefore leave you to the pleasures of meditation."

"Hear me!" implored William, who was now wrought up to a pitch bordering on frenzy.

"You have heard my will," said Sir Julian; "nothing can alter it."

"Oh! villain! villain!"

"You will be rewarded for all these gratuitous compliments, depend upon it, anon," remarked Sir Julian. "For the present, adieu; we shall see each other again, *brother*; ha! ha! ha!"

Thus saying the smuggler chief and Sam Raker quitted the cabin, leaving William in a state of mind which we feel at a loss to pourtray. This information, and he had no doubt but that it was true, was the severest blow of all; he threw himself disconsolately on a seat, and thoughts the most horrible crowded upon his brain. Despair settled upon his heart, and at that moment it would have been a mercy to the young mariner had he met with his death.

CHAPTER XII·

SAILING OF THE DEVIL'S SKIPPER.—THE LOVERS.—THE PIRATE'S TALE.—THE ATTACK. — THE MOMENT OF HORROR. — THE SENTENCE.—WALKING THE PLANK.

"WELL," observed Sir Julian, as he and Sam Raker quitted the cabin in which William was confined, "I think I triumph now."

"Indeed you do, captain," replied Sam; "you have tor red the mind of the young mariner rarely, and I do not think he will be able to sleep much after the interview."

" His misery is food to my soul," said Sir Julian ; " but keep a safe watch over his actions."

" You know that you have no reason to caution me, captain," replied Sam ; " you intend to let him live then ?"

" For the present."

" Is he also to be conveyed to the Death Rock ?"

" He is ; but should necessity require it, consign him to the deep," said the villain.

" I will."

" But I would rather that you should preserve his life for the present, until I can join you at the Death Rock, as I wish further to gratify my malice against one whom I so thoroughly detest."

" Am I allowed to let the lovers see each other ?"

" Yes," answered Sir Julian, " it will convince him that I have spoken the truth, and add to his torture."

" It will soon be daylight," said Sam Raker, " and we had better weigh anchor as soon as possible."

" True, but I wish I could have seen the girl."

" There is no possibility of that," observed Sam ; " but what time do you expect to join us at the Death Rock ?"

" In a fortnight at the latest," replied Sir Julian ; " I do not think it would be safe to leave this neighbourhood before."

" No; it might excite suspicion, and prevent you returning to this part of the country again."

" Let every attention be paid to the girl."

" Your orders shall be strictly obeyed," said Sam Raker.

" No doubt the disappearance of the lovers will cause the greatest excitement, and every inquiry will be made, to endeavour to find what has become of them."

" That there is sure to be," said Sam Raker, " but suspicion cannot well light upon you."

" I know not," said Sir Julian, " but even if it should, I am perfectly safe, as there is no one can prove that their suspicions are correct. But I must be going. Farewell, Sam, till we meet again. As soon as I have gone weigh anchor immediately."

" Aye, capta'n," said Raker, " that shall be done, for I am most anxious to get away from this neighbourhood."

" How astonished they will all be when they find that the Devil Skipper has quitted the harbour."

" They will, and perhaps then suspicion being excited, a pursuit may be commenced."

" It may, but they must be fast sailers that can overtake the saucy Devil Skipper."

Sir Julian now put by his disguise, and, accompanied by two of the smugglers, got into the boat, and was rowed to shore. He walked quick, and soon arrived at the Hall, without having been observed by any one.

" So, I triumph—I triumph," he soliloquized, when he had reached his own chamber ; " all those whom I had cause to dread are removed, and the girl is securely in my power. A short time only will elapse when I shall obtain the full gratification of all my desires, and Flora Clarendon will become the bride of the Smuggler King. Oh ! how anxious am I for that moment to arrive, when those pleasures which I have run so much risk to obtain, will be consummated."

In the meantime William was enduring the most acute mental anguish ; the events of the last hour, the disclosures that Sir Julian had made as to his birth, although the name of his father was still involved in mystery, filled him with the most extraordinary and conflicting ideas. That the villain had spoken the truth in some respects he had no doubt, for there were many parts of the narrative that he had given which corresponded with the statements of Marian; but he could not bring his mind to believe that he was the offspring of an illicit intercourse, neither could he scarcely credit that himself and Sir Julian were the children of one father. In the confusion of the moment, and the astonishment which the disclosures of the smuggler-captain had caused him, he had forgotten to endeavour to elicit whether Marian was really his mother; but it was more than probable that Sir Julian would not have satisfied him on that point. All these thoughts, however, were made to yield to the agonizing one that Flora was in the power of the miscreant Sir Julian, and the fate with which he threatened her, and which he would no doubt put into execution, unless some accident or intervention of Providence should rescue her from his power. How terrible must be the agony of the poor girl's mind at her situation, especially when she should be made acquainted that he was also the prisoner of the Smuggler King! He felt that to her death would be far preferable than her present hopeless situation.

Another thought that tormented his mind was, who the smuggler really was. When he had first spoken to him, the tones of his voice, as we have before shown, forcibly struck him as being familiar to him, but where he had before heard them he could not imagine, and the more he reflected, the more deeply did he become involved in doubt and perplexity.

He hurriedly paced the cabin, clasped his forehead, and gave vent to the feelings that predominated in his bosom in the most grievous exclamations. Then he uttered a prayer to the Almighty, that whatever might become of him, he would mercifully watch over and protect poor Flora from the evils by which she was surrounded, and to avert that dreadful fate with which she was at present threatened. His agitation increased instead of abating, and he sincerely and keenly felt for the sufferings of his friends at the mysterious disappearance of himself and Flora.

He was suddenly aroused from these thoughts by the confusion that prevailed on deck, and the voices of the smugglers, as they answered the commands that were given them by Sam Raker, and it was not long before he ascertained that they were about to weigh anchor. This certainty greatly augmented his anguish.

"Oh, gracious Heaven!" ejaculated the youthful seaman, " protect but my poor Flora from the danger with which she is surrounded at present, and whatever may be the fate in store for me, I am ready to submit to it without murmuring. Poor, dear, innocent girl, what must be your anguish? This fatal vessel is now under weigh, and before her departure is discovered, the wretches will be far out of the reach of pursuit. Mother, father,— for such I must still call ye, and as you have ever proved yourselves to me— Harry, Fauchette—all so endeared to me—alas! what will be your sufferings?—what the sufferings of the parents and sister of my soul's treasure? Oh, God! what a wreck will this act of villany cause!—and that from my brother!—brother! no, I discard the association. He is a miscreant, unworthy of the claims of kindred! It is impossible that the same being can have been our father. Reason revolts at the idea. A murderer by nature! —yes, did he not attempt my life when but a boy? His own admission, and the statement of my foster parents prove it, and his after actions prove that his delight is in bloodshed, in the misery of his fellow-creatures, for, had he not wealth in abundance, to prevent the necessity of his sinking to crime?—Yes, yes—oh, villain! But surely the avenging arm of an all-just God will overtake him—will prevent his triumphing over so much innocence and virtue! Flora, dear Flora, I will still hope that you will escape his atrocious designs, and could I be assured of that, death would to me present no terrors! Who can he be? I am certain that we have met before, but under different circumstances, and when he appeared in a far different character. He called me bastard! My heart spurns the vile aspersion! He calls himself bold, then why are not his acts of villany conducted without disguise? No, no—he is a cowardly wretch, and I still entertain a hope that he will be unmasked, and that he will not be allowed to triumph! Flora, my own Flora, would that I could be permitted to see you, to pour the balm of consolation into your afflicted bosom! Great God! she can never support this heavy trial; her reason must sink under it. My mother, too!—yes, an instinctive voice tells me that Marian was her who brought me into the world—oh, what a terrible fate has your's been! Mother, I shall be choked with the power of my emotions. Poor sufferer—poor injured one, for such I am certain you were, oh, may your sainted spirit intercede for your son, and those he loves, at the Throne of Grace, and avert the dreadful evils with which we are threatened."

Once more the youth threw himself upon a seat, and gave free vent to the intense agony of his feelings, and the thoughts that, like burning coals, rushed upon his brain. Again he started up, beat his breast, and paced the narrow confines of his cabin. With all the manly fortitude that he possessed, the tumultuous rush of feelings that poured like a cataract upon his mind, almost drove him to phrenzy.

The vessel was now gliding swiftly before the wind, and, before the morning, there could not be the least doubt but that she would be far out of the reach of pursuit. Each wave that he heard dash against the vessel's sides sounded more awfully to him than a death-knell, for it announced the certainty of Flora's misery, and the prospect of triumph to the villain in whose power she was.

"Lost! lost!" he exclaimed, in tones of the utmost despair; "the pirate barque glides over the blue waters like a phantom. She will reach her place of destination in safety, and then all chance of discovery is at an end. The Smuggler King, as he calls himself, has hitherto been perfectly successful in all his villanous undertakings, and there is every prospect of his being so in this. Oh, Heavens! sooner would I that a tempest should arise, and engulph us all in a watery grave, than that my poor Flora should survive to become the victim of such a monster."

He mounted on a chest, and now looked out of the cabin window, which was strongly barred, so as to prevent his escape that way, had he been inclined to have consigned himself to the deep, in preference to remaining in captivity, and meeting with the torturing fate that he had every reason to imagine the smugglers would consign him to. It was now broad daylight, and the golden monarch of the day was shining with unusual splendour, upon the broad expanse of waters. It was a magnificent scene; Nature was sporting in all her splendour, and, at any other time, the young seaman's susceptible heart would have bounded in delight and admiration at the glorious sight; but now, under his present melancholy circumstances, all that his eyes could rest upon appeared to wear an aspect of gloom. He sighed to gaze upon the unlimited scene of liberty, and know himself, and her he held far dearer than his own life, bound in the chains of a bondage than which nothing could be more terrible. He saw several vessels at a distance, and when at moments his heart would receive a faint beam of hope, it was immediately overclouded by the certainty that the pirates would be certain to have made use of such precautions as to render all suspicions of her real character impossible. To all appearance, she was a fair trader, and on an occasion of this kind it was not at all improbable that she would attempt any action that might prove her to be the contrary. She was a very fast sailer, and well constructed to brave the wind and the tempest.

"There is no hope," said William, "there is no hope; all is lost, and the fate of myself and my poor Flora, I fear, alas! is sealed. Would to God that a tempest would arise; such a fate would be far preferable than that to which we are doomed."

Away the Devil Skipper scudded on her rapid course, skimming the surface of the vasty deep like a thing of light and magic. It would seem as if it was the far-famed Flying Dutchman, and fully sanctioned the name which had been given to her by her villanous commander and his desperate crew. The heart of William drooped more every moment, as hope seemed further to recede from him. Naturally determined and firm as his heart was, he now became completely inactive, and gave way entirely to the power of despair, and the effect of the awful circumstances under which himself and Flora were placed. His thoughts alternately flew to home, to the home of Flora, and the anguish they crowded upon his brain is more than any language of ours can pourtray. The misery their friends, he was certain, were suffering, must be far worse than death; for they were in that dreadful state of suspense, doubt, and uncertainty, which corrodes the heart, and ulcerates the vitals more than all the horrors of certainty. What could they suppose had become of them? What course could they adopt to ascertain their fate? His imagination could point out none. The generous mind of the young seaman would not permit him to indulge in any selfish regret, his feelings were all excited for the sufferings of others, and those he pictured to his glowing imagination in the most awful characters. Never before had he experienced such thorough agony of mind.

At length he became somewhat more calm, and in the piety of his nature, he offered up a prayer to Heaven, in which he implored its protection for his lover, and that it would enable those friends that were so dear to them to meet the heavy trial to which they were then subjected, with fortitude. He was interrupted by the noise of the smugglers, who were evidently in high glee, from the frequent roars of rude laughter that escaped them, and occasionally oaths of the most awful description would meet his ears, coupled with the coarsest allusions to himself and Flora. The bosom of the young mariner glowed with indignation, and he had the greatest difficulty imaginable to support it with anything like patience, especially when he reflected on his own incapability of preventing or resenting it. He walked backwards and forwards in the most disordered manner, and then beating his breast, threw himself once more upon the seat he had before occupied, and gave way to all those intense feelings of indignation, agony, and shame, that rushed tumultuously upon his mind, and nearly drove him to madness. Had he but the means, he felt that he could at that time have braved the whole of the lawless and merciless wretches, and willingly would he have lost his life in hurling retribution upon their heads.

He was interrupted in these reflections by hearing the smugglers singing, and immediately afterwards he distinguished the following words :—

> " Over the deep, over the deep,
> The pirate's barque doth boldly sweep
> Fearless alike by night or day,
> She seeks her sure and destined prey.
> Merry and bold are the hearts we hold,
> Our stimulant the glittering gold ;
> And gold to our coffers we e'er must bring,
> While the subjects are we of the Smuggler King
> Over the deep, over the deep,
> The pirate's barque doth boldly sweep.

" Merry are we, merry we'll be,
 While we rule the empire of the sea ;
 No danger we fear, all power we dare,
 And the greatest of foes are we to care.
 And never so happy by half we feel,
 As when we are handling the cold bright steel ;
 And our foes to our feet we e'er must bring,
 While the subjects are we of the Smuggler King !
 Over the deep, over the deep,
 The pirate's barque doth boldly sweep.

" Merry we glide o'er the ambient tide,
 And danger we fearlessly deride ;
 With courage we're rife, we glory in strife,
 And the ocean we prize above all in life.
 The land-sharks may growl, at them we scowl,
 While after our prey we dauntlessly prowl ;
 We laugh and we sing, while care takes wing,
 For the subjects are we of the Smuggler King !
 Over the deep, over the deep,
 The pirate's barque doth boldly sweep.

GENERAL CHORUS.

" Over the deep, over the deep,
 The pirate's barque doth boldly sweep ;
 Fearless alike by night or day,
 She seeks her sure and destined prey.
 Merry and bold are the hearts we hold,
 Our stimulant the glittering gold ;
 And gold to our coffers we e'er must bring,
 While the subjects are we of the Smuggler King !
 Over the deep, over the deep,
 The pirate's barque doth boldly sweep."

The most uproarious applause followed this chorus, and it seemed as if the smugglers were determined to keep up their revelry to the utmost pitch. William listened to the wretches with feelings that we have no occasion to attempt to describe, and his fears for the situation of Flora in the power of such ruffians, notwithstanding the strict injunctions which their captain had given them to behave with kindness and attention to her, increased. What would they not hesitate to do ? No crime, however base ; and all that would, he felt convinced, restrain them from going to the greatest extremity, was the fear they entertained of offending their commander.

We will now return to the deck of the Devil Skipper, where Sam Raker and the principal portion of the other smugglers were assembled, and enjoying themselves in the manner we have described.

" Bravo, my lads," said Sam, " I like to see you merry."

" Merry," returned Hemlock. " What is to prevent our being so, now we are once more ploughing our native element ?"

" Yes," observed another of the ruffians ; " but I would much better prefer it if we were allowed to be in actual service, instead of conveying this young seaman and the girl to the Death Rock."

" Pshaw !" ejaculated Sam Raker, " we ought not to grumble at anything we are performing in the service of our captain."

" I do not grumble, Sam, but —"

" There," interrupted Sam, " let us have no buts ; let us have another allowance of grog, and then, if it is agreeable, I will give you the story I promised you."

" Aye, aye, the yarn, Sam, the yarn," exclaimed several voices.

" It is rather a long one, " observed Raker, " and I must well whet my whistle before I begin. It may serve to while away the time, while our saucy craft is gliding on her way to the place of her destination."

The grog was served round, and then Sam Raker commenced his narrative, which we give below, though not in the same words as he delivered it :—

THE PIRATE'S TALE.

" On the coast of England, some years since, there resided in a beautiful little cottage, situated in a most romantic spot, an old officer in the army, Lieutenant Freegrove, who had retired on half-pay, and who had an only daughter, as fair as Hebe, about seventeen, named Eugenia. She was all that could be wished for in woman, lovely, accomplished, gentle, and virtuous, and the comfort of her father's declining years. He had been a widower for some time when this narrative commences, and he looked up to his daughter as the only charm which held him to life.

" It was on the occasion of Eugenia's birth-day, when her father had caused it to be celebrated by a little rustic festival, that she was introduced to a young man, who called himself Edward Somerton, and who made himself so agreeable, and won so much upon the good opinion of the lieutenant, that he was warmly invited to renew his visit to their residence on the following day. This he accepted with evident pleasure, and from that time he became a frequent guest, and insinuated himself not only into the esteem of Mr. Freegrove, but that of Eugenia. He was, indeed, a most prepossessing and intelligent young man ; he had been at sea, and the vivid descriptions he gave of naval engagements, and the various countries to which he had been, quite charmed the ears of his listeners. Day after day elapsed, and Edward Somerton was almost a constant visiter at the residence of Lieutenant Freegrove, and every time he came he became a greater favourite with Eugenia. They wandered to the woods together, picked shells from the sea-shore, and watched the moon's rising and the sun's setting together ; and the result was that Edward soon loved her with the most impassioned ardour, and although she could not feel the same warmth of sentiment, she promised him that if he would treat her tenderly, no other person should ever possess her affections.

" We should have mentioned that there was an inmate of Lieutenant Freegrove's house, a young man, whom the former called Raymond, and whom he had brought from abroad, and adopted as his own son, as he knew not his origin. Raymond's sole pleasure was the society of Eugenia, and he felt a delight in studying, to the best of his power, to gratify her every wish, but since the stranger had visited there he had been supplanted in his attentions, and those feelings he had formerly entertained had been converted into those of the most bitter hatred and revenge against Edward. The latter had sought, by every means in his power, to conciliate his friendship, but in return he met with nothing but scorn, and his not being a nature to bend, the attempt was not again repeated.

" Thus went on affairs, when one day Edward informed his friends that he must, for a few weeks, leave them, as he was about to proceed to France.

" Lieutenant Freegrove could not help expressing his regret at this determination, and he endeavoured to persuade him to consider his house as his home whenever he thought proper to remain in their neighbourhood. The grief of Eugenia at this separation was very great, and before they parted he extorted from her an oath that, should he be absent for months, or even years, she would never love another ; and he further added, that she should know no happiness in her broken faith, no peace in his bosom for whom she might reject him. She had no sooner sworn than Raymond stood before them, his features distorted with passion and with some expression inarticulate from rage, he rushed forward to where Edward stood,

encircling the waist of Eugenia. He raised his clenched hand as though to strike, but his arm was seized, and he was hurled back by the muscular grasp of Edward. Presently he again sprung to his feet, and was about to re-commence the attack, when Eugenia interfered, and upbraided Raymond for presuming to insult the guests of her father; he made some savage reply, and he then retired from the garden, casting a look of hatred upon Edward, which the latter returned with one of scorn.

"Raymond passed that night upon the sea-shore. He scowled around on the tranquil night; his heart cursed the bright moon and the twinkling stars; all externally was calm, whilst within his bosom all was anarchy and strife. He threw himself on the sands, in the shadows of an immense rock, to indulge the thoughts that agitated him, when he was suddenly surprised into watchfulness by a shrill whistle that broke through the silence of the night. He directed his eyes towards the spot from whence the sound came, and saw a boat, with several rowers in it, which had just rounded a headland, and lay in the very shadow that concealed himself. The whistle was repeated, when two men, enveloped in large naval cloaks, emerged from amongst the rocks into the broad moonshine. One was silver-headed, and the other, a young man, wore a tasselled cap, hanging down on one side, whilst from the other, his hair, which was black as jet, hung in curls. They were buried in profound conversation, but it was some time before Raymond could overhear what they said, although, his curiosity being greatly excited, he listened attentively.

"'It is no use going on in this manner any longer,' at last said the elder one to his companion. 'We want money, and money we must have, that's all about it; we haven't had anything like a run for months past; so I advise that we make a prize of the first vessel we can lay hold of, and turn pirates.'

No. 21

"The other was about to make some answer to this, when, as he was stepping into the boat, he felt himself suddenly seized from behind, and immediately afterwards he was struggling in the water. The elder one fired his pistol at the figure, and, springing into the boat, dragged his companion after him, at the same time exclaiming,—

"'Away, my lads, we have no time to lose. Pull away; the land-sharks are on to us.'

"They needed no second command, but plying themselves briskly to the oars, they cleared the headland in an instant. In a few minutes, a small white vessel expanded its white sails to the breeze, and bounded across the moonlit waves.

"Some weeks passed away, and Eugenia experienced all the melancholy that a separation from her lover could possibly engender. He had not returned, and she had now no companion in her solitude; for Raymond was almost constantly by the sea-side, and nothing could induce him to accompany her in her rambles as he had before done.

"She was sitting one morning in the garden, when her father entered with an open letter in his hand, and informed her that they must instantly hasten to France, where his sister was lying at the point of death, and who had something of importance to communicate to him. At first Eugenia expressed a wish to remain behind; but, remembering that was her lover's place of destination, she changed her mind, and most gladly consented to accompany her father. The following afternoon found them, with Raymond, between a scowling sky and a rolling sea. The vessel was crowded with ladies and gentlemen hurrying to France. The wind lay dead against them; dark broken masses of cloud rushed madly on, the rain descended in torrents, and the waves ran mountains high. It was not long ere night overtook them. Eugenia was sitting in the cabin, pale with terror; her father had just left her to go upon deck, when she suddenly felt a shock as though the vessel had struck and every plank was rending; then a confused noise above her head, trampling of feet, blows and groans smote her ears. The hatches were opened and closed again, as though the descent was disputed. Raymond rushed from the cabin, Eugenia, with several of the passengers, followed. It was some minutes before they could get upon deck, and when they did, their eyes encountered a scene of the utmost horror. The night was pitchy dark; the white-crested waves were hurrying by, and breaking over the bows of the vessel, which was held fast on the larboard side by the grapnels of a small schooner, from which twenty or thirty men, with torch and cutlass, had rushed on board. A man tried to seize Eugenia; she eluded him, and running towards the stern, nearly fell over the body of her father, who lay bathed in blood. By this time all the passengers had left the cabin, and were plundered indiscriminately. Some men approached Eugenia (who was endeavouring to restore her father, he having only fainted from the loss of blood) with the intention of plundering her; but Raymond defended her heroically; one he knocked down with his fist, and another he felled with a marline-spike. A pistol was levelled at his breast, when a dusky form, leaping from the schooner, dashed it down, and, in a voice of authority. ordered all instantly on board. Eugenia sprang upon her feet, and rushed forward to the speaker. A gleam from a torch fell on his features, and she uttered a loud shriek on recognising the features of Edward Somerton. With the ferocity of a wolf Raymond bounded forward, and fastened on his throat.

"'Idiot!' exclaimed Edward, as with the hilt of his cutlass he struck him from his hold. 'Aboard, every one of you.'

"In a moment the grapnels were cast off, and the private vessel dashed impetuously through the whirling gulph of the black waters.

"In a short time Lieutenant Freegrove recovered from the effects of his wound ; he found Mr. Emmett, his brother-in-law, partially restored, but still in imminent danger. Since the death of his wife, Mr. Emmet had held no correspondence with the lieutenant, and was now only induced to write because he had no other person in whom he thought proper to confide, and whom he could trust to fulfil his request. He seemed fearful every moment his end should arrive before he had time to divulge the secret which weighed upon his mind, and, therefore, he lost no time in making Lieutenant Freegrove acquainted with every particular. He informed him that he had a son, who was left in his infancy without a mother; that he took him with him to India, travelling under an assumed name, to avoid his creditors—as he was at that time much embarrassed—and leaving behind him a poor girl, whom he had ruined, with another son. As a punishment to him for his treachery, his favourite was stolen from him, as he supposed, by a wandering tribe, and he could never learn anything of him. He amassed wealth, but it could not render him happy, and he soon quitted India to return to England, resolved to make atonement to her whom he had abandoned ; but he searched for her in vain. He then became a perfect misanthrope, and wrote to his brother-in-law only fearing the approach of death, and to beg of him, should he by any possibility obtain news to lead to the discovery of his children, to restore to them the property he had so long possessed with a breaking heart. The only clue he could give to his favourite child, were the initials S. M., the initials of the name he had adopted, pricked in his neck by the sailors of the vessel that carried them to India, and which he had expressed a wish to have done ; but what the name was he went by he forgot to mention, and Lieutenant Freegrove, at the time, forgot to ask. Of the other he entertained a very slight recollection, but his mother was a tall, handsome woman, of the name of Emily Mortimer. The lieutenant promised to do all that Mr. Emmet required of him. Eugenia, a few days after this disclosure was made to her father, was rambling along the beach, when she was suddenly accosted by some woman, who was habited as a gipsy, and who requested that she would accompany her, as she wished to impart something particular to her. Eugenia, feeling no apprehension, complied, and she led her from the beach through a deep wood, and descending some distance a dark and narrow dell, completely shadowed by bushes and trees, she pushed aside the dark foliage, and bidding her companion follow her, they soon found themselves at the door of a little thatched cottage, the dark branches nearly concealing it from view. One half of it was embedded in a huge rock, and before the front two trees grew to a prodigious height, their giant arms forming a screen above it.

"This dismal spot filled Eugenia with some alarm, and she now, for the first time, began to entertain some suspicions of her guide's intentions ; but it was now too late to recede, and she therefore followed the woman into the cottage. She was greatly astonished on beholding the elegant manner in which it was furnished ; mirrors hung round the painted walls, a carpet, that would have graced a drawing-room, covered the floor, and ornaments were profusely, though tastefully arranged round the apartment. Her surprise was increased, when the female, throwing off her disguise, appeared habited in a rich dress, and adorned with many articles of jewellery.

"Having suffered Eugenia to indulge in her astonishment for some time, the woman asked her if she had a wish to see into her future fate ; to which Eugenia replied, that the woman had told her she had something to reveal, and that if she really had, to let her know it, and not trifle with her by asking her if she had a wish to learn what it was not in the power of mortal to divulge.

"The gipsy told her that she would quickly convince her to the contrary, and went on to say that her uncle had two lost sons, whom he wished to find, but that when he did so, it would be a wretched day to him. She then, in forcible language, related the story of the ruined damsel's wrongs; that she had tracked her seducer over the many leagues he had traversed, filled with feelings of revenge. She followed and purloined his son, but lynx-eyed as she was, the stolen boy eluded her, and filled with disappointment and revenge, she reached France. Yet, in the bosom of her own son, she instilled those bitter feelings of vengeance that inhabited her own, and he vowed to revenge a mother's tears in a father's blood. To effect this he herded with men from whom he might never fear to hear a word of contempt. He embraced the hazardous life of the deep, and lived like the gull in the midst of storm. Having stated this much, a silence of some minutes ensued, during which Eugenia evinced considerable alarm. The gipsy then informed her that she too had a lover, whom she found where she least expected; but that Eugenia's vow of fidelity should be broken to him; that the sea was his home, his ship his bride, and that although he loved her, he loved vengeance better.

"She had scarcely given utterance to these words, when Eugenia was startled by a rustling sound at the further end of the apartment, and the next moment, Edward Somerton stood before her. He wore a surtout of blue, buckled round the waist with a rich belt, and open on the breast, which was covered with an embroidered velvet vest. A rich hilted sword hung by his side, and gold-mounted pistols were in his belt. He strove to take her hand, but she withdrew it.

"'So cold, so disdainful,' he said; 'what is the meaning of this? Remember your oath, and come to a neighbouring chapel, where we will be united.'

"'Never,' answered Eugenia, 'never will I become the bride of a man who revels in the plunder got by his myrmidons, who shed the blood of the innocent to obtain it,—those very wretches who cut down my own father to get his gold, and, as an atonement, I suppose, an offer is made to his daughter to share it with their captain.'

"Edward could no longer restrain the expression of his rage at this speech; he strode hastily across the apartment several times, and then, turning to Eugenia, he said,—

"'Headstrong girl! of what utility is this opposition to my purpose? Are you not in my power, and at one word from me, you would be conveyed on board my vessel, in which you would be wafted many miles beyond the reach or knowledge of your friends? And even should they discover you, where is there one who would be hardy enough to attempt to rescue you?'

"'Villain! I would!' exclaimed a loud and well-known voice, and the next moment the room-door was forced back upon its hinges, and Raymond entering the cottage stood boldly before the pirate.

"This turned the current of Edward's fury; he saw before him the man for whom he believed he had been rejected, and whom of all others he thoroughly detested; and with an exclamation of revenge, he rushed upon him, and grappled with him. They long struggled, and pressed each other's throats till their eye-balls started, their lips turned purple, and the blood trickled from their nostrils. At length the gipsy sprung forward, and snatching a pistol from Edward's belt, and seizing Raymond by the collar, she levelled it at him, and was about to discharge the contents, when the action having exposed his throat, her eyes fell upon the letters S. M. on his neck.

"The pistol fell from her hand, and dashing in between them, she said,—

"'Ah! behold! the lost one is found! 'Tis he! 'tis he!'

" Edward quitted his hold; Raymond fell back, and looking on her, seemed to be endeavouring to recollect some long forgotten circumstance.

" With the utmost astonishment, Eugenia looked on, but recollecting the letters her father had mentioned, in Raymond she discovered her long lost cousin.

" The gipsy gazed on him in sorrow; she stood in the middle of the room, her hands pressed to her burning temples, whilst the big tears rolled thick and fast from her fixed eyes; she swung gently backwards and forwards, one foot advanced, and her black hair, with here and there a streak of silver, wildly hanging on her shoulders.

" While they thus stood, a whistle was heard to proceed from the outside of the cottage. Edward gazed upon the gipsy, who still stood in the same position, then advancing towards Eugenia, in a bland manner, he said,—

" ' Dear Eugenia, I pray you to forgive me, for behaviour so culpable, and which the impetuosity of my passion alone hurried me into; if you wish now to depart, Elspa will attend you.'

" With these words, having bowed to her, and casting a look of the utmost hatred on Raymond, Edward retired to the back of the cottage and immediately disappeared. A few moments of silence followed, when the gipsy habiting herself as she had before been, led them from the cottage. After proceeding to some distance along the dell, she pointed the path out to them, and taking the brooch from her bosom, placed it in Eugenia's hand, and whispering, ' Let Mr. Emmet see it,' left them, and plunged into the thickest part of the wood.

" It was now dusk, and therefore they made what haste they could to reach home, Eugenia in advance, the path being too narrow to admit of them walking abreast; when, as she was emerging from the wood, she turned round and missed Raymond. She called, and went a short distance back, but being afraid to venture far, she hurried home, and made her father acquainted with what had happened to her.

" The lieutenant felt the greatest surprise that the youth he had so long sheltered, and who had saved his life in a skirmish in Egypt, should prove to be his brother's son. He frequently had questioned him about his parents, but all that he could recollect was, that his father's name was Marchmont, and had resided in India, and said he had been stolen by gipsies from a woman, who had previously purloined him when very young, from his father; but he had escaped from them, and begged Lieutenant Freegrove to accept him as his servant. He instantly sent servants in quest of him, but no tidings could be heard of him that night.

" The following morning the lieutenant contented himself by merely saying to his brother he thought he had gained a clue to one of his sons. He then proceeded, conducted by Eugenia, to endeavour to find the cottage; but all their efforts were entirely unsuccessful; the bushes were so impervious, that they baffled all their attempts.

" They were compelled to return, although it was not without the greatest reluctance that they did so. Mr. Emmet very anxiously inquired whether they had succeeded, and he expressed the greatest disappointment when he was made acquainted with the result of their journey. Raymond he had never seen, as the lieutenant had not introduced him, in consequence of his illness, and the great objection which he always expressed to seeing strangers.

" In the course of the morning, Eugenia, according to the gipsy's instructions, showed her uncle the brooch, but no sooner had he cast his eyes upon it, than he snatched it from her eagerly, and gazing at it minutely for some minutes, he exclaimed,—

"' Almighty God! what miracle is this? Oh! well do I remember this trinket; it was my gift to the deeply injured Emily on the night when we separated. But, oh! this is torture beyond endurance; after discovering the son I have so long lost, to be thus again deprived of him. But it is a punishment I justly merit, although it is severe.'

" Ever after that day, Mr. Emmet rapidly improved in health and spirits, and was so far recovered as to be able to walk round his grounds. Accompanied by Eugenia, he was sitting in an arbour looking on the brooch and listening to her oft-repeated account of her interview with the gipsy, when suddenly he was startled by observing the shadow of a person pass the window of the arbour, and in the next instant the form of the gipsy, Elspa, stood before them, although her countenance was carefully concealed by the hood of her cloak.

"' That bauble seems to attract your particular attention,' she said, addressing herself to Mr. Emmet; " but what see you so remarkable in it? Does it pourtray the woes and trials the receiver underwent? Does it tell of the morning tear that she has shed, or the midnight vow of vengeance that she has breathed? Tells it of the tireless animosity with which she followed your footsteps from her native country, to the home of the savage and uncivilized? Does it tell how she has watched and followed you step by step, with the untiring zeal of a sleuth-hound, with the vengeful, vigilant eye of the eagle,—and what for? Shall I tell you? It was for vengeance! Yes, it was a deadly revenge she sought on the destroyer of her virtue, the blaster of all her prospects; the destroyer of her peace of mind; the fell witherer of all her joys. Does it tell of your own base perfidy to a poor orphan whose only crime was love? Tell me, does your own conscience acquit you of unkindness to Emily Mortimer?'

" As she gave utterance to these words, in the most vehement tones, she threw by her cloak, and revealed to her penitent seducer, the being he had so deeply wronged.

"' Oh, Emily!' ejaculated Emmet, as he sank upon one knee, ' pardon, I beseech you, pardon me; all I have in the world, I freely offer you as some atonement for the wrongs I have done you; do not, oh, do not reject my offer. Name your will, and whatever it may be, should it be in my power, I swear to grant it.'

"The greatest pleasure and exultation now appeared to sparkle in her eyes, and her bosom heaved with delight, when she gazed at her repentant lover kneeling in humble and earnest supplication at her feet. In a few moments her countenance changed, and as a scornful smile played around her lips, she muttered forth,—

"' Ah! then, my prayer has been heard. The proud bends to the humble.'

" And now Mr. Emmet attempted to take her hand, but she stepped back, and in a voice, which showed the real nature of the feelings that were passing in her mind, she said,—

"' Touch me not! I command you, touch me not. This is the land of the stranger; yonder is England. There, where my poor cot stood, do you repair, and on that spot shall you do justice to her whom on that spot you injured; till then my revenge will be incomplete. There you will find your offspring, my offspring, I should say; but shun him, avoid him, as you would a pestilence, for I have instilled in his mind the direst revenge, day and night, and should he discover you, your blood will be shed to wash out the stain you have cast upon him.'

"' For the love of Heaven!' cried the distracted gentleman, 'let me but behold him, and I will submit to be his slave for the rest of my days. I, his father, will bend to him, if he will but grant me his forgiveness. Tell me, Emily, know ye aught of my other, my fair-haired boy?'

" A look of malice and hatred passed over the strongly marked features of Emily as she replied,—

" ' Yes, that boy was the favourite, and for him mine was abandoned, and his mother left to misery and shame; and if you gain but him, I and mine may still wander on neglected. It was I who purloined him from you in India, but lost him again shortly afterwards by the same means. Once more he has fallen into my hands, and now for the vengeance I have so long sought.'

" ' Oh, Emily !' cried the deeply agitated father, ' you surely will not, cannot harm him.'

" Most remarkable was the expression of Emily's countenance, as she repeated,—

" ' Harm him ! you yet know not Emily; no, mine will be a nobler revenge.   Behold !'

" She stepped from the arbour, and the next moment presented Raymond to his father.   They rushed into each other's arms, and both evinced the greatest emotion, which choked their utterance for several minutes, while Emily stood by and gazed upon them with feelings it is beyond the power of any language to describe.

" When they had partially recovered from their transports of joy, Emily inquired how it was that Raymond found her in the cottage, and left her so mysteriously in the wood ?   He informed her that he was near her when she was accosted by Emily, and being somewhat surprised at her following her, and apprehensive lest any harm should come to her, he proceeded cautiously after them, and listening at the door of the cottage, he over-heard the whole of the conversation that passed between them.   On their leaving the cottage, Raymond heard some whispering among the bushes, and stopped to listen, when he was suddenly seized, gagged, and hurried into the presence of Edward Somerton.   He threw him down a cutlass, and told him to defend himself; but Emily once more interposed, parted them, and then disclosed to Raymond the secret of his birth.

" Mr. Emmet now once more most cordially and gratefully thanked Emily, and again offered to take her hand, but she withdrew it.

" ' Never !' she said, ' in this country; in the land of my birth, should we ever reach there, I am yours; but, oh ! we have a sea to cross, over which skims a fearful and revengeful spirit, which it has been my greatest care and delight for years to foster ; but now my heart, which I had flat-tered myself was tutored sufficiently in revenge to exclude all tender emotions, breaks forth in its former folly, and tells me that it still inhabits a woman's breast—yet there is the only spot where we can be again reconciled.'

" ' I will agree to anything you propose,' said Mr. Emmet, ' and am prepared to go to England immediately.'

" ' To England, away then,' cried Emily, as she darted from the arbour, and swiftly threaded the winding paths of the garden.

" Mr. Emmet immediately made up his mind, and fixed upon the day of his departure.   It proved wild and stormy, and so high did the surf run, that although he offered a liberal sum, he could not prevail upon any of the men to run him over to Dover.

" While he was thus hesitating, and in doubt whether he should be able to succeed in commencing his voyage, a man, whose countenance was not of the-most prepossessing character, being nearly covered with black whiskers, and whose costume consisted of a huge slouch hat, pea jacket, and very wide canvass trousers, undertook to convey them to where they wanted to go.

" In a short time they were buffeting about in the sea, with three or four stout seamen, and a good boat.　Their pilot was a very taciturn man, scarce deigning to answer a question put to him, and his men partook of their leader's lack of loquacity.

"When they had proceeded nearly half way across the channel, and it was becoming more dark every minute, though the waves were somewhat less turbid, a vessel suddenly appeared, bearing down upon them.

"Lieutenant Freegrove inquired of the pilot, what he thought of her, and if he supposed her to be a fair craft; to which he very coolly made answer, that he believed her to be a free-trader.　He then asked what her object might be?　'Plunder,' was the answer he received.　'But,' asked Mr. Emmet, 'is it not possible for us to avoid them?'

"'It is not,' answered the pilot; and by this time the vessel had approached close enough to hail the little boat, and, in a few minutes, was alongside.

"Mr. Emmet cast his eyes aloft, and saw its crimson flag bore the figure of an eagle, with outstretched wings, and bending its fierce eyes below, seemed ready to pounce upon him.

"'Ah!' he ejaculated, 'what means this?'

"'Means!' repeated the pilot, 'I will tell you; it means that the eagle sees quarry.　Yon vessel is a pirate schooner, and I, Edward Somerton, am its captain, and your sworn enemy.'

"At the same moment he threw by his disguise, and appeared habited as Eugenia had seen him in the cottage.

"'Alas!' said Mr. Emmet, 'what have I done to make you my foe?'

"'Villain!' shouted the pirate, in a voice of thunder, 'what have you not done?　Have you not slurred my fame—made me an outcast—a victim to my passions, and amenable each instant to the laws of my land?　I have lived a life of hardships and of scorn, contemned by those who could boast of what I had never known; contemning all who were not branded as myself, for this one sole moment of bliss, for this one glorious moment of vengeance.　What, are you craven-hearted, too?　Would you mould your lips into an expression of mercy?　For the mercy you showed to the unprotected orphan, Emily Mortimer, I thus reward you.'

"Instantly the dreadful dead was perpetrated, and before any one could interfere to prevent him, the pirate's murderous dagger was buried to the very hilt in the breast of the unfortunate Mr. Emmet.　Not contented with what he had already done, he was about to repeat the blow, when at that moment a female form leaped from the schooner, and arrested his arm, and, while she gazed, horror-stricken, on the fast ebbing tide of life, she exclaimed, in a voice dreadfully calm,

"'Wretched, wretched being, you have murdered your father!'

"'The dying man was immediately roused by these words, and suddenly looking up, he faltered out, in a faint voice,

"'Father!　Is this my son?　No, no,' he said, 'his name was ——'

"'Yes,' interrupted Edward, 'I would not be beholden for a name to a mother's weakness, or a father's perfidy, and so I chose for myself.'

"In a moment a more ghastly expression than before overspread the countenance of the ill-fated Mr. Emmet, and his head sunk upon his breast, as he murmured out,

"'Wretched, miserable parricide.'

"Then, turning to Emily, he, with difficulty, said,

"'Emily, adieu!—my death approaches—forgive, and pray for ——"

"He could say no more; his eyes closed, and after a slight tremor, that was for an instant visible over his frame, his soul was summoned before the awful tribunal of his Almighty Judge.

"The expression of Edward's countenance was almost fiendish, and he

gazed upon the body of his murdered victim with the most dreadful and unnatural feelings of delight.

"'Oh! this is a moment of glorious triumph—more sweet than any I have before experienced.'

"'Alas!' said Emily, 'you have fulfilled the task allotted to you too truly. I long since repented of the lessons I had given you, or long ere this I could have enabled you to take your revenge; but you have discovered him, and, as I feared, so it thus ended. Yet do I not hate you. Why should I?—you did but as I had instructed you, and though my foolish heart still clings to its ruin, it cannot surpass the strength of maternal affection.'

"For one moment she quitted the body of the murdered man, to embrace and kiss her son, then turning to where the body of Mr. Emmet lay, she raised him in her arms, and in a moment, and before any one could start forward to prevent her, she sprung into a huge billow that seemed to have rolled itself purposely by the side of the bark to receive her.

"It would be impossible to describe the feelings of all present, especially Raymond, while this dreadful scene was being enacted. With looks of distraction he saw the waves receive the body of that parent whom for so short a time he had known, and then, turning to the murderer, he said,

"'Villain! since you have taken my father's life, yield your own, or augment your guilt by adding to it that of a brother.'

"'I agree to your suggestion,' boldly answered Edward, 'and let he who survives possess Eugenia for a bride.'

"Immediately the combat commenced; they struggled desperately, and once more the dagger was raised; but Lieutenant Freegrove wrenched it from the grasp of the pirate, and the boat lurching at the same time, Somerton lost his footing; Raymond caught a shroud whilst falling, and thus

No. 22

jerked Edward from his hold into the sea. It happened, fortunately, that the sailors who were on board the boat had quitted it for the schooner; as it was, a musket was pointed down upon them, but before it could be fired a sail was announced, bearing down. All in a moment was bustle on board, which enabled Raymond and his uncle to get clear of the schooner. Soon the voice of their captain was heard giving orders to clear away the guns; and, in the course of a short time, a broad sheet of flame showed that the work of destruction had commenced.

"Quickly Lieutenant Freegrove and Raymond reduced their sail, when at some distance off, and lay to, to witness the result. Quite astounding were the tokens of the desperate engagement. Broadside followed broadside, and the cheers and the splitting of the timbers were quite deafening.

"Several times could Raymond and his uncle observe Somerton leaping about the deck, and cheering on his men, as though invulnerable to the balls that came pattering down like hailstones.

"At length the last broadside which the pirate fired struck her opponent betwixt wind and water; she lurched, the seamen gave a fearful shriek, and down she sunk. The next instant it was discovered that the pirate's vessel was on fire. Soon the flames spread around, and rapidly ascended, in spite of all the exertions that were so actively made. They curled around the masts and spars, and shot up their forked tongues to Heaven, as if enraged at finding nothing else to wreak their vengeance on.

"At last the men took to their boats, all but one individual, who paced about the quarter-deck with folded arms, while the thick smoke wound round him, and the flames flashed full upon him, as though to warn, but loath to punish him for his temerity. At last he was seen to plunge into the sea, and instantly disappear.

"While their eyes were still fixed upon the blazing vessel, momentarily expecting the explosion, a wet, dripping figure crawled into the boat by the gunwale, and, bleeding and exhausted, threw himself at the feet of Eugenia.

"It was Edward Somerton. He raised his eyes to her; his looks indicated the utmost anguish and despair.

"'Behold!' he exclaimed, in a melancholy voice, 'behold where sinks the pirate's glory! All my brave fellows are scattered, my gallant vessel sinking, and I with my death-wound: yet there soars my proud eagle still—that is a gratification—one thrill of pleasure amid the throes of pain. Not ignobly has she sunk, but, like a phœnix amidst the destruction that surrounds her, she casts her proud and scornful look below, as though glorying in the desolation that would make others quail.'

"High at this moment shot up the devouring element, and lit up the figure of the vengeful eagle, and then came the explosion, the bursting and scattering of that vessel once so powerful and so daring. At the sight, the pirate groaned.

"'See, see!' he cried, 'down she goes!—she sinks, she sinks in victory! The eagle's bright plume has been sullied by the wave; the sea-gull skims above you now, and every petty craft may sail over the once Daredevil free-trader.'

"Exhausted by the power of his emotions, the pirate remained silent for a few moments, and then, addressing Lieutenant Freegrove, he said,

"'Should you not thoroughly hate and despise me, listen to my words, and turn not a deaf ear to the acknowledgments I have to make for your kindness to me, when I was entirely unknown to you. Eugenia, my heart has long since reproached me for having endeavoured to gain your affections, knowing what I was; but I had never loved woman before, and yet so wild, so resistless, and sweet was that passion, that I tried to conquer it in vain. But now I acquit you of your promise, and my sincere, last wish is, that wherever you may next place your affections, they may be on one more deserving and less unhappy than I am.'

"He again paused, and endeavoured to gain strength to say something more that he wished. At length he said, but in tones much weaker than those he had spoken in before,

"'This life I embraced on account of its better enabling me to procure the vengeance I thirsted for; I joined these smugglers—for they were but defrauders of the revenue then, though subsequent misfortunes and poverty compelled them to feed their wants from the purses of all mankind;—their captain took a fancy to me, and, at the time I left your house, he made me an offer of the command of his vessel, which I accepted, and, although with reluctance, turned pirate.'

"'And,' observed Raymond, 'on the night you left Mr. Freegrove's house, I overheard your conversation, and it was I who seized you, and created the consternation which made your men retreat so hastily.'

"'Ah!' ejaculated the dying man, ' you were ever my foe, but that is over now, I trust; I hope we are foes no longer. Let me, then, dying, press a brother's hand in friendship, which has been raised in enmity so often.'

"Immediately the brothers joined hands, and then, once more, did Edward look towards the few burning spars and planks of his vessel, that shed a faint gleam in a direct line with the boat, and saw floating, within his reach, his broad flag, under which he had sailed so often. Eagerly he seized it, and fervently he ejaculated,

"'My bold eagle, we will sink together; 'you have been with me in my prosperity, when my gallant crew have chanted the Smuggler's Glee, across the broad billows, and death shall not sever us now.'

"Quickly he wound the flag round his neck and breast, and spreading forth his arms he stood up in the boat, and falling back, his native home, the green waters, closed over the body of the pirate.

"Nothing more remains to be added, but that, in the course of a few months, Eugenia, having partially forgotten these exciting events, finding the affections of Raymond to be sincere, with the consent of her father, became his bride."

"Well," said Hemlock, when Sam Raker had finished this narrative, "that is a long yarn, at any rate."

"Yes," exclaimed Raker, "but it is one that I thought would not prove uninteresting to you."

"And, for my own part, Sam, I can say that you judged quite right," observed Hemlock. "The pirate-captain was a brave fellow."

"He was," said Sam Raker; "that I can answer for, as I happened to be one of his crew."

"Indeed?"

"Yes."

"His character was so much like that of our's, that I should almost have thought you had drawn it for him," said Hemlock.

"Yes," returned Sam, "never did two persons resemble each other more than Edward Somerton and the Smuggler King."

"The circumstances of their lives, too, if I have heard aright, are very similar," remarked Hemlock.

"They are; but our vessel has been making way gallantly, and we are now out of fear of all pursuit."

"I never entertained many fears upon that score," said Hemlock; "the Devil Skipper is so fast a cutter, that she can outstrip any other craft upon the ocean."

"How long do you reckon it will be before we reach the Death Rock?" inquired another of the pirates.

"If the wind continues in our favour," replied Sam Raker, "we shall doubtless reach there by to-morrow night. But come, let us to business, my lads; I must pay our prisoner a visit, to see that he is all safe."

The pirates moved off to their different duties in the vessel; and Sam Raker, who, with the heart of a fiend, delighted to witness the miseries of his fellow-creatures, hastened to the cabin in which William was confined.

He found him seated in one corner of the place, in a most disconsolate mood, with his elbows resting on his knees, and his face buried in his hands; but, on the noise which Sam made on entering, he jumped up, and beholding who it was, he fixed upon him a look of the utmost disdain and most haughty indignation. Sam Raker smiled ironically.

"I come to congratulate you on the prosperity of your voyage," he said, "and the cheerful prospect before you."

"If you have come to mock me in my misfortunes," returned William, "I will tell you at once that you will be defeated in your object, as I look upon you with the most thorough contempt. I place my reliance on ——"

"There, no preaching," interrupted Raker; "we do not sanction sermons on board the Devil Skipper. I would congratulate you on the discovery you have made of your brother, and the honour you must feel it to be connected with so celebrated a character."

"Villain!"

"Ha! ha! ha!" laughed Raker; "but I would have you beware what you say, and to use better language, or we may find a way to punish you."

"I despise you and your threats," said William; "leave me."

"That I shall do when it pleases me," returned Sam; "you will recollect that you are a prisoner in, and not the commander of this vessel."

"The sight of you fills me with horror and disgust—murderer!"

"Were it not that I am in a particularly merciful mood this morning," exclaimed the wretch, "I should feel inclined to give you two or three round dozen for that compliment. The woman was a babbling fool, but she is quiet enough now."

"Avenging Heaven! am I to stand here and hear the assassin of my poor, long lost mother ——"

"Your mother!" interrupted Sam Raker, with a look of astonishment; "who told you you were her son?"

"She imparted it to me with her own lips," answered William; "and then, to meet with so terrible a fate!—oh, God! it rends my heart."

Sam Raker paced the cabin for two or three minutes, and muttered something to himself, while William gave way to the painful thoughts that crowded upon his brain. At length, the pirate turned to him, and said,

"The woman was a maniac, and knew not what she uttered."

"She was in her senses when she revealed that secret to me," returned William.

"You do believe what she said, then, to be true?"

"I do."

"And did she disclose to you your real name?"

"She did not."

"That is well."

"And what if she had?" asked William.

"No matter," returned Sam, "but you are securely in our power, and, therefore, it is not of much consequence what you do know."

"But I may escape, and if there is justice in Heaven, I shall not be suffered to fall a victim to such wretches."

"But you may chance to find yourself mistaken," said Sam Raker; "there is not much chance of any one escaping who falls into the power of the Smuggler King and his daring crew."

"And what is it you intend to do with me?"

"You have heard what our captain has said," answered Sam Raker; "but it all depends upon your own conduct, for, should you offend me, I have the power to settle your business immediately."

"You would not dare to do so," said William.

"Not dare!" repeated the villain, scornfully—"what is there that Sam Raker would not dare to do?—is not his power almost as great as that of the Smuggler King himself? Give me cause for it, and, like many a bold fellow before you, you will quickly be given as food to the fishes, the same as that old fool, the *honest* lawyer, Mr. Fitzpatrick, was served."

"Mr. Fitzpatrick?" exclaimed William, with the utmost astonishment.

"Ay,", returned the pirate, "you seem surprised; but such was the old lawyer's fate, and such will be the fate of all those who threaten danger to the Smuggler King."

"Unfortunate man," said the compassionate young seaman, "what could he possibly have done to offend that monster of the deep?"

"That is best known to those concerned in it," returned Sam; "but it will perhaps serve, my young spitfire, to teach you a lesson, that the crew of the Devil Skipper are not to be trifled with."

William remained silent for a short time, reflecting upon the fate of Mr. Fitzpatrick, and the consequences that could have led to it, and the probability of the doom which was in store for himself. At length he turned to Sam Raker, and, in different tones to those which he had before assumed, although they were not from fear, he said,

"Tell me, I beg of you, if you have one spark of manly feeling or humanity within you left, is it true that Flora Clarendon, my Flora ——"

"Your Flora, ha! ha! ha!" laughed the pirate, sneeringly; "she is the property of our captain."

"Is it then true that she is really within this vessel?" asked William, eagerly, "or was it only the boast of your captain merely to torture me?"

"Our captain," replied Sam Raker, "is not in the habit of indulging in such jokes; they are invariably practical ones."

"Then the poor girl is indeed in his power?"

"She is."

"God protect her then!"

"I will shortly convince you that the damsel is on board," said Sam Raker.

"How?" eagerly demanded the young seaman, and his feelings were wrought up to the highest pitch of agitation.

"I will indulge you with an interview with her," said Sam Raker.

"An interview with her!" repeated William, and his heart bounded at the thought, and then sunk again, when he reflected what would be her agony, her distraction, when she should find that he too was in the power of the pirates. "Alas!" he added, "poor girl, the scene will drive her mad."

"No doubt, if she loves you," said the villain, sarcastically, "she will be delighted at the meeting."

"Under such painful circumstances, I fear it will break her heart."

"I doubt much whether her heart is made of such tender materials," said Sam Raker.

William's heart swelled with indignation and grief; he frowned upon the pirate, but returned no answer.

" You see," said Raker, after a pause, " that I can be indulgent some-times."

" Pirate," exclaimed William, " I plead not for myself, do with me as you like ; punish me, torture me, or do what you please, but as you would escape a terrible retribution, which some day or other will assuredly over-take you, do not attempt to harm that innocent girl. Do not venture to insult her by your coarse language, or a curse, a dreadful curse will fall upon you."

" Harm her," returned Sam ; " oh, no, she is the chosen bride of our captain, and must be well taken care of. He must be a bold fellow, or a rash fool, that would attempt to disobey the injunctions of the Smuggler King. But are you prepared for the interview ?"

" I dread, yet long once more to behold her, whom I am afraid is doomed to such misery," said William.

" Misery !" repeated Sam Raker ; " it must be her own fault if she ex-periences it ; any damsel should think it an honour to become the bride of the Smuggler King."

" The bride of a pirate, a robber, a murderer !" exclaimed William ; " oh, the idea is too dreadful to be entertained."

" But will certainly take place," was the pirate's answer.

" Never !"

" What is to prevent it ?" demanded Sam.

" That Almighty commander who ever watches over the good and inno-cent !" answered William, firmly, and with confidence.

" Then why did not that Almighty commander prevent her falling into our clutches ?" asked Sam. " But this is idle talking. I will go to the girl, and in a short time you may expect to meet her on deck."

" May Providence give her strength to support the meeting," said Wil-liam, raising his eyes to Heaven fervently.

The pirate returned no answer, but immediately quitted the cabin. Wil-liam was now in a greater state of agony than he had even been before ; anxious as he was to see his lover, and to endeavour to impart a few words of consolation and encouragement to her, he dreaded the effect which the shock might have upon her, and the consequences that might follow. The interval that elapsed during the absence of Sam Raker, was passed by him in a state of the greatest suspense, and when he reflected on the great misery of mind which Flora must be in, even at her own situation and the fate with which she was threatened, he pictured in the most alarming colours the additional trial it would be to her feelings to know that he also was a prisoner on board the pirate-ship, and the torture that their friends must be in at this double calamity. The rude remarks of Sam Raker had filled him with the utmost resentment, and it was with difficul y, during the brief interview we have been describing, that he could refrain from springing upon him, and inflicting upon him summary punishment. But the certainty that he was completely powerless, and would only excite the ruffian to greater severity, restrained him from so doing. He now endea-voured to compose himself, so as to be able to meet Flora with becoming fortitude and self-possession, upon which so much probably depended, and in a short time he had succeeded much better than might have been ex-pected.

In the meantime Flora had passed a most miserable night, never having ventured to retire to rest, although Maud, at her earnest request, had told Sir Julian that she had, so that she might be saved the pain and disgust of meeting him. During the time that she knew the pirate captain to be on board, she was in a state of the utmost alarm, and the noise and confusion that prevailed in the vessel, convinced her that something unusual was going forward, although she knew not then that her lover was also a prisoner.

When Maud returned to the cabin, Flora, finding her more inclined to be communicative than she had before been, questioned her as to what had taken place during the time that the smuggler captain had been on board; but although Maud was in one of her loquacious humours, she evaded those questions, and declined giving any information upon the subject.

"But I would advise you to compose yourself, young lady," said Maud, "and all may yet turn out better than you at present anticipate."

"Alas," returned Flora, "of what use is it talking to me of consolation situated as I am? What can I expect, in the power, as I am, of a man of such dreadful and desperate character?"

"Nay," returned Maud, "terrible as our captain undoubtedly is to his enemies, you will find that he has not forgotten how to be gallant to the fair sex."

"Can that man possess any feeling of humanity, who can drag a defenceless woman from her friends and home?" demanded Flora.

"But he loves you, miss, and it is only the strength of his passion that has tempted him to the course he has adopted."

"Love!" repeated Flora, with a feeling of disgust; "oh, couple not the sacred name with such a villain."

"I again warn you," said Maud, "to refrain from applying such epithets to our captain."

"Does he not richly merit the title?" asked Flora. "Do not his actions prove him to be a villain of the blackest die?"

"But to you he will be all that is kind and affectionate," said Maud, "if you will but endeavour to return his passion."

"Never!" vehemently returned the damsel. "The very thought is horrible."

"You surely will not be so obstinate as to oppose it?"

"With my very life I will," said Flora.

"But what power have you to oppose him?"

"That of the Almighty, in whom I put my trust, and who will, I have no doubt, assist me through the painful struggle," devoutly answered the maiden.

"He will make you his lawful bride."

"By Heaven, never! I would sooner die first."

"He has wealth."

"I despise it."

"In his real character he has rank, and moves with the noblest of the noble."

"And yet pursues the dreadful career of a pirate?"

"Yes."

"Oh, how naturally base and cruel his heart must be, when, from a mere wanton delight in cruelty and crime, he follows such a course," said Flora.

Maud could not make any reply to this.

"And what is the real name of the smuggler captain?" asked Flora.

"That I must leave to himself to divulge to you, miss," answered Maud; "but no doubt you will be greatly astonished when you hear it."

"When does the vessel sail?" asked Flora, paying no attention to the last observation of Maud.

"Almost immediately," replied Maud.

"So soon! Oh, God; then all hope of my deliverance is at end," exclaimed Flora.

" It would be madness to entertain such an idea."

" And what is the place of her destination ?" inquired Flora.

" The Death Rock," replied her companion.

Flora shuddered at the name.

" The Death Rock stands in the midst of an arm of the ocean," continued Maud, " and on the top of it stands an old tower, which was formerly used as a prison, but has long been deserted, except by our captain and his crew, who make it one of their depositories, for which it is admirably calculated."

" And in that awful place I am then to be confined ?" said Flora.

" You are, as I before said, to be conveyed thither, miss ; but you will find, although its external appearance is not very prepossessing, the interior is fitted up with every comfort."

" Alas !" ejaculated Flora, " what will become of me, imprisoned in that fearful building, and far away from my friends, and at the mercy of a set of wretches who know not what pity is ?   Better were it that I should die, than have to endure a fate far worse than even ten thousand deaths."

" But it will be your own fault, miss," observed Maud, " if you are not happy."

" Happy !" repeated Flora, " oh, how can I be happy, when torn from my friends, from all those dear to me, and they in a state of ignorance as to the fate which has befallen me ?"

" Become the wife of our captain," answered Maud, " and I am certain he will do all in his power to render you the happiest of human beings."

" Become the wife of that monster !" indignantly exclaimed Flora ; " the very thought chills my blood with horror."

" But you have not seen our captain yet, in his real character," said Maud.

" I have experienced sufficient to know him to be a most atrocious villain," retorted Flora, " and never can the impression be eradicated from my mind."

" It will be well for you, if you endeavour to efface it, miss," said Maud.

" Never ! it is impossible !"

" Ah ! that is only your opinion at present."

" It will ever be the same."

" I hope not, for it may be that it will subject you to that state of misery, which I am certain it is not the captain's wish to inflict upon you."

" Then why has he adopted his present course ?"

" Because he had no other," said Maud.

" How so ?" demanded Flora.

" He felt fearful, I suppose, that if he had pressed his suit to you, you would have rejected him, as he knew that you had another lover, and he could not endure the thoughts of tamely resigning you."

" Alas !" exclaimed Flora, her anguish increasing, " where can I look for consolation ?"

" Do not give way so violently to grief, I pray, miss," said Maud, whose manners were greatly changed from what they were when she had first been introduced to Flora ; " it will not alter your situation, and cannot effect you any good."

" But how can I avoid it, under the painful, the dreadful circumstances in which I am placed ?" asked Flora, with a deep sigh.

" I will do anything, I am sure, to comfort you, miss."

" I thank you ; but, alas ! comfort and I will be henceforth strangers, while I am placed in this alarming situation."

" The captain strictly enjoined me to be kind and attentive to you,"

observed Maud, " so that shows that he intends you no harm, if you do not oppose his wishes."

" Poor William," ejaculated Flora, and heavy sobs almost choked her utterance, " poor William, what is now your anguish—the distraction of mind under which you must labour, at my mysterious disappearance? Shall I never behold you again?"

" You may behold him sooner than you expect, miss," observed Maud.

" What mean you?" eagerly demanded Flora.

Maud, however, bethought herself, and evaded the question.

" And what was the reason that the captain did not remain on board?" Flora inquired.

" He has powerful motives for not so doing," replied Maud; " but in the course of a few days he will join us at the place of our destination."

" And then will the acme of my misery commence."

" You must endeavour to think otherwise, miss."

" Alas! how can I?"

" As I have before said, the captain will afford you every indulgence," replied Maud.

" And what indulgence can he show me, when he deprives me of my liberty, and will persecute me with his hateful importunities."

" You must endeavour to learn to think them otherwise than hateful, miss."

" Maud," replied Flora, impatiently, " you advise me in vain; never can I look upon the Smuggler King, as you call him, with any other feeling than that of horror, and the recollection of his actions will make me deem him a perfect fiend in human shape."

" You will say different, I think, when you see him, miss," said Maud; " he is one of the handsomest men in the world."

No. 23

" And think you, Maud, that I estimate any being by their external perfections ? No, it is the mind, the pure and virtuous mind that can alone gain my admiration and esteem. The deformities of this smuggler captain's mind must be more hideous than even the imagination can form any idea of."

" He is one of the most elegant and accomplished men of the day," said Maud.

" And one of the most hardened and atrocious villains."

" I would advise you, miss, to reserve your opinion, until you have had an interview with him."

" Which I hope to God will never take place !" fervently ejaculated Flora.

" There is nothing to prevent it," said Maud.

" Yes, there is," returned Flora.

" What ?"

" The interposition of an all-wise and merciful Providence," replied the damsel.

" Well, well, miss," said Maud, " that may be, to be sure, although I confess I do not know much about such matters; but of one thing I can assure you, that, if you think to escape from the tower of the Death Rock, you will find it impossible."

" There is nothing impossible to that Supreme Power I have appealed to," piously returned Flora.

" But trust me, miss, after all you have said, when you have seen the captain in his private character, you will alter your opinions, and have no wish to escape from him."

" Maud," said the damsel, with a look of indignation and offended virtue, " you disgrace yourself and your sex by thus advocating the cause of a monster !"

" Well, miss," said Maud, who looked considerably abashed, " I am sorry if I have offended you, but I'm sure I meant no harm. It is my duty to urge the cause of ——"

" Had you studied your duty to your fellow-creatures, Maud," quickly interrupted Flora, " you would never have been found on board a pirate vessel, the willing associate and assistant of those bad-minded and lawless men."

Maud could not return any immediate answer to this keen rebuke, but her confusion was greatly increased, and Flora could perceive a tear starting in her eye.

" Ah ! miss," said Maud, " you little know the stern necessity that drove me to this; I was not always what I am now."

" I am sorry," said Flora, " if I have said anything to wound your feelings; but it must indeed have been powerful motives that could drive a female to such a desperate course of life, and to become a voluntary witness to scenes that are revolting to human nature."

" Ah ! miss," observed Maud, whose tones and manner were strangely altered, " I have had my share of misery in this world, although I am obliged now to disguise my real feelings, and to give utterance to words that are quite foreign to my principles. At some future opportunity I may, perhaps, if it is agreeable, relate to you my history, and you will then probable be ready to grant some excuse for my present extraordinary and apparently culpable conduct."

Flora was about to make some observation in reply to this, when they were aroused by a noise upon deck, and then the voice of Sam Raker was heard giving instructions to the pirates.

" They are about to weigh anchor," said Maud.

" Alas ! then it is all over; there is no hope," said Flora, " unless suspicion of my being on board this ship should have entered the minds of my friends, and a pursuit should be commenced."

"There is no chance of that," observed Maud. "Why should any suspicion of the real character of this vessel be excited now when she has been so long in this port, without being thought otherwise than a fair trader?"

"Lost! lost!" cried Flora, in despair, and wringing her hands, as the motion of the vessel convinced her that she had set sail. "Parents, sister, William, farewell!—farewell; I am lost to ye all for ever!"

"There is a favourable wind," said Maud, "and we shall soon be far from this place."

Flora covered her face with her hands, and sobbed aloud, and Maud, who really commiserated with her, did not offer to interrupt her, well knowing that this indulgence in grief would greatly relieve her oppressed heart. The voices of the pirates on deck, singing their rude chorusses, and indulging in revelry, now met her ears, and every tone that vibrated in them filled her with additional dismay. It was quite evident to her that all hope was at an end, and that nothing could save her from the dreadful fate which threatened her but the intervention of Providence, and to that Almighty Power she mentally breathed a prayer, and resigned herself to its keeping, as all other hope was at an end.

"Poor girl," thought Maud; "if her sufferings now are so great, how much more severe will they be when she is made acquainted with all, and that her lover is really on board the same vessel with her?"

But she did not attempt to give utterance to these reflections, and stood gazing at the poor, disconsolate damsel, without seeking to interrupt her.

Flora remained for some time wrapped in meditation, and completely abstracted from everything else; but at length the heaving motion of the vessel, as it flew like lightning over the vast waters, carried on by a favouring gale, aroused her.

"Is there no hope?" she sighed, clasping her hands, and looking most piteously at Maud.

"It would be useless to flatter you with any, my poor girl," answered her attendant. "This vessel is a fast sailer; the wind and everything is in its favour, and before daylight we shall be far on our voyage."

"Oh, God!" exclaimed our heroine; "then, indeed, am I lost. Oh! my parents—my beloved William, what are now your feelings?"

"Do not thus violently agitate yourself," returned Maud, "but endeavour to gain sufficient fortitude to meet all that may threaten you."

The damsel shook her head; her tears flowed fast, and then clasping her burning temples with her fair hands, she once more relapsed into that state of utter despair and apathy which was truly pitiable to behold.

Maud looked on, and really felt for her. At length she ventured to approach her, and, addressing her in the kindest accents, endeavoured to persuade her to lie down for a short time, and try to gain a little rest, which she so much needed.

"It will do you so much good," she added, "and you need not fear that any harm will come to you, for I will remain with you, and watch by your side."

Flora stared at her vacantly for a moment or two, as she did not comprehend what she meant, and then in a state bordering on unconsciousness, she suffered Maud to lead her to the place allotted to her for repose, and throwing herself upon it, notwithstanding the agony of her feelings, so much was she exhausted, that she quickly fell into a sound sleep.

Maud seated herself as she had promised, by her side, and gazed at her pale and lovely face, with sentiments of the deepest compassion, notwithstanding the uncouth manners she had at first evinced towards her. Her sleep, however, was evidently disturbed by the most painful dreams, and she frequently started, and uttered half-broken sentences, of the most melancholy description, and with which the names of William and her parents were mingled.

Thus passed away more than a couple of hours, and Maud remained at her post, for, independent of the promises she had made to the poor suffering girl, she so detested the wretches among whom a hard and evil destiny had thrown her, that she dreaded to be in their presence.

And now the first streak of day beamed in at the cabin windows, and the vessel was still pursuing its swift course, and she could hear the smugglers were busy about the deck, and the different parts of the vessel.

Suddenly Flora awoke, and starting wildly from her pallet, she gazed vacantly around her, as if still labouring under the influence of some frightful vision.

"Where am I?" she exclaimed; "what dreadful place is this? and for what vile purposes am I brought hither? Woman, who art thou? Ah! I remember all now; it was no dream! My reason convinces me of the horrible reality and despair closes around me."

"Be calm, my dear young lady," said Maud; "no harm shall come to you."

"No harm," repeated our heroine; "and in the power of such heartless wretches? Woman, you mock me; you are as destitute of feeling as those whose creature you are."

"Indeed you wrong me," returned Maud; "I feel for you, and pity you."

"Feel for me—pity me!" cried the poor forlorn damsel; "oh, what words of mockery are these!"

"Oh, no, they are not," answered Maud, "and so you will find. But come, will you not partake of some refreshment? It will revive you."

Flora gazed at her with a melancholy expression, and shook her head mournfully.

"No," she replied; "no refreshments can revive the spirits of a broken heart. Oh! my parents! oh, William!"

Maud was about to make some reply, when she was prevented by the sound of footsteps approaching the cabin-door, and Flora hearing them at the same time flew towards her, and clinging to her, with looks of the most unspeakable agony, she exclaimed in frantic accents,—

"Oh! shield me! save me! protect me from the ruffians! Do not let them approach me; oh, do not!"

"My poor girl," returned Maud; "would that I could assist you, but I cannot. Fear not, however, the smugglers will not dare to insult or harm you; it is the strict injunction of their captain that they should not. Be firm! be firm! Hark! they come!"

"Oh! God!" exclaimed the despairing damsel, and she had scarcely thus spoken when the cabin-door was thrown open, and Will Hemlock and two other smugglers appeared. Flora shrunk back with horror and disgust, and clung still more closely to Maud.

"You must come with me on deck," said Hemlock, addressing Maud.

"For what purpose?" demanded the latter.

"That you will learn afterwards," returned the ruffians. "The young lady must accompany us also."

"Oh! spare me!" supplicated Flora; "I am a poor defenceless girl; I never harmed you, why then should you seek to injure me?"

"Oh, we do not mean to harm you," said Hemlock; "but come."

"Oh, for the love of Heaven let me remain here!" implored the damsel; "what would you with me?"

"We have a joyful surprise for you," answered the smuggler, with a disagreeable sneer."

"You mock me, mock a poor helpless woman," said our heroine; "your looks alarm me."

"I tell you again," observed Hemlock, "that we mean you no harm."

"Muster courage, miss," said Maud, in gentle accents, "and all will be well. Come, lean on me; I will not quit your side."

Flora raised her eyes towards Heaven, and mentally supplicating its protection, she suffered Maud to lead her from the cabin, they being preceded by Will Hemlock and the other smugglers.

On reaching the deck our heroine beheld a greater part of the crew assembled, and their bold and ferocious looks filled her gentle bosom with the utmost terror. Her limbs trembled, and it was not without the greatest difficulty that Maud could support her. Notwithstanding the assurances of Will Hemlock, her heart foreboded some approaching dreadful calamity, and sunk with despair; but at length she put her trust in the Almighty, and re-assured, she awaited the issue with more fortitude than any one might have expected.

She was led to the centre of the deck, and a pause of a moment or two succeeded. But it was soon interrupted by a confused noise in another part of the vessel, and Flora, casting her eyes instinctively in the direction from whence it proceeded, beheld the hateful forms of Sam Raker, and two more of the smugglers, appear from one of the hatchways. Her heart palpitated when she saw the shadow of another form; she strained her eyes when it appeared on deck; a giddiness seized upon her brain; her heart's blood ran cold. She gazed again! Could it be real? or was it only some fearful delusion? No— no—she could not be deceived in that well-known, that much loved image.

"William!"

"Flora!"

Burst simultaneously in distracted tones from their lips, and rushing frantically towards each other, the lovers were locked in each other's arms.

The smugglers gathered round them.

Oh! what language can describe the delirium of that moment? Convulsive sobs of the most bitter, heartfelt agony checked the utterance of William and Flora, and pressed firmly to each other's hearts, they could not for some moments speak a word.

"Flora, my poor, wronged, gentle girl," at length exclaimed William; "to meet thee thus! Oh, this, indeed, wrings my heart to its very core. Flora, my loved one; my gentle craft; oh, look up, and behold the anguish of your lover!"

"William!" sobbed Flora, while her heart was ready to burst; "but surely it is all a frightful dream! I could have borne any sufferings; but this— this—oh! ——"

She could no more, but gazing for an instant with looks enough to melt a heart of adamant, in her lover's face, she again sunk, sobbing hysterically, on his bosom.

"This is too much," ejaculated the young seaman, whilst the most dreadful agony heaved his manly bosom. "Flora, my love—oh! villains, can you gaze unmoved on a scene like this?"

"Come," said the hardened villain, Sam Raker, "better language, my young spark, or you may repent it."

"Monsters! heartless miscreants!" exclaimed William, pressing the damsel closer in his arms, and fixing looks of the utmost disgust and indignation upon the crew.

"Ah!" cried several of the crew in a breath, fixing their hands upon their weapons, and darting the most furious looks upon William.

"Beware!" shouted Sam Raker; "or this meeting may be a fatal one to you. I brought you together merely that you might convince yourselves that the Smuggler King's triumph was complete; you had better make the most of the meeting, for the time allowed you is but short."

"They shall not part us, William," exclaimed our heroine; "we have met once more, and death shall only separate us."

"There, that's enough of this palaver," said Raker; "convey them to their separate places of confinement."

Hemlock and two or three others made a motion to advance towards the lovers; but William, supporting Flora firmly with one arm, clenched his fist, and his determined looks and demeanour for a moment seemed to daunt the villains.

"Hark ye!" cried William, "if you are men—if you have still one spark of feeling or humanity left within ye, ye will not attempt to interrupt this melancholy meeting. But if one of ye attempt to lay a hand upon this poor innocent girl, I will fell him the same as if he were a dog!"

"Fools!" cried the infuriated Sam Raker, "why do you stand and tamely listen to the boy's menaces? Part them, I say."

"Oh! no—no—no!" cried Flora; "you shall not tear him from me. I will cling to him with all the strength that woman's love can empower her with. He is mine!—mine in the face of Heaven; and fiends shall not separate us!"

"Tear them asunder!" shouted Raker, furiously, and two or three of the smugglers advanced for that purpose; but no sooner had the first one approached than the young seaman, with a tremendous blow, felled him senseless on the deck. In a moment a dozen of the crew rushed towards him with their weapons in their hands, but Flora clung more closely to him, and shielded him with her fair form, and Sam Raker, in a tremendous voice, commanded them to hold.

"Hold!" he repeated; "we must not harm the girl, but for this daring act he shall be severely punished. Tear them apart."

"Villains!" cried William, worked up to a pitch of frenzy, "I am a desperate and determined man; I struggle in a just cause, that of injured innocence, and by the Almighty God above, if you pollute my Flora with your touch the consequences will be fatal to some of ye, unarmed as I am."

"Monsters!" exclaimed the distracted damsel; "what have we done to merit this? Oh! spare him—spare him. Slay me, but not my William."

"My poor Flora," said her lover, "appeal not to wretches who know not what humanity is."

"Cowards!" cried Sam Raker, "are you all afraid of this daring stripling? Are my orders to be obeyed? Again I command you to tear the girl from his arms."

Once more several of the ruffians advanced, but immediately they came near to him, another was felled by the powerful fist of William; the next moment, however, he was surrounded, and the screaming Flora was torn from his grasp. Worked up to madness, the young seaman struggled violently, and at length managed to release himself from those who had held him, and at the same moment he wrested a sword from one of the other smugglers, and stood upon his defence.

The villains were so completely astounded by this act of daring and bravery, that they stood transfixed, as it were, for an instant, while William rushed upon the man who held Flora, and attempted to tear her from him; but the fellow stoutly resisted, and others flying to his assistance, William, aroused to a pitch of madness, dealt furious blows around him with the deadly weapon he had secured, and two of the wretches were speedily stretched dead upon the deck.

Uttering curses and threats that were dreadful to hear, the other smugglers now rushed upon him, and William being disarmed, sunk upon one knee, and the next moment a dozen weapons would have been plunged in his defenceless body, had not Flora with a loud scream suddenly extricated herself from the hold of the smuggler, and darting forward, rushed in between the smugglers and her lover. They drew back, and arrested their murderous purpose.

"Stand back, all of you," commanded Sam Raker, advancing; "he must meet with another fate. For this, boy, you shall die the death of a dog."

"Oh! mercy—mercy!" shrieked Flora, as several smugglers, by the command of Sam Raker, seized upon her lover, who was overpowered by numbers, and the great exertion he had undergone. "Spare him, save his life; take mine, but, oh! spare that of my lover."

"Bear her hence!" cried Raker, and immediately the poor distracted girl was seized by two of the heartless villains.

William gazed at her with the most dreadful feelings of despair, and then turning to Raker, he said, in a voice choked with emotion,—

"What you do with me I care not; but, oh! unless you would meet the most terrible vengeance of Heaven, harm not that beauteous innocent."

"Your doom is sealed," returned Raker; "bear the girl away."

"Monsters, murderers," shrieked Flora; "you shall not, dare not take his life! Unhand me! let me fly to the arms of him my soul holds dearer than my own existence."

"Away with her," again commanded Raker.

In vain the frantic girl struggled.

"William," she screamed.

"Flora, Flora! we shall meet in Heaven. Farewell, oh, farewell!" groaned William.

"William!" once more shrieked Flora; it was her last effort, and completely overpowered by her emotions, she fainted, and was borne from the deck, followed by Maud.

The villains still retained their hold of William, who remained gazing upon the place where his lover had disappeared, powerless and passive as an infant. Oh, God! what feelings did at that moment rend the young man's heart; they were too powerful for the most eloquent pen to do justice to them by description. He felt assured that he had gazed upon her for the last time, and even the thought of the terrible death which he felt certain awaited him, sunk into insignificance before that reflection.

Not long, however, was he allowed to remain in thought; he was aroused by the voice of the miscreant Sam Raker, who commanded the men who held him to bring him forward.

William became firm, and gazed with a look of hatred and defiance upon him.

"Well, my daring stripling," he said, "you have made fine work of it, and what think you will be your reward?"

"I know it," answered William, "and ask not your mercy; wretches as ye are, I know I can expect none. But beware, you will not always escape, and should you dare to harm the poor girl who is at present in your power, the most dreadful vengeance will overtake you."

"Ha! ha! ha!" scornfully laughed Raker; "but we waste time. Messmates, what does he merit who bids defiance to our power, and slays our comrades?"

"Death!" shouted the whole of the smugglers in a breath.

"Then death be his doom," said Raker; "and that immediately."

"Oh! will you not give me a little time?" asked William; "but a few moments to ——"

"Not an instant!" interrupted Raker. "The death plank! the death plank!"

"Ay! the death plank!" repeated two or three of the smugglers, as they hastened to procure it.

William clasped his hands in agony.

"Oh, God!" he cried; "to die thus, and leave my Flora in the power of such monster, surely 'tis a cruel fate. Had I perished in fighting the battles of my country ——"

"Hold your whining noise," interrupted Sam Raker; "I thought we should soon find the way to tame your lion heart. Prepare yourself to become food for the sharks."

The ruffians now entered with the plank, which they placed for the execution of the unfortunate young mariner. He clasped his hands, and raising his eyes towards Heaven, he invoked blessings on the heads of his foster-parents, and her to whom his whole soul was devoted, and then turned his gaze towards his murderers.

"Your time is come," said Raker; "comrades, conduct him to the death plank."

Two of the miscreants laid hold of his arms, while the others with pistols levelled at his head, and at the point of their swords, urged him towards the fatal plank. One foot he placed upon it, and then once more clasping his hands, he ejaculated in tones that could never be forgot by those who heard them :—

"Parents! friends! farewell! I am going a long voyage, but trust we shall all cast anchor together in the port of Heaven! Flora! loved Flora, adieu! May all good angels protect and bless thee!"

Then turning a solemn look upon Sam Raker and the rest of the smugglers, he added :—

"Mark me! My death I pardon ye; but, if ye injure one hair of that poor girl's head, my dying, my most bitter curse, and that of Heaven, be upon ye!"

"Urge him to his fate," shouted Raker.

William turned upon him one bitter look of scorn; again raised his eyes towards Heaven, and walked firmly along the plank. There was a crashing sound, a heavy splash, and the smugglers rushed to the side of the vessel and gazed eagerly over it.

"It is all over with him," cried Sam Raker.

"Ah! by hell!" said Grampus, "he rises again—he struggles hard. He is an excellent swimmer, and may yet escape us!"

"You should have secured his arms," said another of the villains; "see how he buffets with the waves."

"Fire at him," shouted Raker; "why do you stand like fools prating there?"

A dozen pistols were in a moment discharged at the unfortunate youth.

"Ah! that has settled him," said Raker; "he sinks to rise no more. That job is settled, and now to consign the bodies of our comrades to the deep."

This order was immediately obeyed.

"Well, so much for that business," said the miscreant Raker.

"It was a very bad one," returned Hemlock, with some feeling of compunction.

"Why so?" demanded Raker.

"He was a brave young fellow," returned Hemlock; "and it was a pity he should lose his life in such a manner."

"Did he not slay our comrades?"

"True."

"Then he merited his fate."

"Our captain may not approve of it when he comes to hear it," said Hemlock.

"He empowered me to do as I have done," answered Raker; "if necessity required it."

"But his fate may prove fatal to the girl," observed Hemlock; "and then the Smuggler King ——"

"Ah!" interrupted Raker; "there is something in that; but we must conceal it from her."

"And how can that be done?"

"Maud must be cautioned. Let her attend me instantly."

Grampus departed on this errand, and quickly returned, accompanied by Maud, the horror of whose looks plainly shewed that she was aware of the fate of William.

"Come hither, Maud," commanded Raker.

Maud obeyed, trembling violently, and unable to conceal the feelings of abhorrence and disgust with which she viewed the miscreants.

"How is the girl?" demanded Raker.

"Still insensible," answered Maud; "poor thing, she ——"

"There, we want none of your nonsense," interrupted Raker; "then she knows not of the fate of her lover?"

"No; oh, Raker, it was a bloody—a hellish deed, and ——".

"Bah! be cautious what you say, or we may silence your clack in a similar manner. You must keep her in ignorance of William's fate; make her believe that he still lives. Do you hear?"

Maud, who well knew that it would be useless for her to offer any resistance, replied in the affirmative.

"And you will obey?" demanded the ruffian.

"I must," replied Maud.

"Ay, you know you must," said Raker. "And mind, that you pay every attention to her recovery."

No. 24

"I need no mandates to make me do that," answered Maud.

"Then, begone."

Maud also obeyed this, glad to escape from the presence of the villains, and to rejoin her unfortunate patient.

She found her still in a state of insensibility, from which, for a time, she was afraid she would never recover; she applied all the remedies she could think of, and, at length, her efforts were rewarded, by our heroine opening her eyes.

She stared vacantly around her for a moment or two, and seemed to be almost entirely unconscious of the presence of Maud; but at length, clasping her temples, she exclaimed :—

"William, my own, my fond William, where art thou? Why do you not come to me when I am so very ill? It is unkind, very unkind of you. Come to me—no, he cannot ;—they withhold him from me; the wretches, the monsters! Ah! I recollect now! they slew him, the murderers, and only because he defended his poor Flora from insult. But they shall not keep me from his cold and mangled corse; no; they shall not; I will go to him and bathe him with my tears. Let me begone! let me begone!"

With those words the poor girl endeavoured to start from her pallet; Maud, however, who deeply felt for her, was on the watch, and she gently held her down, and at the same time, observed,

"Pray endeavour to compose yourself, my dear young lady; you may be labouring under a delusion; your lover may not be dead, and ——"

"Not dead! not dead!" interrupted our heroine; "why attempt to deceive me? Did I not see him fall? Did I not see his frightful yawning wounds? Is he not there standing to confirm it? Look at his bright shade, how angelic it looks. Keep me not from him. I will join him! wretches, why would you divide those in death that have so loved in life? Stand back! stand back! you shall not keep me from him; William, I am thine, and who dare alter the will? Woman—fiend!, why do you grasp me thus?"

Again the poor girl attempted to arise, but Maud prevented her, and at length, once more exhausted she sunk back, and again for a short time she remained silent.

Maud gazed on the pallid countenance of the sufferer, and the more she did so, the greater she commiserated in her malady; at the same time she marvelled that she could herself have endured such miseries without experiencing the same.

It was now daylight; the sun was shining brilliantly through the cabin window, and all was calm and beautiful upon the ocean : how different to the hearts that pined and groaned within the precincts of that frail and floating tenement. But a few timbers divided them from eternity, and yet men could venture such crimes that to reflect upon would make human nature shudder.

Maud looked out upon the waters, and when she saw the beauty of the prospect around, she could have wept, and the reflections we have mentioned occurred to her. Often she wished that she might behold some vessel near at hand that might be likely to be able to contend with her, but as far as the eye could stretch, all was clear, and no hope of relief apparent.

The smugglers, confident in their safety, and still anxious to wile away the time, had once more become merry, and were singing the following chorus :—

"Gaily we go, gaily we go,
　Let whatever wind may blow;
　Over the vast and boundless deep,
　Like a thing of light we gaily sweep.
　Blow high, blow low, we fearlessly go,
　That phantom called danger we none of us know;
　Whatever the peril, we still can sing
　In praise of our captain, the Smuggler King!

The foe may advance, we'll soon make him prance,
And the Devil Skipper will lead him a dance !
With pistol in hand, we are all at command,
And those who'll not yield, will our strength understand ;
The land-sharks we fear not, to attack us they dare not,
Or if they do, we care not a jot,
For ' peccavi' we shortly will make all sing.
Who oppose the crew of the Smuggler King !"

"Alas !" ejaculated Maud, "too well do I know the power of the Smuggler King and his desperate crew. Oh ! what a dreadful fate has mine been ; to be forced into a connection with these wholesale marauders and murderers, and to be looked upon with the same impression as the basest amongst them, while, Heaven knows, how foreign my heart is to their principles. This poor girl, too; should she even regain her senses, what will not her sufferings be, exposed as she will be to the insults of the crew, and the persecutions of that desperate man, their chief. Oh! how sincerely do I pity her."

"Pity me !" repeated our heroine, who had been insensible to all but the conclusion of the sentence, "pity me !" and she fixed upon Maud a look which penetrated to her very soul ; "oh! if you sincerely pity the poor bereaved one, why prevent her from joining the spirit of him who formed the principal link in the chain that attached her to life? Pity ! the word is mockery. There is no pity in this world. Man delights in preying upon and sporting with the feelings of his fellow creatures. His course is that of blood; his victims, the innocent. Look at that pale shade that even now glares upon me. Do not his looks confirm what I say? pity! pity! if you pity me sincerely, plunge a knife in my heart, and let me hasten to meet once more my William, where we shall never more be separated. But you too are base, cruel ; you would deceive me ; or why tell me that my William still lives? Did I not see him fall? Did I not behold his bleeding form? Did I not see his body plunged into the deep, and yet you tell me he lives."

"Wonderful !" thought Maud, "that an impression so like the reality should have gained possession of the poor girl's mind. Oh! how it grieves me to have to act the hypocrite, and yet 'tis a mercy to deceive her."

"You are silent," observed Flora, fixing her eyes keenly upon her, "and yet you commune with yourself. Ah! that convinces me that I have spoken the truth, and yet you would endeavour to convince me to the contrary. If you are really my friend, why not acknowledge the fact, and then will I listen to you, and feel grateful for the sympathy you may evince in the untimely death of my poor William ?"

Maud paused, for there was so much reason in the madness of our heroine that she was at a loss how to answer her without divulging the truth, and in her present state, and after the manner in which she had been bound down by Raker and the other smugglers, she was afraid to do so.

"Still silent ! still silent !" ejaculated Flora. "Ah ! that is indeed an admission of the truth of what I have asserted. Why, then, longer act the hypocrite? Why not admit the fact, and then shall I be ready to listen to your advice and consolation with some degree of confidence ?"

Maud again hesitated before she ventured to return an answer, for the fact was, she was perfectly at a loss what reply to make. She was willing to reveal to the poor girl the whole of the dismal truth so far as she knew it, but fear, and apprehension lest the revelation should be productive of fatal consequences to her whom she now really as much esteemed as if she had been her own sister, prevented her. Wildly wandering as was the mind of our heroine at that time, she fixed her eyes with such a keen expression upon the countenance of Maud, that shewed she could penetrate her most inmost thoughts, and after waiting for several minutes without Maud returning any reply, she said :—

"Ah! I see it all! My mind has not been wandering as you would make it appear to me; he is no more, he is no more; the heartless butchers have murdered him; murdered him who was dearer to me than my own existence. Why, then, keep me here? Let me arise and plunge myself into the deep. Let me join my love in his ocean grave. Oh! William! dear William, what is life now to me since thou art gone,—murdered?"

"My dear girl," said Maud, "pray let reason again assert her sway."

"Reason!" reiterated Flora, with difficulty held in her pallet by Maud, and her eyes flashing with frenzied wildness, "who dares to talk of reason to her who has lost every hope? Go, utter your words to the roaring winds, that even now seem to convey the dying moans of my slaughtered William to my ears; they will but return the hollow echo of despair. He is gone, he is murdered, and you know it; what is the use of attempting to deceive me?"

"Believe me, my dear young lady," said Maud, hesitatingly, "I wish not to deceive you, but——"

"But," repeated our heroine, with all the quietness that madness often assumes; "you hesitate; ah! that more and more confirms what I have said. You know that he is slain, yet would you persuade me to the contrary. Oh! William! Can I live after knowing your hapless fate? No; I should prove myself to have been unworthy of your love could I do so. Let me escape from this bondage; do not attempt to detain me;—see, see, my William's shade once more beckons me to join him! I must obey the mandate! Wretches, if you separated us in life, who shall dare attempt to divide us in death?"

Again the poor heart-stricken damsel attempted to arise, and it was as much as the strength of Maud, who was a powerful woman, could do to prevent her.

"For Heaven's sake," said Maud, "do become more composed. Would you rush unbidden into the presence of your Maker?"

Flora glared at her wildly for a second or two, and then replied,—

"What business have I now in the world, since he is gone? Heaven will pardon the deed."

"But you know not that your lover is no more," said Maud. "You saw him not perish."

"But my heart tells me, convinces me that he died," returned our heroine.

"You heard but the threats of Raker when you became insensible," said Maud.

"The threats," repeated Flora—"ah, true—true; and does any of the crew of the Smuggler King threaten without fulfilling what they promise?"

Maud was again at a loss for an answer.

"I see—I see," ejaculated our heroine; "I see it all plain enough. You know that I have surmised the truth, but would deceive me. Oh, God! this is torture. You may call me mad. So I am. Who that has loved as I have loved—who that has lost one who so fondly, so sincerely loved, could live and retain their senses? You have never loved, or you could not thus act towards me. Let me arise and follow my love to his ocean grave. The voice of angels are inviting me. The looks of my murdered one reproach me with my tardiness. Off—off! I will not be detained. Off—off, I say!"

Again the unfortunate maiden exerted all her strength to arise, and it was as much as Maud could do to prevent her. The powerful struggle, however, quite exhausted her, and she remained afterwards for some time passive. Her suffering, notwithstanding, it was evident, was most intense, and the heavy and heart-drawn sighs that frequently escaped her bosom, deeply affected the compassionate Maud, who was anxious, yet knew not how, to impart consolation to her.

Several hours passed in this manner, and at length a loud shout from the smugglers aroused Maud, and convinced her that they were rapidly approaching the place of their destination. She went to the cabin window, and looking out, found that her surmises were correct; the Death Rock was in sight.

It was a gloomy looking place. Upon a black and lofty rock, which stretched itself far into the sea, stood the tower which has been before mentioned. It was a strong built fabric, blackened by time, but which, although it had already stood for ages, seemed to bid defiance to the destruction of many future generations. It was built entirely of stone, and seemed to frown upon the vessels that at different times approached it. For many years it had been used as a prison, and many an unhappy wretch had breathed his last sigh in its horrible dungeons, or swung from a gibbet which had formerly been fixed upon the rock.

For some time, however, it had been abandoned, though for what reason never had transpired, and it was looked upon with a feeling of dread by the inhabitants of an adjacent island, it being generally supposed to be haunted by the spirits of those unfortunate beings that had perished in its cells. For years it had remained unoccupied, but at length the Smuggler King and his daring crew seized upon it as one of their principal depositories for the booty which they obtained by their lawless proceedings; and they could not have chosen a better place, situated as it was, and with such a superstition attached to it, there was very little cause to fear detection. Fitting haunt it was for wretches like the pirate-captain and his daring crew, and they so soon fortified the tower that they were in a condition to resist any force which might be sent against them. Many a deed of blood had they perpetrated within its walls, and many a crew had been enticed to that place of death, to be consigned to a most horrible fate. It had never been suspected by any of the inhabitants of the island we have before alluded to by whom the tower of the Death Rock was occupied, for they all most sedulously avoided it; and there, then, the Smuggler King reigned as despotic a monarch, and with as much security, as any absolute monarch in his own palace.

Although the exterior of this awful place was most repulsive, the interior, at least the apartments that were usually occupied by Sir Julian, when he stayed for any period of time at the tower, were fitted up in a style of the most profuse elegance. Rich carpets covered the floors; splendid mirrors and pictures adorned the walls; and the other portion of the furniture corresponded, and showed the taste of the mind that had directed its arrangement.

Such was the place to which our heroine was approaching, and where she was doomed to be confined, unknown to her friends, and without any possibility of their ascertaining where she was.

They had now arrived very near to the rock on which the tower was situated, and, while Maud was consulting within herself whether or not she should not inform Flora of the circumstance, she received a summons from Sam Raker to attend him on deck. She quitted the cabin, having first satisfied herself that Flora had no means of laying violent hands on herself, and, going upon deck, she found Sam Raker alone.

"How is your patient?" inquired Sam.

"Still in the same state," was the answer which Maud returned.

"Still raving?"

"Yes."

"And does she still entertain the same impression that her lover is dead?" asked Sam Raker.

Maud replied in the affirmative.

"It is strange," observed Raker, " and yet you are certain that you have not intimated to her that such is the fact?"

" I have not."

" You had better be cautious, for should you drop the slightest hint, you will have cause to repent it sorely."

" I need not your warning," replied Maud ; " you have hitherto had no occasion to suspect that I would act contrary to orders."

" No," returned Raker, " but I am certain that your obedience to our rules has only been caused through fear."

" True."

" Well, we are now near to the place of our destination," said Sam.

" I know it," answered Maud, " and for what purpose have you sent for me ?"

" The girl must not remain on board the vessel. She must be removed into the tower."

" Well ?"

" By some means or the other you must get her to arise and assist her to dress."

" That will be a difficult task," said Maud.

" But it must be done."

" I know it."

" Think you not that you can by some means tranquillize her mind, and do away with the impression that has got possession of it ?"

" I have tried every means, but without effect," answered Maud.

" Curses on the girl's weakness !" growled Raker.

" It was a cruel deed," observed Maud, " and no good can come of it." Sam Raker frowned.

" Woman," he observed, " did he not slay our comrades ?"

" And who provoked him to the deed ?" demanded Maud.

" Psha !" angrily exclaimed Sam Raker, " would you attempt to advocate his cause ? know you not that death is the certain portion of those who injure or oppose the crew of the Smuggler King ?"

" Alas !" said Maud, in reply, " too well I do. But he had no right to have been seized in the first instance."

" It was the will of our captain, and would you presume to question that?"

" I may question it, but dare not oppose it," answered Maud.

" You oppose it," said Raker, scornfully ; " but, psha ! why do I listen to this whining nonsense ? Begone, and do as I have ordered you."

Maud departed without saying another word, and having returned to the cabin, she found our heroine in a much more tranquil state than she had expected. Still her mind wandered, and she had considerable difficulty in making her understand what it was she wished her to do. At length, however, she arose, and Maud having assisted her to dress, held her in conversation of the most soothing description until the vessel had cast anchor beneath the rock on which the tower stood.

When Flora was taken on deck, and beheld the gloomy looking place to which she was about to be consigned, she clasped her hands, and looked the very image of despair. Sam Raker and Hemlock approached her, but no sooner had she beheld them than she uttered a scream of horror, and shrunk away.

" Away, murderers ! monsters !" she ejaculated, " there is blood upon your hands ; they still reek with the blood of my poor William. Off ! do not attempt to touch me ; it is contamination !"

" Be calm, young lady," said Sam Raker, " this wild raving will do you no good. Besides, how know you that the person you speak of is no more ?"

"What is the use of speaking to her in that manner?" said Hemlock, "is she not mad?"

"Mad! mad!" reiterated Flora, "yes, yes, I am mad; I must be less than woman could I retain my senses, after the barbarous murder of one that was dearer to me than my own existence. Monsters, what did he to you that you should take his life?"

"But how know you that he is dead?" again demanded Sam Raker.

"Villains!" answered our heroine, "you cannot deceive me. If he is still living, convince me, by producing him before me."

"No," said Raker, with a half satirical grin, "you must not see him again."

"Ah!" exclaimed Flora, "your words convict yourself and convince me that my surmises are correct. He is no more; he is murdered, savagely murdered, and oh! if you have still one spark of mercy left in your bosoms, slay me also, and rid me of an existence that is now a misery and a burthen to me. My soul yearns to join my William! take, then, my life, and I will freely forgive ye the deed, and with my dying breath bless ye for the happy release from a life that is now rendered intolerable to me."

"Psha!" impatiently ejaculated Sam Raker, "enough of this nonsense; we cannot afford to comply with your wishes, young lady, just yet. Our captain and you must be better acquainted first."

"Miscreant!" cried Flora, "for this a curse, a heavy curse, the curse of the bereaved one, of broken-hearted parents, will assuredly alight upon your head. William! dear William, they will not suffer me to join you, but the time will soon come; my heart must break, it cannot long support this painful struggle. My God, let the moment quickly arrive that it shall please you to release me from this scene of misery."

"Oh! you will be comfortable enough by-and-bye, young lady," said the villain Hemlock, "and will learn to forget these heroics, especially when you become the bride of the Smuggler King."

"The bride of a pirate and a murderer," ejaculated our heroine, "never! Heaven will not suffer such a revolting event to take place."

"Well, we shall see," observed Raker, coolly, "but I fancy you will find the power of the pirate and the murderer, as you call him, greater than you at present perhaps anticipate."

"I scorn his power," said Flora, whose reason was now somewhat restored; "there is a power, an Almighty power above, that will shield me from all that he may attempt, and which will overtake him and ye with its terrible retribution sooner than you expect. The perpetrator of crimes so atrocious cannot long escape the vengeance of an offended God!"

"Why listen to this whining cant?" again remonstrated Hemlock; "it is but the wild raving of a giddy, headstrong girl."

"We have now arrived at the place of our destination," ed Sam Raker, "and therefore you must prepare to accompany us to the r."

Flora raised her eyes despairingly towards the building, which seemed to frown upon her, and then turned towards Maud, who had accompanied her on deck, and had been listening with feelings of pity and disgust to the conversation that had passed between her and the villains.

"It is no use attempting to resist them, my dear young lady," she said; "but endeavour to regain your fortitude and tranquillity; I shall be constantly with you, and will be unceasing in my endeavours to afford you consolation in the midst of your troubles."

"Consolation!" repeated Flora, "alas! what consolation can be imparted to a heart so seared as mine. Restore to me my William, ere you talk to me of comfort."

"Remember your orders," said Sam Raker, addressing himself to Maud; "you understand me?"

"I do," answered Maud.

"Then you will do well not to break them," added Raker; "you know the certain consequences that would follow."

Maud returned no answer to this, but devoting her whole attention to our heroine, she took her arm, and followed Sam Raker and some of the other smugglers from the ship.

They passed beneath an opening in the solid rock, which conducted them into a long passage, until they arrived at an iron door. This Sam Raker unlocked with a key which he had brought with him, and after traversing several passages, they arrived at last in the tower. They now passed through numerous apartments, in which were piled numerous bales of goods, and chests, the booty which the smugglers had obtained in their several lawless proceedings, and at length they came to an elegant suite of rooms, one of which contained a very extensive library, and the furniture of them all was costly in the extreme. Our heroine now felt quite exhausted, and sunk upon a sofa, Maud placing herself by her side.

"These are your apartments, young lady," said Raker, "and very handsome ones they are, I think you must admit. Fit for a princess; and if you cannot make yourself happy here, why it will be your own fault."

Flora scarcely understood what the ruffian said, for her heart was full, and her mind was too much occupied with other thoughts, but she gazed at him with a vacant stare for a minute or two, and then covering her face with her hands, she dropped her head upon the shoulder of Maud, and burst into a flood of tears, which the latter made no attempt to interrupt, knowing that it was calculated to afford relief to her overcharged heart.

"I will send some refreshment from on board," said Sam Raker, as he turned towards the door; "probably the young lady, when she has recovered a little from her fit, may feel inclined to partake of it. Come, Hemlock, we must return to the vessel. Here are the keys of the apartments, Maud, and mind you keep a watchful eye on your charge, or you know the consequences that will accrue to you."

"I require no further caution," said Maud, with a disdainful look, and Sam Raker motioning to his companion, they quitted the apartment together.

When they had departed the grief of Flora became more violent than ever, and she was completely deaf to all the remonstrances or consolatory observations of Maud.

"I am here, then," she sobbed, "in the lair of the tiger. Oh, God! protect me, or take me speedily to yourself, for I have no longer any wish to live. Why should I, indeed, wish to live, since my William is no more?"

"Pray be calm, my dear young lady," said Maud. "Providence is good, and although your prospects at present appear sad, something may, when least expected, occur to release you from the Smuggler King's power, and restore you to happiness."

"Happiness," repeated Flora, with a deep sigh; "is it not madness, mere mockery to talk of happiness to the heart-stricken? Can you restore my William to life? If you can, then talk to me of happiness."

"Banish such an idea from your mind," said Maud, "and endeavour to think the best. You know not that your lover really is no more."

"But every circumstance convinces me of the fact," returned our heroine; "or why did the villains refuse to produce him? You know that he is dead, yet would attempt to impose upon me by false and delusive hope."

"I am your friend," returned Maud, "and happy should I be if I could contribute in any way towards restoring you to peace."

"Peace," returned Flora, with a melancholy smile, "that will never again be mine."

"Oh, say not so, miss," said Maud, "you know not what fortune has yet in store for you."

"I know that all my hopes are buried in the ocean deep," sighed our heroine; "would that its green waves now covered me."

"But," observed Maud, "there are others for whom you should wish to live. Parents, dear, fond relations, who ——"

"Ah!" interrupted Flora, "speak of them; oh, continue to speak of them, for it will break my heart the sooner, and rid me of this existence, which is now such an insupportable burthen to me. I shall never, never behold them again."

"Do not despair," interposed Maud; "Providence is kind and merciful, and may restore you sooner to them than you anticipate."

Flora shook her head despairingly, but returned no answer at the moment.

"Alas!" she sighed, at length, "what must now be their anguish?—what the anguish—the maddening torture of the dear friends of my ill-fated William, at our mysterious disappearance? Oh, God! what misery, what a wreck has the villany of the miscreant in whose power I am, occasioned!"

She burst forth into a paroxysm of grief as she uttered these words, and her heartrending sobs were quite piteous to hear.

Maud viewed her in silence, and with feelings of the utmost commiseration, but she felt gratified to find that she was restored to reason, and hoped that in time she would become even more composed, and be able to meet with fortitude the persecution of Sir Julian, should nothing occur to release her before he arrived at the tower. She would willingly have run almost any risk to have restored her to liberty herself, but she saw not the slightest chance of it, situated as the tower of the Death Rock was, and so well guarded as it was

No. 25

by the creatures of the Smuggler King; but still she could not entirely banish from her mind a hope that something would occur to save the unfortunate damsel from the fate with which she was threatened.

She was interrupted in the midst of these reflections by the entrance of one of the smugglers with the refreshments that Sam Raker had promised, and which she immediately spread upon a table, and pressed our heroine to partake of them; but her heart was too full to suffer her to eat, and they remained untouched, Maud also having no appetite. Flora soon afterwards got Maud to assist her to undress, and feeling quite exhausted, she retired to bed, where, worn out, Maud was gratified to find that she shortly afterwards dropped off to sleep, which was more composed than, under all the circumstances, might have been expected. Maud continued to watch her with anxious looks, and felt a great relief that she was not interrupted by Sam Raker or any of the other smugglers, who had returned to the ship, and were most of them engaged in carousing.

"Well," observed Raker, "we have arrived at the place of our destination."

"Yes, and glad enough I am of it," replied Hemlock.

"And we have got the girl here in safety," added Sam.

"And what's more," observed the other, "contrary to our expectations, she is restored to her senses, and I am much deceived if she does not very shortly recover altogether."

"I hope that your surmises may prove correct," said Sam Raker, "for it would have been a troublesome job had she remained in the same state as she was only a few hours since, when our captain arrived."

"It would," returned Hemlock, "for our captain is not one of the mildest of tempers, and no doubt would have been much exasperated at his disappointment."

"I have no doubt he would," said Raker, "but still he could not have blamed me for what I did, after what had taken place, and the authority he had invested me with."

"Certainly not," observed Hemlock, "but it is much better as it is."

"Very true; and I trust, by the time Sir Julian reaches here, the girl will have quite recovered."

"Of course we cannot expect her to be in very good spirits," said Hemlock.

"No," replied Raker, "neither can our captain."

"Much depends on Maud."

"It does."

"Think you, you can depend upon her?"

"I am certain of it," answered Raker; "she dare not disobey our injunctions."

"And yet it is evident that she sympathises with the girl," observed Hemlock.

"She does," returned Raker, "and no wonder, she possesses naturally a tender heart, and you know well that she is not amongst us from choice, but necessity."

"True," said Hemlock, "and I am of opinion that she would gladly avail herself of an opportunity to escape from us, and probably betray ourselves and our captain to the land-sharks."

"Her death would then assuredly follow."

"Yes, if we had the opportunity," added Hemlock.

"If we had any means of ascertaining that such were her actual thoughts, she would not be suffered to live another hour."

"No," said Hemlock; "but leave Maud alone, she is no fool, and will ever conduct her designs with greater ingenuity."

"But still I do not think that we have anything to fear from her," said Sam Raker.

"Why, for that matter, the Smuggler King and his crew are not to be easily intimidated, especially by a woman. Think you our captain will disclose to this girl, this Flora Clarendon, who he really is?"

"I know not ; but should he not disguise himself, of course she will immediately know him, as she has often seen him as Sir Julian Mordlington."

"I think," observed Hemlock, "that, if he acts with his usual caution, he will not make her acquainted with his real character."

"It would, I am of opinion, be bad policy in him to do so," returned Raker ; "for, should she at any time make her escape, of which, however, I do not see much chance, she would not hesitate to divulge all, and there would be an end to our captain's baronetcy."

"To be sure there would," coincided Hemlock. "But think you our captain really intends to make her his bride?"

"I do."

"Well, she is a pretty lass," said Hemlock ; "but I imagine it will be a long time ere Sir Julian will be able to reconcile her to such a fate."

"It may," answered Sam Raker ; "but fear not but he will succeed in time. The captain is a fine, handsome man, and has eloquence at his tongue's end, and ——"

"True," interrupted Hemlock ; "but Flora is, they say, a virtuous girl, and never will consent to link herself to a pirate-captain, and one who has so often shed the blood of his fellow-creatures."

"But of what use will be her resistance? Will she not be compelled?" demanded Raker.

"Ay," answered Hemlock ; "but still, although she may be forced to become his bride, depend upon it she will never look upon him with any other feelings than those of hatred, horror, and disgust. And when she is made acquainted with the fate of her lover, which she must be, her sentiments will be increased rather than abated, if she ever survives the shock."

"Oh," returned Raker, "these women are strange animals, and turn like a weathercock. Deeply affected as Flora may now appear to be, the pleasures and luxuries that will be so abundantly lavished upon her by the captain, will, I dare say, soon work a wonderful change in her, and, when she finds that there is not the least chance of her escaping, she will, if she be wise, rather voluntarily consent than by any obstinate resistance perhaps provoke him to violence and revenge."

"But think you our captain really loves the damsel?" interrogated Hemlock.

"Love her?" repeated Sam Raker ; "no—such a passion as that is a stranger to the breast of the Smuggler King. The only sentiment he can feel for any of the sex is that of wild desire. Any other he would consider to be a weakness. But come, we have other work to do than to be standing talking here."

They separated, and Sam Raker re-entered the tower, in order that he might ascertain how our heroine was. He was glad to be informed by Maud, that, although she had been so poorly as to be compelled to retire to bed, she continued to get more tranquil.

"But I am afraid," she added, "that, when she is made acquainted with the actual death of her lover, she will suffer a relapse, from which it will not so easy to restore her."

"But have I not cautioned you not to hint even to her that William is dead?" asked Raker.

"And I will keep my promise," returned Maud.

"You had better."

"You have no occasion to threaten me, Raker," said Maud ; "but still I do not see how it is possible that she should long remain ignorant of it."

"Oh, yes ; she has no occasion to know," observed Sam Raker ; "some excuse must be concocted to quiet her apprehensions. It must be stated that William has by some means contrived to effect his escape."

"And think you the poor damsel will credit the falsehood ?" demanded Maud.

"You seem to wish that she may not."

"I sincerely wish that she may be able to escape from the fall which threatens her."

"Ah !" hastily exclaimed Raker ; "do you then advocate her cause ?"

"I sincerely pity her," answered Maud.

"Beware that your pity does not go too far," said Sam Raker.

"I need not your warning."

"Would you assist her to escape, had you the means ?"

"Why ask me that question ?" said Maud ; "am I not bound by an oath, a dreadful oath, to be faithful to the Smuggler King and his crew ?"

"Beware that you do not break that oath !" said Raker, with a stern look.

"Would that it had never been extorted from me !" exclaimed Maud. "But, alas ! mine has been a cruel destiny."

"Bah ! no more of this," said the smuggler ; "you know I hate sermons. Mind your behaviour towards the girl, I say again ; for I shall keep a watchful eye over you, and, should you deviate in the least from the line of conduct I have marked out for you, depend upon it you shall not go unpunished. Treat her with every kindness and attention, but be careful that you divulge not any of our secrets, or —— "

Before Sam Raker could finish this sentence, Maud, tired of his observations, and disgusted with his presence, turned upon him a look of ineffable contempt, and abruptly quitted the apartment.

Sam Raker bit his lips.

"That woman," he growled, "is a very she-devil, and I am afraid that some of these times she will bring us all into trouble. I must watch her narrowly, and, should I see anything to arouse my suspicions, she may yet learn to tremble at the power of Sam Raker, although she has hitherto treated him with such scorn. After the death of her husband, did she not reject my advances, although I am sure I was his equal any day ? However, that is all over now, and I have other things to think about than to trouble myself with the caprices of a silly woman. Love and I never properly understood each other, and that's the truth of it, so I have long since made up my mind to leave the cultivation of that passion to others more capable of the task than I am."

Thus saying, the smuggler hastened to join his companions in one of the large apartments below, where he had appointed to meet them, in order that they might enjoy themselves, which they did by giving way to the most boisterous mirth, singing, and drinking, and carousing in the most extravagant manner.

Notwithstanding all that Sam Raker had said to himself, he was actuated by feelings of revenge against Maud, and he would have been pleased to have an opportunity afforded him of gratifying that feeling, and was determined that the first which presented itself, he would not fail to seize upon without hesitation.

Maud well read his thoughts, but she treated him with contempt, certain as she was that the captain placed confidence in her, and that, however Sam might threaten, he would be afraid of going to extremities, lest he should offend the former. No one could view Raker with greater detestation than she did ; and, when he had presumed to press his hateful suit, she had felt a sensation of horror and disgust which we feel entirely at a loss to describe. But she rejected him boldly, and, although he continued to persecute her for some time with his loathsome importunities, he was afraid to proceed to violent means, and was ultimately constrained to give up the attempt. He could not, however, disguise the real sentiments of his mind from the penetrating eyes of Maud, and she marked them with the most thorough contempt, yet caution.

CHAPTER XIII.

THE BARONET.—THE ACCUSATION.—THE DISTRACTED FAMILIES.—THE ABRUPT DEPARTURE.

SIR JULIAN, after retiring to rest in the morning after he had separated from Sam Raker, slept but little, for his thoughts were too much occupied by the events of the night, and his exultation was so great at the success of his diabolical schemes, that he could scarcely keep it within the bounds of reason. The interview that he had had with William, and the manner in which it was evident to him he had excited and tortured his feelings, filled his bosom with the most fiendish delight, and he determined at no distant period to complete the gratification of that bitter hatred with which the young seaman had inspired him. Although he had given full authority to Sam Raker to dispose of him in any way he thought proper, should it be found necessary, he hoped that that necessity would not occur, for the villain had a wish still further to torture him, by keeping him a prisoner in the tower of the Death Rock, and making him become a witness of the union he intended to enforce between himself and our heroine.

"Ah!" he soliloquized, "the Smuggler King is again triumphant; who shall dare dispute his power? Those I hated are disposed of, and she whom I love is also in my power, and cannot now escape me. It will be useless for her to oppose my passion, for mine she must be, and nothing can prevent it. Love, did I say? Yes, stern and cruel as my heart is, the sentiment that I feel towards Flora, is so different to the passions that have hitherto been excited in my breast towards the sex, that I am certain it must be that feeling which now excites all my energies. She shall be my bride, and on the wide ocean with her pirate lord soon learn to forget those friends and connections from whom she has been taken. But a few days, and my eyes shall once more feast themselves upon her transcendant charms; but a few days, and the whole of my wishes shall be consummated. Oh! she will make a fair companion for the Smuggler King."

The villain basked and luxuriated in the ecstacy of this thought, and each moment grew more and more impatient for the time to arrive when he could take his departure from the hall, and rejoin his companions and the unfortunate victim of his persecution at the Death Rock. There were moments, however, when a fear would steal over him, that Flora would not be able to support the heavy affliction in which she must be placed at her abduction, and the alarming situation in which she found herself placed, and he was most anxious to know whether the smugglers would reach the place of their destination in safety, and the state of mind in which our heroine was. Of course, he could not but expect that she would be involved for some time in the greatest grief, and he was apprehensive of the effect which that grief would have upon her constitution. Should he be deprived of her by death, after all the trouble he had taken to get possession of her, he felt that it would be a disappointment which would require all his patience and fortitude to support. He also felt rather uncomfortable at the excitement which he was certain would be created in the neighbourhood by the strange disappearance of William and his lover, so soon after that of Mr. Fitzpatrick, the lawyer; the most rigid inquiries would be made, and yet he knew not why he should fear that any suspicion should attach itself to him, as he had never shown anything, particularly by his conduct, for such being the case, unless it was in the outrage he had once committed on the damsel, and which had evidently prejudiced the minds of her friends and relations against him. Besides, if even it did, what evidence could they possibly be provided with against him; and would not his power, and the station he filled in society, sufficiently protect him? He felt that to encourage such apprehensions was a weakness, and he determined to abandon them.

The abrupt departure of the pirate schooner would, no doubt, create considerable astonishment, and suspicion of her real character would be excited; but that could not affect him, as he had never, as he imagined, been seen to go on board of her, nor could it be known that he was in any way connected with her. Probably, it would be imagined that the lovers had been conveyed on board the vessel, and, in that case it would, he believed, entirely exonerate him from any impression to his prejudice that might have taken possession of people's minds.

Revolving these thoughts in his mind, kept Sir Julian awake for some time after daylight, and he then only slept for about an hour, when he arose, and prepared to await the issue of the events of the day.

He had seated himself in his study, and had taken up some documents to peruse, when he was aroused by hearing a confused noise of voices in the Hall below, and he was about to ring the bell in order that he might inquire into the cause, when there was a knock at the door of the apartment, and on his ordering the applicant to enter, Simon made his appearance, with his usual vacant stare and stupid grin, and after a variety of gesticulations, all indicative of his having some important intelligence to impart, he made a very low and obsequious bow to his master, and attempted to speak, but was interrupted by Sir Julian demanding, in his usual abrupt manner, what it was he wanted.

"Two strange men below, Sir Julian, who want to see you," answered Simon, again making a low bow.

"And what is their business with me?" inquired the baronet.

"Very strange business, I dare say, Sir Julian," replied Simon, "but they would not tell me what it was."

"What are their names?" asked Sir Julian.

"Very strange names, I have no doubt, Sir Julian," said the simple attendant, "but they would not disclose them to me."

"Tell them, I am engaged," said the baronet, "and cannot be disturbed."

"I did venture to tell them so, Sir Julian," returned Simon, "for I did not think you had arisen; but they would not take that for an answer, and said they must and would see you."

"Consummate insolence!" said Sir Julian.

"Very strange behaviour, indeed, Sir Julian," coincided the sensible domestic.

"Tell them, then," observed the baronet, "that unless they send up their names, and the nature of their business, I will not see them."

"Very well, Sir Julian," returned Simon, and once more bowing, he was about to leave the room, when his master called him back.

"Shut the door," he commanded.

"Yes, Sir Julian," answered Simon, doing as he was ordered.

"Come here!" ordered the baronet, sternly.

"Yes, Sir Julian," replied Simon, trembling, and slowly approaching his master, at the same time wondering what it was he now wanted with him.

"What time did you retire to rest last night?" demanded the baronet.

"Dear me, Sir Julian," said Simon, "why do you inquire?"

"Answer the question."

"Why, Sir Julian, Molly and I, in the servants' hall ——"

"Damn Molly and you!" impatiently interrupted his master; "cannot I have an explicit answer from you?"

"Ye—ye—yes, Sir Julian," faltered out Simon, "I was going to give you an *illicit* answer, only you would not give me time. I was going to say that Molly and I, in the servants' hall, were amusing ourselves, by talking about that terrible pirate and smuggler, the Smuggler King, when ——"

"Scoundrel!" exclaimed the baronet, furiously, and grasping the terrified Simon by the collar, "dare to repeat that name again and I will strangle you."

"Lor' bless me, Sir Julian," said Simon, very much alarmed, "oh! do not —I—I—beg pardon. But certainly that—that—he is a terrible fellow, and some say he is the very devil himself; he ——"

"Will you answer my question, sirrah?" once more demanded Sir Julian, with a menacing look.

"Oh, yes, Sir Julian, I was going to say, that Molly and I sat talking about that—that—I won't mention his name, until we were both frightened, and so we separated, and went to rest."

"And what time was that?" asked his master.

"About ten o'clock, Sir Julian," was Simon's reply.

"And had all the other servants retired to their chambers?"

"I believe they had, Sir Julian."

"Then you heard nothing?"

"No, Sir Julian."

"And saw no one pass in or out of the Hall?"

"How could I, sir," said Simon, "when I was in my own room?"

"True. You remember this caution I gave you before, that whatever you may see or hear in this Hall, you must say nothing, as you value your life."

"Oh, yes, Sir Julian," said Simon. "I will be certain not to disobey you; I will not say anything even to any one about that strange-looking black-whiskered gentleman that used to visit you, and who I used to think ——"

"Be careful, sirrah," interrupted his master, "you must not even presume to think."

"Very well, Sir Julian," said Simon. "I will be sure to obey you."

"Well," said the baronet, "now begone and deliver my message to the persons below."

"Yes, Sir Julian," observed Simon, and he was advancing to the room-door, when a sudden thought appeared to strike him, and he hesitatingly turned back.

"What now, fellow?" sternly demanded his master, "why do you not go, as I have ordered you?"

"Pardon me, Sir Julian," said Simon, "but I could tell you something very strange, indeed, if you would only allow me."

"What nonsense have you to utter now?"

"Indeed, Sir Julian, it is no nonsense, but something very serious and important, in my opinion."

"What is it?"

"Why, you must know, sir, that this morning being very fine, I thought I would take a walk to the harbour."

"And what then?" hastily demanded Sir Julian.

"Why," replied Simon, "when I got there I saw a great number of people assembled; and that black-looking vessel which has been lying so long in the port ——"

"What of that?"

"Why it was gone," answered Simon; "it had disappeared suddenly in the night, and it is now generally believed that she was a pirate ship, and some say it could have been no other than the ship of the Smuggler King, the terrible Devil Skipper, as it is called."

"Fools!" exclaimed Sir Julian, with some confusion, and he then added, "what reason had the idiots for supposing her to be a pirate?"

"Because she disappeared so suddenly, and many people now recollect that some of her crew were very suspicious-looking fellows, and ——"

"Beware, Simon," interrupted his master, "let me never more hear you utter a word of this, whatever you may think. If you do, you will incur my utmost displeasure."

"Oh! no, Sir Julian," answered Simon, who was greatly bewildered at his master's manner; "I will not say a word, depend upon it; but if I had known I had been so near the terrible Smuggler King, I should have been naturally frightened out of my seven senses."

"Fool!" impatiently exclaimed Sir Julian; "begone, and do my bidding, and remember well the warning I have given you."

"I will, Sir Julian," said Simon; "oh! dear, to think ——"

"Away!" commanded the baronet, in a voice which made Simon jump. He went to the room-door, but no sooner had he opened it, than two persons walked unceremoniously into the apartment.

"How now? What is the meaning of this insolent intrusion!" said the baronet, but perceiving that it was Mr. Clarendon and Backstay, he in a moment changed his tone, and in accents of affected politeness he added, "to what cause, pray, may I attribute this visit?"

"We came to demand justice, candour, and truth," replied Mr. Backstay, firmly.

"How, sir?" proudly inquired Sir Julian, and concealing his confusion as well as he was able. "This is a strange way to address yourself to me, sir; in what way can I assist you in obtaining the objects you have mentioned?"

"By having the honour and manliness to acknowledge the truth," returned Mr. Backstay, in the same determined manner as before, and eyeing Sir Julian narrowly.

"This language, sir, is bold, and such as I cannot, and will not, submit to even from my equals," observed the baronet; "but since you seem in no mood to do so, perhaps Mr. Clarendon may have the kindness to explain for what purpose you have visited me?"

"Sir Julian Mordlington," said Mr. Clarendon, in a voice almost choked with emotion, "you behold before you a broken-hearted man."

"What mean you?" inquired the baronet, "what has occurred to distress you thus?"

"My child, my poor girl, my Flora!" ejaculated the farmer.

"Ah! what of her?" asked Sir Julian, with well assumed astonishment and interest.

"Since yesterday afternoon she has been missing," answered Mr. Clarendon, and we have not been able to ascertain what has become of her."

"Flora Clarendon missing?" repeated the baronet.

"Yes," answered Mr. Backstay, "and so has my son, William Backstay."

"This is strange, and I am sorry to hear of it," said Sir Julian; "but were they both missing at the same time, say you?"

"They were," answered Mr. Backstay, "and my poor boy I am afraid has been murdered."

"Murdered?"

"Yes; in the hovel in which Crazy Marian sometimes seeks a shelter, we found a pool of blood, and this locket, which William always had suspended from his neck, and which I am certain he would not have parted from only with his life."

Sir Julian took the locket from the hand of Mr. Backstay, and when he cast his eyes upon it, and recognized it, he could with difficulty repress the expression of his emotion.

"This is indeed mysterious," said he; "but what cause had any one to murder him?"

"I firmly believe that he has lost his life in the defence of Flora Clarendon from outrage," answered Mr. Backstay.

"Or more probably," observed Sir Julian, "he has eloped with the damsel, and ——"

"Sir Julian Mordlington," indignantly interrupted Mr. Clarendon, "add not to the misery of an already distracted parent, by suspecting the innocence and virtue of his child. What reason had they to adopt such a guilty course, when they were honourably betrothed to each other, and would in the course of a short period have been united? Alas! I fear that my Flora has fallen into the hands of some villain, and that William Backstay has lost his life in her defence."

"This may be," said Sir Julian, with as much coolness as he could assume; "but what have I to do with the event? What is your object in calling upon me?"

"Sir Julian," returned Mr. Clarendon, and he fixed a keen and penetrating look upon the baronet, "I will not deny that a suspicion has entered my mind that you ——"

"Suspect me!" interrupted Sir Julian, and he frowned indignantly; "dare you, sir, thus attempt to insult me? Think you I am a murderer?"

"I pray you be calm, Sir Julian," answered Mr. Clarendon; "if I wrong you, may Heaven forgive me; but you remember that my daughter was once subjected to insult from you, and ——"

"And for which I have made you an ample apology," said the baronet.

No. 26

proudly; " but now, because the girl is missing, I am to be suspected of taking her away. This is intolerable, it is not to be endured, and I must desire you immediately to quit the Hall, both of you. Had you not been in your present state of trouble, I might have felt inclined to punish you for this unwarrantable libel on my character."

" Sir Julian Mordlington," ejaculated Mr. Clarendon, with increased emotion, " if I have wronged you, from the bottom of my soul I am sorry for it; but, oh, if you have the smallest spark of pity for the distracted parents of that poor innocent girl, you will not attempt to deceive us, but acknowledge your error, restore those who are at present lost, and here we are ready to swear that we will pardon you all that has taken place."

" Mr. Clarendon," said he, at last, " I can make every allowance for your feelings, under the excitement of the circumstances, or I should resent your unwarrantable and unpardonable insolence, in a far different manner to that I am now about to do. Am I tamely to submit to be accused of all the misfortunes that occur in the county? An old lawyer is missing, whom, it is said, but falsely, that I was acquainted with, and that my house was the last place he was known to go to; I am accused of having some knowledge of what has become of him, and on my conscientiously and truly denying the same, I am subjected to an examination by a magistrate. Now a girl is missing from her home, with a young fellow, of whose intentions, character, or designs, I know nothing, and I am to have my privacy abruptly broken in upon, and accused of knowing what has become of them also. This, of course, I cannot endure, and I must therefore desire that you retire from this Hall immediately."

" Hear me, Sir Julian," said Mr. Clarendon, who was more deeply affected than ever, and who began to fear that he had been too abrupt.

" I will hear no more," replied the baronet, sternly, and ringing the bell; " should you again appear here under similar circumstances, you may have cause to repent your temerity."

" Sir Julian Mordlington," observed Mr. Backstay, fearlessly, " depend upon it this affair, and that of Mr. Fitzpatrick, will be sifted to the bottom, and the guilty party, whatever his station may be, shall not be suffered to escape punishment."

" Am I to be threatened and bullied in my own house ?" said the baronet, with the greatest rage—(at that moment a servant made his appearance) —" show those persons down stairs,' commanded he, " and on no account admit them to the Hall on any future occasion."

Mr. Clarendon and Mr. Backstay were both about to observe something, but Sir Julian, after beckoning to the servant in a peremptory manner, retired from the room, and left them to themselves.

When the baronet was alone, he gave vent to his rage without restraint.

" Curses light upon them all," he said; " the bold varlets ! they have already dared to raise their suspicions towards me; and for why should they do so?—what is there in my conduct that has been seen by them that should render them suspicious of me? I would that I was away from this place, and rid of the Hall, for it seems as if I were to be perpetually annoyed while I remain here; I should have thought that my station in society, and the character I have assumed, would have shielded me from everything of the sort, but these lowly hinds have shown me to the contrary; but let them do as they please, they cannot harm me. Did they but know my real character, they would tremble to approach me. In spite of all, the Smuggler King ever has and will still triumph."

He traversed the room as he spoke, and then, in order that he might endeavour somewhat to regain his composure, he walked from the Hall into the garden, before he partook of his morning repast.

He reflected maturely upon all the circumstances, and what was best to be done; but he could not think of any other plan than the one he had already adopted, and in the absence of all proof of his guilt, what had he to apprehend?—nothing. He regretted, however, that he had made a purchase of the Hall, and wished he could as readily dispose of it again, for he was heartily tired of the place, and, after once quitting it, it was quite uncertain when he should be able to return again, engaged, as he would be, on the boundless deep, and in that lawless traffic which he had not himself for so many months mingled in. He was resolved, as soon as possible, to put the Hall into the hands of an agent, to obtain a purchaser for it with all possible dispatch.

In the meantime, the state of mind in which the friends and relations of the missing lovers were in was of such a powerful nature that we must fail in any attempt to describe it. Mrs. Clarendon was so overcome by her emotions, that her senses entirely wandered, and she was compelled to take to her bed, and the condition of Flora's sister was scarcely any better. At the house of Mr. Backstay all were involved in the same description of intense grief, and despair began to settle upon their minds.

Amidst it all they could not do away with the impression that Sir Julian knew something about the disappearance of the lovers, and the interview which they had had with the baronet, the reception they had met with, and the confusion and agitation he so frequently evinced, had not lessened those surmises.

When Mr. Clarendon and his companion quitted the hall, they immediately hastened to the house of Mr. Inglefold, the worthy magistrate we have before mentioned, and, as well as their emotion would permit them, made him acquainted with all that had happened. He listened to them with the greatest astonishment and commiseration, and when they had concluded, he promised to assist them all that lay in his power, and to lose no time in endeavouring to discover what had become of the lovers—although, in the present stage of the proceedings, he was not prepared to offer any opinion as to the probable fate of William and Flora. The blood which they had seen in the hovel, he said, certainly looked suspicious, but still they had no proof beyond the locket of the young seaman, that he had been there; but a strict search must be made after Marian, who, if her senses would permit her, might be likely to give them some light upon the subject.

With respect to the suspicions that Mr. Clarendon and Mr. Backstay entertained towards Sir Julian Mordlington, he could not for a moment agree with them, and he certainly blamed them for having been (out of mere supposition, and without the least evidence to support them) induced to obtrude themselves into the baronet's presence, and abruptly to lay such serious charges to him. He advised them not to adopt such a course in future, but to leave it to Providence and their own vigilance to unravel the mystery.

These alarming events, and in such rapid succession, created quite a sensation in the neighbourhood, and everybody was at a loss to whom to attribute them. Not the least clue had been gained that might lead to the discovery of Mr. Fitzpatrick, and Marian was also nowhere to be found.

The search after all the missing parties was continued with unabated vigilance, but it was all to no purpose; day after day elapsed, and still no better prospect presented itself. Mrs. Clarendon still continued in the same deplorable state, and in the minds of the others, immediately interested, all was anguish and despair.

The sudden disappearance of the Devil Skipper, had also created no little sensation; it was now almost generally believed that she was a pirate, and many attributed the alarming occurrences we have related to the wretches belonging to her. The authorities were greatly blamed for not having made more inquiries concerning her, and it was even hinted by some that they were acquainted with her real character, and winked at the same; and certainly it appeared like it, or the pirate never could have been so daring as to put in at that port. However that might be, they could gain no satisfactory proof of the truth of these surmises, and the whole circumstance remained in a state of the most inexplicable mystery, and all were lost in astonishment and alarm.

Two or three days after the disappearance of the lovers and Marian, it was publicly announced that the Hall was for sale, and it was understood that the reason Sir Julian Mordlington had come to that resolution was, in consequence of his having made up his mind to reside for the future abroad.

In less than a week after this, the Hall was found suddenly untenanted; Sir Julian had departed, no one knew when or where; but it was understood that the estate was sold, and that it was supposed that the baronet had departed immediately after the purchase had been made.

The abrupt manner in which he had quitted the place created no little surprise and speculation for a time, but at length it wore away, and Sir Julian was never more thought of or spoken about, unless it was by Mr. Clarendon, Mr. Backstay, and their families, they still entertaining the same suspicions of him as those which had first entered their minds.

A month had now passed away, and nothing could be heard of the unfortunate persons who form such prominent characters in this narrative; although every possible inquiry was set on foot, and officers were dispatched to all parts of the country to endeavour to unravel the painful mystery, and to ascertain, if possible, what had become of them. It was now almost generally believed that they had met with an untimely death, but who the monsters were that could have perpetrated such atrocious crimes, and what their motives could have been, no one could form the slightest conception.

Mrs. Clarendon continued much in the same state, and it was feared that the poor old woman had received a shock from which she would never more recover. As for Mr. Clarendon, Mr. Backstay, and the others, the unceasing anguish of their minds may be easily conjectured, and, indeed, a blight had fallen upon all their prospects, which it seemed that nothing whatever could remedy.

EPOCH III.—CHAPTER XIV.

THE STRUGGLE WITH DEATH.—THE BARREN ROCK.—THE SUFFERING SAILOR.—" A SHIP! A SHIP!"—SAVED!—THE VOYAGE.—THE SHIPWRECK.

FOR a moment after William's plunge from the fatal plank, into what was intended to be his ocean grave, he felt the waters gurgling over his head; deafening peals of thunder seemed to rattle in his ears, mingled with the hoarse shouts of exultation from the wretches on board the pirate vessel—his senses reeled, and death seemed about to claim his victim, when he arose once more to the surface of the waters, and with that tenacity of human life which is inherent in us all, even though surrounded with danger and despair, he determined to make a powerful effort to save himself. But, alas! what prospect was there of his being able to do so? There was nothing, as far as his eyes could stretch before him, but a boundless sea, and no symptoms of any relief at hand from some friendly vessel who might pick him up, and take pity on his situation. Nothing could be more dismal and hopeless than his prospect; yet still he resolved to struggle while life still remained within him.

These thoughts flashed across his brain with the same rapidity as the rolling waves that ever and anon buried him in their white crested bosoms, and seemed to carry death in every motion. William was an excellent swimmer, and he battled with the billows manfully; he still could hear the shouts of the pirates, and once turning his head he beheld them gazing after him anxiously. Fearing that they might put off a boat in pursuit of him, this stimulated him to fresh exertions, and most vigorously he struggled on, until he could hear their voices no more, and again looking back, he perceived that he had got to some distance from them, in a contrary course to that which they were pursuing; at that moment a huge wave swept over him, engulphing him entirely in its bosom, and it was then the pirates thought he had sunk to rise no more.

Once more he arose when the wave had passed over him; but he was now almost exhausted; breathless and panting he still struggled hard to preserve his life, but he was every moment getting weaker, and despair began to settle upon his heart. In that awful moment of trial, he mentally uttered a prayer to Heaven, and invoked the protection of the Almighty for the preservation of his beloved Flora from the diabolical machinations of the miscreants in whose power she was. The receding waves gave him a short respite, and in that brief interval his strength became a little recruited. Desperate were his efforts, and his courage became somewhat reanimated when he beheld, at some distance, what appeared to be an immense chain of rocks, stretching themselves far into the ocean.

Like the distant ray of light, that gives hopes to the benighted and way-worn traveller of human habitation, did those rocks appear to the struggling young mariner. Could he but gain them, he might still be rescued, at any rate from immediate death, and have a chance of seeing some vessel pass, that might rescue him from the untimely fate by which he was at present enthralled.

Again encouraged by even this faint prospect, he struck out with more than human strength, and seemed to defy the furious waves that dashed and hurled him with frightful velocity along.

Suddenly his hands came in contact with some large substance. It was a raft formed out of planks and spars, and which had been doubtless used by some unfortunate beings in a recent wreck. Rendered desperate by the horrors of his situation, he threw himself with wonderful agility upon it, and, with a length of rope, which he found attached to it, he lashed himself to it, and then breathing another prayer, he committed himself to the care of Providence, and resigned himself to his fate, whatever it might be.

The raft was a very strong one, and braved the waves that had now become more calm. It was fortunately, too, hurried in the direction of the rocks, which now every moment became nearer; but William hoped to find some creek into which he might run, and save himself from being dashed to pieces against the rocks.

For more than an hour our hero continued to float in this manner, and was so much exhausted by the extraordinary exertion he had undergone, that it was not without the greatest difficulty he could prevent himself from going to sleep, in which case his death must have been inevitable.

As he approached the rocks nearer, he was gratified to find that his prayer had been heard, and that he was going exactly in the direction of a little creek, or armlet, between two of the loftiest of them, and where he might probably find some means of ascending to a place of safety.

Another quarter of an hour brought him immediately to the rocks, and the raft floated smoothly and gently into the creek. Releasing himself from the rope with which he had lashed himself, and clasping his hands fervently together, he uttered his gratitude to the Almighty, for the preservation he had thus far experienced. But when he looked up at the lofty and apparently totally inaccessible rocks, there seemed to be but little hope of his being rescued altogether.

While these thoughts were crowding rapidly upon his mind with the most torturing influence, the raft had floated some considerable way ; and, as his eyes wandered eagerly in search of some place where he might make an attempt to save himself, they suddenly rested upon a portion of one of the loftiest and most extensive of the rocks, where a flight of steps, formed by the master-hand of nature, presented themselves. With an exclamation of gratitude and delight, William immediately leaped from the raft, and swam towards them. He gained them in safety, and, grasping firmly at one of the small, craggy projections, he pulled himself up by main force, until he got a firm footing. To clamber those niches or steps, however, was no easy task, tired as William was, and sore with the struggling he had undergone, and he could proceed but very slowly indeed. At length he gained a small ledge, just capable of holding his body, and, seating himself on it, resolved to rest himself for a few minutes, and befit him for the completion of his task. He was now safe from immediate danger, and although, of course, he was ignorant of what ultimate fate awaited him, he felt at that moment like the respited culprit on the scaffold.

But even then his principal thoughts were directed to poor Flora, and the probable misery she was at that time enduring, and the torture of his mind was almost too great for endurance. Twice or thrice, so intense was his anguish, that he was almost induced to plunge at once into that fate he had lately struggled so hard to escape from ; but an instinctive power withheld him, and, dark as at present was the prospect before him, a sudden hope sprang up in his bosom, and led him on to fresh energy and exertion.

"Dear, dear Flora," he soliloquized ; "shall we ever meet again in this world ? Shall we ever again be pressed in happiness to each other's bosoms ? Oh ! yes ; in spite of all our misfortunes, notwithstanding the utter misery of our present situations, something whispers to me that we shall. And yet, what frenzied torture will fill the poor girl's breast, should she become acquainted with my supposed fate, which the heartless wretches will, no doubt, exult in telling her? She will never be able to survive the shock ; or, if she does, what but a state of worse than death can she expect from the monsters who hold her in their power? Beloved friends, parents of my Flora, to ye now my thoughts must turn. Oh ! what a wreck has this event, no doubt, caused in those two once happy homes. My more than parent, Fauchette, Harry, all so dear to me, methinks I see ye in all the wildness of your uncertainty and despair. These reflections are maddening. I that once was so happy and so cheerful, am now a wretched being, clinging to that life which probably will only be prolonged for me to endure, if possible, still greater misery. But, let me not entirely banish hope from my mind. The Almighty commander above, when He has, in his own all-wise will, buffetted us sufficiently in the storms of adversity, will, I trust, anchor us safe in the port of happiness at last. Yes, I will not entirely abandon the anchor of Hope. Bless you, my Flora, bless you, my friends, and may all good angels sustain you in this hour of trial."

He felt greatly relieved by having thus given vent to his feelings, and once more prepared to ascend the rock. It was a most tedious and laborious task, and it seemed as if it was almost impossible that any human being could gain the summit of that stupendous and lofty eminence ; but, nothing daunted, William proceeded, although his feet were very much cut with the labour he had already undergone, and the blood streamed from them, from many a wound he had received from the sharp points of the rocks they had come in contact with.

He advanced but slowly, for the holes in which he had to place his feet, were, in some instances, at a considerable distance apart, and it was not without the greatest difficulty he could succeed in climbing to them. Several times he nearly missed his foot-hold, and narrowly escaped being precipitated into the deep beneath ; but at length, having reached a second ledge, he once more seated himself to recruit his strength, and looked around him.

The day was beautiful, and the ocean now calm and lovely ; brightly did the sun glisten upon that boundless mirror, and not a cloud obscured the clear blue sky ; at any other time the susceptible mind of the young mariner would have been delighted, and even now his soul rose in admiration of the magnificent works of nature, which his eyes contemplated.

He had now ascended to an immense height of the rock, but he had still nearly as far to go. The sight was quite enough to dishearten the stoutest and most determined ; but William remained firm and undaunted. Hope sustained him, and the thought that he should yet behold Flora, and those so dear to him, urged him to deeds that at any other time, bold as he was, he would probably have shrunk from with horror and despair.

Having now once more recruited his strength, and marked the safest way for him next to pursue, he resumed his task, his perilous situations being at times truly frightful, and such as would turn the head dizzy to gaze upon.

At length, after almost superhuman exertion, he gained the summit, and throwing himself down, quite worn out, he fell fast asleep before he could gaze around him, to observe the situation in which he was now placed.

When he again awoke, somewhat refreshed and invigorated by the slumber he had had, but very cold, he found it was night, and the moon was shedding her full lustre on all around, aided by countless myriads of twinkling stars.

He now arose and gazed around him ; the prospect was cheerless in the extreme. He found himself on an expansive surface of rock, which, as far as his eye could penetrate, was quite barren. He already felt the gnawings of hunger, without having the means of appeasing its cravings. Here, then, he must remain to perish of want, unless Providence sent some vessel near the place to rescue him. Had he not better have met his fate in the ocean, he reflected, than to be left to meet a death of so dreadful and lingering a description? He folded his arms across his chest, and for a few moments stood absorbed in deep and painful thought, and unresolved what course to pursue, to leave his fate to chance, or at once to put an end to his sufferings, by plunging into that ocean he had but lately taken such trouble to escape from.

" No!" he at last exclaimed, "that would be cowardly ; that would be unworthy of him who has braved so much. I will not rush unbidden into the presence of my Maker ; but still live, and trust to His mercy to rescue me from the jaws of death."

He felt more confident after having given utterance to these words, and that confidence was increased when he had offered up a prayer to that Supreme Being to whom he had before appealed.

He walked to the side of the rock, and looked over it on to the sea ; it was a sublime sight, such a one as must have filled even the most insensible mind with the most unbounded feelings of admiration and wonder. The ocean appeared like one vast expanse of liquid silver, and reflected back the bright face of the moon, and her companion orbs, as clearly as in a mirror. A refreshing breeze just gently rippled the waves, and all was so calm and tranquil that it imparted a heavenly feeling to the mind, and for awhile was calculated to blunt even the keenest darts of anguish and care.

William continued to gaze upon this scene for some time, and during that period he was lulled into a happy forgetfulness of the loneliness and wretchedness of his own situation. But this was only transient. Once more he stretched his eyes as far as they could penetrate across the ocean ; but he saw not a speck upon the horizon, not the least signs of any vessel, and if he even had, he should have despaired of making known his situation, as, brightly even as the moon shone, he feared that those on the watch would not have perceived any signal of distress which he might hoist, and it was not at all probable that the vessel would approach anywhere near the rocks.

He now walked to some further distance, and was suddenly startled by beholding what appeared to be the dark shadow of something on the ground. He hastened towards it, and then perceived that it was a rug or blanket, which was spread upon the earth. There were the remains of some beef, several biscuits, and a broken bottle, which contained a small portion of rum. Near this spot, some embers indicated that a fire had not long since been kindled there.

"Some unfortunate, or unfortunates have been here as well as me," said William ; "shipwrecked, doubtless, but, perhaps, they are still on the rock ; oh! should they indeed be, I shall still not be left entirely lonely in this barren place. Let me search."

He took a sup of the rum, which seemed to put new life into him, and he then set off on his search, hope being once more revived in his bosom. He took the whole circuit of the place, and examined every spot, but he could discover no traces of a human being.

"They are gone," he said ; "they have been rescued, and I am still left alone."

He returned to the spot he had just before quitted.

"But," he observed, "what could have induced them to leave these refreshments and this blanket behind them ?"

Most welcome, however, were they to him, and he sat down, and ate two of the biscuits, and a small portion of the beef, reflecting upon the necessity of his eating sparingly, not knowing how long he might be destined to remain on the rock. Never had he partaken of any meal that seemed half so sweet, and when he had done, after having returned thanks to Providence for this unexpected meal, he rolled himself in the rug, and resigned himself to sleep.

Notwithstanding the long sleep he had had in the afternoon, he had undergone so much fatigue both of body and mind, that he soon again slept soundly; but his imagination was haunted by dreams of the most conflicting and agitating description, and he felt but little refreshed by it, when he awoke, which was not till the morning.

That day passed away in a similar manner, William being almost constantly looking on the sea, but without seeing anything to excite his hopes. Although his appetite was very keen, he partook still more sparingly than he had done the evening before of the provisions that had so providentially been placed in his way. The third day of the young seaman's being on the rocky, barren island, also expired, and still no hope. The spirits of William began to droop more and more ; the food was all gone, and now all the horrors of starvation stared him in the face, and his brain became bewildered. He continued to watch with the same eager eyes as he had before done, on the following day, but with no better success ; and his hunger was hourly becoming so intense that he could scarcely endure it.

He clasped his hands in despair, and then traversed the spot with a wild and distracted mien.

"God!" he exclaimed, " what have I done to merit such a cruel destiny

as this?   Oh! do not let me die of the gnawing pangs of hunger, and my cold remains left on this barren spot to be devoured by birds of prey.   The thought is too horrible to dwell upon; why should I thus linger on in misery and despair, when I have the means of ending it?   Heaven pardon me the crime, but I can endure this no longer."

As he spoke, he rushed wildly towards that part of the rock by which he had ascended to its summit; frenzy lit his blood-shot eyes, and despair urged him on.   He had reached the edge of the rock, and was about to commence descending it, when some secret power held him back, and the gentle reproving voice of Flora, seemed to breathe in his ear "Forbear!—Forbear! there is yet hope;—still live for her, who shall yet be restored to your arms."

"'Tis the voice of an angel that speaks; madman! coward! what was I about to do?" he ejaculated, stepping back;—"yes, dear Flora, for thy sake, I will yet struggle with my destiny.   But yet 'tis dreadful to be thus left alone on this barren spot, and with these dreadful pangs gnawing at my vitals.   God of Heaven, send me relief! or speedily end my misery by death!"

He returned to the place where he usually watched, and pacing backwards and forwards, he kept his eyes firmly fixed on the broad expanse of the glittering deep, but nothing to alleviate his anguish met his observation.   His throat was parched, and burning with thirst, and his brain was racked as with a torturing fever.   In vain he searched for a spring.   There was none to be found; oh! for one single draught of water—it would have been as the balm of Heaven to his soul.   Madness, he feared, would seize upon him; he tore his hair, and then bit the flesh from his arms, and greedily sucked the thin blood, as it slowly oozed from his veins.   This but increased his anguish, and made his thirst more intolerable; he groaned aloud in the bitterness of suffering and despair, then raved from end to end of the rocky island with the air of a

No. 27

maniac. At length he threw himself on the hard and sterile earth, quite worn out, and resigned himself, as well as he could, to his fate, which he now believed was fast approaching. But he was deceived; nature was not yet quite exhausted, and sleep gradually stole over his eyelids. It was a happy but brief relief from the terrible agony he had been enduring.

He awoke in the morning in a state too dreadful to think upon. His eyes burnt like two balls of fire, and his tongue protruded from his mouth with fever and insupportable thirst. His hunger was so great that he could have gnawed the flesh from his bones, but some inscrutable power prevented him, while his heart felt as though a thousand wolves were gnawing at it. He was too weak to rise, but with difficulty crawled on his hands and knees to his old place of watching. Had any person have seen his cadaverous countenance at that time, they could never have recognized in him the happy and handsome sailor, who was the theme of admiration to all who knew him. Full twenty years seemed to have passed over his head during the few days he had been on that dreadful rock.

"All merciful God !" he exclaimed, in a hollow voice " oh, why did you ever suffer me to awake again ? Why not have let that sleep be eternal, and not have called me back again to this most insupportable misery? No hope ! no hope ! and I shall go mad ! I am enduring even worse than the torments of the damned ! Oh, spare me ! spare me, Heaven !"

As he gave utterance to these words, his eyes wildly wandered once more over the sea. He sees a dark shadow on the horizon ; he stretches his eyes to their utmost limits, yet fears to encourage that fond hope which might prove delusive, and render his despair yet more unbearable. The object becomes more distinct ! It approaches nearer ! God ! it is no cruel phantom of the brain !

"A ship ! a ship ! Saved ! saved !" he shouts, with a wild hysterical laugh, and in an instant with suddenly renewed strength, he sprang upon his feet, and shouted and laughed alternately, like a madman ! Then he called aloud for help, but the vessel was yet too far for the sound of his voice to reach her. Next he tore with frenzied haste his neckerchief from his neck, and waved it in the air, then raved from one end of the rock to the other, shouting and calling as before.

The vessel was sailing with a favourable wind in the direction of the rock, and rapidly approached, but she was still a long way off, too far, indeed, for any one on board of her to observe the signal of the half frantic William, or to hear his shouts ; and at length tired and exhausted, he abated the violence of his actions, and with folded arms and form erect, he more calmly awaited her approach.

On, on, she came, and at last she got so close, that William was enabled to discover her build. We cannot do justice to the unspeakable delight with which he beheld that it was an English frigate ; and he had, therefore, not the least doubt of being rescued from his awful situation. And now he again arose, and with renewed strength, and renewed by hope, he dashed along the rock, shouting and calling, and making use of every frantic gesture.

Nearer and nearer came the frigate, and at length had arrived so near the rock that William felt confident that those on board must see him. Again and again he waved his handkerchief in the air, and called as loud as he possibly could. It was a moment of painful, of the most dreadful, suspense and anxiety ; and it was enough to madden the young man's brain, uncertain as he was that he should be seen, or left to meet the fate with which he had been so long threatened. Several minutes more elapsed, and the misery of William increased, and despair began once more to settle upon his heart, as there was no notice taken from the vessel of his repeated shouts and the signal which he was waving. He called more frantically than ever, and at last he had the satisfaction to behold that a boat was being put off from the ship, into which two seamen jumped, and pulled towards the rock. With clasped hands and upraised eyes, William sunk upon his knees, and uttering a grateful prayer to Heaven, overpowered by the violence of his emotions, and completely exhausted by the exertions he had undergone, he became insensible.

When he recovered, he found himself placed in a snug berth, and being attended to by the surgeon of the ship, who had been using his utmost skill towards his restoration. He was about to return his thanks, when the surgeon requested him to remain silent, as he was not then in a fit state to talk. Such refreshments were then adminstered to him as he was capable of receiving, and being then somewhat more composed, the surgeon left him in the charge of one of the seamen, desiring him to endeavour to compose himself to sleep. This William did, and exhausted nature soon brought that refreshing balm to his wearied frame. But dreams of the most painful description disturbed the imagination of the young mariner: all that had occurred within the last few days rushed upon his mind's eye ;—the death of Marian, whom he believed to be his mother, the interview with the Smuggler King, the meeting with Flora on board the pirate vessel, his subsequent cruel sentence, and the horrors of hunger and despair he had undergone on the barren rock. Then busy and torturing imagination conjured up scenes of the future sufferings he was destined to meet with, and the probable fate of her to whom his whole soul was so fondly devoted. He saw her in the power of the dreaded pirate ; he beheld her subjected to all those insults which the base and evil passions of the villain could urge him to. He heard the soft and plaintive voice of Flora appeal to the monster for forbearance, in vain ; he saw him encircle the trembling form of the maiden, and press loathsome kisses on her blushing cheeks, while he stood by, bursting with indignation and shame, loaded with fetters, and unable to render her any assistance. God ! what mingled feelings of rage, torture, and despair at that moment William imagined he was enduring. It was all the suffering of dreadful reality, at the same time the pirate crew stood around, and laughed at his anguish with demoniac exultation. He felt as if he had more than human strength, and struggled with the fury of an enraged giant to burst the fetters that bound him. He struggled in vain, and at every effort that he made the miscreants laughed louder and more exultingly than before. And oh ! the looks of Flora at that time ! How she groaned aloud in the anguish of her offended virtue, and implored Heaven to save her. At length, exhausted with her struggles, William imagined that the poor girl fainted, and being raised in the arms of the pirate captain, was borne from the place, amid the shouts of his cruel and daring crew.

Suddenly, William imagined that the scene changed, as if by magic, and he then found himself in a kind of chapel, chained to a pillar. There was no one in the place at the time but himself. It was hung around with black drapery, on which were numerous fearful devices, such as skulls, cross-bones, &c. In the centre was a kind of altar, from each end of which stood forth two human skeletons, holding in their long, fleshless hands a lamp, from which glimmered a sickly light, that imparted an aspect of additional horror to the dismal revolting place. The atmosphere of the apartment was oppressive and sickening, and William found a difficulty in breathing. All was silent as death, and he could almost imagine himself in a sepulchre.

Some minutes, William imagined, elapsed in this manner, and without any interruption ; but suddenly confused sounds smote his ears, the door at the further end of the apartment was thrown back on its hinges, with a loud clap, that resounded through the place in dismal and hollow echoes, and a procession of the pirates, attired in the costume of the crew of the Smuggler King, entered; they walked three abreast towards the altar, singing a rude chorus of rejoicing, of which the following were the words :—

> " Crew of the Smuggler King rejoice,
>   In tones of gladness raise each voice,
>   Let us be gay, dull care away,
>   For this is our monarch's bridal-day.
>   Hail to the bride!   Hail to the bride!
>   The bride of the king of the ocean tide,
>   Merrily sing, merrily sing,
>   In praise of the bride of the Smuggler King.
>
> " To the altar let's away,
>   And there let homage each one pay,
>   To him who rules on the bright blue sea,
>   And to her who our future queen shall be.
>   Oh! this is the pirates' day of joy,
>   And nothing shall our hearts annoy;
>   Merrily sing, merrily sing,
>   In praise of the bride and our Smuggler King."

As they shouted in coarse tones these words, the desperate crew of the Devil Skipper advanced up the centre of the place, and arranged themselves on each side of the altar.   Next appeared the villain Sam Raker, bearing the black flag of the Smuggler King, and supported on either side by two of the most desperate of the crew, after which came the smuggler-captain, attired in a most costly suit, but still masked.   He led, or rather dragged, the trembling and almost dying Flora towards the altar.   Oh, how pale and piteous were her looks, as she turned her despairing eyes upon William, while, had a thousand demons been worrying at his heart, he could not have endured half the torment that he did at that moment.   He groaned aloud in all the bitterness of soul-rending agony; then he struggled powerfully to release himself from the place to which he was bound, but he tried in vain, and at every effort which he made the shouts of exultation that escaped the wretches increased.   His brain burned, and his bloodshot eyes seemed ready to burst from their sockets.

Flora was attired in white, and on her head she wore a splendid tiara of diamonds and brilliants.   They reach the altar, and then the shouts of the smugglers were repeated, in tones of the most boisterous mirth and triumph.

And now there appeared standing behind the altar, the form of a man dressed as a minister, but wearing a black mask, the same as the Smuggler King.   The latter forced Flora to the altar, and the priest muttered some unintelligible words, at the end of each sentence of which the smugglers shouted—

"All hail to the bride of the Smuggler King!"

Then the priest went through some curious and mysterious ceremonies, in which he was joined by the others; he next forced the fair hand of Flora into that of the pirate-chief, the black flag was waved in triumph over their heads, the loud shouts of the smugglers rent the place, and once more forming themselves into procession, they moved from the apartment, Flora, having fainted, being carried in the arms of the Smuggler King.   As they departed, they sang the following chorus :—

> " 'Tis done, 'tis done! let all rejoice,
>   And hail our queen with heart and voice;
>   Let these walls with gladness ring,
>   On the nuptials of the Smuggler King.
>   Rejoice! rejoice! rejoice!"

Again in the frenzy of despair did William struggle to release himself, and when the last of the procession quitted the apartment, in frantic and delirious accents did William exclaim :—

" Fiends! wretches! my soul denies the unholy ceremony! Innocence like
hers must not, shall not be sacrificed to such a monster. Heaven will not
permit it! bring her back, I say, and restore her to these arms! she is mine!
she is mine! release me, and restore to me my deeply injured Flora!"

He became hoarse with the frenzy of his agony; but still he struggled violently; he heard the shouts and laughter of the pirates; they rung in his ears
like the voices of so many demons; his heart seemed ready to burst from its
tenement; his brain whirled round, and in the insupportable torture of that
moment, the spell of sleep was broken, and he awoke.

Cold drops of perspiration stood upon his temples, and every limb trembled
with the horrors of that dream. It was almost more than the exhausted
strength of William could support, and it required the prompt attendance of
the surgeon to restore him to anything like composure. All that day and the
two succeeding ones, William continued in a very weak and dangerous state,
while his thoughts were dreadful and racking in the extreme. The dream
continued to haunt his imagination, and he could not but entertain the impression that what he had there seen, was destined to be realized. He also
recalled to his memory the dream which Flora had related to have occurred
to her, and when he reflected upon the manner in which most of the events
that had been presented to her imagination in that vision had been fulfilled,
it added strength to his apprehensions.

At length by the unremitting attentions and skill of the surgeon, the young
mariner gradually recovered, until he had gained strength sufficient to leave
his berth, and was then introduced to the captain, to return his thanks for the
kindness and humanity he had experienced from him.

Captain Sherwood, was an excellent man, and as brave an officer as any in
the navy. He expressed the greatest sympathy in the misfortunes that had
befallen William, and proffered him all the assistance in his power. He informed him that the name of the vessel was the Dauntless, and that she was
going on a three years' station at Malta, and that on their arrival at that place,
he had no doubt but that William would be able to obtain a passage in an
homeward bound ship, as he had no doubt he would be most anxious to be
restored to his friends.

William again repeated his acknowledgments to Captain Sherwood for his
kindness, and the prospect of his being restored to his friends served to tranquillize his mind, and render him more resigned than could have been expected
in so short a time, and under the circumstances.

Several days elapsed, and the ship proceeded on her voyage prosperously,
and William had so far regained his strength, that he was enabled to take
his share in the duties of the vessel. But on the ninth day after William had
been taken on board, the weather changed, and became very squally, heavy
showers of rain descending. The gale increased, and in the evening, which
was as dark as a funeral pall, the thunder and lightning were awful in the
extreme, and the wind varied from S.W. to S.S.W. Then the storm continued
with the most unabated fury, and rather increased. About one o'clock in the
morning it blew tremendously, and William, who at that time was in his
hammock, was suddenly awakened by a great shock, and a confused noise
of men on deck. Immediately he ran up, thinking that they had come in
collision with some other ship; but before he could reach the quarter-deck,
the ship gave a great stroke upon the ground, and a frightful sea broke all
over her.

William could now perceive the land rugged, rocky, and uneven, about
three cables' length from them. And now as the ship was lying with her
broadside to windward, the masts soon went overboard, carrying several of the
unfortunate crew with them. Awful and most distressing was now their
situation, while the tempest raged with terrific fury, and death presented itself

whichever way their eyes were directed.   The masts, rigging, and sails, were hanging alongside in a confused heap.   Violently was the struggling ship beating against the rocks ; the waves curled to an almost incredible height, then dashing down with such force, that they could expect nothing less than that the ship would be split to pieces every minute.

Every person was thrown into the utmost confusion, and it was several moments before they could recover from it ; but when they did, they found it necessary to get everything over to the larboard side to prevent the ship from heeling off, and exposing her deck to the sea.   And now, in the terror of the moment, some of the crew, in spite of the captain's commands to the contrary, eagerly wanted to get the boats out, and, in defiance of all, and deaf to every entreaty, one of the boats was launched, and six of the ablest of the crew leaped into her in a moment, braving one of the most terrible seas that had ever been known ; but they soon paid the penalty of their rashness, for scarcely had the boat got to the ship's stern, when she was whirled to the bottom, and not a soul escaped.   The gale still continued to increase in fury, and the vessel continued to drive at the mercy of the waves, minute guns of distress being fired.   It was a dreadful scene, and death appeared to be inevitable.

At length the unfortunate ship struck upon a reef of rocks, broadside to the shore, heeling on her larboard side towards the sea.   The terror of all was now greatly increased, and many of the crew, in the frenzy of despair, leaped overboard into the sea, and anticipated that death which seemed certain to overtake them.   But the worst part of their danger was yet to come.

During this time William remained calm and resigned, acting with the greatest promptitude, and executing all the orders given to him with the greatest skill and quickness.   He mentally offered up a prayer to Heaven for the preservation of Flora, and then prepared to meet that fate which seemed approaching him every minute.

While they were thus occupied, loud cries of horror and distress were heard from another portion of the vessel, and it was then ascertained that a fire had broken out in the gun-room.   It was found that the manner in which this accident was occasioned, was by some matches communicating to some powder scattered about at the time the signal guns were fired.   The flames soon became most fierce, and the smoke issued in such a manner from the different hatches, that it prevented any person from going below to attempt to extinguish them.

Fortunately, that which no human exertion could have performed, was in about ten minutes effected by the incessant seas that burst over the ship.   In about half an hour, the orlop deck suddenly gave way, and the larboard side of the vessel fell in, when the officers and some of the crew were washed off, and instantly drowned ; and among the rest, the first lieutenant, who perished in an attempt to reach the bow of the ship.   Despairing of assistance, several of the crew now leaped overboard ; but, from the eddy caused from the wreck, they were carried out, in spite of the aid which those on board endeavoured to render them.   About half-past nine o'clock the poop was washed away, and seventy or eighty of the crew, jumping overboard, with difficulty succeeded in reaching it.

They had nearly gained the shore, when a heavy sea, striking the after part, it went end for end over, and every person upon it perished.   The wreck soon afterwards heeled in towards the shore, and, upon heeling off again, it rent fore and aft, and parting in two places before the main-chains, and abaft the fore-chains.

Language must fail to do justice to the horrors of that moment.   A horrid yell was heard for about a minute, after which all was silent, the wreck having dashed to pieces most of the unfortunate sufferers.   About thirty or forty seamen and marines still remained on the bow, where tremendous seas were incessantly breaking over them, and threatening immediate destruction. The only hope of preservation depended on a single gun, whose weight, they flattered themselves would prevent the bows from being upset. Incredible as it may appear, at this critical moment, several of the men were fast asleep, or in a kind of stupor, with their hands fast locked in the chain-plates. From this situation, however, they were soon awfully aroused. The timbers of the bows, incapable of resisting the fury of the tempest, suddenly opened ; the gun went from the side, and all the unfortunate survivors were instantly precipitated into the body of the wreck.

In this moment of horror, William, who had become quite exhausted from the extraordinary exertions he had made, was nearly insensible. Studying only to keep himself above water, he floated in a direction parallel with the shore, and thus escaped the fragment of the wreck by which all his companions, who made directly for the shore, were dashed to pieces.

His strength was soon exhausted ; as a last resource to save his life, he caught at a small piece of timber, a nail of which wounded him in the breast. He instantly fainted away.

CHAPTER XV.

THE CONTINUED SUFFERINGS OF WILLIAM.—THE DISCOVERY.—THE DEAD ALIVE.

FORTUNATELY William continued to float, but he was soon aroused from the state of insensibility which had come over him, by receiving a sudden shock. He immediately caught hold of some weeds, which he held with a convulsive grasp, and at length repeated surges drove him and the weeds (which he still continued to hold fast) over some small rocks, which bruised him exceedingly in several places. Fortunately, however, these rocks served as a barrier to the sea, they broke the force of the waves, and enabled him to crawl to the craggy shore, which, after many painful efforts, he effected.

Now he found himself above the reach of the sea, worn out with fatigue from the bruises he had received, and also with hunger and thirst, and cold. Quite overpowered with the severe struggles he had had to encounter, and so soon after his former sufferings on the barren rock, the senses of William soon became benumbed like his body, and he fell into a death-like sleep. It was a great mercy to the poor shipwrecked mariner, who seemed destined to experience nothing else but the most painful misfortunes in rapid succession.

It was not until the following mid-day, that William recovered from this torpid state ; and probably he never would, had it not been for the happy influence of the sun, who darted his genial rays upon him, and gradually life and animation were rekindled.

But, alas ! to what a sense of renewed horror and suffering was he awakened ; he gazed with astonishment and terror at the prospect around him ; the clouds indeed were dissipated, but the gradually subsiding surge lashed the shore, and exhibited many of his poor mangled shipmates, stretched and breathless on the beach. To the susceptible mind of William, nothing could be a more harrowing sight than this. For a time he forgot even the keenness of his own miseries in the contemplation of this piercing spectacle. He could scarcely refrain from tears, but at length summoning all the strength and fortitude he could, he at intervals conveyed each of them beyond the reach of the sea, and covered their bodies with sea-weeds.

And now he seated himself on the earth, and gave way to all that bitter misery of feeling which his situation naturally excited. It seemed as if he was doomed to perpetual misery, or why one calamity so quickly succeed another? Never, never, did it seem that he was fated to see his native land again, and if Flora had met with the fate which had been hanging over her head, and which the fearful dream he had had would seem to prognosticate, he had little reason to cling to life.

He was aroused from these reflections by feeling the urgent want of nourishment. He had then fasted two days and a night. He therefore arose, and started off in quest of some food. Not far had he wandered before he found some shell-fish, which had been thrown up in great quantities by the late gale. Most delicious was the flavour they had; William fared most sumptuously upon them. He was equally well supplied with water, for the rains which had accompanied the storm had filled the cavities of the rocks, and afforded him ample draughts. Never had he enjoyed anything half so much. But although he was greatly refreshed by this meal, his mind was oppressed with an almost insurmountable weight of care. That evening, and the greater part of the next day, William passed with little rest, and full of the most gloomy and painful reflections on his past disasters and present situation. Greater, however, was his anguish at the uncertainty of the fate of Flora; and loudly he bewailed the evil destiny that had torn her from him, and placed her in the power of such merciless wretches.

"She is lost to me! lost to me, for ever!" he ejaculated, beating his breast; "and even now is doubtless suffering the most cruel anguish, if not shame. But no; surely the monster will not be allowed to triumph in his base and and unnatural designs. There is a just God who will prevent it, and bring him to that punishment which outraged innocence calls for. And yet that wretch has called himself my brother, Brother! My heart revolts in abhorrence at the consanguinity. And yet, what motive could he have for the assertion, if it were not true? What a hard fate is mine; but, brother or no brother, should the opportunity ever be afforded me, by Heaven, I will wreak a terrible vengeance on his head."

He paced backwards and forwards for a few minutes, in a state of the wildest disorder, and immersed in the most tormenting reflections.

At break of day, however, he became somewhat more composed, and began to be more reconciled to the little spot which had preserved him; trusting the time might come when Providence would further befriend him, or suffer him to breathe his last in quietness on the rock; for death he thought preferable to the lingering state of suffering to which he had been for some time past subjected.

The place did possess some little signs of vegetation, and here and there a lofty tree or two reared their heads; but altogether it was most lonely and wretched, and the more so, as he had no companion to whom he could communicate his thoughts, and there seemed to be no prospect of his being rescued.

He had now been here four days, and had in vain endeavoured to solace himself in his forlorn situation; he wanted not for provisions, as there was an abundance of fish, and a species of wild fruit, which was very pleasant and palatable. He had also erected a tent from the sails and spars of the wreck, which happened to be washed ashore, and thus he had a shelter from the inclemency of the weather, which had, however, been hitherto very fine. The melancholy fate of the captain, who had been so kind to him, and the rest of the unfortunate crew, greatly affected him, and preyed upon his spirits, and he deeply regretted that not even one had been saved from the wreck to be to him a companion in his solitude.

He would frequently walk all over the place to amuse himself, and for

exercise, and one day when he had been on one of these perambulations, feeling himself tired, he sat himself down beneath the shade of some trees in order to rest himself, and to indulge more deeply in meditation.

While he was thus occupied, he was suddenly startled by beholding the shadow of what appeared to be a human form, on the ground. Astonished, he immediately started on his feet with an exclamation of surprise, but in an instant the shadow was gone, and he could hear the footsteps of some person on the ground, as if hastily retreating. Quickly William rushed towards the spot where he had seen the shadow, and there beheld the form of a man, flying with the speed of lightning, and already at a considerable distance.

The feelings of delight that he experienced at the sight of a human being can readily be imagined; but of what character the man might be, of course he was at a loss to conceive. He had nothing on his person but a light pair of drawers, and his hair hung long and loosely over his shoulders. The thought immediately occurred to William, that he was some unfortunate shipwrecked mariner like himself, and filled with the hope of a companion in his solitude, he shouted aloud, and called upon him to stop. The man, however, continued to retreat with unabated speed, and never once ventured to look back. He was making his way towards a small cluster of trees at the farther end of the island, and before William could gain upon him, he plunged into the midst of it, and immediately disappeared from his sight.

Disappointed and astonished, William continued to run towards the place, for he was still not without a hope that the stranger could not elude him in an island whose extent was so limited. Having at length reached the cluster of trees before mentioned, William examined the spot most minutely, but could not discover any place which could afford concealment. It was the furthest extremity of the island, and William was quite at a loss

No. 28

to imagine where he could have retreated. He felt greatly vexed and dis-appointed, and yet he was not without a hope that he should discover him, and after once more examining the place, he prepared to retrace his steps to his tent.

This event occupied his mind the whole of the night, and he was unable to get but little rest through it. That his eyes had not deceived him he was certain; but who the man could be, and his motives for being evi-dently so alarmed, also where he had concealed himself, he could not form even the least idea. He could only entertain the same notion that he had at first—namely, that he was some unfortunate person, who, like himself, had escaped from shipwreck; but then if he was so, he could not account for his conduct, in flying from him, when it might have been imagined that the sight of a human being would have inspired him with a hope of relief being at hand. However, notwithstanding he had this time avoided him, he did not believe he could long do so, and he determined to try every means in his power to find out the place of his concealment, and ascer-tain who he was.

He had not the least apprehension that he was an enemy, or that he had more companions on the island with him, or he would not have fled from him thus; but what surprised him most was, that he had not discovered his tent, in which case, as he had evinced such a dread at the sight of a fellow-creature, it was not likely that he would have approached so near the habitation of a human being. Perhaps he was some unfortunate man, who, tired of the world, had taken up his residence there for choice, and not from accident, and if so, his shunning all intercourse with mankind was not so surprising.

The more William reflected on this subject, the more anxious did he be-come to unravel the mystery; and by the break of day on the following morning he started forth on his examination, sanguine with hope that he should be able to meet with some favourable result. He took a complete circuit of the island, and examined every nook and corner that was likely to shelter a human being. but without success. He then made his way to-wards the cluster of trees from whence the man had so suddenly and unac-countably vanished from his sight, going to it from a different way. He had arrived within a few paces of the place, when he fancied he heard the sound of a human voice. He paused and listened, and his heart palpitated with hope. All was silent, and he began to fear that he had suffered his imagination to deceive him, when he again heard an exclamation, and was then certain that he was not mistaken. Cautiously he advanced, fearful of alarming the man, and thus again depriving himself of the opportunity he sought. Looking between the foliage of the trees, to his unspeakable de-light, he beheld reclined upon the earth the very object of his search; it was the same individual he had seen the day before.

His back was turned towards him, therefore he had no opportunity of observing his features; but the figure was that of a robust man, nearly naked, and whose skin was browned with the heat of a scorching sun, to which he had probably been long exposed.

While William thus stood, in a state of mingled astonishment and plea-sure, the stranger once more spoke:

" I was foolish to fly from him, very foolish, but my fears suggested that he was one of my enemies, who threatened me with slavery. There is no vessel to be seen, and from what I have this morning observed on the shore, it is more than probable that he is some unfortunate seaman who has been wrecked in the late gale, and Heaven has at length sent me a companion in my solitude. I will seek him out, and chance whether I meet with in him a friend or a foe."

"Those tones," thought William, "surely, I have heard them before. Yes, their peculiar accent is quite familiar to my ears."

The man now arose from the earth, and turning round, William beheld his features: no sooner did he do so, than he uttered an exclamation of the most unbounded astonishment and pleasure, and bursting in between the trees, he confronted him.

For an instant only, the man gazed at William with an expression that no language can describe; then, with a loud and frantic cry, he rushed forward and enclosed him in a vehement embrace, while mingled tears, laughter, and sobs, evinced the power of his emotions. It was Mr. Fitzpatrick, whom our readers have been led to suppose had met with so horrible a death at the hands of the smugglers.

CHAPTER XVI.

THE DISCLOSURE.—MR. FITZPATRICK'S NARRATIVE.

MR. FITZPATRICK had recognised the young mariner at the same time that he did him, and such was their joy and astonishment at the meeting that it was several moments before they could either of them utter a syllable. Again and again did the unfortunate lawyer embrace William, with all that warmth and sincerity, so characteristic of the Irish, and, in the fulness of his heart, wept abundance of tears.

William was no less deeply affected; from the first moment he had beheld Mr. Fitzpatrick, he had been prepossessed in his favour, and, notwithstanding the pleasure he felt at having again met with him, it was not unmingled with the deepest regret at the alteration he observed in his appearance, and the suffering he had no doubt undergone.

Mr. Fitzpatrick, independent of the pleasure he felt at once more meeting with William, could not help gazing upon him with a still deeper degree of interest, from the likeness he bore to one whom he had so greatly esteemed in life; and the strong hope which had sprung up in his mind, that in him he might discover the being whom Sir Julian had informed him still lived, but who had so long been supposed to be no more.

"Och hone! och hone!" at length exclaimed the noble-minded Irish gentleman, "and faith, did I ever expect to live to see this day? And is it your own-silf, darling, now? Och! but I shall go stark, staring mad with joy. Never, never, did poor Patrick Fitzpatrick expect to see human being again. And you are the honest farmer's son, who behaved to me with so much kindness and hospitality! I can scarce believe my eyes; and yet, faith, and I am sorry and glad, all in the same breath; for you have been unfortunate or else you would not have been here."

"My dear sir," returned William, "this meeting with you has quite bewildered me. Your mysterious disappearance caused us all the greatest alarm, and every inquiry was made after you, but without success; but as Sir Julian Mordlington's was the last place you were known to visit, and, as you had thrown out hints that you and he were not on very goods terms, our suspicions lighted upon him."

"Faith, and nothing could be more correct," said the lawyer; "he was the villain who did it all. He it was who sought my life, because I would not become as great a scoundrel as himself. But you look sad, boy! arrah! and I am afraid you have had your full share of trouble since we last met."

"Yes, sir," returned William, with a sigh; "that home you beheld so happy has been made a wreck of, and this mind, which once knew only joy, is wretched and desolate. Villany has been at work to destroy all that was once so fair and lovely. I have but just escaped from pirates, while my fair, my gentle craft, she who was the sheet anchor of my hopes, the rudder and compass of all my wishes, is even now within their power, and probably by this time consigned to a fate that is even worse than death itself."

These thoughts quite unmanned the young seaman, and he dashed the tears of anguish from his eyes.

"Tunder and turf!" cried Mr. Fitzpatrick, "and can you spake the truth? What? that young damsel, with the two beautiful eyes, twinkling like diamonds, and the voice of such heavenly sweetness, that it was enough to transport a person with rapture to listen to it, taken from you, from her home, her parents, and friends?"

"Alas, 'tis true!" answered William.

Mr. Fitzpatrick gave a peculiar whistle, and then suddenly laying hold of William's arm, without saying another word, he pulled him hastily after him, and, after proceeding some little distance to the right, he began raking away a quantity of weeds, of which William, in his search, had taken no notice, removed some boards, and then revealed a cavity, just sufficent to admit a human body. He dropped into the opening first, beckoning William to follow, which he did, and then found himself at the entrance of a passage, which seemed to lead to some extent under the rock, and which was lighted through several natural fissures.

Having proceeded along this to some distance, they descended into a large and spacious natural cavern, which received light in the same manner as the passage they had traversed, namely, from apertures in the rock.

In one corner was a heap of leaves and weeds, which formed Mr. Fitzpatrick's bed, while the rocky projections answered the purposes of seats. Mr. Fitzpatrick pointed to one of them, which the young seaman, astonished at all he beheld, seated himself upon, and the former placed himself by his side. After a short pause, during which the lawyer eyed William with increased interest, he said,

"Faith! and what you have stated, young man, has given me the greatest pain; and is it pirates you say you have escaped from, and that your lover, that fair girl, you fear is still in the power of?"

William answered in the affirmative.

"And their vessel?"

"Was lying in the port, in the neighbourhood where my friends reside, unknown and unsuspected."

"Ah! the Devil Skipper," said Mr. Fitzpatrick, "and the captain the terrible Smuggler King?"

"The same," answered William; "but you appear to know him?"

"Arrah! now, be aisy—be aisy," replied the eccentric Irishman—"all n good time. Answer me one question."

"Name it?"

"Are you the actual son of Mr. Backstay?"

"Why do you ask the question?" inquired William.

"Do not be after bothering me now," returned Mr. Fitzpatrick, eagerly. "Och—och! and I'm all impatience—I am all doubt, hope, and fear. Again I ask you, are Mr. and Mrs. Backstay really your parents?"

"They are not," replied William.

"Hurrah!" shouted Mr. Fitzpatrick, and he arose from his seat, and performed such strange antics about the cavern, that his companion began to fear that his intellects were affected. "We are coming to it," he continued; "my heart tells me we are coming to it, and that all will yet end well. Och! and the very moment I saw you, my heart assured me that you—but do not keep me in suspense, but tell me all the particulars you know about yourself."

"My dear sir," observe the astonished William, "surely my history, so far as I know of it, cannot be of any interest to you."

"Not of interest to me!" repeated Mr. Fitzpatrick. "Tunder and turf! darling, and you cannot say of what interest it may be to me, and to you to let me know it. Do not be after tasing me now."

William, whose astonishment the more and more increased, at last complied, and related all that he knew of the manner in which he had been saved by Mr. Backstay, when a child, from the wreck, and what had subsequently occurred. Mr. Fitzpatrick listened to him with the utmost attention, and frequently interrupted him with exclamations of the most curious and unaccountable description, and when he had concluded, he eagerly inquired,—

"The name of the shipwrecked vessel? Quick—quick!"

"I do not know it," answered William.

"Och! bother—bother!" he cried; "but let me look at your neck."

William unbared his throat, and no sooner did Mr. Fitzpatrick behold the marks that have been before mentioned, than he once more uttered a strange cry of delight, and vehemently embraced William, tears of ecstacy tracing each other down his benevolent cheeks.

"Och, hone—och, hone! 'tis he—'tis he!" he shouted. "I have found him at last. My hopes are realised. Och—och! and whoever thought Mr. Patrick Fitzpatrick would ever have lived to see this happy day? Yes, it is the darling honey! The son of the best friends—the—the—oh! joy —joy!"

"My dear sir," said the greatly-surprised William, "what is the meaning of all this?"

"The meaning is it you ask?" said Mr. Fitzpatrick. "Faith! and it is this that I have discovered all that I wish to know."

"Did you then know my parents?" demanded William.

"Know them!" repeated Mr. Fitzpatrick; "och! sure and I did then. Och! this is illegant—this is famous. And it's the day of triumph over the guilty that will some time arrive."

"Their name—their name?" said William, with looks of the most earnest supplication.

The lawyer paused a moment and reflected, then replied,—

"No, it must not be; it might frustrate my plans. Nay, do not be after putting yourself out of the way, honey. Sure and it's for your own benefit that I decline revealing to you the names of your parents at present."

"You torture me," said William. "Why delay making me acquainted with all?"

"I have told you that it might thwart the plans I have in view for your benefit."

"How can it do so?" demanded the young man. "Oh! if you knew the sensations you have created in my breast by what you have asserted, you would not thus keep me in suspense."

"Faith, darling!" said the worthy lawyer, "and nothing can grieve me more than to thus afflict you; but I promise you that, in due time, you shall be made acquainted with all, and it shall not be the fault of Mr. Fitzpatrick, if you are not restored to your rights and your proper station in society."

"This mystery is unbearable!" said William.

"Patience—patience, honey; it is all for your good."

"Were my parents noble?"

"They were."

"Am I the child of shame ?"

"The child of shame!" indignantly repeated Mr. Fitzpatrick; "bad luck to the spalpeen that would dare to say so."

"But are my parents living?"

"Your poor father," replied the lawyer, with much emotion, "I fear, perished in the wreck fiom which you were so miraculously preserved, but your mother, for aught I know to the contrary, poor lady, may be still alive."

"Was she then unfortunate?"

"She was deeply wronged," answered Mr. Fitzpatrick, "bad manners to the wretches who worked her so much misery."

"Had I a brother ?" asked William.

"You had," answered the lawyer, "by the same father, though not the same mother."

"And lives he still ?"

"He does; he is a most atrocious villain !"

"And his name ?"

"That also have I powerful reasons for not revealing," replied Mr. Fitzpatrick, "but, by and bye, he shall know both me and you to his sorrow."

William traversed the cavern for a few moments in silence, but with the greatest emotion.

"Oh! why," he said, at length, "should I be thus kept in a state of such painful mystery ?"

"Be calm, darling," said the lawyer, "and rest assured that it is necessary for your own safety and the furtherance of my designs, that you should bear with this yet a little longer; but all shall, by and bye, be explained, no doubt to your satisfaction. In the meantime, let us for the present change the subject, and I will relate to you the particulars of my disappearance, and what brought me in the situation in which you now find me."

Impatient as William was to have the mystery unravelled in which his origin was involved, he was still anxious to hear the particulars which Mr. Fitzpatrick mentioned, and he therefore endeavoured to calm his feelings, and requested the lawyer to fulfil his promise, which he did, as the reader will find below, omitting, as will be seen, such facts about the will and the real character of Sir Julian Mordlington, as it might not answer his purpose to reveal at present.

"After leaving the house of Mr. Backstay," commenced the lawyer, "I repaired, according to my intention, to the Hall, in order to have an interview with Sir Julian."

"Why," interrupted William, "the baronet has stoutly denied that he has any knowledge of you, or that you ever visited him."

"No doubt of it, the villain!" said Mr. Fitzpatrick, "but that he has spoken falsely may some day or other be proved to his shame and confusion. But to proceed—the facts that occasioned that interview it would not now be prudent for me to disclose; let it suffice, that he endeavoured to bribe me to a most villainous deed, which I rejected with scorn and disgust. The consequence was, that high words ensued, and in the midst of them several ruffians rushed into the room, seized me, and conveyed me to another apartment, where I was kept confined until night, when I removed on board the Devil Skipper."

"Ah!" ejaculated William, with astonishment, "then Sir Julian and the pirates were in some way connected ?"

"That will probably be seen by and bye," returned Mr. Fitzpatrick, "but allow me to proceed with my narrative—I was sentenced to death, and two or three hours afterwards, being secured in a sack, so that all hopes of my escape seemed futile, I was conveyed in a boat by several of the ruffians to some distance out at sea, and, in spite of my entreaties for mercy, I was precipitated to what, at that time, I thought inevitable death. It was a dreadful moment when I was plunged to the bottom of the deep, to hear the waters gushing over me, and the shouts of triumph from the wretches, as they rowed away from the scene of death."

"Monsters!" exclaimed William.

"Ay, monsters indeed," returned Mr. Fitzpatrick; "but Providence ordained that they should be foiled in their designs. Owing to the heavy plunge which my body made in the water, or the mouth of the sack not having been properly secured, the rope which bound it burst, and I was enabled to release myself from my perilous situation, and rose once more to the surface of the deep; but the prospect around me was most hopeless. I was far out at sea, and could not perceive any sight of land, or a boat or any other vessel that might pick me up. To attempt to reach the place from which I had been brought would have been madness, as I was at too great a distance from it, and would, in all probability, have fallen into the hands of the pirates again, if even I should have been able to do so.

"Having practised it early in life, I am an excellent swimmer, but not knowing any place on the coast, I knew not whither to direct my course, and therefore all chance of my being saved from a watery grave appeared to be at an end. However, with the tenacity with which we all, even in the most hopeless cases, cling to life, I determined to make a desperate attempt to save my life. But every effort I made seemed likely to prove ineffectual, for the sea at that time was running very high. I buffeted on, notwithstanding, with all my strength, sometimes swimming, and sometimes floating on my back, and by the force of the waves was driven at an immense rate along for more than half an hour, but still without any prospect of relief from the jaws of death, nothing but one vast expanse of ocean appearing around me. I perceived several small vessels pass within a short distance of me, but when I attempted to call to them for assistance, my voice was stifled with the waters, and I was left to despair.

"I was now almost exhausted, and thinking that there was no possibility of my being saved, I breathed a prayer to Heaven, and was about to resign myself to my fate, when, by the light of the moon, I beheld something tossed about on the waves, and which was rapidly being dashed towards me. With the frenzy of despair I caught at it, and it proved to be a boat, turned bottom upwards, and in which some unfortunate individual or individuals had probably perished. It righted, as the wind at that moment changed, and into it I crawled more dead than alive. My situation was now very little more cheering than it had been before, for the boat was hurled along with frightful rapidity at the mercy of the waves, and it seemed impossible that it could live. I sat myself down in the boat, and viewed my desolate condition with despairing eyes. The moon and the stars were shining most brilliantly above, while the wind and the waves were raging at the same time with the most fearful violence; still, although the boat was tossed about like a straw, she continued to weather the gale, notwithstanding she was driven far out to sea, and I knew not in which direction she was being carried.

"Dangerous as was my situation, the fatigue I had undergone, caused me to feel completely overpowered by sleep, and after having once more committed myself to the care of Providence, and never again expecting to awake in this world, I stretched myself at the bottom of the boat, and almost immediately sunk into a deep sleep or torpor.

"When I recovered, I found myself lying in a cabin, and learned from the persons who were attending me, that after I had been picked up by them, I had remained in a state of insensibility for twenty-four hours, and that they had the greatest difficulty in recovering me. I felt myself very ill, as may be expected, and at that time, and for some hours afterwards, had not strength sufficient to ask any more questions. Every attention was paid me, but my mind was in a great state of agitation to know what would become of me, as the ship was proceeding at a rapid rate.

" At length, when I had become somewhat more composed, I was informed that I was on board a merchant vessel, bound to the coast of America, and the captain, after being informed of my singular misfortunes, and ascertaining my name, very humanely promised me all the assistance in his power to return home, from the first port we might touch at; in the meantime he endeavoured to persuade me to make my mind contented, as, if even I should be compelled to proceed the whole of the voyage with him, I had been saved from a dreadful death, and should receive every kindness and attention from him.

" I thanked him for his humanity, but dreaded the idea of having to proceed the whole of the voyage, as it would cause the most serious dis-- arrangement in my affairs, and I knew not what might happen previous to my return. Fate, however, had conspired against me: the following morning, the wind began to rise, and in the course of an hour it blew a perfect hurricane, which lasted for some time with great fury, and the ship was driven far out of her latitude. The storm continued throughout the day, but towards night the wind began to shift and abate, and suddenly became calm, so that we could make but little progress.

" The captain having ascertained the latitude we were in, expressed some alarm lest we should encounter some of the Algerine corsairs, who often ventured on that part of the ocean, and committed the greatest cruelties. This idea created the most serious apprehension in my mind, as our vessel was but ill adapted to resist such wretches, and on her being a very fast sailor rested our every hope. In case of an attack, however, the captain ordered every preparation that it was possible to be made to receive them, and being a good vessel, and carrying six guns, while all the crew and the passengers (of which they were about twenty-eight in number), being resolved to fight boldly, we did not entirely despair.

" For my own part, unused as I was to such scenes, although, I believe, not naturally timid, I dreaded such an event, and trusted that the fears of the captain would not turn out to be correct. In this hope, however, it was my fate to be disappointed, for, after the lapse of about four hours, and just as daylight was beginning to appear, the man who was on the look-out, vociferated that he saw a sail, and presently afterwards, when the light became stronger, two large gallies full of men, were perceived coming towards us. As we saw that all hope of avoiding our approaching enemies was at an end, and that we must come to an encounter, of course we made up our minds to the worst, every person on board being resolved to sell their lives dearly, rather than linger in a state of slavery, that would be even worse than death.

" At this moment I felt endued with double courage, and knowing the desperate state of the ship, I determined to use all my energies, and immediately offered my services to the captain, at the same time informing him that I was unused to warfare, but was resolved to exert myself to the utmost on the present exigency. He thanked me, and having provided me with pistols and a cutlass, I went on deck. I forgot to mention that we had two bow-chasers, and, unfortunately, the ship not having steerage way, we were compelled to bring them to bear upon the corsairs.

" The wretches approached, and, as they did so, we very smartly saluted

them with grape and cannister shot, and this caused amongst them considerable destruction. Right on board ran the leading galley of the corsairs, and carried away our spritsail-yard. Then did they immediately, or at least a portion of them, board our crew ; but, after a sharp and severe struggle, they were repulsed. They were forced backwards, and many of the most desperate, who contrived to escape the slaughter that was created by the bravery of our men, were plunged into the deep, and, as you seamen would call it, were consigned to Davy Jones's locker.

" And now the galley becoming entangled with the bows of our ship, and swinging broadside to, the corsairs found it an advantage, for they had an opportunity of pouring in a larger number of their crew. By this time, too, the second galley had got to the scene of action, and ran us on board on the quarter, by which means our force was divided.

" But still undaunted remained our crew, notwithstanding this occurrence, and noble was the resistance they made. The slaughter which they caused amongst their foes was most terrible. Becoming desperate, at length the corsairs rushed on board, and with their captain leading them on, like an infuriated demon, they seemed determined to have their revenge, or to a man perish.

" At this time I was in the cat-head, by the side of the captain, and after having snapped his pistol at me, which failed in its object, the pirate captain drew another from his belt, and aimed it at the captain. That also failed, and becoming desperate, he made a determined blow at him with his sabre. Our captain, however, was an experienced swordsman, and when the corsair made the blow, he most skilfully parried it off, and at the same time, watching the confusion into which his antagonist was thrown, he rushed forward with a short boarding-pike, and before his enemy could offer any resistance, he plunged it into his body. The corsair gave one hideous yell, and fell back into his own galley a corpse.

No. 29

" Notwithstanding the bravery of our men, the numbers of the enemy quite overpowered them, and many of our crew defending the quarter deck, in consequence of the loss of their gallant companions (who were either killed or wounded) were obliged to give way; while the corsairs, who were desperately enraged at their chief's death, made such a desperate attack, and in such numbers, that we were compelled to run to the hatchway, to make good our retreat from their fury.

" But our cruel enemies pursued us ; and now resistance was of no avail whatever against the heartless assassins who had attacked us. In this dreadful dilemma, we solicited quarter, which was granted to us, not from a principle of mercy, to which their inhuman hearts are callous, but from a hope of gaining a good booty by ransacking the vessel, a desire to increase the misery of the surviving wretches, and by disposing of us as slaves to enrich themselves.

" When quarter was thus granted us, we were commanded to come on deck, and, no sooner had we done so, than the monsters tied our arms behind our backs, and in this manner we were dismissed. However, no sooner had this been done, than we heard a great confusion and noise among the corsairs, which we afterwards found was occasioned by the plunging violently of the galley against our vessel.

" As it appeared afterwards, when the galley first boarded our ship, they had started a plank forward, and injured her bows most materially in other respects. However, they had found means to stop the leaks, and soon freed her by having set to at the pumps.

" And now the corsairs, having secured all their prisoners and divided them, it was my lot and that of the captain to be put on board the very vessel that had received the injury. The captain was immediately recognised as the one who had slain the corsair chief, and I, being his companion at the time we were taken, was set down as equally guilty, and we were both, consequently, treated with a greater degree of inhumanity than the rest.

" The first thing they did with us was to drive us to the chains, where we were spit upon, scoffed at, and abused in every shape, after having been first fettered, and then lashed as if we had been a couple of dogs. Cruel, nay barbarous as was this treatment, we bore it with fortitude and resignation ; but at the same time we could not help the most painful and indignant sensations taking possession of our souls.

" The weather continued calm, and thus every advantage was afforded to the corsairs, which they took. The two galleys shot a-head, and took the prize in tow. As our vessel was heavily laden, she was obliged to *treble-man*, and the current running contrary to their destined port, the rowers, from the excessive fatigue of the oar, were quite exhausted, and soon began to drop off.

" And now approached the moment of the most severe trial. The chains that bound us were ordered to be knocked off, and we were placed as substitutes for the rowers.

" With all our strength did we try for several hours, and it was no use to offer any resistance, as the lash was inflicted in its most goading barbarity to any that attempted to murmur.

" We were all of us stripped of our shirts, our backs severely galled, and for want of nourishment, and with toil and severity, were so weak, that life could scarcely be said to remain within us. In vain were all the sighs and groans of agony we uttered ; they had no more effect than the murmurings of the idle wind upon these monsters in human shape.

" But the Almighty heard our prayers and sent us some relief. A breeze sprung up, and as it continued to increase, to row it was no longer safe nor necessary. In consequence of this we cast off, and as it was still favourable, we were ordered to lie on our oars. Oh! what a release from worse than death was this to us all. But long our hopes were not suffered to endure, for soon the elements began to gather, and, as the evening drew on, a violent gale arose, which, with the roughness of the sea, permitted us no longer to use our oars. This was certainly, in one respect, a respite, but at the same time, all the horror of a tempest was before us, and we felt certain that, in a case of necessity, the corsairs would consign us to the deep. This even might have been considered a mercy, as the prospect at present before us was still more dreadful, namely, a wretched life of slavery and torment; but human nature under any circumstances, and with whatever prospects, still clings tenaciously to existence, and so was it, I believe, generally with us. The clouds threatened a heavy storm, and these portentions were ultimately realized. Dark as pitch became the night, and we soon lost sight of the other galley and the prize. The sea rapidly increased, and, as it did so, the leaks of the galley that had not been sufficiently stopped, gained upon us in a most alarming degree. All our efforts to preserve the galley in which we were, were without success. Everything showed that she was quickly about to founder—she was sinking fast. And now in this critical moment, when all hopes of the galley being saved from her perilous situation were at an end, the corsairs began to clear their boat, and to hoist her out, which was done accordingly, with as little delay as possible. As many as the boat could hold, got in, which was about one-half of the crew, the remainder were left to take their chance in the fast sinking and crazy vessel. Among that number was I.

" No more did we see of the boat, and in a few minutes over the leaky vessel the sea made a breach, and I must confess that at that moment my thoughts were too much occupied in my own preservation, that, with the selfishness of all human nature, in times of imminent peril, little or no attention did I pay to the condition of my fellow creatures in misfortune. It is astonishing, with the best feelings that human nature can contain, this one passion should so strongly predominate, but I dare say you have experienced it, and therefore I have no occasion to apologise for entertaining it, especially as I should be guilty of hypocrisy, were I to attempt to deny it.

" I plunged into the sea, observing a rocky island at some distance, and after much exertion, was enabled to reach it, and clambered with great difficulty up its craggy sides, until I reached the summit. Here, quite exhausted, I threw myself down, and remained in a state of unconsciousness for several hours.

" When I awoke, I sought for some means of allaying my hunger and thirst, which I fortunately found, and then returning to the spot from whence I had arisen, I looked over the edge of the rock, and beheld a couple of bodies that had been washed on to the lower ledge. Humanity prompted me to descend, and getting possession of them, to give them the best interment that I could. This was a task of no little difficulty, and it was not without hazarding my own life that I was enabled to bear their bodies, one by one up the rock, and there I gave them such burial as the place afforded. After this I remained a night and a day, without any prospect of relief, and almost dreaded the idea of a vessel approaching, lest it should turn out to belong to the corsairs, such was my dread of a life of slavery and the torture which I was certain I should experience from these barbarians.

" My terrors were shortly doomed to be realized; on the third day of my being on the island, I was alarmed by the unwelcome appearance of a sail bearing round the rock, which I was not long in discovering to be the other galley that had come in search of her consort. The pirates on approaching the rock observed pieces of the wreck; they, therefore, hoisted out their boat, and getting under the lee of the rock, they landed in smooth water, with perfect safety.

"You may guess what a state of apprehension I was in; all the horrors that I had already endured from the wretches, rushed upon my recollection, and those which I might expect, if retaken, were depicted in still stronger colours to my imagination; I, therefore, as soon as the galley met my sight, endeavoured to find out a place of concealment; but in vain did I seek, nothing of the kind presented itself to my eyes; the rock (if so I may designate it) offered nothing of the kind to me; and it was almost wholly covered with shells and sand. I had not a moment to lose in reflection; but in desperate situations like mine was, the invention is prompt, and almost immediately my mind suggested a project.

"Without being observed, I crawled on my hands and knees near the water's edge, and stretched myself at full length on my face, affecting to have been drowned. In that brief interval I offered up a prayer to the Almighty for preservation; but it was His all-wise decree that it should not be granted. In a few minutes the corsairs began to explore the beach, and observing the sand turned up where I had placed the remains of my companions, they particularly examined it, and, no doubt, when they discovered the bodies of their unfortunate victims, they were not a little surprised. These interments, however, it, no doubt, immediately occurred to them, were the work of human hands; and, in consequence, they renewed their search, and at last discovered me stretched as a feigned corpse in the manner I have described. My feelings at this moment were more horrible than can be conceived by the imagination; but I was afraid almost to breathe, lest I should be detected. Alas! it was soon my fate to be so. The wretches turned me face upwards, and that I was warm and still breathed, they, of course, soon discovered. The plan they adopted to banish my dissembling was a ready one. Several times they shook me, and afterwards bestowed upon me some heavy kicks, so that, unable to endure the torment, I was compelled to throw by all disguise, and to rise up. The miscreants indulged in loud laughter of exultation, and then immediately conveyed me on board the galley, where they closely interrogated me regarding the wreck. Knowing that any disguise would bring upon me their vengeance, and could effect no good, I made them acquainted with every particular. My information was communicated to them by a foreigner who was connected with them, and who understood English very well. No sooner had they received it than the two galleys set sail, I having first been placed in heavy irons, and confined under hatches."

"Your sufferings have been very great," remarked William, who was deeply interested with the narrative of the lawyer.

"Great, honey," repeated Mr. Fitzpatrick, "you may say that same thing; but hold your whist while I finish my story, and, by the holy Saint Patrick, the devil a bit do I care about the sufferings I have had at all at all, since I have met with you, and made the illegant discovery that I have. Och, hone! and it's a happy man that Patrick Fitzpatrick will be again. But hear me out. Dreadful enough was the mental anguish I endured when I was left alone, and as the vessel in which I was confined quickly made its way from the barren rock on which I had been cast, terrible and hapless as that situation had been, I felt more truly wretched, and gave way to all the horrors of despair.

"My fate seemed certain; the wretches in whose power I was, if they did not take my life, would be certain to consign me to a fate still more to be dreaded—that of slavery; and, although I am rather old for service, I had no doubt that they would find purchasers for me, as I was strong and hearty.

"Oh! liberty! liberty! under the greatest possible privations, what a jewel it is! It is the brightest ray of sunshine that lights upon our souls, and death itself, in all its everlasting gloom, is sunshine compared with the prospect of being deprived of freedom.

"I had not been many hours confined when the miscreants, who seemed determined to torture me all they could, brought me forth, and stripping me, flogged me, until completely overcome by the dreadful agony inflicted, I became insensible. I was then reconveyed to the cabin where I had been previously confined, and leaving me a couple of biscuits and about half a pint of fresh water, suffering from the anguish of my poor lacerated back, but more from mental agony at the dismal prospect before me, I was left alone.

"Most fearful were the thoughts, the anticipations that crowded upon my brain; and I would at that moment have viewed death as a mercy. But I was reserved for still greater sufferings, and, I trust, to be made the humble instrument in the hands of a merciful and all-wise God, of bringing down retribution on the head of the guilty, and placing the son of my own dear, esteemed friend, in that station of society, and restoring him to those rights to which he is so justly entitled.

"The galleys, I had been given to understand, were bound for Tripoli, but, on the second day, the wind veered, and we were driven out of our latitude. I had been left during this time with nothing more than the two biscuits and the small quantity of water I have before mentioned, and these being soon consumed, I was in a most wretched condition, feeling all the horrors of the most gnawing hunger and thirst; but hope sustained me, now that the wind had changed, as there was a prospect, however faint, of our coming into contact with some British vessel, and my thus being rescued from the fate which appeared at present to be inevitably impending over me.

"And now the wind freshened, and my hopes increased. It came on towards night a violent storm, and it seemed impossible that the vessel could live. Even this, with death before my eyes, was far preferable to the life of slavery I was sure to be consigned to, if we escaped.

"The gale strengthened, and for several hours we were tossed about with great fury, the corsairs expecting every moment that we must founder.

"They had thrown overboard a considerable quantity of bales of goods, of which they had plundered the vessel I had formerly been in; but still, although the vessel was much lightened, there appeared to be but little chance of its being enabled to weather the storm.

"And, now, from the situation in which I was placed, I could hear the conversation of the crew, and the frightful maledictions they uttered, as the storm increased; but what more particularly engaged my attention afterwards were the remarks of the foreigner I have before mentioned as interpreting my information to the pirates, and which I could understand from a word here and there, alluded to me. He was, with that bloody mind which was ingrafted in his nature, advising the pirate-captain, in order to lighten the galley, to make a sacrifice of the lives of some of the persons on board, and proposed that I, and four other Englishmen, whom I now found to have been secured by the pirates, be the first victims.

"Hitherto I had contemplated death with comparative indifference, but now, when it immediately stared me in the face, I shrunk from it with the instinctive horror which is natural to us all.

"I will not attempt to describe my feelings minutely at that moment of horror ; however, at length I became somewhat more tranquil, and raising my hands and eyes towards Heaven, I resigned myself to its will.

"I had scarcely done so when the door of the cabin in which I was confined was thrown open, and two or three of the corsairs entered. They fixed upon me looks of the most savage ferocity, and seemed to exult in the agony I was evidently enduring. My limbs were manacled, and therefore I had no power to offer them any resistance, if even I had been mad enough to make such a futile attempt under the circumstances. They seized me roughly by the hair, dragging me along like a dog, and spitting in my face, seeming to take a pleasure in offering me every sort of indignity ; but despair had done its work towards me, and I had made up my mind for the worst ; consequently I could suffer no more from the treatment they bestowed upon me.

"Oh ! in that moment who shall describe the multiplicity of thoughts that crowded in such rapid succession upon my mind ? All my past life passed in retrospect before me, and eternity already seemed to break upon my vision ; but there was something at my heart—my conscience, which whispered consolation to me, and assured me I could meet that dread eternity without fear. I became calm, and, by the time I was dragged upon the deck, was perfectly placid.

"The pirates were most of them assembled, and it was evident from their looks that fear was upon their stubborn hearts.

"Tremendously rose the waves, and awful were the dense black clouds that rolled across the horizon. It was a scene altogether that I can never forget ! I looked upon the foaming sea, gurgling and roaring, and already anticipated it as my grave ; calmly I anticipated it, and yet I could not help feeling the most painful, the most acute regret, and a sensation of revolting horror, at such an untimely end, and so far from my native land ; without one sympathising friend or relative to close my dying eyes, or to receive my parting blessing.

"The pirates stood sullenly around, most of them with their arms folded across their broad chests ; but, in spite of their efforts to the contrary, it was perfectly evident that the fear of death was strong within them.

"Two of the unfortunate Englishmen, strongly fettered, like myself, were standing on the deck ; their countenances ghastly pale, their hollow eyes rolling with despair, and every limb trembling with the most powerful and pitiable emotion. I sought to encourage them by a look, but it was all in vain ; it was quite clear, miserable as their situation had been, that they looked upon death with the most unbounded consternation. In their sufferings at that moment I absolutely forgot my own, and would willingly have made any sacrifice, had it been in my power, to have saved them from the fearful and untimely fate which awaited them.

"We had not much time, however, given to us to reflect ; the pirates, at least, two or three of the principal of them, consulted together for a few seconds, and the looks they fixed upon us, shewed plainly the subject they were conversing upon. For my own part I had made up my mind for the worst, and had committed my soul to the Almighty God ; but as for my poor doomed companions, nothing could equal their horrible despair ; the ghastliness of their looks, the quivering of their lips, the convulsive trembling of their limbs, the painful throbbings of their bosoms.

"The consultation between the pirates did not last long ; suddenly four of the stoutest advanced towards my unfortunate companions, and raising them in their arms, they instantaneously precipitated them into the raging ocean.

"Never shall I forget the frightful yell of agony which escaped the poor fellows as they were consigned to their hapless doom ; ever will the awful splash of their bodies, as the raging waters rolled over them, ring in my ears.

They arose again, however, on the bosom of the billows, and, with convulsive agony and shrieks of despair clung to the rail of the vessel and endeavoured to save themselves; unfortunate wretches! A dozen pistols were immediately discharged at them, and they sunk to rise no more.

" Appalled at the dreadful fate of my companions, I now stood, transfixed with horror, expecting my own. I had, as I have before stated, become, in a manner, completely callous to it; but I was doomed to be reserved for another destiny. The blood of the murdered seamen was scarcely washed away by the foaming surge, whose frothy whiteness it had discoloured, when the pirates again turned to each other, and held a conversation in a whisper. I expected that it was tending towards my execution. Two of the villains approached me, and, raising my hands and eyes towards Heaven, I resigned myself to my fate, and offered no resistance. But how surprised I was when, instead of being tossed overboard, as I had expected, they laid hold of my arms, and forced me back to the place of my former confinement, where they left me to myself.

" I cannot say that I felt much joy at this circumstance, notwithstanding I returned God thanks for my present preservation; for the storm still raged so violently, that death appeared inevitable; and, if not, I expected a much worse fate, that of perpetual slavery, and the savage treatment consequent upon it.

" A short time after I had been placed in the gloomy and limited cabin which formed my place of confinement, I was visited by one of the pirates, who brought me another small portion of water, and two coarse and hard biscuits, and immediately left me to myself.

" The storm continued to rage violently for the greater part of the night, when the wind again changed, and it gradually abated, and towards morning it had entirely subsided, and the galleys were going steadily on their course.

" And now were my thoughts more harrowing than they had been before, as the prospect of slavery, and unimaginable tortures, such as I could only expect from such remorseless and blood-thirsty savages, rushed upon my mind. The sufferings of my companions were over; but I had yet, I feared, the worst of all to encounter, and I envied them their fate.

" I traversed the confined limits of my cabin, and gave utterance to the most bitter and painful lamentations. 'Dear England,' I thought, 'I shall never behold you again, and my friends will ever remain in ignorance of my fate, and neither shall I be permitted to discover the innocent and oppressed, and to be the means of restoring them to their rights, and bringing down just retribution on the heads of their oppressors.' I thought of all I had seen and heard at the residence of the good old Mr. Backstay; I thought of you, William, and the resemblance which nature had stamped upon your features, of one so dear to me, and the more I reflected, the more did I become convinced that you were that dear individual whom I sought, and I reproached myself for having neglected to make further and immediate inquiries about you, by which I might have had the means of restoring you to your rights, and of defeating the diabolical machinations of our mutual enemies. But regret was useless, and I sunk into the utmost despair by giving way to it.

" The wind continued favourable, and, in the course of a few days, we arrived at the place of our destination. In the meantime, the pirate who attended upon me, and who was the person I have before mentioned, who had acted as interpreter, informed me that it had been agreed between the two galleys, in case a separation should take place in the night, or by the means of another storm, that they should make for a small island in the Gulph of Mahomet.

" This intelligence I found to be correct, and there they accordingly touched; but not finding the other galley, proceeded in quest of her, and, at length, judging she was irrecoverably lost, the search was abandoned.

" Miserable and wretched as the imagination can depicture I was, when we were anchored in the harbour, for the consummation of my cruel destiny seemed fast approaching, and I was not long kept in doubt and suspense upon the subject. However, we remained for a period of four days longer on board the galleys, when accounts reached the place of the total loss of the prize, and all hands on board, excepting three, the pirates not being sufficiently skilled in tactics, and the English manner of rigging, could not manage the ship ; she, therefore, run at the mercy of the storm, and was soon dashed to pieces on a rocky lee-shore.

" This circumstance, I was certain, would tend to aggravate my fate, and it was not long ere my surmises were confirmed. Nothing could equal the disappointment of the pirates at the loss of so valuable a prize. Soon the galley became in an uproar, and nothing was to be heard but the most vile jargon and execrations.

" And now the moment arrived when my two unfortunate surviving companions and myself were conveyed on shore, and sold without discrimination. To my lot it fell to be purchased by a Jew merchant, who immediately hired me out by the day, with many others, who were Englishmen, and had been at different times captured by the corsairs, to drag stones for the repair of the tower walls.

" I need not attempt to describe to you how galling was this new employment to me. The immense weight of the pieces of rock I had to drag, encumbered by my chains, and the excessive heat of the sun, were almost insupportable. It is remarkable, old as I am, how I could survive it, and hourly did I pray for death to relieve me from my sufferings.

" Whenever I was tempted to alleviate my relaxed frame, I was compelled by the galling lash, to resume the hard toil ; and my lamentations were only met by abuse, mockery, and increased punishment.

" The repairs of the wall being at length finished, my Jew master, not finding immediate employment for me, sold me again to a native merchant, who was immensely rich. I was now obliged to carry water, remove the dust of the place, and perform all kinds of drudgery, yet never received for all my labour one kind look or a civil word.

" Dreadful was the misery under which I groaned, but I will leave it to your imagination. At length, such was my steady attention to business, that I gained the confidence of my master. He frequently had occasion for my attendance upon him abroad. It happened one of these times, that the merchants were summoned to a sale of slaves, which turned out to be the crew of a Portuguese polacre, just brought into the harbour. I was informed that the crew of the polacre made a desperate resistance, which occasioned the death of their captain, and one half their crew ; the remaining part seemed to be young and healthy men, and, therefore, sold well in the market. My master and two other merchants bought six of the youngest, whom I was ordered to convey to the prison.

" The following morning early, I was ordered to convey the six men to my master's house. On our approach we found the outer gate wide open, and the first object that struck me, was the under gaoler, lying dead, and stretched in his gore.

" Alarmed at the sight, we hastily withdrew to the outer gate, and called for assistance, which, having obtained, we re-entered the prison, but found that the six men had escaped. By this time the news reached my master, who immediately went on foot to make a strict search. They were found on the third day hidden amongst the rocks, close to the sea, waiting an opportunity to seize on the first boat that they could find.

" The prisoners being brought back, they were immediately ordered before

the cadi, and after a very short examination, the ringleader of them was ordered for execution the next day.

"As it is a general rule for all the slaves to be sent to such exhibitions, in order to warn them, my master was not backward in sending his, especially as he was so deeply interested. The workmen having finished the platform where the unhappy culprit was doomed to suffer, a frame of wood like a gallows was exhibited. As soon as the malefactor ascended the platform, he was ordered to climb up the ladder with the executioner, who thrust a sharp hook through one of his hands, and hung him thereby to the top of the gallows, fastened by an iron chain. The ladder was then placed on the other side, where also the wretched culprit was dragged up by a hook similar to that which held his hands, and which was drove through the sole of his foot, and fastened also by a chain.

"You may judge what were my horrors at this frightful exhibition, but I had now made up my mind, and that was to escape from this abominable country, at all risks, on the earliest opportunity. We devised many schemes, but one in particular seemed most approved. We had received orders to attend on the following day at the place of execution, when another wretch was doomed to undergo the fatal sentence. We accordingly met at an earlier hour on the following morning, when, on further consultation, one of the party proposed that we should attempt to escape as soon as possible. He acquainted us that, adjacent to his master's house (which was situated five miles from Tripola, and one from the sea-coast), he was employed in gardening and digging, except when he was sent to Tripola with the produce of his labour, and that he was well acquainted with a small creek near his master's house, at the top of which were two or three huts, occupied by fishermen, who always moored their boats, during the night time, near the huts, and, for a safeguard, had a large dog chained on board them, as the men always slept on

No. 30

shore. He, therefore, proposed poisoning the dog that evening, to prevent giving an alarm.

"This proposal appeared to us all to be a very reasonable one, and we unanimously agreed to it; but on second reflection, seven men rushing into an open boat, (for that was our number,) without food, water, or other necessaries, having also a vast sea to contend with, and which, in all probability, we must encounter for many days, threw a momentary damp upon our spirits, and I looked upon it with very little hope. But at length another idea occurred to us; the present day being the last of August, and approaching the feast of the prophet Mahomet, for which the greatest preparations were then making, I proposed that every man should save from his allowance of food each day, a certain portion, and deposit it in a certain place.

"As this feast of the prophet would be a general holiday, there was no doubt but that all classes of people would be deeply absorbed in their religious duties, and it was equally certain that the fishermen before-mentioned would come to Tripola on that day.

"All my companions declared these observations to be very just, and readily consented to be guided by me. A certain place, some distance from the town, and a certain hour, were now appointed for our meeting. In the interim each promised to save all the provisions and necessaries he could, in order to add to the general stock.

"Having concluded this consultation, and matters being thus arranged, the unfortunate seaman who was the subject of this execution began his lamentations and struggles. He seemed to bear his fate with less resignation than the other, and the executioner was compelled to have recourse to force before he submitted to his fate. It was supposed these two men that suffered committed the murder, but, as there was no fair trial, this was all a matter of conjecture.

"As soon as this unhappy man ceased struggling, and was released by death from his torments, which was near sunset, the spectators began to disperse, and the corpse was left to hang until a certain hour on the following day. I and my companions having shaken hands, now separated, filled with the pleasing hope of soon quitting this country of barbarity, and beholding once more our native land, the land of liberty and civilization.

"My suspense and anxiety were now incessant; every hour seemed a month, until the happy day, the 5th of September, arrived, on which evening, at the time and place appointed, we punctually met, and proceeded with all speed to the creek, which had been mentioned by one of my companions. Having boldly entered the huts, we found in them two old women, and a child, about ten years old, the rest having gone to the gala, as we had expected.

"The women, alarmed at our intrusion, and conscious as it seems of our design, fell on their faces on the earth, and prayed for mercy; the child, who appeared the most courageous, was making dexterously towards the door, but having stopped this little one's egress, who would, in all probability, have given the alarm, and thereby defeated our purpose, I held her in my arms, while my companions endeavoured to soothe the old women. Prudence, however, obliged us to secure them with cords, and, as necessity has no law, although my heart naturally revolted from the deed, we commenced ransacking the place, and supplied ourselves with all the necessaries that fell in our way. Of these we found a pretty ample supply, which, in our situation, and the desperate and dangerous undertaking we had in contemplation, were most welcome to us.

"The women continued all the time to utter loud exclamations of lamentation, and to implore our mercy, and we in vain endeavoured to persuade them that we intended them no harm. It hurt me much to behold their emotion, and I was heartily glad when this disagreeable business was at an end.

"Having taken all that we could find, or that we required, we hastened to the boat.

"The dog now flashed across my recollection, and I began to fear that in him we should find a dangerous enemy. Thinking that he would be sure to be acquainted with the child, I considered it would be advisable for me to bring her with me in my arms, as by that means we might obtain the creature's favour, and quiet him. I therefore took the poor little thing up, and carried her away.

"This was the signal for the women to renew their cries; but I assured them we intended the child no harm, and that she would quickly be suffered to return. This somewhat pacified them, and I bore the child away.

"Having thus prepared against the expected danger, I was the first person to enter the boat, and made the child speak to the dog, which made him kind and quiet, and thus my scheme answered well.

"We secured the dog to a long chain, and, watching an opportunity, we threw him overboard. We then desired the girl to return to her friends, and, having set her ashore for that purpose, we shoved off the boat.

"The dog swam well, soon reached the shore, and joined the child, who remained for some time where we had left her, watching our motions.

"It fortunately so happened that we found a cask of water in the boat, which contained about ten gallons, and which we returned thanks to Providence for, for it was a complete treasure to us in our desolate condition.

CHAPTER XVII.

THE NARRATIVE OF MR. FITZPATRICK CONCLUDED.

"Our situation was now as miserable as could be, but the thoughts of escaping from that barbarous country, and the dreadful atrocities we had witnessed, and which I have described, inspired us with hope, and added energy to our exertions.

"Some distance we rowed incessantly, before a favourable breeze sprung up; but we knew not the way we were steering, and our only hope was in meeting with some vessel which would receive us on board, and take compassion on our misfortunes. Should we encounter any of the corsairs we knew that our fate would be certain, and we shuddered with horror when we reflected on it.

"At length fortune sent us a propitious gale, and we set sail, and shaped our course, as well as we could guess, for Malta, and as we got further and further from the dreadful country in which we had been enslaved, our hopes strengthened, and whatever fate might be in store for us, we all considered that it could not be half so terrible as the one from which we had released ourselves.

"All that day the gale continued favourable, but still we saw no signs of a ship, and all around us was as desolate as could be, one vast expanse of ocean, and the immeasurable sky above us.

"I was much more composed than any of the rest, and endeavoured to animate the spirits of my companions, in which I ultimately succeeded better than I had anticipated. We partook but sparingly during the day of the water and provisions we had with us in the boat, and feeling greatly refreshed, we continued on our way with better spirits.

"And now all the scenes of my past life rushed upon my recollection, and afforded me a vast field for thought and painful reflection. I ruminated upon the surprise my sudden disappearance must have caused, and the alarm and consternation it would cause my faithful servant in London, when he should become acquainted with it ; and the uncertainty of my ever seeing him again, and the confused state in which my affairs would be placed, caused me considerable uneasiness. Then the triumph of my bitter enemy recurred to my mind, and caused me, if possible, still more anguish than all. But, in the midst of all, I put my trust in the mercy and goodness of the Supreme Being, and my hopes revived. I trusted that I should yet be permitted to return again to England, and then I should have the opportunity, which I was determined not to miss, of revealing who he was, of bringing him to justice, and thus wreaking upon him a terrible but just revenge for all the crimes he had perpetrated. And that time will come ; yes, wretched and lonely as is now my situation, I will not despair. God has hitherto been most merciful to me, in the midst of the most imminent dangers, and when my life seemed to be not worth a tenpenny, and I trust that He will not forsake me now. We shall both see the white cliffs of old England again, William, and oh, won't that same be a glorious day to Mr. Patrick Fitzpatrick !"

"Heaven send that your hopes may be realized," said William. "But my poor Flora !—Oh ! what hope is there for me, when she is in the power of the villains."

"Hold your whisht, man," said the warm-hearted Irishman ; "and do not be after casting yourself away on the quicksands of despair, as you seamen would call it. The lovely honey, and sure it's bad enough, and dreadful enough that she should be in the power of them same devil rapscallions ; but her innocence will protect her like a coat of mail, and ——"

"Her innocence !" repeated William, with a look of the most poignant anguish ; "alas ! what regard have such wretches for innocence ? She is lost ! lost ! My fair and gentle craft, with whom I had hoped to have cruized so happily over the ocean of life !—lost ! lost ! I shall never behold her again !"

"But I tell you, darling," said Mr. Fitzpatrick, "that you will see her again. You shall see her again ; you will be happy ; you will be married ; she will be lady —— no, mistress—that is—but whisht !—whisht ! Mr. Fitzpatrick ! not now—not now—only I mean to say once for all, and positively that you will be married to Flora Clarendon ; you will be happy ; her parents will be happy—your foster parents will be happy—we will all be happy— and och ! ain't it myself now that will dance a real Irish jig on your wedding, and bespeak myself godfather to the charming little honey that will soon afterwards be smiling upon you, to cheer you, and recompense you for all your past troubles."

In spite of the melancholy thoughts that crowded upon his mind, William could not forbear smiling, and after a pause, Mr. Fitzpatrick resumed his narrative.

"On, on, we proceeded, but still no signs of a vessel met our anxious sight. Towards evening, however, the dark outline of what appeared to be rocks, appeared upon the horizon, and we now began to apprehend that we were steering in a different course to that which we wanted. The wind also changed, and drove us rapidly in the direction of the rocks. Still I endeavoured to keep up the spirits of my companions, and, in the course of a couple of hours, we had neared the rocks, which we perceived to be very lofty, and to extend to some distance. We were now obliged to act with the greatest caution to prevent the boat from being dashed against the rocks, in which event we must all inevitably have perished ; but after a short time, the moon, arising over the ocean in great brilliancy, disclosed to us a small creek, or rivulet, which ran in between the rocks, and we determined to make towards it, with the hope of finding some small island, where we might obtain more fresh water, and perhaps fruit or fish, to help to eke out our provisions until a change took place in our fortunes.

"To accomplish this, it needed the utmost caution, to avoid the dangerous rocks that frowned above us; but, at length we did, and, entering the creek, found, after proceeding a short distance, that it narrowed, and when we had advanced a little farther, we found that the rocks on one side appeared considerably lower, and were easy of access.

"In a short time, the shadow of some tall trees convinced us that our conjectures were right, and that we were near some island, where we might obtain what we required.

"At first we made up our minds that we would make our way on to it, but then again the dread of meeting with the savages entered our thoughts, and we hesitated, and were undecided how to act.

"However, as the night was far advancing, and our course was so uncertain, we mustered up resolution, and determined to venture to get on to the island.

"We steered our boat towards the lowest part of the rocks, which we soon reached, and secured the boat by a rope to a point of one of them; we provided ourselves with a small portion of the provisions, and taking the cask, we ascended the rock with little or no difficulty.

"Upon gaining the summit, we looked eagerly around us, and were pleased to see, at no great distance, the signs of vegetation, and, therefore, proceeded towards it; making up our minds, if we could find a convenient place, to remain there during the night, and endeavour to obtain some rest, to recruit us for our labours of the following day.

"Having arrived at the place where the trees reared their lofty heads, we perceived that they were barren of fruit of any kind, and the island was of very circumscribed extent, and had but a wretched appearance. It certainly was not inhabited, and probably had seldom, if ever, been trod by human foot before.

"We now held a consultation one with another what was to be done; some were for returning to the boat; but we were all so much fatigued, that, at length, it was agreed that we should stretch ourselves under the shade of a cluster of trees, and endeavour to gain two or three hours sleep, which would much refresh us, and at daylight we could take a better survey of the island, and ascertain whether we could procure any fresh water or fruit.

"Before we did this, however, we agreed to return to the boat, and bring on shore the remainder of the provisions, in case we might want to use any portion of them; and it was fortunate we did so, as will be seen by the subsequent part of my narrative.

"We soon reached the boat, which we further secured, and having procured what we wanted, we returned to the spot we had quitted, where we cast lots to see which of us should keep watch, while the others slept, so that he might apprize us of any danger that threatened us. The lot fell upon me, and my companions, having stretched their weary limbs upon the earth, soon fell asleep.

"For my part, I seated myself on a stump of a tree, and casting my eyes vacantly upon the dreary scene around, I gave myself up to the most dismal reflections.

"Worn out with thinking and fatigue, however, exhausted nature could hold out no longer, and at length I fell asleep also.

"How long slumber had closed our eyelids, I cannot say, but at length we were all suddenly aroused by heavy peals of thunder, that rattled through the Heavens, and the most terrific flashes of lightning, that darted across our eyes.

"We started on our feet, and looked with horror around us. The whole place was awfully illuminated by the glare of the electric fluid, and the earth seemed to rock again with the fury of the contending elements.

"Never had I witnessed a more awful storm, and it presented a fearful contrast to the lovely evening it had preceded. During the intervals that the lightning sent not forth its forked glare, the darkness was most terrific and intense; while the roaring of the raging ocean, coupled with the deafening peals of thunder, increased the perfect horrors of the scene.

"The boat! the boat!" was the first thought that occurred to us all, and filled with the most dreadful apprehensions, we rushed towards the place where we had secured it. What a terrible certainty we were doomed to encounter. Our worst apprehensions were realized; the boat had been forced away by the turbulent waters, from the place where we had secured it, and was probably dashed to pieces against the rocks.

"Never shall I forget the terrors of that hour; we stared at each other for a moment, with wild and bloodshot eyes, and then we clasped our hands vehemently and groaned in the intense agony of our despair.

"We were now completely lost, and such was the violent grief and despair of one or two of my wretched companions in suffering, that had it not been for me and the others, they would immediately have precipitated themselves into the raging deep, and thus have anticipated their fate.

"Left alone on this wretched island, without any prospect of relief, what but death was before our eyes; and surely fate seemed very cruel to us.

"For a few moments we all continued to gaze over the stormy ocean with the most agonised feelings, and then overcome with our emotions we could not help bursting into tears.

"I was the first to arouse myself, and speaking to my companions, I implored them not to give way entirely to despair, but to submit with patience to the will of the Almighty, who in due time would doubtless send us relief, and that, perhaps, at the very moment when we thought all hope was at an end.

"This advice, however, was much easier given than taken, and I had the greatest difficulty in bringing them to anything like a degree of tranquillity.

"With dreary steps we retraced our way to the place where we had slept; but the fierce lightning rendered it dangerous for us to remain any longer near the trees, and we were compelled to move into the open space, where we were exposed to the heavy pelting of one of the most violent rains I had ever experienced.

"Never, never shall I forget the horrors that we then endured; they were too powerful, too dreadful, for any language to do justice to them in description. We were soon wet to the skin, cold and shivering, while despair weighed upon our hearts like a heavy load of lead. Death at that time would have been almost a mercy, and yet we clung to life with that tenacity, which is natural to most persons, even under the most trying circumstances.

"The storm continued with unabated fury during the remainder of the night, and we were nearly worn out. It was indeed wonderful how we could support it, but man never knows what he can endure until he ascertain it by painful experience.

"By the time the daylight dawned, however, the storm had entirely abated, but the wind still continued very high, and the ocean was still disturbed in a most frightful manner.

"The aspect of the island appeared to us very little better than it had done at night, but worn out with fatigue, and freezing with cold from the rain, we kindled a fire beneath the trees, by the means of a tinder-box, which one of my companions fortunately had about him, and huddling together around it, we partook but very sparingly of our provisions, and then, quite overpowered by what we had had to undergo during the night, we involuntarily, all of us, fell off to sleep.

" We must have remained in this happy state of unconsciousness for several hours, for when we awoke the sun was at the full, and the earth was nearly dried up from the effects of the late tempest.

" We were greatly refreshed, but when we looked around us, and viewed the cheerless aspect of everything that presented itself to our observation, our despair was not in the least abated.

" At length, by dint of effort, we partly aroused ourselves, and agreed to examine the island, in the hope of discovering some means of support, or fresh water. We went all over the island, but nothing of the sort presented itself, and we now indeed saw no other prospect than of famishing of hunger, unless Providence should send some speedy relief. Then we walked again towards the sea, but there nothing to relieve our anguish met our gaze. We saw nothing of the boat, which doubtless had been dashed to pieces, or driven far out to sea, and thus all means of our quitting the island were cut off.

" Again and again we regretted that we had been tempted to leave the boat; but it was now too late, and even if we had not done so, we reflected that we must all have met a watery grave, for it was utterly impossible that we could have weathered out such a dreadful storm as that of the previous night.

" What was to be done we knew not ; the only chance we had of relief was by some vessel nearing the place ; but even of that there seemed to be but little prospect, as all ships would be cautious to keep clear of those dangerous rocks, unless they might put off a boat with the hope of obtaining fresh water.

" We had provisions enough, with economy, to last us for several days yet, but our fresh water was almost exhausted, and when that was gone and our food, starvation appeared to us to be inevitable.

" I will not attempt to describe to you the anguish of mind we endured, as day after day elapsed, without any change in our circumstances, and our provisions continued getting less. Our water was entirely gone, and the parching thirst that was upon us made us turn from the food with a kind of nausea.

" We had now been on the island for four days, and our food was all consumed, and nothing else, but a dreadful and lingering death of starvation stared us in the face. We looked at each other in despair, and two of my companions were so overpowered by their feelings and illness, that they laid themselves on the earth, and became completely inactive. As for the others, they rushed wildly about the island, calling on God to rescue them, and uttering the most phrenzied and blasphemous expressions by turns. For my own part, I was the calmest of them all, and committing myself to the care of the Almighty, I gave myself up entirely to a fate which now appeared to be inevitable.

" A dreadful day and night passed away, and still no food, no water, nor any prospect of relief. Most of my companions became frantic, and uttered the most piteous cries and lamentations. Never had I expected to experience such troubles as these, and much less after what I had suffered in only my trifling voyage to and from France, when I made a vow that I would never venture myself on salt water again. But we none of us know what we are destined to undergo in the course of our lives ; and, therefore, it is silly and sinful for us to make any rash vows.

" The two poor fellows whom I have before mentioned, died on the following morning, and we immediately consigned their bodies to the deep.

" And now every hour did our sufferings increase ; the pangs of hunger gnawed upon our vitals, and our thirst was intolerable. I felt a burning fever raging in my veins, and was certain that I could not hold out much longer.

" The ocean was perfectly calm and lovely ; but how little did it correspond with the wretched hearts that throbbed in the bosoms of myself and my companions.

"In the course of this day it rained pretty heavily for some time, and we hailed it with transport. We soon obtained a cask full, with which we eagerly slaked our thirst, and then seemed somewhat more revived; but it was only transitory, for now the pangs of hunger became more unendurable than ever. The rain water, too, was also soon exhausted, and then the most horrible despair again settled upon our hearts.

"Another night and a day passed without any food, or a prospect of relief, and we had all of us become so weak that we could scarcely move. In that dreadful situation, I wonder how I retained my senses; but most fervently, mentally, did I pray for death to release me from my sufferings, since all hope appeared to be entirely at an end.

"Night came on—a dreadful night it was; it will be impressed upon my recollection in the most vivid colours, the longest day I have to live.

"We were huddled together upon the earth around our wood fire, whose red glare shone awfully on our pale and ghastly countenances, giving them an awful appearance that was quite frightful to look upon. We had none of us spoken for some time, and the silence rendered our situation still more solemn and impressive; but the wild and bloodshot eyes of my companions spoke much more than words could have done. Suddenly, however, I observed Mark Redfield turn to Sampson Marston, and mutter something to him in an undertone. My heart misgave me, for it foreboded what was coming, and I could see from the expression of their countenances that they had quickly agreed with each other upon whatever it was they were whispering about.

"I was not long kept in suspense, and my forebodings were verified. Mark Redfield turned to me and the others, and, after a short pause, he observed:—

"'Messmates, we have now been here many days, and no prospect of relief opens to us; our food is all consumed, and we are famishing with hunger; say, shall we at once resign ourselves to our fate, or adopt means of allaying the ravenous demon that is preying upon us? I, for one, propose the latter.'

"'Ay, and I, for another,' said Sampson; 'anything is better than to remain in this horrible state of misery.'

"'I understand you,' said I, with a horrible shudder of horror; 'but, oh; forbear, and drive such hellish thoughts from your minds. Live in hopes, and ——'

"'Live in hopes! Ha! ha! ha!' wildly laughed Mark Redfield, and his countenance assumed a still more awful expression, which was perfectly hideous to look upon; 'what is the use of talking about hope to men in our desperate situation? Have we not waited long and patiently, and all prospect of relief is as distant as ever?'

"'What would you propose?' demanded another of my companions.

"'That one of us shall die to appease the dreadful cravings of his companions,' answered Mark Redfield.

"A shudder of horror run through my veins, and those of my companions, but not a tongue moved in reply.

"'It is a terrible alternative,' at last said Mark; 'but the desperate situation we are placed in demands it.'

"'It does,' coincided Sampson; 'and, therefore, let us cast lots who shall perish.'

"'And think you not,' I interposed, 'that the vengeance of Heaven would pursue us for such a bloody and unnatural crime? Oh, bethink ye—bethink ye!'

"'It is useless,' answered Mark, and his looks became more eager and determined; 'death is before us, and we have no other means of retarding,

if not preventing its approach. Are ye all agreed? We all stand an equal chance.'

" ' Ay! ay!' said Sampson, and the others uttered a faint assent.

" ' The lots, then!—the lots!' cried Mark, and he tore up a piece of paper into several bits, and a mark was placed on one of them, and whoever drew it was to be the unfortunate victim.

" While all these fearful preparations were going forward, I need not attempt to describe to you, William, what were my mental sufferings. Language, in fact, could but faintly pourtray them; but never before or since (not even when the fate to which the smugglers doomed me appeared to be inevitable) have I experienced such horrors. I could not speak, for my tongue clave to the roof of my parched mouth, and my eyes seemed to burn like two coals of fire in their sockets. From the dreadful crime my every sense revolted in terror and disgust, and I determined to perish with hunger, should the lot not fall on me, sooner than I would partake of the unnatural repast.

" The papers were placed in Mark Redfield's hat, and were shaken up by every one, then one by one drew forth a paper, turning his eyes away from the hat, at the same time. I muttered a prayer to Heaven, when it came to my turn, and I clasped my hands together with an indescribable feeling, when it was pronounced a blank, and I found that for that time I had escaped.

" The fatal paper was drawn by the wretched man who had inquired of Mark Redfield his purpose, and no sooner did he hear it, than he sunk on his knees, and clasping his hands together in all the horrors of despair, he raised his eyes towards Heaven, and his lips moved, but he could not articulate a word.

" The men looked upon him for a few moments with pity and terror, and I then ventured once more to interfere for him, and to implore them to spare his life.

h². 31

" ' What foolery is this ?' said Mark Redfield, whom despair and revenge had rendered cruel ; ' of what use was the trouble we have taken if we now relent ? I pity poor Ben, but he has fixed his doom, and it cannot be altered.'

" ' God have mercy on me,' gasped forth the poor fellow ; ' I do not ask my life, but spare me for a few minutes while I invoke the mercy of Heaven, and then I will resign myself to your hands.'

" ' Ay, ay, poor Ben,' said Mark ; ' we will not launch you into eternity, before you have had time to say your prayers. But we have yet another painful task to perform.'

" ' What is that ?' I eagerly demanded.

" ' To see who is to do the dreadful job,' answered Mark.

" An involuntary shudder ran through the bosoms of all at this announcement, and the poor fellow who was doomed to die looked for a moment from his devotions, and appealed to us all, with an expression of countenance which it would be utterly impossible for me ever to forget. But he quickly collected himself, and with a look of calm resignation, he continued to pray most devotedly.

" ' Mark Redfield,' I said at length, ' and could you become the murderer of our innocent companion, who has shared with us in all our misfortunes ? No, no,—I implore you, let him live.'

" ' Mr. Fitzpatrick,' returned Mark, ' I take credit to myself for possessing as much humanity as you do ; but it has fallen to his lot to die, poor fellow, and, if the chance falls upon me to do the deed, I must not, will not, shrink from it.'

" ' The curse of the Almighty will assuredly rest upon us for the bloody deed,' I said. ' How dare we hope for His mercy after imbruing our hands in the blood of an innocent fellow creature ?'

" ' Are we not starving ?' said Sampson.

" ' And,' returned I, firmly, ' I am content to die, if it be the will of Heaven, but never will I become the murderer of my companion.'

" ' But, if it falls to your lot, you must,' returned Sampson, fiercely. ' This is not the time for squeamish fears ; Heaven will pardon the deed to which we are driven by desperate necessity.'

" ' Think you, Sampson,' I replied solemnly, ' think you that Heaven will ever sanction a deed of blood ?'

" ' It is useless talking,' said Mark Redfield, ' we are all decided, except you, and you *must* consent. Come, come—the lots.'

" Oh, William, what were my sufferings at this moment ? I cannot describe them. I saw that expostulation was useless, and that nothing I said could save him, and, although I was resolved to lose my own life rather than become an assassin, I was compelled, as it were, to become a party in the dreadful task.

" The lots were again drawn, and it fell upon Mark Redfield to perform the inhuman deed."

" But did he murder the poor fellow ?" eagerly demanded William, whose very soul was wrapped up in the powerful interest of Mr. Fitzpatrick's narrative.

" Hear me out," answered Mr. Fitzpatrick, " you shall be informed of all presently.

" All the time that this was going forward, the wretched man continued on his knees, and solely absorbed in his devotions. It was a moment of the most intense horror, and all eyes became fixed on Mark Redfield, with an expression of awful suspense.

" ' It is a bad job,' muttered Mark ; ' the revolting task has fallen upon me, and I must perform it.'

" He took a large clasp-knife from his pocket as he spoke, and felt the edge with a trembling hand. Then he approached the unhappy victim, who bounded in an instant to his feet, with a look of frantic despair. His eyes rolled wildly, and his breast heaved convulsively.

" ' Hold ! villain !' I shouted, arresting his arm, ' what would you do ?'

" 'I am prepared,' calmly remarked the doomed one. ' God of Heaven, receive my soul ! But—but—if I am allowed to choose the manner in which my wretched existence is to be terminated, let me — let me — be — bled to ——'

" He could not finish the sentence, but covering his face with his hands, seemed to resign himself to the horrors of his fate.

" ' For the love of God ! By all your hopes of mercy,' energetically I exclaimed, " oh ! spare him, and ——'

" ' It cannot, must not be,' interrupted the desperate Mark, ' would that it could be avoided. Are you ready, Ben ?'

" 'I am,' with wonderful calmness, replied the latter.

" ' Do you forgive me the deed ?' demanded Mark, in a faltering voice.

" ' I do—I do—God help me,' answered the wretched men. ' 'Tis stern and cruel necessity compels you to do it.'

" ' It is—it is,' said Mark.

" ' Bless you all, my poor companions,' said Ben, shaking us all vehemently by the hand, ' and send you a speedy release from your troubles, when my poor soul has slipped its cable. Do not put me to more pain than you can help, and I shall soon—be—no more. Oh ! all-merciful God, pardon me my sins, and take me to thyself.'

" It was a scene sufficient to move a heart of very adamant, and scalding tears bedewed each pale and care-worn countenance. I felt as if I were choking, every fibre thrilled with double its usual emotion ; hunger, despair, everything was forgotten in the excitement—everything but the critical situation of poor Ben, who, having resigned his soul to his Maker, seemed to be the least disturbed of all.

" What dreadful consequences do sufferings often produce in the human mind ? Despair dries up all the sources of humanity, and the individual who erst has possessed every kindly feeling, urged on by the selfish dread of losing his own life, becomes little better than a savage.

" So it was with Mark Redfield and Sampson ;—they were not naturally depraved or cruel, and in other circumstances would have revolted with horror from the bare contemplation of such a dreadful deed. But the utter hopelessness of our situation ; the ravenous gnawings of hunger, that, like an insatiate demon, seemed to have glutted upon their very heart's blood, had changed them into little better than monsters, and they now were impatient for the execution of the deed, so that they might appease their intolerable cravings in their unnatural and disgusting feast.

" I felt confident that I could not save poor Ben ; but, oh ! how fervently I prayed to Heaven for its divine interposition. I then renewed my supplications, with all the eloquence that the urgent nature of the terrible event could inspire. But, although they seemed to feel keenly what I said, it could not move them from their purpose.

" The poor victim also forcibly and gratefully felt my pleadings in his behalf, and turning upon me a look which spoke with greater force than much more eloquence could have done under ordinary circumstances, he said,—

" ' Mr. Fitzpatrick, deeply do I feel for the Christian sympathy you take in my fate ; but it is the will of Heaven, and I submit, without murmuring. God bless you, and pardon them, as I freely do.'

" I averted my face, for it was bathed with tears, and the violence of my agony almost stifled me. Certain I am that his sufferings at that moment could not be greater than were my own. My very heart appeared to rise in my throat, and my brain whirled round.   I had exhausted all my arguments, and knew not what to say.

" There was a dead, an awful pause of a few moments; and then poor Ben, turning to Mark, said, in a voice which seemed already as if speaking from the grave,—

" ' Mark, messmates, friends ; I am ready to meet my hard destiny, but, before you perform your revolting task, I have one—one last request to make."

" ' Name it,' said Mark.

" For an instant Ben was overcome by the violence of his emotions, and could not speak ; but at length, heaving a deep sigh, he ejaculated, with much difficulty,—

" ' Mark Redfield, you were born in the same village as I was ; we were playfellows together—went to sea together, and left dear, kind friends and relations behind us.   You may return home, Heaven send that you may ; but, when you are gazing upon the sunny hills, the pretty green fields, and peaceful vallies we have so often together sported over, poor Ben's soul will, I trust, rest aloft—I—I—you know—the old churchyard.   Near its ivied porch, beneath the canopy of a shady tree, there is one silent grave, marked by a simple head-stone, bearing the simple initials of E. H.   I—I—my mother's bones moulder there.   Poor old soul ! she died in my arms, on the very day that I returned from my last voyage, and there I deposited her cold remains, the remains of all that was dear to me—that had been left me in the world. I—I could have wished that my ashes might have been deposited by the side of her's—and—but God wills it different, and I submit ; but, should you return home, will you make me one promise ?'

" ' Go on—go on,' said Mark Redfield, in a hoarse, faint voice.

" ' After—after—I am no more—will you endeavour to preserve my heart ; and, bearing it thither, see it deposited in the same grave where rests my poor old mother ?'

" ' I will—I will,' gasped forth Mark.

" ' Then Heaven bless you, as you fulfil your promise,' cried poor Ben ; ' my spirit will rest happy.   Mother ! mother !' he continued, once more sinking on his knees, and raising his hands and eyes towards Heaven, he ejaculated,—' I die contented ; spirit of my sainted mother, may I join thee in realms of eternal bliss !'

" Another silence ensued, and all eyes were fixed upon Ben with the most intense feelings of agony.   It was almost too much for me, and I was nearly overpowered.   At length poor Ben arose, and, with a placid smile on his pale features, he approached Mark, and baring his arm, he said,—

" ' I am ready.   Courage, Mark, courage, and do at once your dreadful task.'

" Mark trembled excessively as he took hold of Ben's arm with one hand, and raised the knife with the other.   I saw how excessively he quailed, and thought this was an excellent opportunity to renew my supplications.

" ' Spare him !' I repeated ; ' you cannot be so cruel as to take his life. Forbear !'

" Sampson muttered some discontented reply, and once more Mark Redfield became more nerved, and wielded the knife with greater determination.   All this time Ben remained quite calm, and appeared to have made up his mind to the dreadful and untimely fate that awaited him.

" ' Be not hurried on,' I continued ; ' be not hurried on by the frenzy of your present feelings to do a deed that you will ever afterwards repent, and for which, most certainly, the curse of an offended God will pursue you.   Let him live ; at least, do not yet perpetrate the crime—but an hour—but an hour spare him, and then ——'

" ' And what is the use of prolonging the poor fellow's misery, when his doom is sealed ?' demanded Sampson.

" ' Something, in the meantime, may occur to render the dreadful sacrifice unnecessary,' I replied ; ' God may interfere to save us from such a bloody and inhuman crime, and to relieve our present sufferings, and I feel something within me which convinces me that He will. But how can we expect His mercy, if we wantonly imbrue our hands in the blood of our fellow-creatures ?'

" These observations appeared to stagger Mark Redfield, and my hopes revived. He drew Sampson aside for a second or two, and whispered to him, and then, turning to me and my companions, he said,—

" ' What say you, messmates ? Who agrees with the proposition of Mr. Fitzpatrick ?'

" ' All—all !' they shouted simultaneously, and Ben sunk on his knees, feeling, at that moment, no doubt, the same powerful emotions as the condemned criminal, who receives a reprieve at the very moment when he is about to be launched into eternity. He then arose, and, grasping my hand vehemently, the poor fellow could not speak, but burst into tears.

" ' Be it so,' said Mark ; ' and Heaven send that the hopes of Mr. Fitzpatrick may not prove fallacious ; for, if they do, at the expiration of one hour, as near as we can guess, no remonstrances or supplications can save Ben's life ?'

" Oh, what a relief was this to me, short as the period of Ben's respite was. Something seemed to assure me that Heaven would interpose to prevent the necessity of the crime, and I felt a heavy weight removed from my breast. I grasped the hand of Mark and my other companions, and we then seated ourselves, and in solemn silence and suspense awaited the issue of that painful interval.

" Ben employed himself in prayer, for he had not suffered hope to take too sanguine a hold of his mind, and as the time seemed to pass away with more than usual speed, the agitation of every one increased, and my heart began to sink again.

" Suddenly the clouds lowered ; the wind arose, and everything portended an approaching storm ; and soon the thunder sent forth its deafening peals ; the lightning blazed on high, and the rain began to descend heavily.

" We started to our feet, and each eagerly, as the rain partially filled the cask, drank greedily at its contents. It was indeed the balm of Heaven to our parched throats, and its welcome influence seemed to revive us immediately.

" All at once one feeling appeared to stimulate us all, and in spite of the fury of the tempest, we hurried towards the sea.

" It was so very dark, that it was only at intervals, by the vivid flashes of lightning, we were enabled to observe anything ; and the howling of the waves, and the roaring of the thunder was truly terrific.

" All at once the lightning ceased, and the thunder no longer sent forth its deafening reverberations ; but almost immediately afterwards we beheld a broad flash of light glaring on the surface of the ocean at a distance, which was immediately succeeded by the loud report of a gun.

" ' A ship ! a ship !' shouted all my companions, frantically, in a breath ; and the next moment another broad flash of lightning revealed to us a vessel apparently not more than a quarter of a mile from the island, tossing about with great fury at the mercy of the ruthless waves.

" ' Despair ! despair !' cried Mark Redfield ; ' she can never weather out this storm ; she cannot make the island !'

" Again the report of a gun was heard, and then the tempest seemed to increase in fury.

" A dreadful silence ensued, only interrupted by the furious battling of the elements, and the dashing of the waves, as they rolled with fearful fury against the rocks. All—all of us were alike excited, and powerful that excitement was. We looked at each other with despair, and then we clasped our hands, and raising our sunken eyes towards Heaven, breathed a prayer for the rescue of the struggling mariners.

"Once more the gun was fired, and almost immediately afterwards a dreadful yell, which rose above the voice of the storm, came across the troubled ocean, and too fatally announced the fate of the ship and its unfortunate crew.

"'She's gone—she's sunk—or gone to pieces,' ejaculated Mark.

"'Heaven receive the souls of the poor sufferers!' I cried.

"'Heaven hath forsaken us!' returned Sampson Marston; 'and refuses us relief, at the very moment it was so near at hand. Death—death alone awaits us!'

"'Forbear!' I exclaimed; 'arraign not the will of the Most High, presumptuous man; rather pray for the souls of your poor unfortunate fellow-creatures, who have this moment been launched into the presence of their Maker, with all their sins upon their heads.'

"'We are starving!' cried Sampson; 'and what is the use of preaching now? Will that appease the gnawings of hunger, or quench the fire that is burning up our very vitals?'

"'Patience!' I remonstrated; 'you know not yet what relief may be in store for us.'

"'Patience!' he repeated; 'bah! Have we not submitted to patience long enough? Food we must and will have; the time is expired, and Ben must die!'

"'I am prepared,' answered the poor fellow, in accents of calm despair; 'do with me as you will, but forget not my dying request.'

"'Ay, it shall be obeyed,' answered Mark; 'if we have the opportunity of so doing. I have given you my word.'

"'Then,' said Ben, once more presenting him his arm, 'I shall die content. Be quick, and despatch your bloody job!'

"'Hold! hold!' I cried, seizing the arm of Mark; 'hear you not the voice of Heaven speaks in thunder against the inhuman deed? Beware of its wrath! Can you, in such a moment of horror as this, Mark, become a murderer?'

"My impressive words had their due effect upon Mark, and he dropped the knife, and trembled. Sampson immediately picked up the knife, and, advancing towards Ben, he exclaimed,—

"'Nay, then, Mark Redfield, since you are so weak, I myself will do the deed! The hour is expired—no relief is ours, and he dies!'

"'Monster! forbear!' I exclaimed, starting in between Sampson and Ben; at that moment the thunder rolled with redoubled fury, and awe-struck and appalled, Sampson was diverted from his bloody purpose, and all of us turned our eyes involuntarily towards the ocean. At the very instant that we did so, it was illuminated by the broad glare of lightning, and we beheld something floating towards us. Another instant and it was dashed at our feet. It was a barrel. Quickly we knocked in the top, and discovered it to be filled with biscuits, not at all damaged by the salt water.

"'Relief! relief!' we shouted in a breath; 'Providence has at length been merciful to us, and the life of our messmate is saved!'

"We sunk on our knees, and in silence returned our gratitude to Heaven, while poor Ben was so overcome, that he seemed to be in a state of complete stupefaction.

"This lasted not more than a minute, however; greedily each seized a portion of the biscuits, and appeased their ravenous hunger. Never had anything appeared half so delicious to us before; and having satisfied ourselves, we once more eagerly cast our eyes over the ocean in the hope of observing something else.

" Nor was it long ere our hopes were realized. Another cask was dashed at our feet, which, as if Providence had so ordained it, we found to contain fresh water.

" Each eagerly slaked his burning thrust, and then once more falling on our knees we poured forth our gratitude to the Almighty Giver of all good.

" ' You see,' I observed, when my companions had become more composed, ' I was not wrong in the confidence I placed in the mercy of Omnipotence, and by my interposition, have saved the life of an innocent man, and probably those of all of us.'

" ' But the vessel is lost!' returned Mark Redfield, despondingly, ' and we still have no prospect of being released from this desolate island.'

" ' But we are saved from present starvation,' I replied, ' and probably something else may be floated ashore from the wreck, to preserve our lives until Providence may send us relief.'

" My companions all agreed in the truth and force of these observations, and we then proceeded to stow away our biscuits and water under the trees which usually formed our place of retreat.

" We all agreed to partake but sparingly of the provisions and the water, in case we should not be able to get any more from the wreck, and the storm having now almost entirely subsided, we returned to the sea-side, in the hope of meeting with something else which might prove useful to us.

" Notwithstanding what had occurred, the melancholy fate of the ship, and apparently all her crew, filled my mind with the most gloomy thoughts, which I strove in vain to conquer.

" Although the storm had now entirely ceased, the night still remained pitchy dark, and we could see very little more than the vast expanse of waters, that were not lighted by a single star. The wind still moaned dismally, like the melancholy requiem over the souls of the departed.

" Feeling cold and cheerless, after having watched for some time, without meeting with any farther success in recovering anything from the wreck, we left the spot, and having arrived at our shady retreat, we once more partook slightly of the biscuits and the water, and then spreading our jackets on the earth, we stretched our weary limbs upon them, huddled closely together, and enjoyed several hours of the most refreshing sleep we had experienced since we had been in our present forlorn condition.

" In the morning we arose with recruited spirits, and our first step was to make our way to the sea-side, to see if we could discover any portions of the wreck.

" What an awful scene there presented itself to our eyes; the vessel had evidently gone to pieces, and portions of her were floating about in all directions, while numerous bodies had been dashed upon the rocks, and, from the clothes of the seamen, we were convinced it was an English ship. Oh! if it had but reached that place in safety, we reflected, we should at once have been rescued, and restored to our native country; but now, alas! it might be a long time, or, perhaps never, before such a chance would present itself to us again. We could have wept with the bitter melancholy of our thoughts, but our attention was speedily diverted to that which was of more immediate importance. On the shore numerous articles had been washed during the night; among the rest a barrel of pork, and a cask of rum, and another large cask of fresh water, all to us most inestimable. Besides these numerous timbers, and spars, and canvass were floating about near the rocks, which we secured.

" We had now a solemn task to perform, and that was to consign the poor fellows who had perished to their watery grave. We first stripped their bodies o their wearing apparel, and then proceeded to read the burial service over them, which ended, with melancholy hearts we tossed them into the ocean. We then conveyed all that we had found to our tree-sheltered retreat, and enjoyed one of the heartiest meals we had had for a considerable time, refreshing ourselves with a small drop of rum each, which made us all feel as if we were different individuals.

"We had now got sufficient provisions to last us for at least a fortnight, and our hopes revived; while the gratitude of my companions towards me, for having saved them from the hideous crime which they had contemplated, was unbounded.

"During the day we recovered several more useful articles from the wreck, and we then set about erecting a tent, which we soon accomplished, under the trees, and became as happy and contented as persons placed in our melancholy situation could possibly be.

"The following day, one of our companions having rambled in a direction which had before escaped our observation, returned to us with the joyful intelligence that he had discovered a spring of pure water.

"This was another blessing that we had not expected, and no poor wretches could be more thankful for it. But I am afraid I am growing tedious."

"Oh, no, indeed you are not, my dear sir," answered William. "I am deeply interested with your story, and notwithstanding all the disasters which I have myself met with, I never imagined that any human beings could undergo half so much as that you have related."

Mr. Fitzpatrick then resumed in the following words :—

"In the manner I have described three days passed away, and still we saw no prospect of being released from the island. At length another idea suggested itself to our thoughts. As there seemed to be no prospect of any relief coming to us, we determined to make an attempt to release ourselves. We had rescued, as I have before mentioned, a vast quantity of planks from the wreck, and with these we resolved to construct a raft, and to make an attempt to leave the island, with the hope of being able to reach some inhabited place, or to encounter a vessel by which we might be taken up.

"About this task we set with a right good will, and it was not long ere we had constructed a raft of sufficient strength to stand against a pretty rough gale, and large enough, with a sail, &c., to carry us all, and such provisions as we might have to take with us; for, I should have told you, that two or three more casks of pork, rum, and biscuits, in a day or two after the wreck, floated ashore, so that altogether we were pretty well supplied.

"We now waited anxiously for the first favourable day, when we determined to put our project into execution, and hope once more reanimated our bosoms with its cheering rays.

"It was a most hazardous undertaking, but nothing could be worse than our present situation, and the dread of being left on this desolate island to perish ultimately of want, and without the chance of ever more beholding our friends, or our native country, urged and encouraged us on. It is so hard to die in a foreign land, estranged from all that is dear to us, and where our ashes must rest, without a tear being shed by those we have loved in life over the cold and lonely grave that encloses them.

"It was, however, several days before we could find the weather favourable to our purpose, and then, having first implored the assistance of the Almighty, we launched our raft, deposited our provisions upon it, and then committed ourselves to it.

"It was as beautiful a day as ever the all-bounteous God blessed his erring creatures with; Sol rode on his golden throne in all his glory; the air was clear, and the ocean calm and lovely.

"Our spirits were exhilarated, as our raft went steadily on, and as the

rocks gradually disappeared from us, we felt as if we had just escaped from a horrible prison. We were upon the bright blue waters, with a favouring breeze, and a cloudless sky; all seemed to smile propitiously upon us, and our souls rose in gratitude to the Most High, for the mercy He had extended towards us.

" We were obliged to go with the wind, but we were satisfied, when we found, as near as we could guess, that we were going in the direction of Malta. We judged that we could not be more than three or four days' sail from it, and should the wind continue favourable, we might reach there in safety; but we were also in hopes that we should before then encounter some ship, on board of which, out of motives of humanity, we might be received.

" All that day everything continued as we could wish, but it being almost a dead calm, our raft was not able to make way.

" At night, which was as lovely as the day had been, two of us took it by turns to keep watch, while the others stretched themselves on the raft and went to sleep, and thus we all continued refreshed, and fully prepared to encounter any exertions which might be called into action.

" The morning, however, came in dark and lowering; heavy black clouds obscured the sun's disc, and the wind began gradually to rise from N.N.E., and our raft was consequently driven out of its former course. Still we kept up our spirits better than might have been expected, and lived in hopes that we might, ere long, meet with some friendly vessel. We stretched our gaze, notwithstanding, to the fullest extent, but nothing met our observation to give the least encouragement to that sanguine hope. The boundless sea met our gaze on every side, and a heavy, black, cloudy sky frowned upon us.

" The wind continued to rise, and at length it blew such a stiff gale, that
No. 32

our raft was driven before it with the most fearful velocity, and it was not
without the greatest difficulty that we could keep ourselves upon it. We
were soon fated to meet with a misfortune, which, under such circumstances, was doubly terrible; the raft made a sudden and violent lurch,
and we were too much occupied in seeking to save ourselves from being
precipitated into the ocean to think of anything else, in consequence of
which, we had the grief to see the whole of our provisions washed off the
raft.

" We clasped our hands in despair, and the hopes that had before cheered
us on, now entirely vanished. Should we remain without being picked up,
or arriving at any island, where we might be kindly received, for any length
of time, nothing but starvation presented itself. We could have wept, in
the bitterness and agony of our feelings, but I still maintained more spirits
than any of my companions, and did all that I possibly could to encourage
them with hope.

" I have often since marvelled at the wonderful coolness and nerve which
I maintained throughout the whole of those trials, unused to similar calamities as I had always been, and totally unacquainted with the perils of
the deep; but so it was, and to that fortunate fact I owe my preservation.

" The wind, instead of abating, began to get more boisterous, and now
the rain descended in torrents, and the dense clouds gathered so fast, that
it was almost as dark as night. Most of my companions crouched down
on the raft, and leaning their heads on their hands, viewed the dismal and
alarming scene around them with the most fearful despair. For my own
part, I stood boldly erect, and with arms folded, I contemplated all around
me with mingled feelings of wonder, awe, and dread. If I may so express myself, it was sublime and beautiful in its horrors.

" I had met with so many misfortunes, my hopes had been so often
crushed, at the very moment when they had seemed to have been about to
be realized, that I was prepared for whatever new calamity might await
me, and I resigned myself to the Divine Will.

" Hour after hour the storm increased in fury, and we were all of us
wet through by the waves that incessantly washed over us.

" Poor Ben, who had been doomed to die, was quite exhausted, and had
stretched himself at full length upon the raft, when a heavy sea washed
him and another of our unfortunate companions away, and we saw no
more of them.

" This catastrophe seemed to make but little or no impression upon my
companions, for they all expected the same fate themselves, and in such
scenes, I found, from experience, that sympathy is a rarity.

" To the wind and the rain were now added thunder and lightning, and
although it was a most terrific day, Mark Redfield, and one or two others,
now began to express themselves in loud terms of regret that we had
quitted the island, and blamed me for it, although they had been the most
strenuous supporters of it; but this I combatted with their own weapons,
repeating the observations they had themselves made, namely, that it was
better to meet with any fate than to remain on that desolate place, in all
probability ultimately to starve. This silenced them, and the terrors around
us soon diverted them from all other thoughts.

" Notwithstanding it was tossed about like a straw, the raft still continued to weather the storm bravely, and I was yet not without hope,
that, if it at all abated, we might be saved from the fate which at present
threatened us. My companions, however, seemed to think very different,
and abandoned themselves to a gloomy and sullen despair.

" I was doomed, however, to be once more disappointed; the storm continued with increased, instead of abated violence, and death appeared

inevitable. I made up my mind for the worst, and employed the short time, which I imagined was left to me in this world, in prayer. Quite different, however, my unfortunate companions; aroused out of their state of apathy, they first uttered the most bitter lamentations, and then proceeded to give vent to their frenzy in the most dreadful expressions and maledictions. I looked at them with horror, but found it was entirely useless to endeavour to pacify them, or to bring them to a proper sense of their awful situation, and the necessity there was for preparing themselves for the fearful change we had all a right shortly to expect. They gazed upon me with savage looks, and even seemed to view me as their enemy, and the cause of their present misfortunes; therefore, you may judge that my situation altogether was one of the most unenviable description. I, however, supported it all with more fortitude and calmness than I had before given myself credit for, and placidly viewed the destiny that seemed fast approaching us.

" The thunder and the rain at length abated, and the clouds dispersed, but the wind continued at its height, and we were tossed about with the most frightful fury.

" In this manner, on the brink of eternity, we continued for about half an hour, when some rocks in the distance met our observation.

" We had scarcely made this discovery, when a tremendous wave rolled over us, and before we had time to say ' God help us,' we were all washed into the boundless deep.

" My senses were for a moment gone, but I arose again on the surface of a huge wave, which dashed me violently against something, which I perceived to be the raft. Frantically I clung to it, and raised myself upon it, then seizing a rope which was, fortunately, left attached to it, I hastily lashed myself to one of its spars, and resigned myself, quite exhausted, to my fate.

" The raft was dashed fearfully along, and the heavy waves that continually washed over me, seemed to bring death with them every instant. I saw no more of my unfortunate companions, and they must all have met with a watery grave, in the midst of their wild ravings and awful execrations.

" I could perceive that I was being driven rapidly towards the rocks, and I fully expected that I should be dashed to pieces against them; but I breathed a prayer to Heaven, and supplicated for its mercy.

" In about a quarter of an hour the wind lulled; the waves sunk, and a comparative calm ensued. The raft proceeded rapidly but steadily, and, unlashing myself, I stood erect, and gazed around me.

" What a relief was this sudden change to me! I cannot describe it. I laughed aloud in the delirium of my joy, and seemed as if I was inspired with new life. Then I remembered the fate of my companions, and, reflecting that I was alone, I became wretched and melancholy, and I could not help viewing their fate as preferable to my own. But it was only for a moment, and then I turned my thoughts once more towards my own preservation from a watery grave.

" Still the raft was driven towards the rocks, and with such violence, that I saw my life was placed in the most imminent danger. I was yet undecided how to act, when, as the raft gradually neared the rocks, my quick eye perceived one of them that appeared to be accessible, and, in a moment, I had made up my mind. I stripped myself of my jacket, waistcoat, and shirt, so that they might not encumber me, and when the raft had got to within a few yards of the rock, after supplicating the assistance of the Almighty, I plunged into the sea, and swam, as well as my exhausted strength would permit me, towards it.

"After some struggling I reached the most favourable point of the rock in safety, and, catching hold of one of its projections, with convulsive agony I held myself up, as well as I could, and gasped for breath. The waves receded from me, and I was enabled to reach a ledge of the rock in safety, where I laid myself down quite fatigued, and being out of the reach of danger, I gradually fell off to sleep.

"How long I had remained in this state, I know not; but I awoke cold and shivering, and, rising to my feet, I gazed around me. Cheerless as was the prospect, miserable and alone as I was, a sensation of hope, and an unaccountable feeling of happiness came over me. I knelt down, and with tears in my eyes, once more returned my thanks to that beneficent Being who had preserved me throughout so many and such terrible dangers.

"The ocean had now become perfectly calm, and the sun (for it was now daylight) was shining with unusual brilliancy upon its surface; but when I reflected upon the vast havoc the recent storm must have done—the number of unfortunate beings who had been taken into the presence of their Maker, with all their sins upon their heads—the melancholy idea suggested itself to me, that it was like sunshine glittering upon the tomb that incloses all our earthly love—our happiness.

"I gazed at the rock above me, and although it was steep, still its sides were craggy, and I thought I should be able to reach its summit with but little difficulty. But when I had accomplished that task, alas! ' What hope was there for me?' I ruminated. Perhaps to find it barren, and only to have my existence prolonged a few hours, to die a death of starvation. For what had I escaped? What chance was there of my being rescued from the jaws of death? Again, it forciby appeared to my mind, that the fates of my companions were preferable to my own, and for a moment my brain whirled round, and I was almost tempted to plunge into the deep from which I had so recently escaped, and at once terminate my sufferings. But an instinctive voice withheld me from my rash design.

"I stood awhile, and contemplated all around me, and then, once more gazing at the rock above me, I commenced my toilsome task.

"It was not without considerable difficulty that I gained the summit, and then I seated myself on the sterile earth, quite exhausted, and my hands bleeding from the sharp and craggy rock.

"I need not describe to you the place, for it was the same rocky island as that we are now upon. I looked around me. All was desolate and barren. Nothing to cheer me but the rays of the sun, which was then shining in full meridian splendour; and my heart was so full, when I reflected that I was _alone_—not one of my poor companions left, to share with me in my solitude—no one to whom I could communicate my thoughts—I could not help weeping like a child.

"This somewhat relieved me, and I walked on, resolved to make the best of my melancholy situation, and to endeavour to find some place of shelter from the inclemency of the weather, while it might please Providence that I should remain upon the island, and also to see whether there was any prospect of my being enabled to obtain the means of subsistence.

"I was gratified to find all that you have discovered, and that the means of living were provided for me in my solitude, and my hopes, therefore, revived, and I endeavoured to submit to my hard destiny without murmuring; but still, it is so terrible to be alone. Anything in the shape of a human being, in situations like these, let him be ever so illiterate, or generally repulsive, affords the mind relief, and we forget the difference of their nature in that temporary relief to the gloomy thoughts which they afford.

"Still the sleep which I had had somewhat recalled my energies, and I walked forward on my melancholy expedition with recruited spirits; this was greatly added to when I reached one of the places which the recent rains had filled with water, and refreshed myself with the welcome libation. Proceeding further on, I discovered some trees bearing a fruit, which at that time appeared to me perfectly delicious; but this I need not attempt to pourtray to you, William, as you have experienced the same.

"'Heaven still is good and merciful!' I exclaimed, 'and though I may remain here for some time, and perhaps for the remainder of my days, I shall not starve.'

"I took a regular circuit of the island, and having, as I imagined, examined every place, and ascertained all that I could, I felt fatigued, and, accordingly, laid myself down beneath the cooling shade of some trees, and once more sleep closed my eyelids.

"Dreams of the most tormenting nature crowded upon my imagination. I fancied myself in happy England, surrounded by my friends, and with every happiness about me; then I thought I beheld you, William, enfolded in the embrace of that excellent man, my old and esteemed friend, the author of your being, and all was bliss and sunshine around. But it was transient; heavy clouds obscured the horizon; a pool of blood appeared suddenly to flow between you and your father, and separated you, and from its centre arose a fiendish shape, which quickly assumed the form of the villain I so well know. His eyes appeared to flash fire; sulphurous flames issued from his mouth and nostrils. The effect upon me was suffocating, and with the dreadful sensation I awoke, to find myself again in solitude—alone! But still it was a relief to me, and, after recovering my senses, I arose upon my feet."

"Oh, my dear sir," interrupted William 'why not make me acquainted with the name of the author of my being?—why not inform me of the real character of my deadly enemy?—why keep me any longer in this dreadful state of almost insupportable suspense?"

"Whisht! whisht! honey dear," replied Mr. Fitzpatrick; "I know it must be very painful to you, and is a great trial of your patience, but you must bear with it a little longer, and rest assured that all will, in due time, be satisfactorily explained to you by myself, Mr. Patrick Fitzpatrick; and a terrible day will that same day of explanation be to some parties; but you may be certain that I have some very particular reasons now for wishing to keep it a secret for the present."

"Of the good intention of your motives, sir," answered William, "I entertain no doubt, but I cannot conceive the reason why you should wish to withold them from me, and to me the mystery is very painful."

"No doubt of it, darling," returned the lawyer; "but it cannot be helped, and it is all for your good, so with that be content, and hear the conclusion of my tedious narrative, to which I have very little more to add."

William was forced to accede, and Mr. Fitzpatrick concluded his eventful story in the following words:—

"Having gathered and eaten some more of the fruit, I moved from the spot towards the lower ledge of the rocks, with the hope of meeting with some fish that might have been washed on to it, in which, as you may be aware, from your own experience, I was not disappointed; and now, indeed, with all my troubles, I considered myself fortunate, and resolved to make my mind as contented as possible under my difficulties.

"I sat myself down upon the brink of the rock, and gazed over the sea, which was rolling and dancing most magnificently in the golden beams of the sun. No vessel met my sight, but yet, amid all my desolateness, I felt a sensation of happiness and resignation steal over me, and could not help persuading myself that God, who had hitherto rescued me from such imminent perils, when all else had perished, would still watch over me, and eventually save me from my present misery.

"These thoughts greatly revived me, and I left the spot, resolved to return to the same place I had so recently quitted, where I had found the fruit, and where I resolved, for the present, to take up my abode under their umbrageous foliage. Having reached the place, I stretched myself on the earth on a spot which was covered with leaves that had fallen from the trees, but I had scarcely done so when I sunk through them several feet, and was much bruised in my fall.

"Having recovered, I found myself in a cavity of some extent, which had been concealed by the leaves and branches I have before mentioned. I also discovered that it winded down into a subterraneous passage below, which was easy of descent, as nature had formed a complete flight of steps in the rock. I descended until I discovered this retreat, and everything as you now see it, which convinced me that some other persons had been wrecked in the place, and had here found a temporary asylum.

"I will not attempt to picture to you my feelings on that occasion—I was completely overpowered. Here, then, was a habitation provided for me, so long as it might please Providence I should remain on the island, and His goodness to me was made even more manifest than it had been before.

"I, of course, immediately took up my abode in this rocky cavern, and having found some planks in it, I placed them over its entrance, in the manner you have seen, and whenever I quitted it I covered them with boughs and leaves, so that no unwelcome intruders might discover it, for I still entertained strange fears that some of the terrible corsairs would find me out, and that I should again fall into their hands, and it was that which made me fly from you so alarmed when you first discovered me.

"I passed whole hours on the brink of the rock every day in the hope of descrying some friendly vessel, but without success, and I had reconciled my mind to remain here in solitude for the rest of my days, when propitious fortune, and yet, on your account, evil destiny sent you to me."

CHAPTER XVIII.

THE RESCUE.—THE UNEXPECTED ATTACK.—THE DEATH.—THE FATE OF THE PIRATE VESSEL.—THE UNREVEALED SECRET.

"And, is it not strange," said William, when Mr. Fitzpatrick had thus concluded his narrative, "that, in all your perambulations, you had not seen the tent which I erected to shelter me?"

"It is," answered the latter; "but what think you, darling, of my adventures since we last met?"

"They have indeed been most wonderful and trying," said William, "and I wonder how you had fortitude to support them."

"True," said Mr. Fitzpatrick; "ay, and it's no coward that I have proved myself to be, I fancy."

"Indeed you have not," coincided William; "but, alas! we have, I fear, many other troubles yet to encounter, and it may be years, if ever, that we are released from this place."

"Och! och! say not so!" rejoined Mr. Fitzpatrick; "live in hopes, honey, as I have always done under circumstances of the greatest trial, and, depend on it, we shall yet see Old England again, and we shall meet our enemies, and we shall bang them, as Paddy did the drum, and, by the Holy Saint Patrick, we shall all be happy again, and you will embrace your pretty Flora, and she will have to call you husband, and much right to it, too—and —— "

" Poor Flora !" interrupted William, his manly bosom heaving with agony, " will indeed that time ever come ?"

" To be sure it will," answered Mr. Fitzpatrick, " have I not before tould you so, and, faith ! I'm as good as a bogle."

" I see but little hopes of it," sighed William, " since she is in the power of those wretches, the smugglers, or pirates, or both."

" But how do you know that she is still in their power, honey ?" demanded Mr. Fitzpatrick.

" Did I not leave her on board the vessel when the villains condemned me to walk the plank ?" said William.

" True," said his companion ; " but there may have been many events occurred since then."

" There may indeed," returned the young sailor, " and poor Flora may ere this have perished. Indeed, I do not believe she could survive the dreadful shock of my supposed fate."

" Whisht ! whisht ! now," said the lawyer ; " do not be giving way to these ideas ; may not Flora have escaped—been rescued by some British vessel, and the smugglers sent to Davy Jones's locker ?"

" But," said William, with a shudder of horror, " if she has escaped, may it not be with dishonour ?"

" Arrah, now !" returned Mr. Fitzpatrick, " do not be after viewing the worst side of the question. What is the use of making yourself miserable with ideas that may have, and I am inclined to believe, not any foundation in truth. Did you not say that the Smuggler King was not on board, when the d——d rascals attempted to take your life ?"

" I did," answered William ; " but there is no doubt that he would join her immediately at the place of her destination."

" And how do you know, boy," remarked his companion, " whether your sweetheart might not have been rescued before she reached that same place of destination ?"

" I certainly do not know," returned William ; " but the chances are all against any such event having taken place."

" And I say no such thing at all, at all," observed Mr. Fitzpatrick ; " suppose the Devil Skipper should have been attacked and conquered."

" Suppositions !" repeated William, with a look of despair.

" Why, that's all we can at present indulge in," said the lawyer, " and it is always better to encourage hope than despair."

" Have not the smugglers ever proved unconquerable to those who have been sent against them ?" demanded William.

" They have now, I believe," answered Mr. Fitzpatrick ; " but that's no reason at all, at all, that they should always be so."

" I cannot encourage hope," said the young man ; " whichever way I turn, despair meets my eyes."

" Och ! bother ! bother !"

" Should my Flora indeed have escaped, and with honour," continued William, " and been restored to her friends, I feel confident that her sorrow at my supposed dreadful and untimely fate, would soon break her heart, and bring her to a premature grave. My Flora, my own gentle and affectionate Flora, never could you survive the loss of him you so sincerely loved. Oh ! the villain, that tore you away from your peaceful home, had I my grappling irons now upon him, I would never leave him until he had expiated his crimes in his heart's blood !"

"Hold your whisht, now, man," said Mr. Fitzpatrick; "hold your whisht, that need never be."

"What mean you?"

"You must never take *his* life."

"And why not? Is he not the only one who has oppressed me, and destroyed my happiness?" demanded William.

"Faith! and that's true now," said the lawyer; "he is a monstrous big villain, that same, and deserves death, but I repeat that he must not die by your hands."

"I do not understand you," said William, with a look of astonishment.

"It is very likely you do not, darling," said Mr. Fitzpatrick, "and it is not fit that you should at present."

"Explain yourself."

"Explain myself, is it you mane?"

"Yes—yes——"

"Bother, bother, now, do not be after teazing me," said the lawyer, "for it's the divil a bit of an explanation you'll get out of me, just now, any how."

"This conduct is inexplicable," said William.

"It may be so," answered his companion, "but upon my soul I cannot help it."

"It is cruel."

"Musha, William dear, say not so," returned the lawyer, "for Mr. Fitzpatrick never was cruel in his life."

"Why then refuse an explanation which you say it is in your power to give, and which is of such infinite importance to me."

"Because it might stay the ends of justice."

"Mystery upon mystery! This is insupportable."

"But you must learn to support it," returned the lawyer; "it may appear hard, but isn't it myself, Mr. Patrick Fitzpatrick, that knows best what's good for you?"

"I believe you to be my friend, but why——"

"Now, don't be after making a Judy of yourself," interrupted the eccentric Mr. Fitzpatrick, "when I am doing everything for the best."

"To me this secrecy appears perfectly unnecessary, if not absurd," remarked William.

"It may do so," said his companion; "but, by the powers, it will not do so by-and-bye."

"Why should I be kept in suspense?" demanded William.

"I have told you."

"Why should not my bitter enemy perish by my avenging hands?"

"I have told you; but more shall be revealed to you in due time. No, no—the spalpeen may die on the public scaffold, or be blown to the devil in one of his own vessels, which, sure enough, he will some day be; but he must not die by your hands."

"I cannot fathom your meaning," said William.

"And I do not wish you to do so just now," said Mr. Fitzpatrick.

William walked backwards and forwards across the cavern for a few minutes in a tumult of bewildering thought and suspense.

"But Crazy Marian," he at length said.

"What of her?" inquired Mr. Fitzpatrick.

"Think you that the tale she told me was true?"

"From the description you have given of her, and the facts she related, I have not the least doubt of it," answered Mr. Fitzpatrick.

"And that she was my mother?"

"Yes."

William sighed deeply as he observed,—

"Mother—unfortunate mother! to be estranged from you so long, and then only to behold you meet with so dreadful a fate, and at the very moment when you were about to impart to me—your son—the secret of his birth."

"Alas! poor, unfortunate lady," said the lawyer, with much emotion; "but still you know not that she was actually dead."

"I could have very little doubt of it," returned William; "besides, if she even recovered, she would be in the power of the smugglers, who would take care not to let so dangerous an enemy live, or to escape from them again."

"The atrocious scoundrels!" said the lawyer. "But they will all be paid out in their own coin by-and-by, depend upon it; and it's Mr. Patrick Fitzpatrick that will have yet the glorious satisfaction of giving them a lift by-and-by, never fear. But come, William, my boy, you must require some refreshment after this long and tedious story of mine, so let us partake of such humble, but wholesome fare, as it has pleased Providence to supply us with in this desolate place. Och! and it's a fortunate thing that we have met, and it's not long that it will be before we both bid adieu this place in company, never fear."

"Heaven send that your prognostications may be verified," said William, "though much I fear, should it be my destiny to return home, I shall find there all a wreck."

"Arrah! now, boy," returned the lawyer, "why don't you be after hoping for the best? Sure, and it's mighty little use giving way to the blue devils, as I have experienced, the blackguards."

William, although he could not help smiling at the observations of his singular companion, seated himself disconsolately in one corner of the cave,

No. 33

while Mr. Fitzpatrick kindled a fire, and placing a couple of fish upon the embers, cooked them, and these, with some fruit, constituted the humble meal of the two unfortunates.

After this William became somewhat more composed, and they entered into a conversation upon their present circumstances, and the gloomy prospect which was before them. But Mr. Fitzpatrick, in his usual manner, endeavoured to inspire William with hope of a speedy release from their present situation, and he so far succeeded as to make him comparatively tranquil.

The day was now far advanced, and the lawyer proposed that they should remove the tent which William had erected, but this the latter opposed, giving as his reason, that should any vessel stop near the place, and the seamen who landed observe the tent, they would naturally conclude that there was some person or persons on the island, and make search for them.

Mr. Fitzpatrick could not deny that this was very reasonable, and, of course, consented; they, therefore, remained where they were, and passed several hours in conversation, when, at last weary, they retired to the humble pallet which the lawyer had formed.

But it was some time before William could obtain any sleep; the singularity of his situation, his meeting with Mr. Fitzpatrick, and the narrative he had related to him, all crowded upon his thoughts, and kept him waking. But more especially did the mystery which the lawyer maintained as to his birth and the names of his parents harass his mind. He could not conceive, for a moment, the cause of his secrecy, and the more he reflected upon it, the more did he become bewildered in doubt and perplexity; but that his eccentric friend was doing everything from the best motives he could not for a moment entertain any doubt.

Then the untimely and dreadful fate of her he believed to be his mother entered his mind, and his torture was increased.

From her his thoughts wandered to poor Flora, and when he reflected upon the situation she was placed in when he was torn from her, and the probable misery, perhaps shame, to which she had since been subjected, his agony became almost insupportable.

Never could he forget the dreadful scene on the deck of the Devil Skipper; the tears, the prayers, the supplications, and frantic exclamations of Flora, when the villains exulted over the misery of their meeting, and tore them asunder. They were impressed upon his memory in such vivid colours, that there they must remain until his dying-day. It was a mercy to her, he reflected, that she had become insensible before she heard his terrible doom; but he had no doubt the villains would make her acquainted with it, and if they even did not, her fears would be sure to suggest what had taken place, and the terror of her own imagination would, if possible, be worse than reality. She could never survive such accumulated horrors; and even now, perhaps, her whom he prized above all on earth was no more.

Yet, with all these harassing and despairing thoughts, a hope would at times spring up in his breast that they would meet again, and that happiness would yet be their portion; but that, indeed, seemed so extravagant, that it was but transient, and then he would sink into all the wretchedness of utter despondency.

At length, however, balmy sleep alighted on the young seaman's eyelids, and he did not awake until a late hour in the morning.

He found that his companion had already arisen, and was preparing the humble repast for the morning. Of this they both partook, William with a much better appetite than he had latterly done, and they then walked from the cavern towards the sea-side, where Mr. Fitzpatrick proposed that they should constantly watch during the daytime, and for which the tent which William had erected afforded them every facility.

The day passed away without anything particular occurring, and so did the three successive ones. They had an abundant and constant supply of fish, fruit, and water, but no prospect opened to them of being released from their melancholy situation.

William had repeatedly urged his companion to reveal to him the secret of his birth, which he was acquainted with, the names of his parents, and the cause which had led to their separation; but it was in vain, the lawyer persisted in not disclosing more than he had done for the present, and William was thus left in the same painful state of doubt, suspense, and perplexity.

Mr. Fitzpatrick pitied his anguish, and did all he could to soothe him, but with little or no effect; and, as day after day vanished, and still no chance appeared of their being rescued from their situation, his melancholy increased.

It was on the fifth day after William had met with Mr. Fitzpatrick, that they were walking as usual on that point of the rocky island nearest the sea, William with his eyes cast to the earth, and wrapped in deep thought, when Mr. Fitzpatrick suddenly gave him a smack on the shoulder that startled him, and giving a regular bound into the air, shouted at the very top of his voice,—

"Hurrah! hurrah! brogues and buttermilk! By the Holy Saint Patrick, it's come at last. Hurrah! and whack for ould Ireland!"

"What's the matter?" demanded William, looking with astonishment at the singular capers the Irishman was cutting, and imagining, for the moment, that he had actually taken leave of his senses.

"Hurrah! hurrah!" again bawled the lawyer, "och hone! och hone! See—och! och! hurrah!"

"For goodness sake explain yourself," said William. "Are you mad?"

"Mad! Mad!" repeated Mr. Fitzpatrick. "Yes, mad with joy. Look—look—William, dear. A ship! a ship!"

"A ship!" cried William, in a tone of unspeakable delight, and gazing in the direction to which the lawyer had pointed. His joy was scarcely less than that of Mr. Fitzpatrick, when he distinguished in the rays of the sun the white sails of a vessel at a short distance.

"We are saved! we are saved!" said the lawyer, almost delirious with joy. "My heart tells me that we shall find friends in that vessel. The signal! the signal! They cannot help seeing us!"

Quick as thought, they kindled a huge fire on the rock, and, not contented when it sent a lofty column or flame into the air, they tore their handkerchiefs off their necks, and waved them aloft, and shouted aloud in their delirium of transport.

No notice was taken of their signal, but, after the lapse of a few moments, the report of a gun boomed across the deep, and Mr. Fitzpatrick again cried, in a tone of ecstasy,—

"Hurrah! hurrah! By the Hill o'Howth, they have seen our signal; that is the answer to it, and is to assure us that they will assist us. Hurrah! hurrah! We are all right now, William, honey; we shall see ould England again. Did I not tell you so?"

William's feelings need not be described, and the more so, as, the vessel getting nearer, he was enabled to discover her build, and soon found that she was a British merchantman, so that every prospect of their relief was before them.

Again the vessel fired a salute, in answer to the signal which William and his delighted companion had made, the latter of whom was capering about the rock with all the grotesque antics of a wild Indian, and uttering divers peculiar expressions, all demonstrative of the excessive joy he experienced at the speedy prospect of relief.

The vessel was bearing before the wind, in a contrary direction to the rocks, but in a few minutes after the report of the different guns had been heard, a boat was put off from her, which bore away towards the rocks. Mr. Fitzpatrick renewed his capers with redoubled energy, shouting at the very top of his voice,—

"Och! by the holy Saint Patrick! and who will ever be spalpeen enough to give way to despair again? It is farewell to this desolate rock, we may say, honey, and now won't you see your own beautiful little Flora again?"

"Alas!" sighed William, as a deadly blight seemed to fall upon the hopes he had so recently formed, from beholding the ship; "what is there to make me so anxious to cling to life—to revisit England? Shall I not find all wretched there? My friends—my more than parents—perhaps broken-hearted, or, probably, their cold remains resting in the silent grave? My poor Flora, too, perhaps already called to her last, long home; dead —dead of a broken heart—if not still in the power of the miscreants who sought my life; or escaping, now wandering about, the wretched victim of shame—her mind a wreck, and ——"

"Bother, bother, man," interrupted Mr. Fitzpatrick; "faith, and you will persist in overclouding all hope with your dark despair and imaginations. Sure, and may not that great Providence who is so kind to us at the present moment, have rescued the damsel from all harm, and, when you return to England, you will find that lovely face you admire so much, ready to greet you with the radiant sunshine of its smiles. Then, hurrah for a wedding! and farewell to all troubles."

William shook his head.

"My dear sir," he observed, "you advance that which is improbable; in the first instance, the villain in whose power she was when I was torn from her, would take good care that she should not escape from it; in the next, it is not at all likely that he would long delay putting into execution his diabolical designs against her, and, even if she survived her shame, she could never live after the dreadful fate to which she must imagine I was consigned, and ——"

"Arrah, now, honey!" interrupted the lawyer; "no more of it; you would give a man the vapours in the very midst of his joy and his hopes. Here comes the boat, and we shall leave this place anyhow. Ah! and now as they approach nearer, their jolly, open, dare-devil countenances, convince me that they are our countrymen, and well worthy of the title. Hurrah! hurrah! Hilly yeo! hilly yeo! Ship ahoy! Don't you be after seeing, that I have become quite nautical?"

The boat now rapidly approached the rocks, and the three men in it had evidently seen them, and heard the shouts of Mr. Fitzpatrick, for they replied to them with another hearty cheer, which made the rocks re-echo again, and then they directed their boat to that part where there was no danger, and where the lawyer and his companion could reach them in safety.

"Praised be Saint Patrick," said the lawyer; "it is as I thought, they are Englishmen, and we are all right. Och, and it's when we reach that same darling place, which—barring ould Ireland—is the finest country in the world, won't there be a bit of a fillaloo? Won't we astonish our enemies and delight our friends? Och, hone! och, hone! I am so pleased that I could ——"

At this moment, the men had brought their boat immediately under the ledge of rocks which we have described, and were looking up with astonishment and sympathy at the lawyer and his companion.

" What ship, honies ?" demanded the former.

" His Majesty's brig, Thunderer," answered one of the men, " homeward bound."

" Hurrah ! hurrah !" shouted the lawyer. " England for ever !"

William now spoke to them, and briefly described to them who and what they were, and the circumstances that had placed them in their present situation ; and then, at the invitation of the seamen, they immediately descended the rocks, and entered the boat, which put off with all possible speed with them towards the vessel, which had lain by to take them on board.

The joy of Mr. Fitzpatrick approached delirium, and afforded much amusement to the seamen ; but that of William, though not the less great, was not so extravagant, and, when they reached the ship, they were most kindly received by the captain and the other officers, and every attention was commanded to be paid to their necessities.

The account which both William and Mr. Fitzpatrick gave of their adventures and misfortunes to the captain and officers of the brig, excited their deepest astonishment and sympathy, and they expressed the great satisfaction they felt in having been sent by Providence to their rescue at so critical a moment.

Nothing could surpass the kindness with which they were treated, and could William have encouraged the hopes with which Mr. Fitzpatrick endeavoured to inspire him, he would have been happy ; but, in spite of all his efforts to the contrary, his mind entertained the most melancholy forebodings ; and anxious as he had before been to reach England, he now almost dreaded to land there for fear of hearing his worst surmises verified. Even had Flora, by some miracle, escaped from the power of the Smuggler King, which he considered almost impossible, he felt confident that her gentle nature, and the unbounded love she bore him, would not permit her long to survive the dreadful shock which his supposed death must have occasioned her, and that before now she must have perished of a broken heart ; and then the misery and distraction of Mr. and Mrs. Clarendon, and his foster-parents, at their double loss, imagination could scarcely depicture how terrible it must have been ; and the young mariner's heart throbbed with the most bitter anguish, when he reflected upon the sufferings they must have undergone. What a dreadful wreck did he expect to find those two homes that had hitherto been so happy ! What must be the misery of all at the loss of those so dear to them ? He was confident that nothing whatever could impart any consolation to them, and therefore, even the prospect of returning home was darkened by that reflection. Fain would he have banished such ideas from his mind, but, alas ! it was completely useless to make any such attempt, for reason told him that he imagined no more than what must be the result of the misfortunes that had taken place.

In these melancholy ruminations William passed more than an hour, having pleaded indisposition, so that he might commune with his own thoughts, when he was interrupted by the appearance of Mr. Fitzpatrick.

" By the powers," said the honest Irish gentleman, " the captain of the Thunderer is nothing else but the regular broth of a boy; and as everything is in our favour, a fresh breeze, a favouring gale, we have nothing to look forward to but a prosperous voyage, and a speedy return to old England."

" That is, if we do not encounter any fresh squalls," remarked William, smiling.

" Och, bother ! bother, now," remarked Mr. Fitzpatrick, "there you go again; what a divil you are for always putting the blackest side upon everything."

"I would fain encourage hope," said the young man, "but I have so often split upon the rock of despair and disappointment, that ——"

"Psha!" interrupted the lawyer; "and think you a man is always to be unlucky? Mark my words for it, we shall yet see old England again, and be happy too, as I have told you before."

"Happy!" repeated William; "alas! what happiness can there be for me without Flora?"

"Psha!" again exclaimed Mr. Fitzpatrick, "I tell you once more, that you will find her there, and merry, too, I'll be bound for it."

"Merry!" returned the young sailor, "and think you the poor girl can be merry, uncertain as she is of my fate; or, at least certain as she will feel, that I was sacrificed to the vengeance of the smugglers? Did she not behold me felled to the deck, and after what had transpired, would she not feel confident that my life was doomed? Oh, yes, my poor Flora, I am certain, could never survive that dreadful shock."

"Then I am certain you know nothing about the matter, at all, at all," said the lawyer, who, although he was far from entertaining the sanguine hopes he expressed, was anxious to inspire his young friend with hopes.

"Besides," continued William, "should she survive, think you she is not dishonoured—a poor, degraded, broken-hearted being to herself, and a wreck only of what she formerly was?"

"Now then," answered Mr. Fitzpatrick, "I must tell you that I think nothing of the kind whatever."

"Why so?"

"Why so? why, because, according to your own showing, the man whom she had most cause to dread was not aboard when the events you have described took place; and something might occur (and Providence ever kindly watches over the innocent and the lovely) to rescue her before he had the opportunity of encountering her."

"My dear sir," replied William, "I am afraid that these are all fallacious hopes."

"Then, by the powers!" remarked Mr. Fitzpatrick, "do not be afraid of anything of the kind, until you are certain it is so."

William again shook his head, but, at the same time, he thanked the kind-hearted lawyer for his good intentions and the pains he took to comfort him.

The captain of the brig (Mr. Elphinstone) shortly afterwards made his appearance, to whom William repeated his thanks for his kindness in receiving them on board, and the manner in which he had since behaved towards them, and expressed himself willing to repay it by all the humble services that were in his power.

The captain was an Englishman in every sense of the word—blunt, free, and open-hearted, and repeated the pleasure he felt in having been sent to the relief of William and Mr. Fitzpatrick, at the very time, too, when all hope seemed to be at an end.

Mr. Fitzpatrick remained in conversation with William for some time after the captain had left, and still endeavoured to impart hope and consolation to his mind, and our hero, although he really felt it not, sought to appear contented, merely to satisfy him.

"Och!" cried the lawyer, with all his usual buoyancy of spirits, under the most trying difficulties, "and it's won't we be happy when we reach darling England again; and it isn't a small drop o' the crature we'll have neither; and it isn't a small bit of a jig we'll have, when we've made our enemies dance to 'Tantarara Rogues all!' and it isn't a small bit of a song that myself will come out with on that occasion—a bit of a favourite of mine, that I haven't sung for many a long day. And, by the powers! if it's not disagreeable to you, honey, as you've got the blue devils, I'll sing it to you now."

William, with a smile, humoured the whim of the good-tempered Irishman, who, in a voice rather more jovial than musical, immediately sung the following,—

SONG.

"Drink of the flask, you'll find there's a spell in
Its every drop 'gainst the ills of mortality;
Talk of the cordial that sparkled for Helen—
Her cup was a fiction, but this is reality.
Would you forget the dark world we are in,
Only taste of the bubble that gleams on the top of it;
But, would you rise above earth, till akin
To the immortals themselves, you must drain ev'ry drop of it.
Then drink from the flask, you'll find there's a spell in
Its every drop 'gainst the ills of mortality;
Talk of the cordial that sparkled for Helen—
Her cup was a fiction, but this is reality.

"By my sowl," observed Mr. Fitzpatrick, "and it's all a fiction that I'm singing now, since we haven't got the reality, in the shape of a small drop of poteen. But 'never mind, I'll go on in the promise of it, just to give it an extra flavour by anticipation when we get it.

"Never was liquor form'd with such power,
To charm and bewilder that we'll be quaffing;
Its magic began, when in autumn's rich hour,
As a harvest of gold in the fields it stood laughing.
There having by nature's enchantment been fill'd
With the balm and the bloom of her kindliest weather,
This wonderful juice from its core was distilled,
To enliven such hearts as are now met together.
Then give me the flask, you'll find there's a spell in
Its every drop 'gainst the ills of mortality;
Talk of the cordial that sparkled for Helen—
Her cup was a fiction, but this is reality."

In spite of the anguish of his feelings, William could not help smiling at the jollity with which Mr. Fitzpatrick sang the above song; but the recollection of Flora and his friends soon returned to his mind, and superseded entirely all other thoughts. Again that once happy name he had so loved, with the smiling faces that ever illumined his appearance and greeted his return after the perils of the deep, rushed forcibly on his recollection, and racked his brain to distraction. The beauteous and affectionate glances of his adored Flora, her simple but sincere vows of constancy, all came fresh upon his mind, and seemed as if they had been but the events of yesterday. Was such happiness ever again in store for him? Alas! he feared not. In spite of all his efforts and those of his ardent, but eccentric friend, Mr. Fitzpatrick, he could not entertain any other feeling than that of despair. True, the vessel they were aboard of was homeward-bound, and, at present, everything seemed to be in their favour; but he had lately met with so many disappointments, that he was fearful to encourage hope. And then should they indeed be able to reach England, what kind of a reception could he expect to meet with?

Should he behold her to whom his whole soul was devoted, smiling and happy as she was ever wont to be? Oh! no. Should she have escaped from the power of the smugglers, which to him appeared utterly improbable, would it not be with a broken heart—degraded in her own estimation and that of the world, and rendered a poor, forlorn and wretched being for ever? The thought was dreadful, and yet it was too reasonable for the young sailor easily to reject it. Besides, even should she have escaped altogether the danger which had threatened her, could she survive the knowledge of his fate? He felt confident that she could not, or, if she even did, that her mind would for ever be a wreck, and that she would, consequently, in a manner of speaking, be entirely lost to him in the world. And then her friends—his more than parents, too, alas! what would be their misery?—what desolation must their mysterious and unfortunate disappearance have caused to all! That old Ben Backstay, his wife, Fauchette, and all of them, loved him as dearly as if he were actually their own dear relation, he felt confident; for had he not experienced every proof? and, therefore, he was equally as certain that they would be inconsolable for his loss, and, probably, it might hasten them to a premature grave. This thought tortured his mind sadly, and he was glad when the lawyer, who found that all his remonstrances and humour were in vain, quitted the cabin, and left him to his own reflections.

"Alas!" he reflected, "why did Mr. Clarendon and his foster-father refuse their consent to their immediate union? then might all that had since taken place have been prevented. But still might the Smuggler King have persisted in his villanous designs, and, powerful as he was, would have been just as likely to have succeeded as he was under the present circumstances. Besides, his friends, he could not but acknowledge to himself, had acted with perfect prudence, in consequence of the uncertainty of his birth, to delay the union, inasmuch as the disparity of their stations in society might prove an insurmountable barrier to its ever taking place. A barrier! Oh, no! should Flora be still living, what power on earth should prevent him from loving her?—what earthly power should prevent their becoming united?—None—none! That which he felt convinced was sanctioned by Heaven, no mortal power should ever frustrate; nor could he believe that his parents, should they indeed be living, which he at present had every reason to believe they were not, could be so insensible to the virtues and beauty of such a damsel as Flora Clarendon, as to consider her even a match unworthy of a prince.

This thought naturally suggested to him the fate of his parents, and William became doubly harassed and bewildered in his mind. Could it be really a fact that Marian was his mother? The story seemed so wild and improbable that he could scarcely bring his mind to believe it, and yet she was perfectly sensible when she thus claimed him, and he could not conceive what purpose it would have answered her to have deceived him. She had nothing, that he could imagine, to gain by inventing a falsehood of that description; and the melancholy fate she had therefore met with, which, under any circumstances, and had she not been related to him by the nearest and dearest ties of consanguinity, would have excited his utmost sympathy, now caused him the most poignant anguish, and he mentally vowed that, if Providence ever granted him the power, he would bring down a terrible but just retribution on the heads of the murderers. When he recollected what her dreadful sufferings must have been—miserable, wretched, deserted—his heart bled for her, and he could not help reproaching the memory of his father in some measure, either for the weakness or the harshness he must have exercised towards her. Mr. Fitzpatrick had assured him that she was honourably the wife of the author of his being; that she had been injured, calumniated; and surely there must have been something very powerful indeed so far to have blinded and prejudiced his father against the woman he had at the altar vowed to love and protect, as to cause him to abandon her, and tear her own offspring from her fostering bosom. The idea caused

him much uneasiness, and he felt the most painful sympathy and commiseration in her fate. Oh, yes! the voice of Nature—that holy voice, that some time or other speaks with the most irresistible eloquence to the most insensible breast, appealed to him powerfully; it could not be hushed; his heart acknowledged that Marian had spoken the truth, and that she was indeed his mother. What a strange and unnatural destiny, then, had been his, and that of all those in any way connected with or related to him; it seemed as if they had been marked out by evil Fortune to be the sport of Fate—buffeted about on the rude ocean of life, like a vessel in a storm; and, even now, the same hard and cruel lot pursued him with remorseless severity.

"Oh! curses, eternal curses!" the young sailor vehemently ejaculated, "light upon the wretches who in the first place caused so much misery to my poor mother; and tenfold curses, if possible, descend upon the heads of her brutal, her monstrous assassins. But they shall not escape me! No, spirit of my murdered mother; thy son swears to wreak his vengeance upon them, to have a terrible retribution upon their heads, even though he lose his own life in so doing. A just God will suffer me to live for so righteous a cause, and yet place the bloody-minded miscreants in my power!"

He clenched his fists in the determination of the thought, and paced the cabin backwards and forwards in a state of the greatest agitation. For a time these ideas banished even his beloved Flora from his memory, and he gave himself up entirely to the anguish of the feelings they excited.

Then he could not help feeling dissatisfied, vexed, and surprised at the secret which Mr. Fitzpatrick persisted in maintaining regarding the history of his parents, the particulars of which he had positively asserted, and which he firmly believed he was acquainted with. What motives could he have for so doing, and keeping him in suspense? To him it was perfectly

No. 34

inexplicable. Who was more worthy of having these important secrets confided to him than their own son; or, if, as he had declared, that there was no shame attached to his origin, why should he hesitate to make him acquainted with every particular? He was completely bewildered and lost in fruitless conjecture and anxiety. Why should he delay for a moment letting him know everything it was in his power to communicate? Surely it could not retard or prevent any just ends he might have in view? From the short time that he had been acquainted with the lawyer, however, he had ascertained too much of his character to imagine for a moment, that he would deviate in the least from the precise and singular course he had laid down for himself; that it would be useless to urge him any further, for that nothing would at present induce him to become more communicative. He had, therefore, nothing left but patience, which to him, and in his present situation, was a task of no easy description.

Tired of thinking, and being unable to come to any satisfactory conclusion, he left the cabin and hastened to the quarter-deck, where he found Captain Elphinstone engaged in conversation with Mr. Fitzpatrick, and apparently much amused with and prepossessed in favour of the eccentric manners and warm-heartedness of the lawyer.

William now more fully returned his thanks to the captain for his kindness, and expressed his willingness to make himself useful as soon as the former might think proper to avail himself of his services.

The captain appeared pleased with the appearance of our hero, and treated him with every respect, assuring him again of the gratification he felt in having so fortunately been the means of rescuing him and his companion from their perilous and wretched situation; and at the same time he uttered a hope that they would have a prosperous voyage to England, and that they might be restored to their friends.

William once more acknowledged the sense he entertained of his sympathy and good wishes, but, at the same time, he could not entertain the same sanguine hope, when he reflected upon the deplorable situation his friends must have been reduced to at the loss of himself and his beloved Flora.

"Och, now!" observed the lawyer, "and you will persist now in giving way to the mullygrubs; and, by Saint Patrick, it is enough to give a person the cholic to see you. Isn't it a beautiful vessel we are now in? and sure don't she ride before the gale, like a whisp of straw in a whirlwind? and isn't it a match that we are for all the pirates and smugglers that may be bold enough to come athwart of us? And what the devil more is it you would be after wanting?"

"Your friend says right," observed the captain, smiling at the plain and curious manner in which Mr. Fitzpatrick expressed himself; "there is not a finer vessel in all his Majesty's service than the 'Thunderer;' and, if it pleases our Commander aloft to continue the favouring breeze we have at present, we shall be in England in the turning of a handspike. But if we should happen to come athwart hawse of any of those sea-gulls, the pirates, why, we must do our best to give them a drubbing, and make them cry 'peccavi,' that's all."

"You will find William Backstay can play his part among the swabs, your honour, I dare say," answered our hero; "and not a man on board your craft will go into them with better spirit."

"And the devil a one at all, at all, that shall take the shine out of Mr. Patrick Fitzpatrick for that matter," said the lawyer; "och! and isn't it myself that would play the very devil among them for the honour of ould Ireland, and I would afterwards do a little kindness for them in the law way, just to help them to a hempen cravat. Always an eye to business."

"I have no doubt of the courage of you both," remarked Captain Elphinstone; "but I trust it will not be put to the test. You have then, it seems, weathered some rough gales, my lad, although you are young in the service?"

"I have, your honour," answered William.

"And do you mean to say that the piratical swabs, pirates, or smugglers, as they call themselves, dared to serve a British seaman in the manner you described to me?"

William replied in the affirmative.

"And to lay their grappling-irons on your fair craft?" added the captain.

"Yes, your honour," answered William, "and I am fearful that she will never escape from their power again."

"And this was performed, you say, by the lubber who calls himself the Smuggler King?" asked Captain Elphinstone.

"It was," replied William.

"The terror of the seas, as he is called?"

"True."

"I should much like to encounter this same terror of the seas, in his Devil Skipper, as he terms his vessel," remarked the captain.

"Bother! bother, darling," exclaimed the lawyer; "you may meet with him sooner than he may prove his visit to be agreeable."

"You seem to know him."

"I know him to be a very devil," answered Mr. Fitzpatrick; "the same as he has christened his vessel."

"But," returned Mr. Elphinstone; "if he once comes within hail of the 'Thunderer,' I flatter myself that I shall be able to blow him and his vessel to their namesake."

"Say no more about it, honey," said the lawyer; "sure, and hasn't he beat all the force that has bitherto been sent against him?"

"His power certainly appears to be most extensive and extraordinary," said Captain Elphinstone; "at least, he has hitherto been enabled to elude the vigilance of those who have been sent in quest of him."

"Not always, your honour," said William; "for he has had some sharp bouts with the enemy; but, as fortune seems to favour the devil sometimes, he has always managed to defeat them. I am told that he has vessels engaged in smuggling and pirating all over the globe; and such an adept is he in the villany he practises, that he is seldom known until he scrapes acquaintance with his victims, and they do not often want a second correspondence. But let me but once again encounter him, and, may I never go aloft if I ever leave him until I have had his heart's blood, or he mine."

"Bravely spoken, my lad," remarked the captain; "but has no one yet been able to discover who this much dreaded Smuggler King really is? I am told he is here and there, and everywhere. His Protean career is notorious; it is wonderful that none of the wretches who sail with him, have ever been tempted by the large reward which is offered for his detection and apprehension, to reveal his real name."

"He is, in despotic sway over the miscreants of the ocean, in every sense a monarch," returned William; "and his myrmidons dread him as much as they revere him."

"Faith! and it's myself who know the spalpeen well enough," said Mr. Fitzpatrick.

"Ah!" exclaimed Captain Elphinstone, with a look of astonishment, "surely that cannot be a fact?"

"By the Holy Saint Patrick, and all the toads and frogs, barring none, that he scouted, whether it's a fact or not, it's the truth, and the whole truth, and nothing but the truth," exclaimed the lawyer.

"And you have never unmasked the miscreant?" said the captain, with a look of amazement and suspicion; "know you not, sir, that you are running yourself into criminal danger by concealing such a villain from that justice and punishment he so richly deserves?"

"Hold your whisht, now, honey," replied Mr. Fitzpatrick, "and it's not screening the villain I'd be after, at all, at all; faith! and didn't he seek to murder me dead?"

"And you knew him before that?"

"I knew him to be an infernal scoundrel, but not the Smuggler King."

"And you are positive that this Smuggler King, and the fellow you allude to, are one and the same party?"

"To be sure I am."

"Then why not now reveal his real character?" demanded Captain Elphinstone.

"Be quiet, darling," said the Irishman; "all in good time. And sure, and isn't it a fact that, if I was to mention his real name just now, it would retard the ends of justice, and the spalpeen might escape altogether?"

"I do not understand you," said the captain.

"Perhaps not," answered the lawyer.

"Explain yourself."

"I cannot, at the present moment; but leave me alone for dealing out plenty of justice to him; but, were I to let you know more about him at the present time, it might be the means of letting him escape, and retarding justice being done to those, compared with whom he is not worth so much as a counterfeit tenpenny bit."

The captain looked at him attentively for a second or two, and then observed;—

"You are an eccentric man, but still I believe you act from the best of motives."

"Faith, and you may say that, honey," returned the lawyer, "without cracking your jaw in telling a falsehood. Och! and it's my own dear self, Mr. Patrick Fitzpatrick, who will make the spalpeen dance to the tune of the devil's tattoo, but that will be upon nothing at all, at all. Leave me alone for giving them plenty of law. Always an eye to business."

"And this pirate vessel, this Devil Skipper, as it is called, you say, was lying up in port, without her real character being suspected?" inquired Mr. Elphinstone.

"She was, sir," answered William.

"That is strange," remarked the captain.

"It is, your honour."

"Surely some of the authorities must have been to blame, in not keeping a better look out."

"Why, that, sir," returned William, "it is not my place to undertake to say; but at any rate, it looked very suspicious."

"It did, indeed. And on board that vessel you was trepanned?"

"I was, your honour."

"And there met with your sweetheart?"

"Alas! poor girl."

"The rascals!"

"So I say, sir," replied William, the blood mantling with indignation into his cheeks; "and, oh, that I could have but fair play with the captain or the rascal who acts as his lieutenant, I ——"

"What do you say was the name of the latter?" interrupted the captain.

"They called him Sam Raker," answered William.

"Faith!" observed Mr. Fitzpatrick, "and sure enough he didn't belie his name; for the very raking of the bottomless pit he was, and is now, if his old master, the evil one, has not claimed him. That was the same infernal villain who gave me the *sack*, and consigned me as bait for fishes; but it's strange if I do not *hook* him yet."

" This Smuggler King always appears in a hideous black mask, I am informed."

" By Saint Patrick he does," said the lawyer; " but it must be a stout mask, indeed, that would hide his villany."

" Then you have not seen his features ?"-said Captain Elphinstone, addressing William.

" I have not," answered William ; " and very few, besides his own crew, I am told have."

" Och! and it's myself that has, though," said the lawyer.

" You have ?"

" Sure, and I have now."

" Is he a young or an old man ?"

" Young in years, but old in sin."

" I cannot conceive your motives for concealing him."

" It's myself that will unmask him by-and-by, darling," returned the Irishman ; " and, och! won't that be a glorious day ; and the injured shall have their rights, and the guilty shall have their's too, and then it shall be seen whether Mr. Patrick Fitzpatrick is an honest lawyer or not."

" It is to be hoped that the miscreant will, indeed, be detected," observed Captain Elphinstone, " and no longer be suffered to carry on his crimes with impunity."

" Och! and it's himself that will nap it, sure enough," said the lawyer; " and all the rest of his dirty, blood-thirsty, cowardly crew."

" But did you not hear whither the villains intended to carry your sweetheart?" asked the captain of William.

" To the Death Rock, which I am informed is one of his haunts," answered the latter.

" It is a rock on which stands a tower, and which is situated in the midst of the ocean, is it not ?"

" So I have heard."

" A place of great danger."

" True; and there is that superstition attached to it, that no one will venture to approach it," answered William.

" If I am myself permitted, I will not be afraid to approach it," remarked the captain, " and endeavour to hunt the villains from their lair."

" And in that enterprise will I gladly become your companion," said William: " My soul thirsts to meet the miscreant, and to have an opportunity of wreaking my vengeance on his head."

" Bravely spoken, my lad," said the captain; " his day of triumph, I trust, will soon be at an end."

" Faith, yes," remarked Mr. Fitzpatrick, " and that of his punishment will shortly arrive, never fear."

" But," said Mr. Elphinstone, turning to William, " did he not state his reasons for seizing you ?"

" Jealousy and hatred were, no doubt, his principal reasons."

" But think you he had no other?" asked the captain.

" Yes; he taunted me, and called me brother," said William.

" Brother !"

" Yes."

" There is some mystery in this."

" Which my companion states that he is able to unravel," added William ; " but he declines to do so at present."

" All in good time, honey," said the lawyer.

"This is, indeed, strange; I cannot unravel it," remarked the captain.

"Likely enough, for the matter of that," said Mr. Fitzpatrick; "but, by the Holy Saint Patrick, I am doing everything for the best, and all will be explained by-and-by."

"I trust it will," observed the captain; "and that you will prove sincere in your professions."

"Sincere, now, is it you mane?" repeated the lawyer, "faith! and who is it now, that would ever be bold enough, or unjust enough to accuse Mr. Patrick Fitzpatrick of insincerity? By my sowl! and it's my day of triumph that will come by-and-by, any how; and then it's no small praises I expect to get, and two or three hearts that I expect to make joyful."

Captain Elphinstone could not help admiring the blunt and unsophisticated manners of the Irish gentleman; at the same time, he was, like William, lost in amazement at his delaying the revelation which he could, and which he had no doubt he would, make.

"But do you know it to be a fact," he demanded, "that this terrible pirate of the seas is in reality this young man's brother?"

"By my sowl and it's as true as I'm a sinner," answered Mr. Fitzpatrick; "his own brother by the same father, God rest his sowl, but not by the same mother."

"And you know him?" he inquired of William.

"I have told you I do not, sir," replied the latter.

"That adds to the mystery. But do you feel convinced that he is your brother?"

"I have only his bare word for it and the assertions of this gentleman," answered our hero, "which I cannot doubt."

"Well spoken, William," observed Mr. Fitzpatrick; "and it's little cause you have to doubt, at all, at all; more's the pity; although I can scarcely believe myself that the same good father belonged to you both. But all will come out by-and-by, and then it's the satisfaction that we'll all get."

"But do you not remember having a brother?" interrogated the captain.

"Myself and a boy, some years older than myself were saved from a wreck, sir," answered William, "by old Ben Backstay and his son, the former of whom I have ever since called and revered as a father."

"And what became of that boy?"

"He abruptly fled, after having attempted my life."

"Is it possible?"

"It is no less wonderful than true," said the lawyer.

"The young monster!" exclaimed the captain.

"Faith! and that's about the truest word you ever spoke, sir," returned the lawyer.

"And that boy, you believe to have been your brother?"

"To be sure he was," answered Mr. Fitzpatrick; "that is, if we are to believe the mother of the spalpeen; and, for the matter of that, she was not one of the most amiable of ladies; sorrow to the day it was that she became his wife."

"And you have said that they were not by the same mother?" said Mr. Elphinstone.

"I have," answered the lawyer; "but it's all the particulars you may probably be made acquainted with in the due course of time."

"From the questions I have put to you, it may appear as if I am inquisitive," remarked the captain; "but I can assure you that no such feelings prompt me; but the statements you have made have excited my deepest interest."

"The humanity you have shown to us, sir," replied William, "entitles you to our confidence, and I trust that something will shortly occur to urge upon Mr. Fitzpatrick the necessity of no longer withholding from me the secret history of my relations."

" Och! and it's that same you shall have, sure enough," returned Mr. Fitzpatrick, " but all in good time, honey, all in good time. I know what I am about."

" I believe that your intentions are all for the best, sir," remarked William.

" You cannot doubt that they are, my boy," said the lawyer ; " sure, and isn't it myself that loves you, as well as if you were my own son, for the sake of your father, my old esteemed best friend, barring your own merits."

" Still I cannot satisfy my own mind, that this miscreant rover of the seas, —the indirect assassin of my mother,—the destroyer of my peace—the villain who has deprived me of all that was dear to me in life, is my brother," said William ; " nature revolts at the idea."

" It does, indeed, seem improbable," said Captain Elphinstone ; " if I am any judge of countenances, and from the short acquaintance I have had with you, my lad."

" I feel proud of your honour's good opinion," said the young man ; " and trust you will find no reason to alter it."

" Sure and it's myself that am certain his honour will not," remarked the honest Irishman ; " and by the powers, it's myself that will guarantee that same. So, now we understand each other, I must once more take the liberty, my lad, of requesting you no longer to give way to the blue devils, but to wait with patience our arrival in England, when the result of your affairs may be very different to that which you anticipate. This same Smuggler King may be found not to be your brother at all, at all; and, faith! glad enough I shall be if it should turn out so. I confess, as I have before said, that I have often had my doubts upon that subject, for sure and he is no more like that excellent man who was made to believe himself his father, than I am like an angel. Won't I play the very devil with him, sure? And, as for your pretty Flora——"

" Alas !" sighed the young seaman, " I shall, I am afraid, never behold her again, or if I do, she ——"

" There, there, now," interrupted Mr. Fitzpatrick ; " I know what you would say, honey; but let's have no more of that, if you please ; it's time enough to make yourself miserable when you have a cause, or, at least when you are certain that you have good reason to be so."

" Your honest friend here, is perfectly correct," said Captain Elphinstone ; " and although it was a hard thing for the young lass to fall into the power of such a villain, I am not so old a seaman as ever to disregard the sheet anchor of hope, and to place my reliance on the great Commander who watches all our actions, and will ever defend the innocent from the evil machinations, and wicked designs of the guilty."

William bowed to the observations of the humane captain, and felt grateful to that Omnipotence who had placed him and his companion under his protection. But still, in spite of all his efforts, he could not divest his mind of the most dismal forebodings, and he was afraid that his troubles were far from yet being at an end. Could he but have been certain that his beloved Flora was safe, he could yet have been prepared to encounter any fresh dangers with fortitude that might be in store for him ; but, alas ! there was something so improbable in that, when he called to mind the dreadful situation in which he had left her, that he scouted it almost as soon as it was formed. Fearful, however, of offending the captain, he exerted all his energies, and succeeded much better than might have been expected.

" And now, my lad," said Captain Elphinstone; " hasten to the forecastle, where you will find some of the crew, and there you may enjoy yourself over a glass or two of grog. You and I shall soon understand each other, and it strikes me that we shall not part company for some years to come."

"I can but repeat my thanks to your honour for your good opinion," said William, "and it shall be my study to deserve it."

"I believe you, my lad," said the captain ; "you must introduce me to this honest old Ben Backstay, as you call him, for no one honours a veteran tar more than I do."

"My more than father, if he is living, sir," said William, "will, I am certain, feel proud of the honour, more especially to receive that distinction from the preserver of him whom he has ever looked upon, and behaved with as much affection to, as if he were his own son."

"Well, well, avast, avast, young man," said the plain-spoken officer ; "enough of compliments. I also hope that it may yet be my fortune to encounter this terrible sea-monster, this Smuggler King, as he is called, and if I don't pour such a broadside in upon him as will spoil his sovereignty, may I never encounter the enemy again."

"I trust your honour's wishes will be gratified," returned our hero, "and most happy shall I be to have the satisfaction of being your companion in so worthy a cause. The villain has too long carried on his cruel and daring deeds with impunity."

"Faith, and he has," remarked the lawyer ; "but it's my own dear self that will be the man to tackle him. I'll unmask the spalpeen, and it will not be my fault if I do not bring him to justice. Sure, and the day of triumph for Mr. Fitzpatrick, and those he esteems, is not far off."

"Well, I hope it may be as you anticipate," said the captain ; "for a more daring villain, or more heartless scoundrel, never merited the gallows."

"Faith, and your honour may say that," returned Mr. Fitzpatrick, "and no libel on his character neither."

"I hope, my lad," continued Mr. Elphinstone, "also yet to have the honour of being introduced to your fair craft, and to find her in happier circumstances than you anticipate."

William shook his head, at the same time that he replied,—

"I thank you, sir, for your good wishes, but I cannot be so sanguine upon that painful subject. My poor Flora could expect no mercy from the miscreant in whose power she was, and never could she survive the reflection of the cruel fate to which she has doubtless believed me to be consigned."

"Well, well ; it is no use to talk further on that subject at present, although I have little doubt that something very different will occur to what you expect."

William bowed, and the captain having left them, himself and Mr. Fitzpatrick did as he had desired them, and retired to the forecastle, where they found a number of the crew assembled, and were greeted by them with all that generous warm-heartedness which distinguishes at all times the British seaman's character.

The day, which continued fine, passed away without anything occurring worthy of particular notice, the ship continuing to proceed swiftly on her course ; and, as they got farther and farther from the place they had so recently escaped from, the spirits of the lawyer became more and more exhilarated, and he endeavoured to inspire hope in the bosom of his companion. But this was a task of no easy accomplishment, and, although our hero tried all that was in his power to be cheerful and to encourage those sanguine hopes that filled the mind of his friend, there was something perpetually came across his mind to damp his ardent spirits ; and the probable fate of Flora, and all that were dear to him, arose to his imagination in such vivid colours that he found it absolutely impossible to remove the impression.

Notwithstanding he was confident of the sincerity of the friendship which

Mr. Fitzpatrick bore towards him, and that he acted from the best of motives, he could not help feeling vexed and impatient with him, for the manner in which he persisted in declining to make him acquainted with all the particulars of his family, for the present. It was a suspense almost too painful to be endured, and neither could he conceive any reason why the secret should be withheld from him. That the pirate captain, or the Smuggler King, as he was called, was related to him, he could not for a moment bear to entertain a thought; it was revolting and disgusting, and yet had he heard the assertion made by the lips of his murdered mother, the villain himself, and also by Mr. Fitzpatrick; but then might not his father himself have been deceived? Might not the hints and suspicions which the lawyer had uttered be verified, and the miscreant afterwards be proved to be the offspring of shame, that which he had called him? With this hope William endeavoured to reconcile himself; but one thing he was determined upon, and justice he felt demanded it of him, that was, notwithstanding it might after all be proved satisfactorily that he was related to him by the nearest and dearest ties, he would banish all such ideas from his mind with disgust and loathing; and should he ever encounter him, if it cost him his own life, he would wreak his most deadly vengeance upon the monster's head, the miscreant who had been the cause of the assassination of his mother, and probably the destruction of Flora, and all his hopes and happiness. No earthly power should withhold his hand, and there was something within him that assured him the opportunity would yet be afforded him.

Night arrived, and although the moon shone bright and clear, and myriads of stars twinkled in the Heavens, the all but calm that had hitherto prevailed subsided; the wind got up, and quickly blew pretty fresh from the S.W.

It was about the mid-watch, and William and Mr. Fitzpatrick had retired to their hammocks, when they were suddenly aroused by a confused noise

No. 35

above their heads, and presently afterwards the man on the look out shouted at the top of his voice :—

"A ship to larboard!"

"Can you distinguish her clearly?" demanded the officer of the watch.

"Ay, ay, your honour," answered the man. "By the light of the moon I can perceive that she is a suspicious looking craft, and is bearing down heavily upon us, with the wind in her favour."

"Her build?" eagerly inquired the officer.

"I can't exactly say, sir; but she may be a cruiser."

"Her burthen?"

"She may be about four hundred tons."

"Yes, and she may be a free-trader," observed the captain, and hastening upon deck, said, "give me the glass, Mr. Vivian."

The answer returned in the confusion that prevailed on the deck, and the roaring of the wind and waves, neither our hero nor Mr. Fitzpatrick could distinguish; but the former immediately sprang out of his hammock, and prepared to hasten on deck in order to see what was the matter.

"More danger," observed Mr. Fitzpatrick; "och! och! and sure we are never destined to see old England again. What think you has happened, William?"

"I can't say," replied the young man; "you have heard that a vessel is approaching us, but whether friend or foe, of course, I cannot form any idea."

"Och, now, bad luck to it, and sure and this is a great misfortune," observed the lawyer "for should it be a pirate ——"

"Of that we must take the chance."

"But can we not avoid her?"

"From what we have heard, I should say it is not likely we can," answered William. "Hark!"

At that moment the loud report of a gun was heard.

"She has seen us," remarked William, "and that is a signal for us to lay to. I fear she is no fair craft to speak in such a tone of authority."

"But if it is a pirate, surely the brig may be found more than a match for it?"

"It may, but the stranger places pretty good reliance on its own powers, otherwise it would not be so bold upon the point."

"Bad luck to him, whoever he is," said the lawyer; "and it's no very pleasant matter to be called out of a snug sleep in the middle of the night, probably to receive a bellyful of cold steel. Och! and it's a most unfortunate man that you are, Mr. Patrick Fitzpatrick."

"Courage—courage, my dear sir," remonstrated William, "it may turn out better than you imagine."

"And courage is it you're talking about? Sure, and it's not deficient of that same commodity I am; but it's so very vexatious that we should be again disappointed in our hopes, and at the very time when they seemed so certain of being realized."

"This is no time to waste in useless regrets," said William; "hark! the confusion increases; let us hasten on deck, where our assistance may be required, and trust to Providence for a better termination than that we now expect."

"Well, I am ready to attend to you," remarked Fitzpatrick, "and I shall endeavour to do my duty with credit, if my services should be required; but I am sorry that this strange vessel has been so extremely polite as to greet us on this particular occasion. Bad manners to their civility, say I."

"Stay," said William, as a sudden thought seemed to flash upon his mind; "before I leave this place I have something to say to you."

"And what is that, darling?" asked the lawyer.

"It is this," answered William; "should this vessel really prove to be an enemy, we know not what may occur to one or both of us."

"Och! mercy! now do not be after talking like that," said the lawyer.

"Nay," returned William; "it is necessary, for I may not have another opportunity."

"Well, my lad," said his honest companion, "pray, be quick now, and do not keep me any longer in suspense. What request is it that you have to make?"

"Should we come to an engagement," said William, "I may be destined by fate to fall."

"Och! bother—bother!" cried Mr. Fitzpatrick, with much emotion.

"It is not impossible," continued William; "you may be saved and return to England; you may meet with my poor Flora, and my dear friends. Give them my last blessing: kiss my beloved Flora for me, and presenting her with this trinket, tell her ——but—but 1 have no occasion to instruct you further; you know all that I would say, and I know you will not neglect to perform my wishes. There—there," placing the bauble in his hand, and, at the same time, evincing the most powerful agitation.

"My poor boy," answered his companion, with no less emotion than himself, "should the Almighty so will it, I will do all that you desire; but—faith! and I trust it will be many a long day before such a circumstance as that takes place."

A second gun now fired.

"Ah!" said William, "they are upon us; but before we go, Mr. Fitzpatrick, I have another request to make you, most solemnly to make you."

"Be quick, my dear fellow," returned the lawyer; "what is it?"

"My dear friend," answered our hero, "we may both soon be laid under hatches, or it may only be the fate of one of us to be so. The secret you possess concerning me, should you fall, may be lost to me for ever; and, therefore, I beg of you now to inform me what is my real name, and who my parents were, their station in society, and the real name of that villain who is known at present only by the title of the Smuggler King. Justice to me, to all of those whom he has injured, demands this, and I am certain, in a moment of peril like this, you will not refuse me a wish that may be of such importance to me."

The lawyer was about to make a reply, when there was a loud shout on board the vessel, and Mr. Fitzpatrick, whether excited by alarm or astonishment, rushed precipitately from the place, followed by our hero.

They found the decks cleared for action when they reached them, and every man at his post; the captain and other officers were busy issuing their commands, which were as promptly obeyed, and the enemy, having hoisted the red flag, left no doubt as to its real character. Quickly William had seized a cutlass, and was ready to take his part in the conflict; but in the confusion which prevailed he had lost sight of the lawyer, who had also, with more courage and intrepidity than could have been expected from him, armed himself, and mixing with some of the hardy crew, was ready to obey the orders given to them.

And soon the thundering roar of cannon was heard, the Thunderer having refused to strike to the lawless foe, and the dreadful slaughter commenced with equal determination and courage on both sides. William breathed a prayer for Flora, and was quickly afterwards engaged in the bloody strife, the pirates having succeeded in boarding the brig. Again and again they were repulsed with much slaughter on both sides, and again the desperate villains boarded the English vessel, and the situation of the latter became alarming. Still Captain Elphinstone, and the officers and men under his command, lost none of their cool intrepidity, and seemed determined to sell their lives dearly, and to stick by their gallant vessel while she had a timber left to float with.

At this moment the quick eye of William, who had performed wonders, beheld Mr. Fitzpatrick hotly engaged with a tall powerful ruffian, who appeared to be one of the officers of the pirate crew. Notwithstanding the inequality of the contest, the lawyer had succeeded in disarming his adversary, but the latter grappled with him, and raising him in his arms, with as much ease as if he had been an infant, before William could reach them, he had thrown the unfortunate Mr. Fitzpatrick into the deep, at the same instant the pirate received William's weapon in his body, and with an hideous yell the miscreant fell over the side of the vessel, following his victim to a watery grave.

The conflict became more frightful than it had been before ; the pirates, becoming perfectly ferocious when they beheld the fate of their superior, shouted fiercely, " No quarter—no quarter ! Down with the swabs !" At the same moment the wretches on board the lawless vessel hoisted the well known flag of the Smuggler King !

" Ah !" shouted Captain Elphinstone ; " on—on, my lads, you see the enemy you have to contend with, and let us show them that they have British seamen to contend with."

These commands were issued in a great hurry, and the brave crew of the Thunderer acted upon them promptly, and dreadful was the destruction they dealt among their fierce assailants. The dead and the dying strewed the deck in all directions, and the roar of the cannon, the groans of the dying, mingled with the curses of the pirates, formed altogether a scene of surpassing horror.

The pirates were at length daunted, seeing their companions falling so thickly around them, and plunging over the side of the ship, sought their own vessel in the utmost confusion, most of them perishing in the deep.

The Thunderer, which had been lying yard-arm and yard-arm with the enemy, poured a parting broadside in upon her, and scarcely had she cleared from her grapnels, when loud cries were heard on board her. This was followed by a fearful crash, accompanied with a dense column of black smoke, and the pirate-ship was blown into the air, appearing to lift the Thunderer out of the water with the force of the convulsion which the terrific shock occasioned.

There was an awful pause of a second or two among the crew of the Thunderer, and when the smoke had dispersed, the shattered fragments of the ill-fated ship, mingled with the memberless trunks of the crew, were seen tossed about on the white surge of the waves. Captain Elphinstone immediately ordered out the boats in order to rescue any of the stragglers who might still survive ; but not one was saved ; all had perished in that frightful scene of carnage.

The next painful duty they had to perform was to consign the bodies of their unfortunate messmates to the deep, and to attend to those who might still survive their wounds.

Among the missing were William and Mr. Fitzpatrick, and although the fate of the latter was well known, it was not at all doubted but that the unfortunate young seaman had met with a similar one.

In a short time afterwards, the decks having been cleared and cleansed from the awful effects of the late engagement, the Thunderer was again on her course, having sustained but comparatively little damage from the conflict to what might have been expected ; but many were the sorrowful hearts that succeeded to that dreadful and impressive affair.

CHAPTER XIX.

FLORA IN THE TOWER OF THE DEATH ROCK.—HER UNBOUNDED GRIEF.—
COMMISERATION OF MAUD.—STORY OF THE LATTER'S SUFFERINGS.

WE left poor Flora in the most inconsolable grief and distraction at the
tower of the Death Rock, in which state, notwithstanding the remonstrances
and gentle soothings of Maud, she continued for several days; her dreadful
situation, the fate which threatened her, and that which she firmly believed
her lover had met with, were subjects, coupled with the sufferings, too fearful
to admit of any consolation, and alternately she continued raving of her own
destiny and the untimely end of William, in a manner which it was quite
lamentable to hear, praying for death, for what had she now to wish to live
for? Was she not deprived of all that could render life endurable to her
Had she not lost all—everything—with nothing but misery before her.

It wrung the heart of Maud to listen to her, and no one could strive more
than she did to soothe her. It also hurt her much to think that she was constrained to deceive her as regarded the fate of her lover, but, in her present
state of mind, even that deception was a misery to her.

At length the ravings of the damsel ceased, and her grief settled down into
calm despair. One thing that tended to relieve her greatly was the fact that
she was left almost entirely to the society of Maud, the smugglers seldom intruding upon her, though their wild revelry and riotous mirth frequently met
and shocked her ears. Her persecutor also came not, but she looked forward
to his arrival with the utmost dread and horror.

Maud, in order to amuse her, took her over several of the apartments
of the tower, and under any other circumstances, the taste and even magnificence with which they were furnished, would have created her astonishment
and admiration, but, as it was, she gazed at them with listless indifference.

One day, when our heroine had become more calm, Maud, in order to keep
her in the same state of mind, and to divert her thoughts from the painful
subjects that continually engrossed them, gave her the history of herself, which
she had promised her, in the following words:—

THE HISTORY OF MAUD.

"My narrative will present a painful warning to too confiding women, and
convince you that I am not altogether worthy of that prejudice, which, on a
first acquaintance, you naturally imbibed towards me. Alas! mine has been
a life of trouble, brought on, I must admit, in a great measure, by my own
weakness and indiscretion, but which, taken altogether, I trust, is not unworthy of commiseration.

"I lost my parents in early childhood, and my brother, who at that period
had arrived at years of manhood, became my guardian. He had a moderate
competency, and brought me up with as much attention as if I had been his
own child instead of his sister. He never married, and my early days were
passed in every happiness. Alas! the memory of that dear brother is treasured in my heart's inmost core, where it must ever remain while that heart
shall continue to beat.

"I had an aged aunt, who, from her penurious habits, had ever kept herself
apart from her relatives, and lived a life of comparative seclusion.

"It happened that particular business called my brother to London, and
during his absence I was left under the protection of Mrs. Montrose, who
had been a particular friend of my late mother, and was a woman possessing
all the graces of mind that could be attached to the sex. She took the
greatest pains to cultivate my mind, and delighting in her conversation, and

esteeming her character, I readily acquired the excellent precepts she instilled into it.

"At this period I was sixteen, and was considered handsome and accomplished. Alas! that I had not afterwards been too open to flattery, what numerous troubles would it have saved me.

"Months rolled on, and my brother returned not, although we received several letters from him, in which he informed us that a law-suit, in which he had unfortunately become involved, detained him, and it was uncertain what time he should be enabled to return to the country, but he was contented, knowing that I was in safe hands, and hoped that all would be shortly settled to his satisfaction. Six months, however, passed away, and still he came not, and Mrs. Montrose and her husband had just made up their minds to go to London, taking me with them, when the former was suddenly seized with an alarming illness, which baffled all the skill of her medical attendants, and she breathed her last in three days from the time of her first attack. I need not describe to you my grief upon this melancholy occasion, and intelligence was immediately sent to my brother, apprizing him of the calamity.

"It was not long ere we received an answer, in which Mr. Montrose was condoled with on his irreparable loss; but one part of the letter greatly afflicted me; my brother informed me that the litigation he was engaged in had taken an unfavourable turn against him, and it would consequently greatly prolong his absence. He, however, requested that Mr. Montrose would still continue his protection towards me, thinking that I might prove a solace to him in his heavy affliction that had befallen him. Unfortunate confidence! but who could suspect that any one could be so base as to take advantage of it?

"Mr. Montrose expressed himself delighted with the proposal, and I therefore became his constant companion, and, in the innocence of my heart, did all I could to ameliorate his grief. For this he appeared very grateful, and was never happy when I was absent from his society.

"No one could be more amiable in manners than was Mr. Montrose. He was not at that time more than thirty, being two or three years younger than his late wife, and was possessed of every grace of person and accomplishment.

"In a very short time the memory of his wife was banished from his mind and his attachment, his fatal attachment towards me was daily more powerfully evinced. I could not long remain insensible to it, but, innocent of wrong, I knew not that there was any harm in it, and therefore felt honoured instead of alarmed at the distinction which he paid to me. Fatal error! Sadly have I ever since had reason to repent of it. I should have made my brother acquainted with it, and then he would have flown to have aided me with his advice and protection, and snatched me from the base and cruel snare which was laid to entrap me.

"He endeavoured to convince me, and in which he succeeded but too well, that having always lived on the best terms with the friends and relatives of his late wife, decency and the respect he bore them, constrained him from making known, at present, the attachment he bore towards me. He had inspired me with the warmest affection towards him, and which his uniform kindness had almost unconsciously instilled into my mind. Never could I for a moment suspect the honour of his intentions; my heart could not have entertained such a thought, for it was all his own. Upon him I looked as my friend and my protector; my heart was a stranger to deceit, and the purity of its sentiments placed it far above the meanness of suspicion; and from that unfortunate credulity I have to date all my misfortunes, and thus having me in his power, he used that power for the basest of all purposes. Under the most specious mask of deception, he gained my most unbounded love, and then taking advantage of the ascendancy he had gained over my weak soul, that honour which he was bound to protect, was made a sacrifice to his villanous designs and passions."

Maud paused for a moment or two, and gave vent to the bitter grief which the remembrance of the past recalled to her mind. Flora deeply commiserated with her, and, in listening to her painful narrative, for a time lost much of the keenness of her own sorrows.

"When reason returned," at length resumed Maud, "to what horrors, to what bitter anguish was I awakened! I now saw plainly the fatal error into which I had fallen, and I dreaded to meet the reproachful eye of my brother, although I so much needed his protection. Alas! what excuse could I make for the heavy offence? How dare to ask his forgiveness for the disgrace I had brought upon his name. In vain did I remonstrate with the heartless destroyer of my peace; dreading my brother's vengeance, and convinced that he would never pardon the insult offered to his family, my timid bosom tamely consented to conceal its anguish, and patiently endured the miseries of despair, heightened by the deep wounds of neglect and insult.

"I will not seek to describe all that I suffered, for I find that I should fail, were I to attempt the task, to do adequate justice to my feelings on that occasion. My destroyer seemed now to view me with very little regard, and that I had entertained for him began gradually to sink into disgust. I would that I could have escaped from him; but where hide my shame and misery? Alas! the time was shortly to arrive when the fatal disclosure was about to be made, and when my misery, if possible, was to be increased. We received a letter from my brother, in which he informed us that having lost the law-suit, he was nearly a ruined man, and that we might expect his return in a day or two. The terror and grief I felt at again meeting with him were increased by the fatal intelligence of his misfortunes; and now that he most wanted consolation from me, oh! in what a condition was I to give it him.

"Montrose heard of the unexpected return of my brother with comparative indifference, for he was confident I would not make known to him what had taken place until such time as it could no longer be concealed, and, in the meanwhile something might occur to prevent the unpleasant results that might spring from it. I verily believe that the misfortunes of my brother afforded him satisfaction, inasmuch as he would thus be more likely to escape from his wrath, he being rendered comparatively powerless.

"The time mentioned by my brother arrived, and with it he returned to the house of my destroyer. Wretched, pale, and careworn was his face, and his form had become so altered with anxiety, that he looked not like the same individual. I know not how I found courage to meet him; my heart sank within me, and my bosom melted with shame and confusion. But no doubt, at the time he attributed my emotion to the sorrow I felt at his altered appearance, and the troubles that had befallen him, he being nearly a ruined man; and, while he affectionately embraced me, he endeavoured to soothe me, and to convince me that, though our circumstances were so much reduced, we might still be happy, and find sufficient, with economy, to support us in comfort. Oh! my bosom was wrung while he thus spoke; I could with difficulty refrain from throwing myself on his neck, acknowledging my error, and supplicating his forgiveness; but I caught the eye of Montrose, and I trembled, while my bosom at the same time experienced all the feelings of the most unbounded disgust.

"The manner in which Montrose greeted my brother convinces me more than all of the base hypocrite and villain he must be, and I felt surprised at myself for having been so easily deceived by him. He pretended for my brother the most unabated friendship, and the deepest commiseration in his misfortunes, and pretended to endeavour to prevail on him most cordially to remain for some time at his house; but I was well convinced how much he meant to the contrary, and when my brother declined his offer, and expressed a wish to retire to the solitude of his own residence for a few months, and to take me with him, I being now the only solace he had in his afflictions, the satisfaction he felt could not escape my own keen observation.

"I was anxious to escape from the presence of a man whom I could now only look upon with a feeling approaching to abhorrence; but still did I look forward with horror to the time when I must make my brother acquainted with my fault, which I feared would be the means of hastening him to the grave so worn down by care and anxiety as he then was.

"I struggled with my feelings, however, and when the time arrived that we were to quit the house of my seducer, I acted with a fortitude I had never given myself the credit of possessing.

"We arrived at home, that home which was now rendered doubly wretched and melancholy from the change in our circumstances and the reflection on my own errors.

"Shortly after this, we received a letter from Montrose, in which he informed us that business of the most urgent importance had caused his abrupt departure for the continent, and it was quite uncertain when he would again return.

"I well knew the scheme he had in this, and while I could not but feel more satisfied that an encounter should be avoided which might have proved fatal to both or one of them, perhaps that one my brother, I felt the utmost contempt and detestation for the cowardice of the man who could thus inflict an injury, a dreadful, an irreparable injury, and who then had not the moral courage to meet that retribution it so justly merited.

"And now that dreadful time arrived when I could no longer conceal my shame from my brother. He perceived it, and with bitter tears I threw myself on my knees, admitted my crime, and implored his forgiveness. He heard me with a look of horror, and his heart seemed ready to burst from its tenement with shame and anguish.

"I supplicated him to place me in some asylum where I might hide my shame and guilt from the world, and, after he had made a powerful effort to conquer his grief and emotion, he reproached me not; he forgave me, but on the head of my base destroyer he heaped his execrations, and vowed if ever he returned to England again that he would never rest until he had had all the satisfaction that could be obtained for the irreparable injury which had been inflicted upon me. How earnestly did I pray that that opportunity might never be afforded him.

"'But you shall return to me, my poor unfortunate sister,' he said; ' you shall return to me, and I will constantly pray to Heaven for forgiveness for you, and that we may yet again be happy.'

"I threw my arms around his neck, and wept upon his bosom. Long had I marked, with a feeling of horror indescribable, the canker-worm of consumption upon his pallid cheek, and now trembled for that time to approach which should take him from me, and mentally prayed that the same grave, at the same time, might receive us both.

"An asylum was found for me, where my *accouchement* might take place privately, and shortly afterwards I was delivered of a child, which fortunately breathed its last only a few hours after it was born. How I thanked Heaven when the little innocent was taken from me; for, situated as I was, alas! what could I have done with it?—how have shielded it from the snares and vices of the world?

"Having recovered, my brother came to fetch me home, and exhibited towards me all the same kindness that he had ever done; but my brain was racked to distraction, when I beheld the sad havoc that, even during my short absence from home, illness had made in his countenance and his frame. He

was wasted to a complete shadow, and his sallow cheeks, and hollow, sunken eyes plainly showed that his time in this world was but short. What poignant anguish did this cause me! Alas! what would become of me when I had lost his protection, his affectionate soothings!

"My poor brother at length became so bad that he could not leave his chamber, and with what anxious solicitude did I watch over him, and minister to his wants. The dreadful moment at length arrived, and, calling me to his bed side,—

"'My poor Maud,' he said, 'do not give way to violent grief, when the green grave shall wrap my cold remains, it is sinful; and I trust that we shall soon meet together again in another and a better world, where we shall never more be separated. All that I regret in quitting this life is, that I shall leave you, my dear sister, unprotected, and without one friend to console or advise you. But God, I trust, will be your protector, and guard you from those snares by which you have already suffered.'

"He paused—exhausted, and the cold perspiration of death bathed his temples. I pressed his damp hand to my heart, to my lips, and then turned away my head, completely convulsed with grief. Let me hasten over that trying scene, which, whenever I recal it to my memory, renews all the bitterness of my anguish. After a few minutes he resumed,—

"'Maud, there is one thing I would impress upon you with my dying breath—I need not name it—for you must understand me. That man—I cannot mention his name, although I freely pardon him for all the injuries he has done to you and me,—avoid him, cross not his path, and, should you ever again encounter him, oh! shun him, my sister, as you would a poisonous serpent. I—I—ah! that pang—it will soon be over—my eyes grow dim, my dear Maud. I—I—cannot see you—come closer—closer—let me kiss you—bless you—bless you, Maud! Father of Heaven—into thine hands I commit my——'

No. 36

"And, ere the poor soul could finish the sentence, his soul had departed to its native Heaven."

Maud was compelled to pause—she was overpowered by the feelings these afflicting recollections produced in her mind, and the interest and sympathy of Flora increased. At length the former resumed her melancholy narrative.

"With a bursting heart I consigned the remains of my poor brother to their final resting-place, followed only by the two ancient domestics that had formed the whole of our domestic establishment, and a few of the persons who resided in the immediate neighbourhood, and by whom my brother had ever been looked up to with the greatest possible regard; and many were the bitter tears I shed over the spot which contained his silent ashes, and then returned, perfectly inconsolable, to that home which had now become wretched to me.

"Oh, God! how melancholy, lonely, and deserted, was my heart when I entered it, and, completely deaf to all the remonstrances of my kind domestics, I was so overpowered by my emotions, and was compelled to be conveyed to my chamber, which I was totally incapable of leaving for several days. Alas! little did I then imagine the other troubles I was destined to undergo!

"In about a week I was enabled to leave my couch; but, so much reduced in strength was I, that I was scarcely capable of walking. How sad and dreary did everything appear around me, for still was that voice that had ever whispered consolation to me in the hours of my affliction! Alas! he was gone, never more to return, and I was left alone in the world.

"I should have mentioned, that my aunt had some months before quitted the place where she had formerly been residing, and had gone, no one knew whither; and if I had ever been acquainted with the place in which she was dwelling, she was the last individual from whom I could think of asking for friendship or consolation under the heavy afflictions it had been my lot to encounter.

"My thoughts, in spite of me, would often wander to Montrose; but they were now accompanied by disgust and detestation. I remembered the dying injunctions of my poor brother, and was fully determined most strictly to adhere to them, should fortune ever place me again in his way, which I prayed to Heaven it never would."

"And have you never seen the villain since?" inquired Flora.

"You will hear miss," answered Maud, "in the course of my narrative. I now come to another melancholy part of my story. My brother had not been dead more than three months, when I received notice from his late agents in London, that another portion of the lawsuit he had been engaged in, and which had since been pending in one of the courts of law, was decided against the estate, had altered the aspect of my affairs altogether, and that the whole of the little property I now possessed, must, in consequence, pass into other hands.

"This was another severe blow to me, as, in a moment I had become a beggar, and was thrown friendless and penniless on the wide world; but I received the intelligence with more patience and resignation than could possibly have been anticipated. My prospect was dismal enough, but I had been so inured to misfortune that I bore it with most remarkable calmness, and set about considering what was best to be done, as I had only a few days allowed me to quit the premises, when the place would be occupied by strangers, and I knew not a friend in the world to whom I might apply. There was no other chance for me to obtain a living than by going to service, which, humbled as I was, I was willing to do; but how was I to obtain one? and the few trinkets and small sum I had by me in cash would soon be exhausted. Besides, where could I seek a present asylum, where gain a shelter for my weary head? Oh! my poor brother, I reflected, if your sainted spirit is permitted to look down upon me, how will you pity me, and pray to Heaven for relief from the many troubles and difficulties by which I am surrounded. Would that I might be permitted to join you in those blissful realms where trouble never enters.

" The two old domestics I have before mentioned, I thought would have broken their hearts when they heard of the fresh calamity which had befallen me, and to think that they should be compelled to separate from me. In the generosity of their honest old hearts, they offered me nearly every farthing they had been enabled to scrape together after many years, which, of course, I declined; but my heart was too full to speak my gratitude as I could have wished. However, when the day arrived on which I was to quit the home of my parents, and a brother who had devoted his whole soul towards the promotion of my happiness, I yielded to the earnest persuasions of old Deborah, and agreed to accompany her to her brother and sister, who resided a few miles off, and who, she said, she was certain would be glad to receive me, and where I could remain until Providence should supply me with something better, or my tide of fortune might be turned.

" I could never be sufficiently grateful for this offer; for what should I have done without it? But never shall I forget the sorrows of that day; the prayers I uttered,—the tears I shed, as I knelt by my mother's grave, and after half an hour spent in that manner, was with difficulty forced from the spot, and I bade farewell to my home for ever.

" Old Timothy accompanied us to the inn, to carry my bundle; and my parting with the aged man I shall never forget. Had I been his own child he could not have felt more; the big tears chased each other down his furrowed cheeks, and it was not without extreme difficulty I could tear myself from him. We mounted the coach, and were driven off; but the old man stood in the road till it was out of sight, and the last object that met my gaze, was his withered hand motioning to me a last adieu.

" Nothing particular occurred on the journey, and, in a very short time we arrived at the place of our destination, where Deborah's relations received me very kindly, offering me all the accommodation their humble means afforded, and appearing to commiserate with me greatly in my misfortunes.

" The cottage consisted of six rooms, and was much more comfortable than the generality of such places, while the degree of neatness and cleanliness which distinguished everything in the place, showed the industrious habits and taste of Priscilla, the pretty daughter of old Martin and his dame.

" Martin Cressfield and Dame Alice were very intelligent people for their station of life, and were remarkably comfortable and respectable. The former was only a labouring man, but his wife having a small annuity, they were much better off than their neighbours. I was also informed that they had a son at sea, who always assisted them every voyage he returned from sea, and whom they expected home at that time, in the course of a few days.

" Nothing could surpass the attention and kindness with which these good people behaved to me, and had it been under any other circumstances I might have been happy; but what happiness was there for me? and my heart revolted from the thought of being under an obligation to any one, especially to those who could so ill afford it, and which I must be, if I did not obtain anything before my money was exhausted.

" Priscilla was a simple, good-natured girl, who took a pride in being in my society, and who, in her own artless manner, expressed the sincere sorrow she felt for the many troubles it had been my unlucky destiny to undergo.

" But I will not detain you longer, miss, with any particulars that may appear unimportant and tedious, but come at once to other matters.

" After I had been here about a week, Arnold Cressfield returned from sea, and brought with him a well-laden purse, a large portion of the contents of which he liberally distributed to his parents, and also some baubles to his sister. He was rather a good-looking young man, but still there was a certain levity in his manner, and an expression in his eyes that was far from prepossessing.

"I know not how it was, but I could not help an involuntary shudder when I first beheld him, and I was not at all displeased when he proposed to lodge at the neighbouring inn, while he remained at home, as there was not sufficient accommodation in the house of his parents. The expression of familiarity with which he eyed me, was very displeasing to me, and when he heard my name mentioned the start of astonishment he gave, and the curious expression of his countenance altogether did not escape my observation.

"Arnold had only arrived a couple of days, when he said he must be absent from the village for a short time, as he had somewhere particular to go, and at this I was not at all displeased, though the exact reason of my prejudice against him I did not know. He departed, and I felt much more easy after that.

"The young man was gone three days, when he returned and informed his parents that he must be off to sea again on the following Monday, as the vessel would then be ready for sailing.

"His parents were astonished at the abruptness of his departure, and repeated their questions as to the cause, but he evaded them, and seemed not a little confused when they were put to him. As for my own part, I must confess that I was heartily glad at the circumstance, for the more I saw of him, the more did I feel an unaccountable dislike towards him, and I could never look into his countenance without a secret shudder. I know not how it was, but whenever he gazed at me there was a peculiar and certain expression about his eyes which made me shudder, and I invariably averted my countenance, and whenever he spoke to me, it was with the utmost difficulty only that I could return him an answer with any degree of composure.

"Priscilla had frequently asked my opinion of her brother, Arnold, for, as was perfectly natural, she was very fond of him; but I always evaded her questions, and returned such answers, that while they might satisfy her, could not give her the least suspicion of the prejudice I entertained towards him.

"I had almost forgotten to mention, notwithstanding it is very important to my narrative, that, during the time I had been with Martin Cressfield and his wife, I had formed the acquaintance of a Mrs. Normanby, a lady who had been in very good circumstances, but was much reduced; she had still enough, however, to live frugally upon, and to retain one female attendant.

"Mrs. Normanby had been much struck with the virtues of the humble but amiable family with whom I now resided, and frequently visited them, and it was on one of those occasions that I became acquainted with her.

'She was a lady of the most amiable manners and elegant accomplishments, and, on my making her acquainted with my melancholy history, she became deeply interested in me, and offered me not only her friendship, but an asylum at her house, if I would make her so happy as to accept of it. Of course I made her every acknowledgment for her kindness, but I could not make up my mind to become a burthen to one with whom I had become so recently acquainted; I had, therefore, requested a little time to consider of her proposals, to which I was further urged from not wishing to appear ungrateful to my humble friends, by leaving them so abruptly. With this Mrs. Normanby seemed satisfied, and there the matter, for the present, rested.

"The place in which Mrs. Normanby resided, was called Rosemore Cottage, and was situated about half-a-mile from where Martin and his wife dwelt, and frequently did I ramble to it with delight, for, independent of the charms of the society of the amiable hostess, the scenery by which the cottage was surrounded, was the most lovely the imagination could depicture.

" The cottage stood upon the declivity of a hill, a long and lofty chain of which sheltered it from the keen blasts that sometimes howled with fury around, bordered with trees and shrubs, the growth of many centuries. Rising above a canopy of luxuriant foliage, was to be seen an ancient building, known as the old manor, whose lofty turrets cast their long shadows across an extensive lake, that partly overspread the neighbouring valley.

" Nothing, as I have before said, could equal the beauty of this truly prolific spot; wildly romantic indeed it was, and seemed rather the works of enchantment than the earthly habitation of anything mortal. No wonder that I should be charmed with it, or that a lady of the refined and cultivated taste of Mrs. Normanby, should have selected such a spot for her abode. But I am afraid that I am becoming tedious.

" The Monday came, and with it Arnold Cressfield took his departure. At going he bade me farewell with much more respect than he had before shewn in his general conduct, and added that he hoped, if ever we met again, it would be under very different circumstances. I took no particular notice of this at the time, attributing it merely to a friendly feeling, and returned my acknowledgments for his good wishes; but bitterly, as you will find, had I afterwards reason to discover that he had a wicked and sinister meaning in what he said.

" The family, as might be expected, was very dull for a day or two after Arnold had departed, but this gradually wore away, and his absence, as I have before said, afforded me an unaccountable gratification; but still I could not help thinking that something was yet in store for me, which would add to the misery it had already been my lot too late to undergo.

" Having been rather indisposed for a day or two, I had not left the cottage, and in that time Mrs. Normanby had also neglected to call; but one evening Estelle, the female attendant of that lady, made her appearance, with a message from her mistress requesting that I would immediately accompany her to Rosemore Cottage as her lady was too ill to come out, but wanted to speak to me on a matter of importance.

" This message, at the time, rather surprised me, but it was sufficient for me to hear that Mrs. Normanby was ill to induce me immediately to comply with her request and, therefore, hastily putting on my hat and cloak, I left the cottage and accompanied Estelle towards the residence of my friend.

" On our way thither, I questioned the girl most anxiously as to the nature of the illness of her mistress, and I could not help thinking that the answers she returned me were rather confused and singular, but, of course no suspicion of treachery for a moment entering my mind, I attributed her manner to her ignorance, and walked at a quick pace, anxious to see Mrs. Normanby as soon as possible.

" The evening was rather gloomy, so that I could not perceive objects before me very distinctly, and the wind blew very keenly; but, all at once, looking up, I found that we were not proceeding in the same direction that I always took to Rosemore.

" I questioned the girl concerning it, thinking that, owing to the darkness, she had mistaken the way.

" ' Oh, no, miss,' she answered, ' I have not made any mistake; this is the way that I always go, and it is considerably nearer than the other; we shall soon be there now.'

" I was far from being satisfied with this reply, but still, of course, no suspicion that anything wrong was intended could possibly enter my mind. When, however, we had advanced amidst the most gloomy scenery, and which was quite unknown to me, for a considerable distance further, and no signs of Rosemore cottage met my sight, I once more paused and urged upon Estelle the question, whether she had or had not really mistaken the way.

"Before the treacherous girl could return any answer, I was startled by hearing a shrill whistle, and ere I had time to look round a large mantle was suddenly thrown over my head, and drawn so tight that I could scarcely breathe, and I felt myself in the rough grasp of apparently two men who carried me along at a rapid rate, in spite of all my ineffectual struggles to the contrary. I now saw clear enough that it had all been a plot to waylay me, and that Estelle had most cruelly deceived me; but I could not for a moment suspect the amiable Mrs. Normanby.

"My feelings were most horrible at that moment, and I felt certain that I was the victim of some dark and insidious plot, but by whom concocted or executed, I could not form even the most remote conjecture. The mantle was drawn so close over my head, that I could not utter a sound beyond a whisper, and I felt confident that, even if I could, it would have been of no avail, for the villains who had me in their power would have been sure to have taken effectual means to quiet me; and if they did not, it was a great chance if there was any one in that lonely part who would have been willing or had the power to render me any assistance.

"That such cruelty could exist in one of my own sex, I could scarcely believe, but yet the dreadful proof was too certain for me to entertain any doubt.

"I was hurried along at the same rapid rate for some distance, when I felt myself suddenly lifted up into something which appeared a vehicle, and which was immediately driven off as fast as possible.

"When we had proceeded for some distance, the mantle was removed from my head, and you may judge of my astonishment, terror, and indignation, when I found myself seated between Arnold Cressfield and another man, of the most savage and forbidding aspect.

"'Villain!' I exclaimed, choking with resentment, 'for what purpose am I here? What is the meaning of this abominable outrage?'

"'Come, young lady,' replied the ruffian, 'you may as well spare your reproaches and indignation. It is no use with me.'

"'With you,' I repeated; 'who are you?'

"'Arnold Cressfield,' he answered, with a vulgar smile; 'Arnold Cressfield, or Sam Raker, as I am more familiarly called among the crew of the Dragon.'

"'The Dragon?'

"'As daring and gallant a free-trader as ever skimmed the surface of the deep,' he replied.

"'A pirate!' I exclaimed, with a shudder of horror.

"'Ay!' returned he, 'a pirate or smuggler if you will, for I am both. Oh! a merry life is mine; it produces the bright yellow gold, and every one is as free as the element over which he sails.'

"'Monster!' I cried, shrinking from him, with a look of the most indescribable horror; 'and can you thus deceive the best of parents?'

"'Ha! ha! ha!' he laughed, "the old people are happy in being deceived, for were they to know what I really am, it is a chance if they would accept the glittering ore which I every now and then teem into their laps.'

"'And what would you with me?' I demanded, 'oh, tell me, and —'

"'Oh! I want nothing with you,' he interrupted, 'although those sparkling little twinklers of yours might almost tempt a man to mutiny. I would merely take you to an old friend and acquaintance of yours.'

"'Explain yourself, I beseech you,' I cried; 'who is your employer?'

"'My superior,' he answered; 'with that reply you must be satisfied for the present.'

"'Oh! Heavens! what will become of me?' I exclaimed.

"'What will become of you?' repeated the heartless miscreant; 'why, in less than a couple of hours you will find yourself on board the Dragon.'

"I clasped my hands in agony, and gave myself up to despair. Then I implored his mercy, but I might as well have appealed to a block of marble. Finding, therefore, that all was useless, I resigned myself to my untoward destiny, and mentally committed myself to the care of Providence.

"Nothing more, worthy of notice, happened until about an hour afterwards, when the vehicle stopped, and, on alighting from it, I found myself on the sea-coast, with a few dismal-looking huts here and there, which at a subsequent period I learned were inhabited by smugglers.

"To one of these my uncouth conductors led me, and, on entering a wretched room, in which were two robust-looking men, apparently father and son, a squalid, repulsive-looking woman, and several half-naked children, they led me to a seat, and, as I felt convinced it would be fruitless to make any appeal to wretches such as these, I remained silent, and covering my face with my hands, I gave free vent to my feelings of anguish and despair in a copious flood of tears.

"Arnold approached me, and offered me a glass of some kind of beverage to drink, which I, however, declined, for my heart was much too full to seek refreshment, and I remained in the same state of misery and dread until one of the ruffians who had accompanied us, and who had left us when we entered the hut, returned, and informed Arnold that the boat was waiting. The latter immediately arose, and advancing towards me, said that we must be going.

"Trembling, I arose, and, Arnold taking my arm, we departed from the hut, followed by the other men who had attended us on the journey. Having reached a retired part of the beach, I perceived a boat there waiting, into which I was handed, and my companions having steered it round the jutting rock, the pirate vessel, for such I had no doubt it was, met my view.

"How dreadful were my feelings at that moment! I am certain I need not attempt to pourtray them, for you can judge of them sufficiently by what you have yourself experienced. We soon reached the vessel, and I was lifted on board, where I was conveyed half senseless to a cabin.

"I had not been there many minutes, when the door was opened, and the tall figure of a man entered, habited in all the gaudy trappings of a pirate chief, and armed with a couple of pistols in his belt, and a cutlass by his side.

"I trembled at his approach, and fearfully raising my eyes to his countenance, my blood chilled in my veins, as I gasped forth,

"'Montrose.'

"'Ah! my fair Maud,' returned the villain, 'I see that you have not entirely forgotten me. But it is no longer Montrose that stands before you, but Walter, the free-trader.'

"'Sunk so low,' I could not help repeating.

"'Ay, Maud,' he returned; 'the land-swabs fleeced me of every penny, so now I have become prowler upon mankind at large, and I have benefitted much by the change, I can assure you. Welcome, Maud Herbert to the Dragon, and your old lover.'

"'Destroyer of my peace, of all my hopes,' I cried, looking at him with a feeling of the most indescribable disgust; 'what would you with me?'

"'Make you the future bride, in all but the word, of Walter, the free-trader,' he answered.

"Overpowered by my feelings at the time, I sunk senseless at his feet.

"When I recovered, I found myself in the cabin of Montrose, a poor, degraded, wretched, broken-hearted woman.

"For some time after this my senses wandered, but when I recovered, being entirely in the monster's power, I was forced to submit to my

dreadful fate. I will not harrow your feelings, by relating all the sufferings I afterwards underwent; it would shock your ears to be made acquainted with them; suffice it to say that, from that time I was entirely
lost to myself and the world, and hourly prayed that death would release
me from my sufferings. Several times I thought of ending my wretched
existence, but then some secret power arrested my purpose, and I continued to linger and suffer on in the same state of misery as before."

" But could you never find an opportunity to escape from the power
of the miscreants?" inquired Flora.

" Alas! no, miss," answered Maud; " it would be madness for any
person to attempt to escape from any of the vessels who own for their
monarch the Smuggler King?"

Flora wrung her hands in despair, and Maud continued,—

" Besides, could I have regained my liberty, what was to become of
me, friendless, fallen, as I was? No, I was compelled to yield to my hard
destiny, and unceasing was the anguish and horror I was compelled to
endure, at the awful scenes I was often obliged to witness, and the wretches
with whom I was constrained to mingle. All these sufferings do I trace
from that fatal confidence and weakness that made me, in the first instance,
the victim of the villain Montrose; but surely there was some excuse to be
offered for my youth and inexperience, and I have often, in my moments of
wild distraction, been daring enough to arraign the justice of the Supreme
Ruler of all.

" At length, in an engagement with a king's cruiser, my persecutor lost
his life, and I was then removed, with several of the crew, on board the
Devil Skipper, the principal ship of the Smuggler King. Amongst others
who were promoted to this ship, was Arnold Cressfield, or Sam Raker, as
he was then, and is now called, and it was not long after this that he dared
to persecute me with his odious passion, and which, however, I managed
successfully to defy, and the captain, into whose favour I managed to in-
gratiate myself, protected me from his violence."

" And is the present king, as your smuggler chief is called, the same
who at that time held that distinction?' asked Flora.

" He is," answered Maud.

" And yet, after suffering what you have, and the sympathy which you
have expressed, and which I believe you to feel for me, you refuse to
reveal to me his real name?" said our heroine.

" Believe me, I would readily do so, miss," returned Maud, " but it
could not benefit you anything; besides, I am, as I have before told
you, bound by a terrible oath, which I dare not break. Were I to do as
you desire, my own destruction and that of yourself would be sure to
follow."

CHAPTER XX.

THE MEETING OF THE SMUGGLER KING AND FLORA.—THE AVOWAL.—
THE ENTREATY.—THE REFUSAL.—THE DETERMINATION.—THE MOMENT
OF DANGER.—THE ALARM.—THE ATTACK.—THE DESTRUCTION OF THE
TOWER ON THE DEATH ROCK.—THE UNCERTAIN FATE OF FLORA.

THUS had Maud finished her interesting and eventful narrative, to which
Flora had listened with every attention, and for awhile forgotten her own
troubles in the sorrows it recited.

" You have certainly experienced the greatest misfortunes," remarked
the damsel, when she had arrived at the termination of her story, " and
deeply do I pity you; but, alas! are not mine, if possible, even more
dreadful?"

"I admit, miss, that your trials have been severe," returned Maud; but ——"

"Ah!" interrupted our heroine, "I know what you would say; but how can I encourage hope, situated as I am, in the power of this merciless smuggler chief, and from whose power you have before assured me so frequently there is no chance of escaping?"

"But something may occur—some accident to the smugglers, by which you may be released at the very moment when you least expect it," remarked Maud; "and surely Heaven will watch over your safety."

"Oh, it would be a mercy to me were I no more."

"Say not so, my dear young lady; I trust you will yet live to see happier days."

"Alas! what prospect is there for me, since he I loved is no more?—no, no—life would be only a toilsome—an insupportable burthen to me."

"But," said Maud, "as yet you are not certain that your lover is not living."

"You will not undertake to swear positively that *he is not?*" said our heroine, eagerly and emphatically.

Maud remained silent.

"Ah!" cried Flora, "your silence convinces me the savages have murdered him—him who was all to me, to whom I was all! Oh, the blood-thirsty wretches! But a terrible retribution will overtake them; yes, the all-just God will not suffer his avenging arm to remain idle for a crime so monstrous. Who talks to me of life, when my William—my beloved William, is no more,—slaughtered in the bloom of youth?—no, no!—let me join him. For what should I be reserved?—to become the victim of this fiend in human shape?—Oh, never—never!—rather let me suffer the most horrible of deaths which human cruelty can invent, than be submitted to a

No. 37

fate so dreadful, so revolting. Oh, William, William, pray for me at the throne of grace that I may rejoin you, and that speedily."

She sunk into a chair, with a burst of agony that was pitiable to behold. Maud approached her, but she scarcely knew what to say, for she had exhausted all the arguments she was mistress of in endeavouring to tranquillise her, and felt most keenly the awkwardness of the situation she was placed in.

"My dear young lady," she at length said, "let me once more entreat you to be calm. This violent grief is all of no use, and something may yet transpire to better your condition."

"Then it must be in the cold and silent grave," returned the damsel, mournfully.

"Still hope—still hope."

"What mockery it is to talk to me of hope," said Flora; "have you not represented the wretches in whose power I am as the most dreadful that exist? and what hope—what mercy can I, therefore, expect from them?—No, no; it is all a mockery—all a mockery!"

"But something might happen to prevent the captain from coming hither?"

"And think you the villains, on that account, would give me liberty?" asked the damsel.

"They might think it no longer necessary or politic to keep you in their power," observed Maud.

"That idea is absurd," returned our heroine; "would they not be fearful that I should betray them?"

"They would consider that you entertain too much dread of them to do so," answered Maud.

Flora was about to make a reply, when she was interrupted by the abrupt entrance of Sam Raker. She turned ghastly pale at the sight of this villain, and trembled violently in every limb; then she clung to Maud, as if she was fearful that Raker was about to inflict some terrible punishment upon her.

Sam Raker stood gazing at her for a minute or so, in sullen satisfaction.

"What, still weeping, young lady," he said, in his usual disagreeable tones; "this is all useless, and, for my own part, I cannot see what you have to cry so much about in this place, where all is as grand as a palace. Have you not everything you can wish for?"

"Everything but liberty and peace of mind," sighed Flora, turning upon him a look of the utmost horror and disgust.

"As for liberty," said the villain, "it is not very likely you will have it beyond the limits of this tower or the vessel of the Smuggler King, after the trouble we have had to get you in our power; but, as to peace of mind, why, we must leave that to the skill of our captain to restore to you, and I dare say he will be able to accomplish that feat with his usual ability."

"Monster!" cried the damsel; "leave me; the blood of the innocent is upon your hand. Away!"

"How!" cried Raker, looking sternly and suspiciously at Maud—"But," he continued, "I see you have not quite recovered from your raving fits yet; but, as to the commands you have just issued so peremptorily, you must recollect that you are not yet mistress here, although most likely you will be so by and by. Follow me, Maud; I must speak to you in private."

Maud looked at Flora with her usual kindness, and then, attending the villain in silence, left her to her own most painful reflections.

When they had got into another room, Raker closed the door, and after gazing narrowly into the countenance of Maud for a few moments, he said,

" Maud, your patient has not yet got over her raving fits, I perceive."

" And is it likely that she should after the terrible scene which she witnessed on board the vessel ?" demanded Maud, with a look of disgust.

" She did not witness his death," said Raker, hastily.

" But she saw him struggling with you and the others."

" Maud, beware ! Are you certain that you have strictly obeyed my mandates ?"

" If you doubt my word," answered Maud, calmly, " I cannot add anything to what I have asserted."

" You have not given her the slightest hint ?" said Raker.

" I have not."

" Beware that you do not deceive me."

" The villain and deceiver always expect to be deceived."

" You speak boldly, woman."

" You have known my firmness before to-day," answered Maud.

" Psha !" exclaimed Sam, " this is all useless talk."

" Then, why did you broach the subject ?   What want you with me ?"

" Listen to me, Maud.   To-morrow we expect our captain to arrive at the tower."

" Ah !" exclaimed Maud, with emotion.

" You tremble," observed Raker.

" I am not the only one who trembles at the mention of *him !*" returned Maud, with the utmost coolness.

" Ha ! ha !ha !" laughed Sam ; " true, true ; but now mark me, Maud."

" I am listening to you."

" The captain must of course be made acquainted with the fate of the young seaman ;" said Sam Raker.

" Of course he must," returned Maud.

" He will also be sure to make every inquiry about it."

" No doubt of it."

" He may question you," said Raker.

" True."

" Be careful how you answer him."

" I shall speak nothing but the truth," said Maud.

" Be sure you speak *no more* than the truth ; do you mind me ?"

" I hear you."

" And will obey ?"

" Because I must," answered Maud.

" 'Tis well," observed Raker ; " be cautious that you act as you promise, or ——"

" You have no occasion to threaten me. Is that all you sought this interview for ?"

" No."

" What else, then ?"

" You must endeavour to prepare the girl for the meeting. Seek to calm her feelings, and ——"

" That, I think, will require greater skill than mine," rejoined Maud.

" You must exert it to the utmost," observed the ruffian.

" I shall do all I can, for *her* sake," said Maud.

" And for that of our captain, too, I should imagine," added the smuggler.

Maud returned no answer, and, having once more learned from Raker that that was all he required of her, she left the room.

On her way back to the apartment of Flora, she reflected with pain upon what the villain, Sam Raker, had imparted to her, and was at a loss in what manner to divulge it to the damsel.   She knew well the anguish it would cause her, but still she was aware that it must take place, unless something should have happened to the smuggler captain, and, therefore, that the task must devolve upon her some time or other.

When she arrived at the apartment, she was glad to find that our heroine, probably tired out with thinking, had reclined herself upon a sofa, and fallen off to sleep ; therefore, in the interval that should elapse ere she might awake, she would have time to collect her thoughts, and to consider the best manner in which she should impart the disagreeable intelligence to her.

It was more than an hour before Flora awoke, and, looking round, and perceiving Maud near her, the first question she put to her was what Raker had required an interview with her for ?   In the best manner it was possible for her to adopt, Maud informed her.   Flora turned more ghastly pale than she had been before, and sinking back with terror upon the sofa, had not Maud promptly applied a glass of wine to her lips, she must have fainted.

" Oh ! Maud," she frantically cried, " kill me, slay me, in mercy do, rather than let me encounter that dreadful being.   But no matter—no—no —that task will be readily accomplished, for well do I know that the sight of him will be my death blow."

" Dear Flora," said Maud, in her tenderest accents, " pray endeavour to assume fortitude, for at present I am convinced that the captain will not attempt to harm you."

" At present !" gasped Flora, with a look of unutterable anguish.

" Something may occur to save you from his base intentions," added Maud.

" Alas !" cried the distracted damsel, clasping her hands.

" Innocence and beauty such as yours, must—it will arrest his evil designs," remarked her sympathising companion.

" Oh, no !" exclaimed our heroine, " if all that has been reported of him be true, he must be insensible to their power.   Spirit of my murdered William, look down upon me, and watch over me in this approaching dreadful hour of trial."

" That God above, who ever watches over and protects the guiltless, will," solemnly ejaculated Maud.

Flora burst into tears, which Maud was glad to see, and did not attempt to interrupt her, as she knew it would greatly relieve her ; and in that idea she was not mistaken, for in a few minutes our heroine looked up again, and her lovely features were more calm and placid.

" Pray with me, Maud, pray with me," she said impressively, and taking her hand.   " Let us both pray to that Supreme Being you have mentioned, and then I feel assured that I shall be more calm, if not entirely armed with fortitude to encounter every danger that may threaten me."

Gratified at beholding this change, Maud gladly knelt down with her, and they both invoked the mercy and protection of the Almighty for several minutes ; after which they arose, and Flora, with a faint smile, observed,—

" I am happier, much happier and firmer now.   Yes, God is good, and can save his creatures from the wicked designs of the evil, even when the most imminent peril threatens them."

In this confidence, Maud, with all the skill she was mistress of, encouraged her, and, after some further conversation, as the night was wearing apace, they retired to rest.   But, as may be supposed, our heroine slept but little, and when she did, the thoughts that occupied her mind, conjured up the most painful dreams to her troubled imagination.   All the terrors of the following day were presented to her vision, and the Smuggler King appeared to her, if possible, in ten times more horrible characters than those in which he had been generally represented. Then the scenes of her once happy home, now doubtless rendered desolate, were brought to her mind's eye; she saw her weeping wretched parents, her sister, and all that was dear to her; she stretched forth her arms to embrace them, and they receded from her sight, and, in the terror of her feelings, she awoke. Cold drops of perspiration, caused by her dreadful anxiety, stood upon her temples. She looked around her, and could scarcely believe but what those so dear to her were still present, and calling aloud on their names, in frantic accents, the delusion was banished, and she was aroused to all the consciousness of her lonely and dreadful situation.

Again she slept, and then the scene was changed to one of horror. She beheld, in imagination, that awful scene re-enacted, which had taken place on board the Devil Skipper, at the interview between her and her lover. She saw his wild emotion on discovering that she was on board the same lawless vessel as himself, and in the power of the villains from whom he knew she had everything to dread and nothing whatever to hope; she heard repeated his affectionate words, felt the warm pressure of his lips upon her cold pale cheek. She heard his manly words of resentment; saw the fire of his eyes, as they flashed their just indignation on the miscreants. She marked the exultation of Sam Raker and his companions, at her lover's agony and her own; and fancied she still heard the coarse and fierce voice of the former as he commanded them to be torn asunder! She witnessed again the dreadful combat that ensued; she beheld her lover felled to the deck, and the deadly weapons of the smugglers pointed to his breast; she marked his last fond looks, the next moment she beheld him falling on the deck, the red blood gushing from many a yawning wound; human nature could no longer endure the strength of horrible imagination, and shrieking aloud, she awoke.

Rushing from the couch, she sunk on her knees in the middle of the apartment, and, clasping her hands together most vehemently, she cried,—

"Save him—spare him! Monsters! you have shed his heart's blood, and now plunge your deadly weapons into mine. I cannot, will not, live without him! Let me die—in mercy let me die. Oh, God!"

Maud, who slept in the adjoining apartment, was aroused by her cries, and rushing into the room, she caught the poor distracted damsel in her arms. She raised her from her knees, and, in accents of her utmost tenderness, she said,—

"My dear young lady, be calm—be calm; do not thus agitate yourself. It was but a dream—it was but a dream."

"A dream!" repeated our heroine, looking wildly upon her; "true—true—it was but a dream; but, oh! such an hideous one, Maud; a picture, a true, an impressive picture of the horrible reality. Oh! I can never forget it; I saw him fall bleeding from the ghastly wounds the fiends had inflicted; his fast glazing eyes were fixed upon me, and his faint voice articulated and blessed my name, and implored for me mercy. But they were deaf to the poor murdered one's supplications. Deaf! Yes, what pity, what mercy could be expected from demons such as them? And then they tore me from him; they laughed at my sufferings, exulted in the crime they had perpetrated, and—oh! dreadful—horrible!"

She covered her face with her hands, and gave way to the horrors which the reflection excited in her breast.

Maud scarcely knew what answer to return to her, how to expostulate with her. Deeply, most keenly did she feel for the sufferings she was convinced the poor girl must be enduring; but how to ameliorate them? That was a task she knew not how to set about, and she was completely bewildered. She did not immediately reply, and Flora, misconstruing her silence into an acquiescence with the wild and distracting ideas she had formed, thus continued,—

"Ah! you do not speak; your silence convinces me—you cannot deny the truth of what I have all along conjectured and asserted, although, in your kindness of heart, you have sought to pacify me. They have murdered him—murdered the young and the guiltless; the generous youth, who never injured mortal being, but who would willingly have laid down his life in the cause of humanity. Oh! it was a cruel, a bloody deed, and avenging Heaven will surely deeply punish the merciless assassins. William, dear William, when shall we meet again? How long will your own Flora be suffered to remain in this wicked world behind you? Had the wretches slain me also, methinks I could have pardoned them; but no, they kept me behind to let recollection inflict worse than a thousand deaths; they suffered me to live that they might still further gratify their base designs and wishes. And yet, when did either I or my beloved William do aught to injure them or any mortal being?"

She again paused, and appeared to be communing with her own dismal thoughts; and Maud was still too much affected and overcome by the effect of the scene, and the words the poor unfortunate damsel uttered, to interpose.

"But I will weep no longer," resumed Flora; "the sources of my grief are almost dried up, and I will henceforth pray alone to Heaven to take me to him. Mother—father—sister!" she frantically continued, "did I say the sources of my grief were dried up? Oh, no, they are not; I must still weep for you. Alas! what has become of ye? Are ye still living, or has death claimed ye as his victims? Living! oh, no—no—no! The loss of her ye so fondly loved must ere now have broken your hearts, and she alone is left to weep and wail, to mourn in utter hopelessness and despair."

"My dear Flora," at length observed the affectionate Maud, "to give way to this violent grief is all to no purpose. Your imagination has only been tortured by some frightful dream, and, notwithstanding the misery with which you are at present surrounded, and the trouble which appears to threaten you, all may yet be well."

"Well!" repeated our heroine, "and my William in the cold and silent grave—his watery grave. Oh, no; it is mockery all."

"Still the terrible powers of imagination work upon your brain," remarked Maud. "Come—come, strive, my dear miss. Be firm, and bid defiance to the persecution of your enemies. Your lover may yet be in existence, and something seems to whisper me that you will yet behold him again."

"Behold him again!" returned Flora—"yes, in Heaven, but never upon the earth. You would flatter me with false hopes, which are as futile as they are well intended. But I speak falsely; have I not again beheld him? Yes, but a few minutes since I saw him, bleeding and ghastly as he appeared in his last moments. Oh, God! to see him thus!"

"You will yet behold him and your friends once more in happiness," said Maud, who spoke sincerely, for an impression had taken a most powerful hold on her mind that William had really escaped the dreadful fate to which the smugglers had consigned him, though why she should entertain such a thought she could not for the moment form the least conception.

"Oh, forbear!" cried Flora; "if you are really a friend of mine, you will not thus seek to flatter me with false and delusive hopes."

"Indeed, my dear Flora," answered Maud, "I speak only as my feelings prompt me, and not from any wish to lead you astray. On the contrary, I would induce you to resign yourself with fortitude to any painful certainty that may be made apparent to you."

Flora shook her head, and Maud continued,—

"If it should afterwards be made manifest that your much-injured lover is indeed no more, his fate cannot be recalled, and it will be sinful for you to repine against the all-wise decrees of that Supreme Being who does all things for the best, and in his own time alleviates the sufferings and anguish of such of His creatures as He deems fit for awhile to afflict."

Flora looked at her for a moment with more calmness, then passing her fair and delicate hands across her forehead, she burst into tears, and dropped her head on Maud's bosom. The latter was pleased to see this, for she well knew that this ebullition of grief would greatly soothe the anguish of her feelings, and she therefore seized the opportunity to observe,—

"There, my dear girl, you will be better now. Providence ordains everything for the best, and only inflicts temporary troubles upon us to try our fortitude, and to learn us the better to appreciate the many blessings it sends us."

Flora heaved a deep sigh, and replied,—

"You are right, my dear Maud, and I am a poor, weak, foolish girl."

"Remember," added Maud, "not many hours since, we both prayed to the Almighty, and you then said that you felt yourself more tranquil—that you would no longer murmur, but was prepared to meet with resignation and fortitude whatever might befal you."

"I did—I did," sighed our heroine; "but mine is a hard fate."

"It is; but a change in your destiny may shortly take place, and, if you put your trust in Him, rest assured that, sooner or later, it will."

"I will—I will; I will be guided by your advice dear Maud," ejaculated the damsel, affectionately embracing her; "and stifle my feelings as much as possible, hoping that my future prospects may be better than what I now anticipate."

"Well spoken, my good girl," remarked Maud, "and all the humble assistance I can afford you, you are certain you may command."

"I know it—I am convinced of it," said Flora. "You, too, have had severe trials, Maud?"

"I have."

"And therefore are capable of teaching me a lesson of resignation?"

"Who so well as those who have bought dear experience in the school of adversity?" said Maud.

"True," returned her fair companion, "and oh, how weak am I, thus to murmer and complain."

"Do not upbraid yourself, my dear young lady, but endeavour to acquire more strength of mind for the future."

"Oh! Maud," ejaculated the damsel, "amidst all my heavy troubles, how fortunate was I to meet with one like you; and yet, at the same time, most deeply do I regret, that one so well calculated to be an ornament to society, should be placed in such a situation. But I do trust that something will yet occur to remove you from it, as well as myself."

Maud affectionately returned her thanks for the maiden's good wishes.

"Never can I be sufficiently grateful to one who has acted with so much kindness towards me," added Flora.

"Do not mention it, I beseech you," said Maud. "I have done no more than my duty, and most happy am I to think that I have been made the humble means of, in some degree, alleviating your sufferings."

"Alas!" exclaimed our heroine, "what would have become of me, had I been left among such wretches, without one sympathising friend to console or advise me?"

"But had you not better once more seek repose?" asked Maud.

"I do, indeed, still feel weary," replied Flora. "What is the time?"

"It is now past midnight," said Maud, "and a few hours' rest would greatly refresh you, and prepare you for to-morrow."

"Alas!" sighed the damsel, as the Smuggler King, and the much-dreaded meeting she expected to have with him, recurred to her thoughts.

"As I do not feel inclined to go to sleep again," added Maud, "I will select a book, and remain in your chamber, and watch while you sleep."

"No, Maud, I cannot permit that," said Flora. "There is nothing to apprehend, and therefore why should I be so selfish as to wish to deprive you of your regular rest? Retire to your chamber, and I will hasten to my couch, and, with the blessing of Heaven, will seek repose till the morning."

"Be it so, my dear young lady," coincided Maud. "Good night, and may all good angels guard you."

They embraced, and Maud, having seen the damsel once more retire to bed, re-entered her own chamber.

Flora had certainly become more calm after this brief interview with Maud, and, having once more committed herself to the keeping of Heaven, after a few minutes' thinking, she again fell off to sleep.

Not long had slumber closed her eyelids, when busy imagination, never at rest, conjured up the following vision.

The open sea was now revealed to her view. A tempest raged, and the billows were violently agitated, and rolled their white crests to a tremendous height, while dense clouds, like so many funeral palls, hung upon the horizon; but vivid flashes of lightning, ever and anon darting across the surface of the boundless deep, revealed, in ghastly shape and aspect, the horrors that raged around. This tempest, however, was but transitory. Suddenly the wind lulled, the lightning ceased to flash, the clouds dispersed, the waves became calm, and the moon, arising, as it were, out of the very bosom of the ocean, brought every object clearly to her vision. She thought that she was wrapped in a sweet and delicious transport, and could not remove her eyes from the lovely scene, which floated like a scene of fairy land before her.

Suddenly, a distant object met her sight, which was struggling in the waters, and, as well as her eyes would permit her to distinguish, appeared to be a human form. It rapidly approached to the place on which she was standing, which, she imagined in her dream, was a small rock on an island in the middle of the ocean, and, as it came nearer to her, she plainly perceived that her first conjecture had been right, namely, that it was a human form, and she had no doubt but that it was some unfortunate shipwrecked mariner. And now her whole interest was absorbed in the fate of the struggling man, and she imagined that she felt a much deeper interest than if it had been any ordinary individual. Her heart throbbed violently, and the blood seemed to circulate with unusual and feverish rapidity through her veins. She strained her eyes to catch a clearer view of the struggling man, and then she stretched forth her arms, as if she would save him from the fate he was buffeting with. She endeavoured to call, but all her efforts in that respect were fruitless, for the sounds died away in her throat, before she could articulate them.

And now the man disappeared beneath the billows, and she thought he was gone for ever, but a second or two sufficed to undeceive her; again the man appeared, and seemed to be within a very short distance of the place

on which she was standing, and again did she stretch forth her hands, and almost imagined that she could reach him, and that she had strength sufficient to rescue him from his perilous situation; but, when she found she could not, and that the unfortunate seaman was still struggling in the waters between life and death, and evidently nearly exhausted, her despair and anguish were powerful indeed.

Suddenly the man raised his head above the waves, and the full light of the moon shining on his countenance, she recognised the features of her lover. She tried to scream with mingled feelings of delight, astonishment, and horror. He beheld her at the same moment, and seemed to smile encouragement upon her. More violently than ever throbbed her heart, and its every fibre was strained to a pitch of phrenzy. Making a movement towards the brink of the rock on which she stood, Flora imagined in her dream that some invisible power seemed to arrest her purpose, and she remained fixed and immoveable as a statue; but, at the same moment, her lover once more disappeared beneath the billows.

Horror now enchained her every faculty; she gazed wildly and despairingly on the spot where William had sunk, and then clasped her hands in agony. An instant after, a silvery light, which was far more dazzling and brilliant than that of the moon, illumined everything around, and excited in her bosom feelings of astonishment, awe, and delight. Before she could recover herself, she felt herself enfolded in an ardent and warm embrace, and, looking up, beheld herself in the arms of her lover.

"Weep no more, dear Flora," she imagined he said, in his most affectionate accents; "weep no more—I am saved—I am living, and we shall yet be happy!"

She felt his rapturous kisses on her cheeks; she saw his eyes sparkling with life and love; she felt his heart throb responsive to her own, and in he delirium of her transport she awoke.

No. 38

She passed her hands across her eyes, looked eagerly around her chamber, and such was the impression this sweet vision had made upon her, that it was several moments before she could convince herself but that it was reality. But when the truth burst upon her—when she discovered that it was indeed all a delusion, her disappointment and agony were so great that she burst into tears.

These feelings were, however, quickly succeeded by those of joy and hope. She believed that the vision was conjured up to her imagination by the Almighty to ease the torturing pangs that afflicted her distracted mind, and that he still lived, her lover really yet existed, and would yet be restored to her.

Daylight was now just beginning to peep in at the casement of her apartment, and with spirits more exhilarated than they had been since she had been torn from her home, she arose, and hastening to the chamber of Maud, aroused her also.

Maud quickly left her pallet, and gazing earnestly at our heroine, was surprised and pleased to behold the favourable change in the aspect of her countenance, and in her whole demeanour, and she eagerly inquired the cause. Flora, as well as her agitation would permit her, made her acquainted with it, and related, as minutely as possible, all the particulars of her dream, to which the former listened with evident feelings of equal astonishment and pleasure.

" Ah!" she exclaimed, when our heroine had concluded, " we know not the wisdom and goodness of Providence, my dear Flora, to those who put their trust in him. That vision has been presented to your imagination to appease the dreadful anguish which has hitherto tormented your mind, and ought to teach you a blissful lesson of patience and of resignation."

" And it shall, Maud—it shall," eagerly and emphatically answered our heroine. " Oh! I will in future endeavour to be calm and patient, and to entertain the blissful hope that my William lives—that we shall be restored to each other—that the dream I have just detailed to you will be realised."

" It will be realised, my dear young lady," with energy returned her companion; " I feel confident that it will be realised in every respect."

" And yet," remarked Flora, suddenly altering her tone, and looking earnestly at Maud, " and yet you have the power to end my doubts and apprehensions at once, dear Maud, for I am convinced that you must know whether my lover lives or not. Oh, tell me—do not keep me any longer in suspense; tell me all you know, and the blessings, the eternal blessings of Heaven light upon you for it."

Maud was much agitated, and scarcely knew how to reply, or in what manner to evade the questions so pointedly put to her.

" My dear Flora," she at last answered, " you must by this time be convinced of the sincerity of my friendship and sympathy towards you, but do not, I implore you, put to me questions that I cannot answer, and which only torture me."

" You do know, then?" said our heroine, in reproachful accents, " and yet you refuse to ease my doubts and dreadful fears. Oh, cruel—cruel, Maud."

" Call me not cruel, lady," said Maud, " for Heaven knows it is foreign to my nature. I cannot—dare not answer you; my own life would have to pay the penalty if I did; but, if that were all, believe me, I would not for a moment hesitate, but your destruction would be the probable consequence and ——"

" Oh, study not that," hastily interrupted the damsel, " death—anything would be preferable to this intolerable—this cruel state of suspense."

"Do not urge me," said Maud; "I am bound by an oath—a powerful oath."

"And what oath, think you," returned Flora, "what oath, think you, can be binding which is extorted in injustice and cruelty?"

"That may be true, miss, and ——"

"You seek to evade me, Maud," interrupted the damsel, "and, after what has taken place between us, I did not think it of you."

"You judge me too harshly, Flora," said Maud, "indeed you do; it is more out of mercy to you, that I ——"

"Mercy to me!" interrupted our heroine, "what, to keep me in this deplorable state of doubt and uncertainty?"

"I have told you, I believe, that your lover lives," said Maud.

"True," returned Flora, "but that, I am afraid, was a mere subterfuge to try and quiet my apprehensions. Besides, what you have just admitted, that you are bound by an oath, convinces me that you know more than you choose to reveal, and rekindles all my worst fears."

"Oh, say not so, Flora," remarked her companion; "let those sweet hopes, and that firm reliance on the goodness of Providence, which you just now declared to have taken possession of your mind, once more re-animate you. Believe me, I act from the best of motives, and that time will unravel everything."

"Know you whether my William—since you say you believe he lives," eagerly demanded the agitated damsel, "whether he is an inmate of this tower?"

"He is not," answered Maud, after a moment's hesitation.

"And was he on board the vessel when we quitted it?" breathlessly inquired Flora.

Maud remained silent, and appeared much confused.

"You do not answer me," said our heroine, with extreme agitation; "your silence confirms my most dreadful fears; my poor William is no more—is murdered—and what remains to me but misery and death?"

"Oh, forbear, forbear, I implore you, " said her companion, "remember the dream you have just been relating to me, and still encourage the bright sunshine of hope. There is something convinces me that your lover is not dead, and let that satisfy you. The time will come, depend on it, when you will meet again, for God is just, and watches over the worthy of his creatures with a vigilant and a merciful eye."

The gloomy cloud of doubt and apprehension which had for a few minutes shaded the countenance of our heroine vanished, as Maud gave utterance to these observations, and the bright sunshine of hope once more illumined its loveliness.

"Yes," she cried, "I will indeed endeavour to be patient, as I before said, and not to give way to the gloom of despair. The recollection of that sweet vision has rekindled all the hopes I recently entertained in my bosom, and re-inspired me with courage. Could I be convinced that my William has really escaped the power of the savages who sought his life, situated even as I am, methinks I could be comparatively happy. Did I not see him struggling with the waves?—did I not behold him sink and rise again, and when I had given him up entirely for lost, and despair had settled upon my heart, was he not suddenly restored to my arms? Did I not gaze upon his manly and handsome countenance, lighted with joy, and, as he pressed me to his heart, did he not bid me to weep no more, for that he still lived, and we should yet be happy? Oh! yes; I saw—I heard it all as plainly as if I had been in my waking senses, and dream as it was, I will hope that it will be realized, and, in that thought, amid my sufferings, my loneliness, and persecutions, I will luxuriate."

Maud smiled her approval, and confidence being restored to the friends, (for such we must now call them) they embraced, and remained for a short time silent, giving indulgence to the feelings that crowded upon them.

"Well, my dear Flora," at length said Maud, " well can I interpret that dream. You saw your lover tossed about by the billows?"

"I did," eagerly returned Flora.

"Sometimes he sunk beneath them, and seemed as if he would rise no more?"

"True, true."

"And he was ultimately restored in safety to your arms?" demanded Maud.

"I have told you so," answered our heroine.

"What can be more clear?" continued Maud, who, finding that she had now got the damsel in the right vein, was mercifully anxious to encourage her in it. "Thus I read it; your lover will be buffetted by fate through many difficulties and vicissitudes, at times will be nearly sinking beneath them, but possessing patience and fortitude, he will ultimately be able to surmount them, and, at the very moment when despair seems encircling him on every side, he will be restored as from the grave to happiness and his dear and faithful Flora. Is it not so? Does not your own heart assure you that I have interpreted your dream correctly, dear Flora?"

"Maud! Maud!" exclaimed our heroine, while her fine eyes sparkled with more than their usual brilliancy, and her bosom heaved violently; "you will drive me mad with such blissful, such sanguine anticipations. Yes, yes, my heart does indeed tell me that you have read my dream correctly."

"Then," added Maud, "banish all corroding thoughts of care from your mind, and, by exerting a proper energy and courage, set the persecutions of your enemies at defiance, and put your whole trust in a power above them."

"But, alas!" said our heroine, "what can I, a poor defenceless female, do against the determined villany of such a miscreant as this pirate-chief?"

"How often is the most savage and hardened villany abashed and thwarted in its diabolical purpose by resolute innocence?" demanded Maud.

"But am I not entirely at his mercy?" said Flora, "and what will my resistance avail against him? After the trouble he has taken to secure me, and, knowing how completely he has me in his power, it is not likely that he will long desist from enforcing his brutal designs."

"But," answered Maud, "by calling prudence and caution to your aid, you may thwart his plans until relief may arrive, and rescue you from his power."

"That hope," returned the damsel, "I am afraid is fallacious; but, by my soul's eternal welfare, I will suffer death ere I will submit to a connection so odious. Become the bride of a smuggler, a pirate,—never, by Heaven! The bare idea of it freezes the very blood within my veins, and chills my heart with horror."

"Compose yourself, my dear Flora," said Maud; "I admire your fortitude, but let not your energy overcome your prudence, for that would indeed be giving your terrible enemy an advantage. Come, let us partake of our morning's repast, and then endeavour to meet your enemy, when he arrives, with firmness and resolution."

"That terrible meeting," sighed Flora, with a shudder, "how my heart revolts at it!"

"The world believe him hideous in person as in mind," returned her companion; "but few would say so were they to see him in his real character, and that is the reason that he is enabled to mingle in society without suspicion, nay, even to have his society eagerly courted by the gay, the wealthy, and the fashionable. He is young, handsome, and accomplished, and few would imagine that beneath so fair a guise could lurk the heart of a demon.".

" Were he even perfection itself," returned Flora, " I should look upon him with horror and disgust. To my eyes crime would be stamped on every feature, however they might be embellished with all the soft blandishments that are formed to captivate. I should imagine murderer written upon his forehead, though on it sat all that was fine and manly ; and the fire of the demon would flash from his eyes, though they be ever so brilliant and intelligent. The wily allurements of the deceiver and the betrayer would be apparent to my ears in every sentence he uttered, and abhorrence would fill my heart in all that he might say or do, though he might use all the craft that experienced hypocrisy and consummate villany could imagine or concoct. He cannot, he shall not deceive me ; he will stand before me in all his hideous deformity, as the greatest monster that ever preyed upon his fellow creatures."

" You have in your imagination, drawn a just picture of him, Flora," said Maud. " Alas! too well have I reason to recognize it."

" And yet in such a miscreant's power I am," sighed Flora, with a look of unspeakable anguish ; " alas! what hope is there then for me? How can I expect to escape the doom that is awarded to all his unfortunate victims? God of Heaven, protect me, for it is only Thou can avert his dreadful purpose, and sooner than I should meet a fate so horrible, let me cease to exist."

" Be firm, be firm, and put your trust in Him," said Maud ; " maintain your self-possession, and who knows, but even he, monster as he is, may be constrained even to relent, at least, as I have before said, until some fortunate and unforeseen circumstance may interpose to rescue you from his power altogether, and bring him to that punishment which his numerous and abominable crimes so richly deserve."

" Oh! for some means to escape from this dreadful place ere he arrives," ejaculated our heroine.

" I have before told you, my dear Flora," observed Maud, " that such a thought is utterly preposterous, and you must be aware that it is yourself, situated as this rock is, in the midst of the sea, well guarded by his myrmidons, and avoided by every one in dread."

" Alas! I see it is," returned the damsel ; " but is it not known to any of the inhabitants of the island by whom this place is inhabited ?"

" It is not," answered Maud, " and even if it was, he possesses sufficient power in his stronghold to set at defiance all their efforts to rout him or take him."

" And you think it is not suspected by the British authorities ?" interrogated our heroine.

" I do not believe it is," returned the former, " or probably they might make the attempt, though even they, I think, would fail ; and even should they succeed in destroying the place, he possesses such facilities, that he would be certain to make his escape, unless there should be treachery ; but of that he has no cause to entertain any apprehension among his desperate crew. They all obey him as their absolute monarch, and the sovereign of the seas, and look upon him with a feeling of awe, almost amounting to superstition."

" Then, after having thus represented his power," said our heroine, with a look of despair, " what chance is there for me of rescue ?"

Maud could make no reply, and Flora, with a sigh, gave herself up for a few moments to the most gloomy and agonising thought.

"All that you say," she at length observed, "serves to show me more painfully the horrors of my situation, and to banish hope still further from my mind, at the very time when my bosom would gladly receive its most cheering rays."

"Let us talk no more upon this subject, my dear Flora," said Maud; "but prepare yourself for a meeting which evidently must take place."

"Alas! that it should be so," sighed the maiden; "but tell me, has the pirate any more haunts besides this?"

"This is his principal," answered Maud, "and where he stores the most valuable of the booty he obtains; but he has other places in nearly all parts of the world, and is equally unsuspected in all."

"Wonderful!" exclaimed Flora; "it seems scarcely possible that a human being should thus be able to succeed in his cruel and nefarious designs."

"It does indeed, miss," said Maud; "but it is nevertheless true."

"I have heard that, independent of the ill-gotten wealth he has acquired by his lawless traffic, that he is rich."

"He is a gentleman by birth and property," replied Maud.

"What could have induced him to take to such a dreadful course of life?" demanded our heroine.

"I know not, unless it was a natural propensity to prey upon his fellow-creatures, and to glory in working the misery of mankind," answered Maud.

"Were I not too fatally convinced of the fact," remarked the damsel, "I could scarcely believe that such a monster could exist in human nature. But surely a terrible vengeance will some time overtake him."

"No doubt of it, miss," coincided Maud; "for justice, though sometimes tardy, is sure ultimately to descend with terrible force upon the heads of those who offend her laws."

This discourse took place while they were partaking of their morning's repast; but our heroine's heart was too much racked to permit her to partake of anything but sparingly, and, ever and anon, she started when the sound of the waves, as they lashed the rock on which the tower stood, reached her ears, fearing every moment the vessel to arrive which bore the terrible pirate-chief.

When the meal was concluded, Flora and her companion walked to the casement, and, seating themselves on either side of it, looked forth upon the ocean, of which it commanded a boundless view.

The morning was a lovely one, and the sea was glittering in the beams of the sun, while the horizon was beautifully clear, unspeckled by a single cloud. All around was fresh and fair; how our heroine envied the freedom that was displayed to her eyes through her iron-barred casement—that liberty which she might probably never again enjoy. Once more the form of William darted upon her imagination; but he was never absent from her thoughts; and when she reflected that, perhaps, that bright blue ocean flowed over his cold remains, her tears flowed fast, and she mentally prayed that her soul might be quickly permitted to join him.

Then she thought of her home, her parents, her sister, from whom the vast expanse of waters divided her, and her anguish arrived at a height that was almost insupportable. What had become of them? Did they still live? Alas! she could scarcely imagine it was possible that they could survive her loss, beloved as she was by them, and uncertain as was her fate; and, if they had, how lonely and desolate they must be. She pictured to herself her beloved parents, now bent with age and sorrow, their silvery locks blanched by the hand of time; the furrows in their venerable cheeks, rendered still deeper by the ruthless hands of care and anxiety, and the heavy calamity which had fallen upon them. She beheld them, in imagination, tottering to those places that had been her favourite resorts, and weeping bitter tears at the reminiscences they recalled. She heard them in the anguish of their hearts call upon her name, and breathe their plaints to the Most High at the terrible bereavement they had experienced ; and then her heart sickened at the picture her imagination had drawn, snd she endeavoured to find some ray of consolation, one cheering beam to alleviate her sorrows, but in vain ; all was dark, gloomy, and cheerless as the most dreary night.

Maud aroused her from these melancholy ruminations, and endeavoured to divert her thoughts by conversing on different subjects. Our heroine felt grateful to her for the feeling which prompted it ; but, in her present state of mind, it was utterly impossible for her to enter with any degree of spirit into the discourse, and Maud, finding all her endeavours of no avail, at length became silent, and suffered her to relapse into thought, trusting that mature reflection would do more for her than all the arguments she could adduce.

The smuggler's vessel was riding at anchor not far from the rock, and, dark and dismal, it seemed to frown defiance upon all to approach it. Flora shuddered when she thought of the scene that had been enacted on board of that terrible ship, and could almost imagine she saw her lover as he was disarmed and at the mercy of the wretches, with a dozen glittering weapons ready to be plunged into his defenceless body, at the moment when she was torn from him. The recollection was too dreadful, and she endeavoured to banish it from her mind, and to turn her thoughts to some other subject, but in vain ; it would steal upon her, in spite of all her efforts, haunting and harassing her brain to distraction. Now and then her keen eye would discern a dark figure or two pacing the deck, and horror chilled the blood in her veins when she reflected that in them she might behold the assassins of her lover.

But we will leave her and Maud for a short time, and hasten to another scene.

Sam Raker and several of the other smugglers were assembled at an early hour in one of the spacious apartments of the tower, on the morning of which we have been writing, and it was evident from the countenances of all that they were in expectation of some important event. Early as it was, such good friends were they to the choice spirits they managed always to have in abundance at hand, that they were already partaking largely of the intoxicating drink, more particularly Sam Raker, whose libations were frequent and deep, and there was something in the restless expression of his keen and penetrating eyes which showed his mind was far from easy.

" So," said Hemlock, " you expect our captain here to-day, Sam ?"

" Ay," answered Raker, " so I have received secret intelligence ; but I would much rather he would delay his visit for the present."

" Why ?" demanded Grampus.

" Because I am not exactly prepared to meet him," returned Raker.

" Ah !" cried Hemlock ; " do you then fear ——"

" Fear !" interrupted Raker, sternly ; " what mean you by that, Will Hemlock ? You ought to know, from the time we have cruised together, that fear and Sam Raker have long since parted company, if, indeed, they were ever acquainted."

" Avast—avast, Sam," cried Hemlock, " do not mistake me ; I did not mean to insinuate that you are in want of courage, for we all know Sam Raker to be as daring a villain as ever stepped on board a free trader, or stabbed an enemy."

"Ha! ha! ha!" laughed the latter; "well, that is a compliment, any how, and I think I may return it to you, Hemlock, without running much danger of being accused of flattery."

"Thank you for that, Sam," returned the other; "you and I understand each other pretty well, I think."

"It's time we did," remarked Raker; "we have now been acquainted for some years."

"We have."

"But what was it you were about to say when I interrupted you?"

"Why," answered Will Hemlock, "I was merely about to observe, that perhaps you might fear that the captain would not take the death of the young seaman so well as you at first expected."

"No," observed Sam Raker; "on the contrary, I have no doubt that he will be glad to get rid of him."

"Had he reason to fear him, then?" asked Will Hemlock.

"He had," answered Sam; "but that is not business for us to talk about now. I have before told you that the young sailor was left entirely under my charge, to dispose of him as necessity might require."

"You have," said Hemlock.

"And that stern necessity compelled me to the course I adopted."

"Why, as for that matter," remarked Grampus, "the young fellow was aggravated."

"Aggravated! how?" demanded Raker, fixing on the other smuggler a fierce look.

"Why," replied Grampus, "you should not have irritated his feelings by introducing him to his sweetheart, and showing him that she was a prisoner on board our craft, as well as himself."

"You will not dare tell the captain so?" cried Raker, his eyes flashing fury upon Grampus, who, however, stood cool and undaunted, and appeared to view Sam with the utmost contempt and hatred,—"you will not dare ——"

"Dare!" interrupted Grampus, with a look of scorn; "ha! ha! ha! and think you, then, that Sam Raker has all the daring to himself? ha! ha!"

Raker bit his lips, and clapped his hand upon the hilt of his sword, but Grampus at the same time grasped one of his pistols.

Hemlock now interposed.

"Come," he said, "we are not going to get to quarrelling over this affair."

"I suppose I may make my remarks as well as the rest of ye," said Grampus, doggedly; "I speak nothing but the truth, and am not to be intimidated from doing so, for all the Sam Rakers, or rakers of hell, in the world."

Sam looked more stern than before, but he made an effort to keep down his rage, and said,—

"Grampus, you have never borne me any good will."

"Nor do I think that I owe you much for what you have bestowed upon me," returned Grampus.

"Well, this is not the time to quarrel," said Raker; "the time will probably come when we can settle all our little differences."

"Whenever you please," retorted the other, coolly, "you will find Grampus always ready to settle his accounts, and to rub off old scores with all his creditors."

"Enough of this," remarked Hemlock; "no one doubts your courage, Grampus, but we must not have mutiny on board, at the very time when we expect our captain."

Grampus made no audible reply, but he muttered something to himself,

and walked to another part of the room. It was evident that he owed Raker no good will, and the latter eyed him with looks of equal hatred and suspicion, determined at the first opportunity to rid himself of one who might prove dangerous.

"What were you going to say, Raker," inquired Hemlock, "when this bit of a squabble ensued?"

"First of all," said Raker, "let me ask you if the young sailor did not slay our comrades?"

"He did," answered two or three of the smugglers.

"And you know the penalty of that is death?" added Raker.

"It is," assented the others.

"He acted only in self-defence," once more interposed Grampus, coming forward, and meeting the glances of Sam Raker, with looks of stern defiance.

"In self-defence!" repeated Sam Raker; "was he not our prisoner?"

"And was it not cowardly," returned Grampus, "to taunt and irritate one who was powerless, and when his feelings were excited beyond endurance, and he boldly slew those that opposed him, and attempted to tear him from the embraces of his sweetheart, to condemn him to the plank?"

"Cowardly!" cried Raker, knitting his brows, and again biting his lips; "beware what you say, Grampus."

"Oh! I am unused to care much about threats," replied Grampus; "I repeat, it was cowardly, and our captain would say so too, if he were to be made acquainted with all the particulars."

"And yet you took an active part in the proceedings," observed Raker.

"But an unwilling one," returned the other; "though, of course, I must obey orders, I suppose, while our captain thinks proper to give you the power to command."

No. 39

" Well then, as you seem to understand that, you will do well to obey them now ; and those orders are, that you remain silent, and when you do speak, keep your jawing tackle within the compass of civility."

" Bah !" growled Grampus, " for the present, I suppose I must ; but you cannot prevent me from thinking, and I tell you, once for all, that I think it was a d—d unnecessary and harsh proceeding altogether ; he was a brave young fellow, and might have been induced to join us, and we should have found him of much more service than making him food for sharks."

" And think you," demanded Sam Raker, " that we could ever have depended upon him ? he would not have joined us willingly, and at the first opportunity would have betrayed us, and brought us all to destruction."

Grampus muttered something to himself, and then abruptly quitted the room.

" I like not the conduct of that fellow Grampus, of late," observed Raker, when the former had left the apartment ; " he must be closely watched."

" He is rather bold in speech, and takes strange whims at times," answered Hemlock ; " but I do not believe that he means any harm."

" Well, he may not," said Raker ; " but I will keep my eye upon him, and if he gets the weather-gauge of me, he has only one more to deceive, that's all I have to say about it."

" Then you think the captain will be satisfied with the course you have taken ?" said Will Hemlock.

" I have no doubt of it," answered Sam ; " you know he places every confidence in me, and knows that I never act without a cause."

" True."

" Besides, do you think he would ever degrade himself by sanctioning the destruction of any of his crew ?"

" No."

" Well, then, what is there to apprehend ?" demanded Raker.

" Nothing," returned Hemlock ; " but, what is it you apprehend from his early visit ?"

" That the girl will not be prepared to meet him."

" That," answered Hemlock, " she would not be prepared to do at any time, and there are many stouter hearts than usually beat in a woman's breast, who would be in the same situation."

" You are right, Hemlock," said Sam ; " but leave our captain alone for soon conquering her scruples, and quieting her fears, and you know he must expect to find her a little squeamish."

" He must ; but when she is made acquainted with the actual death of her lover, the effect may prove fatal."

" It cannot be much worse than her imagination has already caused," said Sam.

" But think you, you can depend upon Maud ?"

" She knows better than to disobey orders," answered Sam Raker ; " but I must see her presently, and learn how the girl is this morning, and how she received the intelligence of the captain's expected arrival to-day."

" In what manner do you expect the captain to reach here ?" asked Will Hemlock.

" He will travel in his private character as far as B——t," answered Raker, " at which place our little spy craft, the Raven, will be ready, under false colours, to receive him and carry him hither."

" But may not the appearance of two of our vessels here excite some suspicion in the minds of the inhabitants of the adjacent island ?" asked Hemlock.

" Psha !" cried Raker ; " I am surprised at your putting such a question, Hemlock, when you know the fears of the lubbers. They look upon this place with dread and superstition, and would not approach it for the world ; and as for our vessels, were they indeed the devil's ships, as they call them, they could not view them with more terror. The swabs have never ventured to interrupt us, long as we have had possession of the Death Rock Tower. They know better—leave them alone ; they would have to pay dearly for it, if they were."

" But we might not be quite so lucky if any of his Majesty's ships of war were to arrive off this place," said Hemlock.

" No ships but our own ever approach this part, for it is always avoided as a place of great danger; and if they were, we have the means of deceiving them, or of giving them a pretty warm reception. You know that."

" Ay, ay !" observed Hemlock ; " and I do not care how soon our captain does join us again, for we are always becalmed when he is absent from us."

" True."

" But will he appear in his real character to the girl ?" demanded Hemlock.

" That question I am not prepared to answer," returned Raker ; " but, of course, he cannot always remain disguised to one whom he intends to make his wife."

" His *wife!* ha, ha, ha !"

" Yes ; by the rites of the crew of the Smuggler King." said Sam, "and I do not know but they are as binding as those performed by the canting parson."

" Ay, ay, Raker," coincided Hemlock, " you are right; and a handsome bride she will make him,—fit partner for an emperor."

" Yes, the girl is well enough," said Sam ; " but for my own part, I am for mirth as well as beauty ; and long faces, and melancholy yarns constantly ringing in my ears, do not suit my fancy at all. However, I suppose she will answer our captain's purpose for awhile, and when he is tired of her ——"

" I suppose he will send her adrift, you mean to say ?"

" What ! suffer to slip her cable, after having been an inmate of the Devil Skipper and this tower," returned Sam Raker, " and become acquainted with our real characters ; oh, no, leave our captain alone, he is too good a judge for that, she would be certain to betray us. He would adopt other means to quiet her."

" Why," ejaculated Hemlock, and his countenance assumed something of a look of terror, " you do not mean to say that he would have the heart to murder one so young and beautiful ?"

" For the matter of that, Hemlock," replied the other villain, " you know he has the heart for anything, and we ourselves are not over and above particular ; but I do not mean to hint that he would take the girl's life."

" What then ?"

" Why, that he would resign her to one of the crew."

" A very pretty prospect for her," observed Hemlock ; " however, I should certainly not feel the least objection if she should happen to fall to my share."

" I dare say not," said Raker ; " but come, you and some more of the lads had better away to the ship, and see that everything is in readiness against our captain's arrival. He may feel inclined to inspect it."

"Very well," answered Hemlock, "I am ready to attend; I suppose we shall have a rare carousal when he arrives."

"Of course, we must give him a reception worthy of the Smuggler King," answered Sam Raker.

"Ay, ay," said the other smuggler; "there's nothing that suits me better than fighting, plundering, and carousing."

"And I ——"

"Nothing better than ——"

"I know what you would say," interrupted Sam Raker; "well, that is the readiest way of getting rid of your enemies."

"Certainly. I go to the vessel."

"And," added Sam Raker, "as you pass by the door where the girl is confined, look in and tell Maud to attend me immediately."

Hemlock nodded assent, and departed. Sam Raker stood for a few minutes after he was gone, and reflected.

"And yet, after all," he said, "I wish the life of the youth had been spared; I do not know how the captain may take it. No matter—he knows better than to quarrel with me; I know too many of his secrets, and, besides, he cannot afford to lose my services. No, no; and then the young seaman would never have been of any use to us. His mind was too honourable to suffer him to associate willingly with smugglers and pirates; or, if he had done so, he would have escaped from us on the first opportunity, or caused a mutiny on board. No, no; it is best as it is, and so the captain will be inclined to think, I imagine. He had better reason to hate and to dread him, but now he is quieted for ever; all his other enemies are put out of the way, and Flora Clarendon is at his disposal, so there is an end to the matter, and what more can he want? That Grampus, I cannot help thinking of his boldness and the observations he made to me. I know he envies me the confidence which our captain reposes in me, and the authority I possess in the ship; but though the snake may hiss, he dare not attempt to sting. I will watch narrowly the lubber, and the first cause I see to excite my suspicion, shall sign his death-warrant."

He was interrupted in this amiable soliloquy by the entrance of Maud, who had left our heroine more composed than she had been for some time.

"You sent for me," she said, with a look of hatred and disgust which she could never repress when in the villain's presence.

"I did, Maud," answered Sam Raker, in tones less harsh and repulsive than he was accustomed to make use of.

"And what would you now with me?" she again demanded.

"How is the girl this morning?" inquired Raker.

"How can you expect her to be in her present wretched situation?" asked Maud.

"Psha!" cried the smuggler, "I want none of that nonsense. Answer my question plainly and at once; are her spirits any better?"

"That you have the power of judging of yourself."

Sam Raker contracted his large shaggy eyebrows.

"I have often told you that you may repent the boldness and freedom of your language to me," he said.

"And," returned Maud, with a look of the utmost contempt, "I have as often told you that I set your threats at defiance."

"Have you made the girl acquainted with the expected arrival of the captain here to-day?" hastily demanded Sam Raker, taking no notice of the former observations of Maud, after he had walked two or three times across the apartment.

"I have," answered Maud.

" And how did she receive the information?" inquired Sam.

" Not with a smile of joy, you may be sure," answered Maud, in a tone of bitter irony.

" Bah!" exclaimed Raker, " you had better not presume too far on my patience, in thus mocking me."

" You waste your time in thinking to alarm me, *Arnold Cressfield*," returned Maud.

" Ah !" cried Raker ; " mention not that name again."

" I will not," answered Maud. " It belonged to those who were honest, good, and virtuous ; you deserve it not."

" What mockery is this, Maud ?" said Sam. " Why talk to me thus, at such a time ?"

" Because it suits my temper," replied Maud, " and I like to torture you."

" D——n !" exclaimed the villain, passionately ; " but I will be calm with you. How is Flora Clarendon prepared to meet our captain ?"

" As innocence and virtue should," returned Maud, " with firmness and resolution. That sort of resolution which at any time is more than a match for all the villany in the world ; that virtue which can sink the greatest monster into insignificance."

" Ha ! ha ! ha !" laughed San Raker. " A very pretty sermon, to be sure ; but I think she will find her innocence, and virtue, and resolution, and all that sort of thing, of very little use against the power of the Smuggler King."

" That is to be seen," observed Maud.

" It is useless her attempting to oppose him," said Sam Raker. " She must be his. There is no power can save her."

" There is," returned Maud, firmly.

" And what power is that, pray ?" demanded Sam Raker.

" That Power above, who ——"

" Bah !" interrupted Sam Raker. " Begone, mad woman ; but let me advise you to act with more circumspection in the presence of our captain, or, he may chance to take it in his head not to deal so patiently with you as I have done."

Maud made no reply, but fixing on the villain a look of the utmost scorn and detestation, she quitted the room, and hastened to rejoin our heroine.

During the absence of Maud, Flora had been endeavouring to abstract her thoughts from her own miseries in the perusal of a book ; but the task, of course, proved an ineffectual one ; nothing could drown the remembrance of what she had undergone, the situation she was placed in, and what she had, in all probability, yet to endure. Her eyes fell listlessly on the pages of the volume, and she was unable to distinguish a letter. At length, tired with the useless effort, she threw her book aside, and then once more cast her eyes across the boundless deep beneath her.

She could perceive that there was much bustle and confusion on board the smuggler's ship, and her heart misgave her, and she made sure that the anticipations of Sam Raker would be realised, and that the much dreaded smuggler or pirate-chief would arrive at the tower that day, and that his crew were preparing accordingly for his reception.

Notwithstanding all the endeavours she had made to the contrary, as the time passed rapidly away, and every moment seemed to bring her nearer to that interview she so much dreaded, her heart sunk, and it was with the greatest difficulty only she could support herself.

She awaited the return of Maud with some anxiety, and it was not long she was kept in suspense. Maud made her appearance, and, to the eager inquiries of Flora, made her acquainted with the conversation which had passed between her and Sam Raker at the interview. Flora listened to it with indifference, for there was nothing at all new in it, to excite her, and she then directed her whole discourse to the subject of the Smuggler King's expected arrival, for which event Maud still tried her utmost to fortify her, and so far succeeded as to bring her to something like composure.

While they were yet seated at the casement, they beheld Sam Raker and two or three other of the smugglers descend the rock, and put off in a boat towards the vessel, and this circumstance the more convinced them that the pirate-chief, unless anything should have happened to him, would arrive that day. Indeed, Maud expressed her astonishment to our heroine that he should so long have delayed coming, while Flora was unable to form any conjecture of the reason he had not come in the same vessel. But Maud did not dare to satisfy her on that point, although she wished to do so, and therefore she evaded her questions as much as possible.

Hour after hour wore away in this manner; afternoon arrived, and still the smuggler came not. The hopes of our heroine revived, but Maud thought it prudent not to encourage them, as she felt convinced he would not fail, and then all the trouble she had had to prepare her for the interview would have been lost, and her anguish might be more excessive from disappointment.

There were moments, however, when even she could not help encouraging a hope that something had occurred to detain him; but they were only transient, and she forebore to entertain such thoughts for the future.

They continued seated at the casement until the afternoon waned apace, and, engaged in conversation, the time seemed to wear away more rapidly. The sun was just sinking into the bosom of the ocean, when they were suddenly both startled by hearing the report of a gun, which was immediately succeeded by a loud shout of joy, which echoed across the deep, and evidently came from the smugglers' vessel, for it was immediately answered by a louder one still from the wretches in the tower; and then a great confusion followed, the rattling of feet, the hasty banging of heavy doors, and shortly afterwards several of the smugglers were seen running down the craggy sides of the rock on which the tower stood, and appeared to be hastening to that part from whence they could obtain a view of the approaching object which caused their excitement.

Flora turned ghastly pale, and, trembling, she clung to Maud, and looked up piteously in her face. The latter also evinced considerable agitation, which plainly showed that she considered the fears and conjectures of our heroine to be correct.

"Be firm, my dear girl," she said; "be firm, and place your reliance on Him who never deserts the innocent. Depending on Him, you may safely bid defiance to the most powerful earthly enemies."

"He is come," cried Flora; "the monster, the murderer has come to claim his unhappy victim, and I am lost! Oh, God! what will become of me?"

"Believe me, you will yet be saved from his diabolical designs," said Maud. "It would be folly in me to attempt to deceive you, for that gun, and the excitement among the crew, convince me that the smuggler-captain has arrived. Come, come—be calm and firm, as you promised me you would, and fear not but you will yet be triumphant, and the nefarious designs of the heartless miscreant will be frustrated."

Our heroine made an effort to conquer her emotions, but it was a most arduous task, and her heart again failed her.

"I will endeavour to do as you advise, dear Maud," she said; "but——"

She was interrupted by another report of a gun, which sounded near the tower. A second shout from the ship returned the salute; another gun was fired, and our heroine and Maud, straining their eyes, beheld a vessel rapidly approaching the Devil's Skipper.

"Ah! a ship!" cried Flora; "then, indeed, are my worst fears realised."

"It certainly is one of the smuggler's vessels," said Maud, "and no doubt contains the captain. But do not tremble so, my dear Flora; you cannot avoid the meeting, and there is one consolation to you, that the pirate-chief is not immediately coming to the tower. It will give you some time to collect your thoughts, and to prepare yourself to meet him."

"Oh! Maud!" cried our heroine, turning from the window with a sickening feeling, and throwing herself into her companion's arms, "pity me! pity me!"

"Pity you, miss," replied Maud; "you know how sincerely I do indeed pity you; and, would to Heaven, I could save you from the severe trials you will have to undergo; but you know it is impossible, and much depends, indeed everything, I may say, depends upon your own firmness."

"Alas!" sighed the damsel, "what maiden could acquire fortitude placed in my situation?"

"But you must struggle, my dear girl," returned Maud. "If you give way to this weakness, you will be entirely lost."

"I am lost—lost, already!"

"Say not so, Flora. Providence may raise you up friends when you least expect them," observed Maud. "Shew the villain the strength of female virtue, and a firm reliance on that power which he despises, and he, daring as he is, will be abashed, and will fear to use violence to effect his diabolical wishes."

Our heroine shook her head, and after a fruitless attempt to stifle her emotions, she threw herself in the arms of Maud, and giving herself up entirely to her feelings, wept bitterly.

Maud did not attempt to interrupt her for a few minutes, and then she exerted all her skill to soothe her, in which, at length, she partially succeeded.

In the meantime Sam Raker, as has been described, had gone with several of the other smugglers on board the Devil's Skipper, to see that everything was prepared for the reception of their captain, whither it was expected he would repair, previous to going to the tower. They had waited with the utmost impatience, (for the wretches paid as much homage and veneration to Sir Julian, as if he had really been a monarch), but, when hour after hour vanished, and still he came not, they became all in a state of the greatest excitement and anxiety, and various were the conjectures that were formed as to the cause of his delay. Sometimes they were afraid that some accident had befallen him, and that he had fallen into the hands of his enemies, for the weather was favourable, and if he set sail at the time he had apprised Sam Raker, he would have been able to have made the Death Rock in the course of a few days.

At length, all their suspense and apprehensions were banished by hearing the report of a gun, and immediately after a swift sailing vessel shot round the angle of the rock, which they immediately recognised as the Raven, one of their own ships, and which they had no doubt contained their captain.

In a moment a number of the smugglers manned the yards of the Devil Skipper, while others flocked on the deck, and their deafening shouts rent the air.

Again a signal was fired from the Raven, which was answered by another from the Devil Skipper, and succeeded by a second loud shout, as we have before described.

Swift as an arrow the Raven came alongside the other vessel, and amid the heartless and lawless miscreants whom he called his subjects, the Smuggler King stepped on board the Devil Skipper, the far-famed terror of the bright blue waters.

Sam Raker, attended by all the principal of the smugglers, were waiting on the deck, and received him with all due homage.

Sir Julian shook his creature cordially by the hand, and the deafening shouts were repeated. But no person who had been ever so intimate with the worthless baronet could have now recognised him, so completely had he metamorphosed himself.

He was attired in an elegant officer's uniform, which set well upon his graceful and commanding figure. He wore false whiskers of a jet black hue, moustachios and wig of the same, the latter of which descended in long and graceful ringlets over his shoulders, and gave an additional interest to his appearance; a velvet cap, with a gold band, and an immense diamond, set round with brilliants, in the centre; a rich belt, studded with jewels, encircled his waist, from which depended a beautiful sword, with a costly and curiously worked handle.

The hearty greeting of the smugglers having subsided, Sir Julian was escorted to the principal cabin, and then turning to Sam Raker, he said,—

"Well, Raker, lad, I am glad to meet you again. You see I have arrived safe, notwithstanding the suspicions of the land-lubbers."

"And did the swabs then suspect you?" asked Raker.

"Not of being the desperate character I am," answered Sir Julian; "but the parents of Flora Clarendon and old Ben Backstay had the impudence to suppose that I knew something of their disappearance, and pestered me most confoundedly; so, as I began to fear that it might become rather too hot to hold me, I managed to get a customer for my ship, that is, my mansion; weighed anchor one fine morning, when the lubbers were all in their hammocks, spread every sail, and here I am."

"Ha! ha! ha!" laughed Sam Raker. "And glad enough we all are to see you again."

"But where is the girl?" demanded the captain.

"Safe in the tower, captain," answered Sam Raker.

"And William?"

"Made a meal of by some shark ere now, captain," replied Raker.

"Ah!" exclaimed Sir Julian, in astonishment, "how,—no more?"

"True," returned Sam; "he will trouble you no more."

The baronet could not help evincing much surprise and agitation at this unexpected statement; and he commanded Sam immediately to make him acquainted with all the particulars that had led to the necessity of this event, which Raker related in his own way, taking good care to omit all those facts that were likely to redound to his discredit in the opinion of Sir Julian, and applying to his own invention to make the conduct of William appear such as fully to authorise all that had taken place.

Sir Julian listened to him with the greatest attention, and when Sam Raker had concluded, he paused a few minutes, during which time several conflicting emotions and reflections passed in his mind.

"He was a brave youth," at length he said, "and deserved a better fate; but I have no doubt you acted for the best."

"You may depend upon that, captain," said Raker, well pleased to find that Sir Julian was so easily persuaded. "Besides, he slew our comrades, and deserved his fate."

"True," observed the baronet; "besides, he might afterwards by some accident, or other, have become troublesome to me."

"He might," remarked Sam Raker, "and you cannot forget that he was the favoured lover of Flora Clarendon."

"Ah!" exclaimed Sir Julian, "for that I hated him more than all, and all that I regret in his death is, that he was not left for me to exercise my torments upon him; the torment of disappointed hopes; and the horror of seeing me lead to the altar that fair damsel on whom all his affections were placed. But we will talk no more about him. Does the damsel know his fate."

"She does not," answered Sam; "but she strongly suspects that he is no more."

"And has suffered from grief and distraction?" asked Sir Julian.

"Why," returned the smuggler, "of course such ideas were likely to grieve her a bit; but, no doubt, with your usual ability, you will soon be able to banish her sorrow."

"No doubt of it," said the captain, "she is a lovely creature, Sam."

"A fine craft, indeed, captain."

"Well worthy of becoming the Smuggler King's bride," added Sir Julian.

"True," answered Sam, "and with her on board, the Devil Skipper will be more successful than ever."

"No doubt of it," answered the baronet; "but I do not wish her to recognise me as Sir Julian Mordlington; think you this disguise will conceal me?"

"I am certain of it," said Sam; "I should not have known you myself, had I not been apprised of your coming hither. But will you to the tower, captain?"

"I will," answered the baronet; "I long once more to behold her who has cost me so much trouble to obtain; to clasp her to my heart, and steal warm and luxurious kisses from those lips that breathe alone of nectar. This evening shall be devoted to mirth in the grand saloon of the tower, at which, if possible my future queen shall preside. Come, order the boat to be got ready, we will immediately to the tower of the Death Rock."

This order was promptly obeyed, and, in a few minutes, Sir Julian, Sam

No. 40

Raker, and a few of the other smugglers were making their way to the gloomy edifice in which our unfortunate heroine was confined.

Flora had, as we have previously stated, become somewhat more composed, and was once more seated with Maud at the casement, engaged in conversation, on the untoward fortunes that had attended her, when suddenly casting her eyes across the scene she uttered a loud scream, and immediately fainted in the arms of Maud.

The latter was not long in discovering the cause of this emotion, when she beheld the approaching boat, and, having supported the inanimate form of the poor girl to the couch, she applied such restoratives as she happened to have handy, and, in a very short time our heroine opened her eyes, and looking wildly around her, she cried :—

"Do not let him approach! the fiend! the monster! keep him off! He shall not, dare not come near me; I have more strength than he imagines, and will exert it to oppose the villain! Off! off!"

"My dear Flora," said Maud, "there is no one here but me; do not be alarmed, but try and meet with energy that which is now unavoidable."

"Energy!" repeated the damsel, "the word is mockery; is he not there? Did I not see the boat approach the rock, which doubtlessly contained him? Can you deny that?"

"I will not attempt it, my dear girl," answered Maud; "your enemy has arrived, and is at present in this tower; probably, however, he may not seek your presence this evening, and if he should I will plead that you are ill, as an excuse, and by the morning you may be able to recruit your strength; and meet him with that fortitude I have advised."

"Oh! I can never, never, accomplish that painful task," said our heroine; "I shall sink with terror in the miscreant's presence, and death ——"

She was interrupted by a loud knock at the room door, and more terrified than before, and apprehending the worst, she clung to Maud, and trembled violently in every limb. Maud did not answer the knock, and after a short time it was repeated more violently than before, and Flora's fears increased, and she looked aghast towards the door, as if she expected some frightful spectre to enter. Maud, by a look of encouragement, endeavoured to soothe her, and to inspire her with fortitude, and then gently releasing herself from her hold, she walked to the door, opened it, and Sam Raker entered.

At the sight of this remorseless villain, the blood chilled in Flora's veins, and had she at that moment been about to be led out to assassination, she could not have felt more real terror than that which she at that moment experienced.

The ruffian looked round the apartment, and, as his eye rested on the unfortunate damsel, a frightful sardonic grin overspread his features, and he seemed to triumph and exult in the misery which he witnessed. Turning to Maud, he then observed,—

"I suppose you know what I've come for?"

"Oh! save me! spare me!" exclaimed the wretched and distracted damsel. "Death is preferable to me; let me suffer anything, but oh! do not let me encounter that dreadful being!"

Maud fixed upon her an expressive look of caution; and Sam Raker fixed a ferocious glance upon the former, while he observed,—

"The captain requests the presence of the lady in the grand saloon of the tower, where everything is prepared to receive her. You can attend her, if you please, and Miss Flora will find that the Smuggler King has the means, and knows how to receive his destined bride."

"Oh! God protect me!" ejaculated our heroine.

The ruffian smiled contemptuously.

"Are you ready?" he demanded, "for the captain will be impatient at this delay. I will escort you thither."

"Raker," replied Maud, as she noticed the ashy paleness of Flora's countenance, and marked the trembling of her frame, "you surely are not yet deprived of all sense of humanity and feeling, however rough your exterior may be?"

"Humph!" muttered the villain, with a satirical look. "You have only, I suppose, just discovered that. You have strangely altered your tone within this hour or two. But what would you? Be quick, for I have no time to stand parleying here, and I do not see that it is likely to prove a very profitable business. I always like to gain something by my *condescension*. Ha! ha! ha!"

With what feelings of disgust did the maiden view the smuggler; but she awaited with impatience and anxiety the reply of Maud, and also the result, which was at length given in the following words,—

"Raker, you perceive that the young lady is not in a fit state to see the captain this evening, but by the morning ——"

"What!" interrupted Raker, "disobey the orders of my commander! that will never do. They were peremptory, and she must attend."

"Oh! for Heaven's sake!" cried our heroine, clasping her fair hands together, and looking so piteously in his countenance, that it was sufficient to melt even the most stubborn heart, "spare me to-night; and in the morning, I—I ——"

"Do not be cruel," further urged Maud; "do not be quite insensible to the appeal of oppressed innocence; tell the captain that she is ill—any-thing, and that she will attend him in the morning, but that ——"

"Well, well," said Sam Raker, who was really moved, "I will see what I can do; and—but no matter—there, there; mind you keep in the same story in the morning, and it will be all right."

"Oh! thanks, thanks," cried the grateful Flora, who felt as if a heavy weight was removed from her heart, but before she had finished, Sam Raker had quitted the apartment. Flora then flew to the arms of Maud, and although she was yet uncertain whether the captain would yield to her request, she felt so much relieved, that she wept tears of joy upon her bosom. Maud embraced her tenderly, and remarked,—

"My dear Flora, did I not tell you, that if you put your trust in the Almighty, something would be certain to occur, to relieve you; and short as this respite is, I am confident, that if you still exert your energies, you will yet be able to surmount all the difficulties that at present beset you, and to render the diabolical designs of the captain abortive."

"Heaven send that your predictions may be verified," returned our heroine; "but, alas! of that I entertain but very little hope; and even now Raker may not succeed in the request he has promised to make to the captain."

"I have no doubt that he will, though," replied Maud; "for the captain, desperate as his character is in other respects, is too gallant to refuse such a request from a female. It is a great pity that he should have taken to such a course of life, for in manners and mind he is most accomplished, and his person is commanding and handsome."

"Alas! that nature should place so base a heart, in such a fair form," said Flora; "but still do I tremble to meet him; his deeds of darkness have stamped him villain and monster, and all his personal attractions and accomplishments sink into insignificance before his real character."

"Let us hope, my dear miss," said Maud, "that in your case he may, at any rate, prove that he is not so bad as he has been represented."

Our heroine was about to return an answer, when she was prevented by hearing another knock at the door. Her heart palpitated, her breast heaved with violent agitation, and she was compelled to lean on Maud for support. The latter opened the door, and Sam Raker once more made his appearance.

" The captain will excuse the lady to-night," he observed ; " but he bade me inform her, that to-morrow, he shall expect an interview with her in the saloon, when he may require it."

" Oh ! thanks, thanks !" ejaculated Flora ; and her sparkling and lovely eyes beamed with gratitude upon the ruffian.

" You see," said Sam Raker, " I can do a good turn now and then, although I am such an infernal scoundrel. Ha ! ha ! ha ! you should only have heard me plead. Why, I'm one of the best advocates in the world. ha ! ha ! ha !"

Thus saying, the smuggler quitted the room, and left Flora and her companion to their own reflections.

It has before been shewn that Sir Julian Mordlington was a man of the most consummate and luxurious taste ; and he had therefore caused the principal apartments of the tower to be fitted up in that style of elegance which has been described, and which rendered them fit for the reception of a nobleman,—black and unprepossessing as the exterior of the edifice appeared. Frequently had he conveyed the unfortunate victim of his base passions thither, and therefore had he fitted up some of the apartments especially, with every degree of elegance,—all that might captivate and lead the senses astray was to be found there. Rich hangings, silken ottomans, lofty mirrors, magnificent carpets, splendid chandeliers, chaste vases, filled with every scarce exotic that could be met with in Nature's most beautiful works. There was also a collection, in one apartment, of the most valuable paintings ; and another contained a library of classic books, selected from the best authors.

The saloon which has been alluded to was a most spacious and brilliantly ornamented apartment,—one that might have vied with that of a monarch. Though all the other rooms we have mentioned were decorated with well-furnished elegance, they were inferior in point of magnificence to this. The floor was of inlaid marble, four gothic windows looked out upon the vast expansive ocean, commanding a boundless scene. These were furnished with curtains of pink silk, the fringe of lilac and silver, with cords and tassels to correspond. The ceiling, of an octagonal form, was painted in compartments, with an allegorical representation of the seasons. The arches on the opposite sides of the room, and corresponding with the windows, were lined with white marble, and supported by pillars of the same, round which were carried rows of crystal lamps, of various colours, whose glow, when they were lighted up, was peculiarly relieved and softened by intersections of the choicest flowers, running in the same spiral manner between the lights. Alternate rows of lamps and flowers depended likewise from the cornices, and above the doors. The upper end was distinguished by a canopy to match the window curtains, and ornamented with a yet greater profusion of brilliant decorations. Tables, chairs, and stools, arranged with equal taste, and of surpassing beauty, finished the superb grandeur of the whole, and was sufficient to captivate and bewilder the most fastidious taste, and might have been mistaken for a fairy temple, or the palace of some genii, instead of the fiend in human shape to whom it belonged.

Here had the pirate-chief often (when he had steeped their senses in a delirium of sweet entrancement) triumphed over the virtue of the lovely and the innocent ;—here had he wrought the destruction of many of Nature's most lovely works, and afterwards exulted in his fiend-like triumph.

It was by the brilliancy of this apartment, and the other allurements he had designed to throw out, that he hoped to delude the senses of our heroine, and to gain a conquest over her innocence, without having recourse to violence. This he resolved to endeavour to accomplish by the mockery of a marriage, performed after the mystic rites that had been established among the smugglers; and such was the vanity which he possessed, and the knowledge of his power, and that she was entirely left to his mercy, made him entertain very little doubt but that he should succeed.

Seated on the throne beneath the canopy, and surrounded by the principal portion of the crew who were at the tower, or had arrived in the Devil Skipper, Sir Julian was resting on the evening we have mentioned. The smugglers were all arrayed in the most fancy and elegant costumes, which they had for peculiar occasions like these, and altogether the scene was a most imposing one, and had more of the effect of a representation in a drama than anything else; and the imagination could scarcely perceive anything more romantic.

The lengthy table was covered with goblets of silver, and the rich decanters sparkled with the choicest of wines. Sir Julian had removed the cap from his head, and a crown, formed of all descriptions of precious stones, ornamented his brow, which glittered with dazzling brightness beneath the rays of the chandeliers that were suspended from the lofty roof. His whole appearance was in strict accordance with the scene, and could not be gazed on without astonishment, not unmixed with a feeling of admiration.

During the time that Sam Raker was gone to the apartments of Flora, the baronet had commanded that mirth should prevail; and immediately after each quaffing heartily from the contents of the goblet, Hemlock sung the following, to which all the smuggler's present lent their aid in the chorus :—

SONG.

" Old Neptune, they say, is the king of the deep,
　　But that I will stoutly deny,
For a mightier king o'er its billows doth sweep,
　　Who his rival doth proudly defy !
He's a king who gives freedom to all that he rules,
　　No minister's tricks need they fear;
The follies of state he will leave to the fools,
　　While the wide ocean-deep is his share !
　　　　Then fill up your goblets, and loudly sing,
　　　　Hurrah ! hurrah ! for the Smuggler King ?
　　　　　　CHORUS :
　　　　The Smuggler King !—the Smuggler King !
　　　　Hurrah ! hurrah ! for the Smuggler King !

" Proudly he'll ride o'er the bright blue tide—
　　No monarch so proud as he ;
Gold he must have ; and woe-betide
　　Those who his flag shall see !
'Tis vain to oppose him in deadly fight—
　　To yield he will all soon bring :
Oh, nothing can equal the power and might
　　Of the dreaded Smuggler King?
　　　　Then fill up your goblets, and loudly sing,
　　　　Hurrah ! hurrah ! for the Smuggler King !
　　　　　　CHORUS :
　　　　The Smuggler King !—the Smuggler King !
　　　　Hurrah ! hurrah ! for the Smuggler King !"

Every proper effect was given to the singing of this song and chorus and the applause which followed had not subsided, when Sam Raker returned to the saloon.

" How now, Sam ?" demanded Sir Julian, " where is the girl ?"

Raker immediately delivered his message, to which the baronet listened with attention.

"And do you think she is really ill?" he inquired.

"Why a little so-so-like, captain," replied the smuggler.

"Humph!" muttered the captain, "it seems as if I am always to have my hopes deferred, and my wishes ungratified."

"Your pardon, captain," remarked Raker; "but the lass no doubt is rather flurried at your arrival, and I think if you were to yield to her request, and postpone your interview with her till to-morrow, it would be likely to make a little impression upon her. I know what the fair craft is, although I am a smuggler, and leave Sam Raker alone for getting the weathergauge of them at any time."

"You say right, Sam," answered Sir Julian, after a pause; "it would appear rather harsh and cruel of me to insist upon seeing her, if she is indisposed; so I will e'en take your advice, and defer my interview till the morning. This night, in the meantime, we will devote to revelry, and pass the wine-cup merrily round."

"Then I am to say that you will expect to see the damsel to-morrow?" said Raker.

"Yes," answered the captain, "and deliver the message in your best style, and just let her see what intelligent and gallant fellows the Smuggler King owns for his subjects."

"I will weigh anchor immediately, captain," said Raker; "and if I don't deliver my message in a manner worthy of any page, why, may I never go aloft again."

"A very pretty page, too; ha! ha! ha!" laughed Sir Julian, when Sam Raker quitted the room, in which joke the smugglers all joined with hearty laughter.

Sam soon returned, and took his seat on the right side of the captain, beneath the throne—Will Hemlock occupying the left. The goblets were now replenished, and emptied, and replenished again, and the utmost revelry prevailed, Sir Julian setting the example. Toast followed toast, and chorus succeeded chorus, until an early hour of the following morning, when the smugglers, overpowered by the deep libations they had partaken of, staggered to rest, and Sir Julian, who was more sober than any of the rest, although he had quaffed as deeply, hastened to the gorgeous chamber which was prepared for him.

"So," he exclaimed, when he found himself alone, "I have completely triumphed; all my enemies are removed, and here am I, in my stronghold, where no power dare molest me, and the beauteous Flora Clarendon is entirely at my disposal. Glorious triumph! Other monarchs than the Smuggler King might well envy the rich prize I possess. Her beauty inflames my passions, and her innocence but stimulated me to the consummation of all my wishes! Oh! I will shower upon her all the luxuries that wealth can produce, and if the most consummate flattery and impassioned vows can win woman's love, in a very short time I will have her heart as securely in my power as I have her person. Sir Julian Mordlington likes not a ruffian's conquest, and, therefore, by all the soft arts of which I am master, would I win her to my purpose. That would render my triumph more complete, and she must be more than woman if she be able to resist the means I will adopt to captivate her affections. If I fail it will be the first time. Wealthy maidens have yielded to my powers of fascination; damsels lovely as eastern houris have succumbed to the golden snares thrown around them by the rover of the deep; and, by old Neptune, I swear that she shall be added to my long list of conquests. The memory of her lover may, for a time, render her obstinate, and the *good* character the world has given me, and which

I glory in deserving, may alarm her gentle nature ; but these difficulties I do not despair of being able to surmount ; and then, with his fair bride (bride, ha ! ha !) how doubly proud and daring will become the much-dreaded *Smuggler King!*"

Filled with the extacy of these thoughts, Sir Julian felt not inclined to retire to his couch, and he paced the chamber, brooding in sanguine anticipation upon the *pleasures* he would shortly experience in the destruction of female innocence and purity. He thought not of the power that reigned above him, and which in a moment could thwart all his infernal plans, and level him with the dust. He thought not of the terrible retribution, which, sooner or later is sure to overtake the guilty, and in the very moments when they think themselves most secure, and their triumph most complete. He reflected not on the dreadful desolation his awful crimes had doubtless caused ; the broken hearts of the unfortunate relations of that fair and lovely thing whom he held in his power, and whom he had made up his mind to lay waste, and wretched, and degraded. Inured to every species of atrocious crime, he thought not of these ; and yet Sir Julian was not insensible to the feelings of a man ; he was not, amidst all his hardihood and cold-blooded recklessness, deaf to the terrible voice of conscience, which "speaks trumpet-tongued," and there were times when he trembled beneath its powers with all the weakness of the veriest coward. But his moments of compunction were but few, and too brief to suffer him to do any good. He was steeped so far in guilt that he knew it was useless to recede ; and so many were the deeds of blood he had from time to time perpetrated, that he was well convinced there was no mercy for him in this world, and thus he continued his infamous career, regardless of that mercy which is shewn to the repentant sinner in the future. If he abandoned his present course of life he was certain that those fellows whom he would thus forsake, would be sure, out of revenge at losing one who had led them with such daring through every danger, and by his skill and bravery rendered them wealthy, with that ingratitude which is generally the accompaniment of villany amongst themselves, be the first to reveal his character, and the punishment of the law would be certain to follow. To be exposed—to undergo an ignominious trial, and to die upon a public gallows, amid the triumph and execrations of a gaping crowd, his proud spirit shrunk from with a feeling of disgust and determination ; and he, therefore, resolved to pursue the same desperate course he had for so many years followed, until his evil star should predominate, and some accident betray him to, and place him in the power of those laws he had so often and so greatly offended.

Such were part of the reflections of Sir Julian Mordlington, on the morning in question.

"Yes," he exclaimed, "I will ever continue the same ; on the sea the bold pirate and smuggler, dreaded by all, unknown to all but my own brave lads, and conquered by none. Never will I strike my flag until compelled to do so by that powerful enemy, evil destiny. But what should I fear ? Have I not hitherto been triumphant, and may I not continue to be so until old Admiral Death has "laid my mizen topsail to the mast?" Yes, yes, the bold Smuggler King will continue his reckless career, and, whenever he dies, it shall be on board his own gallant vessel, surrounded by the stout hearts that have so bravely stuck to him in every danger. Oh, a gallant life is that of the free-trader ; it is so sweet to be feared, to reign an absolute monarch over monarchs ; to laugh at their boasted power, and to set them and their satellites at defiance. Give me the rover's life in preference to the hollow and flimsy pleasures of the fashionable butterfly, and I experience both. Give me the ocean wide, with its broad billows disporting in the gale, to all the luxuries to be found on *terra firma.* Let me breathe the atmosphere of my gallant ship, in preference to the sickening perfume of the drawing-room or the court. The roar of wind and waves, the rattling of cannon, before all the fulsome flattery from fashionable hypocrites, that it were possible to pour into mine ears. Again I say, a rover's life for me, and a rover I will continue to be, while I have a timber left to float with!"

The villain once more traversed the chamber with hasty strides, as he thus gave utterance to his feelings, and he smiled in savage exultation at the thought. Any one who had beheld his countenance at that moment, flushed as it was by the extraordinary excitement of his feelings, might have taken him for one of those monsters of the deep which are read of in fabulous history. He clenched his fist with determination, and his large black eyes were lighted up by an unusual fire. The Smuggler King was there, in all his fierce deformity, and well did he realize the character which had been given of him.

After a pause, during which he had been giving free indulgence to the feelings which these thoughts engendered, he changed his tone, and thus continued :—

" The disguise I have adopted I think is a wise one; it would not be so well for Flora to know me as Sir Julian Mordlington, although she has not at present any power to do me harm, but there is no knowing what at some future period may happen. She cannot discover me, at least, if I am to place any confidence in the opinion of Sam Raker, and he is a pretty good judge in these matters; and will know me only as the Smuggler King, by which title she must learn to love me; and she will, too, or I have lost all my powers of fascination. She must not yet be made acquainted with the actual fate of her lover, or it is doubtful whether it would not cost her her life; then I should lose my fair bride, and all my trouble into the bargain."

He again paused, for a feeling of compunction suddenly came over him, and he found himself inadequate to the task of conquering it.

" And yet," he said, " I regret that Raker was so hasty, and that the life of William was not spared. I do not like the thoughts of having shed his blood, although I once myself attempted it. He was a brave youth, and—but no matter—it is done now, and cannot be recalled; and, perhaps, it is all the better; for, should I have confined him, he might ultimately have escaped, and having discovered that we were related, become rather annoying, if not dangerous to me. Yes, yes; it is better as it is; it is better as it is! The old lawyer, too, he is removed, and I am quite safe!—quite safe! I have the possession of all my father's wealth; I rule master of the seas; I have faithful, hardy companions, and as fair a craft as ever sailed the ocean of life, at my disposal, and what else can I require? Nothing! Nothing! Away then, with gloomy thoughts; henceforth nothing but joy and blissful anticipation shall occupy them. I will be as reckless in mind, as I am in spirit and in conduct, and leave all that may happen to me to chance, and be prepared to die like a man whenever ill fortune comes. But a few short hours and I shall behold her, who at first sight completely ravished my senses; I shall hear the music of her voice, and bask beneath the radiant sunshine of her eyes, which, like golden beams of Sol breaking through an April shower, will glitter through her tears; pearly drops that it will be my task to kiss away, and to cewnether I cannot ultimately replace them with smiles. Oh! it will be a purous task. and my very soul revels in the thought! She will not weep ng; no, it shall be my power that will teach her to forget the memory of the one she has lost, and give up her whole affections to me. For while she may be coy, and retiring, and reproachful, she may probably shew off a few heroics—have some dozen or two of fits; but after a stiff gale very frequently comes a calm, and so I anticipate it will be with you, my dainty fair one; I

never knew a woman yet who was proof against a flattering tongue, and a handsome person, and both these great requisites I believe myself to possess in an eminent degree."

It will have been seen ere now that among all the numerous faults of the guilty Sir Julian, self-conceit was not the least, and therefore the reader will not feel astonished that he should thus soliloquise. He had a very powerful opinion of his own person, and indeed nature, as we have often before said, had greatly favoured him in that respect; and were it not for the dark, lurking, sinister expression of his eyes, his countenance might have been called handsome. His wit was also abundant, and his mind, notwithstanding the lawless life in which he had so much mingled, was most accomplished.

All these were of great assistance to him in the villanous transactions he carried on, and many were the unfortunate families who had fallen beneath their spell.

At length, immersed in these pleasing reflections, Sir Julian retired to his couch, and dreamt of the pleasures he anticipated in the course of a few hours. It will have been seen from his soliloquies, that he did not intend to put his diabolical designs into execution immediately, but to try all the powers of his eloquent persuasion to win the maiden to his purpose. This was, indeed, a mercy to the damsel, for, however painful his advances might be, it afforded her a chance of retarding his violence until something might occur, ultimately to release her from his persecutions.

After Sam Raker had left Flora and Maud, not feeling inclined to retire to rest, they passed the dreary hours in conversation, in the course of which, Maud tried her utmost endeavours to compose the poor girl, and to prepare her for the interview, which it was evident must take place on the following day.

"But," remarked Maud, "I do not think it will be so terrible, my dear Flora, as you seem to apprehend; in allowing you to remain to-night un-

No. 41

molested, it would appear as if the captain intended to act with some forbearance; and, if you exercise proper firmness and self-possession, all may yet be well, and you may finally be restored to liberty, and from the power of your dreaded enemy."

Flora shook her head.

"Alas!" she observed, "that hope, I fear, is futile. Villain as the pirate chief is, it is not likely that he will suffer any opposition to his wishes, but that he will have recourse to violence, and then I am lost! Who—who can save me? Have I a friend at hand, who will stand forward in my behalf,—and, if I had, what could it avail against the power of such a miscreant?—Lost! lost! entirely lost!"

Maud still endeavoured to soothe her, and to induce her to hope for better things, but she had a most difficult task to perform, and it was a considerable time before she in any degree succeeded. They had taken their seats, as before, at the casement, and in contemplating all that their eyes could gaze on, they both became somewhat abstracted from the gloomy thoughts which it was natural should crowd upon their brains at that time.

The moon was shedding her full lustre over the sea, which was perfectly calm, and reflected back her silvery face with even increased splendour. The wind only whispered in gentle murmurs, and nature smiled in all her happiness.

At a short distance were seen the two pirate vessels, the Devil Skipper, and the Raven, and their long dark shadows were reflected in the deep, while there they seemed, with the daring of their guilty commander, to bid defiance to all around.

The sounds of revelry from the captain and his crew, now reached their ears, and as Flora listened to them, she trembled violently.

"The wretches," she observed, "will become inebriated, and then what restraint will they have upon themselves? They may break in upon us, and forgetting the promises that have been made to us, before long I may be dragged into the presence of their guilty chief. Oh! God protect me."

"And he will, my dear Flora," said Maud. "He will most assuredly protect such innocence as thine. But fear not, the captain is a man of his word, and this night, at any rate, you are as safe as if you were at liberty. As for his fellows, they hold him in too much dread to venture to disobey him. It would be immediate death to those who should attempt it. Of this truth you should be assured from their conduct previous to his arrival."

"These sounds shock my ears," sighed our heroine; "oh! how different to the peaceful quiet of my happy home, which the wretch whose destined victim I fear I am, has rendered desolate."

"Perhaps, my dear Flora," observed Maud, "it is not so bad as your worst fears anticipate."

"Not so bad," repeated our heroine; "how can it be otherwise? Oh, Maud, you can form no idea of the affectionate parents and sister that I had—Heaven knows only if I have them now—or you would not talk thus. Broken-hearted, worn down by grief and horrible uncertainty, methinks I see them now; broken-hearted I know they must be, and how can I hope or look for consolation under such a dreadful certainty?"

"Heaven will support them through the dreadful trial," said Maud, "and you may yet behold them again."

"Oh! never—never! on this earth," ejaculated Flora; "my prophetic heart tells me I shall not."

"Have not others, similarly situated to yourself, and in the midst of their despair, when they least expected it, been restored to happiness?" asked Maud.

"True," replied our heroine; "but, alas! what can I think,—what can I hope, so situated as I am? Confined in this horrible prison, with only you as my friend, and you entirely powerless, what prospect is there of my restoration to liberty, or of ever beholding my dear friends again?"

"Providence often interposes when all hope seems lost entirely," remarked Maud; "but come, let us retire to rest, and hope for better events than those you forebode."

"No—no," answered Flora; "the contemplation of this calm and beautiful moonlight may serve to remove my thoughts from the point to which misery at present directs them. How lovely is all around! See how majestically the queen of night sails through her silvery ocean of clouds! How tranquil is everything we gaze upon, and yet how different to the state of my harassed mind! How can mankind contemplate a scene of happiness and glory like this, and yet, in spite of the Great Being who guides all these wondrous works, delight in deeds of crime and cruelty, and tyrannize and trample on the happiness of their fellow beings? One would think that they could never, in the face of all that is lovely and sublime, seek to deprive their fellow-creatures of the delight of enjoying them, and lifting up their souls in awe and admiration to Nature's God!"

"Wretches who could act thus," observed Maud, "must be insensible to the feelings you have described."

"They must, indeed," said our heroine; "lovely moon! Perhaps at this moment my dear parents, if they be yet alive, are gazing upon thy bright face, and beseeching rest and eternal happiness to the soul of her whom they must think no more. Oh! may thy chaste beams smile happiness upon them, and enable them to bear with fortitude the heavy calamity which has befallen them."

"See! what is that?" suddenly exclaimed Maud, pointing to the dark shadow of some object, which all at once darted from beneath the rock on which the tower stood, into the more open part of the ocean.

"It is a boat," returned Flora, straining her eyes in the direction to which Maud had pointed.

"It is," said the latter, "and contains a man."

"Doubtless, it is only one of the smugglers proceeding to one of the vessels," said Flora.

"No, he has taken a contrary direction," remarked Maud, "and appears as if he wanted to avoid them."

"And is there anything remarkable in that?" demanded our heroine.

"I know not," replied Maud; "but it is something very unusual for a single smuggler to venture forth alone in those parts. See, he pulls hastily, and his errand is evidently one of moment."

"Can you recognize his figure?" asked Flora.

"No," answered Maud; "although the moon shines brightly, he is at too great a distance for me to do that."

They now watched the boat more narrowly, until turning round an angle of the rock, it was hidden from their view.

"What think you of this circumstance?" asked our heroine, whose thoughts were for a short time diverted from the melancholy subjects that had before engrossed them.

"I know not what to think of it," replied Maud; "but, as I before said, I cannot help considering it as something remarkable."

"Well, for my own part," said Flora, "I cannot conceive that there is anything extraordinary in it at all. You say there is an island not far from hence?"

Maud answered in the affirmative.

"Then it is more than probable that the man has been dispatched thither by his captain on business."

"It may be so," returned Maud ; " but still it has made an impression on my mind which I cannot divest myself of."

"I do not understand you," said Flora ; " I see nothing at all exciting or remarkable in the event."

"What's that ?" demanded Maud, hastily, as a sound like something knocking against the casement met both their ears.

Flora started back amazed, and somewhat alarmed.

"It could only have been the wind which shook the window frame," she said, at length.

The sound was repeated, and it then seemed to proceed from something like a pebble striking against one of the squares of glass.

"That was not the wind, I am certain," observed Maud ; " this is most extraordinary."

A third time they heard the sound, and then imagined they distinguished the voice of some one in a suppressed tone.

"That was certainly a human voice," said Maud.

"Some one is below," said Flora.

"What a pity it is that these iron bars prevent us from looking out."

"Let us open the casement," suggested Flora, who trembled with mingled feelings of surprise, anxiety, and revived hope.

Maud thrust her hand between the bars, and opened the casement with very little difficulty. She had scarcely done so, when something was thrown into the room.

They took the light and examined it, and their astonishment and agitation may be well conceived, when they found that it was a stone, to which was fastened a folded paper.

The emotion of them both was so great, that they stood for an instant gazing at it, and unable to move a limb. At length Flora, in breathless haste, picked it up, and was completely thunderstruck when she beheld that it was a note, and addressed to herself in an unknown hand.

She trembled so violently that she could not read it, and, unable to speak, she presented it to Maud, and motioned her to do so. The latter complied, and read the following words :—

"Fair lady, be not daunted ; dangerous as is your situation, you have a friend, who now goes to endeavour to save you. Meet the approaches of the pirate captain with firmness, and he will be thwarted in his plans. In a few days you may expect such relief as will secure your liberty, and bring the wretches in whose power you at present are, to punishment. After you have perused this note, burn it, to prevent all chance of detection."

No sooner had Maud read these lines than our heroine sunk on her knees, and raising her eyes towards Heaven, uttered an exclamation of gratitude.

"Can this be possible?" she cried, " or is it only done to torture me, and sport with my feelings?"

"Oh, no, my dear young lady," remarked her companion, " what motives could any one have for so doing? Hope, bright sunny hope, should be revived in your bosom ; for should this generous unknown be successful in his endeavours, your deliverance may be near at hand."

"The thought is too blissful to be encouraged," observed Flora, " and yet —oh ! Heaven bless the generous being who has written these lines."

"It must be one of the smugglers," observed Maud ; " no one else would have ventured so near the tower of the Death Rock?"

"Then he has perilled his own life in the undertaking?"

"He lives, and should he be caught and detected, nothing but a death of torture awaits him," answered Maud.

"Heaven send that he may be successful," cried Flora ; " not only for my sake, whose cause he apparently so disinterestedly espouses, but for his own."

"God grant that he may," reiterated Maud.

"But, know you the handwriting?"

"I do not remember ever to have seen it before."

"It was doubtless the man whom we saw in the boat."

"That is most probable," returned Maud; "and that he has seized the opportunity while the other smugglers are engaged in their revelry, to seize upon the boat and make his escape."

"And whither do you think he will shape his course?" inquired Flora.

"To the nearest place where he may expect to fall in with some vessels of war," answered Maud; "to whom he will make known your situation, the real characters of the smugglers, and their present haunt; and should he succeed, we may shortly expect such aid that even the Smuggler King and his desperate companions may not be able to stand against."

"But will not the poor fellow's own life fall a sacrifice, should it be discovered that he is also one of the smugglers?" demanded our heroine.

"No," replied Maud; "there is a large reward offered to any one who will discover and be the means of bringing to justice the Smuggler King, and a free pardon to the person giving the information."

"This circumstance is so extraordinary, that it seems scarcely possible," observed Flora; "it is like a dream."

"Does it not prove to you the truth and force of that which I have often endeavoured to impress upon you, my dear Flora," said Maud; "that we should never entirely abandon ourselves to despair, for, in the midst of our most imminent dangers relief often comes from the very quarter least expected?"

"It does, indeed," answered Flora; "and I will henceforth endeavour to follow your advice. But still, we must not be too sanguine; this kind stranger may be unsuccessful, and then the disappointment would be greater than all the misery I endured before."

"Follow the counsel of your unknown friend, miss," said Maud; "be not daunted; if you can but muster spirits and self-possession to endure your meetings with the captain for a few days, all may be well."

"A few days," repeated our heroine; "alas! what may not happen in that time? But, tell me, have you no suspicion, Maud, of who this individual really is?"

"I have not," returned her companion; "indeed, I did not think that there was one among the crew of the Smuggler King, who possessed such humanity."

"But in that open boat, he will never be able to reach the place of his destination in safety," said Flora.

"The weather is at present in his favour," remarked Maud; "and no doubt he well knows how to proceed, and is guarded against all consequences, or he would not have undertaken the cause."

"What can have induced him to take such an interest in me?" demanded the damsel.

"It is, indeed, remarkable," said Maud; "but, perhaps, he may be urged on by the thoughts of the reward, more than from any real feeling of humanity towards you."

"Maud," remarked our heroine, "that is an ungenerous observation which I did not think you were capable of uttering. Had such been his motives, why did he take the trouble of sending the note to me? Why not depart on his errand without running the risk of making any one acquainted with it?"

"Pardon me, miss," replied her companion; "I did not think of that; it was wrong, very wrong of me to make use of such remarks."

"But should the smugglers miss him," said Flora, "their suspicions will perhaps, be excited, and following in pursuit of him, may overtake him before he has been able to reach the place of his destination."

"In the confusion of their revelry, it is not likely that they will think of him," answered Maud; "besides, their numbers are so strong that they cannot easily, for a time, at least, miss one individual, unless he holds a prominent station among the crew."

"Again, I pray to Heaven that he may be successful," exclaimed our heroine; "and surely, whatever his crimes may have been, in so worthy an undertaking Providence will crown him with success."

"Rest assured, my dear young lady," returned Maud, "it will. But who he can be, I cannot form the least conjecture."

"Whoever he be," observed our heroine, fervently, "may the blessings of Heaven descend upon his head, even if he fail in his efforts."

"To that prayer I heartily respond," said Maud; "and most sanguine are my hopes that he will be successful. No person would venture on such an hazardous undertaking unless it was well concocted, and they were pretty confident that it would succeed."

"The tone of his note also speaks his confidence," added Flora.

"It does," said her companion, "and also shews that he takes a deep interest in your welfare."

"True; and, therefore, am I lost in mystery to conceive who it can be. But still the power of the smugglers, as you have represented it, is so great that, after all, they may be able to defeat those who are sent against them. The situation of this tower, too, is also greatly in their favour."

"That is true, miss," answered Maud; "but not suspecting treachery, they will be taken by surprise, and unable to make such a resistance as they otherwise would."

"Ah!" exclaimed our heroine, as a sudden thought flashed across her brain; "but when the pirate-chief finds that he is attacked, may he not in revenge, immediately sacrifice my life?"

"He could not surely be that monster," said Maud.

"If that which you and the world have repeated of him be true," answered our heroine; "he is monster enough for anything. Still have I but little room for hope. Alas! my fate is, indeed, a dreadful, a torturing one."

"Do not, I beseech you, Flora," interposed her companion, "already once more sink into despair. The miscreant may be defeated, and in the power of his enemies, before he has the power to perpetrate such an inhuman crime, even if his black heart could encourage such an idea."

"But you have told me he has the means of immediate escape, should danger surround him," said the damsel, "and if so, may he not be said to be almost unconquerable? Might he not, with a few of his chosen companions, secretly leave the place, when he found his case was thus desperate and hopeless, and bear me with him?"

"My dear Flora," said Maud, "you will persist in always entertaining the most gloomy apprehensions, even when hope shines upon you. If they can muster a force strong enough, this place will doubtless be surrounded, and all retreat cut off."

"Yes, yes," cried our heroine, after a pause, "I will still hope; and all-merciful God surely will not suffer me to fall an innocent victim to such unparalleled atrocity."

"He will not, my dear miss, depend upon it," remarked Maud; "the day of retribution for the wretches, I trust, is at hand; that terrible day when they will have to pay the penalty of all their crimes."

"And shall I then be restored to sweet liberty once again?" ejaculated the beauteous damsel, her eyes filling with tears; "shall I once more see my dear native village? my beloved parents? Ah! gracious Heaven! do they still live ? and, if they do, how, oh, how shall I find them ? Perhaps wandering about, their minds a wreck, and—oh! God! the thought is dreadful!"

" Let me beg you not to give way to it," said Maud ; " you only distress your mind, without any actual cause, by gloomy imagination alone."

" Would that I could believe it was imagination only," observed Flora ; "but, alas! though it even be so, it is too probable to resist its painful influence. Such an event as the loss of their beloved child, must have the most dreadful effect upon their aged minds."

" No doubt it would, miss," returned Maud; " but I trust they have been able to bear up against the shock, and when you return to your native home, you may clasp them once more in happiness to your arms, and meet all that are dear to you, never more to be parted from them."

" Ah!" exclaimed the damsel, with a look of distraction ; " where is he upon whom my whole affections were placed ? The young, the noble, the youthful, will he be there to greet me ? Will he be there to meet me, with the smiles of welcome and of love ? No,—no—no. *He* rests beneath the blue waves, and happiness and Flora must ever more be strangers !"

" But you know not that, my dear young lady," observed Maud, " and therefore why give way to such dreadful apprehensions ?"

" I know it not," repeated the damsel, energetically. " No—no—I know it not for certainty; but you—you know it, and yet refuse to satisfy me !"

" How have I deserved this, Flora ?" said Maud, much affected. " Have I not said enough to convince you that, although I have the will, I have not the power to convince you. But the time will come, probably, when my lips may be unsealed, and then, with what eagerness, what sincerity, will I give you all the information in my power."

" Pardon me, Maud," said our heroine, throwing her fair arms affectionately round her neck; " but I know you will. At times I am so distracted that I scarcely know what I say. I will mention that painful subject no more, but keep it confined to my own seared bosom. But, should we really be delivered from here, you will accompany me—will you not, Maud ?"

" Alas !" answered the latter, with a deep sigh, " what will a poor, wreched, friendless creature like I am do again in the world ?"

" Say not friendless," returned the affectionate and grateful girl. " In me you shall ever find a sincere, though a humble friend ; and I will love you as a mother, for the kindness you have shown me, and without which I must, ere now, have sunk beneath the weight of my afflictions."

Maud embraced her.

" But," she observed, " am I not connected with the smugglers, and must share their punishment?"

" Share their punishment !" repeated our heroine, with a look of anguish. " Oh, no—no—no! that cannot—will not be! You are not to blame. You are not guilty of any crime. You hold their deeds in abhorrence, and you have never had the opportunity to escape from them, or soon would you have consigned them to that justice, to those avenging laws they have so dreadfully outraged."

" Heaven knows I would."

" Then why talk of punishment?" demanded Flora. " Justice, humanity, could never contemplate such a thing! No, dear Maud, you shall yet be free as the pure air we breathe, and, in the future esteem of your fellow creatures, receive the reward due to your many years of patience and suffering."

Maud was too much overwhelmed by the power of her emotions to speak, and again the friends embraced, and, for a short time, indulged their thoughts in silence.

Having somewhat recovered from their emotions, they more calmly conversed upon he contents of the note which they had so mysteriously received, and the result was, that they both entertained no doubts of the man's sincerity, while at the same time they encouraged strong hopes that through his means they should both be delivered from their present captivity, which was even more painful than death.

The poignant dread and anguish which before distracted Flora's mind, were greatly ameliorated, and she prepared to meet the terrible Smuggler King on the following day with as much fortitude as it was possible, under the circumstances, to acquire.

The song and chorus of the smugglers now reached their ears, but when that had ceased, and the tumult of applause which followed it, the noise of the fellows' revelry was confined to the saloon, and the night air blowing keen, Flora and Maud retired from the casement, and, after partaking of some refreshment, and securing all the doors to prevent intrusion, they bade one another good night, and retired to rest.

The events of the evening, however, for some time occupied the thoughts of our heroine after she had reclined her head on her pillow, and when sleep descended on her eyelids, she dreamt of them again. Her rest was, however, more calm and undisturbed than any she had enjoyed since she had been a prisoner in the tower, and she did not awake until the golden beams of the sun darted into the casement of her chamber. She found that Maud had already arisen, and was watching affectionately by the side of her couch, and she greeted her with a smile of sweetness which showed the esteem she bore her.

"My dear Maud," she observed, "I have had such sweet dreams. I saw, in fancy, the contents of the letter we last night received in such a mysterious manner, realized. I fancied that we were delivered by our friends, and that the vessel, on board of which we were received, spread its swelling sails, and quickly wafted us to dear England. Soon its white cliffs burst upon my view—we landed—nature was smiling most bounteously—the golden corn fields glistened in the sunbeams; the rich pastures showed the unbounded goodness of the Almighty to the favoured inhabitants of that happy country; the air breathed a delicious perfume, and the lark, carolling its sweetest note, ascended to the clear blue sky, warbling forth its beautiful music, until it died away in the distance. Oh, it was a lovely sight, Maud, and my heart expanded. I seemed to feel new life. My spirits were reanimated with all the buoyancy of childhood. The scenery, the air, the smiling happy faces, the hue of everything, convinced me, if anything were wanting, that I once more trod my native soil, and that I was free—free as the air I respired. But greater extacy awaited me. Accompanied by you, Maud, I approached my native village. All was fresh and blooming as when I was forced away from it. Every spot seemed to smile and welcome me, and it appeared as if I had only for a time undergone the horrors of a painful vision, to awaken to fresh happiness and redoubled pleasure. And now increased transport awaited me. I came near the dear farm in which I first drew my breath. Surely that was a foretaste of the joys of Heaven, and yet, amid it all, my heart palpitated tumultuously between joy, hope, doubt, and apprehension. These feelings were but brief; the acme of my felicity was at hand. I saw the gate of the old farm quickly open, and the next moment my dear parents and sister—William—all that is dear to me, rushed forth, frantic with joy, to greet me. I felt myself pressed alternately to their hearts—I tried to speak, but the feelings of nature were too much

overpowered to suffer me to speak, and, in the delirium of transport, I awoke. Oh! will ever such a delightful dream as this be realized?"

"It will, indeed, my dear Flora," answered Maud; "this delightful vision has been sent to you, to fortify your mind against the persecutions of your enemy, and to assure you that Heaven is watching over you. It will be realized, and ere long, happiness will be restored to you, and you will be rewarded for all the sufferings you have undergone, and the patience with which you have borne them."

"My dear Maud," said our heroine, embracing her, "how much am I indebted to you for your kindness to the poor forlorn one. Without you, what a poor, miserable wretch should I have been, and ere now must I have sunk under the heavy afflictions that have attended me."

"And most happy am I," returned Maud, "that I have been made the humble but sincere means of effecting such a desirable and worthy object. To see you restored to peace and liberty will be one of the greatest blessings that can attend me. Well shall I consider all that I have done, all that I have myself been fated to endure, repaid, if I can see, if I am permitted to witness the restoration to happiness of one I so fondly esteem."

"And never shall I consider that I am able sufficiently to repay by my gratitude, the motherly affection and solicitude you have shown me," returned the damsel. "Alas! how few beings are there in the world like Maud."

"My dear girl," said Maud, much affected, "you far overrate my merits; I have done no more than what common humanity ought ever to prompt us to perform towards our suffering and oppressed fellow-creatures."

"And yet such kindness you have never yourself experienced," remarked Flora.

No. 42

"But why should I murmur?" added Maud; "God has been very good to me, and all that I have suffered has been but a just punishment for my youthful indiscretions."

"Do not thus reproach yourself, my dear Maud," observed the damsel; "your error was excusable, for you fell the victim of designing villany, and not from your own vitiated nature."

"Heaven knows," ejaculated Maud, with much emotion; "Heaven knows that you do me but justice, dear Flora. My heart had been trained in virtue, my sentiments pure, and my mind unsuspicious of deep, insidious guilt; I listened, trusted—what maiden would not have trusted— would not have believed the vows and emphatic protestations of one who was formed to captivate, who seemed perfection's self; thus confiding, I fell, and from that unhappy moment, a curse seemed to follow in my path, and to immolate all connected with me, in its withering influence; from that moment, happiness and I became strangers, and, sinner as I was, it would have been a mercy to have been permitted to die, to be forgotten. Oh! what miseries, what insults, what degradations, have I not endured since that fatal time? Forced into a life, from which every feeling that throbs within my breast revolts; made to herd with monsters of the blackest dye; to appear what I am not; to witness scenes of crime and bloodshed, of debauchery and every vice, you, my dear Flora, may form an idea of what I must have suffered; you can imagine how my heart-strings have been wrung, what scalding tears I have shed; what liquid fire has fallen upon my brain; you can imagine all this, I am fully convinced that you can."

"I can—I do, indeed," answered Flora; "and sincerely do I commiserate in what you have undergone."

"I know you do, my poor girl," said Maud; "and from my misfortunes you may learn a lesson that, however great have been your own sufferings, there are others in the world who have been fated to endure far more. This should learn you a lesson of patience and fortitude, and teach you not to despair entirely, for even I, poor outcast, persecuted, lonely creature as I am, yet put my trust in the goodness of a beneficent Providence, and hope for some future amelioration of my anguish."

"And you will obtain it, my dear Maud," exclaimed our heroine, fervently; "you will have it, and in seeing you happy, I shall be happy myself. Would that I knew who this generous person is, who has promised me his aid to assist in my liberation."

"That could avail you nothing at present, my dear Flora," answered Maud; "no doubt, in due time, you will be made acquainted with him."

"Whether he succeeds or not," remarked our heroine, "oh, what a debt of gratitude do I owe him! A debt that I shall never be able to repay."

"He will be sufficiently rewarded in the approval of his own conscience," observed Maud; "and if pecuniary reward is what he seeks, he will obtain that from the government."

"I will never believe that he acts from sordid motives," said Flora; for if he did, he would never have troubled himself about me, nor run the risk of being discovered, by conveying me that note, which revealed his intentions."

"He does, indeed, appear to act from the best of motives," said Maud.

"He does," answered Flora; "we cannot entertain any doubt of their purity, or why should he take such an interest in a poor, friendless girl like myself, and to whom he must be entirely unknown?"

"True."

"His conduct is his best recommendation, and demands every confidence," added Flora.

"It does indeed," coincided her companion.

"He must be one of the smugglers, I should think," said our heroine.

"Undoubtedly," answered Maud, "or he would not have been near this place; neither could he have been acquainted with the fact of your being a prisoner here. I am at a loss to imagine who it can be, for they all seem ferocious alike, and so attached to their captain, that they would suffer anything, however torturing and dreadful, rather than betray him."

"It is most surprising," remarked the maiden; "and the more we reflect upon it the more must we become lost and bewildered in perplexity and mystery."

"We must."

"But," added our heroine, "he states in his note that it will be a few days before we can expect anything to be done; and, in the meantime, my misery may have been rendered complete by the villain in whose power I am."

"Do not entertain any such apprehensions," returned Maud; "much depends upon your own prudence and self-possession, for I do not think that the captain will attempt to enforce his guilty intentions for some time, unless he is urged to it by some conduct of your own, which might tend to excite him to revenge. He first seeks to win his victims to his purpose by the blandishments of his manner, and then—if that fail—he adopts the desperate course to obtain the gratification of his diabolical wishes."

"The cold deliberate villain!" cried Flora; "but I will endeavour to be be calm, and to meet him in such a manner as may tend to arrest his infernal purpose until Providence may send me relief. Many thanks to you, my dear, good Maud, for your counsel and advice; without it I should have been lost—entirely lost; for nothing could have saved me from the snares the miscreant has laid around me."

"And most grateful am I that I was here to afford you that assistance under this painful trial," answered Maud; "I return my thanks to Heaven that I have been permitted to perform that good; and I trust that the blessing will be increased by being rendered one of the instruments, in the hands of the Supreme, towards your final restoration to the blessings of liberty and your friends."

Thus the time passed away; but Flora, in spite of all her efforts to the contrary, could not help feeling the utmost dread and uneasiness. A most important day was this to her; a day on which perhaps her very life depended; the day on which she was to be introduced, for the first time, to the terrible and much-dreaded Smuggler King; to be compelled to listen to his odious words, and endure his insults. Under such circumstances, it must be admitted, that it was a great trial to the poor damsel to be able to collect fortitude and self-possession; but Maud exerted all the powers of her eloquence and reasoning, and she so far succeeded, that, by the time they had finished their morning's repast, our heroine was comparatively tranquil and firm.

An hour or two passed away, and, as there was no message from the captain, our heroine became still more calm; for every moment of delay was a relief to our heroine, as it all added to the time which her unknown friend needed to complete his designs, and gave her still greater hopes of her deliverance from the power of the wretches whose prisoner she then was. In these hopes Maud encouraged her; and the consequence was, that, in a short time, our heroine was enabled to look forward to the interview with the pirate-captain without any of those feelings of unbounded horror that had before disturbed her.

In the meantime, Sir Julian, having arisen from his couch, summoned the attendance of Sam Raker, who was not long in making his appearance.

"What is it, captain?" inquired the smuggler, as he entered.

"I want to go on board the Raven," answered Sir Julian; "I have left some papers, which I require."

"Cannot I get them, captain?" asked Sam; "and thus save you the trouble of going to the ship?"

"No," returned the former; "they are locked up in my chest, the contents of which, I, of course, let no one know but myself."

"Oh! very well," observed Raker, "as you please; only I thought that perhaps the debauch of last night might —"

"Psha!" interrupted the baronet; "think you I am overcome by such trifles?"

"Trifles you call them, captain, do you?" said Sam Raker; "now I think quite the contrary; I am a pretty old seaman, and can always stow away a tidy allowance of grog,—but I must say, that the quantity I drank last night capsized me."

"And I, you see, am as fresh as a ship newly launched," observed Sir Julian; "but get ready the boat—one or two of the fellows can accompany me."

"Ay, ay, captain," replied Raker; and he quickly made his exit.

"I am rather uneasy upon this subject," soliloquized the baronet, when Raker had left the room; "I am not certain whether I secured that confounded will, which I got from the old lawyer, in my iron chest, or left it behind me at the Hall. If the latter, it will fall into the hands of the present possessor, and probably cause unpleasant consequences. Cursed fool that I was to be so careless! Why did I not destroy it at once?"

He paced the apartment backwards and forwards, buried in thought;—bit his lips—contracted his brows—and was, altogether, in a most violent sate of agitation.

"But still," he resumed, after a pause, "should the will fall into other hands, it cannot work me much harm, since Fitzpatrick and William are both removed. I am now glad that Sam Raker acted as he did, for it has saved me a great deal of trouble. However, I should like to find the will in my chest, for it would not be altogether pleasant to leave it in the power of strangers to overhaul my affairs. I must and will be satisfied upon that point before I shall be in a proper vein to meet my destined, lovely bride. Ah! Sam, how now? You look confused! What has happened, eh?"

"The boat is not at the place where it was safely moored last night, captain," answered Raker.

"Not there?"

"No."

"Why," demanded Sir Julian, "what can have become of it? It was a beautiful calm last night, or I might have thought that the boat had been torn away from its moorings. Have any of the crew had occasion to leave the tower this morning?"

"They have not," answered Sam Raker.

"That is strange."

"I suspect treachery!" observed Raker.

"Treachery!" repeated the captain; "from whom?"

"One of our crew."

"Treachery from one of the crew of the Smuggler King!" exclaimed the baronet; "bah! the idea is madness!"

"I think differently, captain," remarked Sam Raker.

"What mean you?" demanded Sir Julian, hastily.

"I will explain."

"Then be quick. Are any of the fellows missing from the tower?"

"Yes."

"Who?"

"Grampus," answered Sam Raker.

"Grampus!" repeated the captain; "ah! I never half liked that chap."

"He was a sly villain," remarked Raker, "and I have long had my eye upon his actions."

"How long has he been missing from the tower?" asked Sir Julian.

"Ever since last night," answered the other.

"But may he not have gone to the ship?" interrogated the baronet.

"No, it is not at all likely; he had no business at all there; besides, it was his turn to keep watch on the ramparts of the tower."

"And why should you suspect him of treachery?" inquired the captain.

"I will tell you," answered Sam Raker, and he then related to the baronet the scene we have before described to have taken place between him and Grampus, to which the pirate-chief listened with the utmost degree of rage and excitement.

"Ah!" he exclaimed, when Sam had finished, "insubordination among the crew of the Smuggler King; why did you not in a moment send a bullet through the rascal's head, Sam?"

"I did not like to act without your orders, captain," replied Raker.

"Psha!" returned the baronet; "had you not the command of the ship? Did you not at that time represent myself? You were to blame, Sam—you were to blame. But did you ever hear him utter any threats of vengeance against me?"

"I have heard the fellow growl and mutter something," answered Sam, "but I never could distinguish what he said; he took good care of that."

"D——n!" exclaimed the baronet; "the infernal swab has been tempted by the reward that has been offered for my detection, and if he is not overtaken, he will betray my real name, and probably be the means of bringing such a force against us, that we may find it difficult to repel. Order a signal to be fired for a boat to put off from one of the vessels to convey me on board. There must be no time lost in this business. If we are quick, we may overtake the rascal; and if we do he shall be flogged to death as sure as his name is Grampus; quick! quick!"

Sam made no reply, but immediately departed to obey the orders of his captain, who traversed the apartment when he had quitted it, in a state of much excitement.

"The villain!" he exclaimed; "should he meet with any English vessel, my long hidden secret will be revealed, and the world will know who I am. As for the enemy he may bring against me, I fear that least of all. I have hitherto proved myself to be unconquerable, and I trust that I shall continue to do so. It was madness in Sam Raker to suffer him to live another moment after he had dared to grumble, and to oppose the commands of one to whom, in my absence, I had delegated my power."

At this instant the signal gun was fired, obedient to the instructions of the captain, and was immediately answered by another from the Devil Skipper.

The captain now summoned Will Hemlock to his presence.

"Know you aught of the fellow, Grampus?" he demanded.

"No more than that he has been missing from the tower ever since last night," answered Hemlock.

"And what think you is the cause of his absence?" asked Sir Julian.

"Treachery towards us, captain," answered Hemlock.

"And yet you suffered the scoundrel to live, after he had shown symptoms of it?"

"Raker had the command; I had no authority to take his life," returned the smuggler.

"True," said the baronet, "but do you think it is he who has taken the boat?"

"There can be very little doubt of it, captain. I dare say he seized the opportunity while we were all carousing, last night, to slip his cable and sheer off."

"No doubt of it," coincided Sir Julian, "the d——d rascal! And, I am afraid he has got far enough for our chase to be a useless one."

"I know not that, captain," answered Hemlock, "in such a calm he would not be able to make much way, and we may yet be able to overtake him before he has the opportunity of doing us any harm."

"Ah! we may," observed the baronet, "but we must be prepared in case of danger. Every part of the tower must be well guarded, and a strict watch set for any approaching enemy. I will leave those instructions with Sam Raker, he will know what to do; I want you and two more to attend me to the Raven."

"Ay, ay, captain," said Hemlock; "I am ready."

"Follow, then," commanded Sir Julian, as he walked from the room, and hastily quitting the tower, descended the rock, where the boat was waiting in readiness. The captain having given his orders to Sam Raker, stepped into the boat, followed by Hemlock, and was quickly rowed towards the Raven.

On arriving there, and finding that Grampus was neither aboard that vessel, nor the Devil Skipper, the first thing Sir Julian did was to order off two boats, well manned, in pursuit of Grampus, and he then proceeded to to the cabin in which his iron chest was deposited, to make search for the will.

Eagerly he turned over every article and document it contained, but in vain; the will was not there, and it was now but too evident to him that, in the hurry of his departure from the Hall, he had left it behind him.

His rage and disappointment were now almost ungovernable, and he stamped about the cabin in a state of the greatest excitement.

"Fool!—idiot that I was!" he exclaimed, "not to think of this most important document—to leave it behind me, for the prying eye of busy curiosity to peruse, and perhaps be the means of bringing me to destruction! Curses on my folly again and again! What ho, there!—get ready the boat as soon as possible, and take me to the shore again; let both vessels bring up as near the Death Rock as they can without danger; let every man be at his post, and ready to act in any emergency at a moment's notice."

"Ay, ay, captain," shouted a dozen voices, and every man on board was immediately in action to obey his commands. The boat was soon in readiness, and Sir Julian springing into it, followed by Hemlock, was quickly rowed back again to the Death Rock. Having given orders to Hemlock to hasten to Sam Raker, and lend him all the assistance he could, he retired to his own apartment, and flinging himself into a chair, he gave way for a few minutes in silence to the feelings of rage and disappointment which disturbed his mind.

"Everything," he observed at last, "seems at the present moment to have conspired to vex and disturb me. That infernal rascal, Grampus! there cannot now be any doubt of his designs, and I am afraid that my men will be too late to overtake him; but oh, if they should—oh, how dreadful shall be the punishment I will inflict upon him, as an example to the others;

but I do not believe that there is such another traitor among the whole of my crew; and then that will, to obtain possession of which I sacrificed the lawyer's life. For me to be so thoughtless as to leave that behind me, I must have been mad. No doubt it has fallen into the hands of the person who purchased the Hall of me, and, I dare say, has afforded him and others much amusement and speculation. Bah!—the thought is sickening. However, they cannot harm me by it, and not knowing the desperate character that I am, they cannot have any wish to do so. Still would I willingly give a thousand guineas at the present moment could I but once regain possession of it. It must be done; I must adopt some plan to obtain it; and I will not rest until I have succeeded. But how? I dare not make my appearance in that neighbourhood again to demand it, after the excitement that has been caused by the disappearance of the lawyer, Flora Clarendon, and William; for the old fools dared to suspect me of it, and no doubt they would soon get others to be of the same opinion. All these circumstances retard my anticipated pleasure, and it seems I am never to behold again her who is now securely in my power, for at present I am in no frame of mind to see her, and to play the soft and captivating lover. The Smuggler King, amidst all his triumphs, it appears, is doomed to continual vexations and disappointments. But it's no use repining; I must e'en make the best of it I can. What ho! Raker!"

"Here I am, captain," answered Sam, quickly entering; "what would you?"

"Have you made all the defensive preparations I instructed you to do?" asked the baronet.

"I have," answered Raker; "and I think we may set at defiance an enemy who may venture to attack us."

"That is well," observed the captain; "but you still think that Grampus has left the tower with a treacherous design?"

"What other design could he have in view?" demanded Sam.

"Curses on him!" exclaimed Sir Julian; "but he will have many leagues to voyage before he arrives at any place where he may lay information?"

"Unless he falls in with any vessels on his way," answered Sam; "or gives information at the neighbouring island."

"And there they are so superstitious that they would not believe him," remarked Sir Julian; "and such cowardly swabs that they would be afraid to attack us."

"Ay," answered Sam Raker; "or they would have done so before now. I do not think we have much to apprehend."

"Not much, Sam," repeated the baronet; "should the rascal Grampus reveal who I really am, there would be an end to my career on land, and an embargo laid upon my property."

"True; I did not think of that, captain," said Sam. "That certainly would be rather awkward."

"Awkward!" returned the captain, "it would be next to ruin. I cannot bear to think of it."

"I still entertain hopes that the smugglers will overtake the villain," observed Sam.

"The calm was certainly all against him," said Sir Julian; "and they will be sure to pull their very hardest."

"No doubt of it. But did you find what you went to seek on board the Raven, captain?" asked Raker.

"I did not," answered the baronet. "Curses on it; would you believe it, Sam, I have been that egregious fool to leave the will which I took from the old lawyer behind me at the Hall?"

"Ah!"

"It is true," added the captain; "and the circumstance disturbs me much, for it may be productive of some very unpleasant consequences to me."

"True," remarked Sam; "it is an unfortunate job, but still the lawyer and William are no more, and, therefore, what have you to fear?"

"Nothing particular, in that respect, that I know of," answered Sir Julian; "but still I would much rather that the document was at present in my possession."

"Why, certainly, it would be better," said Sam Raker; "but something may yet occur by which you may regain it."

"It may," coincided the baronet, "and when the present circumstances that vex and harass me have become settled, we must see whether we cannot think of some scheme to accomplish that desire."

"No doubt," remarked Raker, "we shall be able to hit upon one with our usual skill. You know that you may command my aid, and I believe I am rather clever in those sort of things."

"I fully estimate your value, Raker," said the captain; "and have always been ready to reward it."

"Ay, ay, captain," answered his ready creature, "I know all about that, and you know, also, that I have never grumbled."

"Right, right, Raker; but I am vexed and disturbed. Hand me the wine."

"Willingly," answered Sam, bringing the decanter and two glasses; "and, as I feel rather low-spirited myself, I do not mind taking a glass or so with you."

As the smuggler spoke, he filled both the glasses, and unceremoniously taking one himself, he exclaimed :—

"Well, here's confusion to all traitors, captain."

"Death to all traitors," vehemently cried the latter, and they both quaffed off the contents of the glasses.

"You have set a strict watch, Raker?" asked Sir Julian.

"I have obeyed all the orders you gave me, captain," answered Sam; "there is not a nook or a corner which is not ready to give any enemy that may venture to approach us a warm reception."

"'Tis well; I can always depend upon your promptitude."

"I have always given you reason to say so," said Raker. "But what of the girl?"

"Ah! have you seen her this morning?" demanded the captain.

"I have not; but when will you have an interview with her?"

"Not at present, not at present, Sam," hastily answered the baronet. "I am too much ruffled by what has occurred to be able to play the part I wish."

"Well, then, I suppose you will defer it till by and bye?"

"Yes; but she is quite safe?"

"How can she be otherwise? She cannot escape from the tower."

"No; that is impossible. Towards the evening, by which time I shall have become more composed, I will see her; my very soul pants for the interview."

"Well, captain," asked Raker, "and is that all you required of me?"

"It is," answered Sir Julian; "keep a sharp look out, and give me immediate notice should you see anything to excite your alarm."

"You may depend upon that, captain," answered Sam Raker, and having helped himself to another glass of wine, he quitted the room. Sir Julian continued in gloomy meditation for some time longer, and then walked forth from the tower to the rock, in order, if possible, to divert his thoughts.

While these events were going forward, our heroine and Maud were occupied in conversation, and expecting every moment the arrival of some messenger from the captain to summon the former to his presence; but when hour

after hour elapsed, and still they received no interruption, their surprise increased, and they could not form any idea as to the cause.

"Surely it is strange that he thus defers the interview after the peremptory commands he issued yesterday," said our heroine.

"It is, indeed," returned Maud; "something must have occurred to have prevented him."

"What can have happened to deter him from the meeting he was apparently so eager to seek?" asked Flora.

"I know not," returned her companion; "but we ought to feel grateful for it, for everything seems to favour our hopes."

"It does," coincided the damsel, "and Heaven send that it may continue to do so, until the generous unknown may have had time to accomplish his designs, and some assistance may arrive to deliver us from this dreadful state of confinement."

"My hopes are now more sanguine than ever," said Maud; "and if you have the ingenuity and self-possession to baffle the designs of the captain only for a few days, all may be well."

"Alas! I fear," remarked Flora, "that if the captain discovers that the smuggler has absconded, his suspicions will be excited; and he may either enforce his base designs or remove me to some other place."

"Nay, my dear Flora," remarked Maud, "you must not suffer such apprehensions to enter your mind, or it will unfit you for the meeting which, certainly, some time or other will take place."

"But do you not think that my ideas are reasonable?" asked our heroine.

"I do not," replied Maud, "for well I know that he has no place of greater security than this tower."

"But, if he thinks that it is likely to be attacked," added Flora, "is it not probable that he will run away from the threatened danger, and take with him in security his prize?"

No. 43

"Think you then the Smuggler King would ever desert his companions in the hour of danger?" demanded Maud; "indeed, you form but a faint and erroneous conception of his character, if you imagine that he would ever be guilty of so cowardly an action. No; he is ever foremost in the ranks of peril, and by his bold example gives his men the courage and ferocity of tigers."

"Oh, how I shudder at the bare idea of the dreadful scene of carnage that would follow were this tower to be attacked," said our heroine.

"It would indeed be terrible," observed her companion; "but I am used to such scenes, and it is not likely that you would witness much, if any of it."

"But you would not be torn from me?" said the damsel, with a look of anxiety.

"No, my dear Flora," answered Maud, "nothing but death should part us. But I do not think the captain would wish it, as he would be well aware how much you would need my society and consolation in that hour of trial."

"True," remarked Flora; "and, oh, how drearily and miserable would have passed my time, had not Providence kindly afforded me your sweet and soothing society."

"And most happy am I to think that I have been rendered the humble means in its hands," said Maud, "of soothing your sufferings; and I trust that the time is not far distant when we shall enjoy each other's company under very, very different circumstances."

"Heaven grant it," ejaculated Flora, "and how happy shall I ever be to call you my dearest friend."

"I know you will, my dear Flora," answered Maud, who was deeply affected at the simplicity yet sincerity of our heroine's manner.

Thus passed the time, and still they heard nothing from the captain; but ever and anon the confused sounds that reached their ears, convinced them that something unusual had happened in the tower. They could hear the smugglers hurriedly running to and fro, and ever and anon the gruff voice of Sam Raker, as he issued his commands, but they were unable to distinguish what he said. Then they heard a rattling sound, like the clashing of swords, or the clanking of chains. This was succeeded by the hasty banging to of heavy doors, and the lumbering noise as if of some ponderous weights being placed against them.

"Something of an unusual description must have occurred to cause all this uproar and confusion," said Flora, trembling.

"It does, indeed, sound like it," remarked Maud in reply, "but do not alarm yourself; no danger will come to us."

"The smugglers have missed their companion," said Flora.

"It is not unlikely that they have," answered Maud, "and that they are making preparations to defend themselves, in case of an attack."

"Heaven protect him from their power," said our heroine, "and assist him in the furtherance of his worthy designs."

"To that prayer I most heartily and sincerely respond," ejaculated her companion. "But if they have not discovered his absence till now, he has certainly had time to get beyond their reach, and may defy pursuit."

"And should he meet with those who have the power and the will to yield to his wishes, in a short time we may expect some assistance," remarked our heroine.

"We may," answered Maud; "and my hopes become stronger every moment."

Two more hours elapsed, and still they received no interruption; the confusion in the tower continued for some time, and then entirely ceased, and all became as silent as if every one had quitted the place. At length, however, they were aroused by a loud and tumultuous shouting outside which attracted them to the casement. They looked forth, and beheld the Devil Skipper and the Raven making their way towards the Death Rock.

"It is now quite evident," remarked Maud, "the smugglers have missed their companion, and are making every preparation in case of the approach of an enemy."

"Much as I dread such an event, at least, the slaughter which will most likely take place," observed our heroine, "it imparts some degree of consolation to me, as it convinces me that the stranger did not attempt to deceive us."

"It does," returned Maud ; "but I never entertained such an idea, for what motive, what interest could he possibly have in so doing?"

"True," returned the damsel. "Oh, how I shudder when I look on that vessel, where I witnessed the ——"

"Nay, my love," interrupted Maud ; "I must beg of you not to think of those things."

"I fain would not, but still it is not so easy to banish them from one's thoughts."

"I admit the truth of that," said Maud, "but it shows a worthy and virtuous firmness when we struggle under difficulties."

The vessels now neared the rock, and took up their positions on either side.

"It must be a powerful force that can defeat these, I should imagine," said our heroine, "and gain possession of this tower. The pirate-chief at present seems to have everything in his favour."

"Do not despair, Flora," observed Maud, "you know not what may happen to render the aspect of affairs very different."

They walked away from the casement, and Maud attempted by broaching other subjects, to divert the thoughts of the damsel from the harassing and bewildering subject that now engrossed them.

The morning passed away, the afternoon arrived, and yet it seemed as if it was not the intention of the smuggler-chief to disturb them that day. The evening came, it was a tempestuous one, and an impenetrable darkness reigned around. Harsh and loud blew the stormy wind, and the waves dashed against the rock with the most deafening sound ; the rain descended in torrents, the thunder rolled over the tower, and seemed to shake it to its foundation, while gleams of blue lightning shot through the casement, and played awfully around the apartment in which the females were seated. Flora clung in terror to Maud, and shuddered.

"How terrible is this storm," said the damsel.

"Fear not," said Maud ; "we are safe from danger, at least from the dangers of the tempest ; Heaven protect those who are exposed to its fury,—the poor houseless wanderer, or the hapless mariner, who now struggles, as it were, on the very brink of eternity."

Flora clasped her hands together, and raising her fine eyes solemnly towards Heaven, showed how sincerely and fervently she responded to the prayer of her companion. They then quitted that apartment, and entered the inner one, where they were less exposed to the vivid flashes of the lightning.

The men who had been sent in pursuit of Grampus had not yet returned, and, indeed, Sir Julian had not expected that they would have been able in the time. He had passed several hours, after he left the rock, and returned to the tower, in gloomy meditation upon the events of the day, and, having maturely deliberated upon everything, he had at last succeeded in bringing him to something like a degree of composure ; he had summoned Raker to his presence, and was about to send him to request the attendance of our heroine, when the storm commenced, and he started from his seat with considerable emotion.

"It is a terrible rough evening," he said ; "should our comrades be still on the ocean, they will certainly be lost."

"Nothing can save them in those open boats," observed Raker.

"Curses on the misfortunes that follow each other in such rapid succession," cried the baronet, fiercely; "it seems as if some infernal spell was upon me."

"Come, come, captain," remonstrated Raker, "it is no use hoisting signals of distress just yet; they may have put in at some place before this storm commenced, and if so, they are safe."

"They would not venture to do so," answered Sir Julian; "they would not be mad enough to do so, for they would be almost sure to be known. I would sooner they all went to the bottom than that. That villain Grampus will escape us, I am afraid, and if he does, we may expect a visit from the sharks in a short time."

"And, if they come, we are prepared to give them such a salute as they little expect, I dare say," returned Sam; "they will find it no easy matter to conquer the Devil Skipper and the Raven, which they must do before they will be permitted even to pay their respects to the tower on the Death Rock."

"Well, well," said Sir Julian, "we must make up our minds for the worst; the Smuggler King and his brave crew have had many a warm tussel with the enemy, and have always been triumphant; their hearts are as bold, and their arms as powerful as ever they were, and therefore it is strange indeed if they are to be conquered now."

"Conquered!" repeated Raker, "never! They must be lions in might, and myriads in numbers, to trample on the tigers of the seas. But that infernal lubber, Grampus, could I but lay my grappling irons upon him, I would never leave him until I had his heart from his carcase."

"You did wrong in suffering him to escape, when he taunted you in the manner you have described to me," said Sir Julian.

"True, captain," returned Raker, "I know I was wrong; but still, as he was an old messmate, and one who had been in many hard scrapes with us, I did not like to act without orders."

"I know not how it is," said the baronet; "but, although he conducted himself at all times with bravery, and ever seemed devoted to my cause, I always disliked that Grampus. There were times when certain observations would escape him that excited my suspicions; but at the very moment when I was about to call him to an account, he had a happy knack of turning the conversation, and appearing so plausible, that I blamed myself for having doubted him, and looked upon him as one of the most devoted of my subjects."

"He was a crafty knave," said Raker.

"He was," coincided the captain; "but by all the infernal host I swear, if ever he again falls into my clutches, he shall pay dearly for all his tricks."

"Of course his portion will be death, captain?" said Sam.

"Death!" repeated Sir Julian; "and that a death of the most lingering torment; there is no punishment that the mind can invent which can be too dreadful for the fellow who dares to turn traitor to the Smuggler King and his gallant crew."

"Confusion and destruction to all such fellows, say I," observed Raker; "and, mark my words, captain, though for a time he may escape us, sometime or other we shall board him, and then we will wreak our full vengeance on his traitorous head!"

"We will," exclaimed the captain; "but there is one thing that disturbs me."

"And what is that?"

"I have told you," answered Sir Julian; "should he meet with any vessel, he will be sure to reveal my real name, and even if we defeat the force that may be sent against us, which no doubt we shall, my private wealth and landed property will be sacrificed and the landsharks will be more upon the alert for me."

" Let us hope for better things, captain," said Sam Raker.

" What room is there for hoping better?" rejoined Sir Julian.

" Well, well," said Sam, " though to be sure that would be bad enough, still if they lay an embargo upon your private wealth, you will be as rich as any nobleman in the kingdom."

" But it will curtail my power," said the baronet, " spoil my glorious career on the land, in which I used so much to delight, and which assisted us so greatly in our other proceedings. It would be a bad job, Sam, a bad job."

" So it would," returned Raker ; " but then you see, captain, you are meeting troubles on the weather bow ; what you apprehend may never take place, and when it does, it will be time enough to complain ; mayhap, Grampus may be afraid to do anything of the kind ; mayhap, he may not be believed, mayhap, he may be caught before he has the opportunity of doing so ; and mayhap, he may have become food for sharks ere now."

" I wish I could believe as you would persuade me," observed the captain, " but I cannot."

" Why, I never saw you so confounded dull before in all the time we have cruised together, captain," observed Sam ; " but, depend upon it, everything will turn out better than you seem at present to think."

" I hope it may ; but that confounded will ; to think that I should leave that behind me, too."

" That certainly was rather a thoughtless affair ; but I do not see that it can do you much harm ; they will only see ——"

" That but a portion of my father's property was bequeathed to me," added Sir Julian.

" And the rest to your brother."

" My *brother !*"

" I know you do not like the title, and I ask your pardon for making use of it," said Sam ; " however, he is no more ; the old lawyer is no more, and therefore you have nought to fear. No one can dispute your claim to the whole."

" That crazy Marian," observed the baronet ; " I have often thought of her."

" And do you think that she was——"

" Lady Emmeline," added the baronet ; " I have no doubt of it."

" Well—she is also quieted," returned the villain ; " and consequently all his safe in that quarter."

" It may be so."

" It is so."

" Well, I admit that it is so," answered the baronet. " How violently the storm continues to rage, and our brave fellows not returned yet. They must perish."

" I suppose it is a fate we shall all come to some time or another—or the gallows," coolly replied Sam Raker.

" That may be," answered the captain ; " but we can ill afford to lose them at the present time ; we may much need their aid."

" I am sorry for them, but it can't be helped," remarked Sam Raker, in his usual tones. " But come—it's no use thus giving way to the horrors. What about the girl ?"

" Ah !" exclaimed the baronet.

" An interview with her might raise your spirits," added Sam.

" You are right, Sam—you are right," said Sir Julian : " I have delayed too long, and she will begin to think me an easy fool. It shall be so. Is the saloon lighted up ?"

" It is," answered Raker.

" Then I will repair there immediately to receive her, and feast my eyes on her transcendant charms. Away with you instantly, Sam, and bring her to me."

"Ay, captain," observed the ruffian, "now you are in the right vein; woman can either cure or ruin us. I will away directly, captain."

With these words Sam Raker departed, and Sir Julian made his way to the saloon, having quickly regained his composure at the thoughts of our heroine.

Flora and Maud had been listening to the roaring of the tempest, which still continued with unabated fury, with feelings of awe and terror, having given up all idea of the pirate-chief requesting an interview that night, when they were interrupted, in the midst of a conversation upon the subject, by a knock at the room door.

Our heroine started and turned pale, and her heart foreboded what was about to take place.

"It is a messenger from—from him!" she ejaculated. "Oh! I cannot —will not, go! I can never support the interview—my courage fails me, and I am ready to sink with terror at the bare idea."

"My dear girl," said Maud; "remember your promise; pray compose yourself."

In spite of all her efforts, a dreadful trembling came over the damsel; and, had it not been for the support she received from Maud, she must have sunk. The knock was repeated, and was followed by the gruff voice of Raker demanding admittance.

"It is useless," said Maud, "to offer any resistance; we must admit him."

Flora sunk into a chair, and Maud, hastening to the door, opened it, and admitted Raker, who frowned as he entered.

"I thought you were going to keep me at the door all night," he observed; "I think we have given you lenity enough. Come, young lady, you must accompany me to the saloon; our captain demands the interview, he has so long delayed, immediately.

"Oh, spare me!—spare me!" ejaculated our heroine; "indeed, I cannot go!"

"Cannot!" roughly answered Sam Raker; "but you must,—there's all the difference. As for sparing you, I have nothing to do with it,—my duty is to obey orders, and therefore you will oblige me by being as quick as possible."

"Not to-night!—not to-night!" gasped Flora, with supplicating looks.

"Not to-night!" repeated the ruffian; "but indeed it must be to-night, and that directly, too. You were accommodated last night till this morning, and you have had all this grace given to you,—therefore, I don't see how you can well object now. But, come,—the captain will become impatient; he is waiting to see you in the saloon."

Flora turned from the forbidding countenance of the villain with a shudder of horror. Maud whispered a few words of comfort and encouragement, and helped her to rise from the chair.

"Be firm, my dear Flora," she said; "trust to the purity of your own heart, and rest assured, though you are surrounded by every danger, no harm will come to you."

"Humph!" muttered Sam Raker, with a look of sarcasm, which Maud returned with one of utter contempt.

"You will not leave me, dear Maud," sobbed our heroine; "you will not—must not—shall not leave me."

"I will accompany you to the saloon," answered Maud; and she then added, turning to Raker, "I suppose I can do so?"

"Why," answered the ruffian, "I do not know whether I shall be doing right; but, as I've no orders to the contrary, why, you may e'en attend the lady; but be quick—heave a-head; I can't stand palavering here all night."

"Come, my love," kindly urged Maud, looking affectionately in the damsel's face.

Flora raised her tearful eyes towards Heaven, and breathed a silent prayer for its pretection. She then felt more firm, and suffering Maud to take her arm, she led her towards the door, the villain, Sam Raker, preceding them with the light. On their way to the saloon, the maiden was several times compelled to pause, to endeavour to regain her fortitude, which alternately failed her; at which times Sam Raker, stamped impatiently with his foot, and fixed a significant, and not very pleasing look upon Maud. The latter, however, viewed him with perfect indifference and contempt, and devoted her whole attention to the poor trembling damsel whom she attended.

At length they reached the door of the saloon,—and here the feelings of our heroine so much overpowered her, that it was not without the greatest difficulty that Maud could prevent her from fainting. No sounds came from the saloon; but there was a dazzling light issuing from the crevices of the door, and the most delightful odour breathed its fragrance around. This, with the soft and gentle soothings of Maud, tended to revive the poor girl,—and, inspired with a sudden feeling of fortitude, she looked up, and with an expression of countenance which renewed the hopes of her companion, she said—

"I am ready,—lead me to the tyrant in whose power I am, and let him see how firmly virtue and injured innocence can withstand his empty allurements, and defy his unprincipled designs."

Raker grinned a grin of fiendish scorn and exultation as he threw open the folding doors of the saloon, and escorted Flora and Maud into that spacious and elegant apartment.

For a second or two, notwithstanding her recent courage, the senses of our heroine appeared to whirl round, and it was fortunate that she had the supporting arm of Maud, or she must have sunk to the earth.

A delightful fragrance filled the apartment, exhaled from the breath of various flowers, that were placed in vases in numerous recesses. But all was silent, and denoted that no one was present. Sam Raker, having fulfilled his task, left them, and Maud took the opportunity to whisper to our heroine,—

"Courage—courage, my dear Flora; exert that fortitude you have just boasted, and all will be well."

"You are still with me, Maud," said Flora, looking affectionately in her face, "and I will not droop. I will indeed be firm, for there is a just God above, who will protect the innocent, and set at nought all the evil machinations of the guilty."

"He will, indeed, my dear Flora," said Maud, "and it pleases me to hear the confidence you feel."

"Why should I feel otherwise?" returned the damsel. "Have I ever injur'd any one? Never! and Heaven is my witness that I have not; therefore can I place a firm reliance on its Almighty protection."

"You can—you can," energetically replied Maud, "and the Smuggler King will shrink abashed beneath its influence, which will speak from your eyes. Remember the note—live in hopes—battle with the tyrant, and his intentions will be foiled, and a few days will see you restored to liberty, and I hope to happiness."

"Oh! Maud," ejaculated the damsel, "without your soothing voice, what a poor, miserable wretch I should be. To you am I indebted for life, for everything. But you will not leave me, Maud?"

"I will not, my dear girl," answered Maud, "if I can help it; but, if I am compelled, let not your courage forsake you, but recollect that your oppressor is but a mortal man, and that there is a Supreme Power watching over you, who will protect you from all the evils that his base mind may contemplate. Be firm, and you will escape unscathed and free."

"But you must not, *shall* not leave me, dear Maud," ejaculated the damsel, in her most fervent manner. "I shall much need your soothing voice, your gentle consolation, your kind encouragement, to support me through this painful trial."

"My dear Flora," observed Maud, much affected, "if it is possible for me to remain with you, you know, full well, I will; but if I should be compelled to leave you, support it with fortitude; let not your energies forsake you; reply to the observations of the captain as virtue and conscious rectitude will be sure to dictate to you, and, whatever his designs may be, rest assured that he will be frustrated, and in a short time you will return to me braced with new courage, and ready to battle with all his future advances, until Providence shall interpose to rescue you from your present situation, and restore you to that state of happiness and serenity from which you have been so cruelly and unjustly taken, my dear Flora."

"Sweet comforter!" exclaimed our heroine, throwing herself sobbing and affectionately into Maud's arms, "I will be guided entirely by your advice, and, as I deserve it, so Heaven protect me."

Maud embraced her, and they remained silent for a few moments, giving free vent to the emotions that throbbed both of their bosoms.

Flora now looked up, and the scene which presented itself to her gaze completely astonished her and dazzled her sight. We have before described the magnificence and taste which were displayed in the arrangements of this saloon, and now being brilliantly illuminated, it had more the appearance of some scene of fairy land, than the residence of mortal being, much more the heartless being who presided over it. Nothing could possibly surpass the taste and elegance with which everything was arranged, and, as the eyes of the damsel hastily wandered over it, she could scarcely believe but that she was under the influence of some delusive vision. But quickly other thoughts darted across her mind, and, when she reflected that all she gazed upon was merely got up by the miscreant in whose power she was, to dazzle the senses and entrap his unfortunate victims, she turned from them with a feeling of sickening disgust, and once more hid her face in the bosom of the affectionate and sympathising Maud, who had watched her countenance with the most deep and scrutinizing interest, and really trembled in anticipation of the moment when the much-feared Smuggler King should make his appearance.

Several minutes elapsed, and still they were left alone, and that interval was one of suspense and agony to our heroine which she had never before experienced.

The manner in which Sir Julian conducted all his proceedings, as has been seen, was most studied and romantic. His first object was to dazzle by all the glitter of show; to bewilder the senses, that he might more readily acquire a sort of feeling of awe and admiration over those whom he intended to destroy; and many were the unfortunate maidens whom he had conquered by these means. But in our heroine he had a far different mind to contend with. No empty show could delude her imagination; she looked upon it with contempt and disgust. Strong in all the virtues that adorn the sex, she felt herself proof against all the allurements that could be held out to her.

preaches the saloon; doubtless it is him. Now, Floff, come show us the

conjure you to be firm, and all good angels guide and protect you through——

A deadly sickness came over the maiden, but still she was inspired with fortitude, and looked upon the countenance of those whose expression which convinced her that she was fully prepared for the event. The footsteps approached nearer, and suddenly the folding doors at the further end of the saloon were thrown open, and Sir Julian Mortlington, attended, appeared, and after pausing for a few moments, he advanced to the centre of the apartment, and gazed with feelings of admiration at the graceful form of the lovely and gentle Flora, who had once more hidden her face in the bosom of Maud.

Sir Julian was attired in the same manner as we have described he was on the previous evening, and his appearance altogether was most commanding and romantic. He looked like one of those ideal characters we so often read of in the pages of a romance, and his countenance was such, which, at first glance, was every way formed to captivate. But the illusion was but brief to the penetrating eye; soon would it detect the lurking demon, in its lineaments, and turn with shuddering disgust from the being they were at first constrained to admire.

Sir Julian approached nearer to our heroine, and then again paused, and fixed his earnest gaze upon her. Never, he imagined, had he beheld so fair a form, and often had he been dazzled by the loveliness of her countenance. A far different feeling came over him than he had usually experienced under such circumstances, and he might be said to feel a mixture of awe, admiration, and ungovernable desire, unable to subdue his compassion.

Flora knew his presence; but yet she dared not look up. Maud whispered to her a few words of encouragement, and the poor girl pressed her hand in acknowledgment of it.

"Beauteous damsel," at length ejaculated the baronet, in the tenderest and most impassioned accents he could assume, "why conceal that lovely face from him who adores thee, is ready to become thy slave?"

"Ah!" exclaimed Flora, starting suddenly from the embraces of Maud; "that voice—those tones!"

"Confusion!" muttered Sir Julian, aside; "she recognizes my voice; I must be cautious. It is impossible she can remember my features, disguised as they are."

He then added aloud,—

"Sweet Flora, why this reserve? Look up, fair girl, and gladden the heart of thy lover with thy radiant smiles."

"My *lover*!" repeated the damsel, raising her head, and gazing with a look of astonishment, yet revolting disgust and horror at the libertine. "My *lover*!" she repeated, emphatically; "he rests beneath the dark blue waves, consigned to his watery grave by thy murderous creatures."

The baronet was unprepared for such an answer, returned with such firmness and point, and it somewhat staggered him, and he shrunk beneath the reproachful glances of her he had destined for his victim. He, however, quickly recovered himself, and making no immediate reply to the observations of our heroine, he turned to Maud, and in an authoritative tone, he said,—

"Quit the room, Maud."

"Oh, sir," exclaimed the latter, "I intreat you to let me remain. Flora is not well, she has suffered much from her imprisonment, and——"

"Begone! croaking raven," fiercely cried the baronet, and stamping furiously on the floor.

"Let me not leave her," again supplicated Maud; "she may need my support, she ——"

"Away!" fiercely interrupted Sir Julian; "you know full well what it is to disobey my commands."

Flora clung frantically to Maud, and looked at the captain with a feeling of horror, which she could not control.

"Maud! Maud!" she ejaculated; "remain with me. "Do not leave me alone with this cruel man."

The baronet bit his lips, but he stifled his rage in a moment, and in a voice of the softest persuasion, but in which, to the keen perception of our heroine, the villain and the hypocrite lurked throughout, he said,—

"Beauteous Flora, you know me not yet, or you would not use these harsh expressions. But I can excuse you; the world, the idle, prejudiced world, have pictured me as a monster, and ——"

"And," rejoined our heroine, with the most astonishing firmness, "my heart convinces me that the world has not exaggerated the portrait. Dare guilt and cruelty like thine contaminate the virtuous and the pure with thy odious presence?"

The baronet was astonished, and knew not what answer to make. He was quite unprepared for such a reception, and his countenance fully betrayed his emotion.

"By Jupiter," he muttered to himself, "I must be upon my guard, or this fair maiden will be more than a match for the Smuggler King."

Flora continued to gaze at him with a look of hatred and contempt, and she felt at the same moment the most unaccountable fortitude take possession of her mind.

"Dear Flora," at length the smuggler captain observed, once more approaching her, and attempting to take her hand, which she withdrew with feelings of the utmost abhorrence, and which seemed completely to abash him; "dear Flora," he repeated, "surely your gentle and generous nature will not humble itself to the prejudice of the world; you will not be influenced by what you have heard, but judge of me by my conduct towards you. Fear not to trust yourself alone with me, for believe me, I intend you no harm."

"You dare not attempt it," returned the damsel, "in the name of that High Heaven, whose protection I invoke, I tell you, you dare not."

"Leave the room," repeated Sir Julian, to Maud, turning to her in a more commanding tone than before; "am I to be obeyed?"

"She shall not, must not leave me," repeated the damsel, still clinging to Maud, and looking disdainfully upon the baronet; "if your intentions are not base, you will not refuse to suffer that kind being to remain with me, during this hateful interview, who has been my only comforter under the injuries and cruelty I have experienced."

"My beauteous girl," observed the captain, who could not, however, without the greatest difficulty stifle his rage, at the cutting observations which our heroine directed towards him, "I have before assured you that I intend you no wrong, and that assurance I now repeat; but we must be alone: I have that to say to you which must be heard by no ears but your own. But a short time, but a few minutes, and our interview will be at an end, and you shall return in safety to the apartments you have quitted. I cannot, must not forego that pleasure for which I have so long panted."

Flora's fortitude almost forsook her, and she trembled; but she knew it was no use opposing the will of the smuggler captain, and mentally committing herself once more to the care of the Almighty, she turned with a look of resignation towards Maud, who smiled sweetly upon her.

"Woman!" exclaimed Sir Julian, impatiently, "have you not heard my commands? Begone, I say; and when your presence is required to conduct Flora once more to her apartments, I will summon you."

"I go," replied Maud, with an air of firmness, the baronet had never before beheld her assume; "I go, sir, but, mark me! If you attempt to injure, or outrage the feelings of this innocent girl, may the vengeance of Heaven immediately descend upon your head, and crush you!"

The baronet started back in amazement, and could scarcely believe the evidence of his senses; to be thus braved, and by a woman, whom he had ever considered as his most abject slave, it was almost more than he could endure with any degree of patience; but prudence told him that, for the present, he must stifle his indignation and dissemble, although he determined at some future period to have ample revenge for the insult which he considered that Maud had offered to his dignity and power.

"I can excuse the boldness of your words, Maud," he, at length, said, "and am gratified that you have behaved with so much kindness to my fair ward; but I tell you once for all, that I intend the damsel no harm, and in less than half an hour our interview will be at an end. Leave us."

Maud embraced our heroine once more, and then slowly left the saloon.

Flora sunk on a sofa, and covering her face with her hands, felt the utmost suspense and dread at the observations which Sir Julian might address to her. She could not divest her mind of the impression which the tones of the Smuggler King, when she first heard them, had made upon her, and she was certain that she had heard them before, but where she could not imagine, and he had since disguised them, so that she had no further opportunity of judging. Of his features, she had also some recollection, but there she was equally at a loss to decide positively where she had seen them before, and she was lost in these conjectures, when Sir Julian approached her, and attempted to take her hand; she recoiled from him with a feeling of the greatest dread and detestation; and had she been in the presence of a supernatural being she could not have felt greater horror.

"Beauteous, all-bewitching maiden," said the hypocrite, "why thus turn away from me as if I were some hideous monster, whom it were instant death to gaze upon? Oh! let me look at those brilliant eyes, and bask in their sunny radiance."

The bosom of the indignant damsel swelled with the power of her emotions; she raised her head, and fixed upon Sir Julian her looks, but they were those of abhorrence and disgust, and, in tones, that thrilled even to his stubborn heart, she cried,—

"Heartless man, why am I brought hither?"

"To hear the vows of one who would become thy slave," returned Sir Julian, sinking on one knee; "to hear the fervent protestations of a man, who wishes to make it his whole study to please thee; to worship thee; to pour forth in thine ears the sincere and fervent acknowledgements of his adoration. Lovely Flora, here, at thy feet, kneels one whose only hope of happiness rests in thee. Turn then not those looks of scorn upon him, which appear to freeze him into ice, and to sap the whole of his vitals."

"Forbear! forbear!" ejaculated the maiden; "shock not mine ears with thine odious vows, in every one of which is pollution."

"Say not so, beauteous creature," said Sir Julian, forcibly taking her hand, and pressing it to his lips; "oh! how little do I deserve such words from one whom I am prepared to love, to adore."

"Love!" repeated the damsel; "and dare the Smuggler King, the robber of the seas, pollute the sacred word of love, by giving it utterance? forbear! I will not listen to thee."

"Sweet Flora," returned Sir Julian; "even in thy scorn there is a sweetness that charms and bewilders my senses. But those rosy lips were formed to utter different words to those; they were formed for love, and to breathe nothing but its fragrance."

"Hypocrite!" ejaculated our heroine.

"Hypocrite!" repeated Sir Julian; "in the wild profession to which fate has destined me, I may deserve that title, but never from thee, beauteous Flora. No; I would lay open to you all my soul, clear, as in a mirror, the countenance is reflected; and there you will behold your name imprinted in characters that nothing can ever eradicate,—that soul which for some time has been devoted to thee, and thee alone. Forms of transcendant loveliness have charmed my senses, and rivetted my attention, but they have all—all failed before thine, and my heart assures me it must be thy slave, until it shall cease to beat."

While the villain was making this speech, the feelings of our heroine may be much better imagined than described. Her heart palpitated violently, and the blood circulated quickly through her veins. Sir Julian still continued on his knee, and the energy of his manner had added eloquence to his looks. His eyes darted forth an unusual fire, but our heroine turned from him with increased feelings of abhorrence, while at the same time she felt endowed with a fortitude which she never expected she should have been able to acquire.

"Sweet lady," at length Sir Julian resumed, "why avert thy looks from me as if I were something loathsome? Will you not bless my ears with one kind word?"

"And can a man like you," replied Flora, "thus dare to talk, thus dare to profane the ears of innocence with your blasphemous language? One whose name is a terror to all the world; whose deeds are those of darkness and of blood? One who prowls upon the defenceless, and delights in the miseries of his fellow-creatures; who mocks at the word honour, and glories in being considered the greatest villain of the day. Away! my blood chills at the sight of you."

"Fair maiden," observed the baronet, "I could bear all these reproaches from other lips than thine; but from thee they fall like liquid fire upon my heart. 'Tis true I am a smuggler, a pirate; unforeseen circumstances, fate, and misfortune, have made me so; mankind have pursued me, and it is but just that I should retaliate upon mankind. But you have the power to change my very nature; and though I may not be permitted to change my wild and roving life, say that you will love me, and, as my bride, you shall reign the ocean queen, over subjects more faithful, though not so numerous, as ever monarch ruled."

"Heartless man!" exclaimed Flora; "cease—cease thus to insult my ears."

"Nay," returned Sir Julian; "believe me, I speak the sincere sentiments of my heart, a heart that, in spite of the character the world has given me, is susceptible to the tenderest emotions, where beauty such as thine strikes its chords. Oh! how I would worship, would adore thee. I have wealth unbounded, no prince possesses greater power or riches; all—all—will I willingly lay at thy feet, and bend alone the slave of thy will. There is not a luxury, not a pleasure that human heart can wish, which shall not be at thy command, and in thy smiles alone will the Smuggler King seek his happiness! Avert not thy looks, for all is darkness without them; but to gaze on thy lovely features is Heaven itself, and worth a life of suffering to enjoy."

Flora still hid her blushing countenance with her hands, and her emotions were almost beyond endurance. She felt the eloquence of the libertine, but her heart revolted from him as if he had been one of the infernal host. All the horrors of the crimes she had heard he had committed arose to her memory, and her blood chilled at the recollection.

"Not one word," at length said Sir Julian; "not one word of kindness to him who would freely sacrifice his life for your sake?"

"Hypocrite!" scornfully retorted Flora, "can you thus talk, you who have torn me from my home, my parents, all that was dear to me, and perhaps left them broken-hearted? Can you thus talk, who have deprived me of liberty, and confined me in this fearful place amongst wretches from whom my nature revolts with horror, and who would not hesitate a moment in shedding my innocent blood at the word of their lawless commander? Dare you talk of love to her, whose love you have murdered. Away—away!—I dare not gaze upon you! Your hands still seem to reek with his blood."

Sir Julian arose from his knees, unable for a few moments to return an answer, and paced the apartment in a state of mingled rage and confusion. His conscience smote him with the justice of our heroine's observations, and being unprepared for so much firmness in one whom he had expected to find all meekness and submission, he was completely confounded. He, however, soon conquered his emotions, and turning to Flora, he observed :—

"Your observations are too harsh, fair Flora, and I deserve them not. 'Tis true that I have torn you from your home; but to that I was urged by the impetuosity of my love, and the fear that you would not listen to my vows; but I could not live without you, and though my heart revolted from the deed, there was no other course left me. 'Tis true that you are my prisoner, but in this tower there is nothing which you may not command, and immediately have, and say that you will become my bride, and that instant that makes you mine, shall also make you free as air. As for your lover, I slew him not."

"But your myrmidons did," answered our heroine; "and, doubtless, they acted by your orders. The wretches! But, oh! the curse of Heaven will assuredly descend upon their murderous heads."

"He is not dead," answered Sir Julian.

"Not dead," repeated Flora, with a look of the most bitter anguish. "Oh! you would deceive me!"

"I would not; William Backstay lives!" answered Sir Julian.

"Lives—lives!" almost shrieked our heroine; "oh, where?"

"I know not."

"Is he not in your power?"

"He is not."

"Where, then, is he?"

"At liberty!"

"At liberty!" exclaimed Flora, clasping her hands. "Gracious Heaven, I thank thee. But still, I cannot believe you; still I am confident you only seek to deceive me by exciting false hopes."

"I do not," answered the captain; "but why continue to think of one who can never be yours?"

"And why not?" demanded the maiden.

"Because," replied Sir Julian, "thou hast won my heart, and never will the Smuggler King permit her upon whom he has fixed his whole soul to become the bride of another."

"Oh! relent—relent!" ejaculated Flora; "restore me to liberty, to my lover, and I will pardon thee all that I have suffered, and though I can never love thee, I will endeavour to bestow on thee my esteem."

"Esteem!" repeated Sir Julian with a look of scorn, "no; the Smuggler King is not to be satisfied with so cool a sentiment. He must have love, free and undivided love, from that being whom in return he is prepared to worship as an angel. But, oh! Flora, why will you persist in refusing to make another and a worthy being of that man who will think no sacrifice too great for your sake? You may find gentler tongues, more prepossessing forms than those I possess, but never one who can love you so sincerely, so ardently as I do."

" What shameless mockery is this," said our heroine, with a look which spoke much more than any language, however powerful and eloquent, could have done; " can I, think you, forget the dreadful crimes you have perpetrated? Can I cease to remember that you are the feared of mankind, existing by plunder, and associated with deeds of blood? Can I ever forget that you heartlessly tore me away from that happy home, which has thus been rendered desolate? Can I banish from my recollection the scene which passed between me and William Backstay on board your vessel? Can I ever believe otherwise, unless I were permitted to see him, that he fell a victim to your cruelty and crime, and that his blood now calls for vengeance on your head? Banish these ideas from my brain, if you can, and then, and not till then, attempt to talk of love to the unhappy and deeply injured Flora Clarendon."

" Dear Flora," returned Sir Julian, " this is but a fruitless waste of time, and will tend to no purpose. You are in my power; my passion is not to be subdued, and ——"

" Ah!" eagerly interrupted our heroine, " you now unmask yourself, if you thought to deceive me before. You stand confessed a heartless villain, and all the revolting tales I have heard of you are confirmed. Miscreant, I will listen to you no longer; your words are odious to me, and your looks inspire no other feelings but those of horror and disgust; death would be preferable to becoming the bride of such a monster as thou art!"

Sir Julian frowned, and bit his lips; he felt keenly the reproaches of our heroine, and, unable any longer to conceal his rage, he said,—

" 'Tis well, young lady, but when you have exhausted all these heroics, you may have the satisfaction of knowing that they have no more effect on me than the idle wind. Again I remind you that you are entirely in my power, and that in a moment I could force you to my will, but that I would win you by softer measures. But of this rest assured,—I have made up my mind, and you never more quit this tower but as the Smuggler's Bride."

His looks were expressive of determination as he spoke, and he traversed the room with hasty strides. Flora was now quite overcome by anguish and despair, and sinking on her knees to Sir Julian, she exclaimed,—

" Oh! sir, if you have any mercy left within your breast, revoke that dreadful doom. On my knees I implore you; I, a poor innocent, defenceless girl, who never injured you, I beg of you to give me death, rather than dishonour."

" It is in your power to command me, and make me thy slave, fair damsel," said the pirate-chief, raising her from her knees, and looking affectionately in her countenance; " why will you obstinately delay the consummation of that happiness? Say you will be mine, my bride,—and the moment that vow is ratified, I swear that I will restore you to liberty and your friends."

" The wife of a pirate, a smuggler!" returned our heroine, shuddering, " never! Whatever my fate may be, I will learn to submit to it, but never will I consent to become the bride of a man I must ever detest."

" Detest!" savagely repeated Sir Julian, between his teeth; " you had better recal those words—you know not to whom you speak."

" I know you for the desperate marauder of the seas, calling yourself the Smuggler King," said Flora, firmly; " what else are you?"

" That you may know anon, and then you will find that I am no low-bred hind, but that my power is as great upon land as on the sea. But enough of this; I repeat, fair maiden, that to you my whole soul is devoted—I would make you happy, and you will find none that can love you better than he whom you have called the marauder of the seas. But to show you that I am sincere in what I assert, I wish not to take any unfair advantage of you. I will give you time to consider of my offers, and endeavour to convince you that I am not altogether deserving of your hatred. Farewell, beauteous Flora, our interview is at an end. I will send Maud to re-escort you to your apartments."

Thus saying, Sir Julian attempted to kiss her hand, but she withdrew it from him, and fixing upon her a look of affection, he retired from the saloon by the same way he had entered.

Flora felt a great relief when he had departed, but for several moments she was lost in amazement and confusion at all he had uttered. Still the tones of his voice, although he had sought to disguise them, were familiar to her, and she could not help thinking that his features she had seen before. That he was a man of superior birth and education she could not but feel convinced; his language and his manners fully confirmed that, and it surprised her that such an individual should ever take to such a guilty course of life. It removed her heart of a heavy weight when this so long dreaded interview was at length over, and although she felt certain from the words of the pirate-chief that he would never voluntarily release her, without she consented to become his bride, his forbearance and the promise he had made to allow her time to reflect upon his proposal, re-assured her, and inspired her with hope that something in the meantime would occur to rescue her from his power.

She was interrupted in these reflections by the entrance of Maud, who rushed into her arms, and our heroine wept upon her bosom.

"It is over, my dear Maud," she sobbed; "the much dreaded meeting is over, and my mind is greatly relieved from the heavy burthen which oppressed it."

"Thanks to Heaven for that," ejaculated Maud; "but come, my dear girl, let us hasten to our apartments, where we may more freely converse, and you may regain composure after the painful trial you have undergone."

Flora made no reply, but leaning on the arm of Maud, they left the saloon, and immediately made their way to the apartments they occupied in the tower, which having reached, they locked themselves in, and Flora sinking into a chair, for some time gave free indulgence to her feelings, in which Maud did not offer to interrupt her.

"My dear Maud," she at last observed; "oh! what a subtle villain is this pirate-chief; but certain I am that I have somewhere seen him before."

"Indeed?" said Maud.

"Yes," added our heroine; "and I cannot help thinking that you know I have."

"My dear Flora," observed her companion, "why should you think so?"

"I know not," returned Flora; "but do you know his real name?"

"I do," answered Maud.

"And yet you refuse to reveal it to me?" said the damsel.

"Flora," observed Maud, "why continue to urge me upon that subject, when I have already assured you that I am bound by such an oath, as I cannot, dare not venture to break, nor disclose it?"

"Well, well," answered the damsel, "pardon me, Maud; I was wrong; I will not speak upon that subject again."

"But how did your interview terminate?" eagerly inquired her companion.

Flora now, as well as she was able, related all the particulars of it, to which Maud listened with an attention which showed the deep interest she took in it; and, when our heroine had concluded, she remarked,—

"Your conduct, my dear Flora, throughout the whole of this interview, is worthy of the highest praise, and from it you may date the forbearance of the

captain. Did I not tell you that such would be the result, if you acted as I advised you?"

"You did," answered our heroine, "and to you, therefore, am I indebted for my present preservation."

"And if you continue to act in the same manner," remarked Maud, "you may baffle the designs of the captain until something transpires to release you altogether from his power."

"Oh! Heaven send that your predictions may be verified," returned the damsel.

"They will—I feel convinced they will," said Maud; "our unknown friend will succeed in his worthy efforts, and in a day or two there will probably be such a force appear at the Death Rock, that the Smuggler King and his ruffianly crew will find it impossible to withstand."

"But he seems to entertain no fear of approaching danger," observed Flora.

"It is not likely that he would exhibit it before you, my dear girl," answered Maud. "However, we have had sufficient proof that he is alarmed, from the precautions he has taken, and the preparations he has made for defence, in case of an attack."

"True," coincided the maiden; "but should the chances be in his favour, as they have hitherto been in all other contests, our situation would then be probably worse off than ever."

"There cannot be much to apprehend from that, Flora," said her companion.

"Rendered desperate by the attack made on him," returned our heroine, "and fearful that something might occur to release me from him, he would most likely remove me to some other place of security, where I might be deprived of your society, and he would enforce the gratification of his diabolica wishes."

No. 45

"You always entertain the most gloomy and fearful ideas, my poor girl," said her companion; "but, for my own part, I fear no such result. Your innocence will keep him in awe, and your firm resistance will be a check upon his brutal passions; but, once lose the latter, he would be sure to take advantage of it, and then indeed would you be entirely lost."

"I will pray to God to continue my strength of mind," answered Flora, "and endeavour to look with calmness and self-possession upon my situation. But he said that my William, my beloved William, lives! Oh, can that be true?"

"Humbly beseech Heaven that it may be so," replied Maud, anxious to evade that question, "and that he may have escaped all the perils with which he may have been surrounded."

"But, no; it cannot be," added Flora, after a pause, during which she passed her fair hand across her forehead, and seemed to be recalling some painful recollection; "that cannot be; had my dear William escaped, I am certain that he would not have rested a day without devising some means to find me out, and to effect my deliverance. Oh, no; he is no more—he is no more!—and never again shall we meet, until we are united to each other in Heaven."

After some other conversation of a similar description, Flora became more composed, and at length was so much recovered, as to be able to listen with some degree of interest and attention to the contents of a volume which Maud read to her, in order to divert her thoughts and alleviate the distresses of her mind. In this manner they passed two or three hours; and, having partaken of some refreshment, they sought repose.

The storm, which had raged so violently, had now entirely subsided, and to it succeeded a similar calm to that of the previous day and night; it was wonderful to look upon the waters, and to notice the change which but a few short hours had wrought. Her mind, released from the dreadful state of anxiety and suspense that had before harassed it, Flora slept soundly, and awoke not until the dawn of day the following morning.

"The obdurate girl!" soliloquised Sir Julian, as he quitted the saloon, after his interview with our heroine; "by Jupiter, she foiled me at every point. I did not expect to meet with such a resistance; but she knew me not, and what has taken place has the more inflamed my passions. She is lovely as beauty's self, and might almost win a man from crime to virtue. Psha! what am I talking about? I am getting a very fool! But she is entirely in my power, and I am determined that she shall become mine. I will not, however, be too hasty, and I do not yet despair but that I shall be able to win her to my will. Oh, the fire of those brilliant eyes!—enough to light up the most insensible soul, and raise it to admiration and love. Never did Nature mould a fairer form! What symmetry—what grace—what elegance! By every power, she is a fit partner for an absolute monarch, and would enslave the most stubborn heart."

He was interrupted by a loud laugh, and, turning round hastily, to see who it was that had been so bold, he beheld Sam Raker.

"Ha! ha! ha! captain," again laughed the smuggler; "you are fairly caught by this fair craft."

"You are right, Sam," returned Sir Julian; "I confess that she has completely bewildered my senses."

"Then, I suppose, from that, you mean to say that the interview you have had with her has pleased you," said Raker, "and that she has given you a favourable reception?"

"Quite different, Raker," answered the baronet; "she received me in a manner that I never expected. She is as invulnerable as a rock of adamant."

"But no doubt, you will soon find the way to make an impression on her, eh, captain?" observed Raker.

"I will strive my best endeavours to do so," said Sir Julian ; "but I do not flatter myself that I shall succeed."

"Well," remarked the ruffian, "you have her safe enough, and, if she remains obstinate, perhaps a little violence may force her to comply."

"I know not how it is, Sam," remarked Sir Julian ; "but I feel a strange reluctance to use violence towards this fair girl ; and, if I could win her by fair means, I should think myself the happiest fellow in existence."

"Psha !" ejaculated Raker ; "why, you used not always to be so nice, captain ; besides, what was the use of taking the trouble to seize the damsel, and bringing her here, if you were not determined in your purpose ? You might have been very certain that she would never willingly consent to become the bride of the Smuggler King."

"True," answered the baronet, "but do not imagine that I mean to abandon my designs, Raker ; no, no—I would sooner resign my gallant ship, the saucy Devil Skipper, into the hands of the landsharks, than I would resign the determination of making Flora Clarendon my bride."

"Ay, captain," observed Raker ; "now you speak something like yourself. But did she recognize you ?"

"At first she seemed to remember my voice," answered Sir Julian, "but I afterwards disguised it, and all passed off very well."

"You acted prudently, I think, in not letting her know who you really are," said Sam Raker.

"I think I did," returned the baronet, "for although there is not much chance of her now escaping out of my clutches, should ever such an accident have taken place, my secret would have been divulged at once."

"It would," answered Sam Raker. "But you see the storm has subsided."

"I am glad to see it," replied the baronet, "and I hope that our brave fellows have been able to weather it, and will shortly return to the tower.'

"Ay, and bring us some intelligence of Grampus," added Sam.

"Bring the rascal with them, altogether, I trust," remarked the captain ; "or my secret will have been already divulged, and my landed property in England not worth a shilling purchase."

"The fellow will never be so daring."

"Daring ! What think you he has left the tower for," demanded Sir Julian, "but to betray me, and secure the large reward which is offered for that purpose ?"

"Curses light upon him," exclaimed Sam Raker, "and place him once more within our power, and if you will only leave the punishment of him to me, I'll warrant that I will do the business to your satisfaction, and feel a pleasure in it."

"It shall be so, Sam," said the baronet ; "and I only hope that I may have occasion to request your services in that respect."

"But what do you mean to do with the girl ?" asked Sam.

"I have before told you," answered Sir Julian, "that I mean to give her a few days to reflect on my proposal, and then if she does not consent, I will force her to compliance."

"That's what I would do at once," said Sam Raker ; "but you know best, it is not my place to dictate to you."

"I do not like to be too precipitate," remarked the captain ; "as I have before told you, the girl has made a remarkable impression upon me, and I am resolved to try what effect my eloquence will have over her stubborn nature."

"Well, captain," remarked Raker, "I wish you much joy with your task ; for my own part, my loving days are almost over, and ——"

"Nay," interrupted Sir Julian, with a smile ; "if I guess aright, you had once a sneaking regard for Maud."

"Ay," answered the smuggler ; "I had, and still have something of a sneaking fancy for her, I believe; but she bears me about as much love as a seaman does a full grown swab of a marine,"

"Ha! ha!" laughed the captain; "and, if all I have heard is true, she has not much reason to entertain a different sentiment towards you."

"Why," answered Sam Raker, "for the matter of that, I don't think she has. You see, captain, Montrose, who was formerly captain of our ship, the Dragon, took a fancy to her; she was staying at the cottage of my parents, and having informed him of that, he got me to bear her away for him, which I did, and executed it in a business-like manner."

"Well," remarked Sir Julian, "that was one way of making love, at any rate, bearing away the object of your affections for another man."

"Why, so it would have been, captain," said the smuggler, "if that had been the case; but you see, the *tender god* had not smitten me then; I did not feel the *pangs* of love till after Montrose was killed!"

"Ha! ha! ha!" laughed the smuggler-captain; "no doubt your susceptible heart suffered most keenly from unrequited love?"

"Suffered! ay, I believe yer; the 'Sorrows of Werter' was nothing to it."

"Well," said the captain; "see that all is right, and meet me early again in the morning."

"Ay, ay, captain," answered the ruffian, and they immediately separated, the captain retiring to his chamber where he passed some time in meditation upon the events of evening, before he retired to rest. In spite of the natural baseness of Sir Julian's character, and the unlawful designs he contemplated against her, he could not help admiring the strict integrity and firmness of her conduct; and he really felt towards her a very different sentiment to that he had experienced for any of his former victims. Her extreme beauty, her innocence, and the forcible eloquence with which she had appealed to him, had made a deep impression upon him, and filled him with admiration. When he reflected upon the untimely fate her lover had met with, and indirectly through his means, he could not help entertaining a feeling of pity towards her, and one of regret that Sam Raker had not spared William's life, more especially when he reflected that there could be very little doubt that unfortunate youth was his brother.

"But away with these thoughts!" reflected the baronet; "I shall become a very coward, as weak as an infant, and unworthy that title for boldness and recklessness of heart which the Smuggler King has always obtained. I will think of it no more, but become again myself. Had he lived, he might have worked me some evil, especially as I have been such an egregious fool as to leave the will behind me at the Hall. It might have fallen into his hands by some strange accident, and then—but what then? He knew nothing of his origin, and, therefore, it would have availed him but little. However, it is better he is gone—he was my rival in the affections of Flora, and that was sufficient for me to wish him dead. But there is one thing that perplexes me, and that is the manner in which the truth can be imparted to the girl;—I have told her that he lives, and when she is made acquainted with the facts which ultimately she must be, I am afraid the shock will be too great for her, and I shall lose the prize I have been at so much trouble to obtain. This is an awkward affair, but I must set my ingenuity to work, and contrive some scheme to meet it. Beauteous Flora! Methinks I could almost wish that I were innocent,—that I had never sinned, so that I might woo thee upon honourable terms, and boldly and conscientiously aspire to thy love. Bah! I am getting weak again! What the devil has come to me that I take these vagaries? The girl is in my power, and mine she must and shall be, either by fair or foul means."

Pleased with these thoughts, Sir Julian hastened to his couch, and sought that repose which so seldom visits the pillow of the guilty.

He arose at an early hour, and had scarcely left his bed, when Sam Raker made his appearance in his chamber.

"Well, Sam, what news?" demanded the baronet, observing from his countenance that he had something to impart.

"The lads have returned, captain," answered Raker.

"Ah!" exclaimed Sir Julian, eagerly; "and all safe?"

Sam Raker answered in the affirmative.

"And have they met with any success?" hastily demanded the baronet.

"They have not," replied the smuggler.

Sir Julian muttered a bitter malediction between his teeth.

"They could behold nothing of Grampus?" again asked the baronet.

"Nothing at all, captain," was the answer.

"By h—l!" exclaimed the captain, as he clenched his fist and walked hurriedly backwards and forwards across the apartment; "by h—l! this is unfortunate. The fellow has doubtless, then, succeeded in his designs, and, by this time, my real name is as well known as Portsmouth Point."

"Perhaps not, captain," remarked Sam; "he might have been out at sea in the storm and perished."

"No, no," observed the captain; "my worst forebodings are all but confirmed; the rascal has been too fortunate. May vultures eternally gnaw his dastard heart! We must keep a sharp look-out, Sam, for, depend upon it, we shall be able to make them dance to as pretty a tune as ever we did in our lives."

"We will have a hard trial for it, at any rate," observed Sir Julian; "and if they do not find that the Smuggler King is as daring and undaunted as ever, may I never handle a pair of pistols again."

"Well said, captain; and if they do not also find Sam Raker constantly by your side in every danger, may it never fall to my lot to cut that infernal scoundrel Grampus's throat; and that is a satisfaction I would not lose for a ship load of guineas."

"They will find something to do to oust the Smuggler King from this stronghold," said Sir Julian.

"They will," coincided Raker; "or to defeat the bold hearts that are under his command."

"They have never yet been beaten."

"And never will—they would die first."

"Well said, my faithful Sam; you are still the same spirit as ever—dauntless as a lion, and reckless of danger."

"And so I hope always to remain while I have a timber left to float with, and that, whenever I am brought upon my beam-ends, it may be fighting the enemy on board the Devil Skipper!"

"Bravo! Sam!" exclaimed Sir Julian; "with such hearts of courage as yours, what has the Smuggler King to fear from any enemy, however powerful?"

"Fear!" repeated Sam, "it has ever been unknown to us all; and our foes will find that we have lost none of our original mettle, to their cost."

"They shall."

"But, after all, I do not think we shall be attacked," said Sam.

"If Grampus has fallen in with any ships of war, we certainly shall," returned the baronet.

"Ah, if he has," said Raker; "but the chances are that the scoundrel is at the bottom of the sea, and if he is, there is an end to the matter."

"True," observed Sir Julian, "and I am confident that there is not another one among all my subjects who would think of acting the same part."

"That I am convinced there is not," said Sam; "sooner, to a man, would they die a most lingering death of torture than they would, by a word or deed, do ought to injure him."

"I believe it," observed Sir Julian; "and when I forsake my gallant crew, may fortune forsake me."

"Avast there, captain, if you please; we know all that; we have not had so many years' experience under your command to doubt you now."

"Well," said the baronet, "there is enough said about that. You will see that there is nothing wanting for defence in case of an attack."

"I have already seen to that, captain, and everything is in readiness for a warm salute to those who may have the courage to claim our acquaintance."

"You have warned all our men to hold themselves in readiness?"

"I have," answered Sam Raker.

"And we have plenty of ammunition?"

"Enough to blow up all the ships in the king's fleet."

"That is well; but I would much rather the enemy would defer their visit for a while."

"Why?" demanded Sam.

"Because of the girl," answered Sir Julian; "a warm engagement would frighten her to death."

"Very true," returned Sam; "but you know we must take the chances of that, captain."

"Of course we must," coincided the latter; "but how are the lads who have returned from the pursuit?"

"None the better for their enterprise, you may be sure, captain," answered Raker; "such a night as it was last night could not be altogether agreeable in an open boat."

"True," returned Sir Julian; "see that they have their skinsful of grog, and as much as they can eat with it."

"I will, captain," replied the smuggler; and he departed to execute the orders of his commander.

The baronet then went over the tower to inspect the preparations that had been made for the defence.

Flora and Maud, in the apartments that had been assigned them, passed the time, after the interview which the former had had with Sir Julian, much more comfortably than they had done before since they had been in the tower. The day following they passed in reading and occasional conversation, and, as no one offered to intrude upon them, our heroine begun to feel somewhat tranquil, and to hope that some relief would arrive before Sir Julian offered to go to extremes. In the course of that day they could hear by the bustle that prevailed in the tower, that they were making preparations for some anticipated event, and they were of opinion that the smugglers, having missed their companion, expected an attack, and were guarding against it accordingly.

Much as the idea of an engagement filled the gentle breast of Flora with terror, she could not but look forward to it with hope, as the only prospect of her being released from her present confinement, and she trusted that Heaven would guard her in the danger by which they would be surrounded.

They were both in a state of the greatest anxiety, as regarded the result of the unknown undertaking; and there were times when Flora entertained strong apprehensions that he had either failed in his object, or that, if he had been on the sea at the time, he had perished in the storm which had raged so violently on the night before. Maud, however, exerted herself to the utmost to banish these gloomy fears from the mind of her fair companion, and, after some trouble, she partially succeeded.

Two days vanished without any change taking place, and they heard nothing of the unknown, neither did they receive any message from Sir Julian. The life they led was dull enough, but they endeavoured to enliven it by reading the books which they had provided for them, being of the most select and interesting kind. But what could alleviate the suspense of poor Flora?—nothing; and the quick lapse of time, without any change, or a prospect of change in her condition, was well calculated to increase her melancholy. In that wild spot it seemed as though they were shut up entirely from the world, and that nobody would take any notice of them, or interest themselves about them, and such a life was one of lingering and most intolerable misery.

Frequently when our heroine was seated at the casement and watching the blue waves, as they gambolled in the breeze, exemplifying liberty in its most vivid colours, she would burst into tears, and wish that death would come as a relief to her sufferings. At such times, had it not been for the soothing voice of Maud, she must have sunk entirely beneath the heavy weight of cares that pressed upon her heart; it was the gentle voice of that kind and attentive companion that alone sustained her, and to her she never ceased to express her unbounded gratitude. To be so near an island, and yet no aid afforded her, was another thing that afflicted her, and she was frequently of opinion that the Smuggler King and his crew were colleagued with the inhabitants, otherwise they surely would have attempted to disturb them. On that point Maud was unable to satisfy her; but the idea was too probable for her to attempt to banish it, and, in fact, Maud herself was strongly of the same opinion.

Three days had now elapsed, and as no enemy made their appearance, the captain was of the same opinion which Sam Raker had formerly expressed, namely, that Grampus had perished at sea, in his attempt to put his treacherous project into execution. Sir Julian had now, therefore, nothing to disturb his mind, but the unfortunate circumstance of his having left the will behind him at the Hall, and his suit with our heroine. The more he reflected upon the charms of that innocent and lovely damsel, the more fierce and ungovernable did his desires become, and he at length determined to have a second interview with her, and to try what effect his eloquence could now have upon her mind.

Flora and Maud were seated, as usual, engaged in conversation, when Sam Raker made his appearance, and delivered the captain's message, for our heroine once more to attend him in the saloon. She trembled when she heard it, but quickly recovering herself, and determined to act with the same fortitude and decision as she had done on the former occasion, she took the arm of Maud, and followed Sam Raker to the magnificent apartment where Sir Julian was waiting to receive her.

He was seated at a table when she entered, with his head resting thoughtfully on his hand, but he arose when he heard her, and advancing towards her with a smile, welcomed her politely, and attempted to take her hand. This she, however, withdrew, and at the same time felt an involuntary shudder of horror steal through her veins, as she fixed her eyes upon his countenance. A slight expression of displeasure passed over his features, as he observed :—

"So cold and scornful yet, fair damsel? Oh, that I could learn the way to obtain your lovely smiles; it would be as the prospect of relief to the shipwrecked mariner."

"Smiles of esteem and friendship are not due to the Smuggler King, but from his own cruel and lawless associates," firmly answered our heroine, and she averted her face, and leant her head on the shoulder of Maud.

"You are again here, woman," said Sir Julian, sternly, addressing himself to Maud; "beware, this bold intrusiveness may provoke my wrath. Get you hence; my interview is with Flora Clarendon alone."

"There is nothing you can have to utter to me, sir," said Flora, "which Maud may not hear; and if your intentions are honourable, you will permit her to remain."

"Fair maiden," returned the hypocrite, "there is nothing that I would willingly deny thee; such is the magic spell thou hast woven o'er my senses, that thy will I am ready to make my law; but I cannot allow any person to be a listener to the vows I have to offer thee, nor suffer the prying ear of curiosity to hear what may pass between us; our interview will, however, be but brief, and the same degree of honour shall guide my actions on this occasion as on our former one. Leave us, Maud."

"I am ready to obey you, sir," returned Maud, in the same tone of boldness which she had before assumed; "but, remember what I before told you, and ——"

"What!" interrupted Sir Julian, unable to conceal his rage, "dare you threaten me?"

"I hold out no threats, sir," answered Maud, "for I am a poor defenceless woman, and unable to carry them into execution, or, Heaven knows that no one has had more cause to seek for vengeance than I have. No, I only warn you that ——"

"Begone!" commanded the baronet, and Maud, knowing that it would be useless to remonstrate, and that her obstinacy might only excite his feelings, and lead Flora into danger, quitted the room, after having embraced our heroine, and encouraged her by a look of confidence.

Flora was now again alone with the baronet, and she awaited in the most trembling state of suspense the issue of this interview.

The pirate-captain remained silent for a few minutes, wrapped in contemplation of the surpassing charms of the lovely being before him, and therefore Flora had sufficient time given her to collect her thoughts, had she not been fully prepared before. At length the sycophant approached her, and, in spite of her resistance, taking her hand, and pressing it to his lips, with a feeling of the most unbounded and indescribable transport, he ejaculated:—

"Beauteous Flora, once more, then, dost thou illumine my path with thy presence, and fascinate my ears with the soft and seraphic music of thy voice. Oh! what an earthly paradise doth that world become where thou appearest. Since I last beheld thee, my heart has been rent by all the pangs and torments of the most insupportable love; let me then hope that its anguish will not be unrequited, but that the idol of my soul is prepared to receive my vows, and to acknowledge a reciprocal affection! You do not speak—you turn away from me!—Ah! how have I deserved this?"

It would be impossible to describe the feelings of the maiden while the libertine was thus giving vent to his fulsome and disgusting vows. Her heart throbbed so violently against her side, that she could not without difficulty maintain her fortitude, while shame and indignation held predominant sway in her gentle and amiable bosom. She still averted her face, and struggled hard to release her hand from the grasp of Sir Julian, who still held it between his own, and, in spite of her efforts to the contrary, her confusion, her blushes, her wounded delicacy and indignation, conveyed it again and again to his lips, and smothered it with his kisses.

"Release my hand, sir," at length Flora ejaculated, in accents of firmness, "it well becomes the boldness of manhood thus to wound and insult the feelings of an unprotected girl."

"Insult thee, sweetest!" repeated Sir Julian; "now, by all my hopes thou wrongest me; sooner would I perish, and by a death of the most horrible torment, than I would offer to insult so fair a creature as thou art."

"If your assertions are sincere," returned the maiden, quickly, "forbear your hated vows, suffer me immediately to retire, and endeavour to make some atonement for the numerous miseries you have caused, by taking immediate

steps to restore me to my parents. Do this, and I will place some confidence in the sincerity of your assertions."

The baronet paused for a moment or two, confused, and scarcely knowing what answer to make, but he quickly recovered himself, and said :—

"Nay, beauteous Flora, thou dost seek to exact too much from me ; say that you love me ; ask me then for my life, and I will freely lay it at thy feet, but to be deprived of thy presence, and know that thou hatest me, would be worse a thousand times than death."

"Cease thy hypocrisy," answered Flora, " you cannot, shall not deceive me."

"Deceive thee !" exclaimed the villain, " by all my hopes, never ! Sooner would I suffer all the mortal pangs that could be inflicted upon me, than I would deceive thee, most lovely girl. But thou, with youth and beauty so transcendent, cannot surely be so cold, so insensible to the divine passion as to turn a deaf ear to the vows of one who lives but to adore thee ?"

"Horrible profanation of the most sacred passion which God hath granted to his creatures upon earth," returned our heroine. "No more ; it shocks my ears to listen to you."

It was with the greatest difficulty only that the baronet could keep his passion within due bounds, but the virtue and dignity of her manner awed him, and, after pausing for a short time to collect himself, he said :—

"Reproaches, sweet maiden, from thy lips, are worse than so many daggers to my heart ; but it shall be my task to convince thee how little I merit them. 'Tis true, I am a smuggler, a pirate, and, what may be called by the vulgar and illiterate, an outcast from society ; but still do I possess a heart throbbing with all the most glowing and ardent passions to which the human breast was ever susceptible ; and I will not believe so unkindly of thee, dear Flora, as to think you can be insensible to them, and be prejudiced by the idle rumours of a censorious world. No—no, that angelic form was never——"

"Oh, spare me! spare me!" interrupted Flora; "do not shock my ears with vows I must not, cannot listen to."

"Am I then so hateful?" demanded the baronet, in a tone of well-assumed melancholy and regret.

"Heaven forbid that I should hate one of my fellow-beings," returned the gentle maiden; "but acts of cruelty and oppression must excite disgust in every bosom."

"And what have I done to merit thy disgust?"

"Can you ask that question, and still behold me a prisoner in your power, —torn from my home, my parents, and confined in this dreadful place, with no other prospect but one of horror before me? Go seek an answer of my broken-hearted father and mother, and then ask me why I should feel disgust and abhorrence towards thee!"

"I have before told thee," answered the smuggler-captain, "that thou hast the power to unlock the gates of thy prison, and to behold thy parents again."

"Oh! how?"

"Endeavour to love me," answered Sir Julian, "consent to become the smuggler's bride, and you are free."

"Love thee! Consent to become thy bride!" repeated our heroine, and she fixed upon the baronet a look in which all her feelings were revealed; "sooner would I at this moment be stretched a corse at thy feet!"

"Not so," returned the wily hypocrite; "not so, most beauteous Flora; "thou must and shall live for happiness and me!"

"Never! An all-merciful God will interpose to prevent it!" cried the maiden. "Yes, I put my trust in Him, and defy thy power."

"It is that I possess that power that you should respect me, since I have acted with forbearance, and taken no advantage of it."

"For that, indeed, I owe you my thanks," said our heroine; "still further, then, increase the obligation by forbearing thus to importune me, and restore me to that liberty of which you have so cruelly and unjustly deprived me."

"You have the means of liberty at your disposal, fair damsel," answered Sir Julian, "on no other terms can I consent to grant it you."

"Oh! cruel, cruel man!" sobbed Flora.

"Say not so," answered the captain. "To others I may be cruel, but not to thee."

"Why then keep me thus confined?" demanded Flora; "why thus persecute me?"

"It is the power of the love I bear thee, which urges me on," replied Sir Julian; "persecute thee, lovely maiden! oh, call not that persecution which is prompted alone by the sincere feelings of the heart. Could I lose thee, and perhaps never more to behold thee again, and then only to see thee the bride of another? Oh, never! There is no fate, however dreadful, to which evil destiny might doom me, which could be half so terrible as that. Here, once more on my knees, most angelic of thy sex, do I kneel, and crave the blessing of thy smiles; say that you will endeavour to love me, and, oh! how happy shall I be!"

"Kneel not to me, sir," returned Flora, fixing upon him a look of the most bitter scorn, "it is mockery! I hear thy words, but they are as the idle wind to me! Think you that Flora Clarendon, innocent as she is, is so blind that she cannot detect the base hypocrisy of one like thee?

Sir Julian bit his lips, and started to his feet. He paced the room backwards and forwards, and great was the difficulty that he had to keep his violent rage and indignation within the bounds of reason. To be thus braved, and by a simple, defenceless girl; he, who had ruled it o'er the hearts of some of the fairest of the fair, and seldom failed in his projects.

It was too much. He could have forced the scornful beauty to his arms, and sought his revenge and gratification at once, in the destruction of all that was beautiful; but there was something about the innocence, the countenance, the language, the whole demeanour of our heroine, which kept his passions under restraint, and awed him into forbearance.

"By the infernal host!" the villain muttered to himself, "this maiden's charms have placed a spell upon me, and hold me in subjection as a very child. I must shake off this weakness, and exert the power I possess to tame her proud spirit. But can I harm her? No—by all my hopes! methinks I could sooner suffer anything than be guilty of that. And yet but a short time since she—but no matter, I will endeavour to win her by fair and *honourable* persuasion, and, if that fail, then she has herself to blame, and not me, for all that may happen."

He now once more turned to our heroine, who had been watching his agitation, and observed,—

"You have called me hypocrite, Flora; villain—all! But you see that I bear it with patience; and yet, methinks, that better words might grace the lips of one so lovely as thou art. However, I will not upbraid you; misrepresented as I have been by the world, I have become used to such treatment, and it therefore affects me not. Still must you love me, and I do believe you will, although at present you treat the rover of the seas with scorn, nay, even contumely."

"Love!" repeated Flora; "oh, that the word should be profaned by lips like yours. To love your cruel heart must ever have been insensible."

"You wrong me," answered the baronet. "I have known what it is to love, and to meet love's return. I have basked beneath the sunny rays of woman's bright smiles, and heard her breathe words responsive with mine own. I have pressed the form of beauty to my heart, and dreamed a dream of bliss in the soft languishment of her looks. I have felt that I am man, and formed to love woman with the most powerful, the most devoted fondness; but it was left for you, dearest Flora, to convince me that I could worship them—adore them as an idol."

"Oh! cease! cease!" exclaimed Flora, her cheeks suffused with the deep crimson blushes of shame and offended modesty, and her bosom swelling with indignation at the boldness of the villain, in whose power she unfortunately was, and who now once more knelt before her, and fixed upon her looks of the warmest admiration, and almost ungovernable passion. However, even at that moment, her fortitude and presence of mind did not forsake her. She knew that her honour—all depended upon them, and Providence seemed to imbue her with a power far beyond her sex. She turned upon Sir Julian a withering look, and such an one that while it surprised him, abashed him, and kept him within those bounds of prudence which his burning passion might otherwise have caused him to overstep. In spite of the opposition she made to his energetic advances—notwithstanding the reproaches which she heaped upon him—the scorn and hatred with which she evidently viewed him—he could not help thinking that she was the most lovely being he had ever beheld; and, as he gazed upon her, and thought upon the extraordinary fortitude her strict integrity and virtue enabled her to maintain, he could not resist the feeling that came over him, and his admiration increased every moment. Never did he before imagine that he could be so completely subdued, as it were, by woman's charms.

He still continued kneeling, and such was the power which our heroine held over him, and the effect which her words had had upon him, that he was for a short time completely at a loss what answer to make her. She saw his confusion, and while it gratified her by convincing her that for the present, at any rate, she was safe from his violence, she wondered at her-

self, and could not account for the possession of that firmness she had
never anticipated she should be able to acquire.

"Lovely being," he at last ejaculated, "again let me repeat those
words which spring from my heart, which are as pure as purity itself, and
beseech your indulgence. Judge me not by what I have been represented,
but as I shall behave to you. You will find me all that woman can desire;
fond, attentive, adoring. There is not a wish that you will have to express;
I will anticipate your every want, and feel the greatest felicity in gratifying
it. All that wealth can purchase, that love can suggest, shall be at your
command. I will be your slave, your most obsequious slave, ready to obey
your every will. Believe me, I speak the truth. Relax, then, in your cold
and freezing behaviour to me, and, by assuring me that you do not hate me,
that you will endeavour to love me,—make me the happiest man in existence. Nay, continue not to avert that beauteous countenance, upon which
I could gaze my life away. Allow me but to sip the honey of those rosy
lips, and feed my thirsting soul on the transport they will afford. But one
delicious kiss, idol of my soul—one balmy kiss, to charm my ravished
senses, and ——"

"Stand off, villain," boldly cried our heroine, as the libertine advanced
towards her, and endeavoured to encircle her waist with his arms, and to
press his lips to hers;—"stand off, nor dare to pollute my lips with your
detested, your unholy caresses! Nay, dare not to approach me, or I will
invoke the heaviest maledictions of the Most High upon your head, and
wither you in the midst of your fancied might."

Again astounded by the energy of her manner, Sir Julian started back,
and stood gazing at her with looks of astonishment, awe, and admiration,
unable to move or to utter a syllable.

Flora, perceiving his confusion, advanced towards the door of the
saloon.

"I leave you," she observed; "after what I have heard, and your conduct at this interview, it is not meet that I should remain here. In my
own apartments I may be at least secure from insult, and ——"

"Stay," peremptorily exclaimed Sir Julian, and losing every degree of
patience, and starting forward, he rather roughly seized her. "Stay,
proud, scornful beauty," he repeated, "I command you."

"You command me?"

"Ay, I, the Smuggler King! your future lord and master," returned the
baronet. "You stir not from hence till it pleases me. You have scorned
all my advances; you have treated me with insult, and now, I, that would
have humbled to you as the veriest slave, will command and exact obedience
from you as a master."

"So then," said our heroine, with bitter irony, yet most astonishing
calmness; "so then the mask has fallen off, and you stand confessed in
your true character. The gentle lover, the worshipper of female beauty,
has sunk into the unmanly ruffian. 'Tis well, sir. If I were before unacquainted with your real character, you have taken great pains to let me
know you now."

Sir Julian bit his lips, and contracted his brows, and it was not without
the utmost difficulty that he could continue to keep his bursting rage anything like within the bounds of reason.

"Proud damsel!" he cried, "be mindful of your reproaches, for you
have goaded me on by your obstinacy to madness, and I may be tempted
to do that which I should afterwards regret."

"What would you with me?" firmly demanded the damsel.

"I would not injure you, unless you provoke me to it," answered Sir
Julian.

" Suffer me, then, to quit this saloon," said our heroine.

" But one word, and your request is granted."

" Name it."

" Can you love me?"

" Monstrous idea!   Never!

" Be cautious what you say."

" My heart is firm, and nothing can alter it," replied Flora.

" You will not consent to become my bride?" asked the baronet.

" Sooner would I perish!" exclaimed the damsel, fervently.

" Then hear me," resolutely observed Sir Julian.   " My mind is made up, that you never more quit this tower but as my bride.   This is my decision, and you know it; I therefore, to show you that I wish not to act with undue harshness, now give you, from this time, three days more to reflect on it; and if, at the end of that time, you do not consent to become mine, I will force you to the altar, and, after the mystic rites of our communion, make you the bride of the Smuggler King."

" Oh! mercy! mercy!" supplicated Flora, sinking on her knees, and completely horror struck; " do not, I implore you, thus sacrifice an innocent, unprotected girl."

" My mind is made up," answered the smuggler-captain, firmly; " you have heard my decision, and must be assured that it is useless attempting to oppose the will of the Smuggler King."

" Cannot the voice of pity reach thy stubborn heart?" cried our heroine.

" Pity!" repeated Sir Julian; " have I not shewn thee every forbearance, and am still ready to shew thee every indulgence,—all the affection which man can bestow upon woman, if thou wilt but promise me that thou wilt endeavour to love me, and, of thine own free will, consent to accompany me to the altar."

" Oh, sir," sighed the damsel; " what conquest could it be to you to fetter a broken heart?   My soul abhors deceit; and therefore do I once more candidly assure you, that I can never love you; and should you compel me to become your bride, I shall never be able to look upon you with any other feeling than that of abhorrence, and the most unbounded—the most unconquerable disgust."

" Then, by all my hopes!" exclaimed Sir Julian, " you shall be mine! and even though every earthly power should interpose to save you, the Smuggler King will claim his bride."

" And," returned our heroine, with increased fortitude, and her mind made up for the worst consequences, " that hour shall be my last!   Never will I survive such shame—such misery."

" Beauteous, but obstinate damsel," observed Sir Julian, " I will take sure means to prevent that."

" You cannot prevent my poor heart from breaking," replied Flora, with a look of the most bitter sorrow.

" Psha!" exclaimed the baronet. " Beauteous Flora, why talk you thus? Why will you reject the happiness which is offered to you?"

" Happiness—and you!"

" Ay," answered the captain; " happiness and me!   Think you, then, it is impossible for us to be associated?   Oh! you can little imagine the charms I have in store for you; how studious I would be of your felicity; or you would never thus obstinately treat my advances with disdain, and lavish upon me your reproaches."

" And think you, then," demanded the damsel, " that Flora Clarendon is that poor, weak girl, to be entrapped,—deluded, by the tinsel show of pleasure?   You form but a poor estimate of her mind, sir, if that is your opinion.   The partner of a man I must ever despise and shudder at! even

were all the luxuries—the enjoyments that the world contains, placed at
my command, they could not lighten the seared heart that would throb
within this breast; could not alleviate those pangs that must shortly bring
me to the grave."

"You talk like a giddy, thoughtless girl," said Sir Julian; "and time,
methinks, will alter your tones. Die!—no! no! fair damsel, you must
live many years for love and joy; to be the Rover's Bride; his pride and
solace, as he roves over the bright blue waters, the queen of as brave a band
as ever paid homage to a monarch."

"A crew of the most remorseless and lawless wretches, whom it would
be a gross libel to call men," answered our heroine; "but I have listened
long enough to your wild discourse; suffer me to retire, and, in the communion of my own sad thoughts, seek for consolation."

"I will comply with your request, fair lady," answered Sir Julian; "and
let me once more advise you well to consider upon what I have said, and do
not, by any foolish obstinacy, provoke my anger. I would treat you with
every kindness, affection, and indulgence—I would fairly woo and win you;
but, if you persist in rejecting my vows, I am determined to enforce the
gratification of my wishes."

"Nothing whatever can alter the resolution I have now formed," answered Flora. "Let the consequences be what they may, never shall my
tongue utter that from which my heart revolts; never will I speak an un-
truth; no, even though my life should fall a sacrifice—nothing, nothing
shall ever force me to speak that which my heart does not approve of."

"Rash girl!" exclaimed Sir Julian, "what will this obstinacy avail you?
—are you not in my power? and whether you consent or not, what is to
prevent you becoming the smuggler's bride?"

"One above!" answered the damsel, raising her hand solemnly, and
pointing towards Heaven; "that Almighty Power which you dare not invoke, and who will interpose to save me from the cruel—the revolting fate
with which you have threatened me."

"Bah!" cried the baronet, "you talk wildly, Flora; but we shall see
who will triumph when the time arrives. I repeat that I will give you two
days to reflect more maturely upon the subject, and, if you are wise, you will
consent to what I have requested, if not, I sue no longer, but will immediately force you to the altar."

"Oh, sir!" ejaculated our heroine, "again let me implore you to repent,
and retract your cruel decree; force me not into that which must break my
heart."

"Your obstinacy but the more inflames my passions," said Sir Julian.
"I have said the word, and, once for all, I tell you that you shall—you
must be mine!"

"And can you expect any happiness from such a deed?" demanded our
heroine; "do you not think the curse of Heaven will pursue you?"

"Mark me, girl," returned the baronet, suddenly forgetting himself, and
changing his tone, "mark me! the Power you have mentioned I scorn,
and believe not. It may do well to gull old women and silly girls with,
but men ——"

"Hold! blasphemer!" interrupted Flora; "do not shock my ears by
uttering words so horrible. Are you not fearful ——"

"The Smuggler King knows no fear," he interrupted; "his heart is a
stranger to the feeling."

"As it is to pity or humanity," added the damsel.

"You wrong me," he answered; "would you but yield to my wishes,
you would find that I can be kind and gentle as humanity, and benevolence
itself. Oh, how I would study to make you happy—what sacrifices would

I not make to insure it! I would have no will but yours, and to win but a smile from you would be the greatest bliss that I could experience."

"Nay," returned our heroine; "your art cannot have the power to deceive or delude me. Alas! how many unfortunate victims have you gained by similar means? My heart shudders when I gaze upon you, and I ——"

"Enough of this," impatiently ejaculated Sir Julian; "I would possess you, of your own free will possess you, and who knows," he added, with a satirical smile, "but that you might be the means of reclaiming me, sweet Flora, and that I might become a very pattern of excellence and virtue?"

The damsel turned from him with a look of disgust, and, after a pause, she observed,—

"I suppose, sir, I am now permitted to return to my apartment?"

"You are," answered Sir Julian. "I will summon Maud to attend you; but first, my sweet Flora, but one kiss, one sweet kiss from those rosy lips, and ——"

"Hold! miscreant! libertine! seducer!" exclaimed the blushing and indignant girl, as she struggled violently to extricate herself from his embraces; "unhand me! or may the curse of Heaven descend upon your head, and ——"

"A kiss! a kiss!" persisted Sir Julian; "I am determined to have one —ay, even though all the devils attached to Satan, were to offer to oppose me!"

"Oh! help! help!" distractedly screamed our heroine, as the villain still continued to encircle her waist with his arms, and endeavoured to press his lips to her's. She was almost exhausted—another instant, and he would have accomplished his purpose; again she screamed and called aloud for help.

"Spare your sweet breath, my angel," he said; "of what avail are your cries here? Surely there need not be so much fuss about one simple kiss? Come, come, I am determined; I must have it, and therefore it is useless to attempt to resist me."

"Oh! mercy! mercy! spare me!" implored our heroine, with looks that were enough to penetrate to the most insensible heart. "You promised me that you would not commit any outrage, and —"

"Call you this an outrage," demanded Sir Julian, as he forcibly pressed the lips of the blushing damsel again and again to his own lips. "It is ——"

"Help! help!" once more screamed Flora, and forcibly releasing herself from the libertine's hold, she made towards the door of the saloon.

"Am I then so hateful?" demanded the baronet. "By Jupiter, then, this moment will I ——"

Before he could finish the sentence, our heroine had reached the door, where Maud appeared, who, alarmed at hearing her cries, had come to see what was the matter. Flora threw herself into her arms, and hid her blushing face in her bosom.

"That confounded woman again," muttered Sir Julian, starting back in confusion, and gazing savagely upon her. "Who sent for you, hag?" he added.

"Hag!" repeated Maud with a look of scorn; "and the hag defies you, Smuggler King, as you pompously designate yourself."

"Ah! so daring!" cried the baronet, fiercely, and being scarce able to believe the evidence of his senses; "this to me, woman? Know you to whom you are talking?"

"Yes," coolly and firmly answered Maud, at the same time she fixed her keen and penetrating eyes upon him, "I know that I am talking to Sir ——"

"Cursed fiend!" hoarsely exclaimed the baronet, rushing fiercely upon

Maud, his eyes inflamed and blood-shot with rage, and his whole frame evincing the power of his emotion; "cursed fiend! dare but to give utterance to that name, and that moment is your last."

Maud still looked at him with the most perfect contempt, as she coolly replied,—

"Your secret is safe! I remember my oath, and will not break it, although you pay very little respect to it."

"What brought you hither, woman?" he demanded.

"The shrieks of this innocent girl," answered Maud; "whom I perceive, notwithstanding your promises, you have dared to insult."

"Psha!" returned Sir Julian, stifling his wrath; "a mere frolic, Maud, a mere frolic, and nothing to make a noise about. I'll warrant me that you would not make such a fuss, if you were insulted fifty times in a similar manner."

"Heartless, licentious miscreant!" thought Maud, for she did not venture to give utterance to her feelings, knowing that it might bring destruction down upon her own head, and that of Flora. She, however, fixed such a look upon the smuggler-chief, that he could not mistake, and he bit his lips in the most unbounded vexation. Our heroine still clung closely to Maud, and while blushes of shame suffused her lovely cheeks, and tears filled her eyes, she ejaculated in a faint voice,—

"Let us begone, dear Maud; my heart trembles in the presence of that unfeeling, unprincipled man."

"Begone!" said Sir Julian, turning to Maud; "begone, and take with you your companion, and mind, against we meet again, you teach her the blessings of submission, for she will much need it, on that occasion."

He turned upon Maud a significant look as he spoke these words, and the latter, without deigning him any reply, conducted the trembling Flora from his presence.

"So much for this interview," he muttered to himself, when they had quitted the room; "it has but the more inflamed my passions, and I will not delay a moment after the time I have given her, in making her mine. I would not forego that happiness for all the gold that Golconda could produce. No, Flora! you may scorn, hate, dread me, as thou wilt, but still nothing can save thee from me; thou art my destined bride, and shall reign sole empress of my heart. That Maud becomes bold and daring; had I not interrupted her, she would have revealed my real name. Curses on her glib tongue, and I have not at present the power to stop it. Should she reveal any of my secrets to the damsel, to whom she seems so much attached—but no, I am alarming myself without a cause. She dare not, she knows full well that her own life would have to pay the forfeit. Still, I regret that I cannot dispense with her services. I have no one else to attend upon the girl, and should I deprive Flora of her society, it might either retard or frustrate my designs, for Flora could never survive without society, and I must be even a worse monster than she believes me to be, to rob her of it. Her hatred, however, I do not yet despair of being able to conquer, and still powerful are my hopes, that she will prove to me all that my warmest wishes can desire."

Thus sanguine with anticipation, the villain quitted the saloon, and rejoined Sam Raker, and a few more of the principal of the smugglers, in another apartment.

When Flora and Maud arrived in their own apartments, the former sunk into a chair, and gave free vent to the feelings that had long struggled in her bosom. Maud offered her all the consolation in her power, and at length having succeeded in tranquillising her, she elicited from her all the particulars of what had taken place at the interview.

"So you see," added our heroine, when she had concluded, "you see, my dear Maud, that all hope is at an end. Two short days only, and the the miscreant in whose power I am, will force me to become his bride. Oh, God! what will become of me?"

"Your situation is truly a painful one," said Maud, in reply; "but short as is the time allowed to you, something may yet take place to frustrate his designs, and to rescue you from his power."

"It is madness to think of it," returned Flora; "whichever way I turn, I see no prospect of it."

"At present, there certainly is not," answered Maud; "but should the unknown, who left us the note, succeed ——"

"Ah, no!" interrupted our heroine, "I see no chance of that; look at the time which has elapsed since his departure from the tower. The poor fellow has either failed in his object, or perished in the deep."

"I cannot bring my mind to think either," observed Maud; "and, from the preparations that have been made in the tower, and which are still kept up, the smugglers, it seems, do yet think of the danger of an attack."

"Heaven grant that some relief may be afforded me," ejaculated Flora, "or that death may rescue me from a fate so terrible. The insults of that heartless monster, for such I still firmly believe him to be, have filled my mind with disgust and indignation. Oh, my poor parents, what would be your anguish, did you but know the shame and misery to which your poor child is subjected; the cruel destiny, too, which is impending over her."

"Still maintain that fortitude that has carried you thus far through your many trials," said Maud; "and I am yet of opinion that you will triumph ultimately over the machinations of the guilty, and that your oppressor will be brought to shame and confusion."

No. 47

"But think you that the smuggler captain will actually put his threats into execution, at the time he has mentioned?" asked our heroine.

"It would be useless to flatter you with false hopes, in that respect," answered Maud; "the captain never breaks his word, and therefore, unless something should take place in the interim, to rescue you from his power, you may rest assured that he will not fail to do as he has menaced."

"Oh, God!" gasped forth Flora, "what a terrible fate, to become the bride of so cruel, so remorseless a villain; a pirate, a murderer. Horror! my blood rushes with maddening fury to my brain at the bare thought."

"But you will be released," exclaimed Maud, after she had reflected for a minute, "I am certain you will, and that Heaven will never permit so monstrous a villain to triumph over so much innocence."

Flora returned no answer, for her feelings were too much excited to suffer her for awhile to speak, and the remainder of the day passed away in as gloomy a manner as it is possible to conceive. Still no change in the tower. The unknown remained absent, and our heroine had given up all hopes that he would ever return, or that he would succeed in his object. This was a severe disappointment to her, after the sanguine hopes she had been naturally led to encourage from such an event. The man could have no motive for deceiving her, as she must be almost an entire stranger to him, and he therefore could have no cause of enmity towards her, no feeling of malevolence (which otherwise might have dictated such conduct for the purpose of harassing and distressing her mind) to gratify. She had very little doubt that he had perished, for had he reached any British vessel or settlement, his story would have been sure to have been paid every attention to, and immediate steps adopted to release her, and to bring to punishment the miscreants, who had for so many years been the terror of the seas.

In these opinions Maud could not but coincide, and having exhausted all the arguments she could make use of, in order to appease and quiet the mind of her companion, their time passed in the most wretched manner imaginable.

As the time approached when her fate was to be decided, the anguish of the poor girl was quite lamentable to behold; her destiny now appeared inevitable, and she passed her time in melancholy bewailings and alternate prayers to the Almighty for relief.

The suffering of Maud was not much less than that which her unfortunate companion endured, and she felt it more keenly, as she had no hope, no consolation whatever to offer her. She well knew the fierce determination of Sir Julian, and was confident that nothing could move him from his purpose. The prayers, the tears, the entreaties of the fair sufferer, would alike be of no avail, for his heart was insensible to their influence, and every other feeling was absorbed in that of sensual desire.

She almost regretted that she had spoken so boldly to the baronet on the occasion of the second interview between him and our heroine, for she well knew, that however he might appear to pass it off at the present time, he would not fail at some future opportunity, to have revenge, and should he deprive Flora of her attendance, the only friend to whom she could confide her thoughts, and look up for consolation, she was certain that it would break the poor girl's heart. But still it was impossible that he could do that, as there was not another female in the tower, and it was not likely, cruel as he was, that he would deprive her of such a companion.

At length arrived the evening of the second day, when Sir Julian had stated that he should demand our heroine's final answer, and a dreadful time it was to the poor girl. Her doom appeared sealed, for what could save her from it? She clasped her hands together, again and again in agony, and wept scalding tears of anguish. Never could she willingly consent to become the bride of such a villain; and, if she did not, it would make no alteration in her destiny, for Sir Julian had determined to sacrifice her to his passions. Maud had no advice to offer her, for she had given her all that she was capable of doing, and therefore there was nothing but despair before her, whichever way she turned her eyes.

The sun had sunk in the bosom of the western ocean, and the shades of twilight were spreading around. All was perfectly still; melancholy seemed to rest upon everything, and the wind which occasionally blew in fitful gusts around the tower, seemed to partake of the solemn tone of everything else.

Flora had just arisen from her knees, having been invoking the protection of the Supreme, when a knock at the room-door announced Sir Julian. Flora clasped her hands, and groaned in the intensity of her anguished feelings. Maud hastened to the door, after having handed Flora to a chair, and admitted the expected Raker.

He had no occasion to announce his errand, for both Maud and Flora guessed it, and the former having, for the last time, begged of the poor damsel to compose herself, prepared to accompany her to the saloon; Sam Raker, however, now interposed.

"It is the captain's command," he said, "that you do not attend her, Maud."

"Oh! for Heaven's sake, do not prevent her," supplicated the damsel.

"I have nothing to do with it, young lady," answered the ruffian, "only to obey the captain's orders, and those I have told."

"Oh! God! protect me!" sighed our heroine.

"Do not despair, my dear girl," said Maud; "the captain's infamous designs are very evident, but although I am not permitted to attend you, I will be near you, and should you need it, will fly to your assistance."

"Ha! ha! ha!" laughed Sam Raker, "and pray what assistance can you render her, Maud? Think you our captain will be thwarted in his plans by a petticoat?"

Maud turned on the smuggler a look of hatred and contempt, but she did not condescend to make him any reply, and once more embracing and kissing Flora affectionately, she followed her to the door of the apartment, and then resigning the trembling and deeply persecuted girl to the guidance of Sam Raker, she re-entered the room.

With faltering footsteps our heroine followed her ruffianly conductor, who did not speak to her, and several times she was compelled to pause and lean against the wall for support. Suddenly, however, a different feeling came over her, and she was endowed with new and remarkable courage. She hastily dried her tears, and pursued her way, preceded by Sam Raker, with a firmer step, until they arrived at the door of the saloon, through which having seen her pass, Raker left her.

When she entered the room she found that Sir Julian was not there, and she therefore seated herself in a chair, and endeavoured to prepare herself for his appearance. She had not been many minutes in the saloon, however, when the folding-doors at the further end were thrown open, and the Smuggler King entered, and immediately advanced towards her. His countenance was even more than usually animated, and he seemed as if he had taken particular pains with his dress.

Our heroine met him with a steady eye, and a look of scorn; but he, seeming to be prepared for that, took no notice of it, but attempted to take her hand; which, as usual, she withdrew with a feeling of the utmost abhorrence, which she took no pains to conceal.

"Beauteous Flora," at length said Sir Julian, "more charming every time thou meetest mine eyes, the auspicious evening has at length arrived, when I call upon you for your final answer to my suit, and I will dare to hope that it is as favourable as I could wish it, and that you, of your own free will, are ready to become my bride?"

"Presumptuous man," answered Flora; "and think you then that Flora Clarendon, of her own free will, will ever become the wife of a murderer; a man, the mention of whose name fills the breast of every one with horror?— never!"

"Bethink yourself, fair damsel," said the baronet, "you have called me murderer; better language, softer epithets would best become those lips, that were formed for love alone; especially as you accuse me only from report."

"Have you not for years been associated with every crime?" said Flora, fixing upon him a look, which was meant to strike home to his conscience; but to that he was at that time quite insensible; his mind was fixed upon other things.

"We met not here to converse upon that subject," he at length said; "love should occupy our minutes, and mutual vows —"

"Forbear!" interrupted Flora; "to such discourse, I cannot, will not listen."

"Still cold and insensible!" he ejaculated; "but surely you cannot be so mad, so infatuated, my dear girl, as to turn a deaf ear to the acknowledgment of my passion?"

"Again I tell you that I shudder even in your presence," answered the damsel; "why, then, persist in torturing the weak and defenceless with an acknowledgment of that passion which you have misnamed love? Once for all, sir, I tell you, that you can never receive any other sentiment from me than that of hatred."

"Obstinate, headstrong girl!" cried the captain, with an air of resentment, and a frown passing over his features; "what, think you, will this conduct avail you? Are you not in my power, and therefore have I not the means of making you yield to my wishes at once?"

"Alas!" sighed Flora, "full well I know you have; but, cruel as I believe you to be, I do not think you can be so monstrous as to sacrifice an innocent, unprotected girl to so dreadful a fate."

"Dreadful fate!" repeated Sir Julian; "what! to be made the ocean queen; to have a husband whose every thought shall be to please you; to be the mistress of wealth unbounded, and the bride of one whose birth is noble, and whose fortune is princely?"

"And what is all that you have enumerated without happiness?" demanded Flora.

"Happiness!" returned Sir Julian; "it will be your own fault if you do not possess it. There is no happiness which this life can afford which I will not purchase you."

"Can you purchase me peace of mind?" said Flora; "that sweet, blissful peace of mind, which attended me in my happy home, and in the affection of my poor parents? Can you ——"

"Psha!" interrupted the baronet, impatiently; "why talk of these, since you reject the means of being restored to them?"

"Oh! how?"

"Freely grant me your hand," answered Sir Julian, "and I swear that, as soon as possible, you shall be restored again to your parents and friends!"

"Oh! base subterfuge," said the damsel, "merely to entrap me. But I will never consent; every feeling revolts from the unnatural connexion; never will I grant my hand where it cannot be accompanied by my heart."

"And that is your final resolve?" demanded Sir Julian.

"It is," firmly replied Flora.

"Then, mark me," returned the former; "by that decision you seal your destiny, for unless you yield to my will, never shall you behold your parents or friends again !"

"Oh! mercy! mercy!" implored our heroine.

"You have chosen your own fate."

"Yes," observed Flora, fixing upon Sir Julian a look of the most bitter reproach; "I might have been certain of that. Heartless and cruel as you are, I might have been sure that to appeal for mercy to you was like talking to a block of marble. But I invoke the protection of that Supreme Power which I have never wilfully offended against,—I call upon the spirit of my murdered William, for murdered I am convinced he is, to interpose for me in this dreadful hour of trial, and, secure as you may think your triumph is, I will not yet despair that your diabolical plans will be frustrated."

"Bah!" ejaculated Sir Julian; "what absurdity is this; what can save you from my designs? Can I not force you to the altar this instant? You have no friends at hand to fly to your rescue, and if you had, what could they effect against the power of the Smuggler King? What can save you from becoming my bride?"

"Oh! sir," ejaculated our heroine, after a pause of the most intense anguish; "you will think better of this; you will not doom me to such insupportable misery."

"Sweet Flora!" returned the libertine, "fain would I make you the happiest of womankind. There is no such sacrifice which I would not make for your sake."

"Then," exclaimed the damsel, eagerly, "if you really love me, you will immediately abandon your wicked designs; restore me to liberty, and not seek to break a heart which can never be your's!"

"Resign you!" cried the baronet; "never! on you are all my future hopes fixed; without you the Smuggler King will never again be happy, and think you then, now I have you at my disposal, after all the trouble and anxiety it has cost me to obtain you, that I will give up my prize? Never, but with my life!"

"Oh! what happiness can a broken heart afford you?" demanded Flora. "What satisfaction can you feel in possessing the hand of her who must ever hate and despise you."

"In vain would be your efforts," said Flora; "the recollection of your lawless and desperate character would ever rise uppermost in my thoughts, and fill my mind with tenfold horror."

"The romantic ravings of a weak girl," said the baronet, unable to control the rage which the observations of our heroine created in his mind; "but we waste time in useless words. I gave you till to-night to reflect upon the proposal I had made to you."

"You did," faintly ejaculated Flora.

"And therefore," continued Sir Julian, "you cannot accuse me of want of forbearance. You have thought proper to remain obstinate, therefore I have nothing left now but to let you know my decision, from which nothing can move me. To-morrow you become my bride, the unwilling bride of the Smuggler King!"

"Oh, relent! relent!" exclaimed Flora, clasping her hands together; "pity me!"

"If I act with what you may consider harshness," remarked Sir Julian, "you have yourself to blame entirely. The Smuggler King would woo and be wooed. You have rejected my overtures with scorn; you have bitterly reproached me, and applied epithets to me that many men would have severely resented; all this I have borne with patience, but I am not to be foiled in anything upon which I have fixed my mind, and I have determined that you shall become my wife. Had you freely assented to have given me your hand. I would have kept my word, and restored you once more to your parents, with whom for a time you might have remained, but as it is, the Smuggler King will never part from his bride, but in this tower, or in his gallant ship, you shall evermore accompany him!"

"Horrible! horrible!" groaned our heroine, as Sir Julian thus spoke, and she covered her face with her hands, and sobbed aloud. The baronet contemplated her for a few moments in silence, but his determination was fixed, and neither tears nor entreaties could now move him from it. But poor Flora, what was her condition? She was completely distracted, for hope was now entirely shut out from her, and she gave herself up completely for lost. Again she sunk on her knees, and with clasped hands and streaming eyes, she supplicated the mercy of the smuggler captain.

"You pray in vain," he replied; "you have heard my decision, and nothing can alter it. The scorn, the hatred, with which you have treated me, but the more increases my desire, and will add to the triumph I shall obtain in possessing you."

"Rare triumph to boast of," returned the damsel, "that you have doomed to endless wretchedness an unprotected girl."

"That I have gained for my bride rather," said Sir Julian, "one of the loveliest of nature's creatures."

"But you will not, you cannot surely persist in this resolution?" said Flora.

"Again I tell you," answered the baronet, "that I am determined. To-morrow prepare yourself to become the bride of the Smuggler King!"

"To-morrow!" repeated the damsel; "is, then, my doom so soon to be sealed? Oh! aid me, Heaven!"

"There are many maidens who would be proud to become the bride of the smuggler-chief!" said Sir Julian; "he whose wealth is unbounded, and whose power is so well known and feared in all parts of the world. No whining, sickly churl is he, but one who boldly dares and boldly wins."

"Fearful man," ejaculated our heroine, with a shudder, "oh! how I tremble to look upon thee."

"But you must learn to love me," answered the baronet; "you must learn to admire my deeds of daring, and to love me for them."

"Oh! monstrous!"

"Nay!" exclaimed Sir Julian, "you will soon be taught to view things very differently, my beauteous Flora."

"Cruel man! think that my nature will ever cease to revolt at crime, and the awful scenes in which it is your delight to mingle?"

"It shall be my fault if you remain so delicate on those points, my sweet girl," returned the villain. "But away to your apartments, and prepare yourself for the ceremony to-morrow, which will make the rover of the seas the happiest man upon whom fortune ever showered her favours."

"To-morrow! no—no—recal that word."

"To-morrow, my angel, I repeat; to-morrow!"

"What will become of me?" exclaimed the distracted Flora; "oh, not so soon; delay it but for a short time, and —"

"Not for another day," firmly and decidedly interrupted the smuggler-chief; "my soul pants for the completion of my bliss!"

"Cannot anything make an impression on your inexorable heart?"

"It is because I love thee, adore thee, Flora, that I am thus precipitate and peremptory," returned Sir Julian.

"It cannot be!" ejaculated the poor girl; "Heaven will not permit the unholy, the unnatural ceremony to take place; and a dreadful curse will pursue you for making the attempt, and thus torturing an unprotected female who never did you any harm."

THE SMUGGLER KING. 377

"Nay, dearest Flora," returned Sir Julian; "certainly that Heaven you appeal to, will never punish a man for loving one of the most beauteous of nature's works."

"Lost! lost!" sighed Flora, as she sank into a chair and wept unrestrained. Sir Julian approached her nearer, and taking her fair hand, pressed it to his lips. At the odious salute, the maiden started, and hastily snatching her hand from him, retreated to the further end of the saloon.

"Stand off!" she exclaimed; "thy touch is more hateful to me than the sting of the most venomous serpent; and hear me, while I declare, in the face of Heaven, that never will I live as the Smuggler's Bride! the night that makes me yours, shall see me a breathless corpse."

"Be calm, fair maiden," said Sir Julian, once more approaching her; "this violent excitement will do you no good. Die!—no—no—you shall live for many years to add to the glory and happiness of that man whose only bliss is now centered in you."

"I will appeal to you no longer," said the damsel; "insensible to pity as you are, it is but a waste of words to talk to you. But once more I warn you; bethink yourself before you attempt to put your diabolical plans into execution, for as you doom me to misery, so surely will the curse and vengeance of Almighty God pursue you!"

"All, everything, will I brave," replied the libertine, "so that I secure that which is now the sunshine of my life."

"Suffer me to retire," said Flora; "I feel as if surrounded by every horror while in your presence."

"To-morrow," observed Sir Julian, as he touched a small silver hand-bell, to summon the attendance of Maud; "to-morrow is the auspicious day that unites our fates; by which time I trust to see my beauteous queen in a far different humour."

Flora returned no answer, for her heart was too full, and Maud now made her appearance.

"Conduct your mistress to her apartments," commanded Sir Julian, with a peculiar look, "and see that you do your best to prepare her for the joyous ceremony which will take place to-morrow."

Maud returned him no answer, but fixing a look of sympathy on our heroine, she hastened towards her, affectionately took her arm, and led her trembling and agitated footsteps from the saloon.

"Yes, to-morrow," soliloquised Sir Julian, when they had quitted the saloon; "to-morrow shall be the day which makes the beauteous Flora Clarendon my bride. No longer will I delay the ceremony; my very soul is wrapped up in her, and I love her as I have never loved woman before. This is one of the Smuggler King's greatest triumphs, and I feel as if I could really worship her with all the strength of the warmest affection. And yet she hates me—she reproaches me with my crimes. I wonder not at that, but when she is mine, I will contrive such schemes to fascinate her, and delude her senses, that I do not despair of finally altering her sentiments towards me. Lovely Flora! I have seen many of the most beauteous of their sex, but you far outshine them all. I have basked in the favours of the wealthy and the lovely, but never did I covet the favours of any one like yours. And yet 'tis hard to render miserable, even for a time, that gentle being. Psha! it is no use reflecting; I am hurried on by the delirium of ardent love, and it is in vain for me to attempt to resist its influence. What ho! Raker!"

"I am here, captain," answered the smuggler (who had been listening to all that had taken place between Sir Julian and Flora) entering the saloon immediately; "how seems the fair craft now?"

"Oh! obdurate as ever," answered the baronet.

"That is no more than I expected she would be," observed Sam Raker. "If you tarry until you win her affections, captain, I think you will have to wait long enough: for my own part, I should not have delayed the gratification of my wishes so long."

"I have decided," answered the captain. "To-morrow Flora Clarendon becomes the bride of the Smuggler King."

"A noble choice, and a prudent decision," said Raker; "for there's no knowing what squalls may arise, and something might occur to release her from your power before you had the opportunity of gratifying your wishes, and then there would be all your trouble and risk thrown away for nothing."

"True," answered the baronet; "but there is not much fear of that; the enemy we expected has not made its appearance."

"But it may do yet, captain," returned Sam Raker.

"I do not think there is much chance of that," remarked the smuggler-chief. "Grampus, I dare say, has met with the fate which all traitors ought to do, and the secret has perished with him, before he had an opportunity of divulging it."

"Very likely," said Raker; "and I only wish that he had been spared, and fallen once more into our hands, that I might have had the pleasure of flogging him to death. But when do you say that you have fixed for this ceremony to take place—to-morrow?"

"To-morrow," answered Sir Julian.

"That is very early."

"Just now you praised the promptitude of my decision," answered the captain.

"True, I did," replied Sam Raker; "but the bridal of the Smuggler King is no trifling occurrence, and should be performed with all due ceremony."

"The arrangements can soon be made," said Sir Julian. "We have everything ready for them, for this will not be the first time that your captain has led a bride to the altar in the tower of the Death Rock."

"A victim, rather, say," returned Sam, with a significant look.

"Ay, victim, if you will have it so," answered the baronet; "it is a matter of the utmost indifference. But I think I have managed this affair very well."

"With my assistance," added Sam Raker.

"Of course," coincided Sir Julian; "you know I fully appreciate your services."

"I believe you do, captain," observed the farmer, "and so you ought; but I did not expect that you would have had patience to have deferred the gratification of your desires so long."

"You must admit that I have acted with prudence," said Sir Julian; "for, had I been too peremptory, the mind of the girl might have sunk under it, and thus I should have been frustrated in my designs."

"True," answered Raker, "and even now I am doubtful whether she will be able to support the destiny you have awarded her."

"That I must leave to chance," returned the baronet; "if my powers of eloquence fail in the present instance, it will be the first time that they have done so. But I do not despair."

"And you say that the impression is still strong upon her mind that her lover is no more?"

"It is," answered the captain.

"And do you mean to make her acquainted with the facts?" demanded Raker.

"That depends upon circumstances," replied Sir Julian; "but I do not see how it is possible for me to deceive her long."

"Nor I."

"I must expect that she will suffer much for some time," added Sir Julian; "but it must be my constant task to endeavour to reconcile her to it."

"Ay," returned Sam Raker, "and, no doubt, you will find it a rather arduous one."

"That I must expect," said the baronet; "but I have had some obstinate tempers to battle with, but have never failed ultimately to come off conqueror, and I trust I shall do so on the present occasion."

"I have no doubt of it," observed Raker; "but I have every reason to believe that you will find it some time before you can erase the memory of her lover from her mind, to whom she was so devotedly attached."

"All that wealth and luxury can accomplish to dazzle her senses shall be put into operation," said the baronet.

"But will you not allow her to see her relations?" asked Raker.

"That will be matter for after consideration," replied Sir Julian, "though I think it would be a dangerous experiment."

"It would," answered the ruffian; "your real character may now be suspected, and were you to make your appearance again in the neighbourhood of the Hall, at present, at any rate, you would have the landsharks down upon you."

"It might be so," coincided Sir Julian, "and yet that confounded will; I must adopt some means to get that once more in my hands. You must endeavour to think of some scheme by which that may be accomplished, Sam."

"All in good time, captain," said the ruffian; "no doubt my usual ingenuity will suggest a plan ere long."

"Ay, I depend on you."

"And, rest assured, you will not find me fail," returned Raker. "Here, then, Flora Clarendon is destined to rule our queen?"

No. 48

"True," answered the baronet; "for awhile, till I have weaned her to my purpose, and then she shall become my partner in the Devil Skipper."

"Ah!" remarked Raker, "and I care not how soon that is, for we have been leading an indolent life of late, and our comrades much need your presence on board our gallant vessel, to stimulate them by your example to their usual deeds of daring."

"And they will find their king rejoin them with redoubled spirit," returned the captain; "and maintain the character he has hitherto so well supported, as the unconquerable and dauntless rover of the seas."

"But you will not make the girl acquainted with your real name?" demanded Raker.

"Certainly not," answered the baronet; "it would be imprudent to do so."

"And what name will she know you by?" asked Sam.

"Sir Vivian Lincoln," returned Sir Julian; "therefore, be cautious that you remember the name, and do not by any accident reveal my real one."

"You may depend upon me, captain."

"You must also warn the lads to secresy."

"I will do so."

"Enough," remarked the baronet; "now be careful to attend to my orders, and see that everything is in readiness for the ceremony to-morrow."

"I will lose no time in doing as you command," said Raker; "but I feel the want of some refreshment; a glass or two of wine would be as well to enable me to drink success to your designs, and long life to your bride elect."

Sir Julian pointed to the wine, and Sam Raker did not require any farther invitation to induce him to help himself, which he did in his usual unceremonious manner.

The baronet had been buried in deep thought for some minutes, while the ruffian was thus engaged, and he at length said,—

"I wish we could ascertain the actual fate of that fellow Grampus, for I have some apprehensions that he may have been able to have accomplished his designs, and that he has had an opportunity of revealing my real name and rank to some of our enemies."

"No," returned Raker, "it does not seem very likely, or we should have had the landsharks down upon us before this. I am still of opinion that he has perished, and that we have nothing to fear from him in future. Besides, as I have before said, we have everything in readiness for their reception, should they be bold enough to attempt to molest us, and we should teach them such a lesson that they would not be likely to get over for some time."

"I have no doubt of our being able to do so," said Sir Julian; "but still, under all the circumstances, it would be much better at present if we should not come into collision with them. It would put us to a very disagreeable inconvenience, and would frighten the damsel to death."

"Well, so it might," returned Sam Raker; "but, as I before said, I do not think we have much reason to apprehend any such event taking place. But is that all you want with me at present?"

"It is," answered Sir Julian; "but I shall expect to see you early again in the morning."

"You will find that I have been prompt in obeying your instructions," observed Raker, "and I shall look forward to to-morrow with anxiety, as a most important day."

"And I as one which which will complete my happiness," added the baronet. "I know not how it is, but this girl has excited a deeper interest in my bosom than I have experienced before under similar circumstances."

"She is indeed a fair craft," observed Sam, "and such a one as any man should feel proud of."

"She is," said Sir Julian, "and I would not like to lose the prize I have captured for a ship's load of specie."

The two villains now separated, and the baronet, having retired to his chamber, remained for some time in blissful anticipation on the victim he had doomed to destruction, and whom he saw no possibility of escaping from his power.

In the meantime the bitter anguish that our heroine was suffering may be imagined, but cannot be properly described. The fiat of her doom was sealed, her fate appeared to be inevitable; that fate so dreadful that it froze the very current of her veins to think of it. Hope was at an end; despair encompassed her on every side, and Maud had no farther consolation to offer her. She could only implore of her to still put her trust in the mercy of Omnipotence, who, even in the last moment, might interpose to save her from the danger with which she was threatened. Flora wrung her hands, and for a short time was completely inconsolable, and the agony of mind which her companion experienced at seeing the sufferings she endured was almost equal to her own. In vain she endeavoured to persuade her to retire to rest; to attempt to sleep she knew would be madness, and she determined to pass the night in giving vent to the painful feelings that distracted her brain.

At length the violence of the poor girl's grief was almost exhausted, and she became somewhat more calm. She sunk on her knees, and with streaming eyes implored the Almighty to assist her, and rather than she should fall a sacrifice to such a heartless and brutal villain as the pirate-chief, to take her life.

In this manner the time slowly vanished, and, as hour after hour elapsed, and the crisis of her destiny approached nearer, she felt the most poignant anguish and horror that the imagination can depicture. So short was the time allowed her, there was no prospect, there was not the slightest shadow of a chance of her being rescued. Hitherto, she had alternately been induced to encourage hope, when she reflected upon the note which she had from Grampus; but now, when so many days had elapsed, and he returned not to the tower, and she heard nothing of him, she concluded at once that he had failed in his undertaking, or had perished at sea. This idea was too probable for Maud to attempt to controvert it, and being, therefore, unable to offer her any soothing advice, she felt the misery of her situation the more acutely.

"Oh! my dear parents!" ejaculated Flora; "what dreadful sufferings would be yours, did you but know the present situation of your unhappy daughter; the awful, the revolting fate which is impending over her devoted head! Oh! what have I done to deserve to be thus persecuted? But I cannot, will not thus be doomed to horror and shame! No—no—my heart will break at the bare thought, and death will release me from that which is still more horrible. Almighty God! I earnestly and fervently beseech thee to receive my soul, but do not suffer me to fall beneath the power of this dreadful man."

She clasped her hands together energetically as she thus spoke, and her fair bosom heaved with the most violent and indescribable agony. Maud could not make use of any observation, but she gazed at her with those deep and expressive looks of sympathy, which she so ardently and so painfully felt.

All was silent in the tower, and it seemed as if all the smugglers had retired to their chambers, or to the two vessels that rode at anchor near the lofty rock on which the ancient building stood. The two friends remained silent for some time, but, at length the old clock, chiming forth the midnight hour, aroused them, and Maud once more endeavoured to persuade the poor girl to seek a few hours' repose. Flora shook her head mournfully, but she made no answer. It would be useless for her to attempt to seek repose in her present state of mind, for the thoughts of the coming day would entirely banish sleep from her eyelids.

The subsequent hours were passed alternately in weeping and praying, and a dreadful night it was to them both. Our heroine now remembered the dream she had had before she had been torn away from her home, and most of the circumstances in which had been realized, and now the whole of which seemed to be on the eve of being completed, and bitter were the pangs that these thoughts occasioned her.

At length the first beams of opening dawn broke through the casement, and never had any day been ushered in with such misery to Flora and her companion. The crisis of her destiny was rapidly approaching, and it seemed as if nothing could avert it. To appeal to Sir Julian for mercy and forbearance, she knew would be useless, for mercy was a stranger to his breast, and the last interview she had had with him convinced her that his determination was fixed. The unhappy criminal awaiting his certain doom, could not have suffered more than she did at that time, and it was most remarkable that she could find fortitude at all to support it. She listened with breathless attention and anxiety to every sound that could be heard in the tower, expecting every minute that she should be summoned to the saloon; but the morning passed away, and still she remained uninterrupted.

Maud exerted herself to the utmost to inspire her with fortitude and resignation, although the despair she felt was equal almost to her own, and she trembled when she reflected on the consequences that might follow the proceedings of that day. At length a different feeling suddenly came over our heroine, and a ray of hope was once more permitted to enter her bosom. Firm in her own innocence, she felt assured that Providence would never suffer it to fall a sacrifice to the atrocious designs and wicked machinations of the guilty, but that something would occur to save her from it, even at the very moment when it appeared inevitable.

It was a great relief to the mind of Maud to behold this change, and she encouraged her in it.

"Be firm, my dear Flora," she observed; "be firm, and all will yet be well. Something seems to convince me that the events of this day will terminate very differently to that we have hitherto anticipated; and that the miscreant in whose power you are, will not be permitted eventually to triumph."

"He shall not! by Heaven, he shall not!" exclaimed our heroine; "he may force me to the altar, but that moment shall my hand terminate an existence that would then be a curse to me."

"I beseech you," ejaculated Maud, "do not entertain such fearful ideas; the Almighty will not suffer you to be driven to such an awful extremity. The designs of the villain will be frustrated, and you will be released from your present danger. But, hark! some one approaches."

"Ah!" gasped forth Flora, "they come; the wretches approach to force me to the place where the hateful and unholy ceremony is to be performed. The moment of trial is at hand. Oh! heart, be firm."

"Courage! courage!" returned Maud, embracing her.

"You will not leave me, Maud?" said the poor girl; "you will not leave me alone to the mercy of these diabolical wretches?"

"I will not, my poor girl," answered Maud; "let whatever may be the consequences, on this occasion, at any rate, they shall not force me from you."

"Oh! thanks, thanks. But they come."

At that moment the voice of Sam Raker was heard outside, demanding admittance, and after a moment or two's hesitation, Maud opened the door, and he entered the room.

He was attired in a peculiar and gaudy manner, and from the expression of his countenance, it seemed as if he looked forward to the events of the day with no small degree of interest. Flora could not help shuddering at his appearance, and averting her gaze, she hid her face in the bosom of Maud.

"Our captain awaits his bride!" said Sam, "and all is in readiness for the performance of the ceremony; so, young lady, I must once more offer you my services to guide you to the saloon."

Our heroine gently removed her head from the bosom of Maud, and raising her eyes solemnly towards Heaven, she mentally implored its protection and mercy. She then took the proffered arm of Maud, and prepared to follow the ruffian with more firmness than she at first expected she should have been able to acquire. When, however, she once more arrived at the door of the saloon, a sickly feeling again came over her, and had it not been for the support of the attentive Maud, she must have sunk to the earth.

A strange confusion of voices met their ears, proceeding from the saloon, and the utmost bustle seemed to prevail within it, as if they were making preparations for the important event that was about to take place. Flora sighed, and as she raised her head, and gazed upon the door, it seemed as if she was about to enter the temple of despair. Again she mentally committed herself to the care and protection of Heaven, and then she felt more tranquil, and her mind made up for the worst that might follow, still placing her firm reliance on the goodness and mercy of that power she had invoked, and trusting that, even when the danger by which she was surrounded seemed most threatening and inevitable, it would interpose to rescue her, and to bring to punishment her cruel oppressor.

Sam Raker having given three peculiar knocks at the door of the saloon, which he had never done on any previous occasion, the voices ceased, and a silence of a second or two followed, during which interval, our heroine was in a state of the most painful suspense, while at the same time, the proceedings filled her with astonishment and a sensation approaching to awe. Maud exhibited little less surprise and uneasiness, but she endeavoured to conquer it, in order that she might be the better enabled to encourage and sustain Flora, under the trial to which she was at present exposed.

The door at length was opened, but all was involved in utter darkness beyond, and Flora's amazement and uneasiness increased. There was something so remarkably solemn about all the proceedings, and the aspect of everything around, that it was sufficient to fill less timid minds than hers with dread, and altogether it bordered closely upon the supernatural.

Raker laid hold of one of our heroine's arms, while Maud gently took the other, and she was led forward a few paces; but still all was buried in impenetrable darkness, and she was unable to ascertain whether or not there was any one present beside themselves, although she had no doubt that there was.

At length a solemn strain of the most impressive music vibrated on their ears, and floated around the spacious apartment, and gradually a pale and sickly light appeared at the farther end of the saloon, and revealed to them a neatly constructed altar, covered with rich crimson velvet, and adorned with numerous curious devices, in gold.

Completely bound up in astonishment and awe, Flora was unable to utter a word, but stood transfixed to the spot, and clinging fearfully to Maud.

Raker now left them, and shortly afterwards the music ceased, and they once more heard the indistinct murmurings of several voices, which convinced them they were in the presence of the smugglers, although they could not see them.

An interval of a few minutes elapsed in this manner, and then the tones of the music once more swelled upon their ears, and was immediately followed by the chorus quoted underneath, which seemed to be sung by at least a hundred voices, and in tones that were remarkably impressive, and in that strain of wild harmony that had a most extraordinary effect.

"Hail! all hail to this joyous day,
Banish dull care far away;
Let mirth o'er everything preside,
To welcome the smuggler chieftain's bride!
She moves the Queen of Beauty here,
No face so lovely, no form so fair;
And care at her presence must take wing,
Fit prize is she for the Smuggler King!
      Hail! all hail, to this joyous day,
      Banish dull care far away;
      Let mirth o'er everything preside,
      To welcome the smuggler chieftain's bride!

"She comes—she comes, the ocean queen,
So bright her face, so chaste her mien;
She comes to rule o'er the ocean tide,
The lovely and fair, the rover's bride!
Then raise the voice, in gladness raise,
And shout aloud our mistress's praise;
Swiftly the hours in mirth shall glide,
Hurrah! for the smuggler monarch's bride!
      Hail! all hail, to this joyous day,
      Banish dull care far away;
      Let mirth o'er everything preside,
      To welcome the smuggler chieftain's bride!"

The chorus ceased—the music was no longer heard; a delightful and intoxicating fragrance seemed to fill the air, and to exhale its powerful influence over the senses. Our heroine, bewildered by astonishment, and a number of indescribable sensations, pressed closer to Maud, but still the power of utterance was denied her, and she was completely enchained, as it were, by some magic spell. Such was the effect of all around, that it seemed scarcely possible to be the work of mortal beings, and appeared more like one of those extraordinary scenes wove by the imagination of a romance writer, than one of reality.

The time, however, that Flora and Maud were given for these reflections, was but brief; suddenly a loud sound, like a blow upon a gong, resounded through the saloon, and made them start with astonishment, and the next instant the whole place became brilliantly illuminated as if by magic, and the scene which burst upon their ears—the numerous persons present—the peculiarity of their dresses, and the magnificence of all the arrangements, completely dazzled them, and held them in mute astonishment, not unmingled with admiration.

If the splendour of the saloon had before surprised our heroine, she was now quite thunderstruck at the costliness and taste of the display. It seemed as if it was impossible that such a change could have been effected in so short a time. It was one complete scene of brilliancy and surpassing gorgeousness. But when the thought occurred to Flora that all this was got up merely to delude her senses, and as a prelude to her future misery and destruction, her heart sickened, and every limb trembled violently with her excessive agitation. She cast her eyes hurriedly around, but they did not rest upon Sir Julian; he was not present.

The smugglers were arranged on either side of the saloon, and around the throne, and their looks showed the deep interest they took in the unholy ceremony which was about to take place. Beneath the canopy of the throne were placed two lofty, and elegantly gilt and carved chairs, while around it were suspended numerous festoons of flowers, all arranged with the most exquisite taste, and which at once displayed the refined mind of the person who had devised them. The steps that ascended to the throne were covered with rich crimson velvet, and bordered with gold lace, and the festive board, at the head of which it was placed, displayed a profusion of the most magnificent gold and silver plate; in short, everything upon which the eye rested had the most overpowering effect, and gave to the whole more the appearance of some apartment in a fairy palace, than that of the residence of human beings.

The altar was arranged with equal care and judgment, and on each side of it were placed magnificent vases, filled with the most rare exotics, of every delicate hue.

Flora, quite overpowered, sunk on an ottoman, and Maud, placing herself by her side, sought to support her spirits, although she was almost as bewildered and agonised as herself. A pause ensued, and then Raker whispered something to his companions, and placing himself at the head of them, they walked in procession past our heroine, and as they did so, they bowed in homage to her, and then resumed their station in the places they had previously occupied. Once more the organ swelled to its fullest pitch of harmony, and then the smugglers repeated the following words of the chorus :—

"Hail! all hail! to this joyous day,
Banish dull care far away,
Let mirth o'er everything preside,
To welcome the smuggler chieftain's bride,
She comes, the queen of beauty here,
No face so lovely, no form so fair,
And care at her presence must take wing,
Fit prize is she for the Smuggler King!"

Scarcely was this chorus finished, when the folding doors were thrown open, and, attended by several of his crew, Sir Julian entered the saloon.

All that art or wealth could accomplish, he had lavished upon his person, and it was impossible to gaze upon him, in spite of his real character, without a feeling of deep interest, if not admiration. He wore a surtout of crimson velvet, glittering with jewels and gold lace, an elegantly embroidered white satin waistcoat, and a kilt, or petticoat, to match. On his breast he wore a brilliant star, and his head was surmounted by a coronet, formed out of diamonds, pearls, brilliants, and other precious stones. His appearance in the centre of the saloon was the signal for the loudest acclamations of joy and greeting among the smugglers, and, while they walked around him, and paid him their homage, they shouted in tones of redoubled gladness the following words :—

"Hail! all hail! to our Smuggler King,
Before whose power the foe takes wing;
Let us be gay! let us be gay!
This is our monarch's bridal day!
He rules with might o'er the ambient tide,
In his floating palace he'll boldly glide;
But there is not a prize so rare to bring,
As his beauteous bride to our Smuggler King.
Then, let us be gay; let us be gay;
Away with care, away! away!
And we'll make these walls right merrily ring,
In the praise of his bride and our Smuggler King."

Sir Julian stood for a few moments after this chorus had ceased, apparently transfixed in admiration of our lovely heroine, his destined victim, who remained with fixed eyes upon all around, and apparently in a state bordering upon apathy. All hope was at an end, and misery and despair seemed to be inevitable. All around her was alike a scene of enchantment, and Sir Julian viewed the effect it had upon her with feelings of brutal satisfaction.

At length the baronet made a signal to one of the smugglers, who left the saloon, and, in a short time returned, accompanied by two others, one of whom had a costly coronet in his hands, and the other a magnificent velvet robe; they advanced towards the place where the unfortunate damsel was seated, and kneeling obsequiously before her, they placed the robe and the coronet in the hands of Maud, with looks sufficiently intelligible to instruct her how to use them, and then once more retired. Maud trembled with disgust and agitation, but she knew that it would be useless to attempt to make any resistance, and while heart swelled with indignation, and she felt the utmost possible sympathy for her hapless companion, she threw the robe across her shoulders, and placed the coronet upon her brow; poor Flora seeming to be entirely unconscious of what was going forward. No sooner, however, was this task accomplished than the place resounded with the shouts of the smugglers, and once more they raised their voices in tumultuous chorus:—

> "Hail! all hail! to the rover's bride,
> Who is destined to rule o'er the ocean's tide;
> With shouts of gladness these walls shall ring,
> In praise of the bride of the Smuggler King!
> Hurrah! hurrah! 'tis a day of glee,
> In homage to her he bent each knee;
> Joy to the hearts of all it must bring,
> To behold the bride of the Smuggler King!
> Hail! all hail! to the rover's bride,
> Destined to rule o'er the ocean tide,
> With shouts of gladness these walls shall ring,
> In praise of the bride of the Smuggler King."

As the chorus proceeded, the senses of our heroine were recalled; she arose from the ottoman on which she had been seated; renewed energy swelled her frame, and added grace and dignity to her whole demeanour; her brilliant eyes shot forth flashes of indignation, and for a moment or two seemed to astonish Sir Julian and the Smugglers present, and a dead silence ensued, during which interval the damsel was collecting all her fortitude to give utterance to her feelings. Maud was completely lost in amazement at her manner, and awaited the result with the most painful suspense and impatience

Flora advanced a few paces; there was firmness in every step, and the most withering command in her manner. Then she paused, and, in a voice which resounded through the spacious apartment, and commanded immediate and soul-absorbing attention, she exclaimed:—

"Hold! monsters! sacrilegious monsters, hold your accursed and blasphemous ceremonies! In the name of high Heaven, I command you to forbear, and on your heads invoke its most terrible vengeance should you dare to persist. Great as is your power, it must sink into insignificance before that of innocence and virtue! Dare not to proceed with your unholy rites; nature, justice, humanity, all forbid them, and revolt from them! Thus!—thus, do I scorn your base and cruel mockery; your insidious arts to ensnare your defenceless victims to destruction. Away! away with these baubled trappings, whose touch is contamination; purchased only by shame, misery, and dishonour!"

Thus saying, the heroic maiden tore the robe from her shoulders, and dashed the coronet from her brow, at her feet; then, while her countenance assumed an aspect almost unearthly, she stood firmly before them all, and seemed to bid them defiance.

Sir Julian and every one present were completely astounded, and could scarcely believe the evidence of their senses. They had never imagined that one so gentle and so delicate, could ever have assumed an air of such surpassing dignity, and the baronet was for a short time at a loss how to proceed; but he soon recovered himself, and then advancing towards our heroine, his countenance assumed the most bland smiles, and he attempted to take her hand; but she recoiled from him in horror.

"Miscreant!" she exclaimed; "do not offer to touch me; prisoner as I am to you, I stand firm in my reliance upon the protection of the Supreme, and I feel confident that He will not suffer such sacrilege—such an unholy, such an unnatural sacrifice. Off, tyrant, lest the retribution of that power you affect to scorn, but to which you must submit, should overtake you, and crush you before my sight, with all your sins upon your head. If you would make some atonement for the many guilty deeds you have already perpetrated, abandon your present diabolical designs, and permit me to return to my apartments."

"Ask me, beauteous Flora," returned the libertine; "ask me to resign wealth, everything I possess; but to abandon you, my queen; my bride elect; you on whom my whole soul is fixed, you on whom it would lavish its most unbounded adoration—oh! there is madness in the thought. No; too long have I delayed the gratification of my desires, and sought by every means to win your love; but now the day has come, and this hour, this instant shall make thee mine!"

"Thine?—never!" cried Flora, recoiling from him, and clinging to Maud; "Heaven will never permit it, and here do I pray that it will take my life, rather than to suffer me to fall a victim to such a monster."

"Dear Flora!" said Sir Julian, "why thus waste your time, and pollute your lips by the utterance of such unfeminine epithets? Resistance is useless;

No. 49

all is prepared for the ceremony; so come, most lovely of all womankind, to the altar, to the altar!"

"Oh, mercy—mercy!" implored the damsel, struggling to release her hand from his hold; "abandon your cruel intentions, and I will freely forgive you all the sufferings you have caused me, all that it may yet be my hard fate to experience from you."

"Sufferings!" repeated the baronet; "I would sooner perish than inflict upon you any future wrong. You shall have all the bliss, the luxuries that wealth can purchase, or the love of man suggest. I will be your slave; you shall command my every will, and ——"

"Cease—cease!" interrupted the indignant girl; "dare you to talk to me of happiness, when you would doom me to shame; when you would make me the mistress of a pirate, a murderer; the associate of wretches, who exult in the miseries of their fellow-creatures, who delight in the shedding of human blood?"

"I will listen to no more," said Sir Julian; "my mind is made up, and no persuasion, no entreaties can move me from it. The time is come, and the rover of the seas claims his bride."

"My God!" exclaimed Flora, her courage almost forsaking her, and turning most ghastly pale; "my God! is there no hope? No means of escape from ——"

"Escape!" interrupted the baronet, with a look of contempt; "what possibility, think you, is there of escaping from my power? No; the decree is irrevocable, and you are only fruitlessly agitating yourself by thus offering any opposition to it. Come then, my love, and believe me you shall have cause to bless the moment when you became the bride of the Smuggler King!"

Maud now attempted to expostulate; but Sir Julian silenced her with a frown; and now, leading the almost powerless and unresisting girl towards the altar, he stamped with his foot three times, and quick at the signal, a door behind the altar opened, and a figure appeared which was enough to strike terror and astonishment in every breast.

It was that of a man, tall and majestic, habited in a long, flowing black gown, on which were a number of curious and mystic devices. A long white beard descended on his breast, and his features were concealed beneath a black mask, similar to that which the Smuggler King usually wore.

At the sight of this mysterious being, Flora started back appalled; but Sir Julian supported her trembling form with his arm, and gently forced her towards the altar. The smugglers all gathered round in an instant, and then the man, having performed several motions with his hands, and muttered some unintelligible words to himself, the organ sent forth a wild, yet solemn piece of harmony, which continued for several minutes; and, having ceased, the mystic priest commanded silence, in a voice of authority, and, having once more uttered some indistinct words, he turned to Sir Julian, who was still supporting the form of the almost unconscious Flora, and said,—

"King of the free roving sons of the sea, art thou willing, in the presence of thy subjects, to make this damsel thy queen and bride?"

"I am," answered Sir Julian; "no other shall be the bride of the Smuggler King."

"Swear!" exclaimed the priest.

"I swear, by all the rules and laws, and consequences that belong us," answered Sir Julian.

"Then kneel, kneel all, while the ceremony which makes her thine is being performed," commanded the man. In a moment the ruffians gathered nearer towards the altar and knelt; and the priest commenced the unnatural rites, by performing a number of curious and extravagant antics, all the time muttering unintelligible words, and in a language which seemed to be peculiar to himself,

All this time our heroine had been bound up in a kind of apathetic horror ; but suddenly, by a powerful effort, releasing herself from the hold of Sir Julian, she exclaimed,—

"Forbear, sacrilegious wretches, forbear ! Heaven forbids the ceremony !"

"Heed her not !" cried Sir Julian, determinedly, once more seizing her hand, and forcing her to the altar ; "heed her not, but proceed ; I, your king, command you !"

Again the priest proceeded with the mystic ceremony ; but he had scarcely uttered a sentence when Flora, overcome by the horror of her feelings, uttered a loud scream, and sunk insensible before the altar.

"Proceed—proceed !" cried the inhuman baronet ; "heed her not, she must, she shall be mine."

Notwithstanding the insensibility of the poor girl, and the tears and supplications of Maud, the priest was about to obey, when suddenly the loud report of a gun was heard ; the smugglers started to their feet, and Sir Julian gazed around him in astonishment and confusion.

"Ah !" he exclaimed, involuntarily releasing our heroine's hand ; "what means that sound ?"

He had scarcely asked the question, when the folding-doors at the further end of the saloon were thrown open, and several of the smugglers rushed in, in a state of the utmost trepidation.

"How now, fellows," hastily demanded Sir Julian ; "what means this interruption ?—what has occurred to alarm ye thus ?"

"Two British men-of-war are bearing down rapidly towards us, captain," answered one of the ruffians ; "quick—quick—to action, for in a few minutes they will be upon us !"

"D——n !" shouted the enraged captain, "to be interrupted at this moment. It is the enemy we have apprehended for the last few days ; but we are prepared to meet them. Curses on the traitor, Grampus, he has succeeded better than I thought he would. Convey the maiden to her apartments, and see that she is well guarded ; then a portion of you follow me to the ships. We will give the lubbers such a salute as they little suspect. Follow me !"

The priest vanished in a minute, and Maud bore the insensible form of our heroine to her chamber, attended by two or three of the smugglers, who were appointed to guard her, and then the rest of the fellows followed their captain to the ships.

What a change had a few minutes caused. All was confusion in the tower, but every man was quickly at his post, ready for the defence, while Sir Julian, having assumed his black mask and his usual disguise, in a very few minutes was on board the Devil Skipper, and promptly issuing his orders to his daring crew, flying about to all parts of the vessel, and seeing that all was in readiness to receive the enemy.

The ships that were approaching them were heavy burthened, and already hoisted the British flag at the main. Sir Julian viewed them with a steady eye, and was prepared to meet them with all his usual determination and reckless bravery ; but yet his soul burnt with rage and indignation at the interruption which had thus taken place to the ceremony. Every one of the ruffians were resolved to fight to the last, and to perish to a man, rather than yield, and they placed every confidence in their own power, and the skill of their lawless commander.

Boldly the pirate hoisted his flag, and, by firing a salute, dared the enemy to approach. This they replied to by one of defiance, and continued on their way, making for the most convenient place to attack the smugglers. In a short time the two ships of war had got so close that the pirates were enabled to speak them, and demand their business. To this they replied that they were two of his Majesty's ships of war, and commanded Sir Julian and his crew to surrender in the name of the king. The pirates answered them by a heavy broadside, which did some execution, but did not appear to disconcert them, and running boldly into the pirate vessels, the combat commenced with the most desperate valour on both sides. And now nothing was to be heard but the loud roar of the guns, and at intervals the loud voices of the different officers in command, as they issued their orders to, and encouraged their men on. Sir Julian was to be seen foremost in every danger, and his fine muscular figure, and the hideous black mask beneath which he concealed his features giving him an appearance of something supernatural.

The fire of each of the contending vessels was well directed, and the damage done appeared to be about equal; but the enemy fought with the most cool intrepidity, and several times baffled the skill of the smuggler-chief. At length they succeeded in boarding the Raven, but a heavy discharge from the batteries of the tower compelled them to retreat again to their own vessels, and the Devil Skipper having forced a favourable point to assist the other, the engagement became fiercer than ever, and it was doubtful which way the combat would terminate, Sir Julian hoarsely commanding the wretches to give no quarter. Again the enemy boarded the Raven, and again were they repulsed, and the most dreadful slaughter took place on both sides.

At length the quick eye of Sir Julian perceived through the smoke, that the enemy had taken advantage of the confusion of the contest, and succeeded in landing a number of men on an accessible part of the rock, up which they were bounding, in spite of the heavy fire which was opened upon them from the tower, and seemed determined, at all hazards, to make an attack upon that place.

The idea of Flora immediately occurred to him, and fearful that there were not sufficient men in the ancient edifice to save her from falling into their hands, he hastily resigned the command of the Devil Skipper to Sam Raker, and leaping on to the rock, followed by about twenty of the crew, he made his way round to a secret entrance, and immediately gained admittance. And now the slaughter outside the tower was dreadful, while that on board the contending vessels continued with unabated fury. The sailors attempted to scale the walls of the tower, but the heavy fire which was continued upon them laid many a brave heart low, and it seemed evident that they would soon have been compelled to retreat to their ships, when they succeeded in forcing a door, and rushed boldly into the tower. The smugglers met them sword and pistol in hand, and fought with the fury of demons; but nothing could daunt the intrepidity of their companions, or the cool courage of their antagonists, the latter of whom seemed determined to lose their lives in endeavouring to exterminate the villains, and to secure the person of the Smuggler King. They were also aware that he held our heroine in his power, and were resolved to leave no means untried that skill could suggest, or resolution accomplish, to restore her to liberty.

For some time Sir Julian fought at the head of his crew, and performed perfect prodigies of valour and daring, but finding that the assailants were fast gaining ground, and that the smugglers were falling on every side, he became outrageous, and resolved to secure Flora, even at the hazard of his own life. He fought his way to the apartment in which she was confined, and snatching her in his arms, he hurried to the battlements, where a number of the smugglers were hotly engaged in endeavouring to repulse the sailors who were attempting to scale the walls.

The presence of their heroic and desperate chief, re-animated them, and with loud shouts and yells of triumph, they surrounded him on every side, while he supported the inanimate form of the maiden with one arm, and fought a lion with the other.

From the walls the unfortunate but brave seamen were hurled one after the other, and immediately slaughtered by the wretches beneath. At this moment Sir Julian, happening to cast his anxious eyes towards the ocean, beheld, to his dismay and confusion, the Devil Skipper and the Raven break loose from the enemy, and sheer off with the rapidity of lightning.

"Hell and furies!" he shouted; "what is the meaning of this? The rascals!—have they turned cowards? The crew of the Smuggler King fly from any enemy? It cannot be! And yet, see, they flee before the wind with impetuous speed!"

Hoarsely Sir Julian shouted, as though his voice could be heard above the roar of the cannon, and the deafening noise of the conflict; but in a moment he became more calm, as a sudden thought flashed across his brain. It was probably a scheme of Sam Raker's to draw the enemy in chase after them, and thus arrest their action upon the tower; but, however such might have been the case, it signally failed, for the enemy, after firing a couple of heavy broadsides after them, suffered them to escape, and it was soon evident that they were about to turn their whole attention towards the tower, for numbers of the seamen quitted the ships in boats, and succeeded in gaining the rock, which they ascended with desperate determination, cutting down all who opposed them.

The situation of Sir Julian was now most perilous, and he saw that nothing but the most determined and desperate valour could save him from falling into the hands of the enemy. They had succeeded in repulsing those who had first gained an entrance into the tower. He rallied his men, and while some of them rushed out like furies to repel the assailants, he kept his position, directing the fire, and stimulating the crew by his example, to fresh exertions. The seamen, however, continued to clamber up the rock, and fought with a valour which it seemed impossible for any one to resist. Sir Julian, seeing the desperate situation of affairs, requested a parley, which, being granted, he came forward, and still supporting the insensible form of our heroine on one arm, he exclaimed in a loud voice:—

"You know you have a desperate man to contend with, who will sooner die than be taken, while destruction to yourselves would almost be sure to follow. However, I give you one fair chance of saving yourselves. Retire immediately to your ships, and leave this place, which you shall do unmolested; refuse, and before your eyes I immediately sacrifice the life of this innocent girl. I give you five minutes to consider, and, if you are wise you will accept of my terms; if you are mad enough to reject them, the consequences that will be sure to follow be upon your own heads."

The officers appeared astounded by these propositions, but they consulted together, while the villain Sir Julian stood calmly awaiting their decision, with a dagger pointed to the bosom of our unfortunate heroine, ready to put his dreadful threat into execution.

Suddenly a shout of alarm was heard among the seamen and the smugglers, followed by a loud report, and the next instant flames and smoke issued from the different casements of the tower, and it was discovered to be on fire.

The utmost confusion now prevailed, and when they looked up towards the battlements again, Sir Julian and Flora had disappeared. A second report was heard in the building, and the seamen had scarcely time to retreat down the sides of the rock to their own ships, when a fearful explosion took place; a column of black smoke ascended to the clouds, and when it had dispersed, nothing was to be seen of the tower of the terrible Rock of Death, but a portion of its shattered walls, and the heaps of ruins mingled with the mangled remains of the dead, which strewed the spot around.

This calamity struck horror into the minds of all who beheld it, and they looked at each other for a few minutes without being able to speak. At length, however, the officers commanded the crew to follow them, in order

that they might examine the ruins, and see whether there were any survivors from the accident, although that seemed to be most improbable. A
scene of awful devastation presented itself to their observation ; but they
could discover nothing of the remains of Sir Julian or Flora, and they returned to the ship with the most melancholy thoughts, occasioned by the
bad success of their designs, and the melancholy fate which they had every
reason to suppose had befallen the unfortunate damsel whom they had been
so anxious to rescue.

Having collected their wounded together, the following morning, before
daylight they left the place, not being in a condition to give chase to the
two pirate vessels, and entertaining no hopes of their coming up with them
had they even done so.

CHAPTER XXI.

THE FATE OF WILLIAM.—THE RECLUSE FAMILY.

WILLIAM had been thrown overboard by one of the pirates just before
the destruction of their vessel, and, from the fury of the engagement, was
unable to regain the English ship. He, therefore, gave himself up for lost ;
however, he still struggled with the waters, resolved to retain life while there
was the least chance, and striking out as well as his strength would permit
him, he soon found himself out of the reach of danger from the contending
vessels.

Almost immediately after this he beheld the pirate vessel explode, and
the next instant he narrowly escaped being killed from the timbers that
fell around him. Quickly, however, recovering himself, he seized one of
them, and securing himself as well as he could to it, he endeavoured to
reach the English vessel. The exertion he had undergone in the engagement, and since, was too much for him, and he became insensible.

The fate of the hapless mariner would now have seemed to be inevitable,
but Providence still watched over him, and destined him to other things.
On regaining his senses, he found himself stretched upon a sandy beach,
and he became conscious of the kind attentions of some person. He looked
up, and was astonished when he beheld one of the most lovely forms he
had ever seen hanging over him, with looks of the greatest anxiety, and at
that moment engaged in bathing his temples with some water, and trying
all means to recover him. He could scarcely believe but that it was some
bright delusive vision ; but when she saw him open his eyes, and that he
breathed freely again, she uttered an exclamation of delight, and the
deepest blushes of maiden modesty suffused her cheeks.

It was a young girl, who seemed scarcely to have numbered seventeen
summers. Her form, which was rather singularly attired, was grace and
symmetry itself, and her countenance was of that surpassing loveliness and
gentleness, that it could not fail to create admiration in the most insensible
breast.

Surprised, confused, and almost incredulous, by a powerful effort of his
enfeebled strength he got upon his feet, and gazed alternately upon the
damsel, and then around him.

"Where am I ?" he exclaimed ; "and, lovely being, who are you, and
how came you here ?"

"Thank Heaven !" answered the fair stranger, in a voice of the most
musical sweetness—"thank Heaven you have been restored to life ! I found
you stretched upon the beach, and thought at first you were dead, but by
great exertions I have been able to restore you, and ——"

"My kind, my lovely preserver," interrupted the young seaman, still gazing with astonishment and admiration at the fair being before him, "to whom am I indebted for this service, and how came you on this island ?"

"My mother and my other relations reside on this island, sir," replied the blushing girl, "and have done for some time."

"Is it possible ?" ejaculated William.

"It is true," returned the lovely girl; "accident brought us hither, and we have long since despaired of ever being released from it."

"Are there, then, no other inhabitants in the place ?" inquired William, looking anxiously around the place, which presented a much more cheerful aspect than he had at first anticipated.

"There are not," answered the young girl.

"Surprising !" observed our hero; "and saw you nothing of any vessel near this place this morning ?"

"I did not," said the former, "although I concluded that you had been washed ashore from some wreck, and wondered that I did not behold any portions of it."

"Wonderful !" once more ejaculated William; "to me it appears almost impossible."

"But come, sir," said the simple and artless girl, "you must need some refreshment and rest; if you will be pleased to accompany me, I know that my dear mother will be most happy to receive you, and to bid you welcome to all the assistance she can render you."

"Many thanks, fair maiden," said William; "I am ready to attend you."

The damsel made no reply, but stepping lightly, and apparently with the greatest inward satisfaction, along, William, bound up in the utmost astonishment, and scarcely able to convince himself that this remarkable adventure was real, followed her. They soon came in sight of a rudely-constructed hut, partly formed of canvass, and the roof covered with the boughs of trees, and from which it became evident to the young seaman that some one had been on the island before the present family, as, from what he had heard from the young girl, he had reason to conclude that they were all females, and would not have been able to have erected such a place, if they had even been supplied with the means. His surprise increased more and more every moment.

The damsel tripped lightly before him, looking back but once to see whether he was following her, and entered the hut before he had time to reach it. He paused for a few seconds to recollect himself, and to gaze around him, and while he was thus occupied, a middle-aged female, of most lady-like appearance, emerged from the hut, and advanced towards him with a bland smile.

William hastened forward, and made a graceful bow; but the singularity of the adventure altogether had deprived him for the moment of the use of speech, and every faculty was enchained in astonishment and satisfaction.

"Welcome, stranger, to the solitary retreat of the recluse and her family," said the lady; "though most deeply do I regret the misfortune which has cast you on this shore. You are the first human being I have seen on this island, with the exception of my own family, and most happy am I to think that my daughter has been the means of saving you from an untimely fate."

"My dear madam," answered William, "if I do not express my sense of kindness as I ought, or the debt of gratitude I owe to your fair daughter, you must attribute it to my astonishment at finding myself in such a situation, and ——"

"Ah!" exclaimed the lady, with a look of satisfaction—"an Englishman?"

"Yes, madam," returned William, "I am an Englishman, and have,
although young, had my share of the perils and storms of life. But recently I was rescued, with an unfortunate companion, from a desolate rock,
and when the hope had just entered my bosom that I should soon return
to my native land, we were attacked by pirates. I was thrown overboard
—clung to a plank, and recollect no more until I was found by your lovely
daughter."

The lady seemed to listen to William with much attention and admiration. Her countenance, which was still very beautiful, was melancholy,
and she frequently sighed, as gloomy thoughts flashed across her memory.
It was evident that she had experienced the trials and vicissitudes of life,
and, indeed, her present situation, with that of her family, was sufficient to
prove that she had had her ample share of sorrow.

The lady now repeated her gratification at the miraculous preservation
of William, and, after once more expressing her willingness to afford him
all the accommodation that their circumstances and the hut would afford,
he followed her into the humble and rudely-constructed dwelling, which he
found to be scantily furnished with such articles as would be likely to
have been saved from some wreck, and on that point his hostess soon satisfied him, by informing him that, just as he saw the hut then, they found it
when they came to the island, which convinced them that some unfortunate
mariner or mariners had been formerly cast upon the place, and had probably at last been rescued from their lonely situation.

The family of the lady (who, it seemed, was a widow) consisted of Lilian,
the beauteous girl to whom William was indebted for the preservation of
his life; another girl, apparently about two years younger than her sister,
a sylph-like little maiden, with luxuriant auburn tresses, and bright, clear,
blue eyes, and a fine youth, whose age appeared to be about eighteen years.

William gazed at this fair group with wonder and admiration, while
they all flocked about him on his entrance, and he seemed no less to excite
their curiosity and interest. Their manners were simple as their life, but
there was something altogether about them which convinced the young seaman that they were of no common origin, and his amazement was the more
increased that they should be brought into such a situation, for, that they
had voluntarily chosen it, he could not for a moment imagine.

He had not much time, however, given him for these reflections, for,
having seated himself on a stool, the youngest girl and Lilian bustled about
to spread before him such refreshments as the place afforded, which consisted of fish and fruits, and a very pleasant wine, extracted from the grape,
which he was given to understand grew in abundance on the island.

The elderly lady pressed him to eat, which he did, and afterwards felt
much refreshed, and eloquently repeated his thanks for the kindness he had
received, and, at the same time, could not help giving utterance to his astonishment at finding the interesting family in such an extraordinary situation, although he could not imagine that they had voluntarily chosen it as a
residence.

"You are right, sir," answered the lady. "We were driven here by the
most untoward destiny, and we have now been the sole inhabitants of this
place for upwards of four years."

"Is it possible?" said William. "And, during that long period, have
you not had any chance of deliverance?"

"We have seen several vessels pass at no great distance from the island,"
replied the lady; "but failed in endeavouring to make them acquainted with
our situation. And, indeed," she added, with a deep sigh, "we have ex-

perienced so many troubles in the world, and have at length become so associated with this place, that we are almost careless of leaving it."

"Your misfortunes must, indeed, have been severe, madam," returned William, "to make you view with patience and content so desolate a life as this."

"They have been most severe," said the lady; "but it is the will of Providence, and we have learnt to submit to it. In the morning, should you feel disposed to listen, I will relate to you the particulars of that eventful chain of misfortunes which have ultimately brought us to a situation so extraordinary. But, after what you have undergone, you must feel fatigued; therefore, I would persuade you to retire shortly. We will endeavour to accommodate you as well as possible, in the little room in which my son sleeps."

William again returned his thanks for Mrs. Grandville's kindness; but begged to make them acquainted with the particulars of his life, merely to convince them that he was not undeserving of their attention and commiseration; to which the lady assented with much readiness, and William then gave a brief detail of the events that had occurred to him during his life; to which they all listened attentively, but evidently none with greater interest than Lilian, who found it impossible to remove her eyes from the handsome young seaman, as he proceeded; and when he mentioned Flora, and descanted on her beauty and virtues, she felt the most violent agitation, and for which she was totally at a loss to account.

William having concluded, and Mrs. Grandville having expressed her sympathy in his misfortunes, he bade them all good night, and, accompanied by Robert, the son, retired to the room in which they were to rest.

The hut consisted of three rooms, and the one which served for the chamber of the young man was as comfortably arranged as, under the circumstances, ~~could have~~ been expected. The bed was formed of leaves, and covered ~~with three~~ or three rugs; but to William, who had encountered so many ~~...~~, even that was most welcome; and, ~~after~~ a short conversation ~~...~~ companion, whom he found to be ~~a very intelligent~~ young man ~~...~~ stretched himself on the rude pallet, ~~and his companion~~ quickly ~~falling~~ to sleep, he endeavoured to follow his ~~example. His~~ mind was, however, so busily occupied with the extraordinary ~~events that had~~ so recently ~~...~~ and in such rapid succession occurred ~~to him, that for some~~ time he ~~felt not~~ the influence of the drowsy god ~~...~~ upon him. Thus, ~~...~~ was he once more cast away upon a desolate ~~island, and the prospect~~ of ~~returning~~ to England, ~~was as~~ far off as ever. ~~The fate of Mr. Patrick~~ ~~appeared~~ certain, and ~~...~~ had perished ~~...~~ birth, ~~which to him~~ was of so much ~~importance; and he could not sufficiently~~ ~~regret the motives~~ that had ~~induced~~ that ~~unfortunate person to refuse~~ ~~...~~ at the time when ~~he requested~~ ~~...~~ above all other thoughts arose the image ~~of~~ his beloved ~~Flora, and when he~~ reflected on the probability of her fate, ~~and the~~ little chance ~~there seemed~~ to be of his ever beholding ~~her again, his anguish became almost insupportable~~, and he regretted ~~...~~ saved from a watery grave, ~~since all his~~ prospects ~~in life~~ ~~...~~ ever blighted.

~~...~~ and her family had excited the deepest interest and curiosity ~~in~~ his bosom, and he waited most anxiously for the morning, when ~~she~~ promised to make him acquainted with her history.

~~...~~ nature being exhausted, sleep came to his relief, and he did not ~~wake till~~ a late hour in the morning, when he found that his young companion ~~had left~~ him, and he had no doubt that he had joined the family, whom he heard bustling about. He therefore arose, much refreshed, and hastened to the room in which they were assembled.

They all greeted him in the most friendly manner; and the humble repast having passed off very agreeably, Mrs. Grandville, at the request of William, fulfilled the promise she had made on the previous evening, in the following words:—

"You see before you, sir, one of the most miserable of women who ever knew the blessings of wedlock, or the misery that its dissolution has occasioned. In me you behold one who has drained the cup of sorrow to the very dregs, and who, it seems, was born alone to be the sport of fate. But I will not repine, since it has been the will of Heaven; only trusting that, when it shall please the Almighty to take me to himself, He will protect and provide for my poor children, whose prospect, at present, is most desolate and dreary indeed.

"I was the only child of an English naval officer; but both my parents dying in my childhood, I was taken under the protection of an uncle and aunt, who were rich, but of most penurious habits, although they had no child of their own. They never behaved to me with that affection and kindness which might have been expected from their near relationship and my orphan state, and being both Roman Catholics, they resolved to educate me in that faith, and, with that view, they placed me at an early age in a convent in France.

"Although the manner in which I had hitherto been brought up by my relations had given me a serious turn of mind, my feelings were far from being in unison with a life of perpetual seclusion from the world, and, as may therefore be supposed, my situation was now anything but a happy one; and I could not but look forward to the prospect before me, with feelings approaching to those of horror and disgust.

"To these walls there were no means of gaining access, except on a certain *fete*, which took place once a year; on which occasion the usual restrictions were withdrawn, the gates were thrown open, and, to view the ceremony of high mass, the public were admitted.

"It was on one of these occasions that I was assembled with the rest of the vestals in the chapel of the convent ; I was then about eighteen years of age. We had performed our sacred harmony, and we were about to arrange ourselves around the altar, when turning my glances towards the auditory assembled, while a secret wish throbbed at my heart, that I was as free and as happy as they were, I beheld the eyes of a handsome young man fixed steadfastly upon my countenance, and when his gaze encountered mine, there was such an eloquent expression of admiration in his countenance, that it made an immediate impression upon me.

"Blushing, I averted my face, but so powerful were the feelings that throbbed at my heart, that I could not resist the temptation to replace my eyes again upon the handsome stranger. He was still standing in the same position as before, and his eyes fully shewed the emotions that at that moment filled his bosom. The elegance of his dress, and his whole demeanour, bespoke him of noble rank, and my admiration and agitation increased every instant.

"At length the solemn ceremony being over, we quitted the chapel, but the image of the noble stranger followed me to my cell, and never after quitted my memory. I beheld him when slumber closed my eyelids, and in my waking moments he was constantly in my thoughts. Strange as I had hitherto been to the feeling, I could not doubt but this was love, and my seclusion became hourly more intolerable and insupportable to me.

"For several months did I remain in a state bordering on perfect misery, and my health threatened to sink under the anxiety of my mind. I heard but seldom from my uncle and aunt, and it would seem as if they were glad to rid themselves from a burthen, which, to their sordid minds, would have been most annoying.

"At length, the abbe, who used to act as the father confessor to the nuns in the convent, was taken ill, and another monk was recommended to officiate in his place. On his entering my cell, I was struck with his figure, and a sensation throbbed at my heart, for which I was unable to account ; I also noticed the agitation of his manner, and which was the more increased, when, on quitting me, he placed a letter in my hand, enjoining me, in a tremulous voice, to peruse it carefully, and to abide by the injunctions it contained.

"When he was gone, my emotion was so great, that it was some time before I could find courage to peruse the letter, but when I did, judge of my mingled feelings of astonishment, confusion, and delight, when I found that it was from the young stranger I had seen in the chapel of the convent, and contained an ardent declaration of love, earnestly requesting that I would give him a positive answer, and thus at once ease the anguish and suspense of his mind. He informed me that his name was the Chevalier Beausanquille ; that his parents were both dead ; that he was possessed of considerable wealth, and had only had one brother, of whom he had not heard for many years, and who was supposed to have died abroad.

"I will not attempt to describe my feelings on this occasion ; but my heart responded to the appeal thus made to it, and it was in vain for me to subdue the passion which had taken such powerful possession of me. My whole thoughts were now more strongly than ever devoted to liberty and love, and I longed for the opportunity to occur of once more beholding Beausanquille, and it was not long before that wish was gratified. I will pass over the scenes which followed at our different interviews after this ; let it suffice that we mutually acknowledged the sentiments we entertained towards each other, and agreed at the first opportunity that should take place, to effect my escape from the convent, and to be united in the indissoluble bonds of matrimony.

" At length chance afforded us the long-wished for and much-hoped for opportunity which we sought. The lady abbess of our convent was taken ill, and, as every confidence was placed in my abilities, I was entrusted with the entire management of the holy building, and all the same rights which a superior possessed; conseqxently, under these circumstances, there was no difficulty presented itself to our accomplishing our wishes, and at length the happy hour was appointed for my elopement from that misery and restraint, so obnoxious to my feelings, which I had so long endured.

" The mind of my lover was too open, his every sentiment too candid and generous for me to doubt his honour, and I afterwards found that he fully merited that confidence; I had long considered myself a victim doomed to eternal solitude; the extraordinary change my lover's proposals presented, the prospect of happiness that opened to my soul, gave energy to hope, and strength to resolution. I entrusted myself entirely to his care; he provided horses, and a convenient disguise—Heaven smiled upon the deed, and the gloomy convent was soon left far in the distance behind us.

"When we had arrived at the nearest post we were united, and the most unbounded happiness became our portion. Alas! that it was fated to last but only such a short period.

"We passed only a few hours at Marseilles, and from thence we made our way, with all possible despatch, to the beautiful city of Florence. In the vicinity of this place we hired an elegant villa; and, possessed of all that mutual affection and mental gratification could afford, we lived a life of calm retirement and enjoyment, having not a wish beyond each other, and our happy home.

" In this manner eighteen months passed away, when, on the accession of the Pope, a regatta was given in celebration of the event, and all ranks and classes of people in, and for miles around Florence, were excited, and nothing was to be seen or heard but busy preparation.

" It was natural that I should have a wish to partake of the amusement, and my husband, who never denied me anything, consented. Alas! that it ever occurred —what years of future anguish and torturing reflection should I have been saved!

" Never was a more lovely day than that on which the festivities took place. Beautifully serene was the Arno, whose silvery surface reflected, as in a gently-moving mirror, the verdant banks, sloping to the margin, enamelled with flowers, and crowded with gay and expectant spectators. Skimming along the lucid current were seen thousands of little boats, decorated with variegated streamers, some containing the most dulcet harmony, and others lightly shading, with their silken awnings, the sparkling eyes, and roseate blushes of all the fairest damsels of Florence.

" Nothing could equal the enchantment of this delightful scene, and never before had I felt my spirits so much exhilarated. I was charmed with everything that my eyes rested on, for its novelty equalled its grandeur.

"My heart was full with rapture, and, as our barchetta was rowed gracefully along, by youths attired as Arcadian shepherds, I could perceive that the feelings of my husband were as delightful as my own.

" After proceeding for some distance, we arrested our course to listen to the delightful harmony which proceeded from a magnificent barge, moored near the margin of the river, when, on a sudden, a young man of commanding figure, and handsome countenance, whose eyes I had for some few minutes before beheld fixed upon me with an intense earnestness of expression that caused me much confusion, darted towards me, and raising me in his arms, in spite of my screams, endeavoured to bear me into a boat alongside of us.

" As I turned my despairing eyes towards my husband, the surprise and indignation which he experienced at this unexpected and daring outrage were plainly visible in his countenance; his eyes flashed fire, and his whole frame was most violently agitated. He was so taken by surprise that he was unable to move; and the stranger, having committed me to the care of his companions, advanced towards him, drew a stiletto from his sleeve, and aimed a stroke at my husband's unguarded breast. He warded off the blow, and, being immediately aroused to consciousness, he sprung upon the attempted assassin, and turned the weapon against himself. The point entered his heart, and he sunk a breathless corpse at Beausanquille's feet; but, at the same moment that he fell, my husband had a closer view of his features; the paleness of death overspread his countenance; his limbs trembled, and his lips quivered, and, faltering out,—'Great Heaven! it is my long lost brother, whom I have murdered,' before any one could prevent him, he seized the weapon, and, plunging it into his own breast, without a groan, he fell dead upon the body of his brother.

"Language, however powerful, must fail to do justice to my feelings; this frightful tragedy was all the work of a few moments, and, filled with the most unspeakable horror, I immediately became insensible.

"In this state I remained for several days, and, when I recovered my senses, I found myself in my own villa, and attended by my domestics. My husband and his brother had both been interred, and a complete melancholy reigned over the minds of the persons in the vicinity, at the dreadful occurrence.

"The unfortunate brother of my husband, who had taken to a military life, had been taken by the enemy, and detained a prisoner for many years; but, having at length effected his escape, he was returning to Lyons, where he expected to find his brother. Having partaken too freely of wine at the regatta, caused him to be guilty of the outrage, which led to so fatal and dreadful a result.

"For some time I was deaf to all expostulation or consolation, and continued in such a deplorable and dangerous state that my life was despaired of; but at length the violence of my grief abated, and, having settled my affairs, I quitted Florence, and returned to England, being resolved to settle there for the future.

"My relations were so enraged at my leaving the convent, that, in spite of my misfortunes, they would not notice me, and for three years after the death of my husband, I led a life of complete seclusion, avoiding society, and incessantly mourning his dreadful and untimely fate; but at length my health was so much impaired, that my physicians declared that my life would fall the sacrifice, if I did not break from the restraint I had so long imposed upon myself. Life was now of little value to me, but at last I yielded to their persuasions, and mingled in the society of a few select and attached friends.

"It was there that I first became acquainted with a military officer, Captain Grandville, a gentleman of the most manly virtues and accomplishments, and it was not long ere he imbibed a most ardent affection for me, and made an acknowledgement of it, soliciting me most urgently to favour his suit.

"Notwithstanding the esteem I felt for him, the love I bore to the memory of my ill-fated husband for some time prevented me from holding out any hopes to him, but at length his unremitting attentions, and his many amiable qualities prevailed over my scruples, and I granted him my hand. I had no reason to repent of my choice, for no man could more ardently love woman than he did me. I bore him four children, and we lived a life of the most uninterrupted felicity for several years; but about five years since the regiment to which my husband belonged was drafted to go to Gibraltar. With his consent, and my wishes and importunity, I, together with my children, accompanied him there. Little did I anticipate the consequences that would ensue. But I should become tedious were I to dwell too long on particulars so fatal to me,

"During the last bombardment, in removing me and my family from Montagu's bastion to the King's, a cannon ball came, and falling by his side, killed my youngest boy, my Raymond,—blew him to atoms before my eyes, and shattered the right leg of Captain Grandville to pieces. Oh! that I should survive such a sight! But I have survived it, I am ordained to survive it, for the sake of these my beloved children. Heaven wills that I live, although it must be to endure the utmost misery and racking thought.

"My husband was immediately conveyed to the hospital, where he suffered an amputation; but a mortification ensued, and three days put a period to his life and my happiness. Sensible of his dissolution, he commanded me to return to England with all haste. This I solemnly promised I would do. The commanding officer promised him, on his death-bed, to procure me a passport through Spain. Alas! he was not permitted the means of fulfilling his promise; he was killed, and with him died all my hopes.

"After I had performed the last sad offices to one of the best and dearest of husbands, myself and these dear children prepared for our sad, sad journey; but we were unable to obtain a passport, and we were therefore compelled to venture all the perils and inclemencies of a sea voyage. It was some time even before we could succeed in taking shipping for England, and we had not been out many hours, when a violent storm arose, and the ship we were in was tossed about with great fury. I will not attempt to describe my sufferings in this dreadful emergency, but my anguish was more excited for my children than myself. They bore it with greater fortitude than any one could have expected, and resigned themselves to the untimely fate which seemed inevitable, with the most unexampled calmness.

"The vessel continued to rock about, between life and death, during the whole of the day, and the tempest rather increased than abated. Night came on, and what a night of horror it was; never can I possibly forget it. The sea rolled mountains high, and all hope seemed at an end, even in the opinion of the oldest and most experienced seamen on board, that the vessel could possibly long weather the storm.

"In this manner she continued until about midnight, when a dreadful crash was heard; the ship had sprung upon a rock, and almost immediately went to pieces.

"The dreadful scene which followed baffles all description; but I need not attempt to pourtray it to you, sir, who have so frequently experienced similar calamities. All was horror and confusion; but suddenly beholding the crew and passengers rushing towards the long boat, I forced my children with me, and made my way to the ship's side. We were assisted by two of the seamen into the boat, and being now full, we pushed off from the wreck of the ill-fated vessel, to which numerous unfortunate wretches were still clinging in all the frenzy of despair.

"Our situation was now, however, very little better than the one we had escaped from, for death only appeared before our eyes, in such a storm, and exposed in an open boat, which was tossed at intervals comparatively to the clouds, and then engulphed again in the foaming deep. The horrors of the scene were too great for the strength of me and my children to support, and we became insensible.

"What occurred after this I have never heard, but when I recovered my senses, I found myself supported in the arms of my daughters, and my son hanging affectionately over me.

"They could not inform me how we had all been so miraculously preserved, as they had been insensible as well as myself, and had not been able to discover any traces of the boat, or the persons that were in it, so we therefore concluded that they had all perished, and the manner in which we had all been saved was consequently the more miraculous and unaccountable.

"The first thing we did was to throw ourselves on our knees, and return thanks to Heaven, but yet our situation was scarcely less dreadful than death. We were wretched, miserable, and alone, in a place unknown to us, where we might not have the means of procuring food, and must consequently die of starvation, without some assistance was speedily sent by Providence to us. But alas! were we not, situated as we found ourselves, without a prospect of being released from so horrible a fate?"

"It certainly was a most extraordinary trial for you and your family, madam," observed William, "and I wonder how you found strength to support it."

"Ah, sir," answered Mrs. Grandville, "Providence never deserts those who rely on him, and so we have experienced, for, in spite of the loneliness, and now apparent hopelessness of our present situation, He has supplied us with many comforts, as you see, and we have, as it were, become associated with this place."

"But in what way, may I ask, did you find the materials with which this habitation is erected?" asked William.

"I have but little more to add to my melancholy and, I fear, very uninteresting narrative," said Mrs. Grandville, "and then all will be explained. After we had in some degree composed our spirits, seeing that there was no hope of present relief, we determined to take a farther survey of the place, and see whether we could not procure some food, or find some sort of a shelter. We travelled for some distance into the island, and were much gratified to find that it was far from being destitute of vegetation, and contained numbers of trees that bore fruit of a most delicious flavour, and of which we partook with much relish. We also found a spring of pure water, which, under all the circumstances, was to us a treasure almost inestimable.

"We had taken pretty well the circuit of the whole island, before we came to this spot, and you may judge of our astonishment and gratitude to Omnipotence, when we discovered this hut standing nearly as it does at present. Our first impression was that it was inhabited, and I timidly approached the door and knocked, for the purpose of appealing to the humanity of the inmate or inmates, under the distressing circumstances in which we were placed. But no answer being returned, as the door was unfastened, I ventured gently to push it open, and to peep in. I then saw that the place was quite deserted, and did not appear to have been inhabited for some time. Still for awhile we hesitated to venture inside, not knowing whether it might really not be the abode of those who might prove to be our enemies, and who might only be absent for a short time, but noticing the materials with which the place was built, and not having met with any human being in the course of our survey of the island, we at last concluded that it formerly had been the residence of some poor persons like ourselves, who had been wrecked on the island, and we resolved to enter it.

"We soon found that our surmises were correct; we discovered a seaman's old chest, several articles of wearing apparel, some old timbers that appeared to have formed part of a vessel, and looking in the chest, that which at once confirmed our conjectures, a diary, written in a plain but illiterate hand, and from which we ascertained that this had been the habitation of four unfortunate seamen, belonging to an English vessel called the Mermaid, which had been wrecked on that coast six months before, and who had been the only individuals that had been saved from a watery grave. From the abrupt manner in which the diary concluded, we imagined that they had at length been rescued from their lonely and wretched situation, and this idea inspired us with hope that before long some vessel might touch near the island, which would release us also. Again did we return thanks to Heaven, which, amidst all the troubles that had befallen us, had yet been so kind to us, and then our spirits felt more exhilarated, and we recommenced our examination of the hut."

" Is it not strange, madam," remarked William, " that the unfortunate men who inhabited this place, did not remove the hut when they were rescued from the island ?"

" Why," answered Mrs. Grandville, " as you perceive, the materials of which it is built, are all useless, and therefore I dare say they did not think it worth while; besides, no doubt, they were too anxious to get on board of the vessel which had come to their relief, to think of anything else."

" Your conclusion is very probable," said William, and the lady proceeded.

" On further examining the place, we found what was to us indeed a treasure, namely, a tinder-box, a flint and steel, and some matches. We immediately collected together a pile of wood, and kindled a fire, the genial warmth of which imparted much consolation to us, for we had been very cold from our imersion in the water.

" Robert then offered to go and gather some fruit, and attempt to find some fish. He was not long absent, and returned with a quantity of fruit and several fine fish, which we cooked, and having also found a quantity of biscuits in the chest, we made a hearty meal.

" After having rested ourselves, and satisfied the cravings of hunger, we all agreed to hasten to the beach, to see whether there were any signs of the wreck, and walked on with recruited spirits, though our prospect, Heaven knows, was then dismal and cheerless enough. When we arrived at the spot, however, we were unrewarded for our pains, for there were not the least signs of the lost ship, and it was evident that it had been entirely washed away. We felt the most bitter anguish for the untimely fate of our companions, and were again completely astonished, and at a loss to conjecture, how we, all one family, had been so miraculously preserved. We returned to the hut, and after having arranged everything in the best manner we could, we secured the door on the inside, by placing the seaman's chest against it, and then committing ourselves to the care of the Almighty, we retired to rest, and notwithstanding the novelty of our situation, slept well till the morning.

" I will not tire your patience by entering into all the particulars of the ordinary events that have occurred to us since we have been on this island; we have daily gone to the beach in the hopes of seeing some vessel which would release us from our situation, but although we beheld several, they were always at too great a distance for us to be able to make them acquainted with our being on the island, although we have kindled daily large fires on the beach for the purpose of attracting attention.

" After awhile we became more settled and reconciled to our fate, and, as we always procured plenty of provisions, and no one offered to interrupt us, whom we had cause to fear, we were comparatively calm and contented. My principal time has been occupied in forming the minds of my children, and inculcating those precepts of rectitude and virtue I have throughout the course of my life endeavoured to act up to.

" Robert busied himself daily in procuring our food, and in making such improvements and alterations in our rude dwelling as he had the means of doing, so that from an almost shelterless habitation, he has made it what you behold it now.

- " Thus have we remained for upwards of three years on this island without any change, or prospect of change taking place in our circumstances, and never expected again to see a human being. You may judge, then, the

pleasure, notwithstanding we regret your misfortune, with which we receive you amongst us."

William returned his acknowledgments, and Mrs. Grandville having concluded her narrative, he observed,—

"My dear madam, yours has been indeed a life of trouble, and I sincerely commiserate in your misfortunes. Heaven grant that you may ultimately be released from them, and that some vessel may touch this spot in which we may all once more be restored to our native land."

Mrs. Grandville and the others most sincerely and ardently responded to this wish. During the time that her mother had been relating her melancholy narrative, the bright eyes of the lovely Lilian had been frequently fixed on the countenance of the handsome young seaman, and when she remembered what he had said of Flora, and the mutual love which existed between them, she sighed, but she immediately checked the feeling, which almost unconsciously had stolen into her innocent bosom, and blushed to think she had ever entertained it.

William, in spite of the gloomy thoughts that occupied his mind, could not look upon the maiden without admiration, and he thought her one of the most lovely girls, with the exception of his own dear Flora, that he had ever beheld. As the name of Flora arose to his memory—but when was it absent from it?—his mind was wrung with the most intense agony, and despair almost entirely settled upon his heart. Fate appeared to have conspired against him, and it seemed as if he was destined never more to reach his native shores; and if he did, what prospect of happiness was there for him? He would perhaps find those who had ever been to him as parents and relations no more. And Flora, what might have been her fate? It was too dreadful and revolting to think upon. A thousand curses he

No. 51

breathed upon the head of the Smuggler King, and prayed that Providence would yet afford him the opportunity of wreaking his vengeance on his head.

Then, again, the unfortunate fate of Mr. Fitzpatrick greatly agitated him; and he more than ever regretted that that gentleman should have considered it necessary to withhold the secret which he said he was acquainted with from him. Fortune the young sailor cared not about, but he would have been rejoiced to have been made acquainted with the names of his parents, so that he might have had every opportunity of paying due respect to their memory. That Marian was his mother a certain feeling within him, as well as her own assertions, convinced him; but he doubted not that was not her real name. The dreadful fate she had met with was ever present to his thoughts, and many and bitter were the pangs it cost him. He could not for a moment in his own mind dispute the claim she had upon him, the assertions she had made use of, and, as he was confident, perfectly in her senses at the time. The fact of her recognising the locket, and the marks upon his neck, all tended to convince him, and his horror and detestation of the being who called himself the Smuggler King, and by whose orders the murder had doubtless been committed, was increased. But surely, he reflected, justice would ultimately overtake the miscreant; an all-just and all-merciful God would not allow such crimes to go unpunished; but he most fervently hoped that He would make him the earthly instrument of wreaking that retribution on the villain's head.

All these thoughts, independent of his situation, tended to make William truly wretched, and Mrs. Grandville and her amiable family perceiving it, and not wishing to obtrude upon his private sorrows, shortly after the former had given her melancholy recital, left him to himself and the free indulgence of his reflections.

After some time, however, he became more composed, and walked from the hut to take a more minute survey of the island. He walked on for some time, and found that it answered, in every respect, the description which Mrs. Grandville had given of it, and that it presented altogether a cheerful aspect, exhibiting signs of pretty, luxuriant vegetation, and fruit trees rearing their majestic heads in every direction.

Having traversed the whole extent of it, he next bent his footsteps to the sea-side, and, as he cast his eyes over the vast deep, his thoughts reverted to his native land, and the little prospect there was of his ever beholding it again. His mind again became gloomy and desponding. It is true he had companions, and those of the most amiable description; but could they compensate him for the loss of liberty, and all that was dear to him? Could they reconcile his thoughts to the terrible uncertainty of the fate which had attended her he so fondly loved, and those beloved friends who would unceasingly mourn his mysterious and unaccountable disappearance? Alas! no!

Filled with these gloomy ideas he returned to the hut, and found that the family had prepared their humble repast, and were awaiting his arrival. Mrs. Grandville tried all in her power to ameliorate the heavy grief under which he was labouring, and the expressive eyes of the gentle Lilian showed plainly how deeply she sympathised with him. Ashamed of exhibiting what might be accounted a weakness, he struggled with his feelings, and succeeded so well, that the remainder of the day passed more agreeably away than under the circumstances might have been anticipated.

The conversation of the young seaman seemed to please Mrs. Grandville, and Lilian and her sister listened with delight to the marvellous stories he told of the spirit-stirring scenes in which he had mingled on the deep. But no one paid more attention, or felt deeper interest in what he detailed than the youthful Robert, and his ardent spirit panted to encounter the same adventures.

Robert was a most intelligent youth, and from the first moment that William beheld him, he was prepossessed in his favour, and no less was the young man attached to him. From that day they were almost constantly together : together they sought provisions, and performed other services that tended to the improvement of the humble dwelling ; and when these duties were over, seated with the rest of the family around their wood fire, they endeavoured in conversation to drive away the melancholy thoughts which their solitude was likely to engender. In those parties Lilian was the most delighted individual, and the more she saw of William, the more did she admire him ; at least, she sought to convince herself that it was only admiration, but when her young heart assured her that the sentiment deserved a much more tender appellation, she trembled at the danger into which her susceptible nature had led her, endeavoured to banish the feeling, and regretted that William had ever been brought amongst them.

Thus passed away a month, William and Robert going daily to the beach, in the hopes of beholding some vessel within hail, but as often returning to their wild and humble habitation without success. Mrs. Grandville and her children could look upon their present situation with calmness, for the length of time they had been upon the island had associated them with it ; but William, when he thought of home, of his friends, of Flora, could scarcely endure it with any degree of patience. Notwithstanding all the endeavours of Mrs. Grandville and her family, heavily the time wore with him away, and despair at length entirely settled upon his heart. But the time was coming which was once more to revive his hopes, and rescue him and the others from their present situation.

One morning as he and Robert were going, as usual, to the sea beach, on emerging from a thicket of trees, their eyes were suddenly astonished and delighted at the sight of three men, who, from their dress, were evidently sailors. This event was so unexpected, that they could not at first believe the evidence of their senses ; but the men beholding them, uttered an exclamation of astonishment, and approaching them nearer, they recognised from their features that they were Englishmen, and immediately addressed them.

The men were no less surprised at meeting them there, than were William and Robert at beholding them ; but our hero having briefly explained to them their situation, the sailors informed them that they belonged to a vessel called the Neptune, which was lying off near the island, and that they had come ashore with the hope of obtaining fresh water. They also informed them that they were on the passage to England.

We need not attempt to describe the delight of William and Robert at this intelligence, and having informed the men where they could procure the fresh water, the latter promised them to make their situation known to the captain, whom, they had no doubt, would immediately consent to take them on board. William having then pointed out to them their dwelling, returned thither with Robert, to make Mrs. Grandville and the others acquainted with what had taken place.

It would be impossible to describe the feelings of Mrs. Grandville and her lovely daughters on being made acquainted with this event, and the prospect of their speedy deliverance ; their first act, however, after their emotion had somewhat abated, was to return thanks to Omnipotence, and they awaited with impatience, some intelligence from the vessel.

They had not to wait long; in about half an hour after William and Robert had met with the men, the captain and two or three of the seamen made their appearance at the hut, and William, to his great satisfaction, recognised in the former an officer with whom he had formerly sailed. The captain expressed his astonishment at the adventures of Mrs. Grandville, and also the misfortunes that had befallen William, and immediately offered them a passage on board his vessel to England.

We need not say that they were all most unbounded in their gratitude to this gentleman, and they, then, without delay, commenced making the trifling preparations that were necessary for their departure.

Captain Mattley informed them that the vessel he commanded was a cruiser, and William was not a little surprised to hear that he had been in quest of the Smuggler King.

After all the preliminaries that were requisite were arranged, William and the others bade farewell to the island, and accompanying the captain, went on board his vessel, which shortly afterwards set sail, and once more the hope of returning to his native land, and of beholding those that were so dear to him, entered the bosom of William.

CHAPTER XXII.

THE ASSEMBLAGE OF OLD ENGLAND'S TARS.—THE SORROWS AND MISFORTUNES OF MR. CLARENDON AND HIS FAMILY.—THE MESSAGE FROM BASILWOOD HALL.

WE must now return to those scenes from which we have so long departed, and where, as may be expected, the events we have recorded had created the greatest misery in the breasts of all those interested, and the deepest commiseration of all those who knew them.

It was a fine autumn evening that a party of seamen were assembled together outside the Sheet Anchor public-house, and were regaling themselves on such good refreshments as the worthy host was always in the habit of serving his customers with. There were several of the veteran tars, whom we have described in the early part of this narrative, as being the frequent guests of Ben Backstay, and among the rest was Ben's old and particular friend, who gloried in the cognomen of "Commodore Jack."

The laugh, the yarn, and the song, had gone freely round, as well as the grog, when their mirth seemed all at once to be suddenly exhausted, and the conversation lagged most dismally.

"Come, messmate," said one of the company, "have yer slewed up all yer jawin' tackle, commodore? Spin us another yarn."

"Avast there, shipmate," returned the old tar, "I think I have spun all the yarns that are entered on the log-book of my memory; and, therefore, it is time that I should cast anchor, and leave it to some one else. Cannot you give us one, Joe Scupper? Summat about that story of yourn, about the baboon that drest himself in the captain's rigging and cocked hat, and, as they say, resembled him so much, that had he been able to speak, none of the crew of the Fire Fly would have been able to tell one from the other?"

"I have spun that yarn so often, commodore," answered Joe, "that it is quite stale. I wish we had poor old Ben Backstay among us; he is the man for setting yer hearts afloat."

"Ah! poor Ben," said the commodore, "the wind is quite different with him now, and I don't wonder at it, since the strange disappearance of that brave young fellow, William, whom he loved as if he had been his own son, though he was not, and he has never been able to discover who were his parents."

"Ah, poor old fellow," observed another of the company, "it was a sad job for him, sure enough."

"And so he has felt it," said Commodore Jack, "for he has never held up his head since; and what has grieved him more, is the uncertainty there is as to what has been the poor lad's fate."

"Why, it is suspected that he has been murdered by some d—d piratical rascals or other, is it not?" asked Joe.

"To be sure," answered the former; "there was blood found in the hovel where Crazy Marian, as they called her, used to reside, and who has never since been heard of, and the locket which he used to wear round his neck was discovered there, which all looked very suspicious; but what should take him to that place? Now I think it is most likely that he has been taken on board that piratical vessel, (for no doubt such it was) which was so long lying off here, and so suddenly disappeared."

"Ah!" said one of the seamen, "is it not strange that that craft should so long have remained in this port without being suspected and over-hauled?"

"It is," answered another of his companions, "and I have often had my suspicions that it was one of the vessels of the Smuggler King."

"Ay, ay," coincided two or three of the company, "and that he has been the cause of all this trouble. The strange disappearance of the old lawyer too who came down to these parts."

"And what's more," added Joe Scupper, "the disappearance of pretty Flora Clarendon, about the same time as her lover."

"The very same night," remarked another of the party.

"Ah! poor Flora Clarendon," said the commodore, "that was a terrible job; she was as lovely a craft as ever was launched; and a shocking blow has her loss been to her family. Her mother, you know, was for some time raving mad, but at last her grief settled into a calm melancholy despair like, which is quite heart-breaking to behold; and as if Providence had not visited them with misfortunes enough, her poor father was shortly afterwards attacked with a violent fever, and his life was despaired of; but although he got the weather-gage of death, he has since been deprived of one of the greatest blessings, his sight."

"Poor Mr. Clarendon," said half-a-dozen voices, and then a pause ensued, and it was evident from the honest countenances of the persons assembled, that they deeply commiserated with the misfortunes of the parties they were conversing about.

"I did not half like the character of that Sir Julian Mordlington, as they called him," at length observed Joe Scupper.

"No," returned Commodore Jack, "depend upon it he was no good."

"He very soon weighed anchor from the Hall, after the disappearance of William and Flora," remarked Joe.

"Ay," said the commodore, "and it would have been no loss to the neighbourhood if he had gone before. We have got a good one in his place; Squire Melford is an excellent man, charitable to the poor, and generous to his tenants; look at the interest he has taken, too, in the misfortunes of Ben Backstay and the Clarendon family."

"Ay," observed one of the company, "and how he has exerted himself to discover what has become of all the parties missing."

"But without success," returned the commodore; "I have often had my suspicions that Sir Julian knew something about the business. Was not the old lawyer known to have visited him on the very day that he was missing? To be sure he was. And didn't the baronet deny that he had ever been to the Hall, or that he knew anything at all about him? All these things look very black, and he seemed to know it, or he would not have sheered off so quickly as he did."

"Ay, ay," remarked Joe Scupper; "it does look very suspicious, and I only hope that the truth may soon be discovered, and the infernal swabs brought to justice."

" Depend upon it, the rascals will not escape," said Commodore Jack; " but see, here comes poor Mr. Clarendon, led by his amiable daughter, the faithful wife of Henry Backstay."

The poor old man made his appearance, leaning on the arm of his daughter. His form was bent, and his cheeks pale and hollow with care. His long silvery hair flowed over his brow, and half shaded his eyes, which were now darkened by the awful visitation of the Almighty. His appearance excited universal sympathy among the rough but honest hearts that were there assembled.

His daughter was pale and careworn, and it was evident that she had suffered, and was still suffering, the greatest mental agony; but she stifled it as much as possible, fearful that it would add to the anguish of her aged parents, upon whom this blow had so heavily fallen.

" Be seated, dear father," said his daughter ; " we have had a long walk, and, at your advanced time of life, I am certain you must be fatigued. Rest awhile, dear father, rest awhile."

" Ah ! my poor child," answered the old man, in a melancholy but affectionate tone of voice, " what a solace art thou to me and thy mother in the heavy afflictions with which it has pleased the Most High to visit us. Bless thee, bless thee, girl. Oh, I ought to be grateful to Heaven that thou art at least spared to us ; for were we deprived of thee and Harry, thy husband, what would become of us ?"

" I hope, my beloved father," answered his daughter, in her tenderest accents, " that it will please God long to continue me with you. But, come, come, here is a seat, and the air is cool and refreshing from the water."

" Where are we, child ?" inquired Mr. Clarendon, " where are we ?"

" Outside the Sheet Anchor, father," answered his daughter.

" Ah ! then I know I am near some of my old friends."

" Yes, yes," replied his daughter, " here is Mr. Scupper, and Mr. Mainbrace, and several more of your old friends and companions."

" Bless—bless, you all," said the old man, holding out his hand, which the seamen cordially shook. " I cannot see ye now ; all—all is dark, but I know that poor old Clarendon is not an unwelcome guest among ye. I will rest myself awhile."

His daughter led him to a seat, and the old man having paused for awhile, uttered a deep sigh.

" Ah !" he ejaculated, " many—many a happy evening have I spent in this place, before misfortune visited me ; but—but, all is over now—all is over now."

" Say not so, Mr. Clarendon," said Commodore Jack ; " the Great Captain is kind and merciful to all His crew, and who knows but there may be happiness yet in store for you."

" Happiness !" repeated Mr. Clarendon, in a melancholy voice ; " ah ! no, how dare I hope for it, deprived as I am of my sight, and that which was so precious to it, my poor child, my Flora ?"

" Father, dear father," remonstrated his daughter, " why will you thus give way to despair ? True, most terrible have been our calamities, but it is the will of Heaven, and we must learn to submit."

" Thou art my gentle monitor," said the poor old man, affectionately ; " I know that it is wrong and sinful of me to arraign the justice of God ; but where is the erring mortal who has been visited by such heavy misfortunes as I am, who can help murmuring? Methinks that if I could but be certain of the fate that has befallen my darling Flora, however awful it might be, I could in time learn to submit to it."

"Dear father," said his daughter, "do not, I beseech you, give way entirely to despair, for something convinces me that Flora will yet be restored to us."

"Yes, my dear girl," answered the old man, solemnly, "in Heaven—in Heaven. Last night, indeed, imagination restored her to me in my dreams; I clasped her to my fond old heart, and pressed my lips upon her cheek. I heard her in her own angelic tones repeat the name of father. It was like the music of Heaven to my soul, and scalding tears chased each other down the deep furrows of my cheeks. But transient only was the bliss afforded me. A deafening peal of thunder reverberated above my head, and I embraced my child no longer; her form had faded into thin air, and I stretched my eager arms alone at empty space. So fade all the hopes I would fain indulge."

"Poor old man," said Commodore Jack to his companions, but looking around him, he suddenly exclaimed aloud, "Ah! see, Ben Backstay is coming full sail this way. What's the matter with him? He looks all—"

"Mr. Backstay," interrupted the old man; "what can cause his hurry? Has any fresh misfortune befallen us?"

At that moment Mr. Backstay arrived upon the spot, and hastily approaching Mr. Clarendon, he said:—

"Ah! I am happy I have found you, my old friend; I have been seeking everywhere for you."

"What is the matter?" demanded Mr. Clarendon, in alarm. "Has anything happened?"

"Nothing that need cause any apprehension," replied Ben. "A messenger has been at my house from Squire Melford."

"From Squire Melford?"

"Ay."

"For what purpose?"

"The squire requests to see both you and me immediately at the hall on business of importance," answered Mr. Backstay.

"Business of importance," repeated Mr. Clarendon; "what can he want?"

"That of course I know not," said Ben; "but take my arm, and we will go there without any more delay."

"Heaven send that he may have something to impart that may tend to alleviate our distress," ejaculated the daughter of Mr. Clarendon. The old man responded to the wish, and then taking the arm of Mr. Backstay, he departed with him for Basilwood Hall, filled with strange doubts and conjectures as to what could be the business upon which Squire Melford desired so particularly to see them.

Mrs. Backstay having accompanied them as far as she was going on their way, took her leave, and made her way home, with a heart fluttering with hope and astonishment.

CHAPTER XXIII.

THE INTERVIEW.—THE DISCOVERED WILL.—THE DOCUMENTS.—THE MYSTERY PARTLY EXPLAINED.

On arriving at Basilwood Hall, late the seat of Sir Julian Mordlington, they were immediately ushered into the presence of Squire Melford, who received them with much politeness, and having requested them to be seated, he commenced:—

"You are aware, both Mr. Clarendon and yourself, Mr. Backstay, that I have greatly interested myself since my residence in this neighbourhood, in endeavouring to unravel the unfortunate and mysterious events connected with you."

" Oh, yes, sir," observed Mr. Clarendon, " and many thanks do we owe you for your unexampled goodness ; the blessing of Heaven ——"

" Nay," interrupted the benevolent squire, " I have but endeavoured to perform a duty which is incumbent on us all. But, hear me ; I think at last, I have discovered a clue to the unravelment of part of the mystery."

" Ah !" ejaculated Mr. Clarendon and his companion in a breath.

" Compose yourselves," returned Mr. Melford, " and listen patiently to me. In the first place, Mr. Backstay, I must beg permission to put a few questions to you."

" Speak on, sir, I beg," said Mr. Backstay, eagerly ; " I am ready to answer you anything that is in my power."

" I have my reasons for the interrogatories I shall put to you, as you will afterwards perceive," observed Squire Melford ; " I believe you have told me that the young man who has disappeared so suddenly and so unaccountably, is not your son?"

" He is not, sir," answered Mr. Backstay.

" And that you saved him and another, a lad apparently some years older, from a wreck on the French coast ?"

" True."

" How long is that ago ?"

" About two and twenty years, if my memory serves me right," answered Ben.

" And you do not remember the name of the vessel that was wrecked ?"

" I do not."

" And the elder boy quitted your hut suddenly ?" asked Mr. Melford.

" He did," answered Mr. Backstay.

" And you have never heard anything of him since ?"

Ben answered in the negative.

" And the other child ?"

" Is he whom I have since brought up as my own son. He could just make us understand that his Christian name was William, and that is all we could make out about him."

" And you never could discover who his friends or relations were ?" asked the squire.

" Never."

" Although you advertised the circumstance in the papers ?"

" I did, sir."

" That is strange," observed Mr. Melford, after a pause. " Now, let me ask you, Mr. Backstay, what was your opinion of Sir Julian Mordlington, the late possessor of this Hall? Speak fearlessly, for justice to yourself and others demand it."

" Well, squire," returned Mr. Backstay, " if I must speak my mind, I must say that I entertained no very good opinion of him."

" He once insulted my girl," said Mr. Clarendon, with much emotion, " and I have often suspected that he is not unacquainted with her disappearance."

" The mysterious disappearance of Mr. Fitzpatrick, in the first instance," resumed Ben, " and then Sir Julian's denying that he knew anything about him, although I am convinced that he visited him on business of importance on the very morning of the day he was missing, added to my doubts, and ——"

" What was Mr. Fitzpatrick ?" demanded Mr. Melford, interrogating Ben hastily.

" From what he informed me, and what was gathered from his own papers in the chest which he left at my house, he was a lawyer."

" And of London ?"

" Yes."

"Then the mystery is at once explained," said Mr. Melford.

"Oh, what mean you, sir?" impatiently asked Mr. Clarendon. "Have you discovered anything that may unravel the probable fate of my poor child?"

"I think I have," answered Mr. Melford; "but first let me put a few more questions to Mr. Backstay. You say you lived near Dieppe at the time of the shipwreck from which you rescued William and the other lad?"

"I did—I did," answered Ben, eagerly.

"And that you were at the time a fisherman?"

"True; my son Henry can corroborate that, and the finding of the two children, for he was with me at the time."

"Then," observed Mr. Melford, "there can no longer be any doubt about the matter. Mr. Backstay, you will be astonished when I tell you that William, whom you have so long protected, is the brother of Sir Julian Mordlington."

"The brother of Sir Julian Mordlington!" repeated both Mr. Backstay and Mr. Clarendon, in tones of the most indescribable amazement and incredulity.

"True," answered the squire; "by the same father, though the same mother bore them not."

"Gracious Heaven!" exclaimed Ben, "can this be possible?"

"It is—it is," said Mr. Melford; "the baronet is the same you also rescued with William from the wreck, and who made his disappearance so abruptly from your hut."

"Then," ejaculated Ben, fervently, "he is a villain, a most hardened, atrocious villain; for, from the marks that were imprinted upon the child's throat, there can be very little doubt, young as he was himself at the time, that he had attempted to murder him."

"Of that I am convinced," observed Mr. Melford; "and, moreover, that he was urged to it from the most interested motives."

No. 52

"Good God!" cried poor old Ben, "I am completely astonished. Oh, my poor William! But who was the parent of these young men?"

"General Sir Clarence Mordlington," replied Mr. Melford, "who had been out to India, and was on his return to England, when the wreck took place by which he perished, his two sons being all that were saved from the watery deep, and by you."

"Remarkable—miraculous!" cried Ben and Mr. Clarendon; "but how know you all this?" inquired the former.

Mr. Melford took a roll of paper from his pocket.

"In examining some of the apartments of the Hall, which I had not before minutely surveyed," answered Mr. Melford; "in a small closet I discovered this—look at it."

Mr. Backstay eagerly glanced over the document, and, to his utter astonishment, found it to be a will, purporting to be that of General Sir Clarence Mordlington, entrusted to the care of Patrick Fitzpatrick, esquire, attorney, London, and executed in the year 17—, in which he bequeathed to his eldest son, Julian Mordlington, certain property in Hampshire, and fifty thousand pounds ; to his youngest son, William Mordlington, and his heirs, all his estates in the county of Westmoreland, and thirty thousand pounds ; but, should he not survive, then the whole to go to Julian, with the exception of five hundred pounds per annum to Lady Emmeline Mordlington, his second wife, with his forgiveness for the indiscretion laid to her charge.

With the most unbounded astonishment did Mr. Backstay gaze at this will, and he could scarcely believe the evidence of his senses.

"But how is this to be proved a valid instrument?" he inquired.

"See you not the names of the attesting witnesses?" demanded the squire.

"True," answered Ben ; "but may they not be all dead?"

"No," said Mr. Melford. "The two principal I am acquainted with, and can have their evidence at any time."

"That is fortunate, indeed," remarked Ben, who could scarcely recover from the astonishment into which this discovery had thrown him. "But," he continued, after a pause, "how came this into the possession of Sir Julian?"

"It is evident," returned the squire, "and, I fear, too fully accounts for the disappearance of Mr. Fitzpatrick and William. To gain possession of this from the lawyer, doubtless, incited him either to remove him out of the way, or to take his life ; and knowing William to be his brother, and that he might afterwards discover the same, and seek restitution of his rights, has also induced him to get him out of the way."

"Dreadful supposition," exclaimed Ben, "and yet too probable. Alas! then, my poor boy, I shall never behold you again."

"Say not so," observed Mr. Melford ; "I have strong hopes to the contrary."

"And my Flora!" in accents of agony, ejaculated Mr. Clarendon ; "oh, what has become of her?"

"Patience, my dear sir," said Mr. Melford, "and all may yet be well. I have good reason to believe that this Sir Julian had formed an attachment towards your poor girl, and no doubt it is he who has borne her away, and that she is still in his power."

"Oh, God!" groaned Mr. Clarendon, "then what hope is there for me?"

"Say not so," returned the squire ; "all may yet be well, and I trust it will."

"Heaven send that it may," observed Mr. Backstay, emphatically ; "but what could have induced Sir Julian to have left such an important document as this behind him, when he disposed of his estate to you, sir?"

"I cannot account for it," answered Mr. Melford ; "but it is certain it must have been done in a moment of great thoughtlessness, and by the wise dispensation of Providence, which, sooner or later, by means the most miraculous, brings the guilty to light, and restores the oppressed to their rights ; but, astonished as you already doubtless are, I have yet more to create your wonder ; who, suppose you, is Sir Julian?"

" You have already informed us, sir," answered Ben.

" Ay," observed Mr. Melford, " I have told you how he is related to William, the foundling of the wreck, but who ——"

"Who then is he really ?" hastily and impatiently inquired Ben.

" The long dreaded and desperate Smuggler King," answered Mr. Melford.

" The Smuggler King!" repeated Mr. Clarendon and Ben, in accents that may better be imagined than described.

" Ay," returned Squire Melford; " the villain is at length unmasked ; he stands confessed, by his own showing."

" The Smuggler King !" cried Ben, " and the brother of my poor William !"

" And who holds in his power my poor Flora, no doubt. Oh, horror !" groaned Mr. Clarendon, and he covered his face with his hands, and rocked to and fro in his chair, in a state of the greatest mental agony.

" There cannot be any doubt of it," said Mr. Melford, " and that the vessel which so suddenly disappeared from this port, was the notorious and much dreaded Devil Skipper."

" Horrible !" gasped forth the unfortunate Mr. Clarendon.

" Nay, my dear sir," interrupted Squire Melford ; " I pray you compose your feelings, and with the assistance of the Almighty, the villain may yet be brought to punishment, and your daughter restored to you."

" Oh, God ! my darling Flora in the power of such a miscreant as that, what hope is there for me ? what must have been her fate ?"

" But," said Ben, " how have you become acquainted with this ?"

" Behold !" answered Mr. Melford, taking from his pockets several letters, which he placed in Ben's hands ; " these I also found with the will, and which have doubtless been left behind by the quondam Sir Julian. Read them — they will explain everything "

Mr Backstay, as well as his agitation would permit him, glanced eagerly over the contents of the letters. One seemed to be the copy of a letter addressed to Sam Raker, on board the Devil Skipper, in which he informed him that he was convinced that Ben Backstay was the same man who saved him and his brother from the wreck of the Terrible, and that William was no other than that brother. It expressed his regret that he had failed to take away the life of the boy in the cottage of the fisherman, and urged Sam Raker, to be vigilant, and endeavour to get the young seaman in their power, to which he was further urged by the love which existed between him and Flora Clarendon, whom, he added, he was resolved, at all hazards, to possess. Another letter purported to come from Sam Raker, and was addressed to Sir Julian Mordlington, in which that ruffian expressed his surprise at the apprehensions of one who had spread such universal terror on the seas, under the title of the Smuggler King, especially when he had secured the will, and the lawyer, Mr. Fizpatrick, was disposed of. The other letters contained matter all tending to show that Sir Julian Mordlington was the actual individual who had so long defied detection as the Smuggler King, and revealing his designs against Flora Clarendon, and all the other persons who had suffered from his nefarious transactions.

Mr. Backstay read these important letters again and again, and could scarce believe the evidence of his senses, while the agitation of Mr. Clarendon was so great, that it required all the eloquence of Mr. Melford to bring him to anything like a degree of tranquillity.

ᵴ "But what is to be done in this fearful emergency?" asked Ben.

"Leave that to me," answered the squire; "I will immediately place these documents in the hands of the proper authorities, and I entertain the most sanguine hopes that the guilty parties will speedily be brought to justice, and those that are so dear to you, if they are still in existence, be restored to you."

Mr. Clarendon groaned aloud with despair, and it was some time before he and Mr. Backstay were sufficiently recovered from the dreadful state of agony into which these extraordinary events had thrown them, to leave the Hall, which at length they did, Mr. Melford promising to¦ see them the next day, and requesting them to be of good heart, as he entertained the most sanguine hopes that all those who were so immediately and fondly connected with them, would be restored to their arms, and that all would yet be well. Mr. Backstay and his unfortunate friend fervently raised their hands towards Heaven, and responded to this wish. They then took their departure.

CHAPTER XXIV.

THE APPREHENSION OF SAM RAKER.—THE TRIAL.—THE ˙UNEXPECTED APPEARANCE.—THE TALE OF OPPRESSION.—THE CONVICTION.¦

WE will pass over the particulars of the anxiety and anguish of the two families of Mr. Clarendon and Mr. Backstay, at the circumstances we have recorded in the previous chapter, and the sensation which was caused in the minds of all the persons in the neighbourhood, by the discovery of Sir Julian Mordlington being the much dreaded Smuggler King. Mr. Melford was indefatigable in his exertions, and the most active measures were adopted by the authorities to substantiate the facts, and to bring the guilty parties to justice.

The two principal attesting witnesses to the will of the late General Mordlington were produced, and proved it to be an authentic document, and among others, Flynn, the confidential clerk of Mr. Fitzpatrick, came forward, and proved the will having been in his master's possession, and the arrangements there had been between him and Sir Julian, in respect to pecuniary matters. Thus far everything was pretty clearly elucidated, and there could be little doubt on the mind of any reasonable person, that William was the son of the late general, by his second wife, Lady Emmeline, he having acknowledged him in his will, although he had appeared to entertain some apprehensions that he was not when the separation took place, although his afterwards taking him with him to India, was sufficient to establish that fact.

In the midst of this suspense, the vessels that had attacked the tower on the Death Rock arrived at Portsmouth, and confirmed the fact of the destruction of that place, and Flora Clarendon being in the power of the Smuggler King, and, as it was feared, having perished in the explosion, with her guilty persecutor. These terrible facts Grampus, who was on board the vessel, corroborated, and also the death of William, and all the circumstances that followed.

It would be impossible to do adequate justice to the terror and despair of all the parties interested, on hearing these dreadful particulars. For some time Mrs. Clarendon and her husband were in a state bordering on madness, and were completely deaf to all the attempts at consolation that were offered to them, and Ben Backstay and his family were in a condition equally pitiable. Their hopes were now entirely crushed, and they looked on all the efforts that were making to fully elucidate these fearful occurrences with perfect apathy.

On the contrary, Mr. Melford still entertained strong hopes that everything would turn out better than at present there seemed to be any right to anticipate, and was unremitting in his exertions and likewise to impart confidence and consolation to the distressed families.

Grampus was detained in custody, until it should be more satisfactorily proved that Sir Julian and the others were no more; and, in the event of their not being so, and being apprehended, he would be admitted as evidence for the prosecution.

Vessels were dispatched in every direction in search of the pirates, and the rewards for the apprehension of the Smuggler King, dead or alive, were doubled. Nothing could equal the excitement which prevailed all over that part of the country, and many were the fervent prayers that were offered up that the hardened miscreant might be detected, and that the unfortunate individuals who were supposed to have been murdered, might yet be found to be alive, and restored to their friends; but few were the hopes that were entertained that such would take place.

Grampus was well acquainted with all the haunts of the smugglers, and could therefore give every instruction for the authorities to act upon.

Six weeks in this manner elapsed, when one day a cruiser arrived in the port, having on board Sam Raker and several more of the smugglers, who had been taken in an engagement which the cruiser had with the pirate vessel, in which Sam Raker had sought refuge before the destruction of the tower. The pirate vessel had been so much damaged that it shortly afterwards went to pieces.

Grampus immediately swore to Raker and the others, and the rage of the villain was indescribable at finding the man whom he so thoroughly detested his principal accuser, and the one who was likely to bring him to the gallows. With a hopeless pertinacity, however, common to such miscreants, he still protested his innocence, and declared his entire ignorance of Grampus, or the transactions of which he accused him.

He was examined before the magistrates, when he still persisted in his innocence, and denied all knowledge of Sir Julian and the fate which had befallen him. He was, after one or two examinations, fully committed to take his trial at the ensuing assizes, on the charge of piracy and murder.

The day of trial at length arrived, and the excitement which prevailed in the immediate neighbourhood, and for miles around, was immense. The court was crowded at an early hour, and Grampus was brought forward as the principal witness against the prisoner. The harrowing accounts he gave of the murder of Marian by the ruffian, and the cold-blooded assassination of Mr. Fitzpatrick and William, filled the bosom of every person present with disgust and horror, and the unfortunate families who were so intimately connected with these terrible events excited universal sympathy. The letters which Mr. Melford had discovered at the Hall, and which so unanswerably confirmed the guilt of the villain, were produced, and the writing sworn to by Grampus; but still he stoutly persisted that he was innocent.

" Are you to take the evidence of a fellow like that," demanded Raker, pointing to Grampus, " who has confessed himself to be one of the crew of the Smuggler King, and most likely is guilty of the very crimes with which I am charged? Again I say I am innocent; who else dare accuse me?"

" I dare, villain!" exclaimed a loud female voice, at the tones of which even the sturdy miscreant trembled and turned pale. A great sensation was created in the court, and the next moment, a female of majestic form, but emaciated appearance, rushed into the witness-box, and confronted the prisoner.

"Crazy Marian!" burst in tones of astonishment from the persons in the court.

"Powers of darkness!" cried Raker, turning ghastly pale, and glaring with distended eyeballs upon the form before him; "is this a delusion, or ——"

"It is no delusion, monster," answered the female. "It is Marian, her whom you thought you had murdered, but whom an all just Providence hath saved to bring you to the gallows."

"How is this?" demanded the judge, in astonishment. "Are you the Marian whom the prisoner is charged with murdering?"

"I am, my lord," answered Marian; "I had sought an interview with William, known as William Backstay, but who is my son ——"

"Your son?" interrupted the judge.

"Yes," firmly replied Marian, "my son,—my only one, of whom I was so cruelly deprived. In me you behold Lady Emmeline, the unfortunate wife of General Sir Clarence Mordlington."

A sensation of the most unspeakable astonishment ran through the court, and all eyes were immediately fixed upon her.

"Look at this paper," said the judge, handing the will to her, over which she hastily glanced her eyes; "know you that handwriting?"

"Oh, yes—yes," she answered with the deepest emotion; "it is that of my unfortunate deluded husband."

"Heed her not," said Raker, eagerly; "she is a maniac, a confirmed maniac."

"Once," she calmly replied, "I own I was, for the injustice I had received, the loss of my husband and my child, was too much for my reason to withstand; but it has once more asserted its sway, and here I stand to bring the guilty to punishment."

"Are there any persons present," inquired the judge, "who can swear to the identity of Lady Emmeline Mordlington?"

The two witnesses to the will, and Flynn, now stepped forward, and swore positively that, although time and trouble had somewhat altered her features, they had not the least doubt but the witness in the box was the individual she represented herself to be.

"Proceed with your evidence, madam," desired the counsel for the prosecution.

Lady Emmeline, having taken a few moments to recover herself, complied, and related what took place in the hovel.

"I had sought an interview with William in the wretched hovel which sometimes sheltered me, and in the course of that meeting I found, beyond doubt, that he was my own son. The circumstance of the wreck, from which he was rescued, with Sir Julian, by Mr. Backstay, the locket, his likeness to my husband, and the three marks on his neck, corresponding with those on my own, and the strawberry on his wrist, all convinced me. Oh! what were my feelings at that moment? I was about to disclose to him the name of his father, when I was shot by yon villain, and fell senseless. When I recovered I found myself in the cottage of one of the smugglers, who happened to pass by the hovel a few minutes after the occurrence, and possessing more humanity than his fellows, secretly conveyed me to his humble home, where his wife attended me, and prescribed such remedies to my wound as her knowledge dictated. I recovered."

"And why did you not before appear and make these accusations?" inquired the judge.

"Because," answered Lady Emmeline, "I was bound by a promise to the smuggler, who was fearful of the vengeance of his comrades, not to reveal myself until a favourable opportunity should present itself."

" Is that witness forthcoming ?" inquired his lordship.

" He is here, my lord," replied Lady Emmeline, and at that moment the man stepped forward, and corroborated all that she had stated.

" My lord," resumed Emmeline, " shall I trespass on the patience of yourself and the jury for awhile, while I give a brief explanation of a few particulars which, although not bearing immediately on this trial, are so important to me, in exoneration of my character?"

The judge bowed his consent, and the court listened with the most breathless attention, while Lady Emmeline thus went on to say,—

" My marriage with Sir Clarence was looked upon with an eye of jealousy by the friends of his late wife. They had ever imagined that he was more attached to me than to her, and they, therefore, sought every means to annoy me, and to work my ruin, which, fatally for me, they were afterwards enabled to accomplish. I had borne my husband a child, and it was but a few months old, when a gentleman, named Hector Longford, introduced himself to our family. Fatal day for me! He had been the friend of the late lady and her relations, and I looked upon him with an eye of suspicion. Not long had he become intimate with us, when the freedom of his manners towards me excited my alarm and disgust, and I avoided him as much as possible. He, however, forced himself upon my society, and, at length, completely unmasked himself, and made proposals to me of the most abominable nature. I repulsed him with disgust and abhorrence, and threatened to make my husband acquainted with his conduct, upon which he assured me, with the most diabolical rage depicted in his countenance, that, if I did, he would weave such a snare to entrap me that my destruction would be inevitable. Alarmed, I promised not to say anything about the matter, on his assuring me that he would never mention the hated subject again. He did promise me, and shortly afterwards he quitted the house, and I saw no more of him for some time. But the demons were at work. Combining with the relations of my husband's late wife, the villain trumped up a charge of infidelity against me, which my husband was too ready to believe, although I know that he loved me as dear as his own existence. The consequences of this was our separation, my child, my darling boy, was taken from me, and taken with his father and Julian, shortly afterwards, to the Indies, whilst I was left a wretched bereaved wife and mother—an outcast—looked upon with scorn by society, and pitied by few. For some years I flew from the scenes in which I had formerly mingled, and wandered to strange parts. Is it to be wondered that my reason should become impaired with all this heavy weight of sorrow, injustice, and calumny upon my mind? For some time I became a miserable maniac, and those years of insanity are like a dream to me ; but my senses are now restored, and ——"

"Ha! ha! ha!" interrupted Raker, with a fiendish laugh; " your senses are restored but to know the extent of your misery. I may swing on the gallows, but the Smuggler King will escape the power of the law, and in my last moments I shall have the satisfaction to know I triumph,—William, your darling William, is no more!"

" Murderer! monster!" shrieked the distracted Lady Emmeline ; " for this may the eternal tortures of the damned light upon thy guilty soul!"

A thrill of horror ran through the court, and Lady Emmeline was borne insensible into an adjoining apartment.

There now wanted nothing more to complete the evidence against the guilty Sam Raker and his companions, and they were accordingly convicted, and sentence of death, in the usual form, passed upon them.

It would be impossible to describe the emotions with which the families of

Mr. Clarendon and Mr. Backstay retired to their homes, and we will, therefore, pass over them. The fate of the lovers now appeared certain, and they had therefore nothing to look forward to but despair and misery.

Lady Emmeline was conveyed to Basilwood Hall, where Mr. Melford ordered every attention to be paid to her that her situation required.

The next night the villain Raker attempted to escape from the place in which he was confined, but he was fortunately detected, and committed to a place of greater security, prior to his execution, which was ordered to take place in three days from the time of his conviction.

CHAPTER XXV.

FLORA AND THE SMUGGLER KING.—EMBARKING ON BOARD THE RAVEN.—THE ATTACK OF THE NEPTUNE.—MEETING OF THE BROTHERS.—DESPERATE ENGAGEMENT.—THE UNEXPECTED DISCOVERY.—DEFEAT OF THE SMUGGLER KING.—THE MEETING OF THE LOVERS.

THROUGH the secret passage which was so well known to him, Sir Julian bore the insensible form of Flora, his mind filled with all the torments of rage, disappointment, and revenge. The outlet from the passage was at the farthest extremity of the rock, and he had only just emerged from it when the fearful explosion of the tower took place. He paused, and gazed on the work of destruction with a wild eye, and then maledictions upon the heads of those who had caused it, and upon Raker and the others who had abandoned him in the Raven, burst from his lips. However, he had escaped, and Flora was yet in his power, and that was some consolation to him. He did not long hesitate whither to go. On the island was a small house, kept by a man and his wife, who were in his secret, and were employed to give notice at the tower when any suspicion of danger occurred to him. Thither, therefore, he made his way, not doubting but that the Raven would in a short time return to learn the fate of the Devil Skipper and himself, and then he could immediately embark with his prize.

On our heroine recovering her senses, therefore, she found herself in a small room, with an elderly but disagreeable-looking woman watching by her, and she then learned the fate of the tower, and the pirate vessel, and that she was still in the power of Sir Julian, whom, however, she yet knew by no other title than the Smuggler King.

Terrible indeed was her agony when she was made acquainted with this, and she wrung her hands in despair. But what had become of poor Maud? Had she perished in the dreadful explosion? Alas! she feared she had, and bitter were the tears she shed for her fate.

It is needless to attempt to pourtray the rage of Sir Julian at the destruction of his favourite vessel and the tower, in which was deposited so much of his wealth. He was some hours in a state bordering on madness, and it was quite dreadful to hear the curses that escaped his lips. He had now lost the principal portion of his treasures, and as his real character would be known in England, his property there would be confiscated. Again he cursed his own folly in leaving the will behind him at the Hall, but even had he not done so, as circumstances had now turned out, it would have been just the same, and he had the fiendish satisfaction of knowing that William was no more, and therefore he could not have the triumph of enjoying that property, he (Sir Julian) had so long usurped.

He felt too much harassed in his mind to seek an interview with Flora, and therefore determined to defer doing so until a future period. This, of

course, was a great relief to the poor girl; and with exception of the pangs she endured from her uncertainty as to the fate which had befallen her lover, she became comparatively composed and resigned to her destiny, still not without a faint hope that Providence would ultimately interfere in her behalf, and rescue her from the troubles she had so long endured, and the terrible fate with which she was threatened.

She often thought of poor Maud; what had become of her? Alas! it seemed too probable that she had perished with the destruction of the tower, and that she would never behold her again. This idea filled her bosom with horror; when she remembered the many acts of kindness she had received from that unfortunate woman, the gentle sympathy she had ever evinced in her sorrows, and the manner in which she had exerted herself to sustain and encourage her under trials that must otherwise have borne her down, she felt for her all the affection of a sister, and lamented her untimely end more than ever.

She could form no idea of what the pirate captain intended to do, since his vessel and the tower were destroyed, and his daring crew scattered, nor did she seek to obtain any information from the people belonging to the place in which she was now confined, as their manners were the most repulsive, and they would never condescend to reply to any questions she might put to them only in surly monosyllables, from which she was not able to elicit anything. Dismally enough her time passed, but yet there were moments when she indulged in the hope that the Smuggler King would not be long able to detain her, injured as his power was, if not totally destroyed; but in that wild and unknown place, what chance was there of her ever being able to return to England? Alas! she saw none. It was to her a matter of astonishment that the pirate captain did not visit her, and she could not imagine what were his motives for not doing so; but it was to her a source of much gratification, and tended in some measure to alleviate the tediousness of her confinement.

From the casement of the room in which she was confined, she had a view for some distance, but it was gloomy and wild in the extreme, and was only calculated to increase her sadness instead of affording her any gratification.

Several days elapsed, and Sir Julian anxiously watched and awaited the arrival of the vessels, and could not account for the delay, sometimes being apprehensive that something had befallen them. In moments such as these, he was almost distracted, and he would pace the beach in the most disordered manner imaginable, no one having any suspicion of his real character, as he had assumed the disguise of a humble fisherman, wore a black patch over one of his eyes, and a grey wig. It would have been quite impossible for any one to have recognized him. But the vessel came not, and he daily returned to the house of the people where he was staying, in the same state of mind; giving vent to his feelings of disappointment and rage in the most bitter maledictions, which almost alarmed them to behold, albeit they were not much accustomed to fear.

Often Sir Julian would venture as far as the rock on which the tower had lately stood, and gaze upon its blackened ruins, while the feelings of a demon raged within his breast.

" Ruins of the Tower of the Death Rock," he would soliloquize, " ye stand there as if to mock me with the remembrance of your former strength, and of the d——g blow which has been given to the power of the Smuggler King! Oh! how many a revel have I and my daring crew had within your walls; there the monarch did I reign, surrounded by willing subjects, and piles of treasure. Where are they now? Gone! gone! all destroyed, and here I stand alone to contemplate the devastation which in so short a time has been made. Oh! curses, the most terrible curses, light upon those who have caused this! My floating palaces, too, my noble Devil Skipper and Raven, which struck terror into the minds of all who beheld them, and which had so gallantly and for so many years withstood the fury of the elements and bid defiance to all who were bold enough to attack you, where are you now? Destroyed, blown to pieces, perhaps not a timber of you left for your former commander to gaze upon. Oh! I will have ample vengeance for this;—if I have not hitherto been a fiend in human shape, I will become one now, and pursue my enemies to destruction. I will search them out, I will pursue them, though it be to the remotest corner of the globe, and have a terrible retribution upon their heads!"

Thus saying he clenched his fists, and fixed his eyes with terrible determination upon the ruins.

Sir Julian, accompanied by the man at whose house he was staying, had visited the interior of the ruins of the tower, and had found many valuable articles, and a considerable sum in money, that had not been injured by the explosion, and which they, of course, removed to a place of security, but the principal portion of the contents of the tower were destroyed, and the loss, therefore, to Sir Julian was immense.

How bitterly did he breathe his curses against Grampus, and long to have him in his power, that he might gratify his revenge upon him by a death of the greatest torture, and he did not entirely despair but that the time would arrive when that opportunity would be afforded him.

Three more days elapsed, and still the Raven did not arrive, and Sir Julian began to fear that it would not come, but that Sam Raker and the others, hearing of the destruction of the tower, would conclude that he had perished in it, and that therefore it was no use, and might be attended with danger for them to make their appearance in that quarter again, or, at least, for some time to come.

This idea filled him with despair, and again and again he regretted that Sam Raker had quitted the scene of action, when he reflected that they might ultimately have conquered the foe, and the tower still have remained uninjured. But he had no doubt that Raker had acted from motives of the best policy, in order to divert the enemy, for he well knew his fidelity, and that he would lose his life sooner than act with treachery towards him. But should his fears prove correct, and he be left on that island without the means of escaping from it, what was to become of him? His power would be entirely at an end, for he knew of no means of making the pirates aware that he was still alive, and where he was.

Never had Sir Julian felt such anxiety and fear before, and the misery he was then enduring was a just punishment for the many crimes he had committed, the long career of guilt he had experienced.

So much was his mind occupied by these reflections, that he scarcely ever bestowed a thought upon Flora, and she was thus left to the uninterrupted indulgence of her own meditations, and saved the horrors of a meeting with her cruel persecutor. Painful enough were those meditations to the poor girl, for whichever way she turned her thoughts she could see no prospect of hope at present, and the mysterious behaviour of Sir Julian, in not visiting her, filled her with alarm, as the idea suggested itself to her that his present forbearance would be succeeded by the worst her imagination could depicture. She was entirely in his power, and had no means of offering any resistance to him, or, if she did, what could it avail her? Would it save her from his diabolical designs? Reason—despair told her that it could not.

And now, more than ever, did the poor girl miss the society of Maud, to soothe, to counsel, and sympathise with her, and then the certainty of that unfortunate woman's fate impressed itself more powerfully on her mind. Home next recurred to her imagination, and when she reflected upon the desolation that had been there spread around, and that her parents were probably no more, madness almost seized upon her brain, and she paced the apartment in which she was confined, in a state of agitation which needs no description from us. William, too, was he not lost to her for ever? Oh, yes, too well did she know the cruelty of the wretches in whose power she last beheld him, to expect that they would permit him to live, especially when they were aware that he was the object of her affections, and after the scene which had taken place on board the Devil Skipper. As for the assertions of the pirate-chief, that he still lived, she placed no confidence in them, and firmly believed that he had only given utterance to them for the purpose of quieting her apprehensions, weakening her abhorrence of him, and thus affording him a better opportunity of effecting his cruel and nefarious intentions. William, parents, perhaps, then, she might see no more; what in the world had she to hope for to live? Nothing; and most fervently did she wish that it would please the Almighty to take her to Himself, rather than that she should live to suffer the misery she was at present undergoing, or be consigned to that terrible fate she had just cause to apprehend while she was in the power of the villain, the Smuggler King.

Deprived entirely of society; left alone to the communion of her own wretched thoughts; without books of any kind, in the perusal of which she might have diverted them, the reader may well imagine how heavily passed the poor damsel's time. It was, indeed, all gloomy night with her, and it is wonderful how her reason was enabled to support the heavy burthen with which it was loaded; but, amidst it all, she placed a firm reliance on the goodness of the Almighty, and, with the spirit of a true Christian, submitted to His will. Thus did she find that inward consolation which others would not have done.

Another day, and another day, and still was Sir Julian kept in the same state of almost insupportable suspense and uncertainty, and his patience was now fairly exhausted, and he apprehended in reality that Sam Raker and the rest of his crew had fallen into the hands of their enemies, and that his career was at an end.   But to fall in this manner, he who had for so many years held every one in terror, and bade defiance to all the power that had been sent against him, filled him with deeper rage and regret than all.   Had he perished on board of one of his own vessels, surrounded by his desperate crew, and in the prosecution of the villanous traffic he had ever pursued, he would not have regretted; but to be deserted, to be left powerless, and to die unknown, it drove him to madness even to think of it.

Still he continued his disguise, and never failed to perambulate the beach, with the hope of seeing something of the vessels, and often he ascended the summit of the Death Rock, and stretched his eager eyes across the vast expanse of ocean by which it was surrounded, but nothing met his gaze to gratify his hopes.

Three weeks had now elapsed since the destruction of the tower, and so much was Sir Julian occupied by other anxious thoughts, that he had yet forborne even to seek an interview with Flora Clarendon; not that he had given up his designs against her—no, the villain was determined, let whatever might be his own fate, that she should not escape that doom he had, from the first moment he had beheld her, contemplated.

It was about this period that Sir Julian had been absent the whole of the day from the house, wandering about the beach, and deeply immersed in his own agonized and guilty thoughts.   At length the shadows of evening descended upon the earth, which, however, were quickly dissipated by the light of the moon, which arose in silvery brightness, and illumined everything around with its refulgent rays.   The ocean glittered in its beams, a tranquil silence reigned around, only at intervals interrupted by the low moaning of the wind among the cavities of the rocks, or the gentle dashing of the waves as they laved the shores.

Sir Julian made his way to the Death Rock, and slowly ascending it, stood on its summit beneath the shattered walls of the tower, and folding his arms across his expansive chest, gazed with deep and sullen steadfastness over the deep.

So bright were the rays that Cynthia shed, that everything was clearly distinguishable for miles around, and not long had Sir Julian stood there, when suddenly his keen and penetrating eye caught the shadow of some approaching object in the distance, which he was not long in ascertaining was a ship, which appeared to be steering in the direction of the rock.   His heart palpitated, and his hopes revived; but lest the vessel should be an enemy, and not the one he wished to see, he entered the ruins of the tower, and placed himself in a position where he could observe all without himself being seen.

In a state of the greatest impatience he awaited for more than an hour, before the vessel had arrived near enough for him to have an opportunity of judging from her build what she was; but at length, the wind being in her favour, and the light of the moon assisting him, it got so near that he was enabled to ascertain beyond a doubt that it was a schooner, and that more than ever confirmed him in the supposition that it was one of the long expected pirate ships.

In a short time the schooner had reached to within a very short distance from the rock, and he then discovered that his surmises were correct—it *was* the Raven!

Sir Julian shouted aloud with delight and exultation, and rushing from the place of his concealment, he once more stood upon the most prominent part of the rock, and shouted and waved his arms about in the wildest extacy.

The vessel put in at a small cove, not far from the rock, and presently afterwards he saw a boat containing several men making towards that part of the shore where they could conveniently land. He dashed through the ruins, along the secret passage, and reached the beach just as the men had landed, and whom, with much satisfaction, he discovered to be part of his own crew.

They started on beholding him, but so well was he disguised that they did not recognise him until he called to them, and they then knew the tones of his voice. Will Hemlock and the others hastened towards him, and they raised a shout of joy and exultation when they recognised their desperate captain.

"Hurrah!" exclaimed Will Hemlock; "the Smuggler King is yet alive, and our enemies, therefore, have not gained a complete triumph."

"Hurrah, for the Smuggler King!" shouted the others, and they all gathered around their captain.

"Look at yon ruins," said Sir Julian, pointing to the tower, "and see the ruin that our accursed foes have accomplished. Wealth, all, have been sacrificed in that, and ——"

"True, captain," returned Hemlock, "it is a bad job ; but the ocean deep is yet left for the Smuggler King and his subjects, and we will have more wealth, double the wealth that has hitherto filled your coffers, to make amends for this loss."

Sir Julian shook his head.

"It will be long ere we shall be able to redeem this loss," he said ; "but my soul thirsts for vengeance. Hemlock, what made Sam Raker and the rest of you abandon me in the manner you did ?"

"It was a scheme to divert the attention of the enemy," answered Hemlock, "and to arrest their attack upon the tower."

"Ah! but why did you not return when you perceived that they did not give chase to you ?"

"Sam Raker advised that we should not go," answered Will Hemlock, "as he felt confident in case of emergency you could make your escape, and he thought that you would sooner that the tower should fall a sacrifice than both your vessels to the enemy. Contrary winds drove us out to sea, and prevented our returning at the time we wished."

"Curses on his headstrong folly !" said Sir Julian ; "our triumph would have been certain ; when did he know the Smuggler King fly from the foe ? Better that we had all perished than to suffer this defeat. But where is my bold Devil Skipper ?"

Hemlock's lips quivered, and he seemed to fear to answer.

"Ah! you hesitate !" impatiently cried the smuggler captain ; "you do not answer. What other misfortune has hell conspired to award me ? Speak, quick ; do not keep me in this suspense ; what has become of my ship ? Where is Sam Raker ? Why did ye not return together ?"

"Captain," answered Hemlock, still hesitating, while the cheeks of his rough companions were blanched with fear, as the fierce eye of their much dreaded captain rested upon each of them, and they saw the turbulent passions that were raging in his breast ; "captain, I am sorry to inform you that the Devil Skipper is destroyed, and Sam Raker is in the hands of our enemies, and probably, by this time, far on his way to England."

"Liar !" furiously cried Sir Julian, seizing Hemlock by the throat, and his eyes appearing to flash fire ; "you do but come here to mock me ! Beware, or you know your fate ! My gallant vessel destroyed, my faithful Raker in the hands of the swabs ! 'Tis false ! 'tis false !"

"Captain," said Hemlock, releasing himself from his hold, "I speak the unfortunate truth, as our messmates can prove."

"Gone ! destroyed ! Sam Raker a prisoner !" shouted Sir Julian, in tones that made the very rocks re-echo. "D——n! this, then, is indeed the final blow to the Smuggler King!"

"Nay, captain," returned Hemlock; "we are not yet conquered; we will live for revenge!"

"Revenge!" exclaimed Sir Julian; "oh! yes, I will have a terrible, a sanguinary vengeance! I will become a very demon, and—but my gallant ship! the Smuggler King's ocean palace, destroyed! Sam Raker taken prisoner! It is all a dream! I cannot believe it."

"It is too true, captain," answered Will Hemlock.

A dreadful curse escaped the Smuggler King's lips, and he walked furiously to and fro for a few moments, unable to utter another syllable. The smugglers, daring as they were, trembled for the consequences of their captain's rage, although it was no more than they had expected.

"But how did this happen?" he at length demanded, turning to Hemlock; "tell me quick—my burning brain will not admit of any delay?"

"Two days since," answered Hemlock, "we were suddenly surprised by two British men-of-war, and although we endeavoured to avoid them, they gave us chase, and shortly came up with us."

"Well, and what then?"

"Of course we had no alternative left but to fight," replied Hemlock; "and a desperate and bloody engagement commenced, which for some time continued, and the result appeared very doubtful. But they carried too much heavy mettle for us, and their crew nearly doubled the number of our men. Besides, after the engagement we had had here, our ammunition run very short, so that we laboured under every disadvantage; the enemy boarded the Devil Skipper, and great slaughter ensued. Sam Raker was secured as a prisoner, and it was in vain that I went to his assistance; shortly afterwards the Devil Skipper blew up, and every soul on board the vessel perished."

"The fiends of hell have conspired against me!" shouted Sir Julian; "the star that hitherto guided the fortunes of the Smuggler King is set. Oh, curses—infernal curses! But you escaped?"

"Ay, with much difficulty," answered Will Hemlock; "and hastened hither with the hope of meeting with you."

Again Sir Julian paced the beach, and nothing could equal the rage and agitation which he evinced.

"My poor ship!" he ejaculated, in melancholy tones; "never more shall I sail in you; oh, why was I not present to perish with you?"

"Be calm, captain," remonstrated Will Hemlock; "though misfortune certainly now frowns upon us, the flag of the Smuggler King shall yet float triumphantly over the main, and he shall have ample revenge!"

"Ay, by hell, I will!" cried Sir Julian; "I will have revenge in the heart's blood of all the human race that fall into my hands. To the boat; I must on board the vessel, and by to-morrow's dawn we will set sail on our fearful expedition. I feel prepared for more desperate deeds than have hitherto marked my character, and my soul thirsts to resume my career of plunder and of bloodshed. To the boat—to the boat!"

"But the girl, captain," asked Hemlock, "what has become of her?"

"Oh, she has not escaped me," answered the former, exultingly; "she is safe at the house of Lawrence Brassford. This night she shall be taken on board the Raven; and, when I have recovered from the shock which this unexpected intelligence has caused me, I will see about completing my designs against her. That villain, Grampus——"

"Ay, it is he who has caused all this," said Hemlock.

"The traitor!" exclaimed Sir Julian; "but, by the infernal host, I swear that, if he be living, I will not rest until I have found him out, and had my revenge upon him in his heart's blood."

" Would that we could get him in our power, captain," observed Hemlock ; " but I fear there is not much chance of that."

" Why ?" demanded Sir Julian.

" He is under the protection, or shortly will be, of the authorities in England."

" How know you that ?"

" He was on board one of the vessels by which we were attacked at the tower, was he not,?"

" I know not."

" But I am convinced," said Hemlock, " for I myself beheld him."

" Ah !" exclaimed Sir Julian ; " and yet you suffered him to escape. Why did you not level a pistol at the villain's head, and ——"

" I had not the opportunity, captain," interrupted Hemlock, " though I sought it ; he was always too well surrounded."

" The dastard knave !" cried the smuggler-chief ; " oh ! how my soul yearns to meet him. But, to the boat—to the boat !—my soul is on fire for vengeance ; and, when we are on board our craft, we must consult upon the best means of accomplishing it. It would not be prudent to remain here any longer than possible."

" It would not," coincided Hemlock, " for no doubt some of our enemies will come here again in search of us. Whither think you of directing your course ?"

" That we will decide anon," answered Sir Julian ; " but at present I think of going in search of some of our other vessels, and, when we meet with them, we will close together upon the enemy, and seek a bloody satisfaction for the destruction of the tower and the Devil Skipper."

" Wisely resolved, captain," observed Will Hemlock ; " and no doubt we shall very soon be able to redeem the heavy loss we have sustained."

" Nothing can ever replace that," said Sir Julian ; " the loss of my gallant vessel, the terror of the ocean, the destruction of the tower, and, above all, the confiscation of my property in England, for no doubt every one will shortly be made acquainted with my real character, and the will and other papers I was thoughtless enough to leave behind me at the Hall, will fully prove that. Cursed fortune seems to have turned against me all at once."

" She will smile, captain, never fear," remarked Hemlock, as he led the way to the boat, into which they jumped, and were soon making their way towards the Raven.

In the meantime Flora was still enduring the greatest mental anguish, and was at a loss to imagine what could be the smuggler-chief's future intentions towards her, as he did not offer to interrupt her, or to seek an interview with her. Did he intend to keep her a prisoner in that lonely place. Alas! If he did, all chance of being rescued was equally as hopeless as when she was in the Tower of the Death Rock. Oh! how miserably tedious passed the hours with the poor girl, with nothing to divert her thoughts for a moment from her own melancholy situation, and with no other prospect to gaze upon from the casement of her apartment but the wild and desolate island beyond. Death surely would have been preferable to that she was fated to undergo.

Could she but have obtained some books, by the perusal of which she could have occupied her mind for a few hours, it would have been a great relief to her ; but, when she asked the wife of Laurence Brassford if she could oblige her in that manner, she surlily replied,—they had something else to do than to waste their time over such nonsense, and that they had never been fine folks enough to trouble themselves to learn to read.

Flora therefore was thwarted in all her wishes, and had no means of seeking relaxation from the heavy cares that oppressed her. On the night of the arrival of the Raven she had felt more than usually unhappy, and her heart seemed to forbode that something particular was about to happen, to make a change in her situation. She sat in a melancholy attitude by the casement; and, although she had heard the old clock in the house strike the hour of ten, she did not feel inclined to retire to her couch. Some instinctive power seemed to urge her to remain up, and she listened to catch any sounds that might come from below, while her heart fluttered, and, in spite of her efforts to subdue it, she trembled violently. But all remained perfectly still, and she imagined that Sir Julian had not yet returned.

Another hour passed away in this manner, when she suddenly heard a confused noise from below, then the muttering tones of several voices, among which she distinguished that of the pirate-chief.

At first they spoke in such low accents that she could not distinguish a word they were talking about, although she went to the room-door to listen; but at length Sir Julian spoke louder, and her ears were shocked with a terrible oath, which convinced her that something had happened to excite him greatly. She could also hear the gruff voices of several men, and that circumstance increased her alarm.

" To-night," she at length heard Sir Julian say.

"So soon?" questioned another, in whose tones she recognised those of Laurence Brassford; "this is sudden, indeed."

" It must not be delayed," returned her persecutor; " after what has happened, there might be danger in deferring it. So your wife had better go and prepare her."

" Very well," answered Laurence, and then the conversation again dropped into low murmurs, and Flora could not make out another syllable that was spoken.

" God preserve me!" ejaculated our heroine, clasping her hands; " what can they mean?"

She trembled with apprehension, and before she could in any degree regain her composure she heard a footstep on the stairs leading to her apartment. In a moment or so afterwards, the door was opened, and the old woman made her appearance.

" You must prepare yourself to quit this place, young lady," she said.

" Leave this place?" repeated Flora.

" Yes; it is the captain's orders," answered the old woman; " and I dare say you are not sorry for that."

" When? when?" eagerly demanded the hapless damsel.

" You must be ready to depart in an hour."

" Whither am I going?"

" That is no business of mine," returned the old woman; " but I dare say you will find it out quite soon enough. Here is a cloak, and that will, I dare say, be enough for you, for you will not have to go far before you are lodged again."

" Gracious Heaven!" cried the agitated girl, " for what am I destined?"

" To be the bride of the Smuggler King, there cannot be a doubt of that," answered the old woman. " Remember, I shall call for you in an hour."

" At this time of night?" said Flora; " why, it is near midnight."

" Well, I can't help that; those are the orders I have to give you, and you must not disobey them."

" God help me!" sighed our heroine, " I have no power to do so."

The old woman made her no answer, and having placed the cloak over the back of a chair, she quitted the room. Flora's distress of mind was now beyond all bounds; she should again behold the Smuggler King, and Heaven only knew what were his intentions towards her, or whither he was going to convey her; but, from the voices of the men, many of which were familiar to her ears, she imagined that they were part of the pirate crew, and that she was

once more about to be taken on board of one of their vessels. She could no longer doubt that the captain would defer putting his terrible threats into execution ; she trembled with horror, and gave herself up entirely for lost.

"Oh !" she reflected, "what a mercy would it be to me if it pleased the will of the Almighty now to take me to himself, and thus save me from shame and degradation."

Even the confinement she had experienced in the house, lonely as it was, and revolting as were its inmates, was happiness compared with the change she now anticipated, for she had suffered no interruption, and the Smuggler King had never intruded himself upon her ; but now she was going once more immediately into his presence, and would be continually shocked and annoyed by his hateful importunities, with no faithful and sympathising Maud near her to advise her, and to restrain the boldness of his advances. Tears gushed to her eyes, and she could not help thinking that her destiny was a cruel one, and one which her conduct had never merited. To such a state of despair was she driven, that had she been possessed of the means, she would have laid violent hands on herself, and thus have ended a life which had now become burthensome to her. Then, on a moment's reflection, she reproached herself for the thought, and for giving way to that weakness which could not alter her condition, but, on the contrary, would give an advantage to the villain in whose power she was, and prevent her from being able to offer that resistance to his designs which by coolness and fortitude she might otherwise be able to do.

"Yes," she ejaculated, "I will be firm, and meet my oppressor as I have hitherto done, and which has enabled me at any rate to abash and awe him in the moments of his greatest determination. That just God, who watches with a merciful eye over all His creatures, will not suffer a poor, innocent, and unprotected girl to fall a victim to such villany. To His care will I commit myself, and with fortitude and patience await the result."

No. 54

She knelt down, and solemnly and meekly implored the protection of the Supreme, and afterwards arose with astonishing calmness and resignation, and prepared to equip herself for the journey she imagined she was about to take.

The night she could find was cold, and she therefore considered the cloak which the old woman had brought very acceptable, and enveloping her form in it, awaited the expiration of the hour. It soon passed away, and exactly as the old clock struck twelve, she heard a noise from below, and immediately afterwards the footstep of the old woman once more upon the stairs. Again she silently commended herself to the care of Omnipotence, and she had scarcely done so, when the wife of Lawrence Brassford entered the apartment.

"Now, young lady," said the beldame, "are you ready?"

Flora made no answer, but pointed to the room-door, and the old woman led the way out.

They proceeded down stairs, and entered the parlour, and our heroine trembled, in spite of her previous resolutions, when she perceived Will Hemlock and several other smugglers assembled, and in the midst of them the Smuggler King, whom by his voice she immediately recognized, although he was still disguised in the same manner we have before described.

The villain arose on her entrance, advanced towards her, and seemed to eye her with looks of satisfaction; Flora turned from him in disgust, but her courage returned, and she prepared herself to act with firmness and resignation.

"Beauteous Flora," said Sir Julian, "I am happy to see you once more, though I have deprived myself of that pleasure for some days past; and, therefore, I think you cannot but give me credit for my forbearance. I am sorry to have to disturb you at so late an hour as this, but urgent necessity compels that we should immediately depart from this place."

"And whither would you now convey me?" asked Flora.

"Once more on ship-board," answered Sir Julian, "there to reign the mistress of my heart."

"Oh, God!" exclaimed our heroine, and she recoiled from his touch with a feeling of horror.

"Nay, fair damsel," exclaimed Sir Julian, "you need not express such a fear; there are many who would be proud to be the bride of the rover of the seas."

"Then why not search them out," demanded Flora, "and no longer persecute with your odious vows one who can never look upon you with any other feelings than those of the utmost hatred and abhorrence?"

"Psha!" ejaculated Sir Julian; "you young ladies often talk about hatred and all that sort of nonsense, before you absolutely know the meaning of love. Such beauteous and gentle maidens as Flora Clarendon were never formed to hate any of their fellow-creatures."

"There are those beings in the world," returned our heroine, "whose actions make them detestable to every one who is not as guilty as themselves; those whose actions can excite nothing but terror and disgust; such a being is he who calls himself the Smuggler King, or he would never have torn an innocent girl from her home, her parents, her friends, and thus continue to persecute her."

"But the Smuggler King will make amends for all that he has done, when thou dost become his bride," returned Sir Julian. "He will suffer you then to see your relations, your native country, to ——"

"Then," interrupted our heroine, "I shall behold them no more, if those are the only conditions, for death would I choose, rather than become the wife of a man whose hands are stained with the blood of one who was indeed dear to me."

"You accuse me of that I am not guilty of," said Sir Julian; "you will, however, change your mind ere long, or I am much mistaken."

"Never!" exclaimed Flora, vehemently; "witness me Heaven, never!"

"And suppose I am as determined as yourself?"

"Alas! I know that I have no power to oppose your diabolical will, without one friend at hand to aid me," said the damsel; "but surely, cruel as you are, you will have some pity for me, and act with forbearance."

"Have I not acted with forbearance already?" demanded Sir Julian. "The beauteous Flora should seek not pity where she may command love, adoration; why should she sue for pity to one who is ready to become her slave?"

"Thy words are hateful to mine ears," said our heroine, fixing upon him a look fully expressive of her feelings.

"They may be at present," remarked the smuggler-chief; "but I am much deceived if you will not by-and-bye alter your tones. But this is not the time or place to talk of these matters; we must depart, for the time is waning fast, and the morning's sun must see us far away from this place."

Flora shuddered.

"Oh! must I," she said, "become a prisoner on the wide ocean deep, surrounded by wretches capable of any crime, and without one sympathising soul, without one female near me, to soothe and advise me under my heavy misfortunes?"

"That you will find when you get on board the Raven, fair Flora," answered Sir Julian; "perhaps it may not be so bad as you apprehend."

There was something in the manner in which Sir Julian uttered this, which somewhat appeased the fears and anguish of the damsel, and excited a faint feeling of hope in her bosom; but when she thought of poor Maud, and reflected how unlikely it was that she should ever again meet with one so kind and sincere as her, but instead, perhaps, some creature of the pirate captain's, whose society would be almost as revolting as his, her hopes were crushed, and she could not help feeling the greatest doubt and apprehension. She raised her eyes towards Heaven, and mentally imploring its aid and protection, resigned herself without another word to that fate she could not resist, and to accompany the smugglers on board the Raven.

Sir Julian and Hemlock took Laurence Brassford aside, and made some observations to him in an under tone, to which the latter nodded assent, and the baronet then took the arm of Flora, and with an insinuating smile motioned towards the door of the house. Our heroine shuddered with horror and indignation at the touch of a being she so loathed, but so much dreaded, but knowing that it would be useless to attempt to oppose him, she suffered him to lead her forth, followed by the rest of the smugglers, who had been gazing at her with bold and fearful looks.

The night was very dark, and the wind blew bleakly from the ocean, but Flora heeded it not, so much was her mind occupied with other thoughts that racked her brain to distraction. Sir Julian and the smugglers held no conversation together, but hurried on at a quick pace, as if fearful they should be seen by any one.

In a very short time they reached the place where the boat was moored, and our heroine, as she gazed upon the dark waters of the boundless deep, and reflected that she was so soon to become a prisoner on them, entirely in the power, and at the mercy of villains who mocked its dictates, felt the most powerful sensation of dread steal over her, and she clasped her hands in agony.

Sir Julian having handed her into the boat, was followed by his companions, and they immediately put off towards the vessel, which soon afterwards Flora was enabled to distinguish. In a short time they reached it, and our heroine was conducted on board, and from the deck to a cabin well fitted up, where she was left alone. Unable any longer to restrain her emotions, the poor girl burst into a flood of tears, which somewhat relieved her mind, but still she saw nothing but despair before her.

She once more implored the mercy of the Most High, and then seated herself, and endeavoured to await the issue of her destiny with firm resignation.

She was suddenly aroused from this lethargy by hearing a light and hasty footstep approaching the cabin, and the next moment the door was thrown open, a well known voice repeated her name; she looked up, uttered an exclamation of joy and astonishment, and was immediately pressed to the bosom of the kind and faithful Maud.

Yes, it was Maud, alive and well; she had been saved from the conflagration of the tower, and was once more destined to become the companion of our unfortunate heroine. So overcome was the latter by this unexpected meeting, that she could scarcely prevent herself from fainting, and it was not until poor Maud had again and again embraced her, with the same ardent affection as if she had been one of her dearest relations, and endeavoured to soothe her into composure, that she could believe that it was reality.

"Look up, my dear girl," said Maud, "it is no ideal vision, but Maud restored to you to be the companion of your misfortunes, and to endeavour to re-animate your bosom with hope and fortitude."

"It is, it is indeed my dear, kind, faithful Maud," exclaimed Flora, returning her embraces most fervently; "kind Heaven, I thank thee for this. But, oh, tell me, how has this happened? how did you escape the terrible explosion at the tower, and what has brought you again into the power of your enemies?"

"I will tell you, " answered Maud; "I need not attempt to describe to you what my agony was, when the Smuggler King tore you from me, and bore you to the battlements of the tower. I anticipated, I fully dreaded what your fate would be, and I wrung my hands in despair. With what sorrow I listened to the dreadful clamour of the battle, and between the pauses of the firing and the curses of the combatants, I fancied I heard your voice shrieking to me for help. I approached as near the battlements as I could, and heard the words the smuggler-captain addressed to his enemies; my blood chilled with horror, and I found that nothing now could save you. The shouts of the sailors, and the curses of the smugglers, convinced me that the latter were being defeated, and what at another time would have afforded me pleasure, at that moment filled me with the most serious alarm, for I knew that the captain would keep his threats, and would not fail to sacrifice your life, sooner than that you should fall into the hands of his foes. The misery I then endured, was greater than I remember ever before to have experienced.

"At length I heard a shout from some of the smugglers that the tower was on fire, and presently afterwards heard them rushing towards the place where I was to endeavour to make their escape. That impulse which guides us all in moments of danger, urged me to do the same, and with feelings it would be useless for me to attempt to describe, I rushed from the place where I was standing, and made my way to the secret passage with which I was acquainted. Fortunately I reached it in safety, and dashing along its intricate windings, with a speed which terror gave me, I shortly reached the entrance, and emerged into the open air, just at the moment that the tower exploded.

"What a sight of horror was this to me! I concluded that you, Flora, had perished with the rest, and I stood, fixed as a statue to the spot on which I was standing, and beat my breast in all the agony of despair. For a moment I reproached myself for the selfish feeling which had tempted me to endeavour to save myself, and wished that I had perished with you.

"At first I knew not whither to go, but after I had somewhat conquered the confusion of my thoughts, I remembered a cottage kept by an old man and his wife, whom I had on some former occasion rendered some services to, and having a sum of money by me, I determined to bend my course thither, not doubting but that they would afford me a shelter, until I could find some means to get to England. I was not mistaken in my surmises; the old people received me kindly, and were in a state of great excitement, curiosity, and alarm at the events that had taken place at the tower; but I evaded their questions as to the cause of them, for I did not think it would be prudent at present to make known the real characters of the captain and his crew.

"Several days of the greatest misery I endured, for I had been unable to learn anything of your fate, and I could only come to the dreadful conclusion that you, as well as all those who were in the tower, had perished in the flames.

"I frequently traversed the island, and wandered to the sea-beach, with the hope of being able to learn something that would satisfy the fearful doubts and apprehensions that tortured my mind; but it was not until this evening that anything particular occurred to me, to banish the suspense in which I had so long remained. Walking along the beach, I suddenly perceived the captain standing on the summit of the Death Rock, for his well known figure could not be concealed from me, although he was so closely disguised; and it was then for the first time that the hope occurred to me that you had been preserved, and was either on some part of the island, or that the sailors had succeeded in rescuing you from his power. Oh! how earnestly I prayed that the latter might be the case.

"I continued to watch the captain until he entered the ruins of the tower, and then casting my eyes eagerly in the direction in which he had been gazing, I for the first time beheld the dark shadow of an approaching ship. My heart beat high between alternate hope and fear, and I resolved to watch the result of this event let whatever might be the consequences.

"In a short time the vessel came nearer, and I thought I could perceive, as well as the light would permit me, that it was one of the smuggler's vessels. At length the vessel veered round the rock, and presently afterwards a boat approached the shore. I concealed myself in one of the cavities of the rocks, and had not long done so, when I beheld Will Hemlock and two or three other smugglers step on to the bench; they were immediately joined by the captain, and approached close to the spot where I was concealed, but they could not perceive me, and I was enabled to hear all the conversation that passed between them. Judge my delight when I heard that you had not perished in the burning of the tower, and that, therefore, there was a probability that I should behold you again? I could scarcely help betraying myself, so great was my extacy; but anxious to hear all I could, I determined not to do so for the present. From the observations that passed between the captain and Hemlock, I also learned that the Devil Skipper had been destroyed, and Raker conveyed a prisoner to England."

"Ah," ejaculated our heroine, " one villain, then, at any rate is secured, and the power of the Smuggler King somewhat limited. There may yet be hope."

"There is hope, dear Flora," answered Maud; " pursuit will be made after the pirates, and you may yet be rescued,"

"But, alas!" observed the damsel, " ere that aid arrives it may be too late, and the miscreant in whose power I am, may have enforced his cruel designs, and rendered me a wretched and degraded being for ever."

" Do not give way to despair, Flora," said the affectionate Maud ; " remember that I am with you to console and advise you, and, although my power is not great, I have hitherto been the means of tending in a great measure towards making the captain act with forbearance towards you."

" You have indeed, my kind Maud," returned our heroine, " and, oh ! how grateful am I to you for that, and to Heaven for having restored you to me. But proceed, Maud, with your narrative."

" Being now certain," resumed Maud, " that you were alive, and confident that the captain would have you conveyed on board the vessel without delay, I determined to reveal myself to them, so that I might have the opportunity of again being near you."

" Generous, disinterested-hearted woman," exclaimed our heroine, " when shall I ever be able to repay you for your kindness to me ? But Heaven will reward you."

" Those who conscientiously do their duty," returned Maud, " need not despair of meeting with reward in the approval of the Almighty. But to proceed : before I could carry my intentions into effect, the captain and the others had entered the boat, and were on their way to the boat ; but I was certain that they would not long remain there, and I therefore hurried to the cottage at which I had been staying, and which was at no great distance, to inform the old people who had been so kind to me, that I must shortly leave them, and having rewarded them for their trouble, I returned to the spot I had recently quitted, and awaited the captain and any other of the crew that might come ashore with him.

" In about an hour the boat once more made its appearance approaching the land, and when they had alighted on the shore, I made my appearance before them. I need not attempt to describe to you the astonishment of the smuggler chief when he beheld me, whom he expected had perished in the fearful conflagration of the tower. He could at first scarcely believe the evidence of his senses, but when he was convinced that he laboured under no delusion, he seemed very well pleased to have found me again ; assured me of your safety, and that I should shortly behold you, and then ordered one of the men to convey me on board the vessel, and to return with the boat to the same place, and there await him and the other smugglers. The man obeyed, and I soon found myself once more on board one of the dreaded pirate's vessels. The interval that elapsed before your arrival, my thoughts were of the most anxious description ; but I need not attempt to describe them to you."

" Dear Maud," said the grateful Flora, " and for my sake, then, you have once more deprived yourself of liberty, and placed yourself in the power of the wretches from whom you have already experienced so much misery."

" Oh, name it not," answered Maud, " I am near you, and that is a sufficient recompense for all. To know that you have escaped the dreadful and untimely fate, which I feared had befallen you, is to me a source of gratification which I cannot express."

" Oh, Maud," ejaculated our heroine, throwing herself once more into her arms, and sobbing upon her bosom ; " my tears alone must thank you,—words have not sufficient power to do so. But this cruel pirate chief ! Oh, God ! when I think of him it chills my very heart's blood with horror. That day, that fatal day, when the tower was attacked, will never be effaced from my memory. And now I am still in his power, and from his character I cannot expect that he will long desist from making me his victim. There is nothing but misery and despair before me."

" At present, my dear girl," answered her companion, " I must confess that your prospect is gloomy enough ; but still trust to the mercy and goodness of

Heaven, which has hitherto protected you at the moment of imminent peril, and all I trust will yet be well."

"Maud, my most affectionate, my gentle Maud," exclaimed the poor girl, "for your sake I will endeavour to be calm, and to exert my energies and fortitude to the utmost. You have ever been my kind monitor and soother in moments when, without you, I must have sunk beneath despair."

"The captain," observed Maud, "will for some time, no doubt, be too much occupied in arranging his future plans after the severe blow his power has received from the destruction of the tower and his principal vessel, to prosecute to any extremity his designs against you, and in the meantime help may arrive to rescue you when you least of all expect it."

"But you will not leave me ?" anxiously asked our heroine.

"No, my dear Flora," replied Maud, "I shall be your constant companion, the captain has permitted me to be so, and therefore take comfort."

"I will, indeed," said the damsel, her countenance brightening, "for in your society I can find comfort, even though surrounded by the greatest misery. But, my dear Maud, there is one question I must ask you, and I beg that you will no longer refuse to answer it me, as evil fortune might again separate us, and then my anxiety would not be appeased."

"What is it you would ask, dear Flora ?" said Maud.

"This terrible pirate captain," returned our heroine, "my oppressor ; you know him well ; you have assured me that you do, and I am confident that you must. Reveal to me his real character,—his real name."

"Flora," said her companion, "have I not told you that I am bound by a terrible oath ?"

"Of what effect is an oath extorted by such wretches ?" demanded Flora.

"But should it be discovered that I have revealed his real name and character," said Maud, "not only my destruction, but yours would inevitably follow."

"And what chance is there that such a discovery will be made ?" demanded our heroine ; "you are certain that I will keep it a secret as long as it may be necessary to do so."

"Oh, yes," observed Maud ; "I do not doubt you, unless, in your interviews with the captain, your excited feelings might cause you inadvertently to divulge it."

"Entertain no such apprehensions, dearest Maud," said the damsel ; "caution shall ever seal my lips. Besides, if Grampus reaches England, he will be sure to reveal the secret, and it will soon be known to all the world."

Maud hesitated, and our heroine more forcibly urged her.

"I will trust you, Flora," she at length said, "and Heaven pardon me if I do wrong in breaking the oath that has been administered to me."

"It will, it will !" eagerly ejaculated the maiden ; "oaths cannot be binding that are extorted from the innocent and the oppressed by those who respect them not."

"Suffer not your surprise to overcome you by the disclosure I shall make," said Maud, "for we might be overheard, and ——"

"You may trust me, dear Maud," replied our heroine ; "I will be guarded."

Maud placed her finger on her lips, and then going to the cabin door, she looked out to see that no one was near at hand to overhear them. She then returned to Flora, who was most anxiously and impatiently awaiting the revelation of what she had long been so eager to know.

"Dear Flora," observed Maud, "I have often told you that the Smuggler King, as he is called, is a man of rank."

"You have—you have !"

"That, unknown when on shore, he has mingled with the most fashionable classes of society, and that his company has always been eagerly sought after," added Maud; "and that, possessing the powerful influence of personal wealth, he has always escaped the eye of suspicion, and been thus enabled to carry on his diabolical purposes with a certainty of success."

"True," answered our heroine, "but if he is a man of rank and fortune, what can induce him to proceed in such a nefarious career?"

"His own base mind, Flora," replied her companion, "and his naturally base propensities. You must have observed, in the interviews you have had with him, that he is accomplished, and possessed of those qualities that would enable him to shine with respect in society, instead of being one of its greatest curses, its oppressor, and its dread."

"I have," answered Flora.

"And you have never been able to recognize his features?"

"No. I have before told you, Maud, that they are familiar to me, but still I cannot recollect where I have seen him before I fell into his power."

"But you have seen him, and often," said Maud, in lower and more cautious tones.

"Where?—where?"

"Know you Basilwood Hall?" demanded Maud.

"Oh, well!" answered our heroine; "it is close to that once happy home, but now, I fear, happy no longer, in which I first drew my breath."

"Then you know Sir Julian Mordlington?" said Maud.

"Ah! what of him?" eagerly asked the damsel.

Maud drew nearer towards her, and, whispering in her ear, said,—

"Sir Julian Mordlington and the Smuggler King, in whose power you now are, are one and the same person.

Flora started.

"Sir Julian Mordlington!" she exclaimed. "Gracious Heavens! is it possible?"

"Hush! be cautious!" said Maud. "It is true. Now, dear Flora, you are acquainted with the secret you have so long wished to know, and I hope you are satisfied."

"I can scarce believe my senses," said our heroine; "but now I remember, the features, the tones of his voice, as I first heard them—oh, yes, t must—it must, indeed, be true!"

"It is," returned Maud; "you cannot imagine that I would attempt to deceive you; besides, I could have no interest in so doing."

"Oh, no," observed Flora; "but, abandoned as I believe Sir Julian to be, and much as I instinctively dreaded him, never could I for a moment have believed him to be the monster that he is. He whose name strikes terror to the heart on hearing it mentioned only; whose career has been one of rapine and bloodshed. Alas! how unaccountably does fortune sometimes bestow her gifts."

"True," answered Maud; "but, if Grampus arrives safe in England, all will be revealed, and the wealth which Sir Julian has hitherto possessed, will be forfeited to the crown."

"And he will never again be able to venture to England," observed Flora, "and, therefore, unless I am rescued from his power by some miraculous means, all chance of beholding my native land again is at an end. Oh! misery! misery!"

"Nay, this despair is useless," said Maud, "and is but a poor return for the confidence which, at your earnest request, I have reposed in you."

"Forgive me, Maud," said the damsel. "I will endeavour to control my feelings. But one more question; it is a solemn one, and I hope you will no longer refuse to answer it candidly."

"Name it."

"My poor, my unfortunate William," sighed Flora. "After that scene on board the pirate's vessel, I became insensible, and Maud, dear Maud, as you love me, and would banish the dreadful suspense that has so long tortured my mind, tell me, know you really whether or not he yet lives?"

Maud paused, and seemed anxious to evade the question.

"Oh! do not hesitate!" implored our heroine. "The certainty, let it be ever so fatal, would not be half so dreadful as the state of doubt and apprehension I have been so long suffered to remain under."

"Why, my dear Flora," asked Maud, "do you urge this question?"

"And is it not a natural one?" demanded Flora. "Is it not natural that I should be anxious to know the fate of that dear youth who loved me so sincerely? Oh, Maud, you are my best friend, and when you know the anxiety of my mind, I am certain you will not refuse me."

"How can I answer you?" said Maud.

"You—you must know his fate," said the maiden, "although, from the best of motives, you have hitherto endeavoured to deceive me."

"I have not deceived you, Flora, I saw him not slain."

"Ah!" cried our heroine; "but did he not disappear from the ship? and what could have become of him, how could they have disposed of him, when it was at the time under full sail?"

"We know not that he disappeared from the ship," answered Maud; "all that we know is, that we did not behold him again after the interview which took place between you on board the Devil Skipper. He might also have been conveyed to the tower of the Death Rock."

"Ah! no!" ejaculated Flora. "I cannot believe it; or, if he was, have I not even full as much cause for misery and despair, since he must have perished with the conflagration of the tower?"

"My dear Flora," observed Maud, "again I assure you that have I no certain knowledge of your lover's fate; but I will not deceive you, I will not flatter you with false hopes, which I cannot myself entertain; it would be cruel to do so. Much then do I fear that the unfortunate William has fallen a victim to the cruelty of Sam Raker, who, no doubt, was authorised by Sir Julian himself to do the deed."

"God of Heaven! preserve my senses," cried the distracted Flora, her countenance turning ghastly pale, and her whole frame agitated with the most powerful emotion.

"Pray be calm, dear Flora," said Maud; "it is useless to repine at the will of Heaven; and, after all, it may not be so bad as we apprehend. By some miracle, your lover may have been preserved, and you yet may meet again."

"Oh! no," exclaimed our heroine. "It would be madness to indulge in the hope. Calm! yes, I will endeavour to be so—Heaven help me!—as calm as I can expect to be under such awful circumstances; for it is no more than my worst fears all along anticipated. But surely the avenging wrath of the Almighty will overtake his cruel murderers for their accursed deed."

"It will—it will," observed Maud; "and you will yet live to triumph over your infamous persecutors."

"Live!" repeated Flora. "What should I wish to live for? Triumph! Alas! what triumph can I expect, since he to whom my whole soul was devoted, is no more? Murdered, barbarously murdered, by these fiends in human shape. Oh, God! it would have been a mercy had they sacrificed my life at the same time. But it will not be long; the time will soon come when I shall be released from this mortal coil. This heart must soon break beneath the weight of heavy cares that oppress it."

"Nay, nay," soothingly ejaculated the affectionate Maud, "say not so, you will yet be happy."

"Happy!" ejaculated our heroine. "Oh! the word to a wretched bereaved being like I am, is mockery. Can I, think you, ever be happy with these reflections upon my mind? Can I be happy to know myself to be in the power of this monster of the deep, Sir Julian Mordlington, the murderer of my unfortunate William, with no other prospect than shame and degradation before me? Oh! impossible! God of mercy! I beseech thee to take me to thyself before such a calamity can befal me!"

"Endeavour to acquire fortitude," remonstrated Maud, "and, unfavourable as your prospects at present appear, something assures me that you will yet have to triumph over your oppressor, and to see retribution hurled upon his head."

"Oh! my good Maud," remarked the poor girl, "how can I ever sufficiently appreciate your goodness to me? But, to be firm, how vainly do you advise me. How can I hope to be firm with those dreadful thoughts crowding on my brain, and the awful fate which threatens me?"

"Reliance on the mercy of the Supreme Power, will render you so," answered Maud.

Flora raised her eyes devoutly towards Heaven, and mentally ejaculated a prayer for the merciful interposition of that Power to which Maud had appealed.

"I need not, I am sure, my dear Flora," said her companion, "again impress upon your mind due caution in your future interviews with Sir Julian Mordlington. Should he discover that I have betrayed his real character to you, nothing but the destruction of us both would be sure to follow."

"Need I say," observed Flora, "you may depend upon me? Heaven forbid, that I should place one who has ever been so kind to me, who has been my best friend under difficulties the most trying, and without whose counsel and advice I must have sunk in despair, in danger. But still there is a mystery about Sir Julian's character which you have not thoroughly explained. Observations which I recollect his having made to William, and the peculiar emotion he exhibited whenever he saw him, would make it appear that he had some other motives for wishing to sacrifice his life, than the mere fact of his being his rival in my love."

" Upon that point," returned Maud, " I cannot give any satisfactory answer; although I am of your opinion, that Sir Julian had some other incentive for his conduct than the mere fact of William's love for you. There is a mystery attached to the origin of William, I have heard you say."

" There is," replied Flora. " He is not the son of Mr. Backstay, although he goes in his name. He was taken by the farmer from a wreck off the coast of France, and it has never been in the power of his protectors to discover his parents. There was another boy, dressed as a midshipman, and who appeared to be some years older than himself, and from the resemblance might have been taken for his brother, preserved with him."

" Ah!" ejaculated Maud, " and what became of that boy?"

" He disappeared in a very mysterious and abrupt manner," answered our heroine, " and, from the impression on the throat of William, it would seem as if the other boy, young as he was, had made an attempt upon his life."

" Is it possible?" exclaimed Maud, with a look of astonishment and horror.

" It is true," returned Flora.

" And the friends of your lover have never seen or heard anything of the young midshipman since that remarkable period?" asked Maud.

Flora answered in the negative.

" It is singular," remarked Maud, after a pause; " but now I recollect that Sir Julian is said to have been saved from a wreck when a boy, and that he made his appearance very suddenly to Mr. Fitzpatrick, who had been the soliciter of his father, and represented that all on board had perished, save himself."

" Wonderful coincidence!" said our heroine; " and know you whether Sir Julian had a brother?"

" I have heard that he had," replied Maud.

" And that he was on board the same vessel with him, when it was wrecked?" inquired Flora.

" I have been informed that he was, and that he would at that time have been about the same age that you have represented your lover to have been."

" Good God!" exclaimed the astonished girl, " but, surely, it cannot be."

" What?" exclaimed Maud.

" That William and Sir Julian could have been the same individuals."

" Ah!" ejaculated Maud, " that thought never before occurred to me."

" And yet two beings of such opposite characters," remarked our heroine, " could not, surely, have been brothers?"

" The brothers of whom I speak," answered Maud, " were so by the same father but not the same mother."

" And think you that the Irish gentleman who disappeared in so mysterious a manner, is the same Mr. Fitzpatrick as the one you have mentioned?"

" I have no doubt of it."

" And that Sir Julian knows anything of his fate?"

" He is his murderer," answered Maud.

" His murderer!" repeated Flora, with a shudder of horror.

" Yes," said her companion; " he was forced on board the Devil Skipper, and by the orders of Sir Julian thrown overboard."

" The monster !" gasped forth Flora ; " and why should he seek his life ?"

" " That he had some powerful reason, and was afraid of the unfortunate gentleman, I have no doubt," returned Maud. " I have heard something about a will which he held, and which Sir Julian wished to get possession of."

" The more I hear of him, the more does his character fill my mind with horror and disgust," ejaculated our heroine ; " but Crazy Marian, as she was called, knew you aught of her ?"

" I know that she perished by the hand of Raker, in the hovel, where she used to seek a shelter, on the evening when William was seized by the smugglers," answered Maud.

" Are you acquainted with her real character ?" asked Flora.

" I am not," replied her companion ; " but I have reason to imagine that Sir Julian had some suspicion of her real character, and was glad to get her out of the way."

" She had sought an interview with William ?" said our heroine.

" She had."

" What could be her object in doing that ?" asked Flora.

" I know not," answered Maud, " but it would seem that she had some secret to make him acquainted with, for just as she was about to reveal it, Raker made his appearance, and took her life."

" The cruel villain," said Flora ; " but he is in the power of justice, and will doubtless receive that punishment which his crimes merit. The more I reflect upon every circumstance, the more do I become involved and bewildered in mystery. What could Marian have to impart to William, and why should Sir Julian seek her life ?"

" That is a mystery," answered Maud, " which only time can unravel. But endeavour to compose yourself as well as possible, and to meet Sir Julian as usual, to prevent his suspicions from being excited."

" I will try my best to do so," returned our heroine, " although I fear that I shall find it a difficult task. How can I ever meet the miscreant without a shudder of horror ?"

" It is only by firmness and resolution that you can hope to thwart his diabolical plans," remarked Maud ; " and to induce him to defer the execution of them until such times as you are rescued from his power. But the vessel is now under weigh, and we are pursuing our voyage."

" Alas ! whither are we going ?" said Flora.

" I am not aware," replied Maud, " although I have no doubt that it is the intention of the captain to make for that part where he expects to meet with some of his other vessels. He will, I dare say, seek a dreadful revenge for the defeat he has lately experienced."

" Oh, God ! and shall I again be a witness of more scenes of bloodshed ?" said the poor girl, clasping her hands emphatically together.

" Alas !" remarked Maud, " what else can you expect, while you are in the power of the Smuggler King ?"

" True, true," sighed Flora ; " but surely the vengeance of Heaven will overtake him ; it will not suffer him always to carry on his cruel career with impunity."

" Depend upon it, my dear Flora," said Maud, " depend upon it that it will not ; and even now, his power is greatly diminished, and another blow like the one he has lately received, will be his complete downfall. He can never more venture to visit England."

" Unless he should do so disguised," said our heroine.

" No disguise could conceal him from the searching eye of Grampus," returned Maud ; " besides, his power is at an end there, and he would find it a difficult matter to escape the hands of justice."

" Alas !" ejaculated Flora, " I fear that he will escape too long for me to entertain any hope of being rescued from his nefarious designs. Heaven help me, for mine is indeed a terrible situation."

Maud was about to make some reply, when they heard a footstep approaching the cabin, and she placed her finger upon her lips, to caution her to silence. The next moment the door was opened, and Will Hemlock made his appearance.

"The captain wishes to see you," he said, addressing himself to Maud.

"What would he with me now?" demanded the latter.

"That I know not," returned Hemlock; "but it is his will, and, of course, you will not venture to disobey him."

"I attend you," said Maud.

"You will not long absent yourself from me, will you, dear Maud?" anxiously inquired our heroine.

"I will quickly return, depend upon it," answered Maud.

She then embraced Flora, and fixing upon her an encouraging look, followed Hemlock out of the cabin.

We need not attempt to describe the feelings of our heroine, when she was thus left to herself; she reflected on all that Maud had said to her, and the disclosures she had made filled her mind with the most unbounded astonishment and emotion. The fate of William now appeared to her but too certain, and the terror it caused her, needs no description from us. Alas! what had she now to look for—what to hope? The discovery of the real character of Sir Julian filled her with the greatest amazement, and taking all the circumstances into her consideration, she could not help thinking that William and the Smuggler King were in some manner connected with each other.

The vessel was now making rapid way, and every hour seemed to plunge her into deeper despair. The only consolation she felt in her present lamentable situation, was the restoration of Maud, whom she was delighted beyond measure to find had escaped the awful fate which she feared had befallen her. She looked most anxiously for her return to the cabin, but at the same time she trembled when any noise from the deck above reached her ears, apprehensive that it was Sir Julian who was approaching her, and dreading his presence as much as if he had been some unearthly fiend of darkness. However, he came not; and our heroine was at length gratified by the return of Maud.

"What news?" said Flora, looking most anxiously in the countenance of Maud, on her entrance; "what fresh designs has the villain in contemplation to torture me?"

"Compose yourself, my dear Flora," replied Maud, "and hope for the best. The captain is at present too much occupied with reflecting on his late defeat, to think of prosecuting his designs against you. He merely wished to question me as to the state of your mind, and has ordered me to pay you every attention."

"And has he said nothing about seeking an interview with me?" asked our heroine.

"He has not," answered Maud; "and I do not think that such is at present his intention."

"God grant that it may not be," said the damsel; "for how can I ever endure the presence of that fiend in human shape? and have you not been able to ascertain whither we are bound?"

"I have not," answered Maud.

"But why should I suffer that to trouble me?" said our heroine; "what matters it whither we are going, since I am in the power of the miscreant Sir Julian?"

Maud made no reply to this, and endeavoured to direct the thoughts of our heroine to other subjects, in which she succeeded better than she might have anticipated. The day wore heavily away, and night arrived without anything having occurred to alleviate the distress of Flora's mind. They were now many miles out at sea, and were still ignorant of whither they were going. The night was calm and beautiful, and the moon shone clearly in at the window of the cabin; but, alas! its brightness now had no charms for Flora, and all was as dreary to her distracted mind, as the most gloomy midnight. It was in the conversation only of the gentle and affectionate Maud, that she could find the least ray of comfort, and even that was indeed most limited.

It was late before she retired to rest, and then she would not have done so had not Maud assured her again and again, and with a sincerity which she could not doubt, that she would not leave her, and at length worn out with fatigue, both of body and mind, sleep descended upon her eyelids.

How long she had slept she had no means of ascertaining, but she was suddenly aroused by hearing a loud noise upon deck, and then the voices of the smugglers and the commands of the captain, mingling confusedly together. Maud was up, and was listening attentively at the door of the cabin. Flora hastened from her pallet.

"Something has happened," she ejaculated. "What can it be? What fresh danger have we to apprehend?"

"Fear not," answered Maud; "for I have every reason to hope that relief is at hand."

"Relief! oh, what mean you?" eagerly inquired our heroine.

"From the words I have overheard the smugglers utter," remarked Maud, "I have ascertained that a vessel is bearing down upon us, which appears to be an English frigate."

"Ah," cried Flora; "but should the pirate's ship prove too powerful for it."

"We must hope for the best," said Maud; "the smugglers are desperate men; but Heaven will protect the just, and perhaps at length hurl a terrible retribution upon the heads of the wretches."

"Oh! how I shudder at the thought of this expected engagement," cried our heroine.

"Hark!" said Maud.

"She nears us," the voice of Sir Julian was now heard to exclaim; "it is a heavy built craft, and we shall have our work to do; but courage, my lads, think of our late defeat, and let the thirst of vengeance embolden ye. There is no flinching away from her, but fight like devils, as you have often done before, and I do not fear the result. Clear the decks, and every man to his post; we will never yield while there is a drop of blood left in our veins."

"Ay, ay, captain," shouted a dozen coarse voices, and the confusion that prevailed on deck increased, and it was quite evident that the commands of Sir Julian were promptly obeyed, and that every means was prepared for the sanguinary contest which was about to ensue.

Flora raised her eyes towards Heaven, and mentally invoked its protection, in which supplication Maud joined her heartily, and they then awaited in great suspense, but stronger hope, the arrival of the vessel,

In the meantime the scene on deck was of the most animated and bustling description; every man was steadily waiting at his post the approach of the enemy, while Sir Julian was rushing about issuing his commands, and encouraging his crew to acts of desperation and bloodshed.

The vessel had now gained so rapidly upon them, that in a few minutes she would be upon them altogether. Sir Julian liked not the appearance of her, but, determined to conquer or perish, he awaited the commencement of the engagement with calmness and fortitude. Bold in his defiance, he had caused his flag to be hoisted, and braved the enemy to the combat. Will Hemlock foreboded an unfavourable result, but he did not mention his fears to Sir Julian, but prepared to render all the aid in his power in the coming battle.

And now the vessel had come alongside the Raven, and the captain commanded the pirate to strike his colours, in the name of the king. This was answered by a broadside from the Raven, and immediately the battle commenced with great fury. The smugglers fought desperately, and Sir Julian urged them on with more than superhuman courage. In spite of the heavy mettle which the frigate carried, and the superior number of the hands on board, for some time the result appeared likely to be in favour of the pirates, but at length there was a loud shout of apprehension from the smugglers, when they perceived through the smoke two more vessels bearing down upon them.

"D——n!" exclaimed Sir Julian; "we stand no chance, our game is up. But no flinching. Courage, my lads! die, but never with life yield to the lubbers."

There was madness in these orders, for what chance could the pirates have when they were opposed by such a powerful enemy; but still the wretches fought with redoubled fury, and with a courage and bravery that were worthy of a better cause, and whenever the greatest danger appeared, there was Sir Julian sure to be there, and seemed to be completely reckless of the danger around him.

At length, however, the enemy, encouraged by the approach of assistance, and making sure of conquest, fought with increased determination, and at length succeeded in boarding the pirate. The first object that met the gaze of the astonished Sir Julian filled him with dismay.

"Powers of hell!" he cried; "do my eyes deceive me? Can the deep give up its dead? Fitzpatrick!"

"Faith, and it is myself, you infernal spalpeen," said that gentleman, for he it certainly was; "I have been preserved from the fate to which you consigned me, and I shall do myself the pleasure of seeing you dangle from your own yard-arm."

"Sir Julian Mordlington, as you have hitherto called yourself," observed a tall, elderly man, very much sunburnt, who was standing by the side of Mr. Fitzpatrick, "yield yourself, nor thus madly persist in a combat which must end in your destruction."

"Yield!" shouted Sir Julian; "the Smuggler King yield to dastard knaves like ye? Never! Who art thou that dare to utter such a command?"

"One whom thou wilt shortly know," replied the stranger; "and who has a right to command thee!"

"Daring idiot!" shouted Sir Julian; "thus I silence thy bold tongue for ever. Die!"

In a moment he snatched a pistol from his belt, and discharged its contents at the stranger, who sunk bleeding in the arms of Mr. Fitzpatrick, exclaiming:—

"Unhappy, guilty wretch, you have shot your own father!"

The smugglers involuntarily drew back on hearing this, and Sir Julian gazed at the wounded man with amazement as he said:—

"Who art thou that thus boldly darest to claim affinity to me?"

"Hector Langford," answered the man, "the unhappy author of thy being. I succeeded in seducing the virtue of the first wife of General Sir Clarence Mordlington, and you are the fruits of that criminal intercourse. For many years I have been abroad, but was returning to my native country, when I accidentally met with Mr. Fitzpatrick on board the same vessel. I speak the truth, and with my latest breath will assert it."

"'Tis false!" exclaimed Sir Julian; "toss him overboard!"

Several of the smugglers advanced to obey the commands of their captain;

Fitzpatrick, being surrounded by several of the sailors, kept them at bay, removed the wounded Hector Langford to a place of security, and the next moment the other two vessels bore down to the combat, and almost the first man who jumped on board the Raven, was William. Yes, one of the vessels was the Neptune, in which he and the Grandville family had been rescued from the island.

Had a spirit at that moment have arisen to the sight of the smuggler captain, he could not have evinced more astonishment or alarm than he did at this unexpected appearance.

"Have the powers of hell conspired against me?" he cried; "William Backstay!"

"Ay!" returned our hero; "it is William, whom your wretches doomed to death, but who has been preserved to be revenged for the wrongs heaped upon him and Flora Clarendon, by you, monster."

"Fight on, my lads," cried Sir Julian; "and yield not while life remains to one of us. Daring stripling, thus will the Smuggler King prove how futile are thy threats."

"For Flora's wrongs," exclaimed William, as he rushed, followed by several sailors, on the smuggler chief, and commenced the combat with a determined valour, which it was soon evident Sir Julian would not long be able to resist, while his crew were falling fast around him. At length the cutlass of the pirate captain was broke short in his hand, and he sunk on one knee, and William was about to plunge his sword in his body, when Sir Julian fiercely shouted,—

"Hold, rash fool! I am thy brother!"

"My brother!" repeated William, with a look of amazement, and his purpose was in a moment arrested.

"It is false!" said Hector Langford, whose wound had been bound round with a handkerchief, and he had greatly revived; "'tis false! He is my son, and you, William, are the son of General Sir Clarence Mordlington, who perished in the wreck of the Enterprise many years since. Lady Emmeline Mordlington is your mother, whose fair fame I traduced out of revenge for the manner in which she resisted my infamous importunities."

"Curses light upon the tongue which gives utterance to this declaration!" cried the smuggler captain; "but why stand ye all amazed? Fight! fight! my lion hearts, and die by the side of your king!"

Hastily he snatched a sword from one of his men, and rushed desperately to the combat; but it was useless, the crew fell fast around him, and the seamen from the different vessels pouring in a torrent on board the Raven, Sir Julian and the rest of the survivors were disarmed, and the long dreaded Raven of the seas was at length compelled to yield to defeat. The shout of triumph which arose from the sailors had scarcely subsided, when William's ears were saluted with a piercing shriek, and the next moment he held the insensible form of his long lost Flora to his heart.

CHAPTER XXVI.

THE DEATH OF THE SMUGGLER KING.—THE RETURN TO ENGLAND.— THE SEQUEL.

LANGUAGE, however powerful, could not do justice to the feelings of all parties present at this unexpected *denouement*; again and again did William frantically press the form of his beloved Flora to his heart, and cover her pale cheeks with his kisses. He could scarcely believe but that he was dreaming,

for their unexpected restoration to each other seemed too delightful to be real. Then the meeting with Mr. Fitzpatrick and Hector Longford; the revelation of the long hidden secret, and the singular disclosures that had been made, completely bewildered him, and he could never sufficiently admire the goodness of Providence, who had at last restored them to each other's arms, after encountering so many difficulties. But there was one thought that racked his brain; it was the terrible uncertainty as to what had befallen Flora, who had so long been in the power of the miscreant Sir Julian; but no, he could not, dared not to believe that the villain had succeeded in his diabolical designs, for had he done so, confident he was that the poor girl could never have survived her shame.

Then the discovery that Marian was really his mother, and the dreadful fate he imagined she had met with, caused the most painful emotion in his breast, and in that few minutes he endured more torture than he had experienced even in the moments of his greatest sufferings and dangers.

The smugglers were now all secured, and Sir Julian was guarded by two of the sailors, and stood contemplating the scene before him with sentiments of the most unbounded rage.

" So," he exclaimed, " the reign of the Smuggler King is at an end ; no more shall his name strike terror over the watery deep. Curses light on this misfortune! that the star of destiny, which has so long shone so brightly upon me, should be thus set for ever! William, you triumph, but had not my hand failed many years ago, thou wouldst not have lived to see this day. But unhand me ; I am powerless now, and I would make thee some reparation ; I have that in my possession that will be of service to thee, and make some amends for the injuries I have done thee. Let these fellows unhand me but for a moment while I give it to thee."

No. 56

William, who did not suspect his purpose, motioned to the sailors to release him for a moment from their hold, and Sir Julian pretended to approach our hero, but suddenly darting to the side of the ship, he raised his hands, and excaimed,—

"The Smuggler King will never swing at the yard-arm; thus he boldly consigns himself to that element over which he has so long swayed with sovereign power."

In a moment, before any one could prevent him, he sprang overboard, and a dozen pistols were immediately discharged at his head. Once his head appeared above the ocean; the blood was gushing in a purple stream from his temples, and fearful and ghastly was the expression of his countenance. One loud and hollow laugh escaped him, the next instant the waves rolled over him, and the Smuggler King was seen no more.

It was some moments ere the persons present could recover from the excitement caused by this unexpected event; but the smugglers having been secured, our hero, with the assistance of Maud, bore the still insensible form of Flora on board the Neptune, whither he was followed by the delighted Mr. Fitzpatrick, while Mr. Longford was immediately attended to, and William was very well pleased when the surgeon announced that the wound he had received was not mortal.

From Maud William received every particular relating to Flora, and we need not attempt to describe the extasy he felt, when he was thus convinced that the villain, Sir Julian, as he had called himself, had not succeeded in accomplishing his cruel designs, but that that poor girl, to whom he was so fondly attached, was as innocent as the day when first they met. To Maud, for the kindness and attention she had paid to Flora, he could never sufficiently express his gratitude, and knew not in what manner he could reward that excellent woman as she merited.

Mrs. Grandville and her family felt the utmost satisfaction at the result of these events, and the restoration of the lovers to each other, and their utmost sympathy was excited for Flora, with whose charms they were most forcibly struck.

But it would be impossible to give a correct idea of the scene which took place when Flora recovered her senses, and found herself safe, under the protection of her lover, and learned that she had nothing more to apprehend from the Smuggler King. She could scarcely believe but that she was labouring under some delusion, and wept with joy upon the bosom of her lover, whom she had never expected to behold again, and who now seemed as if he was restored to her from the grave.

When they had somewhat recovered from their emotion, they entered into a mutual explanation, and related to each other the troubles they had undergone, and most heartily did they return their thanks to Heaven, which had protected and supported them under such very severe trials.

The pirate vessel having been taken in tow, the vessels resumed their voyage, and now the almost certain prospect of again beholding that land from which she had been so long separated, filled the bosom of the maiden with the brightest hope; but when she reflected on the uncertainty of what had befallen her parents, and that the silent grave might long since have inclosed their remains, she felt a sadness steal over her heart, which she in vain endeavoured to banish. The change in William's circumstances created the most lively emotion in her breast; to find that his birth was noble, and to see every prospect that he would be at length restored to his rights, gave her the greatest satisfaction, the more so, as she was convinced that no alteration in circumstances he might experience, could ever banish that ardent, that sincere love he felt for her, and that no other would ever become his bride. The unhappy fate of Lady Emmeline, however, filled the mind of the gentle damsel with the deepest regret, for that she had fallen by the hand of Raker she could not entertain any doubt, and that certainly would, she knew, greatly embitter the peace of mind of her lover. Had she but been aware of what had recently taken place in England, how different would her thoughts have been.

The amiable manners of Mrs. Grandville and her family greatly interested our heroine, and the sympathy they expressed for her won her utmost esteem. The manner in which they had behaved towards William, when he was cast on the island, excited her most unlimited gratitude, and she took every opportunity that was presented to her of evincing the same.

Mr. Fitzpatrick had given William every explanation, and related all the early particulars of his parents, to convince him that he was really the son of the late General Mordlington and Lady Emmeline, and there could be no doubt but that they would find no difficulty in establishing his claim on his return to England. Mr. Longford also repeated his confession, as related to his criminal intercourse with the first wife of General Mordlington, and the calumnies he had invented, and which too fatally succeeded in prejudicing that unfortunate gentleman against her,

"But since that time," continued Mr. Longford, " I have never known a day's peace of mind. I was compelled by business to go abroad, where my conscience perpetually upbraided me, and I was pursued by a train of continual misfortunes, that rendered my life miserable to me. At length I determined to return to England, and make all the atonement to her, for the wrongs which I had inflicted on her, that it was in my power to do. I accordingly embarked on board ship, in which I accidentally met my old acquaintance, Mr. Fitzpatrick, who had been saved from a watery grave by the humanity of the captain."

" Yes, by the powers," said the good-humoured Irishman; " I was fished up out of the sea for the third time, and most happy I am to think I was so, since we have all met again in so wonderful a manner, and I do not doubt but that you will quickly be restored to all that happiness from which you have been so long estranged. And it's no Smuggler King that you will now have to fear at all, at all."

" I and Mr. Fitzpatrick," continued Mr. Longford, " as I before stated, had been acquainted some years before, and it was not without considerable emotion that I beheld him again, especially when I knew myself to be so unworthy of his friendship; but I mustered resolution, made a confession to him of my guilt, and, after the disclosure, I felt easier in my mind than I had been for many years. I need not, however, attempt to describe to you my anguish when Mr. Fitzpatrick informed me of the murder of Marian, whom, from the description that was given of her, I firmly believed to be Lady Emmeline, and sincerely grieved was I to learn that you were in the power of the smugglers, for after what this gentleman had related of you, I entertained not the least doubt that you were the son of General Mordlington, and who had been supposed to have perished in the wreck. Could I but behold you again, and be the means of making you some atonement for the injuries I had done to you and your parents, I felt that I could be comparatively happy, but I was certain that if I were not permitted to do so, I could never die in peace. Providence, however, has in a most marvellous way gratified my wishes, and I can never be sufficiently grateful for it."

" Marvellous, indeed, faith! and you may say that," observed Mr. Fitzpatrick; " and it's not a little surprise we shall cause in the world when we return to old England. Och, and it's much joy that is in store for us."

"Could we find that Lady Emmeline is really still alive, and that nothing serious has befallen any of our dear friends," said William, "we might indeed be happy; but ——"

"Hold your whist now, man," interrupted Mr. Fitzpatrick; "faith, and we will have no buts in the matter. It's myself that live in hopes that all will turn out better than we at present anticipate, and that uninterrupted happiness will yet be our portion."

"I hope you may not be deceived, my dear sir," said William.

"Deceived!" repeated the honest lawyer; "it's my own self now that is seldom deceived at all—at all."

"And you really think that I am the son of General Mordlington?" said William.

"Think," answered Mr. Fitzpatrick; "arrah, now, ain't I certain of it? I tell you that you are no other than Sir William Mordlington, as rich as a prince, and that Miss Flora here will be Lady Mordlington, and that I shall do as I said—have the pleasure of dancing at your wedding, and a rare jolly day we will have of it too. Och, and isn't it myself that will be happy on that occasion, any how, on the wedding of the son of my dear but unfortunate friend."

William could not help smiling at the manner of Mr. Fitzpatrick, and the beauteous Flora, when she looked in the countenance of her lover, and there read the sentiments of his heart, felt herself almost supremely happy.

The prospect of returning to her native land, and the hope of being restored to the arms of her parents, restored her spirits, and as the voyage hitherto had been prosperous, she looked forward to the future with the most cheerful anticipation.

Maud was also in excellent spirits; the troubles she had for so many years undergone seemed now to be at an end, and blessed in the friendship of our heroine and her lover, and with the consciousness of having acted as she ought to do, she hoped that her future days would be passed in serenity and peace.

Frequently would William and Flora pace the deck of the ship, and while they gazed with delight on the calm bosom of the boundless deep, and recalled to their memory the many dangers from which they had been so miraculously preserved, their souls rose in gratitude to the Almighty Director of all events, and the thoughts of home and their dear friends arose upon their sanguine imaginations.

Mr. Longford's wound, which was in the arm, gradually healed, and in the course of a few days he was almost entirely restored to convalescence. He was a man of refinement and great intelligence, and his conversation at all times proved very agreeable to our voyagers. He sincerely repented of the errors of his past life, and both William and Mr. Fitzpatrick did all they could to comfort him, and to assure him of their forgiveness. But the recollection of the atrocities his wretched son had been guilty of, and the misery he had caused to so many of mankind, greatly embittered his peace of mind, and cast a gloom over his future prospects, which he felt it would not be easy for him to banish.

Nothing particular occurred on the voyage, and at length they came in sight of the white cliffs of their native country. Oh, what a moment of rapture, yet not unmingled with apprehension, was that to them all. Mr. Fitzpatrick was in perfect ecstacies, and performed such a variety of grotesque antics on the deck of the vessel, that any one to have beheld him might have been inclined to imagine that he had taken a leave of his senses.

But, oh! what mingled hopes and fears filled the bosom of our heroine; it was not without the greatest difficulty that William was enabled to tranquillize her, for he himself felt in that state of mind which it is needless for us to attempt to pourtray.

They reached that well-known part, which they had never expected to behold again, and then the sight of the three vessels caused the utmost excitement in the minds of the inhabitants who flocked to the place to see them come in. When they were informed of the destruction of the Smuggler King, and who were on board the Neptune, nothing could exceed the sensation that it caused, and the demonstrations of delight that were manifested by every one. The news spread like wildfire, and our voyagers were soon made acquainted with all the remarkable events that had taken place— that both families were alive—the trial of Raker—the restoration of Lady Emmeline, and the discovery of the will by Mr. Melford. With hearts bounding with transport they hastened to meet those who were so dear to them, and whom they had never expected to meet again. And here we must draw a veil over the scene which followed, for language is far too weak to do it justice. With what feelings of delight and gratitude to Heaven did the poor old people press them to their hearts; with what extasy did Lady Emmeline embrace that son from whom she had so long been separated, and invoke a fervent blessing on the heads of him and our heroine. There was only one thing that threw a damp upon poor Flora, and that was the awful calamity that had befallen her father, in the loss of his sight.

We need not attempt to describe the astonishment of Lady Emmeline on beholding Mr. Longford; but on being convinced of his sincerity, she readily pardoned him for all that she had suffered through his means, and acknowledged that he had rendered her all the atonement in his power, by making her innocence known to the world.

A few days served to establish the identity of William, now Sir William Mordlington, and himself and his mother were restored to their rights and proper rank in society, Mr. Melford having given up Bazilwood Hall to them, on his being reimbursed for the money it had cost him to make the purchase.

Happiness and tranquillity being restored to them all, the day was fixed for the nuptials of Sir William and Flora, and a day of rejoicing was that in the neighbourhood. The church bells rung their merriest peals, and rich and poor were alike invited to the festivities. There was a ball and fete in the grand and spacious saloon of the Hall, and Mr. Fitzpatrick fully performed his promise of dancing a jig on the occasion, until he was fairly out of wind, and as red in the face as a new chimney-pot.

Ben Backstay and his family were removed to the Hall, where they took up their future residence, Sir William still continuing to look upon them as his parents, and behaving to them with all the affection of a son.

Mr. and Mrs. Clarendon could not be persuaded to quit their old farm; but they were constant visitors at the Hall, and, in the certainty of their daughter's happiness, found their own.

In the course of a few months, Mr. Clarendon underwent an operation which was successful, and the blessing of sight was restored to him.

The faithful and affectionate Maud continued to reside at the Hall, and was esteemed by Sir William and his lady as their warmest friend and dearest companion.

Mr. Fitzpatrick, having retired from his profession, purchased a house in the neighbourhood, and was always a welcome guest at the Hall.

Mrs. Grandville and her family became comfortably settled in London, and often were invited to Bazilwood Hall, which invitation they always felt a pleasure in availing themselves of.

Lady Emmeline lived for many years afterwards, to see her son surrounded by every domestic happiness, and the father of a numerous family of children, who were the pride of their parents, and were esteemed by all who knew them.

Mr. Longford retired into private life, and by a pure life of virtue and benevolence endeavoured to make amends for the errors he had been guilty of in his youth.

The villains who had so long been the terror of the ocean, were in time all either destroyed or apprehended, but history still traces with dread the fearful career of the desperate rover of the seas, THE SMUGGLER KING.

THE END.